To Simon & Karen,

With all my lov

Mum

X X X

X

ONE OF THESE DAYS

ONE OF THESE DAYS

Audrey Jackson

Book Guild Publishing
Sussex, England

First published in Great Britain in 2010 by
The Book Guild Ltd
Pavilion View
19 New Road
Brighton, BN1 1UF

Typesetting in Baskerville by
SetSystems Ltd, Saffron Walden, Essex

Printed in Great Britain by
CPI Antony Rowe

A catalogue record for this book is
available from the British Library

ISBN 978 1 84624 398 1

1

"One of these days, Rosie Byrne, I'll be wearing fur-lined drawers and you'll have to pay ten bob to even *talk* to me!" Chrissie O'Rourke giggled breathlessly.

The two girls struggled up the area steps and into the side alley of Dominic House, carrying the ashes of last night's fires in the drawing-room and study, the sharp handle of the huge tin bucket digging painfully into their cold hands as they shared the heavy load. Huffing and puffing, they made their way along the short distance of the narrow, chilly passage, hopping unsteadily over the icy cobbles. Through their thin-soled slippers they could feel every lump and bump on the frozen surface and couldn't wait to be finished their morning chores.

"God, it's m-m-murderous c-c-cold today!" Chrissie muttered through chattering teeth. Rosie nodded vigorously in silent agreement.

"Come *on* Rosie, or we'll be late for school." Impatient and bossy as ever, Chrissie hurried her panting companion along. "You know old mother Murphy has got it in for us since last week!" she added with a scowl.

Rosie smiled guiltily, remembering the dreaded episode at Mass on Sunday, when they had been sitting together on the hard old benches of St Patrick's, just behind the rigid figure of the darkly clad, fearsome Miss Murphy. Chrissie have given what she thought was a discreet nudge of her elbow to Rosie, nodding her head at their teacher.

"Ouch!" Rosie's surprised cry echoed around the silent church. She clamped her hand over her mouth in horror, as the wild-faced dragon turned to glare at her. Chrissie stared in shock at her friend who was convulsed in silent laughter, her eyes crinkled with mirth and her face as red as a beetroot! As the dumbfounded Miss Murphy turned her back on them, her face set like stone in blind fury to face the altar again, Chrissie cupped her hand over Rosie's ear and whispered,

"Look at her neck! She's got an *earwig* crawling up it!"

"Holy Mother!" Rosie mouthed, her own face screwed up in agony, vainly attempting not to make a sound.

It was no good. Soon they were both clutching their stomachs, their shoulders silently shaking with hysteria, as hot, uncontrollable tears slid down their pink cheeks. It was just impossible; after only a few minutes they could no longer hold back the deluge of laughter.

"Oh Jesus, I've *wet* meself!" Chrissie announced at the top of her voice, to the whole congregation.

Grabbing her open-mouthed, quaking pal, she dragged her stumbling and sweating from the pews, down the aisle and out into the biting winds of the busy Dublin thoroughfare. Her last vision as they fled in terror, on legs that could barely hold them up, was that of the bulging, glittering eyes of Miss Murphy as she turned again to glare at the sound of the clattering feet of her fleeing pupils.

They were to pay dearly for the fiasco in the coming weeks, after the dreaded punishment had been delivered. The two quaking culprits had stood side by side and white-faced in front of the whole school, fiddling nervously at their skirts, awaiting judgement. The other two classes were crowded together in Miss Murphy's room on Monday morning to hear justice done, along with their teachers, Mrs Doyle and Miss Cleary. The children stood squashed shoulder to shoulder, not daring to move a muscle.

Miss Murphy faced the pupils, erect and determined, her jaw working in an alarming manner under the fleshy folds of her quivering double chin, her wiry greying hair dragged severely to the top of her head in a tight bun, her arms clasped beneath her enormous heaving bosom, glaring over the heads of the terrified girls at some point above the clock on the back wall. Through gritted teeth she declared with unconcealed contempt that they were the most brazen girls it had ever been her misfortune to set eyes on and therefore, they would have ... *No* play! *Extra* homework and would stay behind after school each day for a *month* to sweep and tidy the classroom. They would go personally to Father O'Brien at the presbytery and apologise profusely for the obscenities voiced in such a sacred place and would offer their services in the distribution of alms down at the St Vincents de Pauls Society for Waifs and Strays whenever necessary. (That was bad enough, but to have to clean the toilets in the playground at the end of each day was the *final* humiliation!)

Their friends felt quite sorry for them, especially Johnnie and Paddy, Chrissie's younger brothers who had, with tear-filled eyes, witnessed their sisters' and her friend's tortured expressions.

After the punishment had been announced, the rest of the school were dismissed and began to make their way slowly back to their classrooms in terrified silence. Chrissie and Rosie returned quietly to their desks, wishing the ground would open up and swallow them. But as Chrissie turned and saw the smug, satisfied expression on Jimmy Dwyer's cheeky freckled face and his wiry red hair sticking out in all directions where he hadn't bothered to comb it that morning, her narrowed eyes glittered dangerously and she stared unblinkingly into his mocking gaze. With clenched fists she swore silently to herself that she would punish him dearly, for the pleasure he was taking from their disgrace. She breathed slowly and deeply to control her temper as she slid into her seat and opened her desk quietly to get her books out for the lessons, determined not to make a further show of herself that day.

She soon regained her composure and as she looked up to the front of the class, Miss Murphy was writing on the blackboard with her back to them. Chrissie tried to get Rosie's attention by pressing gently at her toes under her chair, but she refused to look at her. Before she knew what was happening Rosie felt a crumpled scrap of paper being shoved into her palm. She clutched the note tightly, not wishing to risk taking even a quick peek at it. After a few moments, however, curiosity got the better of her and she very carefully picked at the piece of paper under her desk until it lay open, flat on her lap. She waited until Miss Murphy looked down at the pile of books on her table and slowly slid the creased message up on to her reading book, where she could see it. She glanced sideways at Chrissie who sat with an innocent expression on her face, angelically concentrating on the book before her. She thought it was probably just a little 'keep your chin up' note, but as her eyes took in the bold print she burst into a fit of uncontrollable coughing, which Miss Murphy, thank the Lord, took for a bout of nerves and immediately ordered her out to the playground to get a drink of water!

Chrissie quickly retrieved the note under the cover of helping her friend out of her desk, but she was not quick enough. Miss Murphy's ever watchful eyes caught her slipping something into her pocket. She marched down the classroom, dragged Chrissie unceremoniously to her feet, shook her roughly and demanded to see what she had put into her pocket. With a shaking hand, Chrissie withdrew the offending scrap from her skirt. Miss Murphy grabbed it and held it up before her. She stared in bewilderment and read aloud:

WHAT DO YOU THINK EVER HAPPENED TO THE EARWIG?

She stared incredulously at Chrissie, shook her head in despair and putting narrow hissing lips very close to Chrissie's burning ear, said very quietly, "Chrissie O'Rourke, I sometimes think you are quite, quite *mad*!"

As they finished emptying the contents of the bucket on to the ever growing pile of ashes down at the bottom of the garden, they heard the kitchen door open and the raucous voice of Mary Flannagan, 'head cook and bottle-washer', as she called herself, summoning them in for a mug of tea before they went to school.

Chrissie flung the bucket haphazardly in the direction of the shed, missing it by miles, and it clattered noisily against a brick wall. They scurried to the back door and wiping their frozen feet quickly on the coarse rug outside, fell laughingly into the bright, warm, welcoming glow of the large busy kitchen and quickly removed their damp slippers. They sat themselves down gratefully on the broad-seated kitchen chairs around the scrubbed table. Cupping their stiff little fingers around the steaming mugs, they relished the luxurious warmth and the delicious smells of Mary Flannagan's domain as they slowly sipped the sweetly flavoured brew, trying not to scald their chapped lips. They smiled across the table at Daisy, Mary's young niece, who had been sent from London into the safe care of her Aunt. After the end of the dreadful war Daisy hadn't wanted to go back home and so, with much soul searching and many letters back and forth between the two sisters, it was agreed that Daisy could stay on with her Aunt for a while longer. Chrissie had plagued the shy girl with question after question about her hometown. Mary would tutt and fuss every time she heard the inquisitive girl, telling her to leave Daisy be and not to be bothering her.

Mary Flannagan was a dear old friend of Maggie O'Rourke, Chrissie's mother. When Mrs O'Rourke had lost her husband three years previously at the age of 36, after a prolonged bout of racking bronchitis and left her with six young children to rear on her own, Mary had tried to do what she could to give her a helping hand, one way and another. She would carefully wrap up pieces of lamb and beef that 'them upstairs' had left over, into clean scraps of linen and give them to the boys when they came tapping at the kitchen door on their way home from school. Sometimes she managed a large jug of creamy milk and half a loaf of freshly made soda bread and, on a few occasions, they even got a bowl of the scrapings from the huge copper jelly moulds. (Raspberry flavour was Mary's speciality!) For a special treat, the ever resourceful Mary would make up an extra amount of a fruity cake mixture to put in the range, when she had been asked by the mistress to bake a birthday cake for one of the privileged children in the family. (It wasn't much, but anything helped when Maggie had so many mouths to feed.)

Now and then she was even able to bundle up a few bits and pieces of old clothing for them, which the young Miss Angela and Master Thomas had grown out of. They were supposed to go down to St Vincent's, but Mary thought she could put them to a much better use and was more than happy to pass them on to Maggie's young family. Chrissie was delighted to get these 'posh' good quality clothes and by the time she had made a few alterations to suit herself, she wore Miss Angela's cast-offs as comfortably as though they had been made to measure.

Chrissie was the eldest of the six. Three boys: Johnnie and Paddy, the twins and Peter the baby of the family and three girls: young Maggie, Mary and herself. She happily took on the responsibility of taking care of the younger ones to help her poor overworked mother, who was getting rather frail and never seemed to be in the best of health.

Chrissie was a bright and happy child with a great sense of humour and made the best of any situation. (Which sometimes got her into an awful lot of bother.) Her thick wavy chestnut-coloured hair, that swung heavily about her shapely shoulders and took on bright burnished highlights in the long summer days, and her wide brown velvety eyes caught the attention of many a male, as she went in her natural, carefree way about her business in the streets and shops of her neighbourhood. She always had a smile and a cheeky laugh for everyone and although she was still only twelve years old, her slender youthful body, full of vital energy and character, held the promise that in not too many years she would ripen into an adventurous, full blooded, voluptuous woman, ready to take on the world.

When Mary Flannagan's scullery maid, Molly O'Shea, had gone off to the country with her family, who had been left a farm in Wicklow by an old uncle, she had had the idea of asking Chrissie's mother if she would let her daughter come in every morning before school and help out with cleaning and setting the fires for the day. She would be paid, of course. Chrissie jumped at the offer, but only if she could bring her friend Rosie with her. Mary agreed and they were paid two shillings each a week, because after all, it was very dirty work and it would mean that they would have to get up even earlier every morning.

Rosie went along with most things that Chrissie suggested, so was happy to take on their early morning job. Chrissie always gave her mother most of her wages, but kept a little for herself for a few treats now and then. Rosie was in a better position, however, than her friend, as there were only two children in her family, herself and little Liam. Her father was fit and healthy and had been in constant work at the brewery since he left school.

Although the two of them swore that *nothing* would ever come between their friendship Rosie was often appalled when Chrissie acted outrageously, or wanted to get up to some mischief or other. But secretly, she really did admire her and longed to be a little bit more like her. She knew she was not as pretty at Chrissie, with her dark gypsy looks and temperament and the way she could turn the heads of young and old alike, but Rosie did have a quiet charm about her that was very appealing. She wore her thin mousy-coloured hair straight to her shoulders. (Chrissie had tried for years to get her to tie it up in rags overnight to make ringlets, but she wasn't brave enough yet.) Her light hazel eyes that tilted a little at the

6

corners, had tiny specks of gold in them that would sometimes shine prettily and brighten up her otherwise plain little oval-shaped face.

Rosie was a loving, kind and gentle girl with a heart as 'big as the sky', as Chrissie would say and she declared solemnly that she would defend her little friend to the death. Many a time she almost did, especially when she nearly flayed Jimmy Dwyer alive with her skipping rope in the playground after he teased Rosie over the two strange-looking spots that had appeared overnight on her chin. She felt triumphant after the lashing she had given him in front of his cronies, but even more overjoyed at not being caught! But when he had surreptitiously sneaked a penny toffee for each of them into their school bags the next day she was even more delighted. (She suspected that he had filched them from Mr Brennan's sweet shop, but didn't really care!)

The two girls worked well together and went from room to room as quietly and quickly as they could, trying not to awaken any of the gentry occupying the luxurious bedrooms of the grand Dominic House. They trod carefully on the thickly piled, beautifully coloured carpets and rugs, peeped into cupboards and pulled out drawers of the magnificent highly polished sideboards and carefully ran their hands lovingly over the beautiful fabrics covering the many sofas and armchairs, smiling wistfully at one another.

One day, when they had almost finished their early morning chores, Chrissie had accidentally made a dirty ashy smudge on the cushion of the tapestry wingchair, which stood majestically by the fireside in the library. She had been sprawling cheekily in the comfortable chair, pretending to smoke a large cigar, slippered feet resting on the shiny brass fender (they had to take their old boots and stockings off when they were working in the house and Mary had kindly acquired a couple of old pairs of slippers to wear around the place) when suddenly, they thought they could hear voices in the hall. She flew guiltily out of the chair and gasped in horror when she saw the tell-tale mark on the beautiful seat. Chrissie almost had a fit when she tried in panic to rub it off with the end of her rough old brown skirt and only succeeded in making it worse.

"Oh, *shite*, Rosie! We're dead! Quick, give us a hand here!"

They heaved awkwardly at the heavy cushion, and managed with great difficulty to turn it over to hide the evidence of the mischief.

7

They grabbed the old newspapers and stuffed them on top of the ash bucket and hauled it off down the hall and the back staircase giggling nervously and almost tripping over their own feet in their haste. They lived in torment for days, wondering if they would be found out and made to pay for the chair to be cleaned, or even be told they had lost their jobs. But thankfully, nothing was ever heard. They thought it nothing short of a miracle and after weeks of lighting candles and saying extra rosaries every night they finally relaxed.

"Come on you lassies, off you go to school, or you'll be getting me into trouble," Mrs Flannagan scolded.

Chrissie and Rosie reluctantly left the comfort of the high-backed kitchen chairs and drained the mugs carefully into the deep kitchen sink. They sat on the stone flags by the back door and crammed their now-warmed feet into their stockings and boots.

"Thanks, Mary, see you tomorrow," Chrissie chirped cheerfully.

"It's 'Mrs Flannagan' to you, young lady. How many *more* times?"

"Thank you, Mrs Flannagan," Rosie said politely.

"You're a real crawler, aren't you, Rosie Byrne?" Chrissie jeered as they set off, shivering, down the alley and into Dorset Street, which took them through to the bustling streets around the colourful Moore Street market and eventually to St Brigids Catholic school. (Rosie didn't take any notice of Chrissie's remark, as she was well used to her friend's comments and knew she didn't mean half the things she said.) "God, this place really *stinks* doesn't it?" Chrissie wrinkled her pert little nose in distaste. She said the same thing most days! But today was Friday, and that meant fish day. So, it was true. It really *did* stink, to high heaven.

The air in Moore Street was always filled with feverish activity. The noise was almost deafening, what with the bellowing barrow-boys, competing with each other for attention, the blue-nosed, blind accordion player, who perched on an upturned beer crate and would play requests for a penny and whose melodious tunes could be heard from one end of the market to the other; *and* the customers who could shout almost as loudly as the traders, in order to get their money's worth.

Sometimes fights would erupt between the stalls, when one or two of the men who had spent far too much time in one of the crowded pubs down on the docks, became boisterous and foul mouthed. Of course, they would be in no condition to work at all, but they knew what would happen if they dared to go home without any wages. Some of their womenfolk were even tougher than they were and what with a house full of young ones, stood no nonsense at all from their unreliable men.

Mostly, the street was full of the rich mouthwatering smells of juicy fresh fruit and the earthy aromas of vegetables that were piled high on the many barrows that lined the way, but sometimes, especially on a hot summer's day, there was the overpowering acrid stench of horse manure! It was always a relief to reach the end of the street where the sing-song voices of the flowersellers vied with one another to sell huge armfuls of sweetly fragranced blooms.

The tinker women, coarse and weary, with their leathery, lined faces, picked their way through the hustle and bustle with screech- ing children hanging off their skirts and, more often than not, a little black curly head peeping out of a thick woollen shawl that was wound tightly across their mothers' breasts and tied at the back in a chunky knot. The shuffling women would smile beseech- ingly at passers-by, coaxing them in whining voices to buy some 'lucky white heather for your drawers, missus?' and if you spent a few coppers with them, they would bless you with all that was wonderful and if you tried, in vain, to ignore them, they would curse you so loudly and colourfully that you would wish you *had* spent those few extra pennies!

On Fridays the whole street reeked so strongly of the mackerel, cod and whiting that had been caught that morning off the coast of Bray, that the girls always held their noses and pushed and shoved their way along the narrow pavement until they reached the far end.They often barely avoided falling headlong on the slippery uneven path and landing among the fish heads and tails that were cast carelessly around by the fishmongers, who wealded their long, shiny, blood-coated knives with relish while obligingly gutting the fish for the fussy housewives and the snooty servants, who came buying for the big houses in town.

This Friday, was the end of the first week of 'punishment', but it wasn't getting any easier, especially for Chrissie. Her rebellious spirit couldn't take much more, but Rosie timidly kept reassuring her that it wasn't that bad really; they *could* have been expelled. Chrissie had already been warned several times, by a seething Miss

Murphy, as yet again, she was found to be the culprit of a further escapade; and was often told, with sorrowful eyes raised to heaven, that if it hadn't been for the 'dear memory of her devoted father', who had been a daily communicant and a saint in her teacher's eyes, she would have been asked to leave the school without further ado.

As they took the shortcut into Bakers Alley, which would lead them to the back gate of the school's small playground, they linked arms and held tightly on to each other as they trod carefully over the icy patches.

"Hey, Chrissie, hope you haven't forgotten your *scrubbing* brush?" Jimmy Dwyers sneering voice echoed down the narrow passage behind them.

"Piss off, you ugly eegi!!" Chrissie spat back.

"Sshh, Chrissie, Miss Murphy *m-m-*might hear you," Rosie nervously warned her fuming friend, knowing there would be even more serious consequences for her if she was heard 'cursing' yet again. "Oh! bugger her and all of them!" Chrissie retorted carelessly. "I've had just about enough of this place. I can't wait to get out of here and I don't care if the old bag *does* expel me!" She tossed her head defiantly as she shoved open the stiff wooden gate.

"One of these days I'll show the lot of them, you'll see." she vowed. "Especially that no-hoper Dwyer!

Jimmy Dwyer had been the bane of Chrissie's young life, for a long as she could remember. It was difficult to avoid him as he only lived a few doors away and it seemed that whichever way she turned she bumped into him. She knew for a *fact*, that sometimes he deliberately lay in wait, to pester and torment her.

One evening as she had made her way to the old lavvy at the end of the garden she had the creepy feeling that someone was watching her. She shrugged it off and went inside the cold dark little building and did what she had to do. As she stood up and rearranged her clothes she thought she saw a flash of light through a crack in the splintered wooden door. As she threw the door open she was caught in the full beam of Jimmy Dwyer's old bicycle lamp as he balanced precariously on top of his garden fence. She knew straight away, of course, who it was.

"I'll get you for that, you fecker!" she screeched, and in one swift movement bent down and picked up a handful of gravel from the path and threw it with all her strength in his direction. Her aim was *good*. The sharp stones caught him squarely in the face and he came crashing down on to a patch of his grandmother's beloved wallflowers, cursing Chrissie loudly as he fell. She felt great for days when she saw the raw grazes on his arms and spindly legs and the huge bump on his scratched forehead.

Jimmy was an only child as his mother had suffered the loss of three children after *his* difficult birth and she had had such a rough time that the doctors warned her she should not even *think* about taking the risk of having any more children. Mr and Mrs Dywer were devoted Catholics and were deeply dismayed when they realised what this would mean. On her frustrated husband's insistence, Mrs Dywer had gone nervously to Father O'Brien one night after October devotions, for advice on birth control, but the spluttering, outraged priest had hurried her away from the presbytery door as though she would contaminate him in some way. His only advice was "to pray to the Virgin Mary for guidance." She had fled guiltily from the doorstep, clasping her thumping breast and thanking God that he hadn't excommunicated her on the spot.

The atmosphere in the house soon became unbearable and the rows between husband and wife increased. They had always been such a loving devoted couple, but the pressure between them now was just *too* much to take and one night when Mr Dwyer collapsed, once more, on to the kitchen floor in a drunken stupor, announcing that he had no housekeeping money for her this week and she could do what she feckin' liked about it! his defeated wife finally accepted the fact that there was nothing left for her here, and looking sadly down at him she knew that this was it. She had had enough. She sighed softly and calmly went into the bedroom, picked her little son up from his cot and wrapped him snugly in one of the warmest blankets. She lay little Jimmy on the bed and took her coat and scarf from the back of the door. She stood in front of the speckled mirror on the wardrobe door and slowly did up the buttons on the worn dark-blue woollen coat. She tied the thin paisley scarf securely around her head, picked up her child and without a further glance at her sprawling husband, let herself out of the house, quietly closing the door behind her and went with a heavy heart through the dark streets, home to her widowed mother.

2

Rosie had been listening to Chrissie's dreams and fantasies since they had first met and had happily accompanied her on her jaunts to the more 'select parts of town', as Chrissie put it, where, on warmer days, she would take her through the tree-lined streets and squares, with their elegant Georgian houses and beautifully kept, sweetly scented gardens, with their neat little daintily coloured borders and clipped hedges. One of Chrissie's favourite places was Stephen's Green, where the two girls would stand gazing at the splendid façades and fashionably dressed folk who came and went about their unhurried comfortable lives. Chrissie was completely entranced by what she considered the 'lap of luxury'.

"One day Rosie, that will be me stepping out of a house like that, wearing furs and diamonds," Chrissie vowed to her best friend.

Rosie secretly thought that she was a bit nuts, but loved her nonetheless for it and hoped fervently that one day, her dear pal's dreams would come true, but couldn't for the life of her imagine how. She was quite content herself to carry on from day to day, quietly going about her mostly uneventful life. (Apart from when Chrissie got them both in a spot of bother, that is.)

Other times if they could get away for a couple of hours they would stroll around town taking in the sights and looking long-ingly into the inviting shop windows. As they passed the splendid façade of Bewleys' coffee house in Henry Street, they would always slow down and inhale deeply the glorious aromas coming from within. Chrissie wished fervently that she would soon have enough money in her purse to be able to treat herself and Rosie to at least one order of the exotic refreshments and mingle with the elegantly clad customers in the wonderfully relaxed atmos-phere.

Sauntering by the shining windows they peered into the brightly lit windows of the exclusive establishments in Grafton Street and watched admiringly as stylish ladies climbed into grand motor cars, their heavily laden chauffeurs carefully placing their purchases into the boot of the gleaming vehicle.

"I know, Chrissie," Rosie would smile at her friend. "One day that will be you!"

"You're right there!" Chrissie would laugh.

The next few weeks followed fairly trouble-free, as Chrissie kept her head down, determined not to get her friend into any *more* trouble. She felt a little sorry for Rosie because she was so inoffensive and tried to please everyone and felt that most of the scraps they got into were all her fault anyway. If only she could keep her big mouth *shut* a bit more often.

Mrs O'Rourke had been mortified when she'd learned of the scene her daughter had caused at Mass and the ensuing punishment had meant she had even more work to do with the children at home, as the extra time Chrissie had spent at school every evening and the Saturday mornings down at St Vincents, meant that she had to contend with everything herself. It was very hard for her, trying to keep the younger ones in order and keeping on top of everything. She had even taken in washing and ironing from Dominic House, on the suggestion of her friend Mary Flannagan, for a few extra shillings a week, but it was still a real struggle trying to find ways of putting at least one decent meal on the table.

Maggie O'Rourke had been a great beauty in her younger days. She was not a very tall woman but always held herself so proudly as she walked, with her head held high and a tender smile on her soft features. She was a highly respected figure in her small community with her gentle nature and kind word for all. She appeared to onlookers as a smartly but simply dressed lady, always in the long black skirts of her generation and immaculate white blouses with meticulously pressed and starched lacy collars and cuffs. Her dark grey double-breasted woollen coat fitted snugly into her small waist. Her ageing little black boots were always highly polished and her narrow-brimmed black felt hat, with its dainty net veil, sat at a rather jaunty angle secured with her treasured jet hatpin over her neatly arranged bun. If anyone had looked more closely, they would, of course, have seen that her clothes had been repaired many times over, but with great skill nevertheless and under those rather thin but dainty black gloves were very red and very raw, work-worn hands. She had been teaching Chrissie her skills at sewing and mending and was pleased to see just how quickly her bright daughter picked it up especially as she realised that the rheumatism in her own hands was getting worse by the week.

At the end of the month's punishment, Maggie decided that she would allow Chrissie to have a little time off for herself before she was once again plunged into the almost never-ending help with the day to day chores at home.

As the weather eased up a little and the biting winds became a little less cruel, Chrissie decided that she would take Rosie for a wander down to the docks and watch the boats loading and unloading. Maybe even go an extra couple of miles along to Dún Laoghaire and watch the mail-boat coming in, as a special treat.

This would mean an extra early start though, as the Princess Maud docked very early in the morning and usually after a rough night's crossing from Holyhead. Rosie had reluctantly agreed, although she couldn't really see what the excitement was in watching gangs of rough boisterous seamen toiling away on the dockside or bone-weary travellers trudging down the gang plank, heavily laden with battered suitcases and grumpy tearful children, but of course Chrissie had other ideas!

She would invent stories of where the boats had come from, what they where carrying and how long it had taken for them to sail here, there and everywhere. She had such an active and vivid imagination you would almost believe that she had been one of the crew or passengers herself. Indeed she often wished she was.

"You know *what*, Chrissie?" Rosie said, as they stood hunched together to keep warm, over the wooden rail that divided the customs hall from the alighting passengers.

"What's that, Rosie?"

"Sometimes I really think that you wished you were a million miles away from here."

"Course I do! You don't think I'm going to stick around *this* place for the rest of me life, do you? I'm not going to end up like me mam, with a string of kids hanging around me and nothing to put in their bellies and on their backs!" Chrissie retorted cruelly.

"Aw, come on, it's not *that* bad and that's a *horrible* thing to say about your poor mam! She works *so* hard and has kept you all spotless and well fed, despite all her troubles. Sometimes I think you are just a bit too mean and ungrateful, Chrissie O'Rourke! I'm sorry I let you drag me out of my warm bed at this hour of the morning! I'm going home!"

Rosie pulled away from the stunned, open-mouthed Chrissie.

"Oh! I'm sorry, I didn't mean it to come out like that Rosie, *honest*!" Chrissie cried, as she ran to catch up with her friend. "It's just that sometimes I just want so much *more*, I want to go to new places, meet interesting people, do exciting things! Don't you, Rosie? Honestly now, don't *you*?"

"No! I'm quite happy, thank you very much!" her friend replied tartly. Rosie quickened her pace along the quayside as Chrissie ran alongside her.

"Hang on a minute, Rosie, don't let's fall out, *please*! she begged. "This is silly."

"I'm not falling out with you, Chrissie, but I sometimes wonder if it's just *me* you want to get away from, with all your high faluting ideas and your mad notions."

Chrissie stopped walking. She stared in astonishment at her friend's back for a long moment and then she ran to her, grabbing her roughly by the shoulders, spun her round and saw with shame, the tears slowly falling down the cold cheeks. She pulled her sobbing friend tightly to her breast.

"Ah, little Rosie, don't say that, please don't *ever* say that!"

"Let me *go*, you're squashing me!"

"No, not 'til you say I'm forgiven."

They were both sobbing now as they clung to one another in the chilly morning air.

"All right, all right, you're forgiven, but I know you'll go away one day and leave me behind!"

They stood looking at each other sadly.

"I can't *lie* to you, Rosie. I will leave Ireland one day, I just *know* I will, but you can come with me. We can *both* go away. We could go on the boat to England and we could get good jobs and send money back home. Maybe *one* day we'll have enough money to send for everyone to come and join us." Chrissie looked pleadingly into Rosie's sad face. Rosie heaved a great shuddering sigh. "I *can't* come with you, Chrissie. I want to stay here where I belong. You should stay here where you belong, too. Something bad will happen if you go away, I *know* it will."

"Oh don't be silly, what will happen to *me*? You know I can take care of meself."

"Well, I heard me mam and dad talking about things that can happen to girls when they go away to England, bad things."

Chrissie threw back her head and laughed.

"Now what on earth is that supposed to mean? Would I get kidnapped or something and sold into slavery! Ha, ha . . . At least it would be more exciting than working down at the mill or in the bloody *jam* factory!"

"Oh, I don't know. It just makes me scared when I think about it . . . and stop teasing me, you're getting to sound like Jimmy Dwyer!"

"Don't you ever put me in the same class as *that* little rat!" Chrissie's eyes hardened in rage.

Rosie sighed quietly. "No, no, you're right, I shouldn't have said that. I'm sorry. Anyway, you're not even *thirteen* yet, so you've plenty of time to change your mind."

"No . . . I'm sorry Rosie . . . you're right. We still have a few years left at school and who *knows* what could happen by then. Come on, let go and have a cup of tea at Masie's Café. It should be open by now."

Chrissie smiled sweetly into her friend's hopeful face, thanking God that Rosie couldn't read her thoughts at that moment.

She knew in her heart, of course, that one day she would leave Dublin, with all its childhood dreams and memories. She did want to do more with her life, other than join the crowds of girls marching off to this factory or that, all doing the same boring things, day in and day out. The hot-headed girl knew she didn't have a lot of patience at times so would have to find herself something intensely interesting to keep her occupied. She would work on it during the time she had left at school and would maybe get another part-time job during the holidays to help with the money side of things. She would continue to try and persuade Rosie to come with her, of course, and she was almost sure she would give in . . . in the end. Chrissie wasn't so sure about her mother though. She had *never* really understood this burning passion that beat in her daughter's young breast.

Chrissie had bravely broached the subject many times with her, as they stood together, arms deep in suds over the old tin bath that was balanced between two chairs in the backyard on wash days or as they sat by the fireside, mending holes in socks and tears in trousers, late into the night. Her mother would sigh deeply and shake her head in despair as soon as Chrissie started to chat about what it would be like to live in another country in a big city and earn lots of money and wear beautiful clothes and so on. To be able to afford to go to the cinema every week or even a theatre! Imagine that!

"Chrissie, dear, you know that's just not *possible*, is it now?" her worried mother tried to reason. "You know I need you here. How on earth would I manage on my own and the young ones love you, you know that. They would miss you terribly and so would I . . . and what about poor little Rosie? She'd be lost without you and apart from all that where would you get the money! We only manage from week to week as it is. Come on now; be sensible. Stop all this idle dreaming. We've a lot to get through and I still have a heap of collars to starch for the big house and you know how early you have to be up in the morning."

"But, mam, I've only another couple of years at school and then Margaret (as the young Maggie liked to be called) can help you more, she does little enough now!" She snorted in disgust. "She's big and strong and Paddy and John can lift and carry and run messages for you. Maybe find themselves a job after school or something to help you out and when I get a *real* good job, I'll be able to send you money every week. It'd be great, wouldn't it?"

Chrissie would regularly go into a dark mood after these frustrating conversations with her mother, but soon came round when she caught the big soft eyes gazing sadly at her. She would smile guiltily and rush and give her worried mother a breath-taking hug.

"Ah, don't worry, mam, I'm not going *anywhere*!" Chrissie would assure her soothingly (not for a while, anyway, she would think to herself).

The next couple of years flew by and by 1950, Chrissie and Rosie had passed their school-leaving certificates, both with flying colours. It wasn't a minute too soon for Chrissie, as she stood excitedly before Miss Murphy to receive her long awaited reward. She took the parchment scroll that had been tied neatly with a thin strip of red ribbon with a trembling hand and noticed with amazement that her teacher's hand was also shaking. She frowned as she looked straight into the pale grey crinkled eyes in the tired face, fearing some untoward remark, which had become so common to her during her school days. To her astonishment she swore she could see a tiny tear in the corner of each eye. She couldn't believe it!

"Must be relief at the thought of getting rid of me at last," she thought amusedly to herself. She turned quickly back to her seat and watched as the rest of the class proudly received their certificates. Jimmy Dwyer was the last to receive his and as he passed her desk, he tapped her lightly on the top of her head with the rolled up certificate and looked down at her with a gloating look in his eyes.

"Bet you never thought I'd be getting one of *these*, did you?"

Chrissie sniffed disdainfully up at him. "Get off, ya big eegit!" she said, "and a lot of good *that'll* do you!"

She had to admit to herself, though, he *had* buckled down and worked well in the past year. Maybe he was getting a bit of sense at last. Chrissie had also noticed that he was almost two inches taller than her now. His hair had toned down from the *woeful* blazing red that it had been into quite a pleasant shade of auburn and was always brushed neatly back. She supposed that he wasn't that badlooking, really. (But she had cringed many a time when she caught him watching her across the playground or had puzzled when he had shuffled past her red-faced in the street, eyes down and without making any of the rude comments that she had become so used to.)

As Chrissie and Rosie heard the loud clanging of their last ever home-time bell, they beamed at each other across their desks. Chrissie gave a huge deep sigh and breathed joyously, "At last . . . freedom!"

The whole class was laughing as they made a noisy exit from the room. Chrissie was the last to leave and as she reached the door she felt the eyes of Miss Murphy on her back. She turned slowly to look at the solitary figure leaning heavily on her desk, watching her. She didn't know why, but she felt herself drawn to approach her. As they stood face to face, Chrissie saw the familiar features begin to crumble.

"Oh. Miss Murphy, I wasn't *that* bad, was I?" she tried to joke.

Miss Murphy tried to look sternly at the girl and thought, "My god! That could be me standing there forty years ago!"

"Oh yes you *were*, Chrissie, you've caused me nothing but grief since the day you walked into my classroom!" After a small pause she added very quietly, "But, Miss O'Rourke . . . I will surely miss you."

Chrissie reached out impulsively and grabbed her dry wrinkled hand. She squeezed it gently, but for once in her life couldn't speak for the lump in her throat that was choking her. Miss Murphy pulled herself together and bade Chrissie a terse goodbye and, as she turned stiffly away, she added in a small, quavering voice, "Oh and Chrissie . . . God bless you . . . and keep you safe till you're home again."

Chrissie ran out of the classroom and into the playground, brushing the tears roughly from her eyes with the sleeve of her cardigan.

Rosie was surrounded by their friends, all saying tearful good-byes and promising to see each other whenever they could and wishing each good luck for the future. Chrissie sped past them and out through the school gate for the last time. As she ran down Baker's Alley she heard Rosie's voice calling her to wait.

"What's wrong, Chrissie?" Rosie gasped as she finally caught up with her distressed friend.

Chrissie slowed down at last. "Nothing, nothing at all!" she gulped.

"Well, you don't *look* like there's nothing wrong. Are you crying? I thought you would be happy to get away at last. Did Miss Murphy say something to upset you?"

"Just leave me *alone*, will you, Rosie. I'm all right!" Chrissie shouted angrily.

"I know, I know . . . it's all a bit much, isn't it? All the excitement and everything," Rosie said soothingly as she caught hold of Chrissie's hand tenderly. "Don't worry, everything will be *fine*, you'll see."

Chrissie nodded her head silently, walking slowly while catching her breath, still thinking of Miss Murphy's sad face. She must have been so *wrong* about her. For so long. Why hadn't she even bothered to take the time to see what a lonely old woman she really must have been and how caring she could be, given half a chance. She must have taken the time to understand Chrissie after all and knew that once she had left St Brigids, it wouldn't be long before Chrissie would leave her and all her family and friends far behind, as she made her own way in the world.

"Maybe we weren't so different, after all," she said, almost to herself.

"What did you say, Chrissie?" Rosie asked cheerfully as she waved goodbye to a group of girls who were standing around Jimmy Dwyer and a few of his friends, giggling and chatting, on the corner of Lambs Passage. Chrissie glanced across the street, waved and smiled brightly through moist, blurred eyes. "I just said, . . . shall we go and get an ice cream before we go home?"

"I don't know about an ice cream, I think I'd prefer a pint of stout!" Rosie exclaimed, laughing mischievously at Chrissie's astonished expression.

"You're a dark horse, Rosie Byrne. Where did you learn such *dreadful* habits?" she scolded haughtily. "Do ya think we'll get away with it?" she added thoughtfully.

"God, Chrissie, I'm only *kiddin'* you!"

"*I'm* not!" Chrissie declared cheekily.

For one minute Rosie almost believed her and as she saw the impudent look in her friend's sparkling eyes, she gave her a quick hug and said,

"Come on, let's go and get that ice cream!"

3

Much to Chrissie's annoyance and frustration, she had *finally* succumbed to her mother's fretful pleading to accept the position of junior seamstress at the local clothes factory that she had been offered on the very first day she had started looking for work. She had only gone in the first place out of curiosity and to stop her mother worrying. She had trekked for weeks around town after that, in a vain attempt to find some other more interesting employment that would suit her ambitious nature, but there was really *nothing* to offer her. In fact, the unemployment in town was getting higher by the week and she realised if she didn't take up *this* job, or any *other* job in fact, very soon, she would never be able to boost her meagre savings enough to enable her to even pay for her *fare* out of this place.

She had gone back to Mr Silverstein, very reluctantly, to ask if the position was still open.

"So you've decided that we're good enough for you, after all then, Miss O'Rourke?" he had superciliously remarked, as he sat in the small cluttered office, leaning casually back in his brown leather swivel chair, his well-fed belly stretching the ash-speckled fabric of his new waistcoat. As he looked her up and down through a haze of swirling cigar smoke, he liked what he saw.

The young woman who stood haughtily before him was dressed smartly in the same light grey two-piece costume and neat white blouse that she had worn when she had first approached him for work. Her matching black handbag, shoes and gloves were obviously not *new*, but he was impressed by the assured way she carried herself, knowing that it must have taken a good deal of gumption to come back again to the factory. He thought "*This* one might be a bit of a challenge". She was different from any of the other girls who had willingly or unwillingly gone through his hands over the years. She had an air of confidence about her that he felt would take her far in whatever she set out to do, but would she come round to his way of thinking? He wasn't sure.

Chrissie had not answered him for fear she would say the wrong thing. She had smiled brightly, wishing she could be anywhere else but there. She knew that all the girls in the factory called him 'Aul Slimy', because of his lecherous reputation, but was determined that it wasn't going to put *her* off! She desperately needed this job.

"Right then, we'll see you at seven o'clock on the dot, Monday morning. Mrs Hogan, the supervisor, will show you around. I'm *sure* you will know some of the other girls working here. I believe most of them come from *your* part of town," he leered.

Chrissie still didn't say anything, but silently seethed at his comment, knowing exactly what he meant.

"Bring your own overall and get that *hair* tied back, we don't want any accidents on the machines," he said, his voice tight as he quickly looked away from the thick glossy waves that tumbled loosely over the curve of her shapely bosom.

"You will be paid piece-work, which is a shilling a completed garment. Take this down to the wages office," he said abruptly as he handed her a note that he had been scribbling. "Good Morning."

"Thank you, Mr Silverstein, and good morning to *you* too," she said, as politely as she could manage.

As she made her way through the buzzing and whirring noise of the industrial sewing machines and through to the back of the factory, where she had been directed by a cheeky young lad who was collecting great bales of garments from each of the workers, her jaws were clenched in frustration.

"What in the name of all the saints have I let meself in for *now*?" She thought angrily to herself.

By the time she had had a cup of tea and a chat with Breda Flynn, who did the wages, she didn't feel too bad. It seemed that most the girls were a good crowd and easy to get on with. There were a few that weren't too popular, it seemed, but that didn't bother Chrissie at all; she could handle herself and besides she was only there for the money. She knew she was capable of turning out good work, as she had proved only too well, when she had come to see Mr Silverstein the first time and had been asked to show what she could do. It had only taken her a couple of minutes to get used to the huge machine and had speedily produced a simple summer frock much to her future boss's amazement.

Mrs O'Rourke had been thrilled to bits when Chrissie told her mother the good news.

"Oh Chrissie, love, that's great! We'll be made up!" She said delightedly as she hugged her daughter warmly and almost danced them both around the small kitchen.

"Well . . . I'll *try*, mam, but I don't know how long I'll stick it there," Chrissie said honestly. "The old devil has a terrible reputation with the girls and you know *me*, I won't be able to keep me mouth shut for too long!"

"Chrissie, now you know that's probably only gossip! You know what those factory girls are like. You have to give him a chance. We can't afford for you to lose the job before you've even started!" her mother warned.

Nevertheless, as she turned back to the boiling pot of potatoes on the top of the range, she frowned thoughtfully. She *did* know all about Mr Silverstein. She had heard plenty of wagging tongues concerning his exploits, but she would pray extra hard to keep her daughter safe and to give her patience with her employer. So it was with some trepidation that she waved Chrissie goodbye on her first day at work the following week.

"Please God, we're doing the right thing," Maggie whispered to herself. She thought about Rosie, who had been taken on full time at Dominic House. She had settled in very well and was happy and at least *Rosie* wouldn't have any problems with her employer.

When Mrs Fitzgerald had proudly told her doting husband that she was expecting another child, he had immediately insisted that they should advertise for some extra help for her. She wasn't too keen to start with, but as the morning sickness and the fatigue didn't seem to be improving, she reluctantly agreed.

Doctor Fitzgerald had called Mary up from the kitchen early one morning and fearing she had done something dreadful to upset him, she stood nervously outside his study door. She hesitated a few moments before tapping quietly.

"Come in, Mary."

"Good morning, sir," she murmured timidly, eyes downcast, anxiously twisting at the front of her spotless white apron.

"Good morning, Mary . . . and how are you, this fine day?"

"Very well, thank you, sir," she answered a little more confidently now at hearing the merry tone in his deep voice.

As she looked up, she saw that Dr Fitzgerald had a particularly happy expression on his face as he stood hands clasped behind him, his back to the roaring fire, rocking on his heels. She smiled back at him.

"We have some good news for you, Mary, and we need a little help from you, too."

"Oh yes, sir, anything, anything at all."

She wondered what the '*good* news' was, exactly.

"Well, it seems that in a few months we are going to have *another* little Fitzgerald in the house."

"Oh Sir!"

"Yes, great, isn't it," he said proudly. "The only thing is, as you may have noticed, my dear wife has been feeling more than a little off colour lately (Mary had *indeed* been wondering about that) and I feel that she may need some more help with the children and such."

"Of course, sir," Mary quickly agreed, but at the same time she thought to herself, Holy Mother, he can't expect me to do any more than I do *now*. I'm run off me feet from morning 'til night as it is!

He must have read her mind. "Don't look so *worried*, Mary, we won't be asking you to do any more than you do already. That would be almost impossible, eh?" he laughed kindly.

"Yes, sir," she smiled shyly.

"What I would like you to do is to suggest some young lass to us, who you think we could all trust here, with the children and so on. You know she would be well taken care of. She could have the little room at the top of the stairs beside Angela and we would supply her with some suitable clothing for her position and of course she would eat with you in the kitchen. She would be well paid and after a few months if we find her suitable and she wishes to stay we would naturally think about increasing her salary. What do you think, Mary?"

Mary was greatly relieved at the thought of not having any more responsibilities thrust upon her. "Well sir, I can think straight away of *one* girl who would be *most* suitable. Young Rosie Byrne. You know, sir," she rushed on. "The young one that comes in every day with Chrissie O'Rourke to do the fires? She's leaving school soon and I know she hasn't found a job yet. She's a good little worker and comes from a lovely family."

"Of course, little Rosie. Now why didn't *I* think of that? Yes a very pleasant young woman. No trouble at all. Well, shall I leave the arrangements to you, Mary? Will you ask her to come and see me as soon as she can?"

"Yes, sir," Mary beamed.

Rosie had accepted immediately when Mary had rushed up to her excitedly after early Mass the following Sunday. Although she didn't really want to leave her family for a live-in job, when she told her mother about the forthcoming interview with Dr Fitzgerald, Mrs Byrne told her she didn't mind at all. It wasn't *really* like leaving home properly, was it? She would only be half an hour away and to live in a grand house like that she would be more than comfortable. She and Rosie's father would be only too happy to know she was safe and well cared for.

So, several weeks before Chrissie had taken her first grudging steps towards her future life, Rosie had presented herself on the doorstep of Dominic House as the new 'children's nanny' in the Fitzgerald household.

4

"Are you comin to the dance tonight, Chrissie?" Moira Reardon called out in her unmistakable nasal voice, over the heads of the factory girls as they stood in line waiting their turn to clock off for the week.

"Course I am, wouldn't *miss* it!" Chrissie yelled back laughing. "Just have to run meself up a snazzy little number first!"

She was always the envy of the other girls at the local dances on Friday nights. Much to their constant envy and amazement, she regularly appeared in a new, fashionably styled and beautifully made outfit. She knew full well how secretly jealous some of them were, but didn't give a hoot. She didn't do it on purpose, more to prove to herself what she was actually capable of achieving in the couple of hours between work and the time she strolled off down to the dance hall and, of course, to see the reaction from a certain person!

She had, at first, begrudged the ten shillings she had to fork out to Mrs Leary for the deposit on the rusty old Singer. She agreed to pay a shilling a week until the machine was paid for, and over the months it had well and truly paid for itself. What with all the new blouses and skirts she had made for herself out of remnants from Mrs Leary's drapers shop on the corner of Bull Lane and with the constant demand from her neighbours to do all kinds of alterations, she was more than satisfied with the few extra shillings she had made for herself.

"I'll see ya outside the Arcadia about eight." She hurried off through the busy streets, praying that Mrs Leary would still have the piece of black satin with the gorgeous gold stripes that she had promised to keep under the counter for her.

At five minutes to eight Chrissie sauntered casually along to the dance hall, humming a little tune to herself. She was very happy with her new outfit tonight. The thin gold stripes on her full black skirt glittered attractively as she swung her hips in a *most* provocative manner. The sleeveless little black top she had made a couple

26

of weeks before was tucked tightly into the waistband of the new skirt and she had carefully arranged a small black chiffon scarf into the plunging v-shaped neckline, so her mother wouldn't be giving her another lecture about looking like a 'loose-woman'. The one and only evening bag that she possessed and which held her precious cherry-red lipstick, a comb, half a packet of Sweet Afton and a couple of shillings for the evening was clutched tightly under her arm.

She could hear Jimmy's contagious laughter before she rounded the corner. Quickly checking her reflection in the nearest shop window, she threw her head back and shook the long, gleaming tresses away from her shoulders. Swiftly whipping the chiffon scarf away and stuffing it into her bag, she strolled casually on to meet her pals.

As she passed the entrance to Brady's bar, she noticed Jimmy and his friends standing by the open doors smoking and chatting, and she heard a low whistle of admiration and grinned in satisfaction, knowing *exactly* who it was. She continued nonchalantly on, hips swinging, ignoring the insolent stares of the young men. Her eyes lit up when she saw Rosie. "Hey, *Rosie*! What a great surprise. What're *you* doing here?"

"I've got the evening off, so I thought I'd come and keep an eye on you." Her friend replied. "And by the looks of you, you *need* it," she added, frowning as she took in the exposed cleavage before her. "For goodness sake, Chrissie, that's a bit daring, even for *you*!"

"Don't be such an old *prude*, Rosie, you sound like me mam!" Chrissie scolded lightly. "Come on," she added, quickly grabbing Rosie's elbow," let's get a good table before those other eegits get in!"

For weeks now Chrissie had pointedly ignored Jimmy, as she gaily danced the night away with every other lad who asked her (even if she did think he was the ugliest thing on two legs that she had ever clapped eyes on.) She was determined to make Jimmy jealous and knew that he was slyly watching her every move as she twirled happily around the dance floor. She hadn't forgotten all the mean things that he had said and done when they were younger and thought this was a good way to pay him back. She needed Jimmy Dwyer to want her so *badly* that it hurt! She had watched him take up girl after girl for every single dance, but he had never approached her once. She always noticed, however, that he didn't ever ask anyone on to the floor for the 'last dance' and felt that very soon he would bring himself to ask *her*! So when he finally *did* make his move, she wanted her rejection of him to be as painful as possible. The only problem was, he wasn't making any moves at all. In fact he always disappeared before the strains of the last waltz had ended. The bravest thing he had achieved was a few wolf whistles when his pals were with him.

Betty Clarke sat heavily down on the seat beside Chrissie, sweating profusely from the rigorous reel she had just finished with her boyfriend Eamon.

"Jesus! That's me finished for the night, Chrissie. I haven't a *breath* left in me!" she gasped dramatically, wiping her scarlet sweating face with an already soaking-wet wrinkled pink handkerchief.

"I'm not surprised, the way you've been throwing yourself around at everyone all night," Chrissie commented dryly as she reached for the last cigarette in the packed on the table.

"What's *that* supposed to mean?" Betty sniggered. "You don't do so badly yourself, Chrissie O'Rourke! And don't think I didn't see you watching me when I was dancing that lovely *slow* number with Jimmy!"

"Hmm! What makes you think I care about what *that* eegit gets up to?" she sneered back.

"Oh, come off it, Chrissie! Stop kiddin' yourself. The whole place knows the way you both sneak looks at each other."

"I think you'd better get your eyes tested, Betty. I don't give a damn about Jimmy Dwyer or who the *hell* he dances with!" Chrissie blazed hotly.

She stood up abruptly from the table, shoving her chair noisily away and stubbing her half smoked cigarette roughly into the over-full ashtray. She shoved her way angrily and roughly through the smooching couples towards the exit.

"Hey, Chrissie, wait for me!" Rosie called out behind her. "Where are you *going* so early? It's not half nine yet."

"Oh, it's too bloody hot in here! I'm going out for a walk," Chrissie replied sulkily.

"I'll come with you. I'm a bit tired tonight anyway."

In the cool evening air the two friends walked along the quiet pavements.

"What's wrong, Chrissie? What's upset you?"

"Oh, nothing really, Rosie, just a bit worn out. We've had a really busy week and I don't feel up to all that jiggin' about tonight."

"Well, I never thought I'd hear you say that!" Rosie laughed. "How is it at the factory anyway? Is 'aul slimy' as bad as the girls say he is?"

"Worse!" Chrissie snorted. "Do you know he has been trying it on with me from the *day* I started there. Always calling me into his office on *any* excuse to lech over me. Dirty old devil! Rubbin' up against me whenever he can. Leaning over me while I'm on the machine, with his stinking hands on my shoulders trying to get a look at me tits and his rotten hot breath all over me. God, he's *disgusting*!"

"Oh, Chrissie, that's *awful*!" Rosie sympathised. "Why don't you get your mam to say something to him?"

"God! your joking me, aren't you? I wouldn't tell me *mam* a thing like that. Anyway I can handle *him* and besides I don't want to get the sack . . . I haven't enough money saved yet for me fare!"

Rosie stopped walking.

"You're not *still* thinking of leaving are you, Chrissie?" she asked in a tiny voice. "After all this time?"

Chrissie turned to her friend. "Yes, . . . yes, I *am* still thinking of leaving, Rosie!" came the determined reply. "It's just taken a bit longer than I planned, that's all."

As she watched her face crumple, Chrissie began to feel a little angry towards her friend. "Don't look at me like *that*! What did you expect? I told you *years* ago that I wanted to do more with me life than you do. Anyway, you're happy enough in your swanky house, you wouldn't miss me at all!" she said spitefully.

"You know, Chrissie, you have really changed. I thought we could always be friends, but you're very nasty sometimes, you know; now I'm not so sure."

"I haven't changed at all! I still want the same things that I always did and by God I'm going to get them!" She shouted defiantly into the face of her astonished friend. She turned on her heel and stormed off down the street away from the dejected figure of Rosie who stood forlornly under the dull yellow light of the old street lamp.

5

The long days in the sweltering factory dragged on and on and Chrissie was becoming more and more bored as the weeks went by. She still produced perfect clothing in record time and was often rewarded with an added bonus in her pay packet at the end of the week. She also successfully managed to ward off the unwelcomed advances and suggestive remarks and looks from her lecherous boss.

She was feeling *very* bad now about the way she had spoken to Rosie and wished she could do something to make it up to her, but she hardly ever saw her. Rosie didn't come to the dance hall again after the night Chrissie had upset her so much. She had even got bored with trying to attract the attention of Jimmy Dwyer, just so she could spurn him!

It was almost Christmas, and Chrissie knew that if she went to Midnight Mass, Rosie was sure to be there. She promised herself she would make a determined effort to speak to her and apologise, she *so* longed to be friends with Rosie again and although they hadn't seen a great deal of each other over the last couple of years because of the hours that they worked, she was never far from her thoughts.

Maggie O'Rourke had not been feeling well for days and really couldn't face the cold dark walk to and from St Patrick's on Christmas Eve, so she asked Chrissie if she would mind terribly going on her own this year. Of course Chrissie insisted that her mother should not even think of leaving the house in her condition and it was no bother at all for her to go on her own. This could be a good opportunity to approach Rosie privately and, if she would accept her apology, she might *even* accept an invitation around to tea over the Christmas holidays. Chrissie knew her mother had been very upset over their 'words' and would be delighted to see them friends again.

As she made her way quickly along to the church, head down against the increasingly bitter wind, she sincerely hoped that Rosie would be there and she would have a chance to speak to her, but as it turned out it was Rosie who came running along the street through the thickening fog, to meet *her*.

"Oh, Chrissie!" she cried, as she gulped in the freezing night air. "Have you heard the news?"

"Oh, Rosie! It's so good to be talking again!" she almost shouted in amazement as she threw her arms open, but stopped instantly when she saw the tear-stained face in the pale moonlight.

"What did you say, Rosie?"

"I said . . . have you heard . . . the news?" her panting friend replied.

"What *news*? What are you talking about?" Chrissie questioned anxiously. "Come in here a minute and tell me," she added, pulling Rosie by the elbow into a darkened shop doorway for shelter against the wind.

"About Miss Murphy."

"What about Miss Murphy? What's happened?"

"Well, you know that she hasn't been well for some time?" Rosie replied, her breath coming a little more evenly now.

"*No*, I didn't, *actually*," Chrissie replied a little tartly, feeling rather put out at not knowing.

"Well, Mrs Phelan sent her little Michael up tonight to tell me mam that . . . that . . . oh Chrissie! Miss Murphy *died* this evening!" she finally blurted out.

"Oh my *God*! I didn't know. I didn't even know she was *ill*! Jesus Mary I feel *terrible*! Rosie, I can't even remember the last time I gave her a thought! What was it? Where did she die? Was she in hospital, or at home? What? We could have at least gone an seen the old devil, for feck's sake, we owed her *that* much!" But for all her bravado Chrissie's eyes filled with sorrow. "Poor old ma Murphy," she said in a whisper.

She glanced at Rosie as she stood beside her, quietly sobbing into a dainty lace-edged handkerchief. Chrissie gave a deep shuddering sigh and after roughly wiping the tears from her eyes, she linked her arm through Rosie's.

"Come on, Rosie, we don't want to be late for Mass, *especially* tonight," she said resolutely.

The two young women joined other straggling groups, as they made their way down to St Patrick's for the long service. They half-heartedly returned seasonal greetings with their friends and neighbours and blinked furiously as they entered the silent church, their eyes adjusting slowly to the brilliant light from the hundreds of candles that shone so beautifully across the heads of the kneeling congregation. The brightly lit church was already crowded with people and the reunited friends weren't even bothered when they realised that they were too late to get a seat and would have to stand at the back of the church along with all the other late-comers.

"Old ma Murphy would love *this*," Chrissie remarked ruefully. "Having to stand to attention here for an hour and a half."

Rosie gave a tiny sad smile and just nodded in agreement.

"Morning, Chrissie, and a *fine* morning it is, right enough!" The cheerful voice of Billy the post boy greeted Chrissie as she flung open the front door in answer to the urgent knocking.

"A fine morning indeed! Have you looked at the colour of that sky," she disagreed with a scowl.

"Well it's all the finer for having seen you, anyway," he retorted cheekily.

Chrissie laughed shortly and asked him what all the noise was about.

"Well . . . it's like this . . . I have a very important-looking letter here for yourself," he answered, drawing himself up to his full five-foot-six, adding "And it needs to be signed for, too," as he waved the long white envelope in front of her pretty face.

"You're a cheeky young monkey, Billy Doyle, give it here!" Chrissie snatched the envelope from him, frowning at the typewritten address.

"Sign here, please," Billy grinned, handing her a grubby sheet of paper and the stub of a pencil.

"Turn round then," Chrissie demanded.

"Turn round? What for?"

"So I can lean on your back and sign the paper, ya *eegit!*"

"Oh, right-oh."

"Sorry, have to rush. I'll be late for work," she called over her shoulder as she slammed the door quickly on the gap-toothed grin. She knew if Billy had *his* way, he would keep her gassing on the doorstep until she really was late for work.

"What was that, Chrissie?" her mother called from the scullery.

"Just a letter for me, mam. I had to sign for it," she called back.

Maggie came in from the scullery wiping her hands on her damp apron.

"Sign for it, indeed, sounds very official."

"Mmm ... I wonder what this is all about?" Chrissie said, holding the letter up to the light and turning it over and back again.

"Well, you won't know until you open it, will you?" Maggie laughed. "Unless you have X-ray eyes, that is! Come on, don't keep us in suspense."

With a puzzled expression, Chrissie slid a knife along the edge of the envelope and carefully removed the headed notepaper.

Mulligan's Solicitors,
O'Connell St.,
Dublin.

Dear Miss O'Rourke,

We would be most grateful if you would be kind enough to keep an appointment, which has been made for you at this office, with our senior partner, Mr James Mulligan. It has been arranged for Friday the 20th January at 2p.m.

There are certain legal matters we wish to discuss with you at some length and in your own interest we advise that you attend at this time.

Yours sincerely,

Miss A. Reilly (secretary)

"Sweet Jesus!" Chrissie cried. "What the feck's this all about?"

"Chrissie!" How many times do I have to tell you *not* to take the Lord's name in vain and stop that cursing!" Maggie shouted, as she hurriedly blessed herself.

"Oh, I'm sorry, mam, it just came out," Chrissie apologised quickly.

"It always *does*, doesn't it Chrissie! Here, give me that, let me see what's going on," her mother replied hotly as she discarded her apron and sat herself down at the kitchen table holding her hand out for the letter. Chrissie listened, bewildered, as Maggie read the draft aloud.

33

"Well, this sounds *most* important. What on earth do you think it's all about?" her mother asked, just as puzzled as her daughter.

"I've no idea mam, honest! But how can I ask 'Aul Slimy' for time off? We're really busy now, what with all the new spring orders and stuff and I'm suppose to be overseeing all the other girls now. I just won't have *time*."

"But you *must* go, Chrissie, you'll be in trouble if you don't. You can't ignore a letter like this. It could be *anything*." Her mother's worried eyes looked up at Chrissie as she asked quietly, "Have you been up to anything I don't know about, Chrissie?"

"What do you *mean*, mam?" she replied indignantly.

"Oh I don't know, this is all very worrying."

"Oh, don't worry, mam, I'll ask him this morning," Chrissie relented, seeing the nervous expression on the lined face of her mother. "If he says no, I'll just go sick."

As Chrissie rushed panting through the factory gates, catching up with Moira Dowling and her sister Masie, who themselves were always tearing down the road at the last minute, she was thinking of what excuse she could give 'Aul Slimy' for taking time off to keep the appointment in town.

"Hey Chrissie, not like *you* to be late," Moira laughed as Chrissie pushed passed her hoping that she would be in time to clock-on before the factory siren sounded. As luck would have it the girls made it in the nick of time and were sitting at their machines a moment before the factory power was turned on for the day.

"Phew! That was close!" Chrissie sighed with relief as she tied her thick mane of hair back roughly into an untidy knot.

When eleven o'clock finally came and it was time for the ten-minute morning break, Chrissie made her way lightly up the short flight of rickety wooden steps to her boss's office.

"Come in," he boomed, answering the timid rapping on his door.

"Oh it's *you*, Miss O'Rourke. And what can I do for you?" he enquired, the ever-present ogling look in his hooded eyes.

"Well, it's like *this*, Mr Silverstein," she began as sweetly as she could, trying to ignore his lecherous appraisal. "I was wondering if I could possibly have a couple of hours off next Friday afternoon."

"What would *that* be for then, Miss O'Rourke?"

"I have an important appointment that I have to keep in town," she smiled winningly.

"An important appointment, indeed?" he sniggered. "And who would that be with, may I ask? One of your male admirers, could it be?"

"No, it's *not* and you may *not* ask!" she blurted out "It's *private!*"

Realising her ghastly mistake, she opened her mouth to apologise, but snapped it shut immediately when she saw the explosive expression on his face that had turned rapidly from pink to scarlet to purple in rage. As his two fleshy fists came crashing down on to the desk before him and the already messy pile of orders cascaded on to the floor around him, he screamed almost incoherently, "Get out of my office, you cheeky little guttersnipe! How dare you speak to me like that!"

Chrissie jumped back in terror, fearing he would leap across the desk and strike her. But she wasn't about to give in.

"Oh, I'm *sorry*, Mr Silverstein, really I am!" she wheedled. "It's just that I've had a letter from a solicitors' office and *they* made the appointment, not me. I have to go you see, it could land me in a *whole* lot of trouble if I don't!" she pleaded.

"I *said* . . . GET OUT!" he yelled back, pointing a quivering pudgy finger at the door.

"But Mr Silverstein . . . *please*! I'm really sorry, *honest* I am. I'll make up the time and everything, really!!" she implored.

He sucked in a deep breath and slumped back down into his chair. They both glared at each other in silence. "Why should I miss a golden opportunity like this?" he thought to himself. "I could teach this stuck-up little madam a thing or two. Always thinking she's better than everyone around her."

Chrissie really thought that she had gone too far this time. She'd *never* get the time off now. Or even worse, she'd get her marching orders!

Pulling a large blue handkerchief from his pocket, Mr Silverstein slowly wiped the perspiration from his face as he collected his thoughts. Chrissie waited with baited breath, fearing an instant dismissal!

"Very well, Miss O'Rourke, you may take Friday afternoon off . . . but, I want you here an hour extra *every* night next week and all day Saturday to make up for it."

"Oh, Mr Silverstein, thank you! Thank you *so* much! You won't regret it!" Chrissie sighed with relief, eyes wide in amazement and almost unable to believe her good luck. As she turned to leave the office she heard her boss mumble, "Oh, I know I won't regret it, but I think you might, young lady!"

Chrissie stiffened, her hand clasped to the smooth wooden doorknob. She gritted her teeth and turning her head slowly she looked back over her shoulder at the crouching figure of her boss, who was gathering up the fallen papers from the dusty floor. As she screwed her face up in disgust, she thought to herself, "You'll have to catch me first, you dirty old bastard!"

6

Chrissie looked up quickly from the magazine she was pretending to read, as the office door opened.

"Mr Mulligan will see you now, Miss O'Rourke," the solicitor's secretary informed her snootily.

Chrissie placed the copy of *Ireland's Own* neatly back on the table in front of her and rose rather unsteadily to her feet.

"Thank you, Miss Reilly," Chrissie replied politely, but as she passed the haughty woman holding the door open for her, she caught the overpowering smell of 'Evening in Paris'. She couldn't resist sniffing a couple of times as she wrinkled her nose in distaste and whispered, "*Lovely* perfume!"

As the door closed a little too loudly behind her, Chrissie was greeted kindly by Mr Mulligan as he stretched out a welcoming hand to wish her good afternoon.

"Please sit down, Miss O'Rourke," he said in a deep cultured voice. "Well, Miss O'Rourke, I'm sure you are wondering what this is all about?" he beamed at the nervous expression on her face.

"Yes-yes I am."

"Don't look so worried, my dear, I don't *bite!*" he assured her, his eyes twinkling mischievously behind the large horn-rimmed spectacles that sat heavily on his bulbous pink nose. Chrissie giggled softly and sat back into the heavily cushioned chair. She watched him shuffling a small pile of papers in front of him on the wide desk.

"Right. Down to business."

"Right," she said immediately, feeling that this was a man she could trust and feel at ease with.

"I'm sure that you are aware of the recent sad loss of your old schoolteacher, Miss Murphy?"

"Yes I am, but what's that got to do with *me*, Mr Mulligan? Apart from her being my old schoolteacher, that is?"

"It has a great *deal* to do with you, Miss O'Rourke. Now be patient please and I will explain."

"Miss Murphy came to me some years ago to deal with a family matter when her only brother died, and then again more recently when she knew she was gravely ill. You see, she has no other living family now and it was her dearest wish that it should be *you* who would benefit from her will."

"Her *will!*" Chrissie exclaimed loudly. "God Almighty!"

Ignoring the outburst Mr Mulligan continued. "Miss Murphy lived very frugally all her life, in a small house, which she rented here in Dublin, but she was actually the owner of quite a large property that her brother left to her when he himself died years ago. It was a run-down old farmhouse but Mr Murphy, Robert that is, had converted it over the years into a very presentable home. He kept a few sheep and pigs and a small herd of cattle which had brought him in a comfortable enough living, but when he became ill himself he had to sell off all his livestock. When he knew there was really no hope of making a recovery, he wrote to me and asked me to come and visit him so he could get his affairs in order. My own father had been their family solicitor before me, that's how he got in touch with me.

"You see, as Mr Murphy had never married himself, it was quite a simple matter to leave everything to his sister. He knew that she had never wanted to live in the country and much preferred the city, but he thought that maybe she could sell off the old house and buy herself a decent one here in Dublin. But as you see, she didn't ever do that. She told me when her dear brother died, that she would have loved to travel when she was younger, but had never had the chance and now it was too late and apart from that she would never think of leaving her beloved St Brigids."

Chrissie was sitting openmouthed the whole time. For one of the rare moments in her life she was speechless.

"So *now*, Miss O'Rourke, I think you will understand why you are here today," he smiled.

"Well—yes—no—yes," she stammered.

"You are now the proud owner of Ballycross Farm, in the garden of Ireland, county Wicklow."

"A *farm!* I own a *farm?*" Chrissie spluttered, pink-faced.

"Yes, indeed you do, Miss O'Rourke, and not only a farm, you have a tidy sum of money coming to you as well."

"*Money?* What, from Miss Murphy?"

"Of course, Miss Murphy," Mr Mulligan laughed. "Who else have we been talking about?"

Before Chrissie got up the nerve to ask him how much, he happily informed her that she would receive the handsome sum of £500 just as soon as all the necessary papers were signed. Chrissie almost fainted in disbelief. She didn't know whether to laugh or cry.

Mr Mulligan rose from his desk and went to a side table by the tall window and poured a large glass of water. Handing it to Chrissie he patted her lightly on the shoulder saying, "You look a little overcome, my dear. Drink this, you will feel better in a minute. I'm sure this has come as quite a surprise to you, but a *pleasant* one, nevertheless, eh?"

Chrissie gulped at the cool drink. "Mmm."

"So, if you would be kind enough to sign these papers for me. Just there at the bottom of each sheet where I have put a little mark," he indicated.

Chrissie put the heavy crystal glass on to a small mat on the desk and reached out to pull the documents towards her. Mr Mulligan handed her his initialled fountain pen to sign with. Her hand trembled as she signed her name three times, slowly and carefully.

"There now, all done. Let me be the first to congratulate you on your good fortune and if you ever need any advice, please do not hesitate to contact me. Miss Reilly will give you your cheque on the way out and, Miss O'Rourke, if you will take my first piece of advice to you, please deposit it as *soon* as possible in the bank. You can't be too careful, you know. Oh, and I will send you the deeds for your house in a couple of days."

"Thank you, Mr Mulligan, *thank* you!" Chrissie replied in a hushed voice. She smiled faintly as he rose from behind his desk and walked to the door to open it for her.

"Good afternoon, Miss O'Rourke, and good luck."

"Good afternoon, Mr Mulligan.'

"I think you'll be wanting *this*, won't you?" the thin reedy voice of Miss Reilly called out as Chrissie was halfway out of the office door.

"What?"

"I said, I think you'll be wanting *this*!" With pursed lips the solicitor's secretary held the cheque out before her, keeping her eyes averted from Chrissie's bewildered features.

"Oh, yes! yes please!" Chrissie answered, suddenly coming out of her trance-like state. "Thank you."

As Chrissie wound her way back home through the busy streets, still clasping the cheque close to her bosom, she tried to come to terms with her luck. She still couldn't quite believe it. Miss *Murphy*, of all people! This could be the answer to her dreams!

Quickening her pace in her eagerness to get home and tell her mother everything, she fell headlong into the muscular arms of Jimmy Dwyer who was turning the corner of Leason Street, scattering the contents of her bag on to the pavement. As she struggled to keep her balance he gathered her possessively to his broad chest. "Well now, Chrissie O'Rourke. Where are *you* going in such a hurry?" he teased, as he pulled her firmly to her feet.

When she didn't immediately pull away from him, he frowned, suddenly a little embarrassed, and slowly released his firm grip on her.

"Are you all right, Chrissie, you look very strange?" he said, holding her at arm's length.

She let her arms drop from the front of his rough tweed jacket, and coughed, more than a little embarrassed herself.

"I'm *fine*, thanks. You can let *go* now," she mumbled, bending down to pick up her belongings from the street.

"Shouldn't you be at work at this time of the day?" he asked, checking his watch as he bent down to help her retrieve a cracked mirror and a few coins that had spilled from her purse.

"Yes I should, but that's none of your business."

"Ha! Still the same old Chrissie! This must be yours, too."

As he passed her the precious cheque he couldn't help glancing down at it. "Jesus, Chrissie! Five hundred pounds!"

"Give me that, you ignorant pig, it's mine!" Chrissie demanded furiously.

"All right, all right, keep your hair on! I couldn't help but see it! Where d'ya get it anyway?"

"That's none of your business, either! Get out of my *way*! I have to get home!"

As he stepped sideways to let her pass, he couldn't help but think what a great looking young woman she had become. Only a few years since they had left school and look at her now!

"Ouch! Me feckin' ankle's broken!" Chrissie yelled, as she tried to shove passed him.

"Here hold on to me again," he offered, adding with a rueful grin, "just for a minute."

Hopping on one foot she grabbed at his outstretched arm for support. "Oh God! this is *all* I need!" she howled loudly.

"Look Chrissie, there's a bar just down there," Jimmy nodded in the direction of Brady's pub. "Hang on to me and we'll go and sit down for a minute and have a look at the damage."

Grudgingly she agreed and leaned into him as he slipped a strong powerful arm around her small waist, holding on to her a little more tightly than she thought was really necessary. Lowering her gently on to the nearest chair, he knelt before her and tenderly raised the swollen foot.

"What do you think you're doing, Jimmy Dwyer?" she demanded, scowling at his bent head.

"Would you ever stop *yelling*, Chrissie. I'm just trying to see what you have done, OK?" he answered, looking up into the near-tearful face. "Can you move it at all?"

"I don't *know*," she sulked.

"Well try a *bit*, will you!"

"Ooohh! no! It really *hurts*!"

Still holding her painful foot he reached out and pulled a nearby chair closer and placed her leg on it. "I'll get some ice."

Chrissie watched his broad back as he made his way over to the bar. "Shite, why did it have to be him, of all people?" she thought to herself angrily. "Look at the feckin' state of me!"

"Here. Let's wrap this around it for a while." Lifting her leg carefully, he sat opposite her in the chair and placed her foot on his knee and taking the scuffed shoe off he wrapped the bar-towel that he had filled with ice around the swelling.

"Ow!"

"Sorry."

They both sat, somewhat embarrassed now, looking at the offending ankle, not quite sure what to say next. After a long moment Chrissie offered a small, "Thank you."

"That's OK," he grinned cheekily.

The barman came over, smiling, and placed two large brandies on the small table beside them.

"Here," he laughed. "On the house. You look as though you could do with it."

"Thanks, Michael, you're a gent," Jimmy smiled back.

"No bother."

"Here, drink up, Chrissie, it'll help," Jimmy said as he put a glass into Chrissie's shaky hand.

She slowly sipped the burning liquid, trying not to let any expression show on her face as the fiery drink caught her breath. She didn't want Jimmy to think this was the first time she had ever tasted such a drink. The warm feeling in her stomach very quickly became *most* comforting. She took another few sips and then, as she drained her glass, she found that the flavour wasn't so harsh now. In fact she quite liked it.

"Hey, slow down, Chrissie." Jimmy warned. "You won't be able to stand at *all* if you keep that up."

"Don't be such an eegit. I can handle me drink," she laughed confidently.

"Right then. Would you like another?"

"Yeah, why not?"

"Right you are then."

Lowering her foot gently to the floor, he couldn't stop his eyes from lingering for a moment on her shapely leg. Chrissie saw what he was doing and tugged her skirt down from where it had ridden up and said with a mocking grin, "And you can stop that right now!"

As he jumped up in a fluster, Jimmy couldn't resist the temptation and said as loudly as he could, "Sorry about that, but you have the biggest tear in your stockings that I have *ever seen* in me life!"

Chrissie's cheeks flamed in temper as she sat glaring at his back, while he chatted idly for at least ten minutes to a pal of his who had just come in. She watched him as he laughed and joked as though she wasn't there, fuming silently to herself. She couldn't bring herself to look him in the eye as he handed her another drink, still angry at herself for agreeing to come into the bar in the first place.

"Feeling better now?" he asked casually, trying not to look at her either.

"Yes, thank you," she answered just as casually. "Me mam will be worried out of her mind though. I think I'll try and walk on it now. I have to get home."

"Well, at least finish your drink and then we'll try again."

Almost throwing her drink down her throat in her haste to get away from him, she coughed and spluttered noisily, causing him to roar and shake with laughter as he rocked back on his chair, which infuriated her no end.

She stood up so abruptly that she immediately fell back, howling like a banshee, into the chair. Her head was spinning and the pain in her foot was unbearable.

"YOU BASTARD, DWYER!" she screeched, her face purple with fury.

The whole bar looked around as Chrissie's curse reached every corner of the pub. It wasn't anything they hadn't seen or heard before and soon turned away to resume their mumbled conversations.

"Oh, *quite* the lady these days, aren't we?" Jimmy sneered. "And here's me thinking you'd *changed*." Pushing back his chair, Jimmy stood before her and with a stony expression on his handsome face, he bowed mockingly and bade her a "Very good evening."

Chrissie sat in astonishment as she watched the departing figure. She couldn't believe he was just going to *leave* her there! He *couldn't*. He *wouldn't* would he? How the hell was she going to get home?

"Lover's tiff?" Michael asked in mock concern as he collected the empty glasses and wiped the table.

"What? No it's *not*! He's just an ignorant *pig*!" Chrissie retorted.

"How's the foot anyway? Have ye far to go?"

"It's *fine*, thanks," she answered ungraciously, unwrapping the sodden towel and prodding the red patch on the side of her ankle. "Look. I think it has gone down a bit."

"Well, it doesn't look too good to me. Would you like me to get one of the lads to give you a lift home?" he asked, nodding over to the group of lads in the corner.

"No, no, I'll be OK. If you could just give me your arm while I stand up and put me shoe back on. I'll be OK, thanks."

Her head was still spinning and she felt decidedly *sick* as she muttered goodbye to the barman and bravely hobbled along the street, holding on to the wall. She made very slow progress under

the inquisitive stares from passers-by. Feeling nauseous and humiliated, she eventually reached the end of her street and was worried
about what she would say to her mother. (With luck she wouldn't
be able to smell the drink on her, otherwise she would be in for a
hell of a lecture!) Still, as soon as she heard the good news from
the solicitor it would take her mind off it, Chrissie thought hopefully. Taking a deep breath and with great effort she straightened
herself up, smiled brightly and knocked on the front door.

Mrs O'Rourke had been waiting anxiously for hours and opened
the door quickly.

"Oh, thank *God*, Chrissie. I thought something had happened
to you. Where have you *been* all this time?"

"Well, I'm *here* now, mam, and I have some great news for you!
You're not going to *believe* what happened at the solicitors'!" She
answered as gaily as she could.

"What are you standing there for, my girl? Come on in, for
goodness sake, and tell me!"

As her mother led the way along the dimly lit hallway, Chrissie
grimaced painfully as she hobbled behind trying with all her might
to walk as though there was nothing wrong, but as they went into
the kitchen her mother turned around frowning. "What's that
smell?"

"What smell, mam?" Chrissie asked innocently.

"Chrissie! Have you been *drinking*?"

"Erm . . . er . . . I . . . I . . ."

"Now don't you lie to me, young lady! That's alcohol I can
smell, and seeing that *I* haven't touched a drop for years, then it
must be *you*, mustn't it?" her mother said angrily as she glared at
the guilty expression on her daughter's face.

Chrissie dropped on to the chair.

"Yes! Yes, I have had a drink, mam, but I had a good reason!
Look at me foot! I bumped into someone when I was rushing
home from the solicitors' office and I twisted it! And Jesus it's
killing me!"

"Chrissie!"

"Sorry, mam . . . but I couldn't walk and he offered to help me
and he took me into a bar and gave me a brandy to help the pain
and put ice and everything on it!" she rushed on, trying to placate
her mother.

"*Who* took you into a bar?" her mother demanded.

"Jimmy Dwyer."

"Dwyer! Huh!" Maggie snorted, as she looked down at the pained face. (She couldn't remember the last time she'd seen Jimmy at Mass and she wasn't even sure that he was working.) "Let me have a look, then."

Maggie soon had the sore ankle neatly bandaged in a clean damp cloth and as she secured it at the side with a tiny gold safety pin she said, "You better tell me what the solicitor had to say, then."

Over a welcome cup of tea and a couple of aspirin, Chrissie told her mother the news. Maggie sat with her arms folded, staring intently across the table at her daughter. Her tea went untouched as she listened silently, not really believing what she was hearing.

"Look, mam, if you don't believe me!" Chrissie cried, as she fished around in her bag for the cheque. "Where the feck is it?"

"Chrissie!"

"Sorry, mam!"

"Oh *noooo!*" she wailed. "I can't find it! Oh *noooo!*"

She tipped the contents of her bag on to the kitchen table and rummaged through the odds and ends in panic. "Oh mam, I don't believe it! It's not here! I've *lost* it!"

She burst into floods of tears and Maggie sprang up from her seat and put her arms around the quivering shoulders.

"Now, now, Chrissie, don't be upsetting yourself," she consoled. "Someone will find it and probably hand it in to the bank or something. It's no good to anyone, if it's got your name on it now, is it? It *has* got your name on it, hasn't it, Chrissie? This cheque of yours! It's not just one of your little *dreams*, is it?" She tried to joke.

"Yes, it's *mine* all right," Chrissie replied despondently. "What am I going to do now?"

Just then, they heard a loud rapping on the front door.

"Drink your tea up, there's a good girl, and I'll see who that is."

"Good evening, Mrs O'Rourke. I was wondering if Chrissie is home yet?" Jimmy smiled.

"Yes, yes, she's here. What is it you want with her, may I ask?"

Jimmy was a little taken aback by the abrupt reply, but continued politely, "Well, it's just that she dropped something this afternoon and I just came around to give it back to her. I'm sorry,

I must have put it in my pocket by mistake and I thought she would be worried about it. It's worth quite a bit to her!" He smiled knowingly.

"Oh, I see," Maggie said quietly, as she realised that it could only be the cheque that he was trying to return, when she saw the folded paper in his hand.

"Who is it, mam?" Chrissie called from the back of the house, wondering why her mother was taking so long to answer the door.

"I *suppose* you'd better come in."

"After you, Mrs O'Rourke."

As Jimmy's large frame filled the doorway, Chrissie looked up in surprise.

"Oh no, not you *again!*" she blurted out rudely. "What do you *want?*"

"Charming as ever!"

"Jimmy has just come to return something to you, Chrissie," her mother intervened quickly, as she saw the colour rising in her daughter's cheeks.

"I thought you might need this," he said straightfaced as he held the cheque stiffly before her.

"Oh *Jimmy*! You *angel*! Thanks, thanks a million!" she gushed profusely, only just managing to stop herself from throwing herself into his arms.

He threw back his handsome head and laughed loudly. "Well, that's an improvement from earlier on!"

"Oh I'm *sorry*, really I *am*," she went on. "It's just that I was in terrible pain and what with the drink and everything . . ."

Her mother looked sternly at her and then at Jimmy. "Well, enough said about *that*, I think!" adding quickly, "Would you like a cup of tea?"

"No thanks, Mrs O'Rourke. Me mam will have the dinner ready and you know what she's like if I don't get home on time? I'd better be off. I hope your foot'll be OK Chrissie."

"Thanks."

"See you then!"

"Yeah, bye, and thanks again!" she smiled shyly up at him.

7

After she'd given the young ones a hurried early supper, washed them and tucked them up for the night, Maggie sat down gratefully with Chrissie beside the small fire in the parlour, exhausted by the day's events.

Chrissie was feeling a lot better now and after having a few prods at her ankle, when her mother wasn't looking, was pleased to see that the swelling had gone down and that the pain wasn't half so bad. The thumping in her head was beginning to clear, too. They chatted for hours about Chrissie's good fortune, still not really able to take it all in as they tried to decide what would be the best thing to do.

"We could go down to Wicklow, mam, and take a look at the old house, couldn't we? If you liked it you could all move down there to live. It would be great, wouldn't it? Get away from *this* place. All that fresh air for you and the little ones." Chrissie rambled on excitedly,

"What do you *mean*, Chrissie, for me and the little ones?" her mother asked, a little concerned.

"Well, mam . . . I been doing a lot of thinking." She wasn't quite sure how to put it, but finally blurted out. "I have enough money *now* to go to England!"

"Oh Chrissie, not that again! I thought you had given up on that years ago!"

"Oh *no* mam! *Never*! I have been thinking about it for as long as I can remember."

"But what about your *job*? You've been doing real well there. You're even supervising the girls now and at your age that's a *great* achievement." Maggie tried to persuade her. "You could be running the place in a few years."

"Yes I know, but it's not what I want. I just can't spend my life working for a devil like Aul Slimy! I can't *stand much* more of him. Oh the work's OK and the girls aren't a bad bunch, but I know I could do better for myself. Please mam, Don't make it *hard* for me!" she begged.

"Make it *hard* for you indeed!" Maggie cried. "I'm only trying to protect you, Chrissie – from *yourself*, mostly!"

"But I'd be fine, honest, mam. I have enough money for the fare now and to find a place to rent. I'd *easy* get a job over there, you know that. I'd *always* write to you and even come back and see you all. Do you think I would forget about you all? Surely not!"

Maggie sat silently gazing into the flickering flames. She knew deep down that she should let Chrissie go and try to make her own way. Her daughter had an ambition about her that she had never really understood and she supposed that maybe she was just being a little selfish in trying to stop her; but she was so young. The house in the country *did* sound good and would be a great life for the rest of her children. Healthy and safe and indeed it would give her lazy younger daughter Margaret no excuses for not doing her fair share around the place, if Chrissie wasn't there. She knew Chrissie would *never* lose touch with them. She was a good girl at heart and had never really let her down.

Chrissie watched her mother nervously, as she sat thinking.

"Oh *please* God! Make her see what an opportunity this would be for me," she prayed.

After a long while Maggie looked up at her daughter's anxious face.

"Shall we take one step at a time, Chrissie?"

"Whatever you say, mam," Chrissie replied hopefully.

"I think we should go and take a good look at this 'Ballycross Farm' and then we'll see."

"Oh, mam, thank you!" Chrissie nearly knocked her mother off the chair as she fell on her, hugging her tightly.

"I haven't said *yes* yet, young lady, so don't get too excited!" Maggie said, with a small smile.

"We could take the bus down and have a look!" Chrissie suggested excitedly. "But I'll have to telephone Mr Mulligan on Monday to find out exactly where it is."

"Well yes, I suppose we *could* Chrissie, but don't forget you have to go to the bank with your cheque first. The workman's bus leaves for Wicklow at seven in the morning and we could get the evening bus back, but I will have to ask Moira next door if she will get the children to school and if she will give them a bit of tea for me."

"Course she will, mam, you've done *her* enough favours in the past!" Chrissie's mind was racing now.

"I'll see her after Mass on Sunday and ask her, but Chrissie, just one thing—"

"What's that, mam?"

"I don't want you to say anything to the others until we're sure about everything, all right? I don't want them spreading it around the street. You know people can get a bit funny sometimes."

"No, you're right, we won't say a word, and it will be a great surprise for them."

"Chrissie, please, nothing's settled yet! Anyway, look at the time," she said, glancing up at the old clock on the mantelpiece above the fire as it gave out its sweet chimes announcing midnight. "You'll have to get word to Mr Silverstein about your ankle or there'll be trouble from him, no doubt!"

"Oh, don't worry about *him*," she scorned (he can stick his job where the sun doesn't shine, she thought to herself). "I'll send our Patrick down to Annie Duffy with a message and she can tell him on Monday morning and then we can go into town about the bank business and we could get the bus down to Wicklow on Tuesday."

"Right, my girl. Off to bed with you, then."

Maggie helped Chrissie to her feet and was relieved to see that she was almost able to walk on her own. "The foot seems a bit better, Chrissie."

"Yes, yes it does, mam, thank God, but I'm so tired I could sleep for a week."

After making the telephone call to the solicitor's from the bread shop a couple of doors down, Chrissie came back home happily to tell her mother that it seemed that 'Ballycross Farm' was just outside Annamore village and was on the bus route. After that she went proudly down to the bank in O'Connell Street with her precious cheque and opened her first ever account. The pain in her ankle was completely gone.

The early morning journey down to the country was a slow, bumpy ride on the hard wooden seats of the old bus, but neither of them seemed bothered as they passed through villages and towns they had never seen before, eagerly taking in the fresh sights and sounds of the country. It was years since Maggie had left Dublin and she was quite excited herself at the unexpected trip.

"Look, mam, there's the sign for Glendalough!" Chrissie pointed out. "We can't be too far now. Mr Mulligan said Annamore was only about half an hour before there."

"Oh, *yes*, I can see it too," her mother smiled. "What are you doing?"

"I'm just going up to ask the driver how long more we will be."

"Don't be mithering him, Chrissie."

"It's all right mam. Don't worry, he won't mind.'

She chatted and laughed for ten minutes with the red-faced chain-smoking driver, clinging perilously on to the back of his seat as the bus wound its way up and down the narrow stony roads, swinging around sharp bends. Returning to her seat, Chrissie was pleased to inform her mother that he would be giving them a shout in about fifteen minutes.

After telling the driver they would be waiting here for him to catch the evening bus later on, they waved a cheery goodbye and watched as the bus swayed around the corner of a whitewashed cottage and over the old bridge and on towards Glendalough.

The air around them was fresh and pure and filled with the delightfully pretty sounds of birds and trickling water and the soft morning breeze carried on it the faint smell of wood smoke and heather. Through the high branches of the thick hedges and tall trees that lined the narrow road, the dappled light fell gently across them and they could see the pale blue of the sky that was becoming clearer and brighter by the minute.

"Oh, mam, it's *beautiful*!" Chrissie sighed.

"Yes, Chrissie, it really is."

"Well, I suppose we'd better find the lane that goes up to the farm," Chrissie said, looking around her. "It can't be far from here. Will we go and knock on that cottage door over there? I can't see anyone else around, can you, mam?" Maggie could only hear the distant sound of a tractor, but had to agree that was the best idea.

Chrissie tapped gently on the low door of the cottage, not wishing to disturb the peace of the place, but after waiting several minutes knocked a little louder. The door opened very slowly and all they could see was a pair of very small blue eyes in a very round pink face peering out at them suspiciously. "Yes?" the soft voice enquired.

"I'm sorry to bother you, but we were wondering if you could please tell us the way to 'Ballycross Farm'?" Chrissie asked.

The door opened wider to reveal the stooping figure of an old lady. She glanced silently back and forth at the strangers as if a little afraid to answer the girl.

"You see, we have come down from Dublin on the bus and we're not sure which road to take now," Chrissie explained, realising the woman was unsure of them.

"There's nobody up there.'

"No, we *know* that."

"Well, what do you want to go up there for?"

"We just want to have a *look* at it." Chrissie was getting a little impatient now.

Maggie stepped forward and held out her hand.

"Good morning, missus. My name is Maggie O'Rourke and this is my daughter Chrissie. We're *sorry* to be bothering you, but we really *do* have to get to the farm today, so if you would be kind enough to point it out we will be on our away."

"From Dublin you say?"

"Yes, that's right," Chrissie said.

"And you want to know the way to 'Ballycross'?"

"Yes, yes we do!"

The old woman ignored Chrissie's indignant stare and looking at Maggie said, "You'd be wanting a cup of tea first then, I expect?" Without waiting for an answer she opened the door wider and walked back into the house leaning heavily on a knobbly walking stick. "Come in," she called over her shoulder. Chrissie looked at her mother and they both giggled. "Come on mam, I could *murder* a cup of tea!"

"So could *I*!"

They followed the old woman through to the back of the house to the small kitchen and were surprised to see how neat and clean the whole place was.

"Do you live here on your own?" Chrissie couldn't help asking.

"No. My grandson John is here with me. The only one left now. He's up in the top field with the tractor since early morning. He's a good lad, stayed with me when all the others went off to England." She took a rather battered-looking tin jug from a hook over the fireplace, dipped it into a bucket of water on the floor

51

and carefully transferred it to the huge black kettle that hung on a long hook over the fire in the hearth.

"Sit down for a minute, will you?" she indicated to Maggie.

"Yes thank you. We're very grateful," Maggie replied as she sat down on the small settle by the fireplace. Chrissie noticed several other large black pots that hung over the fire on hooks as she sat herself down on a little stool by a neat pile of logs.

"Do you do all your cooking over the fire?" she asked, amazed, thinking how hot it must be in the small house in the summer months.

"You're a very inquisitive young one!"

"I'm sorry," Chrissie blushed.

"Well, yes I do. Can't be bothered with all those new fangled gadgets! We manage well enough!"

Maggie watched her, thinking of her own mother so many years ago.

While the kettle was sizzling away, the old woman busied herself getting cups and saucers from the dresser. Chrissie went over to help her.

"Here, let me put those out for you."

"Thanks."

"Is the farm far from here?" Maggie ventured politely as they sipped the strong tea.

"No, not at all. It's only a short walk up Darragh Lane," she replied. "You just go up the road about two minutes past the style over the way and you'll find it, but I did tell you, no one's there now. What would you be wanting to go there for anyway?" Maggie thought the woman deserved an explanation after her hospitality and told her briefly the story behind their visit.

"Ah, so *that's* it! Well I don't know what state it's in now, no one's been near it for years. It was a grand little place before poor old Bob passed away, may his soul rest in peace," she said sadly, blessing herself.

"I think we'd better make our way up there then, don't you, mam?" Chrissie said, as she fidgeted on the small stool trying to catch her mother's eye.

"Let your mother finish her tea and don't be so impatient!"

Chrissie kept silent, not wishing to upset the woman. Maggie drained her cup and stood up to take Chrissie's cup over to the small table in the corner, which was obviously used to do the washing-up.

"Let me help you with these first, missus."

"No, you all right. I can manage, thank you, and me name is Grady, Eileen Grady."

"Well, thank you so much Mrs Grady for the tea, we really appreciated it, didn't we, Chrissie?"

"Oh yes, it was lovely!" Chrissie enthused, only too happy now that they were soon to be on their way.

As they went out once again into the beautiful morning air, Mrs Grady said her farewell to them and told them they would be more than welcome to come in and wait for the evening bus when they were finished their business up at the farm. They thanked her profusely and said they wouldn't *dream* of going home without saying goodbye to her (knowing, of course, that she would be anxious to hear all the gossip!).

Ballycross farm was easy to find and after a short climb up the steep and winding overgrown lane, they came to a four-bar gate that stood slightly open. Chrissie shoved hard to push it wide, trying to free it from the clumps of grass and weeds that had grown up between the bars.

"Be careful, Chrissie, it doesn't look too strong!"

"There, that's got it," Chrissie panted, as the gate flew back against the crooked post with a splintering crunch.

"Come on, mam, here we are!" She tugged at her mother's sleeve impatiently.

"Goodness, Chrissie, let me get me *breath*, will you?" Maggie laughed, but Chrissie had already run ahead past the side of the cottage and into the small yard.

Chrissie held on to her mother's arm and they stood together, silently surveying the forlorn looking house before them. The once whitewashed stone walls of the low building were *hideously* discoloured with dirty green slimy patches and the two windows on either side of the front door were thick with grime and cobwebs and, like the door, the brown paint on the window frames had almost gone and what was left was hanging in dry flakes. The weeds and brambles that climbed thickly and coarsely up the walls looked about to cover the whole house.

"Well, the roofs good, anyway!" Chrissie said cheerfully, as she saw the doubtful expression on her mother's face. "Apart from the bird's nests, that is," she added, pointing up at the straggling chunks of straw and twigs that were wedged under the edges of the corrugated-iron roof. "Shall we go inside, mam, and have a look?"

Maggie shook her head; "Oh, Chrissie, I don't know . . . if it's like this on the *outside* what on earth is it going to be like on the *inside*?" she said frowning. "And how will we get in anyway?" She suddenly realised they hadn't even thought of that!

"It's OK, nobody locks their doors in the country, mam!" Chrissie replied, full of confidence. She looked around the untidy yard until she spotted a thick piece of a branch, half hidden under a pile of rotting leaves and manure.

"Here, this'll do."

She tugged it free and began to struggle with the brambles around the door, knocking them roughly to the ground and trampling on them till they were almost flattened. It didn't take long to clear a small patch and she pushed and pulled on the old door handle, laughing happily when it gave way without much trouble at all. She didn't even notice the scratches that covered her legs and the long rip on the skirt of her pink floral dress.

As their eyes gradually became accustomed to the gloomy interior of the house, they cautiously explored the dark, damp rooms and Maggie wondered just how long it would take to get the place in *any* sort of order at *all.* (If she decided to live there, that was!) As they peered around, their eyes gradually became accustomed to the gloom. It seemed that the place was full of good, solid furniture.

"It doesn't look like anything's gone out of here at all, Chrissie," Maggie remarked in surprise. "Look, there's even a dresser full of Delft."

Everything was just as Bob Murphy had left it so long ago, when he went into hospital for the last time. Thinking that his sister might change her mind and come and live in the country after all, he left all his belongings as they were. Of course, this was some years ago and most of the stuff was quite old fashioned, but Maggie could see that under the heavy coating of dust and what looked like mice-droppings the damp furniture was still in very good condition.

"I can't *believe* it, mam . . . you wouldn't have to buy anything at all for the place."

"Well, I don't think anyone would be sleeping on *those* beds!" Maggie said, disgusted at the thought.

"Oh I don't mean the *beds*, mam," Chrissie scorned, wrinkling her nose. "They're woeful old things. And they stink with the mould on them!"

They went back outside into the welcome daylight, and picked their way around the messy yard and found a well in the corner. From a gap in the densely overgrown hedge, where a partially hidden gate hung on one rusty hinge, they gazed across the wide open countryside.

"Look, mam, you can see the 'Sugar Loaf' from here!" Chrissie cried excitedly. "I've seen it in pictures. That must be it and there, look beyond, it's beautiful!" as she pointed out the majestic out-lines of the Wicklow Mountains, which stood proudly against the misty blue of the morning sky.

"They surely are a sight for sore eyes!" her mother agreed wholeheartedly.

After walking around the house exploring each corner, they wandered back over to the well.

"At least there's fresh water," Maggie said thoughtfully.

Chrissie leaned carefully over the edge of the moss-covered stones surrounding the well and dropped a small pebble over the side and waited for the 'plink' as it reached the water level.

"Ooh, it's quite deep, mam."

"Don't worry how *deep* it is, as long as it's clean and fresh, we'll manage."

Chrissie turned slowly to her mother, her eyes sparkling.

"Does this mean what I *think* it means?" she asked quietly.

"Mmmm ... maybe it could," Maggie answered, as she walked back to the cottage and stood thinking.

Chrissie held back and waited, with baited breath, for her mother's decision. She watched as Maggie paced slowly back and forth, deep in thought. As she sat herself down on a rusty upturned bucket, Chrissie prayed as she had never prayed before. When Chrissie was almost fit to burst, Maggie turned around and looked into the anxious face of her beloved daughter and said, "All right Chrissie, I *will* bring the children down here to live. I think between us, we could make this a grand little place."

"Oh, mam! Thank *God*! I thought you were going to say it would be too much for you! Oh that's great! Great!" Chrissie almost screamed in delight as she grabbed her mother in a tight embrace.

"Now, calm down, will you child! There's a *lot* to be sorted out before anything happens!"

"Oh, I know mam, I know, but I'll help you, you know that! I can pay for all the moving and everything and help you clean the place up. We can get rid of all these weeds and rubbish and we can burn those horrible old beds and paint the walls and scrub the floors. We could drag all that awful filthy furniture outside into the sun and give it a good clean and polish." Chrissie raced on, her eyes sparkling, not stopping to take a breath.

Maggie's face flushed with pleasure as she was caught up in her daughter's enthusiasm. "Come on, Chrissie, let's have a think, shall we?"

They linked arms and walked slowly back down the lane to the road, making plans for the future.

"Let's go and ask Mrs Grady if there's any where we could get a bite to eat," Chrissie suggested. "I'm starving and we've hours to wait for the bus yet."

"Well there's not a lot around here, I don't think," Maggie replied doubtfully as she gazed up and down the quiet road.

Just then, they heard the noisy rattling of an engine. As it turned the bend in the road they saw the tractor and stood as far back as they could on the grass verge to let it pass, and waved back to the cheery, curly-headed, fresh-faced driver.

"Morning, ladies," he called loudly over the noise of the old motor. They watched as he made his way down the side of Mrs Grady's cottage.

"That must be John," Chrissie commented, thinking what a handsome specimen he was. She had taken in the bright corn-coloured hair, the sparkling blue eyes and healthy glow of his skin, not to mention the broad muscular back and shoulders, all in one glance.

As he leapt down from his high seat, John glanced across once more at the two figures watching him and wondered who they were. The young one was a pretty as a picture, he thought.

"You're looking a bit lost, ladies," he called out with a winning smile on his healthy face. "Can I help you at all?"

In two or three long strides he crossed the road.

Chrissie looked up into his handsome face and smiled back.

"No thanks, we're grand. We're just going to see Mrs Grady."

"Oh? That's me Grannie!"

"You must be John then?" Maggie said, holding her hand out to introduce herself. "I'm Mrs O'Rourke and this is my daughter Chrissie. We met your grandmother earlier."

John Grady shook hands with Maggie and then Chrissie. Chrissie felt herself blushing furiously as his solid hand firmly covered hers, for a long moment, in a warm greeting.

"Well it's great to meet you," he replied, a little bemused and wondering what this was all about. "Come on in," he invited. They followed him around to the back of the cottage and waited while he shook his clay-covered boots off and then followed him into the small kitchen, where Mrs Grady was stirring away at a large black pot over the fire.

"We have some visitors, Grannie!" John said, bending to give his grandmother a peck on the cheek.

"Ah, I was wondering how you were doing. Come on in and have a seat. I put a bit extra on for you," she said without looking up.

"Oh no, really we couldn't," Maggie answered. "We couldn't be putting you to all that trouble."

Chrissie gasped and shot her mother a quick glance, fearing that she was about to refuse the meal. Her mouth had been watering from the moment they entered the house and she could swear they could all hear her stomach rumbling. Eileen Grady caught the expression on the pretty girl's face and chuckled to herself.

"It's no bother at all," she said kindly. "Put out some more dishes, will you, John love?"

As John pulled out the old circular table to make room for another couple of chairs that he'd brought in from the front parlour, Chrissie's eyes never left his tall rugged figure.

"There we are, ladies," he said. "Make yourselves at home."

"Thank you," Maggie and Chrissie replied in unison.

While they ate the delicious broth, Maggie explained to John the circumstances that had brought her and her daughter there that day. Feeling as though they had all known each other for years they chatted comfortably for a long while and Chrissie found that she was rather disappointed when John rose from the table and declared that he had better be getting back to work.

"Thanks, Grannie, that was great . . . as usual!" he said cheerily, adding "And it was great to meet you," as he looked down into the soft velvet of Chrissie's eyes.

He shook hands with Maggie and said; "So, it looks like we're going to be neighbours!"

"Yes, yes, it *does*," Maggie replied, nodding her head in agreement.

"You'd better be off then, John, or you'll be up in the top field until dark again like last night," Eileen Grady reminded her grandson.

"It's OK, Grannie, I'm not afraid of the bogey man!" He laughed in reply.

As they all said their goodbyes, Mrs Grady added, "I think you'll have time for another cup of tea and a bit a cake before the bus comes."

"Oh, that would be lovely," Maggie replied, thinking what warm and friendly people Mrs Grady and her grandson were. It would be a real boon to have neighbours like them.

Her heart still fluttering a little Chrissie listened intently to the sound of the old engine fading into the distance. The hours had passed very quickly as they sat and chatted like old friends.

"Will we wait outside for the bus, Maggie?" Eileen asked as they finished washing the dishes. "It should be along in a few minutes and it's always on time these days." The three women stood outside the cottage and Maggie thanked Eileen warmly for her kindness and told her she was looking forward to bringing her family down to the country soon and introducing them to her. "Oh! I'm sure they're a grand little bunch, if *you* two are anything to go by," Mrs Grady assured her new friend with a smile. "It'll be *great* to have a bit of life around here again!"

"Oh, here's the bus now," Chrissie said, as the bus came into sight, swaying slightly as it crossed the little bridge.

"Well, God bless you both now and safe journey," Eileen Grady said as the driver opened the door for them. "The same to you, Eileen, and thank you again for all your kindness today," Maggie replied.

"Yes . . . thank you Mrs Grady," Chrissie added, stepping up lightly on to the small uneven platform behind her mother.

They took their places as the back of the bus, and watched the little figure of Eileen Grady as she waved her farewell, until the bus was out of sight. "Well, Chrissie, I think we're going to be all right, don't you?" Chrissie was silent. "Chrissie! did you hear me?" she added, nudging her gently. Chrissie was staring out of the window, lost in her own thoughts. "Sorry, mam, what did you say?" she said, turning her head.

"I said, I think everything will be fine, don't you?"

"Oh, it will be *great*, mam," Chrissie answered with feeling. "The kids will love it there! So much space to run around and John was telling me that there is a grand little school and a church over in the next village that you can all can easily walk to and there's a van that brings groceries every week and he said that you can get milk and eggs from him every day and there's always someone who can give you a lift if you ever want to go into town!"

Maggie sighed deeply. She had hoped that after today her daughter might have changed her mind about England, but it didn't seem as though that was to be. She had watched her and John Grady chatting and the looks that had passed between them, and had felt sure a little spark was developing between them. She had hoped it would be enough, by some small miracle, to make Chrissie have second thoughts. He was a strong, hardworking and handsome lad, who obviously thought the world of his grand-mother and their home. Just the sort of lad she would have loved for Chrissie. She looked at the thick waves of shiny chestnut hair that hung loosely around her daughter's shoulders half covering her pretty face, and reached over and squeezed her daughter's hand softly. As Chrissie turned, they smiled a little wistfully at one another and Maggie said tenderly; "It's all right Chrissie, I under-stand, I really *do!*"

"Thanks, mam," Chrissie answered quietly, quickly turning to gaze blindly out of the window before her mother could see the little tear that had just escaped from the corner of her eye, "Thanks."

8

"That's right, Mr Silverstein, I think you heard me the first time! I'm giving you more than a week's notice and you're lucky to get *that*!" Chrissie shouted into the flabbergasted purple face, as she stood, hands on hips, defiantly in front of her dumbfounded boss.

"How *dare* you speak to me like that, you young *tramp*!" he screamed back at her.

"I can talk to you any way I want to, Mr Silverstein," she sneered, "And if it wasn't for those girls out there and the mess I'd be leaving them in," she added, throwing a glance through the small glass window that overlooked the floor of the factory, "believe me . . . I'd walk out NOW!"

Mr Silverstein tried desperately to compose himself and he glared back in rage. Who the hell did this little bitch think she was! Through gritted teeth he finally managed to utter; "So what do you think you're going to do with yourself then, Miss high and mighty!"

"That's none of your damn business," Chrissie replied calmly examining her fingernails and relishing every moment of her long awaited glory. "Anyway, I'd better get on with my work. I have a basket-full to finish before Friday . . . Payday!"

As she turned on her heel to leave the office, Mr Silverstein jumped from the chair, completely beside himself in anger. He sent the heavy chair crashing to the ground and when he saw the superior smile on Chrissie's face he could stand it no longer and yelled savagely, "So you've found a job for yourself down on the docks at last then have you, where you belong? *with the rest of the old tarts?*"

Chrissie turned quietly and walked steadily back to stand in front of him. Mr Silverstein was panting loudly as he leant heavily on the wide desk for support. Chrissie saw with disgust, the thick blobs of saliva that dribbled messily from the foaming mouth, the bulging eyes with pink specks and the blotchy red and purple skin. She leaned over as close as she could bear to the open-mouthed ugly face and said slowly and clearly. "Well, *you* would certainly know about 'old tarts', wouldn't you, sir? You've paid enough of *them* in your time!"

Chrissie watched the changing expression on his horrified face with sheer glee. She thought at one point he was about to have a heart attack!

"WWWHAT!"

"I think your hearing is going, Mr Silverstein! Or do you think that none of us out there know what you get up to on Saturday nights?" she spat back spitefully.

This time Chrissie really did think he was going to have a seizure! Almost apoplectic he clutched at his chest, desperately trying to catch his breath. His red-veined eyes were stretched wide with shock and horror. There was an animal-like growl coming from his choking throat.

"And do you really believe that none of us have guessed who's the father of that unfortunate child that poor little Josephine Kelly has in her belly?" she screamed mercilessly.

As the gasping figure began to tremble and sway, Chrissie quickly ran around to the other side of the desk and hauled the heavy chair upright and shoved Mr Silverstein roughly back into it. "There you are, sir, nice and *comfortable*. We don't want you to be taken ill or anything, do we now? What *would* Mrs Silverstein do I wonder? Would you like me to get you a drink of water or something, sir? You look *dreadful* pale!"

Chrissie was delighting in every moment of her triumph. As she poured half a tumbler of water from a small jug on the cluttered table, she watched the defeated, slumped form through her lowered lashes with a tight smile on her flushed face.

"There you are, Mr Silverstein," she said sweetly, as she thumped the glass down on to a crooked pile of papers in front of him.

"*Th – th* – thanks," he stuttered, almost inaudibly.

"Well, I really *must* be getting back to work now. The girls will be wondering what we've been up to up here, won't they, sir? And we don't want to give them any funny ideas, do we?" Chrissie jeered as she turned to leave. Just as she was about to slam the door in a final act of defiance, she heard a mumbled, "Wait . . . just a moment." "Yes?" she said, turning her pretty head. "Close the door and come back here . . . please."

"What do you want?" Chrissie asked harshly, as she stood glaring

61

down at him. "Ahem!" he coughed nervously. "What you said about— Mrs Silverstein. You wouldn't *em, em,* you would'nt . . . er?"

"What? . . . Wouldn't *what?* Tell her about all your filthy goings on? Ha! What do you think?"

"Please, Miss O'Rourke, you wouldn't, would you? It would destroy me! I have a family to think of . . . neighbours . . . not to mention the business . . . Oh God!" he sobbed.

Chrissie watched his bent head in disgust. "Huh! Well, it would be more than you deserve, that's for sure after what you've put all those poor girls through for so long. And God knows what diseases you've brought home to that poor woman of yours. Jesus! She must be a bloody *saint* to have put up with you for so long!"

"Pleeeaase . . . Miss O'Rourke," he begged.

"Well, let's put it this way, Mr Silverstein. It's for me to *know* and for you to *wonder!*" she sneered. "Oh, and I think I've just changed my mind about the week's notice! I'm leaving *now!* You can get my wages and my holiday pay made up and I'll send my *sister* down tomorrow to collect it. I don't think I could bear to see that pathetic face for another minute! Oh! And *another* thing. If I hear that you have dared to give my sister even *one* dirty glance I'll come back and break YOUR FAT FECKIN NECK!"

It took no time at all for the O'Rourke's good fortune to spread around the neighbourhood, due to the fact that Chrissie could contain herself no longer than a couple of days! She couldn't *wait* to tell Rosie all her news and arrived early one morning flushed and excited in Mary Flannagan's kitchen, bursting with enthusiasm with all her plans for the future.

"Well, God bless us and save us!" Mary exclaimed, clapping her hands in delight. "No one deserves it more than your poor mother! But are you *sure* about this England thing, Chrissie? Wouldn't you rather go down to the country with the rest of the family? Your mother's not as young and healthy as she used to be you know, and I'm certain she could do with the help!"

"Oh, *yes,* Mary! I'm sure all right!" Chrissie smiled.

Daisy sat watching the two of them chatting and as she nibbled slowly on a chunk of thickly buttered warm soda bread, she began to feel very homesick. She hadn't thought about home for a long time now, apart from when she read the few and far between short letters her mother had scribbled from time to time.

"Sorry, Daisy, what did you say?" Chrissie turned her sparkling eyes on the young girl across the table.

"Oh, I just wondered Chrissie, when are you going?" she asked timidly.

"As soon as I can, Daisy, just as *soon* as I can!" came the determined reply.

"Well, I was just thinking," she hesitated shyly. "Would, *em*— Would you take *me* with you?"

"Oh, Daisy love, what are you saying!" Mary cried in alarm. "I thought you were happy *here*!"

"Oh, I *am*, aunty! Really! But I just thought . . . well, it's been so *long* now . . . I just thought if Chrissie would take me with her . . ." she trailed off.

Mary's face crumpled as she fought back the tears. She had always known this day would come, but had never really prepared herself for it. They had become very close over the years and she had watched Daisy grow from a pale gawky young child into a pretty and confident girl, and she knew in her heart it would be a tough parting when the day finally arrived for her to return to England.

"I'd better get the kettle on. Rosie will be down for her break in a few minutes and she's in for a *real* surprise now, isn't she?" Mary forced a smile through her misty eyes.

Chrissie looked at the downcast face and felt sorry for young Daisy. "Do you *really* want to go home, Daisy?" she asked kindly.

"Well. I hadn't thought about it so much before now, Chrissie . . . but I think I *would* like to see me mam and dad again . . . and everyone . . . it's been such a long time."

At that moment the kitchen door opened and Rosie gasped in surprise at the unexpected visitor.

"Oh! Chrissie! How lovely to see you! You look *great*!" she cried happily as Chrissie rose quickly from the table to give her a tight hug.

"And it's great to see *you* too!" She replied, holding her friend at arm's length, adding admiringly "and just look at you!" Rosie blushed prettily as her dainty hands smoothed her already neat and glossy hair that was caught up in an elegant roll.

"What are you doing here, Chrissie, shouldn't you be at work?" she frowned, as she took a welcome cup of tea, noticing Mary's shaking hand. "Oh, Chrissie! There's nothing wrong is there? It's not your mam, is it?"

"Oh no, Rosie, don't worry. It's nothing like *that*!" she laughed in reply. Then she blurted out the whole story, hardly taking a breath in her excitement.

"Well, believe it or not, Chrissie," Rosie smiled reaching over to squeeze Chrissie's hand warmly. "I'm very pleased for you. I always *knew* one day you'd be off, but who'd have thought it, eh? Good old Miss Murphy. She came up trumps for you after all."

"Yes, God bless her!" Chrissie replied gently.

"When is your mother moving down to Wicklow?" Rosie asked. "I'll have to go and see her before she goes and say a *proper* goodbye to her and the children."

"Oh, quite soon I think, but I'll be going with her for a few weeks to give her a hand around the place. It's in a real state at the moment and it will need a lot of clearing out and cleaning and everything. We are going down this week for a couple of days to air the place and at least get the old beds out and burn them." She laughed. "I'm going to treat her to new ones as a surprise for her and the kids."

"That will be great, Chrissie. What a nice thing to do," Rosie said.

"Well I can afford it *now*, can't I?" Chrissie answered happily.

"Are you all right Mary?" Rosie asked in concern, turning her head as she heard Mary sniffing.

Mary had been standing with her back to them for some time, gazing out of the small window that looked out on to the blossoming back garden.

"Yes, I'm fine, love, thank you. Just thinking you know . . . about things." As she glanced around Rosie was puzzled when she saw her red eyes. "Oh, Mary, you've been crying!" she exclaimed. "Whatever's the matter?"

When she didn't reply immediately. Chrissie said, "I think Mary is a little upset, Rosie, because Daisy has just asked me if I will take her to England with me."

"Daisy!" Rosie cried in shock. "No!"

Daisy looked sadly around the kitchen at all the eyes that were upon her and didn't know what to say. She was beginning to feel that she shouldn't have said anything at all. They must all think she was *so* ungrateful after all their kindness to her over the years. She pushed back her chair and stood forlornly before them.

"I think I'll just go up to my room for a while, if that's all right," she murmured.

"Just a moment, Daisy!" Mary called to the departing figure.

"Yes?'

"I'm sorry if I sounded unkind, love, but it was just a bit of a shock, that's all! Of course you can go with Chrissie if you *really* want to." Adding thoughtfully, "If she'll take you, that is!"

"Course I'll take her! I couldn't leave her in that state now, could I?" Chrissie assured Mary. Daisy couldn't believe it! Unable to speak, she just flung herself at Chrissie and sobbed hysterically on her shoulder.

When things had calmed down and Rosie had said goodbye to Chrissie and gone back upstairs to finish off her work in the nursery, Mary asked Chrissie if she would like another cup of tea before she left. "That would be lovely, thanks Mary, then I'd better be off and give mam a hand."

"I have a little put by for Daisy," Mary told her confidentially as they sat together sipping the freshly brewed tea, "just in *case* she ever needed it."

"Oh, Mary, don't worry about that! I'll pay her fare and I'll make sure she gets home safely."

"I wouldn't expect you to *do* that, Chrissie! You'll have to take care of your money, you know," she warned her. "It won't last long if you keep spending it so freely."

"Not at all, Mary. I'd be happy to, don't worry. But you can give her a little spending money if you like . . . you know . . . to make her feel a bit independent . . . like me!" she grinned cheekily.

"You'll never change, will you, Chrissie O'Rourke," Mary laughed loudly.

"I hope *not* Mary!"

Mary glanced quickly at the old clock on the wall and exclaimed, "Lord! Will you look at the time? I've a heap of things to do today. You'd better be getting back to your mam or she'll think you've run off and left her already!"

"Yes, I'd better get me skates on," Chrissie agreed. "The house is like a tip with everything all over the place and the kids are going scatty with excitement! Me mam will be getting one of her 'heads' if I don't get back soon."

As they quickly rinsed and dried the cups Chrissie told Mary

65

that she would come around with her mam in the next few days so they could have a good long chin-wag before they all left.

Chrissie said a hurried goodbye to Mary and rushed off home, her feet hardly touching the ground as she wove her way quickly through the bustling streets.

The next few weeks passed in a flurry of excitement and hard work and by the time the last box was loaded into the back of the hired van and the O'Rourke family gathered together on the narrow pavement outside their old home, there wasn't a dry eye in the street, as friends and neighbours came to wave their final farewells to their much loved neighbours. Even Rosie had managed to get an hour off so she could say goodbye to her dear friend.

Their heads were spinning as they were all hugged and kissed and wished the best of luck in their new home. As Chrissie released herself, breathlessly from Rosie's tight grip and wiped her eyes roughly with the back of her hand, she strained her neck over the heads of the crowd gathered around them. She was looking for Jimmy!

"Where the *hell* is he?" she thought savagely to herself. It seemed as though the whole street were there, but no sign of Jimmy Dwyer! Angry at herself now, for even thinking of him, she turned bright eyed to her mother and said loudly;

'Are we ready then mam? I think we've got everything don't *you*"

"Yes love!" her mother replied with a tired smile "Let's load up the children shall we. I think there's enough room in the back for the twins and the rest of us will have to squash in the front with Mick."

"Right we are then Mrs!" Mick Mahoney, the driver, laughed, "Let's see what we can do!"

They finally pulled away from the crowded pavement. The twins waved madly through the tiny windows in the back doors of the old brown van but as Mrs O'Rourke, Chrissie, Mary and young Maggie had to sit almost on top of each other in the front seats beside the driver, they could hardly lift heir arms to wave *their* last goodbyes. Patrick was going to follow them down on the back of his friends' bike, as there just wasn't an inch of space left. When he had first suggested this, Maggie had been horrified at the very thought, but after much persuading from Chrissie, she had reluctantly given in, making him solemnly swear that he would make his friend drive slowly and carefully. Chrissie had told her not to worry, because Brendan Mahoney was a good lad and he would be terrified at the thought of upsetting *her.*

As they craned their necks to get a final glimpse of the old street and as the heavily-laden van slowly turned the top corner, Chrissie smiled with smug satisfaction as she saw the tall bulky figure of Jimmy rushing along in the direction of her old home!!

"Too *late* you eegit!!" she thought bitterly to herself.

Maggie turned and caught the glaring look in Chrissie's eyes.

"Are you all right love?"

"Course I'm all right mam!! Couldn't be better!!" she replied her voice cracking as she, quickly swallowed the huge lump in her throat that was threatening to choke her.

"Come on Mick, put *your foot* down!!" Chrissie cried impatiently. "There's the best pint of stout you've *ever* tasted in your life waitin' for you at the other end!!"

As the whole van erupted into cheers and laughter, Chrissie yelled even louder

"YA BETTER WATCH OUT WICKLOW, COS HERE WE COME!!!!!!!!"

9

During the next couple of months of a warm and mellow summer, the meadows and lanes around Ballycross Farm gradually blossomed into a picturesque tapestry of life and ever-changing colour. Cattle and sheep grazed contentedly on the long sweet grass in the lush fields and around them in the thick brackens and heathers brightly coloured butterflies fluttered gently on the softly perfumed air. Every member of the O'Rourke family joined together in the mammoth task of turning the neglected old house into a habitable new home for themselves. From the youngest to the eldest they busied themselves from morning till night, clearing, cleaning, sweeping and painting.

The forlorn looking building had been coated with several layers of whitewash, the doors and window frames had been scraped and repainted in an attractive shade of dark blue and the windows sparkled and glittered in the sunlight. The yard was neat and tidy now with a huge pile of logs for the fire stacked up by the end wall. Johnny had come over most evenings after work to give them a hand with a lot of the heavy work, which they were most grateful for, especially Margaret, who had been only too eager to give a helping hand whenever she saw him striding through the gate! To her mother's extreme annoyance she flirted outrageously with him and in Chrissie's words 'made a real show of herself!' One evening Chrissie became so enraged by her embarrassing behaviour that she dragged her forcefully through the yard and around to the back of the house, where she gave her a fearful mouthful and ended up smacking her sharply around the face, when she continued to cheek her brazenly. Margaret vowed to herself, however, as she ran weeping in humiliation into the house, that she would pay Chrissie back for that one day!

Chrissie had laboriously painted the walls of every room in the house with a pretty shade of pale primrose, and painstakingly cut and pasted on a delightful border of deep creamy roses along the top of each wall. She also made up pairs of dainty floral curtains for all of the bedrooms and a chic little blind for the small kitchen window. The ceilings were clean and white now and the whole house shone with new life.

The clipped hedges surrounding three sides of the yard, that had been sadly neglected for so long, were now thick and green and were heavy with bright summer berries where hundreds of birds would come to feast. The little outhouse in the furthest corner of the yard, which had been so derelict and covered from top to bottom in thick brambles, had been repaired and repainted in the glossy blue of the front door and window frames and was being comfortably used as the family's privvy.

The lush green meadow that sloped gently down to the back of the house became the younger children's playground. Many a pleasant evening was spent relaxing and chatting, and sometimes they would even take their supper up in a huge basket and lie around on the thick blankets that Chrissie had bought for that very purpose.

It all seemed so idyllic now and Maggie was secretly hoping that Chrissie had changed her mind about going off to England. But of course she had not!

One balmy evening as the sun slipped slowly down in the silvery pink sky behind the distant mountains and the late summer fragrances drifted over them, Chrissie decided it was time to talk seriously to her mother about leaving. She had been answering Daisy's eager letters from Dublin regularly and was happy to know that her family had kindly agreed to let her stay with them in London for as long as she liked and until they were satisfied that she had found herself a good job and somewhere decent to live. (They were only too pleased to help Chrissie out, considering her kindness towards their daughter in bringing her home.)

Putting on a brave face Maggie nodded and smiled gently as Chrissie went over her plans. "So when are you thinking of going, love?" Maggie asked quietly as she began to gather up the plates and cups that were scattered around the blanket.

"Next week, mam," Chrissie answered, as she jumped up to help her mother with a heavy basket.

"Oh, so *soon*, Chrissie!

"Oh mam, please! Haven't I waited long *enough?*" she replied with her usual impatience, "We did agree, didn't we? Just look at the place, mam! It looks a real picture now. It's beautiful and you have enough money that I put aside for you to last for quite a while. Well at least until I can send you some more!"

"All right, Chrissie, calm down, will you. I'm not trying to stop you! It's just that these last few months have gone so quickly and now the time has come for you to go I just feel a little upset, that's all!"

Chrissie sighed deeply as they strolled silently together, carrying the basket and blankets between them. She knew she would miss all of them terribly and wanted to make her parting as easy as possible for everyone.

Later that night when all the young ones were tucked up in bed and sleeping soundly, Chrissie and her mother sat together by the low fire that they had lit to take the chill off the night air. They both knew that there wouldn't be many more nights like this for a long time. Lost in their own thoughts, they both gave a little start as the clock chimed eleven and Maggie said, "Bedtime, I think."

"Yes, mam.'

Chrissie had carefully packed some of her freshly washed and ironed clothes into her new suitcase each day and slipped it quietly under the bed in the evening, careful not to wake Margaret. She had arranged with her mother that she would slip away early on Friday morning before anyone else was awake. She just couldn't bear the thought of saying goodbye to them all, as she knew it would be a long and tearful farewell.

Maggie stood for a long while by the side of the bed in the cold grey of the morning looking down at the peaceful sleeping face of her lovely daughter. She prayed fervently for her to be in God's good keeping till she was home again. As she bent over the slumbering figure and gently pushed a damp curl away from her forehead, Chrissie's eyes flew open and she sat bolt upright in the bed. "Sssh!" Maggie warned as Margaret groaned grumpily and turned over to face the wall.

Chrissie kept her eye on Margaret as she stumbled around the room trying to get herself together. She didn't have time this morning to heat any water to wash, so she quietly poured a little from the jug into the china bowl on the small washstand in the corner and splashed her face and body with the icy contents. Her teeth chattered as she rubbed herself dry and slipped into the clothes she had ready hanging on the back of the door under an old sheet.

As she dragged the suitcase cautiously from under the bed, Margaret gave another little moan but thankfully didn't wake up.

Chrissie went silently down the two shallow steps into the kitchen and saw that her mother was sitting at the table with a pot of tea and a plate of buttered bread laid out for them both.

"Oh, mam, I couldn't eat a thing," she whispered. "I'm sorry!"

"Just have a cup of tea then, love," Maggie answered, knowing that she probably wouldn't eat a thing all day herself.

Chrissie went to the door and opened it, looking out at the brightening sky and shivered excitedly to herself. All she wanted now was to be away as quickly as possible. It wouldn't be long before the early workman's bus would be along.

"Come on then, Chrissie," Maggie said, as she began to pull her coat around her shoulders. "Let's get down to the road."

"No, mam! Please! Please don't come down to the road," she pleaded in a hushed voice. "I couldn't bear it!"

"All right love," Maggie replied, a little relieved.

Chrissie grasped her mother in a tight embrace for a long while, breathing in her familiar sweet scent and feeling her small bony form. As she fought back the hot tears she was unable to utter a single word of farewell. She released the trembling figure quickly, snatched the suitcase from the floor and made a hurried exit. As she made her way out of the yard and down the dew-covered lane she tried not to slip on the damp moss-covered stones as she struggled with her case. Stopping abruptly about halfway down, she drew her breath in sharply. "Oh Jesus! It's the bloody bus!" she cried out loud.

The surprised face of the driver was a picture, as he caught sight of the lone figure hauling the heavy case across the road. He hadn't expected to see anyone along this stretch of the way so early in the day. He pulled up sharply as he saw Chrissie waving frantically at him. Jumping down he ran over and gave her a helping hand. Chrissie thanked him profusely, completely unaware of the inquisitive stares and nudges of the small group of grinning lads at the back of the bus. In her haste she hadn't even noticed the twitching curtains on Mrs O'Grady's parlour window. After Chrissie had paid the few shillings fare to the driver and wedged her case between him and a couple of sacks of peat, she flopped down heavily on the nearest seat and sighed with relief.

"Thank 'feck for that!" she thought to herself. She couldn't begin to imagine what would have happened if she had missed the bus that day, what with all the arrangements and with Daisy waiting to meet her in Dublin. She tried to make herself comfortable on the hard seat and began to feel very drowsy. She hadn't realised how emotionally draining the whole thing would be as she made the first step on her long journey. Her lids were heavy and it wasn't too long before she began to doze fitfully, as her thoughts flitted from one thing to another. After a while she fell into a deep sleep.

Before she knew it, she was awoken rudely from her slumbers by a hard rapping on the window beside her. Her neck was stiff and painful and she jumped with a start and stared through the smeared window, straight into the red face of a very excited Daisy! Chrissie blinked several times and rubbed her aching neck.

"God! I'm here already!" she thought. "Oh well . . . here we go!" Smiling broadly at the driver she bumped her case down the crooked steps and on to the pavement of Stephen's Green. Daisy threw herself at Chrissie with such force that she almost knocked her off her feet.

"Am I glad to see *you*!" she cried in delight. "Look, I have the tickets here! I got them last night and I have me bag packed and everything. Oh Chrissie I can't *wait*!" Her childish enthusiasm was contagious and Chrissie threw her head back and laughed loudly, as she ducked away from the tickets that Daisy was waving in her face. "What? Did you think I'd change me mind or what?"

"Oh *no*! No, of course not. But I'm so excited! Come on, let me help you with that." she said, grabbing the case.

Chrissie felt a little strange as they made their way through the bustling crowds on their way to work in the pale morning sunshine. She had become so used to the peaceful ways of the countryside that she felt a little confused and out of place in the jostling streets. It took almost half an hour before they turned the corner of Dorset Street and back on to her old home ground. She felt better now and when they opened the kitchen door of Dominic House she was more than happy to see the familiar, smiling face of Mary Flannagan who hurriedly dried her hands on her apron as she rushed to greet her.

"You're looking *grand*, Chrissie! The country air must surely suit you! Come and sit down now, I've been keeping the pair of you a bite to eat before you go up and have a little rest before you set off this evening."

Chrissie suddenly realised that she was ravenous and gratefully polished off the huge plate of rashers, eggs, sausages and black pudding that Mary had placed before her.

"That was lovely, Mary, thank you," she said, as Mary poured her another cup of tea and sat down to join the two girls.

"I don't think I'll be able to sleep today though, Mary." She hesitated for a moment. "I have a few little things that I wanted to do."

"What on earth do you have to do today, Chrissie?" Mary frowned.

Chrissie suddenly thought – "Where's Rosie? She does know I'm going today, doesn't she?"

"'Course she does, love, don't fret! She's gone off to the dentist with the little ones this morning. She made an extra early appointment for them so she could get back in time to have a few hours with you and say goodbye to you properly."

"Oh great! I thought for a minute that I'd missed her," Chrissie smiled.

Daisy, who had been sitting bright eyed and happy, asked Chrissie what it was that she had to do.

"Oh, I just wanted to have a little wander around," Chrissie answered evasively. "You know . . . take a little walk and stretch me legs."

"I'll come with you then. I'm not tired either."

"No, Daisy! I really *do* want to be on my own," she replied a little sharply, avoiding the disappointed look on Daisy's downcast face.

"OK, then!" Daisy sulked.

"Leave her be, Daisy," Mary scolded. "Chrissie probably has a few friends she wants to say goodbye to."

Chrissie looked up quickly and was surprised to see the little wink that Mary gave her as she turned to the dishes in the sink. "I'll help you with those, Mary," she offered.

"No thanks, love. You go and have your little *walk* and then you can come back and have a nap later," Mary answered, without turning around, "And *you*, Daisy, can run up to the nursery and keep an eye on baby Gerard while I get this place cleaned up and do the vegetables for tonight."

10

Chrissie stood a little timidly outside Mrs Dwyer's front door. She wasn't sure if she was doing the right thing or not. "Oh! What the hell!" she thought, as she raised her hand to the shiny brass lions' head knocker. She knocked twice and waited patiently. She knocked again, more loudly this time. Nothing. Nobody answered. She looked up at the windows and saw that they had been opened a little to let in the fresh air, so Mrs Dwyer *must* be in. She surely wouldn't go out and leave the windows open like that? "Bad idea after all?" she mused. Just as she was thinking she wouldn't bother trying again, she thought she heard a shuffling sound coming from behind the door. Putting her ear against the heavy wood she knew she was right. Bending down to the letterbox she put her mouth close and called out: "Hello! . . . Hello! . . . Is that you, Mrs Dwyer? . . . It's Chrissie here! . . . Chrissie Rourke!"

"Chrissie! What a lovely surprise! What are you doing here?" Mrs Dwyer exclaimed as she opened the door.

"God! I thought something was wrong when you didn't open the door!" she gasped in relief. "I knew I could hear you inside."

Mrs Dwyer grinned ruefully. "Ah well, it's the old legs, Chrissie. I'm not half as quick as I used to be. What can I do for you? Are you back in Dublin? Is your mam here?"

"No, she's not with me, Mrs Dwyer." Chrissie wasn't quite sure what she should say to her. She had been hoping that Jimmy would be in, but she realised now that he had obviously found himself a job at last. She had desperately wanted to show off to him and let him know that she was off to England. She thought that she could have casually said that she had just called in to say goodbye to his mother.

"Are you coming in, Chrissie? We can't stay here on the doorstep all day, can we?" The door opened wider. Chrissie refused the offered cup of tea as she sat in the small back kitchen with Mrs Dwyer. She thought that she had better give her all the news about the family and what they had been doing all summer and explain about her journey to England. Mrs Dwyer was happy to hear all the good news and a little surprised to hear about London. "London, indeed? I'm fed up with hearing *Jimmy* talking about going to London!"

"*What?*" Chrissie almost shouted in shock. "*He's* going to London?"

"Oh no, Chrissie!" Mrs Dwyer laughed. "He just *talks* about it. He wouldn't leave me here on me own, would he? Not the way I'm feeling these days," she added, screwing her face up and rubbing her sore back.

Chrissie stood up from the small table. "Well, I'd better be going, Mrs Dwyer. It's been grand seeing you and I hope you'll be feeling better soon."

"I doubt that, Chrissie, but God is good! Jimmy looks after me well. I couldn't have hoped for a better son!" she said, thinking sadly of her earlier days with her husband.

"Will you tell him that I called?" Chrissie asked, in a small voice.

"I will *indeed*, Chrissie. God bless you now, love. Safe journey."

Rosie tapped lightly on Daisy's bedroom door, where the two girls had been laying together on the bed trying for hours to catch a few minutes' sleep. Daisy had quickly got over her sulks when Chrissie had gone off on her own earlier and had spent a happy hour or so playing with the new baby in the nursery. They were much too excited for sleep and had lain awake each thinking their own thoughts.

"Are you awake?" the soft voice asked.

"Come in, Rosie!" They both called out in unison and then laughed.

"Mary has made some tea for us and she told me to come up and fetch you down," Rosie smiled, adding "Here, I've brought you up some hot water if you want to freshen up a bit."

Daisy rushed off downstairs to the kitchen without even bothering to run a comb through her tangled hair but Chrissie thanked Rosie and took the heavy jug from her. She stripped off her clothes, unembarrassed in front of her friend, while Rosie turned away a little shyly and made herself busy tidying up the bedclothes. She was taken aback by Chrissie's shapely figure with its healthy glowing skin and long, well formed limbs. She really looked quite grown up now, Rosie thought, and wondered if she herself would ever look as curvy and womanly as Chrissie did.

Chrissie washed herself all over with the delicate rose-scented soap and then dried herself in the warm soft towel that Rosie had brought in for her from the airing cupboard on the landing. After dressing she sat before the little dressing table and took her brush and make-up from her shoulder bag.

Rosie sat on the side of the bed and watched her friend as she brushed her thick glossy tresses. Chrissie pulled up the sides of her heavy locks with two tortoiseshell combs. Her hair was so thick that she always had a problem keeping it tidy and usually got so impatient with it that she ended up tying it back with a ribbon. But today she wanted it to look special. When she had lightly powdered her face and applied her cherry red lipstick she stood before Rosie with her hands on her hips and asked cheekily; "Will I do, then?"

"You look lovely, Chrissie. You really look smart in that suit. Did you make it yourself?"

"No – don't faint!" Chrissie joked. "I actually *bought* this one!"

The navy-blue serge suit fitted Chrissie to perfection and the crisp white cotton blouse with the lacy Peter Pan collar set it off beautifully. She had also bought herself a suede bag and matching shoes in almost the same shade of navy as the suit. She hadn't really intended to spend so much money on her 'going off to England' outfit, but she had gone to Bray one day with her younger sister Margaret with every intention of buying some material to run something up as usual, but when she saw that there was a sale on in one of the better shops, she just couldn't resist it. Margaret had encouraged her all the way, naturally, as she never had a problem spending money, especially on fashionable items. It was mostly imaginary spending, because she hadn't left school yet and hadn't even bothered looking for a few hours' work, but she could always manage to cadge a little from her mother now and then, even if it was only for new slides or hair ribbons. Her secret wish was to bleach her hair blonde, just like she had seen in the glossy film magazines. She would style it exactly like Lana Turner she promised herself.

"Are you two lassies coming down?" Mary's voice floated up the back staircase.

"Just coming!" they called back.

Chrissie and Daisy couldn't eat a thing and anxiously watched the clock.

"Time to be off, I think!" Chrissie announced when she could stand it no longer.

76

"Yes, you're probably right, love," Mary agreed, a little reluctantly. "Let's get you on your way then."

"Where are you going, Rosie?" Chrissie asked, as she saw her friend reaching up to the coats on the rack by the hall door. "I'm coming to the boat with you, silly," Rosie grinned.

"But I thought you were working?" Chrissie said, a little puzzled.

"Well, I got the evening off so I could come with you and see you safely on your way. After all the aggravation you've given about going to England, I thought I'd better make sure you didn't miss the boat!" she said lightheartedly, as she buttoned up her long coat and tied the belt tightly around her small waist. She *hoped* that she sounded lighthearted, because that wasn't exactly how she was feeling. She had an odd feeling inside her that just wouldn't go away. Maybe she was just imagining it, but it felt like fear. She wasn't sure why she was afraid, because she knew that Chrissie was well able to look after herself. At least she was here at home, but she wasn't convinced about that in a strange country. Daisy's parents sounded like great people and she was certain that they would take good care of Chrissie, but she knew that Chrissie wouldn't want to be hanging around with them for too long. As soon as she got the chance she would be off on her own. 'Oh well, there's nothing *I* can do about it now,' Rosie said to herself, trying to shrug off the nagging thoughts.

Mary watched the three young women from the front steps of Dominic House as they walked off down the road laughing and chatting, with a brave smile on her kind face. She had made her goodbyes to Chrissie and Daisy as brief as possible. Over the years that Daisy had been in her care she had treated her just as if she were her own child and had loved her dearly. So it was a very sad parting for her indeed and she couldn't believe how she had kept up the constant good-humoured chatter with the young girls as they got ready without bursting into tears. When they reached the corner they all turned as one, and waving merrily and without stopping disappeared out of sight. The unshed tears fell heedlessly down Mary's cheeks now as she turned on her heel and let herself back into Dominic House.

"Ah well!" she sighed to herself, "that's that, then. God bless them and keep them out of harm's way!"

11

The train journey from Westland Row was only a short one and as the three girls alighted from the train in Dún Laoghaire Chrissie shivered and looked up at the darkening sky. A thin mist was swirling around the docks and shrouding the low buildings and the customs hall in a moving grey blanket. "Come on, Daisy," Chrissie urged with a shiver. "Let's get in out of this."

Daisy gasped as the damp fog parted for a moment and she caught her first glimpse of the Princess Maud anchored alongside. "Oh my God! It's enormous!" she cried, half fearfully, half in delight.

Rosie and Chrissie laughed too, thinking of the many times they had spent down here when they were younger, watching all the boats, big and small, going in and out of the port.

"Don't worry, Daisy! It won't sink!" Chrissie teased.

"I bloody hope not!" Daisy said, wide-eyed.

"Stop being so mean, Chrissie," Rosie scolded, "and stop cursing, Daisy!"

Rosie stayed with them as they made their way with the other shuffling passengers along the dockside and then stood huddled together at the bottom of the gangway. Daisy pecked Rosie on the cheek and hurried up the wobbly gangway gripping her little case tightly.

"Well, you better be going then, Chrissie," Rosie smiled brightly. "They won't wait for you!"

"Yes, yes, time to be off," she answered, a little absently-mindedly as she peered through the mist and over the heads of the last few straggling passengers.

"What are you doing, Chrissie? I thought you couldn't wait to get going?" Rosie questioned her, frowning as she too turned around and looked along the darkening dockside. "Who're you looking for?"

Chrissie didn't answer and instead just dropped her case heavily on the damp ground and grabbed Rosie, crushing her tightly to her. 'All these goodbyes,' she thought sadly.

"That's it then, Rosie Byrne. Take care of yourself now, won't you? Promise me?" she said seriously, holding her friend at arm's length and looking into the strained pale face.

"I'm supposed to say that to *you*, aren't I?" Rosie grinned.

"Oh *me*? I'll be just fine."

"'*Course* you will—" Rosie assured her, hoping that she sounded more confident than she felt. "Will you just look at Daisy up there?" Rosie exclaimed in alarm, pointing at the waving, shouting figure that was hanging over the high rail at the side of the ship. "You'd better go, Chrissie, before she falls overboard!"

The two friends giggled as Chrissie bent and picked up the suitcase. As she stood up slowly and placed one foot on the wooden gangway, she was almost knocked sideways as a tall lumbering form shoved passed her. "Hey! You big eegit! Who the hell d'ya think you're pushing around?" she cried angrily.

"I'm sorry, I'm *so* sorry, my dear. I didn't see you there."

Chrissie found herself staring up into the coldest grey eyes she had ever seen in her life. An icy shiver ran through her but she shrugged it off quickly. "Well, I should think so too," she mumbled uncomfortably and turning to Rosie said, "Bye Rosie – see you soon."

"Bye, Chrissie, be careful!" Rosie warned with a wan smile.

"Please – let me take that for you," the English voice said close to her ear.

"No thanks! . . . I can *manage*?' Chrissie replied vehemently.

"No, really! It's the *least* I can do. Please!" he insisted.

Chrissie let the case fall clumsily to the ground, not really knowing why she had changed her mind so quickly. "There you are, then," she said, a little less tersely. "Help yourself."

She followed the tall darkly clad figure on to the ship and was joined by Daisy who informed her that they should put their luggage in the baggage hold. "Look!" she pointed to a smily-faced seaman. "If you give that man over there sixpence he will take it for you and get it out for you when we reach the other side! Go on, Chrissie, I saw the other people doing it. Oh! Who's this with your bag?" She had just noticed the dark figure beside Chrissie.

"Just somebody who gave me a hand, that's all."

"A bit *old* for you, isn't he Chrissie?" Daisy whispered cheekily.

"Behave yourself, Daisy," Chrissie glared at her. "I don't even know him!"

Chrissie muttered her thanks to the tall stranger and without looking up into those cold eyes again, leaned over to take the bag from him. "My pleasure, my dear," he replied smoothly and as their fingers touched briefly, Chrissie was completely engulfed with the overpowering scent of heavily applied cologne. Turning away smartly he disappeared along the deck and through the nearest entrance leaving a trail of the sickly aroma in his wake.

"God! Is he wearing *perfume*, Chrissie or what?" Daisy laughed, wrinkling her little nose in distaste. "Do you think he's 'one of *those*'?"

"Oh no, Daisy love ... I doubt that *very* much," Chrissie answered, wondering how Daisy knew so much for her age.

They both jumped in fright as the ship's fog horn gave out three deep and shuddering ear-splitting bellows.

"Can I take those for ya girls?" the gravelly voice asked at Chrissie's elbow. "We're sailin' in five minutes and ya don't wanna be dragging them 'round with ya all night, do ya?" Chrissie rummaged around in her purse for a sixpence and smiled her brief thanks.

"I'm freezing Chrissie, aren't you?" Daisy asked hugging herself tightly. "Shall we go inside?"

"No, I want to wave goodbye to Rosie. Come on!" She tugged at Daisy's sleeve and pulled her to the rail, wedging herself between the groups of passengers who were dutifully waving their farewells to friends and relations. Chrissie screwed her eyes up as she tried to make out the faces on the dockside as they disappeared and re-appeared through the floating mist.

"There she is!" Daisy yelled, pointing into the gathering gloom and leaning forward as far as she dare. "Is that someone with her, Chrissie?" she added, squinting her eyes into the gloomy distance below.

"What? Where? I can't *see*!"

"Look! *There!* By that big stack of crates!"

"Oh God! Yes. Yes, I can see her now – *Oh!*"

"*Jimmy!* ... *Jimmy!*" I'm here! Up here!" Chrissie yelled, her lungs fit to burst.

"Bye, Chrissie! Bye, Chrissie! Good Luck!" the strong voice called back, seeming to echo all around her.

With a loud and crunching judder the ship began to inch its way slowly from the dockside and out into the night, and Chrissie strained her eyes to catch a last glimpse of the faceless figures. She cupped her hands around her cold lips and called as loudly as she could; "DON'T FORGET ME, JIMMY!"

And the promised reply came floating across the night, "NEVER, CHRISSIE O'ROUKE . . . NEVER!"

Stifling a sudden choking sob, Chrissie caught the astonished Daisy by the arm and pulling her way from the rail said; "Come on, Daisy. Let's go and get a drink in the bar."

"OK, Chrissie, I'm right with you! I'd love a *real* drink!"

"Not for you, silly, *you're* too young but *I* could surely murder a large Jamesons right now." Daisy scowled as she allowed herself to be led through the entrance on the deck that obviously opened into the bar, considering the noise and smell that emanated from it as they tugged on the weighty brass handle of the door. She kept close to Chrissie as they made their way through the noisy smoke-filled lounge and up to the crowded bar, where a freckle-faced young steward was doing his best to keep up with the orders for drinks that were being shouted at him from all directions. The horseshoe-shaped bar was already awash with carelessly spilt drinks and Chrissie watched in disgust as a gang of boisterous young lads who had no doubt been drinking heavily already jostled with one another childishly, making a nuisance of themselves.

"Will you watch out, you big fool!" Chrissie yelled into the ear of one of the lads, who stumbled backwards into her as he tried to balance four pints of stout on a small tin tray. "Sorry, darlin'," he slurred, grinning down at her through bleary eyes.

As he staggered away from the bar, grinning stupidly, Chrissie wished fervently that he would trip over, spill the drinks and do himself a bit of damage at the same time! She shivered when she felt the hand touch her shoulder and give it a little squeeze. "Here we are again then, my dear. Would you allow me to buy you and your young friend here a drink?"

As Chrissie looked away from the penetrating stare of the grey eyes she had already made a discreet note of the stranger's appearance. The thick silvery hair was brushed smoothly away from the lean face with its high cheekbones and wide mouth. She also noticed a very thin scar that ran from the corner of his left eye, down the side of his cheek to his angular jawbone. To Chrissie's rather inexperienced eye, his clothes seemed to be stylish and expensive but as the sickly smell of his cologne invaded her senses yet again she turned away, sniffing loudly and snootily informed him, "No, thank you, we're buying our own drinks!"

Looking at her intently, he raised a thick dark eyebrow and said "Very well, then, perhaps some other time." And reaching into the inside pocket of his long black Crombie coat with its smooth velvet collar and lapels, he took out a small, white, purple-edged card and silently handed it to her.

Chrissie took it from him and didn't even bother to look at it. She just assumed it was his phone number or something. "Thanks," she muttered ungraciously and stuffed it into her shoulder bag.

"Well! What do you think of that?" a wide-eyed Daisy asked.

"Oh, don't give him another thought, Daisy, just a dirty old man looking for an easy lay!" Chrissie informed her as she saw the worried look on the young girl's face.

"An easy lay? What's that?" she asked in feigned innocence.

"Never mind, Daisy, never you mind . . . Look here's the chap coming over to serve us at last."

As Chrissie found them a couple of spaces on the long seats by the wall, she glanced quickly around. The stranger seemed to have vanished. "Come on, Daisy, sit down here before anyone else gets them."

"Where do you think your man went to, Chrissie?" Daisy asked.

"Who?"

"The one who stank of perfume," Daisy laughed.

"Oh *him*. I told you not to worry about him, Daisy."

"He made me feel – funny! Do you know what I mean, Chrissie . . . Sort of creepy?"

"Yes, I *do* know what you mean, love, but stop thinking about *him* now!" she ordered kindly. "Drink your orange juice and we'll go and see if we can get a berth for the night. I think they have a place where just the women can go for the crossing. It will be cheaper than trying to get a cabin for the two of us."

As Chrissie lay stretched out on the narrow bunk below the sleeping Daisy in the shared women's cabin, her jacket neatly folded around her shoulder bag with its precious contents carefully positioned under her head, she thought of all the things that had led up to this night. She smiled to herself when she thought of the effort that Jimmy must have made to get to the boat on time to say goodbye to her. Lying with her arms folded across her as she stared up at the rusty rivets in the ceiling not two feet from her head, she promised herself that as soon as she was settled in London she would write to him and tell him all about it and thank him for coming to see her off, even if it *was* at the last possible moment!

Her thoughts returned to the stranger who had come into her life unbidden. Jesus! What am I thinking? Come into me life indeed? Just a ship passing in the night . . . Ha! That's a good one!' she chuckled to herself.

The dull throbbing of the engines gave an odd sort of comfort as Chrissie lightly dozed but just as she relaxed, giving in to the rest that she so badly needed, she had the strangest feeling that she was choking. Her throat was tight and her nostrils felt full of a nauseating odour and her stomach began to churn and heave alarmingly. She sat straight up in the narrow bed and banged her head with a sickening thud on the low ceiling. "Oh Christ! me feckin' head!" she screeched at the top of her voice.

Daisy's tired little face appeared almost immediately over the edge of the bunk and gazed in fright at the pale, tearful face of her friend.

"Chrissie! What's wrong? What's happened?"

"Nothing's happened, for Gods' sake! I just bashed me bloody head! All right? Chrissie answered roughly.

"Huh! Well, you don't have to be like that!" but Daisy's irritated expression softened when she saw Chrissie's tears. "Are you sure you're OK, Chrissie?"

"Yeah, sure. Sorry about shouting at you, Daisy," Chrissie apologised, as she rubbed the sore lump on her hairline. "I bet this'll look *great* in the morning!"

"Oh you always look lovely, Chrissie," the younger girl reassured her. "Anyway . . . you can just put a bit of make-up over it and pull your hair down to cover it up! No one will even notice."

"Go back to sleep, Daisy," Chrissie said quietly but firmly, rather embarrassed now at her outburst as she looked around at the other bunks and found that she had disturbed several women who were glaring at her under the dull lighting of the crowded cabin. Pretending not to notice them, she turned over on her side away from the accusing looks. She breathed in and out, deeply and slowly, trying to control the waves of sickness as she clutched at her cramping stomach. 'I can't be seasick,' she told herself. 'We're hardly moving!' Then she remembered what it was that had woken her up with the frightening feeling that she was suffocating. As Chrissie had fallen into her much needed sleep she had almost at once begun to have a strange, muddled dream. Her family, friends, home were all mixed up and made no sense at all. The changing faces were blurred and indistinguishable and floated around in a disjointed dance and jumbled laughing voices were confusing and distant, but as the wavering muddled haze slowly began to clear, the terrifying vision of a pair of icy-grey eyes came slowly towards her out of the mist, carrying with them a heavy cloak of a sickeningly sweet odour that bore down on the sleeping girl as if to crush the life out of her.

Chrissie pulled the thinly woven cover from underneath her and, gripping the rough edges, wiped the cold film of sweat from her brow. She tried to curl herself up into a comfortable position under the cover but she shivered uncontrollably. Her damp hair stuck to the back of her neck and her new underwear and stockings were clammy and cold against her soft skin. However much she tried she just couldn't seem to shake off the horrible feeling that the bad dream had left her. Never in her life had she been troubled with scary dreams, and it frightened her. She began, for the first time, to worry if she was making a big mistake. What if this was a warning that she really *was* doing the wrong thing in going to England and leaving her friends and family behind? Should she have listened to people when they had tried to warn her? And – just who *was* that sinister looking stranger who had dared to invade her life?

After another hour of lying awake, worrying and fretting and going over and over everything from her school days to the present time Chrissie's weary thoughts at last hovered on the brink of sleep. The last image she saw before she fell into a dreamless slumber was that of herself and her mother sitting in the plush red velvet seats in the stalls of the Adelphi Cinema in O'Connell Street, gazing enraptured at the huge screen, where Scarlet O'Hara was uttering the unforgettable words: "Oh! I *can't* think about that today . . . I'll think about it tomorrow!" "Mmmm!" she mumbled in agreement as she slipped into peaceful oblivion.

12

"This looks like a good one, love," Betty Carter smiled encouragingly as she underlined yet another boring factory job in the local paper. Chrissie sat with her elbows on the table across from her with her chin resting heavily in her palms. She didn't even bother to answer. She just sighed despondently and gazed at the top of Mrs Carter's bent head.

Daisy's home-coming had been eventful and tearful and the excitement had lasted for weeks. Nobody could believe that this was the same little girl who had gone off to Dublin nearly ten years ago. So grown up now and almost a woman, they had said and so pretty and what a lovely accent she had acquired.

Mick and Betty Carter had greeted Chrissie with thanks and enthusiasm and had invited the neighbours around for celebration drinks while they tried to catch up with the news from the years that Daisy had been in Ireland. Chrissie was delighted at first with all the attention and the constant buzz of excitement, but when things had quietened down a little, she thought it was high time that she started working. She had hardly any money left now and was feeling very guilty about not being able to give Mrs Carter anything towards the housekeeping, but after trudging around the local streets and scanning the papers for any suitable employment she was bitterly disappointment at not finding the 'good job' that she had been so sure would materialise as soon as she set foot on English soil.

"Here, Chrissie," Betty shoved the newspaper towards her. "You'd better have a look yourself, I have to be getting off to work. I don't want to be late, might get the sack and that wouldn't do at all. What with Christmas only a few weeks away and everything!" she tried to joke. "Anyway," she added, "I want to ask Mr Wilson if he will take Daisy on for a few hours now and then, especially over the holidays, at least until she gets something more permanent."

Giving her the sack was the last thing on Mr Wilson's mind. He had always had a soft spot for Betty, since the first day she had walked into the bakery and nervously approached him asking for work. He would never have let his feelings be known to her, of course, he had far too much respect for her and her family and he had felt so sorry when she had told him that she had sent her little daughter away to her sister in Dublin when the war broke out. He only knew her husband as a nodding aquaintance but knew he was a hard-working man who had worked at a leather factory on Long Lane since he had left school, and when he heard from a delighted Betty one morning about his recent promotion to floor manager he couldn't have been more pleased.

"Good luck, with the job hunting, love," Betty smiled down at the bored expression as she pulled on her dark-brown raincoat and wrapped a multi-coloured scarf around her head. "And don't worry, something will turn up, you'll see!"

"'Bye Mrs Carter!" Chrissie answered in a quiet voice.

Chrissie decided to make another cup of tea before she looked through the ads herself. As she tidied away the breakfast dishes and gave the floor a quick sweep while she waited for the kettle to boil, she tried to shake off the depressed feeling that had been hanging over her head for days.

She got on very well with Daisy even though she was a few years younger than herself and found her good company, but she knew for certain that Daisy was going to end up in a dead-end job somewhere or other as she had no ambition at all about her and couldn't understand why Chrissie didn't want to go into one of the shirt factories down the road. They were always crying out for machinists and everyone knew how talented Chrissie was with a sewing machine. Daisy hadn't been able to find herself any work either because she was just a bit too young to start work properly and too old to go back to school. She passed the time doing a few hours cleaning in the new launderette that had opened down the road and she had joined a local drama group that belonged to their parish church.

Chrissie put the tea on the table and was about to sit down again when she heard three loud raps on the front door. She smiled to herself, knowing exactly who it was.

"Mornin' love! How's your belly off for spots?" the coarse laugh greeted her as she opened the door.

"Hi Silvie, come in."

Silvie Higgins lived two doors away and most mornings she came

86

in for a chat before she went to work as a barmaid in the local pub, *The George.*

"Pour us a cup, will you, love. I'm spittin' cotton!" she said, making herself at home. "You still looking for a job?" she asked, glancing down at the open pages. "Don't worry, you'll find something soon."

"Yeah, that's what Mrs Carter's always telling me."

"Took me months to find something I *really* wanted! Now look at me, practically run the place on me own!" she boasted proudly. "Mind you, what I really want is a decent place of me own."

"Do you, Silvie?" Chrissie asked, as she handed Silvie her tea and sat down again.

"Course I do! Just need a bit of cash! I've got all the experience I need," she joked winking cheekily. "Here, have a fag."

Chrissie laughed. "Thanks." Silvie always cheered her up. It had crossed her mind several times to ask Silvie if there were any vacancies at *The George* for another barmaid, but always thought better of it, knowing that Betty wouldn't hear of it.

"Tell you what! I've just had a great idea! It's me day off tomorrow – why don't we go 'up west' and have a laugh? You look like you could do with it!"

"Up west?" Chrissie frowned. "Where's that?"

"Oh, come off it!" Silvie jeered good-humouredly. "Don't tell me you've never heard of it!"

"Oh! You mean the West End," Chrissie blushed.

"Course, silly, where'd you think I meant? The Christmas lights are on now and you'd love that and we could do a bit of window-shopping and then go and have a little drink and have something to eat later on. Maybe a bit of dancin'," she said wiggling her hips saucily in the chair. "What'ya say then?" she smiled brightly, fluttering her over-made-up eyelashes.

"Well, it sounds great . . . but I'm not sure," Chrissie answered doubtfully.

"What are you worried about? Think I was asking you to go to the bleedin' North Pole or something!"

"Well, it's just that . . ." Chrissie hesitated, sighing, "I can't really afford it."

"Oh, is that all! Don't worry love, I invited you, so it's my treat. OK?"

"Well, all right then," Chrissie brightened up. "But I *will* pay you back as soon as I get a job."

"OK! Whatever you say!" Silvie replied, stubbing her cigarette out. She pulled a small gold-plated compact from her bag and checked her reflection. Chrissie watched as she patted the halo of peroxide-blonde curls and then touched up the scarlet lipstick and added a little more pink rouge to the aheady glowing cheeks. The heavily mascara-ed eyelashes blinked furiously again into the little mirror as another coating was applied. Silvie always reminded her of a doll that she had once seen in a toy-shop window, but she was such a good-hearted girl that Chrissie couldn't help liking her.

"Oh bugger!" Silvie tutted. "Look at the time! better get going." She stood up and adjusted the short black skirt that had ridden up her thighs while she had been sitting. "What ya think of me new blouse, Chrissie?" she asked with a broad grin as she opened her coat and exposed a huge bosom that was barely covered in frilly black chiffon. Chrissie gasped and then laughed loudly. "God! You're a case, Silvie! Go on! Get off to work, will you?'

"Ha, ha!" Silvie laughed. "Your face! Anyway . . . be ready at six tomorrow night!"

"Don't worry. I'll be ready."

When Chrissie mentioned her night out to Betty, she got a long lecture about being led astray etc, but it didn't bother her, she had been expecting it. "Don't worry, for goodness sake! Betty. I don't think Silvie is as bad as everyone thinks she is," she had told her as they cleared the dishes away from supper.

"Chrissie'll be all right mum, she can take care of herself,' Daisy butted in as she folded the tablecloth and put it back into the sideboard drawer. "Wish *I* was going for a night out!"

"Well you can *wish* my girl!" Betty scolded. "It'll be a long time before I let you out in the company of that little tart!"

Chrissie kept quiet. She was always upset when she heard Betty talking about Silvie like that, but thought she better not get into a row with her. Anyway . . . what was so wrong with her? She admitted that she *was* a bit brassy, but that was just her way. At least she was working and always had money in her pocket.

The next morning, when everyone had gone out, Chrissie decided to do an extra bit of cleaning and polishing over the whole house, just to keep Betty in a good mood and to show her that she appreciated her. She spent most of the morning hauling wet clothes from the boiler in the corner of the kitchen to the sink for rinsing, and then out into the backyard to be put through the mangle in the corner. The day was bright and sunny, but freezing cold, so by the time she had finished three loads of sheets and clothes and had them hanging from the two clothes lines in the yard, her hands were almost numb. When she finished mopping the floor she put the kettle on and collapsed into the chair exhausted but satisfied with her efforts.

After a quick cup of tea, she went upstairs to tackle the bedrooms. Of course Betty and Mick's room was always spotless and she was pleased to see that the bed was already made and everything was in order. She tidied up the bathroom and the room she shared with Daisy in record time and swept the stairs down and along the short hallway, and brushed the dirt out of the front door across the pavement into the gutter. Chrissie then set about the business of finding herself something to wear that evening.

Her wardrobe was a bit sparse these days as she hadn't really been able to add much to it since coming to London, but she did have a nice new red swagger coat that she had bought in a ladies' clothes shop in Tower Bridge Road, and a smart pair of black suede shoes. When she had first seen the prices in the shop she had begrudged paying so much money for her new coat, but had consoled herself with the thought that she would soon be working and it *was* getting colder by the day after all! She decided on a black turtle-necked sweater and black pencil skirt. They would go well with the red coat and with the black and red silky scarf that she had bought the other week in Bermondsey market. The outfit would look good, she thought, not as eye-catching as some of Silvie's outfits of course, but attractive nevertheless.

Sitting on the stool in front of the little oak dressing table, Chrissie gazed at herself in the mirror. 'Now, what to do with this lot?' she mused as she pulled her heavy chestnut locks up and away from her face. "I know," she said aloud. Jumping down the stairs two at a time she rushed into the sitting room and pulled out a couple of magazines from the rack by the side of the brown suedette settee. She flicked impatiently through an old copy of *Woman's Own*, scouring it for a picture she had seen a while ago. "Good," she grinned when she found it.

She fiddled fussily with the thick mane of hair for ages trying to achieve the style on the sophisticated model in the picture, but when another length of hair escaped from the back of her French-roll, she almost screamed in frustration.

"Shite!"

She picked her handbag up from the floor where it had fallen and tipped the contents messily on to the freshly made bed and managed to spill most of it on to the floor. She could have sworn there were a few hair clips in there somewhere. "Oh, great, here they are!" she sighed. As she bent down to gather up the rest of the things that had fallen on the bedside rug she noticed the corner of something sticking out of her little address book. She frowned as she pulled the gilt-edged card out and held it before her:

"The Purple Parrot Club" she read, "Exclusive . . . members only. Oh! It's that feckin' eegit on the boat," she realised, stunned. She hadn't given him a thought since.

Her next action was one that she would regret for many years to come . . .

She shoved the little card roughly back into her bag and clipped it tightly shut. Glancing across at the pink alarm clock on Daisy's side of the bed she groaned, "Damn! Look at the time!"

No time now for the luxurious soaking she had promised herself. Rushing into the cold bathroom, she stuffed the plug in the hole and put the taps full on; she guiltily sprinkled a handful of Betty's floral-scented bath salts into the water and, tugging her clothes off, dropped them in a heap on the floor and climbed into the half-filled bath.

At five to six Chrissie thought it nothing short of miraculous that there she was, ready and waiting, perfectly groomed and excitedly anticipating her evening out. As she came slowly down the stairs, feeling like a million dollars, she grinned when she heard the loud knocking on the front door.

"Well, look at you!" Silvie beamed. "You look bloody gorgeous!"

Chrissie blushed at her enthusiasm, but knew she looked good anyway. Just then Betty and Daisy came along and as Betty brushed passed Silvie with a mumbled "evening", Daisy cried in delight, "Oh mum, have you seen Chrissie's hair? How did you get it like that, it's *beautiful*!"

"Yes, of course I've seen it and yes it *is* lovely," Betty replied.

"Here Daisy love, take these bags into the kitchen and put the kettle on, will you?"

"Course, mum," she answered, and added over her shoulder as she took the heavy shopping bags from her mother, "Have a great night, you two!"

"We will, don't you worry about that!" Silvie called down the hall, ignoring the icy stare from Betty.

"'Bye, Mrs Carter!" Chrissie said, giving Betty a quick peck on the cheek. "And don't worry, I won't be late."

Betty turned back to the door and stood on the doorstep watching the two figures walking quickly away from the house and shivered as a cold blast of air blew along the darkened street. The two girls soon disappeared into the night and as she closed the heavy front door behind her Betty couldn't shake off the feeling of dread that had been with her since the night before. She shook herself and muttered softly, "Silly old cow! What's the matter with you? She'll be fine!

"Yeah I know, it's bleedin' 'orrible down there sometimes," Silvie said in sympathy as the two girls emerged from Leicester Square tube station and she noticed Chrissie's perspiring brow. Her first experience of the tube left a lot to be desired. The cigarette smoke and the heat of the closely pressed bodies on the train had been nauseating and a little scary too. She leaned against the wall by the entrance and gratefully gulped in great lungfuls of the crisp night air. "God! That was suffocating!" She tried to grin.

"You need a drink, me girl!"

"You're right there!" Chrissie agreed, nodding.

"Come on, then," Silvie said with an encouraging smile, "I know the very place."

Holding her friend firmly by the elbow she steered her determinedly through the throngs of late night shoppers, street buskers and groups of sightseers and theatre-goers. Chrissie's stomach settled down as they made their way through the crowds in Leicester Square and very soon they turned into a narrow street that seemed to be lined with pubs, clubs and music bars.

"Dave's Place is just down here," Silvie informed her, pointing down the gaudily lit street. "Known him since we were at school. He's done real well for himself, too!"

As they passed darkened doorways unrecognisable blasts of music assailed their ears and Chrissie wondered just what she was letting herself in for. The whole atmosphere of the street was decidedly seedy and just as she was about to suggest that they should perhaps go and have something to eat first, Silvie stopped abruptly. "Here we are!" she announced proudly. Chrissie looked up at the multi-coloured flashing bulbs around the arch-shaped sign of – 'Dave's Place!'

"Come on, dozy," Silvie grinned. "What'cha waitin' for?"

Chrissie followed her friend slowly down into the gloom, stepping carefully on the uneven stone steps of the narrow stairway, and held tightly on to the coarse rope rail to steady herself. Silvie parted the red plastic beaded curtain at the bottom and held it open for Chrissie. "Welcome to Dave's!" Chrissie blinked rapidly as her eyes adjusted to the flickering candlelight. As she became accustomed to the dim glow she was surprised to see that the small bar was almost full, even though it was quite early in the evening.

"Hop up!" Silvie smiled, patting one of the high stools by the bar. "Make yourself comfy." Chrissie perched a little nervously beside her friend as she took in her surroundings. It didn't seem *too* bad. Mostly couples sitting at the little round tables, sipping drinks and chatting quietly. At least the music was playing softly in the background and not screeching out some of the awful sounds they had heard earlier. Silvie called out cheekily to the dark-haired barman, "Hey Georgio! you not workin' tonight?"

"Be right with you, ladies," he grinned back from the other end of the small bar where he had just finished serving two hard-faced girls in very short, black leather skirts and brightly coloured, low-cut clinging t-shirts. One of them glanced over at the two girls at the other end of the bar and winked saucily, as though she knew them.

"Evening!" Georgio grinned broadly as he sauntered over to them, flashing brilliantly white teeth and staring brazenly in Chrissie's direction. She blushed furiously at the open admiration on the young man's face.

"Hey! You can stop that for a start, you cheeky beggar!" Silvie laughed, good-humouredly nudging Chrissie. "He's a right flirt, he is."

"What are you having then, girls?"

"Two large G and T's, sweetheart," Silvie said, and turning to Chrissie added, "That all right with you, love?"

"Yes. Great, thanks," Chrissie said hurriedly.

"Where's Dave tonight then, sweetheart?" Silvie asked, after she had taken a long drink from the tall glass he had placed in front of her.

"He'll be back later, darlin'," Georgio replied. "Don't worry."

Chrissie was shocked, when she glanced down at her watch, to see that they had been in the club for nearly two hours and had been drinking steadily the whole time! She had to admit to herself though, that she *was* having a good time even though her empty stomach had rumbled noisily several times. She had given up long ago trying to remind Silvie that they were supposed to have been 'window shopping'. Silvie had been in her element, of course, flirting outrageously with every man who caught her eye!

Squinting again at the tiny hands of her watch, she decided that she had better try once more to get Silvie to leave the club so they could get something to eat before they both fell off their stools, but just at that moment she was distracted by a commotion at the entrance when a noisy group of lads almost fell through the beaded curtain laughing and carrying on.

"Noisy buggers!" Silvie tittered giving them a quick onceover.

"I'm just going to the ladies," Chrissie tried to whisper in her friend's ear.

"What!" Silvie yelled back over the raucous laughter.

Chrissie was too embarrassed to repeat what she had said because by then they were surrounded by the newcomers, who were giggling like school boys as they tried to introduce themselves and ask the girls what they would like to drink.

"Don't mind if I do," Silvie slurred winking at Chrissie. "I'd like a *large* one!"

"Bet you *would!*" the tall blond one muttered.

"Oi, you *dirty* little devil!" Silvie feigned annoyance.

Chrissie had a feeling that things were going to go downhill from now on, especially when she saw Silvie's eyes nearly pop out of her head when one of the young men pulled an overstuffed wallet from his back pocket and leaned between them waving his arm to try and get Georgio's attention.

"What's this then boys?" Silvie smiled sweetly up at them. "Christmas bonus already?"

"Nah!" he grinned. "Just a little bit a luck on the gee-gees today!"

"Oooh ... lucky you!" Silvie crooned, leaning forward just enough for him to see the mounds of her plump breasts down the front of her flimsy blouse.

"Yep!" he drooled back, licking his full moist lips. Pulling a five-pound note from his worn wallet he said, "Here Chas, get the drinks in mate!"

"Let's sit over there, shall we?" Silvie nodded to the table in the corner that had just been vacated. "OK," he grinned, as Silvie slipped her arm through his and clung on possessively.

Chrissie slid awkwardly from the stool as the rest of merry little group made their way to the empty table in the corner. She hung on to the edge of the bar for a moment as she steadied herself, surprised by her light-headedness and the weakness in her legs. She gave Georgio an embarrassed grin when he asked her if she was OK. "Mmm, thanks," she mumbled.

"Come on!" Silvie cried over the sound of the juke-box that was now playing much louder. "Don't take all night!"

Chrissie tutted as she took a deep breath and made her way over to them trying to walk as sedately as she could, cursing herself silently for getting drunk. Nobody seemed to notice anything odd as she sat down heavily on one of the low stools between two of the lads and breathed a sigh of relief.

Chas was soon on his way back from the bar, precariously balancing a full tray of drinks as he swayed towards his companions. When they had sorted the glasses out and noisily toasted each other the young blond man said, "Hey, we don't even know your names, girls!"

"Well, I'm *Patsy* and this is me mate, *Shirley*," Silvie told him seriously without looking at Chrissie. "Who are you then?"

"Oh no! . . . What the hell's she up to now?" Chrissie wondered to herself as she sipped yet another G and T.

"Me name's Mark and this is Chas and this is Pete!" he slurred, waving his long arms over the heads of the group. Chas and Pete bobbed their heads around as if to acknowledge recognition. Chrissie giggled quietly and prayed she didn't look as bad as they did, especially when Pete's head suddenly drooped on to his chest and he looked at though he had fallen asleep.

Mark was busy trying to get to know 'Patsy' better, thinking he was on to a good thing, as he draped his arm heavily around her shoulders and slobbered noisily over her. Chrissie wasn't so drunk that she didn't notice his hand slipping inside Silvie's coat and his fingers fiddling with the tiny buttons on her blouse.

"Er . . . Sil . . ." she began, tugging at her friend's elbow. "Emm . . . Patsy!"

"What!" Silvie turned red-faced and angry, "What's up wiv you? Jealous?"

"No, I'm not *jealous*!" Chrissie retorted loudly. "It's getting late and I think we should be going, that's all!"

"Oh shut up! Don't be so bleedin' miserable!" Silvie answered.

Chrissie was fuming. Her head was beginning to throb and she was angry with herself now. Why hadn't she listened to Betty! She had no money for the fare home so she would have to wait for Silvie anyway, whatever she was getting up to. Bugger her!

"'ang on a mo, darlin'," Silvie purred, releasing herself from Mark's sweaty embrace. "Just gonna powder me nose."

"Don't be long, sweetie," Mark leered, as ran a sticky hand along her thigh as she tried to get up.

"Oi, you saucy monkey! Have patience, will ya!" Silvie grinned crookedly as she slapped his hand away. 'You'll be lucky mate!" she thought to herself as she pulled her skirt down and grabbed hold of Chrissie's arm. "Come *on*!" she said urgently under her breath.

Chrissie followed her through to the back of the club and down a dingy corridor and into the scruffy little 'ladies'. She couldn't help giggling when she thought what they must look like and she couldn't really blame Silvie. After all, she hadn't forced her to drink so much. They both rushed into the grubby cubicles and relieved themselves noisily.

"Thank God for that!" Chrissie laughed loudly. "I've nearly peed meself twice tonight!"

Silvie tittered stupidly in the next toilet: "Me too!"

As they squinted into the brown-speckled mirrors over the grubby chipped hand basins and tried to repair the damage to their make-up, Chrissie tried to persuade Silvie that it really *was* time that they made a move to go home. Her head was beginning to ache and her empty stomach was gurgling noisily!

"Don't be bleedin' daft, gel, we ain't started yet!" Silvie informed her.

"What *are* you on about, stupid?" Chrissie shook her head and hiccupped loudly. "I've had enough to drink tonight to last a bloody month!"

"Ow d'ya fancy goin' dancing, then?" Silvie asked, as she dragged a damp tissue under each eye, rubbing roughly at the streaks of mascara on her blotchy skin.

"Dancin'?" Chrissie burst out laughing, but winced as a sharp pain shot through her temples. "We can hardly stand up straight. Anyway," she added more quietly, "We can't afford it." Silvie gave her friend a sneaky sideways glance. "What?" Chrissie asked as she caught the sly look.

Silvie tottered over to the door, opened it quietly and looked quickly up and down the dim corridor. She closed it silently and put a finger to her lips. "Sshh!"

Chrissie watched in amazement as her tipsy pal leaned her back against the door, hoisted up her skirt and rooted around up the legs of her black nylon knickers.

"What the hell?" she began.

"Shut up ya silly cow!" Silvie scowled.

Chrissie's mouth dropped open when she saw the scruffy brown wallet emerge from the cheap lacy underwear. "Jesus!" she exploded. "It's that bloke's feckin' money! You shittin' little thief!"

"Oh, shut yer bleedin gob, miss high and mighty!" Silvie griped, adding nastily, "We're goin' out on the town, wever yer like it or not!"

"Well *you* might be, but *I'm* going home!" Chrissie glared defiantly.

"Oh? An 'ow d'ya think ya goin' a do that then, silly? Yer aint even got ya fare back!'

Chrissie snorted loudly, knowing she was stuck. She turned back to the mirror and fiddled with the long strands that had escaped from her carefully styled hair and wanted to cry in temper.

"Look, mate," Silvie wheedled. "They'll never bleedin know, bloody twits! We can be out of here in a couple of minutes, don't worry!"

Chrissie ignored her as she delved into her bag to find her lipstick, desperately thinking of a way out of the situation.

"'Ave ya got a bit a foundation, love?" Silvie asked, as though nothing was amiss. "Me skin's gon a funny bleedin' colour!"

"No!"

"Let's 'ave a look then," Silvie giggled as she made a grab at the bag. "Bet yer 'ave!"

"Get off!" Chrissie yelled, trying to push her away.

Silvie laughed as she shoved her hand into the bag and rummaged around awkwardly. Seconds later the handbag dropped to the floor spilling the contents over the dirty tiles.

"Oooh, what's this then?" Silvie tittered as she picked a small purpled-edged card that had fluttered to the ground. Chrissie frowned. Silvie held the card up to the bare bulb overhead and peered closely at it. "The Purple Parrot!" Grinning stupidly at Chrissie's furious expression she said, "Well, well, well, ain't we the saucy . . . cheeky one, then?"

"Give me that!" Chrissie made a lunge at the waving arm.

"I don't think so," Silvie ducked away. "Think we just found a real 'posh' place to have a bit of a laugh, don't *you*?" she winked.

Just then there was a low murmur of voices coming from outside.

"Shite!" Chrissie exclaimed, a thin film of sweat breaking out on her forehead. "Now what?"

"Follow me!" Silvie ordered gruffly.

Dragging Chrissie behind her Silvie barged passed the two girls who were chatting and laughing outside the door.

"Oi! Ya silly mare! Mind who ya shovin'!" one of them yelled nastily.

"Piss off slag!" Silvie shouted back over her shoulder and she pulled Chrissie along to the fire exit.

Chrissie heard the torrent of abuse behind her as she let herself be led roughly through the heavy door and up the dark steps and into the alleyway that ran along the back of the club and into the street beyond. Silvie giggled nervously as she turned to look into the horrified face of her friend. "Don't worry, love, we'll be long gone in a minute or two."

Chrissie couldn't even reply and she stumbled on trembling legs down the noisy road trying to keep up with the tottering Silvie. She felt as though she was living through a nightmare. This was getting completely out of hand! Just as she got her breath back and was about to tell her drunken friend in no uncertain terms that she didn't care how she would do it but she was off home, when Silvie turned to her smiling, as though nothing were amiss.

"There's a cab over there, look! Just dropping those blokes off. Come on!"

Before she could stop her, Silvie was off across the road and waving the little card under the nose of the grinning cabbie. "Know where this is, love?" she slurred.

"Course, sweetheart, jump in!"

Chrissie stood hesitantly on the kerb watching in disgust.

"What about yer mate then, darlin'?" the driver asked. Silvie tutted as she looked back at the dejected figure.

"Come on, silly! Ya can't stand there all night! Looks like you wanna do a bit of business!" Silvie roared before she tumbled into the back of the taxi. Chrissie flew across the road with every intention of smacking her stupid pal across the face but when she saw a small crowd beginning to gather on the pavement to watch the spectacle with amusement, she quickly jumped in beside the slumped girl.

As the cab pulled away Chrissie leaned back into the comfort of the deep seat and wiped a damp shaking hand over her sweating thumping head. Heaving a heavy sigh of relief she silently thanked God that they were at last on their way home. She couldn't believe what had happened in the last few hours and swore to herself never to have another night out with Silvie. She looked over at the snoring girl and couldn't help grinning weakly at her comical open-mouthed, dribbling pal, with her smudged make-up and corkscrew bleached blonde curls. "You wait 'til tomorrow!" she whispered, "I'm never going to let you forget this!"

Her eyelids drooped sleepily as the cab wound its way expertly through the bright lights and throngs of traffic of London's West End. Chrissie couldn't be bothered to take notice of anything any more; all she wanted to do was to pass out beside Daisy.

She must have dozed off for a moment because she was jolted awake when the squeal of brakes told her that she was home. As the cab pulled up to the pavement she rubbed her eyes wearily and nudged Silvie awake, telling her they were back in Bermondsey. Silvie sat bolt upright, a bemused expression on her crumpled face. She blinked a few times and then grinned cheekily, "I don't think so, love!"

"What?"

Chrissie's eyes bulged in shock as the taxi door was pulled open by a smartly uniformed doorman who greeted them with a polite "Good evening, ladies."

They had arrived at the Purple Parrot club in Mayfair.

"Jesus Christ!" Chrissie fumed as she stepped awkwardly out of the taxi behind the sniggering Silvie.

"Ere are, darling," Silvie threw a five-pound note in the general direction of the driver. "Keep the change." He'd seen it all before. "Thanks, sweetheart, have a good night!"

"We will," Silvie promised as she zig-zagged across the pavement and peered through the thick shiny glass of the entrance door.

"Allow me, madam!" The doorman was at her elbow. Pulling it open for them he smiled automatically. "Cheers, mate," Silvie said, without even looking at him. "Come on, Chrissie. I'm not going in on me bleedin' own!" she added loudly over her shoulder.

With a resigned sigh Chrissie followed her hesitantly across the luxuriously appointed foyer. Their footsteps were silent as they walked slowly over the thick pile of the expensive carpet and over to the enclosed reception desk where a beautifully dressed dark-haired girl sat smiling demurely as she watched the scruffy pair of young women weave their way towards her. 'Looks like a bit of trouble here,' she thought to herself as her manicured fingertips hovered over the emergency button under the highly polished counter. "Good evening," She continued to smile politely. "How can I help you?"

Silvie suddenly felt very brave and said coarsely, "We wanna drink, of course, what'ya think, ya stuck up cow!"

Chrissie hung her head and cringed inwardly. Shite.

"Are you members, madam?" Beth inquired demurely, already knowing the answer. No unaccompanied females ever came to the club. Especially little slags like this one! Silvie ignored her and again demanded loudly and rudely that she should be shown to the bar. Now! Beth pressed the little brass button three times and within seconds Reg Dixon, the club's manager, appeared at the desk.

"Good evening, ladies," he said, in a deep quiet voice. "I think it would be best if I called a cab for you, don't you?" Chrissie looked up into the broad handsome face with its bright blue eyes and wanted to die of embarrassment.

"It's OK, thanks," she tried to smile at him. "We're just going."

Grabbing Silvie's arm roughly she tried desperately to pull her towards the exit, but her furious companion would have none of it!

"PISS OFF!" she yelled into Chrissie's perspiring face, struggling to free herself from the determined grasp.

"How the *hell* did you get mixed up with this little tart?" Reg grinned as he came to Chrissie's aid. "Come on, love. Let's *go*!" he added more firmly to Silvie.

Chrissie gasped as Silvie suddenly pulled herself free, swung awkwardly around and stamped spitefully on Reg's foot with a four-inch stiletto heel.

"OW! You little bitch!" he screamed in pain, hopping on one foot. Chrissie tried in vain to catch hold of the flailing arms as her incensed friend flew at the glowering manager and tried to rake at his face with her scarlet talons, but his reactions were much quicker, from years of experience, and he snatched hold of her stiffly lacquered hair and spun her around towards the door.

"Leave her alone, *please*!" Chrissie begged, tugging on his thick, muscular arm. "She's just had too much to drink! *I'll* see to her."

Silvie fought like a wild cat, kicking and yelling and screaming obscenities at both of them as she tried to fight them off. Then to their utter amazement she somehow managed to spin around and spit viciously into Reg Dixon's astonished face. As Chrissie saw the raised arm with its clenched fist she threw herself at him. "That's *enough*!" she screamed.

Reg ground his teeth and breathed deeply, trying to control his temper. He had never hit a woman in his life! Half-battered to death a few arseholes that were asking for it, of course, but never a woman. In the few moments it took for him to get himself under control again he glared stonily at the two young women.

Everything was happening so quickly that Chrissie's head was spinning frighteningly, but as she looked at the panting trembling girl beside her she knew she just had to get them out of there, right now! Silvie looked as though she was getting ready for Round Two! Her small, bloodshot eyes were glittering nastily in her blotchy, smeared face. "Ya lairy bastard!" she seethed, wiping her running nose across the sleeve of her jacket. "I'll 'ave ya yet!"

Chrissie was horrified as she watched her, as if in slow motion, take a few tottering steps towards the rigid figure, grin stupidly and promptly vomit straight down the front of his beautifully tailored black evening suit. Roaring like an injured animal, Reg Dixon fell upon the fainting girl with a vengeance. At the same time Chrissie tried desperately to get herself between them, but before any of them could stop themselves they had fallen with a heavy thud in a mass of tangled arms and legs.

"Well, well, well!" a softly dangerous voice floated over their heads. "What do we have here?"

"Oh *shite*!" Chrissie groaned to herself, turning her face into the carpet as she recognised the cultured tones.

Charles Latimer looked disdainfully down at the writhing bodies at his feet. "Do get up, Reggie, and get rid of this trash, there's a good chap! We have a busy night ahead of us!"

As the owner of the Purple Parrot turned on his well shod heel to go back to the comfort of his office and pour himself a large drink, he glanced back at the scene. His nose wrinkled in disgust as he watched Reg haul himself to his feet and pull a snowy-white hankie from his pocket and try to wipe away the worst of the congealing mess on his jacket. He was fuming when he thought of the impression that his 'special guests' tonight would get if they arrived early and were confronted with such a spectacle.

"Hurry *up*, Reggie!" Charles called urgently. "Get changed and take a shower, for God's sake!"

"OK, boss."

In swift obedience Reggie turned and made his way across the lobby and disappeared through a door behind the reception area.

Charles Latimer shook his head impatiently as he saw the scruffy blonde girl crawl slowly across to a plush velvet sofa by the wall in the foyer and try to pull herself up, heaving noisily as though she was about to throw up again, with the dark-haired one supporting her around the waist in an attempt to get her to her feet. He frowned. There was something familiar about her.

Chrissie glanced furtively though her lowered lashes at the tall figure who was watching them. "Come *on*, Silvie," she hissed urgently. "You can do it!"

Gripping her weeping friend firmly by the elbow she did her utmost to steer her towards the street, where Harry Black was holding the heavy glass door wide open in anticipation of their exit. He had watched the whole scene in amusement through the highly polished glass. Another little story to tell the wife in the morning! She loved to hear all the gossip from the club. Of course he wouldn't dream of telling her half of the things he'd seen and heard since he took the job after his retirement. She'd never have let him work there if she had known about some of the 'comings and goings'!

Chrissie kept her head down as she held on tightly to the sobbing girl beside her. "Nearly there," she encouraged in a whisper. But it was too late. "Just a moment, please!"

"Bugger!" Chrissie mumbled under her breath. She knew he had recognised her.

"Are these yours?" the voice enquired.

Chrissie turned her head slightly and looked over her shoulder into the cold grey eyes of Charles Latimer.

"Pardon?" she asked haughtily.

"These, my dear!" he answered smoothly, dangling a pair of scuffed black suede shoes before her.

Chrissie looked down at her bare feet and wanted to cry in shame as she saw the tattered runs in her stockings (well Betty's, really!) and the broken toenails that were poking through. She took her shoes from the long, thin fingers in silent humiliation. Just then Charles Latimer tutted in annoyance as he caught sight of a sleek black limousine pulling up silently to the kerb.

"Come here!" he ordered them sharply.

Before Chrissie knew what was happening he had beckoned Beth Andrews over from the reception desk and asked her to take the two young women to the ladies' room to get themselves cleaned up, and in lowered tones told her that under no circumstances was she to allow them to leave the club until he gave his permission. Tonight was very important for him. He had worked for months on the latest deal between himself and his two business associates from LA and he didn't want anything spoiling it at the last minute.

"Certainly, Mr Latimer," she smiled sweetly. "If you'd like to follow me please *ladies.*" Beth added superciliously, without even looking at the two scruffy creatures that were cluttering up the doorway.

Chrissie fumed as she forced Silvie along the plush, low-lit corridors behind the swaying hips of the pretty receptionist. Even in these ridiculous circumstances Chrissie couldn't help but admire the elegant line and fabric of the long, black satin evening dress and the lovely noise it made as it rubbed gently on the silky stockings that covered Beth's long shapely legs.

"Here we are!" Beth opened a door at the far end of the long corridor and indicated that they should go in. "You'll find soap and towels and stuff in there to sort yourselves out," and then added a little more kindly when she caught the forlorn but proud look on Chrissie's pale face. "If you've got a shilling or two there's a perfume machine on the end wall," she pointed into the long narrow room. "Should make you feel a bit more human." Just before Beth closed the door quietly she reminded them that they were not to leave until she came back to get them. Chrissie nodded that she understood. Silvie wobbled over to one of the pink shelled-shaped basins and lowered her head, gulping sickeningly.

"Oh no you *don't*, madam!" Chrissie yanked her back and propelled her into one of the spotless gleaming cubicles, lifted the gold toilet seat and said angrily "You can throw up all you like in *here*!"

Trying to ignore the horrible retching noises that Silvie was making Chrissie took her new red coat off and draped it over one of the dainty little gold chairs that stood in front of each hand basin. She looked around her and wondered for a moment where her new scarf had gone! She splashed her face with the cool refreshing water and trickled handfuls down the back of her neck and across her chest. Wiping herself slowly with a fragrantly scented soft pink hand towel, she stared dumbly at her dishevelled reflection and didn't know whether to laugh or cry. "Oh, mam! Thank feck you can't see me now!" ('Stop cursing, Chrissie,' she could almost hear her mother say.) "Sorry, mam." Pulling the last couple of hair clips from her knotted hair she shook her head and sighed loudly.

Silvie emerged pale faced and silent from the cubicle after flushing the toilet twice.

"Gawd! I feel like bleedin' death!" she grumbled, as she plonked herself down heavily on to a seat.

"Yeah," Chrissie grinned wryly, "and you look it too! Come on, get that coat off and clean it up. It's disgusting!"

"I can't be bloody bovered love, me bleedin 'ed's killing me!" she whined. "Let's just get 'ome."

"*Your* head!" Chrissie snorted. "Mine's lifting off me with the pain!"

"Look, Chrissie," Silvie began. "I really need to get some-thing . . ." she trailed off.

"Never mind what *you need*," Chrissie retorted sharply. "What *we* need is to get smarted up and get home! Now come *on*! Scrape some of that shite off your jacket and wash that muck off your face. Jesus! you stink to high heaven!"

"But you don't understand—"

"Yes I *do*, stupid! You've got a feckin' hangover! And so have I!" Chrissie almost shouted.

Silvie fumbled around in her overstuffed handbag and pulled out an odd assortment of make-up and crumpled bits of paper. "I'm sure I didn't take all of 'em," she muttered to herself as she tipped the contents of the bag all over the black marble surfaces between the basins.

"What are you mumbling about and what are you looking for?" Chrissie asked irritably, screwing up her face in pain as she tugged relentlessly at the knots in her long hair.

"Oh, just a few aspirin or something that I thought I had left," Silvie said lightly.

"Give me one, for feck's sake, will you?"

"I don't know if I got any left!" Silvie answered quickly, looking guiltily up at Chrissie's pained expression.

"Yes you have!" Chrissie cried triumphantly "Look! There!" she pointed. "Stuck to the side of your bloody lipstick, you eegit!"

Silvie snatched at the topless tube that was getting damper by the second in the hand basin and picked nervously at the two little blue pills that were stuck on the side with trembling fingers. "Thank fuck for that!" she gasped.

"Well, at least you could give me *one* of them!" Chrissie almost yelled, holding her temples as a bolt of pain shot through her head. "After all you've put me through tonight!"

Silvie hesitated for a moment wondering if she dare risk it. One would be enough to see her through; but she'd rather have them both!

"Come on then!" Chrissie held her hand out. "Give!"

"OK!" Silvie said casually, not wanting to arouse any suspicion. "But it might be a bit strong for ya."

"Don't be so bloody stupid!" Chrissie snorted. "After what we've put away tonight I doubt that very much."

Before Silvie could change her mind Chrissie took the strangely coloured little pill, popped it in her mouth, turned the cold tap on and bent down to take several mouthfuls of water to swallow it.

Silvie turned her back on her friend as she took her jacket off and tried to scrub at the mess. "Soddin' 'ell, this is vile!" she moaned, as she saw that all the rubbing was making it even worse. Chrissie glanced down at her watch as she reached out to get her coat.

"Jesus Mary!" she cried. "It's nearly one o'clock in the feckin' morning!"

"So?" Silvie asked cheekily. "You gonna turn into a bloody pumpkin or something!"

Chrissie straightened herself up. "Come on, scrub your face and try and do something with that lot!" she almost laughed nodding at the state of Silvie's hair. "We've got to get out of here."

Chrissie almost felt sorry for her pal as they stood side by side gazing at their reflections in the shiny mirrors. "Sight for sore eyes or what?" she grinned.

"Mmm," Silvie agreed as she stared back at the Panda eyes that were looking back at her. As their eyes met they looked solemnly at each other for a few moments and then without warning both fell back into the little chairs behind them screaming in uncontrollable laughter. They were giggling and squealing so loudly that they didn't hear the door to the ladies' room opening.

"Feeling better, then?" Beth asked snootily as she stood behind them watching the fiasco. Chrissie jumped up in fright and embarrassment. "Oh! Sorry about that!" she sniffed, looking around for something to blow her nose on.

"Here," Beth reached into one of the cubicles and pulled off a wad of soft pink toilet-paper and handed it to the shame-faced girl. "Thanks."

"Mr Latimer sent me to see if you would like to join him for a drink before you leave."

"No thanks!" Chrissie said firmly. "We have to get home."

"No!" Beth replied steadily. "I don't think you understand! He wants you to come to his office!"

"No!" Chrissie stood face to face with her; hands on hips. "I don't think *you* understand! We're leaving! Now!"

"Look, dear," Beth's voice softened as she put a warm gentle hand on Chrissie's. "Take a bit of advice. When Mr Latimer invites you somewhere you really should go! Believe me he's not a man to be messing with!"

Chrissie frowned. The girl's words sounded rather worrying. She got the impression that she knew what she was talking about.

105

Perhaps it might be better to just go along and have a small brandy after all; thank him kindly and then leave.

"How's yer 'ed?" Silvie piped up, putting her arm through Chrissie's.

"Not bad. Why?"

"Well . . . why don't we pop along to Mr Whatisnames' place, 'av a few quick ones and then get off 'ome?"

Chrissie shrugged her shoulders as she grinned back at Silvie. "Oh shite . . . why not?"

The two girls made themselves comfortable in the luxurious soft black leather armchairs in Charles Latimer's office, and looked around at the opulence of the beautifully furnished room. From the oak-panelled walls with their sparkling crystal sconces and gold-framed pictures and photographs, to the huge art-deco cocktail cabinet that stood wide open displaying a vast array of twinkling glasses in all shapes and sizes and the neatly arranged bottles containing numerous choices of alcoholic drinks that stood along the three glass shelves. The pink mirrored lining of the cabinet made it look like an Aladdins' cave.

They felt a little nervous as they sat silently, waiting for Mr Latimer. Chrissie felt a lot better now, since she had taken the 'painkiller'. Her head had stopped throbbing and she was begin-ning to see the funny side of things. She knew, of course, it was very late and there would be hell to pay the next day, from Betty. She was already toying with the idea of asking Silvie if she could stay at her place for the night, so that she wouldn't have to be waking the whole household up and face the fury of Betty's rage at coming home at all hours of the morning.

"'Av ya got a fag?" Silvie whispered at last.

"No," Chrissie whispered back. "Course not, you bloody smoked them all!"

Silvie bit down on her lip and she tried not to giggle again. "Oh yeah!"

They both jumped guiltily as the door swung open and Charles Latimer sauntered into his office. "Good," he said, nodding in their direction.

As he walked passed Silvie on his way to the drinks cabinet he wrinkled his nose at the sour smell that was emanating from her stained clothes. "God Almighty!" he thought. "She smells like cats' piss!" Smiling over at Chrissie he asked what she would like to drink. Before she could answer Silvie's shrill voice demanded two large brandies.

"Is that all right with *you*, my dear," he asked Chrissie, completely ignoring the other girl.

"Em . . ." she hesitated a moment and then replied sheepishly. "Yes, please." The sooner they drank up the sooner they would be on their way.

As he placed a small purple coaster on the glass-topped table beside her and then put the large brandy glass down, Chrissie once again caught the heavy cloying scent of his aftershave. She smiled up at him, thinking that somehow it didn't seem so sickening now.

"By the way, my dear, I don't think we've actually been introduced, have we? I'm Charles Latimer," he held a cool hand out. "And you are?"

"Chrissie," She ignored his outstretched hand, "Chrissie O'Rourke."

Silvie was chewing on a broken nail as she watched them and waited impatiently for her own drink. Without looking at her, Charles placed the drink beside a pile of magazines on the small table at her elbow and turned quickly away. He walked over to the wide leather-topped desk and perched on the edge, sipping his drink slowly and watching Chrissie over the rim of his glass.

"'Ave ya got a ciggie please?"

Chrissie was surprised at the polite tone of her friend's voice. He stretched a long arm behind him and took a black marble cigarette box from his desktop. "Would *you* like one, my dear?"

"Thank you," Chrissie took a long filter-tipped cigarette from the proffered box. Silvie tutted as she rose and leaned across Chrissie to take one for herself. "Charmin'," she muttered under her breath.

Chrissie glanced once more at her watch. 'Shite! It's nearly two," she thought to herself. Charles Latimer was watching her every move. "Yes, it is a little late, isn't it!" he smiled as though reading her thoughts. "Mmm!" Chrissie knew it was about time they were on their way, but before she could say anything he was asking her if she had to get up for work early in the morning. Silvie tittered as she blurted out, "Get up for work? She ain't even got a bleedin' job!" She was feeling braver now as the mixture of brandy and her little pill hit the right spot.

Chrissie blushed as he looked at her in annoyance. 'You just wait, you bitch!' She thought as she stubbed out her half smoked cigarette and swallowed the remains of her drink.

"Oh really? What a shame," he said kindly.

"No, not really. I'm sure I'll find something soon enough," she glared again at the smirking Silvie.

"Oh yeah?" Silvie laughed. "Ya bin saying that for the last six months!"

"Look, I think we should go now," Chrissie stood up. "Thanks for the drinks, but like you said it's getting late – or should I say early."

"Just a moment, my dear," Charles replied calmly and then turning to the slouching Silvie he added, "Would you mind waiting outside please?"

"What for?" Silvie asked rudely, struggling to her feet. She didn't dare ask again when she caught the steely glint in his eyes. Charles Latimer covered his mouth and nose with his hand as she weaved her way past him and out of the door. She slammed it shut and stood with her ear pressed up against it. She didn't want to miss anything.

Chrissie smoothed down her skirt and buttoned her jacket. She picked her bag up from the table and ran a hand over her hair. 'God! What must she look like?' Turning to face him she asked bluntly, "What is it? What do you want?"

"It seems to me, my dear, that I could be of some help to you."

"What do you mean?"

"Well," he smiled pleasantly. "It just so happens that I am looking for a new girl to work at the Purple Parrot, and as you are not presently employed perhaps we could come to some arrangement?" He held his hand up to stop her as she opened her mouth to speak.

"I think you would find it a very pleasant experience to work here. All the girls at my club make a very good wage, one way or another, they'll all tell you. Of course, you would find it a little strange at first, but I have a couple of young ladies who have been with me for quite a while and if you would like to come along and have a little chat with them, they will explain a few things and get you sorted out. You could work in the bar for a while and maybe do a few hours with another girl on reception until you get used to it. What do you think?"

"Well, I don't know," Chrissie mumbled half to herself, not quite knowing what to make of it all. "I've never worked in a night club before," she added lamely.

'You think I don't know that, my little Irish rose?' Charles Latimer thought to himself. 'There's no way I'm going to let *you* slip through my fingers, you little beauty!' Trying to sound as relaxed as possible he took her gently by the elbow and led her to the door. "There's no hurry, my dear, really. You take all the time you need, but I'm sure with Christmas coming you'd like to have a few extra pounds in your purse now, wouldn't you?"

Chrissie smiled wanly up into the lean angular face and noticed again the long scar that ran down his cheek. "That's true," she agreed.

"Here take my card . . . and, please . . . give me ring as soon as you make up your mind. I don't want to offer anyone else the position until I know your decision." As he turned the large brass handle to open the door for her, Chrissie slipped the card into her bag and turning her head back to him asked timidly, "By the way . . . what sort of wages are you talking about?"

"Oh, you would have to start at the bottom, I'm afraid, my dear. Don't want any trouble with the other girls now, do we?"

"Well, how much then?" Chrissie demanded more firmly.

"Shall we say fifty pounds a week, just to start with . . ." he watched her pretty mouth drop open and her beautiful soft brown eyes grow wide in disbelief.

As her new boss opened the door wider to let Chrissie through, Silvie almost tumbled headlong in on top of them, an incredulous look on her bright pink face. She had heard every word. "Fifty bleedin' quid? Well *fuck me!*"

Charles Latimer looked down his long thin nose in disgust and sneered, "No *thank* you, my dear . . . I think I'd rather fuck my granny!"

He slammed the door on the two astonished faces.

13

"And just where do you think you're going, my girl?" Betty demanded breathlessly as she caught up with Chrissie before she reached the end of the street.

"Oh . . . em . . . Mrs Carter . . . I . . . emm." Chrissie turned slowly around to face the furious woman.

"Never mind all that!" Betty pushed Chrissie along the street in front of her. "You get back into that house right now, my girl, and tell me just where you spent last night! Daisy *told* me you crept in after I'd gone to work this morning. Guilty conscience, eh?"

Chrissie had already concocted a story about the wonderful job she had been offered the night before in a lovely 'posh' restaurant as a receptionist and was on her way to have a chat with the girl who was leaving, so she could show her the ropes. She told Betty that they had met a girl in a very nice coffee bar and she had told them about the job and given her the phone number to get in touch. She admitted to staying the night at Silvie's place, which she knew would not be very well received, to say the least, but after tossing and turning till daylight on the hard old divan in the front room, she had made her mind up to take her chances at the Purple Parrot. After all, what harm could it do? And there was certainly nothing else she was interested in doing at the moment. At least she could pay her way and finally be able to send a few pounds back home every week. Nobody would have to know.

Betty stood in stony silence, her arms folded firmly in front of her ample bosom listening to Chrissie's explaination of the evening's events. (Well the version Chrissie wanted to tell her anyway.) "Huh! I thought so!" Betty laughed sarcastically. "Bring some of her dodgy mates back with her, did she? Join them for a few drinks, did you? Then get too drunk to even stagger a couple of yards back home? I'm bloomin' disgusted with you girl! What would your mother say?"

Chrissie open her mouth to reply but decided against it. Thank

God she didn't know what really had gone on. Pulling her shoulders back and looking Betty straight in the eye she said as contritely as she could manage, "I'm very sorry, Mrs Carter. Truly I am. We were having such a good time looking at all the shops and the lovely Christmas lights an' all that we forgot about the time."

She watched the older woman's face soften a little as she thought for a moment and then turned to fill the kettle at the sink.

"Where's this place you're going to work then?'

"In Mayfair," Chrissie replied quickly.

"Sounds very posh."

"Oh, *yes!*" Chrissie rushed on, "It's a *gorgeous* place. Very busy and all sorts of rich looking people go there and you should see the fabulous cars they come in. The girl that's leaving told me she gets really good tips most nights and sometimes she earns more on tips than she gets in her wages, can you believe it? And do you know?" she went on, getting a bit carried away, "She drives a sport car and goes abroad on holiday twice a year at *least!*"

"Sounds a bit too good to be true, love," Betty frowned as she reached out for cups from the dresser.

"Oh, sorry, Mrs Carter, I won't be able to stop for tea. I have to be there in about an hour." Chrissie smiled.

"Well, what can I say Chrissie, love?" Betty looked into the eager young face, thinking that maybe this was the only chance she might have at getting a few extra quid towards the housekeeping for a while and God knows she could do with it! "Shall I keep you a bit of sausage and mash for later?" she grinned.

"Mmm, lovely," Chrissie smiled back and gave her a quick hug before she said a hurried goodbye.

"Oh, Chrissie," Betty called out to her before she closed the front door. "Have you got enough for the fare?"

"Yes, thanks," she called back and went quickly down the steps to the street, not waiting for Betty to ask her how she had managed that.

Betty sat stirring her tea for a long while after Chrissie had left, with a nagging thought at the back of her head, that if that little tart down the road had had anything to do with it, maybe Chrissie's excitement over her first job in London would be short lived and may not in fact turn out to be quite what she was expecting. She had read horrifying stories about innocent young girls being led astray and lured into lives of crime and vice, and prayed that nothing like that would happen to Chrissie.

Chrissie pulled out the five-pound note she had taken from the stolen wallet, paid the cab driver, took her change and handed him back a shilling tip. As he pulled away from the kerb the cabbie looked into his rear-view mirror and shook his head knowingly as he saw her smile up at the window cleaner and then go into the club. "Another lamb to the slaughter," he muttered.

The Purple Parrot looked almost ordinary in the daylight. There was no doorman to greet her this morning, just a freckled-faced young man polishing away on the glass and whistling to himself.

"Mornin'," he grinned down at Chrissie from his ladder. "Lovely day."

"Yes," Chrissie answered brightly.

When she just stood there he asked, "You looking for someone, love?"

"No, it's OK thanks, just seeing one of the girls about a job they offered me last night."

Bobby Brown stepped down and moved the ladder out of her way. "Oh right!" he smiled. What a cracking looking bird, he thought to himself. Dresses a bit like an old maid though. He thought she didn't look like the usual type he saw at the club. More like a secretary or something. They weren't a bad bunch of girls really and he earned a few extra quid from some of them, cleaning and polishing their cars. He wasn't daft though, he knew they were all call girls and most of them earned their wages on their backs after hours, but hey, who was he to judge? He had been in and out of the nick himself since he was fifteen. He had built up a nice little 'round' himself in W1 in the last couple of years and was proud to be bringing home an honest living for a change, and so he kept himself to himself. "Good luck!" he smiled again as he gathered up his bucket and cloths. "See you round, maybe."

Chrissie stood in the lobby looking about her and wondering what she should do now. There didn't seem to be anybody around. In the distance she could hear the soft muffled sound of someone playing the piano. Tip-toeing across the thick carpet and through the curtain-draped archway she followed the sound.

Stopping outside a set of double doors with small porthole windows, she waited a little nervously for a moment listening to the gentle rhythm. Then taking a deep breath she pushed on the doors that swung silently open and walked into the piano lounge. In the dim light she could see that the room was full of circular tables with dark purple cloths over them and the dainty chairs around them were covered in purple velvet. In the middle of each table was placed a single gilt candlestick with a tall purple candle in it. Black marble ashtrays sat alongside with a book of matches in each with a parrot design on the cover. At the end of the room was a long, well-stocked bar lined with tall chrome-legged stools. At one end of the bar was a large gold painted birdcage, where a purple feathered parrot perched motionless, staring across the room at her with huge black beady eyes. She looked over to the far corner and saw the small upright piano that was being played by a young woman. Just then the girl stopped playing, looked up and laughed, "God! you scared the living daylights out of me!"

Chrissie moved in and out of the tables until she reached her.

"I'm sorry, I didn't want to interrupt you. That was lovely, you play very well!" She held her hand out to introduce herself. "I'm Chrissie."

Maria nodded and took her hand.

"Hi, I'm Maria. Maria Costello. And you must be the new girl? The boss called me this morning, said you might drop in and if you did I was to explain a few things to you."

"Is he here?" Chrissie asked, looking quickly over her shoulder. "I was supposed to call first, but I thought I may as well come straight over!"

"You're joking!" Maria stood up. "Bet he doesn't even get out of bed til three o'clock!"

Chrissie was surprised to see that Maria was dressed casually in a pair of faded jeans, white t-shirt and a pair of old strappy sandals. Her dark blonde hair was scraped back into a tight bun at the back of her head and her high-cheekboned face was devoid of any make-up. But even in the dull light Chrissie could see the dark circles under her green eyes.

"Would you like a cup of coffee?"

"Yes, *please*," Chrissie answered gratefully. Her throat was parched and her head was beginning to ache again.

113

"Follow me, then."

They went through a door behind the bar into the kitchen and Maria pointed to a couple of chairs by a table in the corner.

"Take a pew," she winked at Chrissie. "You look as though you could do with a little livener. I'll make a pot shall I?"

"Lovely . . . thanks."

As Maria bustled about she wondered what had brought this pretty little thing to the club. She hadn't been working the night before so she hadn't heard the gossip about the scene. She turned to Chrissie, thinking how young she looked.

"Do you smoke?"

"'fraid so," Chrissie grinned.

"Hang on a mo, I'll get us a packet." She was back a few seconds later unwrapping the cellophane from a packet of king-size that she had 'borrowed' from the bar. "Here!"

"Thanks."

As they sat together chatting like old friends Maria found herself getting more concerned about Chrissie as she listened to her talking about her life back home and how she was now living with the family in Bermondsey. She wondered if she should warn her that she might be taking on a bit more than she could handle? She looked such an innocent compared with all the others, in her neat little navy-blue suit and white blouse, and it sounded to Maria that the girl was still a virgin. She *was* lovely though. The punters would be craving to get their dirty mitts on her. Curiosity finally getting the better of her she asked, "How did you know about this place then, Chrissie?"

Maria knew for a fact that the jobs were never advertised anywhere and Charles Latimer relied on word of mouth between the girls and their aquaintances. She couldn't imagine in her wildest dreams this naïve young women mixing with any of the others that worked there. Chrissie quickly explained how she had literally bumped into him on the boat over, months ago, and how he had given her his card, leaving out all the stuff with Silvie of course!

"Oh, I see," Maria smiled and took a deep draw on her cigarette.

"How long have you been here, Maria?"

"Couple of years come Christmas," she answered almost proudly.

"And where did you learn to play the piano like that? You're *very* good, you know."

"Taught myself," Maria blushed. "That's why I come in early every day, to practise. Well, apart from not being able to sleep anyway!"

Chrissie had the feeling that Maria was a sad person inside and wondered what *her* story was. "What do you do here, Maria?" she asked. "Are you behind the bar or a waitress or what?"

"Er ... no. Not exactly," Maria replied hesitantly and then taking a few mouthfuls of hot coffee, giving herself time to think, decided that she should explain a few things to the wide-eyed young girl sitting across the table. At least she could give her a chance to change her mind before she made any commitment. Once *in* it was almost impossible to get *out*, as she knew only too well herself.

Maria had been thrown out of the family home at the tender age of fifteen, because she wouldn't respond to her stepfather's over-amorous advances *and* because her mother wouldn't believe her when she tearfully tried to tell her how she had to put a chair behind the door to stop him from coming into her room. He had been trying it on with her for months. Every night when her mum went off to do her late-night cleaning jobs he would make lewd and disgusting suggestions to her and one night she was so terrified when he had sneaked up behind her and made a grab at her, shoving his fat sweaty hands up her skirt that she had run scream-ing to lock herself in the bathroom until she heard her mother come home.

Maria couldn't count the number of nights she had sobbed herself to sleep after hearing the old bastard taking it out on her poor mum because he couldn't have his way with *her*. It had sickened and disgusted her as she listened to the animal grunts and groans through the thin walls and her mother's cries of pain and humiliation. She had thought once or twice of writing to her brother, Billy, who was doing two years in Wandsworth for yet another spate of burglaries to pay for his drug habit, but decided against it because she knew it would wind him up so much that he would probably end up doing murder when he got out! They had both been through enough in their young lives and she didn't

115

relish the thought of visiting him 'inside' for the rest of his life. When she had finally plucked up the courage to tell her mum Maria had felt shocked and betrayed when her mother had flown at her in a violent rage, calling her all the filthy names she could lay her tongue to. "You're a dirty, filthy, lying little bitch!" she had screamed into the stunned girl's pale face. "You're a jealous little cow, d'ya know that, Maria! Ow *dare* ya say such vile things about my Ronnie! I've bloody 'ad enough of ya! Now GET OUT!"

"What?" Maria had whispered fearfully. "What do you mean, mum?" Already knowing the answer.

"I *said* get out of this fuckin' house! I never wanna see your bleedin' miserable face again!" She snatched her bag from the kitchen table and through gritted teeth muttered nastily, "I'm goin' down the off licence and when I come *back* you'd better be *gone*! Right?"

Maria stood quaking before her and nodded.

"You 'eard!" her mother screamed. "JUST FUCK OFF!"

Maria shivered and reached for another cigarette.

"You all right Maria?" Chrissie asked quietly, noticing the pained expression. She reached over and gave the girl's cold hand a little squeeze.

"Course I am!" Maria smiled quickly, holding the half empty cigarette packet out. "Here!"

"Thanks . . . again!"

"Look," Maria began, taking a deep breath. "Are you sure you want to work here, Chrissie?"

"Well, yes, yes I do," Chrissie answered, wondering why the other girl was looking so worried. "Why?"

"Well, it doesn't seem to me that you had any experience in this line, that's all."

"Oh, that's all right, I'm a quick learner," Chrissie assured her confidently. "Anyway what's to know about serving a few drinks or working at the desk out there? I'm sure I could pick it up in no time. Besides," she added ruefully, "I haven't got a lot of choice. I'm absolutely broke."

"Course you have a choice, silly! You *always* have a choice!"

"No I *don't*, Maria. I really *need* the money! Anyway, you haven't told me what *you* do here yet!"

Maria decided that she would try to shock Chrissie out of

coming to work at the club. "I'm a hostess, Chrissie," she answered flatly.

"A what?" Chrissie frowned.

"I'm a hostess," she repeated calmly. "I sit with the customers all night, drink cheap champagne, dance with them, flirt and talk dirty to them and then if they offer me enough I go home with them and do whatever they want! OK?"

Chrissie shifted awkwardly on the seat, blinking rapidly, her mouth open in surprise. "Oh shite!" she muttered.

"Yes, Chrissie . . . oh shite! as you so aptly put it!"

"But I thought . . .?" Chrissie began.

"No, you didn't think, you didn't think at all, did you?"

Chrissie did begin to think then! She sat motionless for almost five minutes without saying a word. Maria eventually stood up.

"Shall I make us another pot of coffee?" she asked kindly.

Chrissie came out of her trance. "Yes, please!"

"I'm sorry to have put it so bluntly, love," Maria said as she put the fresh coffee on the table between them. "But it was for your own good."

Chrissie watched her as she re-filled the cups and then asked, "If you get wages here, Maria, then why do you have to . . . em . . . do all that other stuff?"

Maria shuffled her feet under the table and picked at the corner of her thumbnail. She kept her head down, not wanting to meet Chrissie's innocent eyes.

"Well?" Chrissie asked again, puzzled.

"The thing is, love," Maria began in a low voice. "I've got a little bit of a problem."

"What sort of problem?"

Maria sighed heavily; what was the point? Everybody knew anyway and if Chrissie did come to work at the club some of the bitches that worked there would be only too glad to fill her in! "A bloody drug problem! What do you think?" she hissed.

"A *drug* problem?" Chrissie answered stupidly. "What are you talking about?" Chrissie was getting nervous now. This was a new world to her. She'd never met anyone involved with anything like this before. She's read about it in the Sunday paper, of course, but as far as she was concerned the people she was reading about might as well live on the bloody moon! She didn't know what to say as she gazed down at the black roots of Maria's bent head.

117

The tear-filled eyes came slowly up to meet Chrissie's. "Well, now you know!" she said softly, adding "Do you want me to call a cab for you?"

Chrissie ignored the question. "You said before that I had a choice, right?"

"Well . . . yes."

"So that means I don't have to do that stuff you were talking about if I don't *want* to, doesn't it?"

"I suppose so."

"So if I just sit and chat and have a dance or two, maybe flirt a bit, I don't have to do any of the other business and I'd still get my wages, right?"

"Well, yes . . . but . . ."

"That's what I'll do then." Chrissie smiled brightly, looking more confident than she actually felt.

"You don't *understand*, love," Maria tried. "Sometimes . . . the boss wants you to meet some of his 'special' customers and believe me it's not as easy as you make it sound to stick to the straight and narrow!"

"What do you mean?"

Maria sighed heavily again. "OK . . . for instance . . . one night I was offered two hundred quid to go up to the Dorchester with a couple of blokes and have a bit of fun with them!"

Chrissie gasped. "Two hundred pounds! Jesus Mary! What did you do?"

"What do you think I bloody did, you silly girl?" Maria managed a smile.

"Oh right!" Chrissie mumbled, embarrassed by the very thought of it and knowing that there was no way on earth she would ever let herself get involved with anything like that! 'Jesus, *two* men!' she thought.

"There is another thing, Chrissie," Maria started.

"What?" Chrissie replied quickly.

"Oh, nothing disgusting!" Maria laughed when she saw the horrified expression. "It's just that you have to pay for your dresses and things out of your wages every week."

"Oh, that's all right then!" Chrissie grinned back, thanking God that she hadn't said anything any worse than she had already told her. Maria looked at the clock on the wall and then back at the young woman opposite. "What are you going to do then?"

118

Chrissie stood up abruptly, brushed her skirt down and smiled. "You'd better show me around, hadn't you?"

Maria took Chrissie up to the girls' room, where they all met in the evenings before they got changed and made-up for work and engaged in noisy gossip and banter. There was not always friendly rivalry between them, however, and who could blame them? Each and every one of them had their own sad and disturbing stories to tell.

The room was messy but clean and was scattered with a hotch-potch collection of big armchairs and several little tables that were piled high with glossy magazines and newspapers. Maria showed Chrissie the rail of long and glamorous eveningwear that she could choose a couple of dresses from.

"Not the ones with the paper name tags clipped on, they're already spoken for," she told her. "Don't want to cause any trouble on your first night, eh? Look, these aren't bad." She pushed some of the dresses along to make a space on the rail so Chrissie could see a couple of the newer looking ones at the end.

"Oh, this one's *lovely*," Chrissie coo-ed, running her fingers over the black satin of the off-the-shoulder dress in front of her. "Looks like my size too!"

"What size are you?" Maria asked.

"I don't know, to tell you the truth. I usually make my own clothes."

"Really?" Maria was impressed. "Try it on."

Chrissie looked around for somewhere to change. Knowing what she was thinking Maria told her to just go behind the rail if she was shy. You'll have to get over that in a bloody hurry, she thought to herself.

Chrissie giggled as she nipped behind the line of dresses and quickly stripped down to her white cotton underwear. She wrinkled her nose as she caught a glimpse of herself in the long narrow mirror on the wall and promised herself that she would buy herself some fancy 'undies' with her first week's wages.

When she emerged from behind the rail, she saw that Maria was sitting on the arm of one of the comfortable looking armchairs flicking through a magazine.

"Wow!" she smiled broadly when she saw Chrissie. "You look lovely!" Too bloody good for this place, she thought.

"Do you think so?" Chrissie asked, knowing full well that she looked absolutely gorgeous. "Can you do the zip, please, I can't quite reach it?" She had never worn anything so glamorous or daring in her life. And she *loved* it! The two girls laughed as Chrissie paraded around the room, holding her head high and thrusting out her shapely bosom with its newly displayed cleavage and swaying her hips provocatively for fun.

"You should wear your hair down, Chrissie, it would look great like that."

"Do you think so?"

"Certainly would."

They carried on chatting while Chrissie took the dress off and following Maria's advice tore a little piece of paper off the top of a magazine, scribbled her name on it and pinned it with a hair-clip on to the front of the dress.

"Where's the toilet, Maria?" Chrissie asked as she hung the dress carefully back on the rail. "I'm bursting with all that coffee!"

"Over there," she pointed to a door in the corner.

While Chrissie was out of the room Maria sat thinking to herself. A sudden idea came to her.

"That's better!" Chrissie laughed, as she came back tucking a few strands of hair that had escaped behind her ear.

"I've just been thinking, Chrissie," Maria said.

"Oh, yes?"

"You know you were saying earlier that you would love to get your own place?"

"Yes?"

"Well, I was just wondering if you would like to share with me. I know its not exactly your *own* place, but it would be a start."

"Pardon?" Chrissie said in surprise.

"It's just that . . ." Maria began, a little embarrassed. "Well you see I have a two-bedroomed flat over in Bayswater and to tell you the truth," she grinned, "I've got a tiny bit behind with the rent and I could really do with a flatmate! What do you think?"

Chrissie couldn't believe it! A job and a place of her own, well more or less, all in one day! She accepted without hesitation and hugged Maria warmly. "That'd be *great*, Maria. Thank you *so much*!"

"Right, then," Maria said when they reached the lobby a few minutes later. "See you tomorrow then. I'll meet you at Marble Arch tube station about ten o'clock and you can come back with me and see what you think." Chrissie gave her a warm hug saying; "Thanks for everything, Maria. See you tomorrow."

Chrissie pushed the heavy door open and let herself out.

She tripped lightly along the busy streets without a care in the world, humming happily to herself as she hailed a taxi to take her back to Bermondsey. On the way back she invented another little yarn that she would spin to Mrs Carter about her good fortune over the flat.

14

"FIFTY BLOODY POUNDS A WEEK!" Better Carter nearly choked on the mouthful of sausage and mash.

Chrissie rushed over to pat her on the back as the poor woman sat doubled over the kitchen table scarlet-faced, as she coughed and spluttered noisily, in shock. When she eventually caught her breath she asked wheezily, "What in the name of God sort of job is that?"

Chrissie got her a glass of cold water and sat down again, trying to explain with an angelic look on her face. "I told you, Mrs Carter. I am going to be a receptionist at the restaurant and maybe sometimes do a bit of waitressing. And, like you said yourself, it's a *very* posh place. Costs a fortune to eat there, too." she added for good measure.

Betty gave her a suspicious glare, her red eyes beginning to water again. "Sounds too good to be true, if you ask me!" she said hotly shoving the remains of her dinner away.

"Sounds great to me!" Daisy piped in goggled eyed with excitement.

"No one asked for your opinion!" Betty snapped.

"There is something else," Chrissie said hesitantly.

"What!"

Chrissie waited for a moment before saying anything as she looked at the pinched expression on Betty's face. Oh what the hell? "I'm going to be sharing a flat with one of the girls there."

Betty pushed her chair back and stood up slowly, her eyes never leaving Chrissie's. She leaned heavily on the table on her broad knuckles. "I can't believe what I've just heard!" she breathed. "After all we've done for you, Chrissie, and now you're just going to up and away without a thought for anyone but yourself!"

Chrissie felt a niggle of anger inside her but she did her best to keep her temper under control. Having a row with Betty was the last thing she wanted to do but she felt aggrieved that she couldn't feel just a tiny bit pleased for her. After all if she had had any notion at all about what had really happening over the last couple of days and what kind of establishment the Purple Parrot truly was, Chrissie was without a doubt that she'd have kicked her backside out into the street and been told never to darken her doorstep again!

When she saw Betty open her mouth to speak again, Chrissie rushed from the room before any more harsh words could be thrown at her. She stayed up in the little room that she shared with Daisy for the rest of the evening listening to the low murmur of voices of Betty and her husband Mick, when he came home late from a hard day's work. She knew that they were talking about her and waited for Daisy to come up to bed to tell her what they had been saying. Her stomach was rumbling noisily as she realised that she hadn't had anything to eat all day, but she didn't dare go downstairs again to get her dinner from the oven.

Chrissie lay on the bed staring at the cracks in the ceiling for hours, wishing away the hunger pangs and wondering if she was doing the right thing working at the club. She had convinced herself she could handle it and in a strange way was oddly excited about it all. Whatever ideas came into her head nothing seems to diminish the thrill of earning such a huge amount of money every week, and the idea of wearing such swish clothes was just a dream come true. Anyway, if things did get out of hand she could just walk out. She was sure Maria wouldn't throw her out of the flat; she seemed such a kind girl, even with her problem. Chrissie couldn't make head nor tail of that side of things, she hadn't liked to press Maria for any more details when she saw the sad look in the girl's tired eyes. 'If it all goes wonky,' she told herself, "I'll just have to admit defeat, that's all, and take any old sort of work to help pay my share of the rent.'

Just as her eyelids began to droop Daisy appeared in the doorway carrying a plate of sausage and mash, swimming in steaming hot gravy, on a small tin tray. "Here," she beamed. "Mum said you'd better eat this or you'll be sick."

"Oh Daisy!" Chrissie almost wept. "You're an angel!"

As they sat together on the side of the bed Chrissie asked Daisy, through mouthfuls of dinner, what they had been saying about her.

"I don't really know, Chrissie, they sent me into the front room," she answered honestly.

123

"Did they?"

"Yeah!" Daisy giggled. "At least I didn't get sent into the backyard like I usually do when they don't want me to hear what they're taking about! Too bloody nippy out there tonight!"

"Stop cursing!" Chrissie said, sounding just like her own mother.

"You can talk!"

"And don't be so cheeky!"

"Huh!" Daisy snorted and then said, "She can't be too mad at you, can she? She *was* going to give your dinner to next door's cat after you stomped off up here!"

The next morning Chrissie got up before anyone else and crept into the bathroom to have a quick wash before they heard her. When she had finished she went back to the bedroom and pulled her suitcase from under the bed. She glanced over at Daisy's peaceful face as she slept on and opening the two drawers of the dressing table as quietly as possible she slipped her few belongings quickly into the empty case. She had decided not to say goodbye to anyone and was going to leave a note that she had scribbled before she went to sleep, thanking them for all their kindnesses to her, and God knows there had been many. She promised to keep in touch with them and send them a forwarding address for her mother's letters, as soon as possible.

Chrissie held firmly on to the bannister as she sneaked down the stairs, carefully avoiding the squeaky ones, and held her breath as she tip-toed into the kitchen with her brief note. As she trod silently along the narrow passage and pulled the front door open without making a sound, something made her look back over her shoulder. Betty Carter was sitting at the top of the stairs with tears rolling down her cheeks. With a lump in her throat and a tight determined smile Chrissie pulled the door wide open and said firmly, "Bye, Mrs Carter!"

"Bye, Chrissie, love," she replied in a hushed voice. "Good luck and God bless."

Chrissie couldn't bear it! She closed the door with a bang and sped down the street with her suitcase banging painfully on the side of her leg and tears streaming from her own eyes now. She slowed down when she turned the corner and putting her case on the pavement beside her leaned against the window of Wilson's bakery, brushing away the tears with the palms of her chilly hands. Mr Wilson was just putting a huge tray of fresh currant buns in the window and looked up at her in surprised concern. "What in heaven's name is going on?" he wondered when he saw the distressed girl. Just as he was about to open the door and ask her what was wrong, she noticed him watching her. Picking up her case she marched off down the street towards Tower Bridge Road without a backward glance. She knew she would find one of the cafés down there open for business and she had just about enough money left now from the fiver, to get something to eat and to pay her tube and bus fare over to the West End. No more cabs for her for a while.

Chrissie relaxed as she sat on a wobbly stool by the window munching on a slice of toast and jam and sipping at a mug of boiling hot tea. The warmth around her was cosy and comforting and as she looked about her at the crowded café one of the burly workmen sitting near caught her eye. Pointing with his knife to her suitcase, he asked pleasantly, "Off on holiday then, sweetheart?"

Chrissie nearly choked on the mouthful of bread. "Yes . . . I'm going to Spain. Got a job there in a big new hotel!" she smiled cheerfully after she had swallowed another mouthful of tea to stop herself coughing. "Grand, isn't it?"

Chrissie met up with the bleary-eyed Maria outside Marble Arch tube station, as arranged. The girl was shivering with the cold, hugging herself tightly in an effort to keep out the chill. She had a long brightly coloured hand-knitted scarf wrapped protectively around her head and the shoulders of her knee-length sheepskin coat. Chrissie looked into the dark-circled eyes and thought that she looked as though she hadn't slept a wink all night (which indeed she hadn't.)

"You OK?" Chrissie asked.

"Yeah, fine thanks," Maria grinned back. "Just a bit tired, that's all! Bloody *freezing* today, isn't it?"

"Mmm. You're right there," Chrissie nodded back as a raw gust of wind blew along the busy street.

"Come on," Maria urged as she linked arms with Chrissie. "We can get a bus to my place over there," she nodded across the wide road.

125

Chrissie was pleased to see that it was only a few stops to the Bayswater Road and was feeling more and more excited about seeing Maria's flat for the first time.

They turned off the main street and hurried along the row of tall and elegant terraced houses. Chrissie was pleasantly surprised when they stopped outside one of them. She looked up at the four-storey house and thought how grand it looked, with its shiny black front door and the gleaming brass of the lion's-head knocker. Almost as grand as the ones around Stephen's Green, she smiled to herself, 'well, *almost*!'

She wasn't so pleased, however, when she had to drag and bump her suitcase up the stairs to the top floor. The first couple of flights had been covered in an expensive looking patterned carpet, but as they climbed beyond the first floor, the carpet disappeared and was replaced by cracked linoleum, and by the time they reached the top floor the steps were just bare boards. The small landing at the top of the house was dark and dingy and Chrissie stood puffing and panting behind her new flatmate as she turned the key in the door, feeling very apprehensive.

As she followed Maria into the tiny flat, Chrissie was relieved to see that it was clean, bright and warm. The cheap furniture was neatly arranged around the small sitting room and there was a light smell of pine disinfectant.

"Put your stuff down, then," Maria said, "and I'll show you around. Not that that'll take too long!" she grinned.

Chrissie put her handbag down on one of the two over-stuffed armchairs and then wedged her case between them. She pulled off her coat and laid it across the back of the chair. Her tour took all of three minutes! Maria showed her the little blue-tiled bathroom, her own sparsely furnished bedroom and the tiny empty box-room that was to be Chrissie's room. Maria giggled when she saw the blank expression on her face as Chrissie stood in the doorway looking at the empty space.

"Don't worry," she laughed, "you won't have to sleep on the floor! I told Gino downstairs that you would be coming and he said I could borrow his spare 'put-u-up'. He works in the Pizza Palace down the road and he's going to bring it up when he comes home later on this afternoon."

"Thank God for that!" Chrissie laughed back in relief, wondering at the same time what a Pizza Palace was!

"I've got a spare pair of sheets and a blanket that you can have as well," Maria told her.

Chrissie sat in the sitting room and waited for Maria to make them some tea. The kitchen was so small that two of them couldn't get into it at the same time!

"I know it's a bit cramped," Maria called out to her, "but we'll manage, won't we? Take our turns in the bathroom and stuff!"

"Course we will!" Chrissie called out more cheerfully than she felt. It wasn't *quite* what she had imagined, but as she told herself, 'beggars couldn't be choosers and she would be silly not to take up the offer and make the most of it. Anyway, with the great wages she would be getting it wouldn't be too long before she could start saving up for a deposit for a proper place of her own. "We'll be fine!"

After helping the curly headed young Gino up the stairs with the folded bed and thanking him for his kindness, Chrissie made up the bed and then brought her suitcase into the small room. Maria had given her one of the wooden chairs from her bedroom and a small pink rug to go alongside the narrow bed. As Chrissie sat deep in thought on the edge of the low mattress Maria popped her head around the door saying, "I've finished in the bathroom, Chrissie. You'd better get yourself 'tarted up', we've only got an hour or so before we have to leave. My hairdryer's in the kitchen if you want to borrow it. It'll take ages to dry that mop of yours otherwise!" she called over her shoulder as she went back into the sitting room and sat down heavily into an armchair. She was exhausted! The night before had been marathon; even for *her*! She glanced back and glimpsed Chrissie in the tiny kitchen as she plugged the hairdryer into the socket on the wall and switched it on. Maria felt around with her fingers under the edge of the chair and pulled out a battered tobacco tin and swiftly rolled herself a thin joint of marihuana. Chrissie was completely unaware of what her new found friend was up to as she flicked her long tresses from side to side and ran a hand through her thick mane, in an attempt to dry her hair as quickly as possible. She was delighted with the power of the small appliance, (the only other time she had used one was when she had borrowed Silvie's one morning, but this one was much better).

When Maria heard the dryer being switched off she guiltily

squeezed the end of the lighted 'cigarette' and put it carefully back in the old tin and shoved it under the chair.

"All done," Chrissie announced a while later, as she stood in the doorway wrinkling her nose. "What's that funny smell?"

"Yes, I was wondering that?" Maria answered as she stood up abruptly. "Must be Gino cooking up something exotic."

"Really?" Chrissie frowned again. "Smells disgusting!"

The two girls arrived breathlessly at the Purple Parrot just before seven o'clock that evening. They'd made a last-minute scramble to get ready for work and a mad dash off down the street to catch the bus to get them there in time.

Chrissie followed Maria quickly through the deserted lobby and up the back stairs to the girls' room. It was full of noisy chatter and as Maria pushed open the door Beth looked across knowingly at Chrissie's uncomfortable expression. "Hello again!" she smirked, as she ran her hands up the length of her long shapely leg and hooked a button up on her black suspenders. Dropping the hem of the silky dress, she turned to a couple of girls who were sprawled out reading magazines, saying, "Have you met our new recruit?"

Chrissie blushed furiously as she met the curious gaze of Ulrika, a strikingly attractive cool, natural blonde Swedish girl and Chloe, a dark-skinned sultry young woman, with a voluptuous figure, full red lips and the most stunning smile Chrissie had ever seen. Another small group of girls were standing together laughing uproariously as they exchanged notes from the previous night's work. They nodded their greetings and gave her a quick once-over and went back to their chatting.

"Evenin' all,' Maria gave a quick general wave around the room and then, turning to Chrissie, asked her in lowered voice how she knew Beth.

"It's a *long* story," Chrissie whispered back. "Tell you later."

A few more girls arrived giving Chrissie cursory glances as she stood awkwardly in the middle of the room fidgeting with her handbag, and not knowing quite what to do next.

"Come on!" Maria grinned. "Get a move on!"

Beth glided past them on her way out, remarking over her shoulder, "Yes, you'd better get a move on, dear, it'll take you all night to get yourself looking even halfway decent!"

Chrissie's face reddened in temper as she open her mouth to answer.

"Oh, leave it, Chrissie," Maria said. "She's just a jealous old bitch! Can't stand to see a new face around here, frightened you will put her nose out of joint!"

"Oh I'd *love* to!" Chrissie seethed.

Maria cackled with laughter. "Yeah, I know how you feel!"

The room was nearly empty now as the two girls hurriedly stripped off, Chrissie behind the rail, of course, and prepared themselves for the evening. Her hands were trembling as she slipped into her long gown and fiddled with her hair.

"Haven't you got any more make-up than that?" Maria asked when she came over to do the zip up for Chrissie and saw the powder compact and the small tube of lipstick on the table.

"No!"

Maria looked at the flushed face and asked her if she was OK. "Haven't changed your mind or anything?"

"No, I'm fine ... really. Just a bit of a headache. Too much excitement for one day." Chrissie tried to laugh. Maria open her bulging make-up bag and pulled out a few bits and pieces offering them to Chrissie.

"Here, put a bit of eyeshadow and mascara on. Do you want me to do you a bit of eyeliner?"

"No, I can manage thanks," Chrissie said gratefully.

Maria felt sorry for her as she saw the amateurish way Chrissie was applying the make-up. She watched the girl's reflection in the wall mirror and thought again of how lovely looking she was, so fresh and innocent and yet in another way so mature for her years. She asked Chrissie again, "You *sure* about all this!"

"Course I am, silly!" Chrissie answered steadily. "I'll be fine when I get started. I'm just a little bit tired that's all! Too much to take in all at once!"

Maria took a glass from the cupboard under the sink and filled it with water. She turned her back on Chrissie and took a small box out of her bag.

"What's that?" Chrissie asked curiously as she saw what she was doing.

Maria coloured slightly as she answered; "Just a little something to get me going! You *know?*"

AUDREY JACKSON

Chrissie reached out and took hold of Maria's clenched fist. "Let's have a look!"

Maria opened her fingers slowly and Chrissie saw half a dozen little blue pills.

"What are *they*?"

"I told you, something to give me a bit of energy."

Chrissie picked one up between her thumb and forefinger and peered closely at it. "I had one of these the other night!"

"No? Where?" Maria frowned.

Chrissie didn't want to launch into the full-length version of her night out with Silvie, so she just said, "Oh, I was out with a friend and we had a bit too much to drink and my head was lifting off me, so she gave me one of her painkillers!"

Maria wondered at the naivety of the girl. Or perhaps she wasn't as innocent as she was making out. "And you felt OK afterwards?'

"Yes I felt great!" Chrissie nodded.

Maria held out her open palm. "Do you want a couple of these then?" she asked cautiously.

"Well, you're surely not going to take *all* of them?" Chrissie hesitated for a moment looking down at the little pile of pills. "Course not!" the girl answered quickly.

"OK then!"

"Might as well," Maria sighed. "Give you a bit of Dutch Courage, and there's plenty more where they came from!" Not wanting to appear as gauche as she was feeling Chrissie took three pills from the outstretched hand and popped them into her mouth. Maria laughed as she upended the glass and tipped the water into the sink: "Oh bugger the water, wash 'em down with this." She pulled a small flat bottle out of her bag and half filled the glass again.

"What's that?" Chrissie spluttered, trying not to let the pills fall out of her mouth.

"Mother's ruin!" Maria giggled.

Chrissie grimaced as she swigged down a mouthful of the neat gin.

"Yuk!"

"Come on, Cinderella," Maria grinned crookedly as she linked Chrissie's arm, "Let's go to the ball!"

* * *

Beth gasped as she caught sight of the two girls sauntering arm in arm down the stairs, chatting and giggling like old pals. They made quite a striking pair! She watched them jealously as they strolled through to the piano bar together, her own pretty face contorted with envy.

"Whew! Quite a looker, eh?" Reg said, giving a low admiring whistle.

"She's OK," Beth snapped back. "Won't last long!"

"Now, now, don't be bitchy!" he grinned.

Beth ignored him and sat back down on her high stool behind the desk and pretended to concentrate on a heap of receipts that she was supposed to have gone through earlier. She had other things on her mind (including how on earth she was going to 're-arrange' the figures to cover her petty pilfering!). Just at that moment Charles Latimer came out of his office and stopped dead in his tracks when he saw Chrissie and Maria going into the bar.

"Good evening, ladies," he nodded as he came towards them.

"Evening, Mr Latimer," Maria called back sweetly over her shoulder.

Chrissie took a deep breath and turned to face him. "Good evening."

"So you decided to join us tonight then, my dear?"

"Yes."

"Good," he smiled, unable to take his eyes from her. Her eyes sparkled with humour and her full red lips curved in an audacious smile. The thick and gleaming hair cascaded over her shoulders and brushed the soft pale skin on her neck enticingly and he longed to reach out and push back the heavy waves that hung down one side of her face, partially covering one of her dark velvety eyes. Licking his dry lips he caught hold of her elbow and nodded to Maria, "You carry on, Maria. I'd like to have a quick word with Chrissie."

Maria looked sideways at Chrissie. "You OK?" she said, almost under her breath.

"Why shouldn't I be?" Chrissie laughed, flicking the weight of her hair away from her face.

"See you later then."

"Sure."

Tripping lightly along beside her boss Chrissie wondered what he wanted to talk to her about. As he held the door open for her to pass, the closeness of her warm body was almost too much to resist, but resist he must! He couldn't believe his good fortune, but vowed to keep his hands off her for the time being. He had some heavy deals going down at the moment with his contacts from LA and, if she was agreeable, which he was almost certain she would be, she would be a real asset to him.

Chrissie perched on the broad arm of the leather sofa and accepted the glass of brandy as though it was the most natural thing in the world to her. She sipped her drink as she watched Charles Latimer relax into his chair smiling congenially. Wishing to appear calm and sure of herself, she returned his smile.

"Well now, my dear," he began as he reached into his pocket for his cigarette case. She sat up straight. "Yes?"

He stood and came around the desk offering her a cigarette. As she took one and he lit it for her he continued, "I have been thinking."

"What's that?" she asked, pursing her lips and blowing a long plume of smoke into the air. Charles Latimer walked slowly around the room as he made his proposal. "I have been thinking, my dear, that you are far too good to be working out there," he indicated towards the door, "and I was wondering if you would like to do a little 'private' work for me?"

"Private work?" Chrissie grinned, her eyes following him. "Now what exactly would *that* mean?"

Her heart began to beat rapidly and she prayed that he wasn't about to ask her to do anything too disgusting.

"For a start, my dear, it would mean that you would be earning an awful lot of money for a young woman of your age and it would involve travelling to some very exciting and interesting places . . ." He held up his hand to stop her when she opened her mouth to speak. "Let me continue!"

"I was only going to ask if I could have another drink!" she pouted.

"Of course!"

Chrissie took a deep breath and exhaled loudly. What on earth is he talking about? she thought. As she stubbed out her cigarette she watched him pouring the drinks and couldn't help admiring the cut of his expensive suit, the style of his handmade shoes and the glint from his gold cufflinks. As she took a mouthful of her fresh drink she gave a little hiccup and giggled, "Oops, sorry!" she put a hand to her mouth.

Charles Latimer stood in front of her frowning. "Listen my dear. I want you to listen *very* carefully . . ."

"I am!" she glared up at him. "I am!"

He looked into her wide over-bright eyes and it crossed his mind to ask her what she had taken that night, apart from the alcohol. He wasn't stupid. He could see that she was a little 'high'. Still, that was her problem! If that was the way she wanted to play it: all the better for him in the long run. He could supply her with anything she needed. He guessed that it was undoubtedly Maria who had given her a few pills for Dutch Courage, but decided against saying anything until he was sure she'd accept his generous offer. "OK, calm down," he said, waving his hand dismissively.

"Sorry," Chrissie mumbled in fake contriteness.

"The thing is, my dear," he started again. "I would like you to do a little trip for me to the states. To LA, to be precise." He grinned when he saw her frowning. "Los Angeles," he explained. Chrissie didn't dare say anything. She was too ashamed to admit that she had never even heard of the place.

"I have some business associates there and they have a few 'packages' that I would like you to pick up and bring back for me, that's all. Simple, eh?"

Chrissie grinned cheekily at him. "Why can't they post them?"

"Don't be stupid, Chrissie!" he snapped back. "Our business is very confidential and everything is carried out on a very personal basis."

"Oh . . . I see."

She didn't 'see' at all, but guessed quite rightly that it must certainly be something illegal. Probably diamond smugglers or something, she thought to herself.

"It would also mean that you would be taking something for them, too," he said seriously, pausing for a moment. "Money. In fact . . . a lot of money!" He studied her expression closely as he came and sat on the sofa. "Come and sit down properly," he patted the seat beside him.

Chrissie obediently slid off the arm of the sofa and leaving a wide space between them she turned and looked at him. "What exactly *is* in it for me?" she asked.

"For a start, Chrissie, I would give you enough money to buy yourself a decent wardrobe before you went." When he saw the pleasure in her eyes, he continued quickly. "Some nice dresses, a few smart suits, matching bags and shoes. What do you think?"

"Sounds great!" she beamed, as she wriggled excitedly.

"And then, if all goes according to plan, I will pay you your 'wages' when you return."

Chrissie hardly dared ask, but she did. "How much?"

"£500!" he replied immediately.

"What!" Chrissie almost shouted. "£500 feckin' pounds!"

"Keep your voice down, my dear," he warned, "and do moderate your language! It doesn't suit you at all."

Chrissie stood up and began pacing around the room. She couldn't believe it! Surely she was dreaming?

Just then the shrill of the telephone interrupted their conversation and as her boss answered the call and spoke quietly into the mouthpiece, Chrissie went unthinkingly to the drinks cabinet and poured herself another generous helping of Courvoisier. This was absolutely unbelievable! But there was no way she was going to turn down an opportunity like this. Her mind was racing with all the things she could do with the money. There would be no stopping her now! Her hands were shaking as she raised the glass to her quivering lips. 'So what, if it's not all above-board?' she thought recklessly. 'Who's to bloody know anyway?'

As he replaced the receiver, Charles Latimer turned and asked, "Well? What do you think, my dear?"

"I think it sounds just fine, Mr Latimer!" she smiled winningly. "Just *fine*!"

"Wonderful!" he rubbed his hands together. "Wonderful!"

He came over to Chrissie and slowly removed the empty glass from her and put it on his desk. He placed his cool hands on to her firm, shapely shoulders and looked deeply into her glowing eyes. "But I must tell you, my dear, that before we go ahead with our little 'arrangement' I have to have your solemn assurance that whatever is said or done between us, or any of my associates in this business, will remain completely and utterly between those directly involved. Do you understand?" He gripped her shoulders a little more firmly. His face was so close to hers that Chrissie had the awful feeling that he was about to kiss her and in a moment of panic she pulled his hands roughly from her shoulders and shot back, "What do you think I am? Stupid? Of course I can keep my mouth shut!"

"Good," he muttered. "Now, my dear," he smiled at her, thinking how lovely she looked as she stood glaring at him, with her flushed cheeks and brazen expression, "I have a little treat for you."

"Really?" Chrissie answered coyly as she brought her temper under control.

"Yes! That was a friend of mine on the telephone, inviting us to dinner."

"Was it?"

"Yes," he nodded. "So if you'd like to run along and get yourself a wrap or something, I'll get Reggie to bring the car around and we can be off!"

Chrissie couldn't take it all in. What the hell was going on? "OK," she said as she floated through the door he was holding open for her. "Won't be long."

As she made her way back down the corridor and pushed at the swing doors into the club, she wiped a hand across her feverish brow. Her head felt strange, light and fuzzy, not quite with it. The piano bar was almost full and as she wound her way through the busy tables she was vaguely aware of the tinkling of the piano in the far corner as she peered though the blue smoky haze for a glimpse of Maria. As she put her hand on the door that led up to the girls' restroom, she caught sight of Maria waving to her from across the dimly lit lounge. Chrissie beckoned to her to come over. Maria rose quickly to her feet and planted a kiss on the bald perspiring head of her first customer of the night. "Back in a tick, sweetheart," she coo-ed. "Just popping out to powder me nose."

As she eased herself past his short bulky figure he grabbed at her small rounded bottom and squeezed it spitefully between his sweaty hands. "Don't be long darlin'," he groused. "Haven't got all night!"

Maria made her way over to Chrissie pulling a tissue from her bag and wiping the vile taste from her lips as she thought, Course you haven't got all night, you arsehole! Probably have to get home to the poor wife and kids with the remains of the housekeeping money!

Following Chrissie quickly up the stairs she asked her friend breathlessly what was going on. What had 'old Charlie boy' said to her?

"Just asked me to go out to dinner with him and his friend," Chrissie lied, keeping her face averted from Maria's inquisitive stare, as she rummaged through the piles of clothes on the chairs looking for something to throw around her shoulders.

"Oh! Is that all?" Maria sounded disappointed. "Thought at least he was going to ask you to entertain some of his mates for the night."

"What?" Chrissie spun around. "I told you I'm not doing all that stuff."

"OK, OK, keep your bloody hair on!" Maria laughed. "What're you doing up here anyway?"

"I'm looking for a shawl or something," she explained, beginning to shake with nerves. "I've only got my coat with me and I can't wear that with this dress," she wailed. "It'll look daft!"

"Oh for God's sake, stop panicking!" Maria tried to sooth her. "I think I've got a black one in my cupboard."

Chrissie breathed a sigh of relief as Maria produced a large square of delicately woven black wool and handed it to her.

"Oh thanks, Maria," she sighed. "You've saved my life!"

"Well, hardly," Maria giggled. "It's only an old thing that I haven't used for ages."

Chrissie quickly folded it corner to corner, swung it around her shoulders and knotted it loosely across her ample bosom. "OK?" she turned to face Maria.

"Lovely" she smiled back. "Where're you going anyway?" she added.

"Haven't a clue to tell you the truth," Chrissie said with a little worried frown.

"Bound to be somewhere posh."

"You think so?"

"Course," Maria assured her. "He knows how to look after himself, that one!"

Chrissie chewed on her bottom lip as she turned to check her reflection in the mirror again.

"You sure you're up for this?" Maria asked her when she saw the shadow of doubt cross Chrissie's face.

"Sure I am!" Chrissie answered. "Just that my head feels a bit woozy."

"Fancy a quickie?" Maria asked, as she went over to the little cupboard under the sink.

"A what?"

Maria stood up and grinned cheekily as she held up a small flat bottle of vodka and waved it in the air.

"Jesus!" Chrissie grinned back. "I think I've had enough already."

"Oh, don't be such a spoil sport!" Maria chided her as she twisted the cap on the bottle. "At least have one snifter with me, before you go off into the wide blue yonder!" After she had taken a deep slug of the neat vodka she wiped the rim with her hand and held the bottle out. "Here." Chrissie took the bottle and tilted it into her mouth. As the biting sting of the liquor hit the back of her throat she almost choked on it and she coughed and spluttered till her face turned crimson.

"For feck's sake, Maria, what the hell are you trying to do to me?" She gasped as the coughing fit finally abated and she rummaged in her bag for a tissue to wipe her wet cheeks and runny nose.

"Oh, stop moaning!" her friend chided, grinning at Chrissie. "You know you love it!"

Chrissie opened her mouth to say something but when she saw the cheeky look on Maria's face she just shrugged her shoulders and grinned crookedly back. "Well I guess I could get used to it!"

Just then the door burst open and a furious Beth stomped into the room. "Lover boy sent me up to get you!" she spat nastily. "Get a move on! He's pacing around down there like a man demented!"

Chrissie refused to be drawn into an argument with this stuck-up little madam, but she mentally filed it away to deal with another time. Anyway she was feeling good about tonight and she wasn't going to let some jealous bitch spoil it for her.

"Thank you" she smiled sweetly into Beth's sour face as she brushed past her and made her way back downstairs. "Don't work too hard."

Beth snorted her disgust as she rounded on Maria. "What's she up to?"

"Haven't got a clue," Maria answered quietly as she thought to herself, and if I did I wouldn't bloody tell you!

Chrissie sat entranced beside her boss in the back of his gleaming limousine and feeling very elegant, even though a little tipsy, as they made their smooth journey towards the restaurant. It was only a few streets away and the excited young woman was a little disappointed that they had arrived so quickly. Reggie pulled up smoothly at the kerb and then opened the door for them with a small smile on his handsome face. Chrissie allowed herself to be drawn from the car by his strong hand and gasped in delight when she saw the plush façade of the exclusive establishment.

"Thank you, Reggie," Charles nodded and he joined Chrissie on the pavement. "I'll call you later."

"Enjoy your evening, Mr Latimer," he inclined his head. "And you too, Chrissie."

"Thanks," she grinned back cheekily. "I will."

As they waited to take their turn through the huge revolving doors, Chrissie's stomach was quivering with excitement. She felt Charles' hand slide firmly around her small waist and gained a little comfort, in a strange way, from its support.

"Ready?" he asked.

"Of course," she answered quickly, straightening her shoulders as she glanced sideways up at him and wondered again about the long thin scar on his angular face. "Can't wait!"

Chrissie slipped her arm through Charles' and clung on tightly as they made their way across the black and white marble tiles in the foyer and took their place in the small queue waiting to be shown to their tables.

"Ah! Good evening, Mr Latimer, sir! What a pleasure it is to see you again."

They were greeted amiably by the *maitre De*, a short and very red-faced Italian, with a thick fat neck and wobbling chins who beamed delightedly at them as he shook Charles' hand warmly.

"Thank you, Antonio."

"And may I also welcome you too, madam, to our humble establishment?" Antonio gave a little bow. Chrissie was beginning to feel overwhelmed – this fabulous place was anything but humble; but she smiled politely back and murmured her thanks. She felt an urge for another drink as she licked her dry lips and gazed around at the elegant decor, admiring the high ceilings and the sparkling chandeliers, the heavy deep-red velvet curtains that draped several archways around the reception area and the huge potted palms that stood so exotically in black marble urns. In one corner of the large foyer was a tall Christmas tree exquisitely adorned from head to foot in gold and crimson shining baubles. Her stomach knotted for a moment as she wondered what everyone at home was doing right know and if they were missing her at all. She was brought abruptly back to the present by the sound of Charles' voice.

"Pretty, isn't it, my dear?" he smiled at her child-like expression.

"It's lovely," she whispered.

"If you'd like to follow me please, sir—madam," a young man indicated towards the dining room. "Your dining companions have already arrived."

Chrissie felt as though she was walking through wonderland as they passed under the marble archway and into the dining room. As they made their way between the occupied tables to the far side of the huge room, where elegantly clad groups sat in low conversation, she could barely take in the opulence of her surroundings as she tried to control her breathing to calm down the rapid beating of her heart. Never in a million years would she have dreamt that one day she would be eating in a place like this! As they neared their own table she saw two swarthy men, in beautifully tailored evening suits and white, stiff-fronted shirts, rise to greet them.

They looked like twins, but one was slightly taller and slimmer than the other.

"Evening, Charles," the taller one said, holding out his hand in greeting. "Good to see you again."

"Good evening, Marco," he smiled. "Alfonso," he shook the other hand that was reaching out. "Great to see you both again."

Chrissie clutched at her small handbag, fiddling nervously at the clasp as she saw the two pairs of black eyes roving her body admiringly.

"May I introduce our companion for this evening?" Charles turned to Chrissie, giving her a warm smile. "This is Chrissie." Charles moved out of the way as the two brothers came around the table to say hello. In turn they took Chrissie's slender hand lightly and raised it to their moist lips in greeting. Chrissie shivered inwardly at the intimate touch but smiled broadly as she politely said 'good evening' to each of them. Her eyes widened momentarily when she caught a glimpse of identical heavy gold rings, with rubies the size of a sixpence set into the centres, glinting up at her.

The young man who had showed them to their table quickly moved around and pulled a chair out for Chrissie. "Madam" he said quietly. Chrissie sat down, fearing that at any moment her legs would give way under her. "Thank you," she smiled up into the good-looking face and almost laughed out loud when he gave her a little wink. 'Cheeky little devil!' she thought. 'Nice, though.' She watched him as he went to a small side table by the wall and picked up several leather-bound menus. He swiftly distributed them, asking if they would like something to drink. Charles ordered champagne, of course, and Chrissie licked her lips in anticipation. Her mouth was becoming drier and drier with nerves and excitement. When she opened the rather heavy, thick menu she drew a sharp breath of panic as she saw that the whole thing was written in a foreign language. She looked across the table at Charles who was staring at her in amusement and who had immediately guessed her predicament.

"Shall I order for all of us?"

Chrissie sighed in relief. "That would be lovely."

After a few glasses of Bollinger and a couple of American cigarettes Chrissie relaxed completely and by the time they had finished their delicious four-course meal, she wanted the evening to go on forever. The wine that had accompanied each course had delighted her with its flavour and heady effect. 'Jesus! If I don't become a raving alcoholic after this lot I never will!' she told herself, amused by the whole thing. She had been more than happy to tuck into the mouth-watering creamy chicken soup, the succulent steak and had just loved the raspberry sorbet. (Her stomach had begun to growl ominously earlier on and she was terrified everyone would hear it!) When the waiter had brought the cheeseboard she sliced herself slivers of the various cheeses to accompany the funny little biscuits and had enjoyed every mouthful. At first Chrissie had been a little put out when the men appeared to be ignoring her as they talked among themselves during the meal, but after a while was glad that she wasn't being included in the conversation, as all they seemed to be talking about was business, boats, travelling around the world and vast amounts of money! When the table had finally been cleared, the waiter asked them if they would like brandies or liqueurs. Charles answered for all of them and said they would, but they would like them served upstairs in the penthouse.

"Of course, sir."

Chrissie's heart lurched violently. 'Oh feck! Here we go!'

Marco pulled Chrissie's chair out for her and quickly slipped a broad hand around her waist when he noticed her wobbling slightly.

"Don't worry, Chrissie." He drawled in his deep American accent. She grinned stupidly up at him as he pulled her shawl from the back of her chair and draped it around her shoulders. "You'll be fine."

As they made their way back through the dining room towards the discreet elevator at the back of the restaurant, Chrissie realised through the haze of her jumbled thoughts that she was desperate to go to the toilet. With all the drink she had had that evening, her bladder felt as though it was about to burst. She was too embarrassed to ask where there was one but reassured herself that there must certainly be one upstairs.

The small lift felt suffocating with all their bodies in such close proximity and for one awful moment Chrissie felt as though she might throw up all over them. The feeling quickly passed as the doors opened smoothly and they stepped on to the thick creamy carpets of the penthouse. Charles was watching Chrissie closely as she tottered over to the nearest sofa and dropped heavily into the soft cushions. He came and stood beside her as he noticed her eyelids drooping and her body splayed out and hoped that he hadn't made a big mistake. "You all right my dear?"

"No! I'm not bloody all right!" Chrissie's eyes suddenly flew wide open and she glared up at him. "I want a bloody wee!"

"God almighty!" Charles muttered in disgust as he yanked her unceremoniously to her feet, glancing over to the tall windows, where Marco and Alfonso were looking down at the bright lights of London and talking quietly together.

"Get up, you stupid girl!" he hissed nastily into her red face, "and go and sort yourself out! If you ruin this for me tonight, believe me there will be hell to pay!"

The vehemence of his expression frightened Chrissie for a moment and she thought better of answering him back. So she obediently allowed herself to be led over to the bathroom door

141

and ushered into the small room with yet another reminder to get herself together, tidy herself up and come back and join them. Chrissie leaned heavily on the shell-shaped pink basin and gazed mournfully at her reflection. She blinked rapidly and shook her head as she tried to clear her thoughts.

"What a feckin' state I've got myself into!" she groaned loudly. "I'll have to take the pledge, that's for sure." She belched loudly as she kicked off her shoes, lifted her long skirt and waddled over to the toilet. She bunched up the length of the material round her waist as she tried to pull her knickers down at the same time. She got them as far as her knees when she suddenly sat down with a thump on to the cool seat. "Shite!" With a wonderful relief she emptied her bursting bladder. "Thank feck for that!" she muttered to herself as she grabbed at a wad of toilet paper and wiped herself awkwardly. Struggling comically with her underwear and dress in a futile attempt to pull her pants back up, Chrissie sighed in frustration and staring morosely down at the old-fashioned underwear, she suddenly got a fit of giggles. "Oh, bugger it!" she said to herself when the tittering had subsided and bending down she tore off the offending article, screwed it up in a tight ball and stuffed it down the back of the cistern. "Fur-lined drawers, my bloody arse!"

After splashing her face over and over with the refreshingly cold water, combing her hair and applying some fresh lipstick, Chrissie didn't feel so ghastly. Her head was aching like mad and apart from the rather pale complexion, she wasn't looking that bad, but a guilty thought of what she wouldn't have done for one of Maria's little 'liveners' right now crept into her mind. She ran her trembling hands over the smooth material of her dress and breathed deeply. "Well, here we go!"

"Oh, there you are, my dear," Charles smiled thinly. "We thought you had fallen asleep in there," he tried to joke.

"No, I'm fine, thanks." She grinned back weakly. "Think I just had a little too much to drink."

"Hey! Don't worry kid!" Alfonso said kindly, as he caught her eye. "We've all done that from time to time. Eh, boys?" They all muttered in agreement.

"Come and sit down, my dear," Charles patted the space on the sofa between himself and Marco. "I've just been explaining to my friends here about our little 'arrangement'."

Chrissie ignored his invitation and perched on the edge of a high-backed cane chair that was shaped like a great open fan by the window and tried to concentrate on the twinkling of the moving lights far down below. She fought the panic that was rising within her and prayed to all the saints above, that they weren't all about to jump on her! The way that they had been looking at her, especially the de Santos brothers, with their hooded eyes and lecherous expressions, had made her skin crawl. Then all of a sudden she remembered. The 'arrangement'. Of course! She visibly relaxed and turning to face them again said, "Oh! I see!"

"Yes," Charles said, rising and coming towards her. "I've told them that you have agreed to work for us." He held out an open cigarette case.

"Thanks."

Just then there was the light swishing sound of the elevator arriving and Marco rose to take the small tray of drinks from the waiter as the doors opened silently.

"Thanks, buddy. That'll be all." he blocked the young man's view of the room with his thick-set frame. "Here."

"Thank you, sir," the waiter replied quickly as he took the crumpled note and shoved it into his pocket.

Chrissie didn't really want any more to drink, but took the small glass of golden coloured liqueur anyway. She sipped slowly at the sweet liquid as she listened to her new employers. So far they hadn't made any suggestive remarks and seemed content enough to merely go over what Charles had already explained to her. She still felt very strange, a bit weary and not quite with it, so she just sat quietly. Her head was fuzzy, but wasn't thumping so wildly now. The warm feeling from her first ever liqueur was soon easing her tense young body.

Alfonso glanced at his wristwatch. "Think we should be making a move soon, Charles."

"Oh? So early?"

"Well we have a few things to do tomorrow," Marco agreed as he rose to his feet. "And besides we still have one or two people to see tonight."

"Why don't we have coffee before you go?" Charles asked.

"Well, OK." Marco sat down again, smiling across at Chrissie. "Guess we could do with an eye opener! But then we really do have to be off."

"And you, my dear?" Charles asked pleasantly. "Shall I order a coffee for you?"

"Yes, please," she answered as she checked the time and was shocked to see that it was almost one o'clock in the morning. For a minute she wondered where on earth the men would be going at this time of night, but by the way they had both exchanged glances she thought that they probably had a couple of women lined up for their entertainment. "Well, as long as it's not me!" she thought.

The de Santos brothers excused themselves to go to the bathroom to freshen up. Charles held his hand out to Chrissie. "Come and sit over here, my dear."

"I'm OK, thanks," she replied quickly.

"Are you feeling all right? You look very pale."

"I told you before," she answered rather tersely. "I just had too much to drink earlier on."

"Are you sure that's all it is?" he asked, as he noticed how nervous she was getting again. She had seemed for a while to be relaxing as she sipped at her drink, but he noticed that she had started to look a little strained again.

"Of course! What else could it be?"

He came and stood over her. "To be truthful, Chrissie," he said very quietly bending closer to her face. "I could have sworn that you were just a little high on something."

"What?" Chrissie fidgeted on the hard seat, pulling away from him. "What are you talking about, for Gods' sake?"

"Oh come on, my dear!" he sneered. "I'm not a bloody fool, you know."

Chrissie chewed on her bottom lip as she held his determined stare.

"Did Maria give you anything?"

"No!"

"Don't lie to me, Chrissie!" he said through clenched teeth. "I won't be lied to! Do you hear me?"

Chrissie tried to get up but he shoved her roughly back on to the chair.

"Get off me, you pig!" she spat.

Charles' attitude suddenly changed. For one moment he felt like slapping that pretty face till it was raw and make her tell him the truth, but having second thoughts, perhaps he could handle

144

this much more successfully in another way. He crouched down beside her and took her small hands into his. "I'm sorry about that, my dear," he wheedled. "It's just that I've been watching you this evening and you were giving me the distinct impression that you had had more than just a little too much to drink."

Chrissie opened her mouth to protest.

"Shh," he said putting a finger to her lips. "Don't get upset. I'm not accusing you of anything, but if you're going to work for me . . . then I will look after you. That's all."

"What do you mean?" Chrissie asked timidly.

"Well, let's say . . ." He hesitated for a moment when he heard the toilet flush in the bathroom. "Let's say, that if you feel the need for a little something . . . you know . . . to give you a bit of energy . . . make you feel more confident . . . well . . . all I'm saying is . . . that you just have to ask me! OK?"

Chrissie nodded dumbly and tried to smile, but it just wouldn't come. 'Feck! He's talking about bloody drugs!' It suddenly dawned on her. All that stuff with Silvia and with Maria and the pills! What a silly bitch she had been! How could she have been so bloody ignorant! She pushed his hands from her lap and got up quickly from her chair and began to pace agitatedly around the room. She had to think. And think quickly, but she was finding it difficult to get her head straight.

The coffee arrived and the two brothers came back from the bathroom. They were laughing and acting the fool and patting each other on the back as though they were sharing a huge joke. Chrissie eyed them suspiciously. What the hell had they been up to?

"Here we are," Charles announced. "Coffees all round?"

He poured the dark steamy liquid from the tall silver pot and asked sociably, "Cream, sugar?"

"Thanks," Alfonso replied, making himself comfortable again in one of the deep cream leather armchairs.

"My dear?"

Chrissie gritted her teeth as she turned away from the impressive modern landscape she was pretending to admire. "Yes?"

She couldn't see what Charles was doing as he had his back to her pouring the coffee into the small white cups that he had arranged on the low table between the seats; so she was completely unaware of the small amount of white powder that he expertly

145

tipped from a thin wrap of paper into the cup nearest to him. "Come and join us, my dear," he beckoned.

Chrissie tried to walk as sedately as possible across the room, but things were still a little out of focus as she sank into the seat beside Alfonso.

"Sugar?" Charles asked her.

"Two," she answered, keeping her eyes lowered.

"There you are," he handed her the dainty cup and saucer.

"Thanks."

Her mouth was dry again and she gulped greedily at the hot drink. "Yuk!" she said ungraciously, screwing her face up. "You didn't put any sugar in it!"

"Maybe it's a little strong for you!" Charles answered quickly. "Here." He picked up two small lumps of sugar from the little bowl, dropped them into her cup and gave it a quick stir.

Chrissie finished the rest of the strong sweet coffee in one gulp and grinned up at him. "That's better!"

The two de Santos brothers were in a very jovial mood as they said their goodbyes. They told Chrissie that they would look forward to meeting up again, in the States. Alfonso was standing in front of Chrissie extending his broad, hairy-backed hand in fare-well, but as she tried to rise from the sofa she fell straight back down and burst into hysterical laughter at her own clumsiness. Her long shapely legs splayed out in front of her in a most unladylike manner and as she tried in vain to rise to her feet she caught sight of her bare toes poking through gaping holes in her stockings. At this point she just didn't know whether to laugh even harder or cry as she found all eyes on her crumpled body and dishevelled clothing. The poor girl groaned loudly as she tried to pull her skirt down in an attempt at decency and wondered for a second where her shoes were. Her head was buzzing like a swarm of crazed bees and her whole body tingled with pins and needles. Running her fingers through the tangles of her so-called glamorous hairstyle, Chrissie felt as though she was giving herself an electric shock. "Jesus, Mary!" she giggled stupidly, staring at the three men with eyes like huge black saucers. It was as though it was the first time she had ever seen them.

"I think I'd better get this young lady home," Charles laughed, thoroughly amused by the situation. "Time for a little shut-eye."

"Sure." Alfonso hung a weighty arm around Charles' lean

shoulders. "You do that! But Charles, old man," he added more seriously. "You just make sure you take real good care of our little investment here." He nodded over at Chrissie who was now sprawled out along the whole length of the sofa on her side, with her head propped up on one cupped hand smiling inanely at them with a vacant expression. Their voices seemed so high pitched and strange to her and everything appeared to be moving in jerky motions. Chrissie was vaguely aware that she was running her swollen tongue around her mouth and lips and couldn't understand why she couldn't feel anything. Something told her that she should try and lie still until she felt normal again but her young body felt like springing up and doing a jig around the room.

'What the feckin hell is happening to me?' Chrissie wondered wildly as she desperately tried to gather her thoughts together and stop herself from bursting out laughing again. She watched the figures of the de Santos brothers disappear into the elevator and waited for Charles to launch into the biggest lecture she had ever had in her life about getting drunk and making a show of herself. But instead of that, he just casually strolled over to the small bar by the wall and poured himself a drink. Chrissie at last managed to pull herself up into a sitting position. She wasn't bothered at all at what he had to say to her. She didn't care about anything at that moment. She had never felt so good in her life!

"Hey?" she called across the room. The sound that came from her throat sounded like a stranger's!

Charles turned slowly to look at her. "What?"

"Where's mine, then?" she managed to mutter smiling broadly and holding out her open hand and wiggling her fingers.

Charles sighed loudly as he poured a tall glass of water for her from the glass jug and came over to give it to her. "Drink this," he ordered, not unkindly.

"What the feck's this?" Chrissie glowered as she took the water from him.

"What does it look like, my dear?"

"It looks like bloody water!" Chrissie frowned as she raised the glass to her almost numb lips.

"Well, that's exactly what it is, my dear!"

"Well I don't *want* water," Chrissie sulked "I want a *real* drink!" The feeling was beginning to creep back into her mouth.

"I think you've had enough alcohol tonight, my dear, don't

147

you?" Charles sat on the edge of the coffee table in front of her. "So just drink it all up, there's a good girl."

Chrissie tutted loudly, but took a few gulps nevertheless.

"OK?" she said cheekily, wiggling the glass at him.

"No! Drink it all!"

"All right! All right!" Chrissie growled up at him. "Bloody misery!"

"Feel better?" Charles asked, ignoring her comments, as he took the empty glass and returned it to the bar.

"Suppose so," Chrissie admitted grudgingly. Her thirst had been quenched for a while but she couldn't keep still, so she got awkwardly to her feet and began to pace around the room. Her whole body was restless and she felt as they she should be doing something energetic. "I *know*!" she grinned over at Charles, who was watching her from across the room.

"What?" he asked.

"Why don't we go dancing?"

"What *are* you talking about, Chrissie?" Charles couldn't help laughing at her. She looked so young and vulnerable as she stood swaying slightly, with her arms outstretched in invitation. Her face was a picture of animated delight as she began to waltz around the room with an invisible partner. Her thick chestnut hair swayed heavily around her shapely shoulders as she came closer and closer to him. Charles Latimer sighed deeply in frustration as he grabbed hold of one of her soft arms and pulled her to him. "No, Chrissie!" he breathed into her ear, his thin fingers sinking into her warm flesh. "Not *now*!"

"Why not?" she shoved him away from her and glared up into his angular face.

"Because it's very late, in case you hadn't noticed." He turned away from her and pulled an initialled handkerchief from his breastpocket and wiped his damp forehead. "I'm going to call Reggie to take you home."

"Oh, don't be such an old spoil sport!" Chrissie stuck her bottom lip out like a spoilt child. "I was just beginning to enjoy myself." She watched him through lowered lashes.

"Yes, I can see that, my dear."

"It's not that late anyway," Chrissie persisted, squinting down at her watch.

"It's late enough!" Charles answered abruptly.

"Well I feel fine and I don't think it's *fair*!" Chrissie pushed her way past him and danced across to the bar.

"Leave that *alone*, Chrissie!" Charles ordered sternly.

"Why? I'm a big girl now and if you want me to do all that 'business' for you, the least you can do is let me have a little drinkie!" Chrissie glared at him defiantly over her shoulder as she reached for the nearest bottle.

"Oh for God's *sake*, Chrissie, you really are the limit!" Charles was getting mad now. He was a little annoyed with himself too. Perhaps he had introduced her to the delights of the white powder too soon.

"Oh go on," Chrissie purred. "Just a little bitty one . . . Pleeease!" she wheedled.

"Give me the bottle," Charles demanded. "I'll do it."

Fearing that she would spill the whole bottle of vodka over the immaculate cream carpet, he gently but firmly removed the drink from her grasp and poured a small amount into a clean glass. "Here. That's all you're getting," he said roughly when he saw the disgruntled frown. "I'm calling Reggie. Now!"

"*Slainte!*" She waved the glass at him and downed the lot in one go and handed it back to him.

"You really are something else, my dear!" He shook his head and wondered again if he was doing the right thing. "Go and sit for a minute, will you?" Charles put the receiver down after making his call to the Purple Parrot, "and calm yourself *down*."

"Why don't you come and have a little dance with me, Charles?" Chrissie called over her shoulder as she swayed around the room, her shapely hips moving provocatively to the rhythm of an imaginary dance band. Her eyes were almost closed as she danced on and on.

Charles strode across the room and just managed to catch her before she collided headlong into the tall window. He dragged her back across the room and pushed her firmly back down on to the sofa. She tried to struggle to her feet, her hair hanging over her glowering face, but he shoved her back down again. Glaring up at him in fury she yelled, "You're a real ARSEHOLE! Do ya know that *MR* Latimer?"

Charles had just about had enough now. Chrissie didn't see the blow coming and the flat of his hand slapped her sharply across the cheek. She opened her mouth to hurl a torrent of vile abuse

149

at him but found she couldn't utter a single word. She was completely in shock. It wasn't the searing stinging pain she felt on her face, but the sudden realisation of what must have happened to make her act like a complete whore. Turning away from his furious expression she slowly rubbed at her reddening cheek as the full horror sank into her befuddled mind. As her thoughts began to clear a little she took great gulps of breath as her anger mounted. 'The utter bastard! What the hell had been in that coffee?' Chrissie knew full well that she had had far too much to drink that night and what with the pills she had shared with Maria earlier on, what a mixture for disaster that must have been! But surely nothing would have made her feel so damn crazy? He must have given her 'something' that she had never experienced before. She thought about what he had said earlier on about helping her out with whatever she needed. Before she could help herself, Chrissie collapsed along the sofa in a heap of utter humiliation and wept bitter tears, calling her mother's name softly into the damp cushions. Her muffled sobs touched Charles a little as he saw her shoulders shuddering in despair. He came and leaned over the back of the sofa and stroked her bent head. "Come on, my dear," he tried to placate her. "It's not that bad. Surely?"

Chrissie inhaled deeply then sniffing loudly she mumbled, "Go away!"

"Come on, my dear," Charles said lightly. "Get yourself together. Reggie will be here any minute."

Chrissie very slowly lifted her head and pushed the damp hair away from her wet forehead with a shaking hand. She uncurled her aching body and sat up as straight as she could. The poor girl felt as though she had been run over by a steamroller, mentally and physically! But, of course, Chrissie being Chrissie still had that certain spark of something inside her that was beginning to come back to life. She felt a white-hot rage starting to gather as she sat motionlessly assessing her thoughts and planning her next move.

At that very moment she could have happily stuck a knife into the cold heart of Mr Charles Latimer for what he had undoubtedly done. But what good would that do her anyway? She wasn't going to let him get away with it though! She could wait! But what could she do now? Not a lot. Giving a juddering sigh, Chrissie looked down at the crumpled state of her lovely evening dress and noticed the dirty grey smudges of cigarette ash and splashes of coffee stains. She brushed at them quickly, as if to take her mind away from her predicament. "Jesus! Look at the state of this!" she grumbled to herself.

"Leave it!" Charles said quietly. "I'll have it cleaned for you."

"You needn't bother," Chrissie answered haughtily. "I can do it myself."

"Don't be silly, my dear! It's the least I can do."

"Is it? Is it really?" she answered though gritted teeth. Before he could say another word Chrissie gathered her strength and pushed herself to her feet. Charles wondered what she was going to do, as he took in the determined expression and the cold hard glint in her beautiful eyes as she stood defiantly in front of him, her arms at her sides, her head erect.

"I'll tell you what you can *do*, Charles," she began.

"Oh yes? What's that, my dear?" he pulled a cigarette from the case offering her one. She shook her head. "Well, for a start, Charles."

He waited.

"You can *stop* calling me your feckin' '*dear*'!"

He almost laughed out loud. "Oh? Is that all?"

"No, it's not *all*!" Chrissie answered smoothly. "You can tell me what the hell you put in that damn drink, you bastard!"

"I don't know what you're talking about, my . . . oops sorry . . . Chrissie?" he mocked.

"Don't take me for a complete eegit, Charles! I may not be twenty-one yet and may still be a bit green around the edges but I'm not such a feckin' fool that I haven't worked out what your game is!" Chrissie continued, her voice getting louder by the minute.

"Keep your voice down!" he hissed, stubbing out his half smoked cigarette.

"Why?" Chrissie whispered back caustically. "Afraid someone might hear what a total gob-shite you really are?"

"I told you before Chrissie! Moderate your language!"

"Moderate my *language*?" Chrissie's voice was full of heavy sarcasm. "You feckin' hypocrite!"

Charles took a step towards her. She didn't move.

"What you going to do?" she sneered. "Hit me again?"

Charles snorted loudly and turned on his heel. "Just shut up, you stupid girl!"

Chrissie's insides were bubbling with rage but she brought her temper under control and stayed silent. It wouldn't do her any good now if she let all hell break loose! She would have dearly loved to launch herself at him, raking his arrogant face to shreds and leaving him with a few more scars to explain! She ran her hands down over her hips as she calmed herself down. As her fingers touched the silkiness she suddenly remembered she wasn't wearing any knickers! "Oh shite!" she muttered.

"What?"

"Nothing," she replied guiltily.

Charles came over to her and wondered at the sudden change in her demeanour. He had been thinking that maybe he had gone too far with her, too soon. He decided to broach the subject before Reggie arrived. Almost humbly he began, "Can I say something, Chrissie? Without you tearing my head off?" he tried a weak smile.

"What?" she met his cool gaze, thinking how close he had come to her very thoughts!

Shrugging his lean shoulders he motioned towards the nearest armchair. "Please. Just sit down for a minute."

Without answering, Chrissie sat on the arm of the seat and waited She was still thinking of how she could retrieve her underwear.

"Can we call a truce?" he asked quietly, as he lit another cigarette and offered her one. This time she took it. As he lit it for her he saw that her hand was trembling. When she didn't answer him, he continued.

"Look, Chrissie! I'm sorry that I slapped you, but really you were getting out of control!"

"How dare you!" she shook her head in disbelief. "And I wonder how that happened?" Her voice was very low and she ran her tongue around the inside of her mouth she realised that at some point she must have bitten a chunk from her cheek. It felt raw and painful and she could taste blood. She began to feel sorry for herself as another headache began. Her throat was sore and she felt weak and stupid. She couldn't understand why; one minute things didn't feel so bad and then the next she just wanted to curl up and sleep for a month.

Charles noticed how she seemed to be wilting and the blazing defiance had almost gone. He went to the bar again and poured her another glass of water and added a few ice cubes. "Drink this."

Chrissie took it from him without comment. She drank half the glass, gratefully, easing her sore mouth a little and passed it back with a trembling hand.

"You OK?" he asked, as if concerned.

Chrissie gazed up at him with bloodshot eyes and took a deep breath.

"Not really," she said quietly.

"What's wrong?"

"Don't start all that again, *please*!" Chrissie shook her head as she looked down and picked at her bitten fingernails and nicotine-stained fingers, thinking how uncared for they seemed. "You know as well as I do, that you bloody doctored that coffee."

"OK. OK," Charles grinned wryly. "I admit I did put a little something in it." Before Chrissie could say anything he held up his hand to stop her. "But I thought it would make the evening a little more enjoyable for you, that's all. And don't keep glaring at me like that!" he scowled back. "Stop trying to act so hard done by! If you ask me, you're not the little miss innocent that you're making out to be."

Chrissie thought back over the evening and indeed the last few days and had to admit to herself that she was fast becoming one of the women that she had always thought so badly of, what with the drinking, the pills and whatever the hell the shite was that he had put in her drink. Her stomach tightened guiltily as her mother's face floated before her and much to her surprise, Jimmy Dwyer's broad handsome features invaded her anguished thoughts. She gave a great juddering sigh; "I need to go home."

"Don't worry, Reggie will be here soon and you can be on your way."

'What, all the way to Dublin?' Chrissie thought miserably. She knew it was too late for that. Anyway she didn't have any money. How could she go back empty handed, after all the bragging about her great job; and to go home in such a state would be more than she could bear. She looked up as the jangling of the telephone interrupted her jumbled thoughts.

"Reggie's on his way up," Charles announced.

"Good," Chrissie murmured as she dragged herself to her feet. "Better find my shoes! I'm just going to the bathroom for a minute," she added as she spotted her shoes on the other side of the room.

"OK, but make it quick, will you, Chrissie? Reggie has to get back to the club."

"Right."

Chrissie couldn't bear to look at herself in the mirror as she felt herself near to tears again. She rubbed her aching forehead as she bent down awkwardly and felt around behind the toilet for her knickers. Her heart beat frantically when she realised that there was nothing there! "Jesus! Mary!" she almost wept. "They're gone!"

"Chrissie!" Reggie's voice called from the other side of the door as he tapped lightly. "You ready, love?"

"Just coming," she called back. She suddenly remembered how the de Santos brothers had been laughing and giggling like a pair of naughty schoolboys when they came back from the bathroom earlier on. She sank to the floor in humiliation. A louder rapping on the door made her jump.

"Come on love!" Reggie called out.

"All right!" Chrissie shouted back and cringed as her head thumped painfully. Struggling to her feet, she caught sight of her bedraggled reflection and groaned loudly. Looking away quickly she turned the little brass handle on the door. "Just coming," she said avoiding Reggie's curious look. "Been looking for my shawl."

"It's here." Reggie held Maria's shawl in front of her.

"Thanks."

Chrissie still couldn't meet his eyes as she let him wrap the shawl around her drooping shoulders. She felt a little comfort as his warm hands gave her a little squeeze of encouragement. When Reggie had seen the state of Chrissie his heart had lurched with anger and he'd hoped that nothing too untoward had happened to her. She was different from all the other girls that he had dealt with over the years he had been at the Purple Parrot. He had promised himself that he would try and keep an eye on her as much as he could. He put a heavy arm around her shoulders and led her towards the chrome doors of the lift. "Soon be home," he said softly and Chrissie just nodded dumbly.

Charles watched them through narrowed eyes as he wondered if he could trust Reggie enough not to interfere with his plans for Chrissie. On a sudden impulse he stepped in front of them before Reggie pressed the lift button.

"Just a sec!" he smiled widely. "Can I just have a quick word before you go, my de— Sorry, I mean Chrissie?"

"What?" she asked, as she looked up into his pale eyes.

"Come over here for a minute."

Reggie folded his arms and turned away, appearing not to be paying any attention to the conversation.

"Well?" Chrissie asked again. "What now?"

Charles slid his hand inside his jacket and pulled out his wallet.

"I thought maybe you could get yourself a little something in the shops tomorrow?"

Chrissie's eyes widened as she watched him count out five crisp ten-pound notes.

"Just by way of a little apology for . . . well . . . you know?"

Chrissie only hesitated for a moment before reaching out and taking the money. A tiny little voice in her tired brain told her to tell him to stuff it up his arse, but she ignored it and weakly smiled her thanks. She folded the notes quickly and shoved them into her bag before he had a chance to change his mind, or before *she* did.

"I take it the deal is still on?" he said, bending more closely to her flushed face.

Chrissie straightened her back and looked him at him evenly. "Of *course*, Mr Latimer . . . Oops! sorry! I mean *Charles*!"

Reggie looked over his shoulder at the pair of them, unsuccessfully straining his ears to hear what they were saying. "Ready, sir?" he asked, as he checked his watch.

"Yes," Chrissie answered before her boss had time to reply. "I'm ready."

"Just one more thing!" Charles grinned as he put his lips to Chrissie's ear and whispered. "Perhaps you may like to start your shopping in Bond Street . . ." Chrissie frowned. ". . . A rather exclusive ladies' wear establishment!" he continued, his hot breath burning Chrissie's soft flesh. "It's called *La Femme* . . . I believe they specialise in hand-made silk underwear."

The poor girl drew back from him as though she had been bitten by a snake, her eyes wide with horror as the truth about her missing knickers flooded into her befuddled mind. "What!" she yelled into the arrogant sneering face.

Reggie just managed to grab hold of her flaying arm as she clenched her fist and launched herself at Charles Latimer. He spun her around and marched her through the door and the now open lift.

155

"Come on, love," he muttered. "It's not worth it! Believe me!"

Chrissie was panting wildly as she struggled to release herself from Reggie's iron grip.

"Leave it!" he said more firmly.

"*Leave it?*" Chrissie seethed, still wriggling frantically. "I'll kill that piss-taking bastard!"

Reggie pushed her into the corner of the lift and leaned heavily against her in an attempt to get her under control. He didn't know exactly what had gone on in the penthouse that evening, but he was pretty sure they hadn't been playing tiddly winks! He also knew that it didn't pay to cross Charles Latimer. "Be *quiet*, for fuck's sake, love."

As the fight suddenly went out of Chrissie she whispered, "You can let go now."

Just before the lift doors closed silently on the penthouse Chrissie caught a brief glimpse, over Reggie's shoulder, of Charles Latimer pulling her stained, crumpled knickers from his pocket, wrinkling his long thin nose and dropping them unceremoniously into the nearest litter basket! Chrissie groaned loudly as a black cloud of despair engulfed her and as her legs buckled under her she fainted away into welcome oblivion in Reggie's strong arms.

15

"Come on!" Maria's strident voice rang out from the door of Chrissie's room. "Get up! We have to get ready for work!"

Chrissie hauled herself into a sitting position and dragged the covers up under her chin. She blinked her eyes, trying to clear her blurred vision. "OK, OK," she groused. "I'm awake! You can stop shouting now!"

"Bloody cheek!" Maria laughed. "After last night's little episode I think you should have been up at the crack of dawn making breakfast for me!"

"Oh . . . God . . .!" Chrissie groaned, scratching her head as she tried to get her thoughts into some sort of order. Maria plonked herself heavily down on the bed beside Chrissie and held out a packet of cigarettes. "Want one?"

"Yuk!" Chrissie's stomach heaved. "Take them away . . . *please*!"

"That bad, was it?" Maria asked lightly.

"Yes!" Chrissie answered, "and worse!"

"Come on then!" Maria encouraged, making herself more comfortable. "Tell!" When Chrissie didn't answer Maria chided, "Well, it's the least you owe me after all I did for you."

"What do you mean?" Chrissie asked with a frown. She desperately wished she *could* actually remember what had happened last night. She had only a vague recollection of being in the penthouse lift with Reggie and nothing more after that till a few moments ago.

"Bloody hell!" Maria laughed again. "You must have had a bloody skinful!"

Chrissie looked guiltily at her friend. "Mmm."

"Come on, you drunken old cow," Maria tried to joke. "Come and have a cup of coffee. I've just made a pot. That'll wake you up a bit." She leapt from the bed and giggled. "And then you might be able to remember where you left your drawers!"

"What?" Chrissie called out as the bedroom door closed. "What do you mean?" As the door shut, Chrissie saw that her new black dress was hanging neatly on the back and it looked as though it had been recently pressed, and her shoes, which had obviously been cleaned and brushed, were placed tidily by the wall. She lifted the covers from her shivering body and dropped them abruptly. Covering her mouth with both hands she smothered an anguished sob. She felt herself blushing from head to foot and her cool skin grew clammy with perspiration. She was stark naked! Scrambling hurriedly from under the sheet, Chrissie grabbed the thin dressing gown that Maria had lent her. She tied the frayed cotton belt tightly around her waist and shuffled out to join Maria in the warm sitting room.

"There you are," Maria pointed to the steaming mug on the coffee table. "Get that down you! Listen," she added kindly when she saw the despondent expression on Chrissie's face. "I was only joking, you know."

"What about?" Chrissie asked as she sat down and reached for her drink.

"You know," Maria tried to keep a straight face. "About the – em – about the knickers and stuff."

Chrissie didn't say anything for a few moments. She was sipping the strong coffee that was beginning to revive her spirits. Everything was gradually coming back to her now. Thinking carefully about what she should tell Maria, knowing that she couldn't give all the gory details, she began by thanking her for cleaning up her dress.

"Oh, don't worry about that," Maria smiled as she stubbed out yet another cigarette."I did it earlier on while you were snoring your head off."

Chrissie smiled back. "I suppose you put me to bed as well?"

"Well, you don't think I'd have let old Reggie do it, do you?"

"No! No of course not!"

"Quite the gent he was really," Maria grinned. "Tell you the truth I've got a soft spot for Reggie," she confided. "Not in a 'lovey dovey' way. It's just that he's a really nice bloke under all that muscle and hard-man act."

"Yes, I thought so too," Chrissie nodded in agreement.

"Carried you in here, like a knight in shining armour, he did."

"How embarrassing!" Chrissie grinned crookedly.

"Not really," Maria said. "I'm sure he's had to do a lot worse than carrying a young maiden in distress up a couple of flights of stairs! Help yourself to more coffee while I go and get some make-up on. You'll have to get a move on and wash your hair. It looks a right blinkin' mess, if you don't mind me saying!"

"I don't mind at all, Maria," Chrissie said quickly. "The only thing is though . . ." she hesitated.

"What's that?" Maria said over her shoulder as she made to leave the room.

"I . . . em . . . I won't be coming to work tonight." Chrissie watched the astonished expression on her friend's face.

"Why not, for God's sake?" Maria turned and sat down with a thump beside her. "You'll get the bloody sack! His bloody lordship won't stand for that, you know!" she finished emphatically.

"Well, the thing is . . ." Chrissie began hesitantly. "He has asked me to go to America and work in one of his friend's new clubs out there." Chrissie glanced away guiltily and picked up a magazine from the table and began to flick through it.

"What the fucking hell are you talking about?" Maria asked in amazement. "You don't know anything about working the clubs!"

"Well, that's what it was all about last night," Chrissie hurried on, wanting to get the string of lies out of the way as soon as possible. "While we were chatting over dinner they asked me if I would go and work for them!"

"Who were they?" Maria asked suspiciously. "Don't tell me!" she added without waiting for a reply, "I bet it was those two greasy, flashy looking brothers that I see at the club sometimes with old Charlie boy!" When she saw the flush of guilt creeping into Chrissie's pale face, she knew she had guessed right. "They are a right pair of villains, those two!" Maria got up and began to pace around the room. "You don't want to have anything to do with *them*! I've heard some right stories about those two bloody gorillas!"

"What do you mean?" Chrissie asked as innocently as she could, without looking up from the magazine.

"They're into heavy drugs!" Maria shouted. "That's what! And I mean BIG time!"

"Well, I don't know anything about all that," Chrissie answered quietly. "All I know is that I will be getting paid plenty to work there *and* I'm getting some sort of allowance before I go to buy loads of new clothes!"

"Believe me, Chrissie!" Maria said seriously. "I do know what

159

I'm talking about. You don't want to get involved with people like that! Anyway," she added tersely, "it's upside down."

"What is?" Chrissie frowned.

"The bloody magazine!" she pointed out.

Chrissie dropped the copy of *Woman* and sighed, as she felt herself becoming annoyed. She didn't want to argue with Maria, she had been too good to her. "You could come with me and help me choose some nice things to wear," she tried. "You could show me the best shops to go to!"

Maria shook her head in frustration. "When's all this supposed to happen then?"

"I don't know for sure," Chrissie answered truthfully. "He said it would be very soon though."

"And what am I to do about the extra rent I was supposed to be getting from you?"

"Oh, I'm so sorry, Maria, I forgot all about that." Chrissie felt awful about letting her down. "But honestly I could do with the money they are offering. I'd be able to save a lot and it wouldn't be too long before I could go home and maybe buy myself my own little place over there."

"I thought you wanted to get your own place *here*," Maria sulked.

"Well I *did*," Chrissie admitted. "But to be honest, I'm missing my family and my friends so much already that I would just love to go back as soon as possible."

"Oh well," the other girl said sadly. "I thought it might be too good to last. Every time I think I've got a good friend they up and vanish."

Chrissie went over and put her arms around Maria and hugged her warmly. She didn't know what to say to her, but she felt as though she was being rather dramatic about someone she had only known for such a short time. She knew that there was no way that she could try and wriggle out of her agreement with Charles. She wasn't so stupid to think that the de Santos brothers weren't every bit as dodgy as Maria was saying, but after all she had left home and come to a strange country to make her fortune and that's exactly what she was going to do. After all, she told herself firmly, when an opportunity like this comes up there is no way in the world that she would let it slip through her fingers. She would just have to be very careful, very careful indeed, not to let herself be drawn into any funny situations.

Maria sniffled loudly as she wiped her damp eyes with the palms of her hands and drew herself from Chrissie's embrace. "At least you can tell me about the knickers then!" she smiled through unshed tears.

The whole thing progressed with head-spinning speed. Before Chrissie knew it she found herself standing in the queue, with Reggie by her side, at the check-in desk for Trans-Am.

All she had had to do was get her photos taken for her passport and it had miraculously appeared in a couple of days. Charles had taken care of everything and not a word was ever mentioned again about the disastrous evening they had spent together. She had even managed a few pleasant hours with Maria going around the West End, picking out new clothes for her trip. Maria had decided not to say any more about Chrissie's new job. It wasn't her business anyway. The truth was, when Chrissie had told her about the offer of the job in America, she had been jealous. She did have a sneaky feeling, though, that there was more to it than Chrissie had told her, but she didn't want to know. She had more than enough problems of her own to sort out.

"That colour looks good on you, Chrissie," Reggie grinned down at the excited young girl by his side.

"Thanks," Chrissie smiled back at him, stroking the soft wool. "It's all the go in the shops this year!"

The dark crimson swagger coat, with its wide sleeves and deep collar, emphasised Chrissie's dark colouring beautifully and she had had her hair done in one of the expensive hair-styling establishments in Regent Street the day before and thankfully the thick coils had stayed put all night (with the help of numerous clips, layers of hair lacquer and a nylon scarf tied tightly around it).

"Next, please." The attractive girl behind the desk smiled. Reggie lifted the heavy new suitcase on to the rubber luggage belt. "Passport and ticket please," the young woman asked, still smiling warmly.

Chrissie's hands shook a little as she handed over the papers. "Thank you."

After a quick flick through the girl stamped the passport, checked the details on the ticket and handed them back. "Thank you, madam," she said. "Please listen out for your gate number to be called and have a nice trip."

"Thank you," Chrissie replied as she carefully put her travel documents back into her new black patent handbag. "I will."

As Chrissie and Reggie walked slowly across the concourse he said, "I'm sorry I can't wait to wave you off, love, but I have to get back to the club. We have an early delivery this morning and if I'm not there to check it in, half of it will probably mysteriously vanish!"

"Oh no, Reggie," Chrissie said firmly. "You must have been up at the crack of dawn to pick me up, as it is."

"That's OK."

"Besides," she added a little shyly. "You've done enough for me already."

"Better go then," Reggie said somewhat gruffly. He bent and quickly gave Chrissie a peck on the cheek.

"Bye, Reggie, and thanks for everything." Chrissie felt as though she was saying goodbye to an old friend. Without another word Reggie Dixon turned swiftly on his heel and headed towards the exit.

Chrissie stood alone for a few moments watching his broad shoulders disappear through the wide doors. Then she looked around and became aware of a group of business men, with their bulky briefcases and smart suits and long dark overcoats, looking in her direction. She gave them a cheeky little smile and without waiting for their reaction walked across to a nearby magazine stand and selected the thickest, glossiest magazine she could find.

Finding herself an empty seat in the long rows of passengers Chrissie made herself comfortable. She was trying to appear as though she was a well-travelled young lady as she flicked the pages and every now and then glanced nonchalantly up at the clock. She had heard several announcements for flights as she sat waiting patiently for hers to be called. Just as she was beginning to get a little worried that she had missed her call, the strange tinny voice on the tannoy announced the number of her flight to Los Angeles. Breathing a sigh of relief she followed the signs to the gate number that had been announced and prayed, not for the first time recently, that she was not making a mistake. She had forced herself to never again think of the mess she had got herself into with those stupid pills and all the concoctions of drinks she had taken in such a short time and promised herself that she would be aware of every situation she found herself in in the future, and never repeat what could so easily have become a nightmare.

Little did Chrissie O'Rourke know, however, that as she excitedly boarded the huge plane, her heart full of ambition and her head filled with the ideas of wealth and glamorous living, that she was taking the first fateful steps into a time filled with terror, bloodshed and inconceivable heartache!

16

LA . . .

As Chrissie stepped on to the tarmac at Los Angeles airport she raised her face to the pale misty blue of the sky and inhaled deeply. She couldn't believe that the sun could be shining at this time of year: two days and it would be Christmas!

At first the idea of her first ever flight seemed so thrilling as she had settled herself into the window seat and gazed around, but as the hours drew on Chrissie began to feel drained and uncomfortable. The service she received from the bright and helpful cabin crew couldn't be faulted, but just as Chrissie had started to think that the journey would never end, the pilot's deep husky voice announced that they would be landing in fifteen minutes. Chrissie smiled brightly at her travelling companions alongside.

Mabel and Fred had kept up a non-stop conversation the whole way. Even when Chrissie had closed her eyes and tried to feign sleep they chatted amiably on and on. At first sight of them Chrissie had been quite alarmed at the bright purple rinse in Mabel's permed hair and when she had seen the size of Fred's rear end she wondered how on earth he would manage to squeeze it into the narrow seat. But they were so friendly and concerned about a young girl travelling all that way on her own to a strange country, that Chrissie didn't have the heart to ignore them. They warned her continually about just about everything she could imagine. If they had only known what she was really up to, Chrissie had thought guiltily, they wouldn't have even started a conversation with her in the first place. She had told them briefly about her new secretarial job and they had to agree that it sounded most respectable. She had emphasised that it was only a temporary position to fill in for a friend of hers who was on maternity leave, so she would soon be on her way back to Ireland to her family. So they shouldn't worry about her, she'd be fine.

They went through immigration and customs together, after collecting their luggage, and Chrissie was deeply touched as the

164

tubby little lady, with her pebble glass spectacles above brightly rouged cheeks, stood on tiptoes and gave her a tight hug to wish her good luck. Fred shook her hand politely and said it was very nice to have met her.

"Do you have someone to meet you, honey?" Mabel asked as she fussed about with her numerous bags and packages.

"Oh, yes," Chrissie answered quickly, hoping the arrangements that Charles had explained to her were going according to plan.

"That's good," Mabel nodded. "We have to go now, sweetie," she added, dropping one of her bags to the floor. "There's our Brad over there waiting for us." Mabel waved wildly at a short young blond man who was standing patiently by the arrivals barrier. "Come *on*, Fred!"

Fred trundled behind her with the luggage trolley and grinned at Chrissie. "Bye now and good luck!"

"Thank you."

As they disappeared into the crowds Chrissie chewed on her bottom lip as she tried to find something she would recognise. There were so many people though. How the hell would she know who it was that was supposed to be picking her up? As she pushed her trolley slowly along between the other passengers, her heart rate began to increase and the palms of her hands felt hot and sticky. 'Oh shite!' she thought to herself. 'What the feck am I going to do now?' Just then the dense crowds parted in front of her and she caught sight of a tall handsome figure leaning with one elbow on the dividing barrier, waving a huge placard that read 'Miss Chrissie O'Rourke'.

Chrissie breathed a huge sigh of relief, but blushed furiously at the same time at the sight of her name being held up for all to see. She didn't realise, at first, that there were several others cards being held aloft in a similar manner for other passengers to recognise. Her legs wobbled as she made her way over to him. "Excuse me," Chrissie said timidly. He turned his head. "I think you're waiting for *me*!"

Matt O'Brien dropped the card to his side and slowly raised a tanned hand and lowered his gold-rimmed sunglasses to look at her. Chrissie smiled shyly up into his deep-blue eyes.

"Welcome to LA, mam," he drawled.

The young girl shivered, as he slowly looked her up and down and ran a wet tongue over his full lips. "*Very* nice." He pulled himself up abruptly and reached out to lift her suitcase off the trolley. "Follow me, please."

Turning quickly he strode off towards the nearest exit and Chrissie found that she was almost running to keep up with him. She followed him through the noise and bustle and out again into the bright sunshine. Blinking rapidly, she shaded her eyes against the glare and almost panicked when she thought she had lost sight of him.

"Over here!" he called.

Chrissie gasped as she saw him standing beside the open door of the longest, shiniest car she had ever seen in her life and beckoning to her. She smiled her thanks as she climbed into the cool luxurious vehicle and made herself comfortable.

"OK?" Matt asked as he slid back the glass partition behind the driver's seat.

"Fine, thanks."

"Let's go then."

As the limousine pulled smoothly away from the kerb, Chrissie pulled a packet of cigarettes from her bag. She had been dying for one for hours. She had been trying to cut down, but her nerves were ragged and she wondered if her driver would mind if she smoked.

"Would you mind if I smoked in here?" she asked quietly.

"Sure. Go ahead," he answered pleasantly. "We have air-conditioning."

Chrissie wasn't sure what 'air-conditioning' actually was; just knew she'd read about it somewhere. "Thanks," she replied. "Would you like one?"

"Yeah, why not?"

Chrissie pulled one from the pack and leaned out and stretched her arm through the small window. "Here."

"Thanks."

As her hand brushed the shoulder of his light-coloured suit she admired the style of his clothes. They seemed very expensive to her. 'Bet that shirt's handmade,' she mused. When she saw him flick open his gold lighter, Chrissie cursed herself for not remembering to buy herself one of the cheap ones she had seen in the market. Her hand trembled a little as she scratched several times with her match on the battered little box. Eventually she managed to light her cigarette and moved further back into the deep seat to make herself more comfortable. After inhaling and exhaling deeply several times, Chrissie became calmer. As she relaxed, she was aware that her driver was watching her in the mirror and wished he would take his glasses off, so she could see his eyes. As if he knew what she was thinking, he removed the shades and smiled at her in the reflection. "Where're you from, Chrissie?"

"London," Chrissie answered, without thinking.

"No," he laughed back. "I mean originally."

"Oh sorry," she giggled. "Dublin."

"Thought I recognised the accent."

"Really?" Chrissie was amazed. "Have you been there?"

"Sure have."

"When?" She was intrigued.

"Mostly for the races at the Curragh. We stay in Charles' place while we're there."

"God, I can't believe it!" Chrissie laughed. "What a small world!"

"Have you been to Charles' place down in the country then?"

"Charles' place?" Chrissie frowned.

"His so called country estate? You know the stables and stuff?"

A little voice warned Chrissie to be careful. She didn't know why, but she merely answered, a little off-handedly, "Oh *there*! No, not yet. I've been a bit busy lately." Deciding to change the subject as quickly as possible she asked him what his name was; after all he knew hers.

"It's Matt. Matt O'Brien."

"No!" Chrissie laughed. "So you're Irish too!"

"Well half of me," he laughed again. "The *good* half."

Chrissie soon felt her eyes drooping as she tried to concentrate on the beauty of the passing scenery; the ever changing roll of the hills on one side and huge expanse of the glittering ocean on the other with the miles and miles of golden sands in between.

It hadn't taken them long to leave the sprawling city and make their way out on to the highway. The whole thing was beginning to feel unreal. Here she was being driven along by her own chauffeur, wearing lovely new clothes and with a suitcase in the back that was full of beautiful things she hadn't even worn yet (including some very sheer and saucy black underwear). She was about to make more money than any one she knew could have earned in years and she was being treated as though it was something she did every day. There was one thing that was bothering her, however. What had Matt meant about Charles country estate? He had never mentioned to her that he had a grand house in Ireland. Suddenly, it sunk in. 'So *that's* what he was doing on the boat!' she told herself; wondering why he hadn't taken the plane, he could surely afford it! Chrissie jolted awake as Matt's voice invaded her muddled dreams.

"We're here, Chrissie!" he said loudly for the second time.

"Oh Jesus!" Chrissie said as she sat upright. "Sorry. I must have fallen asleep."

"Plenty of time for that later," he told her as he held the door open for her to get out.

Chrissie stepped out on to a wide gravel drive and stood before the most beautiful house she had ever seen. The ten bedroomed, pink and white painted villa with its sparkling windows and terracotta tiled roof, stood amidst the most luxuriant, colourful and immaculately kept gardens imaginable. Chrissie was dumbstruck! Now she really did feel as though she was dreaming!

"Jesus, Mary!" she whispered as she gazed around at the myriad of colour, the perfectly trimmed hedges and up at the swaying palm trees that bordered the magnificent property. Sighing deeply, her eyes rested for a moment on the fabulously sculptured dolphin that turned very slowly, spewing iridescent fountains of cool water over the expanse of the velvet lawns in front of Casa Miguel.

"This way," Matt urged. "Senor Miguel is not a very patient man!"

Chrissie followed Matt up the wide marble steps and into the cool interior of the house. She couldn't wait to get out of her heavy coat and wished she had chosen something a little lighter to wear. 'Never mind,' she told herself happily. She had all those lovely new outfits in her luggage! Standing in the spacious hall and looking around, as her eyes gradually adjusted to the rather dim interior she realised that Matt was no longer there. Puzzled she took a few hesitant steps towards the nearest open door.

"Senorita?" A soft voice beside her, enquired. Chrissie jumped with fright! She hadn't heard Rosita Gomez, the short, round-faced maid emerging from another of the many rooms in the wide hall. The little woman, dressed in a neat long-sleeved black dress, with a crisp, white, lacy-edged apron tied tightly around her ample waist, smiled up at her. Her jet-black hair was pulled tightly up on to her head in a neat thick coil and the gold looped earrings glinted as she inclined her head.;

"You like me to show you to your room?"

"Yes, please," Chrissie nodded and then asked. "Where's my suitcase, by the way?"

The woman just shrugged her plump shoulders and said. "This way please, senorita."

Chrissie followed her up the two flights of stone steps and along another wide corridor.

"In here, please."

Chrissie walked into her lovely room and almost clapped her hands in delight. It was beautiful! The four-poster bed, swathed from top to bottom in yards of pure white patterned voile was unbelievable! A true fairy tale! She ran over to the open terrace windows and laughed like a child when she saw the shimmering water in the heart-shaped swimming pool. Turning to thank the woman and to ask her where the bathroom was, she was surprised to see that the room was empty, the door closed and she was alone. "Strange," Chrissie thought. Oh well! Everything's feckin' strange at the moment!

Tugging at the buttons on her coat she pulled it off swiftly and threw it across the bed.

"God!" Chrissie puffed. "That's better!"

Sitting on a pink, damask covered chaise longue, Chrissie kicked her shoes off and rubbed her aching foot. Just then she noticed another door leading off the bedroom. Crossing the cool tiles, she opened the door that led into a huge, sparkling white bathroom. "Lovely," Chrissie smiled. "Just lovely."

Wondering for a moment if she should wait for someone to come and tell her exactly what she was supposed to be doing, her eye fell upon a bathrobe hanging over a gold-plated rail.

"Oh, bugger them!" she laughed. Stripping off quickly, Chrissie looked along the glass shelves that lined the wall and taking a bottle-shaped like an enormous teardrop, removed the glass stopper and sniffed at the thick lilac coloured contents.

"Mmmm!" she sighed. "Grand!"

Perched on the edge of the huge bathtub Chrissie waited impatiently for the scented water to fill to capacity. Tipping the creamy liquid into the running water, she leaned over the side and swished her fingers through the warmth and giggled like a school-girl at the mountains of inviting bubbles. At long last she replaced the half-empty bottle on the shelf, turned the gold-plated taps off and stepping in carefully she slithered down into the softness of the perfumed water. Closing her eyes she lowered herself further till the silky bubbles touched her chin and savouring the delights of the deep, roll-topped bath, it wasn't too long before she succumbed to a light and dreamless sleep.

"Hey?" the deep voice mocked menacingly, close to her ear. "Not sleeping again?"

Chrissie grabbed at the slippery sides and pulled herself to a sitting position, spluttering noisily as she swallowed a mouthful of soapy water. "What the feck?" she coughed, her heart thumping wildly at the sudden awakening. She glared straight into narrow slitted eyes, only inches from her own.

Matt stood up then and stared coldly down at the young naked beauty before him, his hands resting on his slim hips. Chrissie felt her body turning red hot with shame, under the insolent gaze. She wondered just how long he had been watching her. "Do you *mind*!" she yelled brazenly up at him, covering her foam-covered breasts with shaking hands, acutely aware of her nudity. "What the hell do you think you're *doing*?"

Matt O'Brien spun on his heel and walked towards the open door.

"Get dressed and come down to the library!" he ordered sharply. "And move it!"

Waiting a few moments until she was sure that she was alone again, Chrissie scrambled out of the cool water and dragged the bathrobe around her damp body. "Cheeky bastard!' she fumed to herself as she looked wildly around the room for her suitcase. She thought Matt had brought it up to her. She marched across the room and threw open the doors of the huge wardrobe. It was empty. 'What the hell's going on?'

Chrissie sat on the edge of the soft bed and puffed nervously on a cigarette. She couldn't understand what was happening. Why hadn't anyone brought her luggage up? She stubbed out her cigarette and lit another one, frowning when she saw that the pack was almost empty. 'Shite!'

The bemused girl wondered where Matt's friendliness had gone. He had been so charming earlier on, why was he acting so nastily now? She grumbled in frustration as she squashed her cigarette into the ashtray, "Bloody men!"

Deciding to put the same clothes back on again, Chrissie went back into the bathroom and retrieved them from the floor where she had thrown them in a crumpled heap. She couldn't bear to put her dirty underwear and stockings back on, so reluctantly she just slipped into the short light grey skirt and buttoned up the white blouse, hoping that some one would remember in time to bring her clothes up before she made her way downstairs.

"Oh good." Chrissie sighed as she did up the last little pearl button and heard the tap on the door. "Come in!" she called out. The door opened slowly and the little maid popped her head around.

"You come now, senorita?"

Chrissie pulled the door open wide. "Where's my case?" she demanded rudely.

"You come," Rosita said, making to leave.

"Come in *here*!" Chrissie hissed, grabbing the woman by the elbow. "You come in here and tell me what the heck is going on?"

"Take your hand off me please, senorita," Rosita replied calmly.

Chrissie felt ashamed at the way she was treating the older woman and mumbled an awkward apology. 'Sorry.'

The maid looked quickly up and down the empty corridor and then walked swiftly past Chrissie and into the room.

"I think the senor is angry," she whispered, her black eyes wide with fear.

"What are you talking about?" Chrissie whispered back.

"I hear them in the library, senorita." Rosita wrung her hands. "And they were shouting and cursing! I couldn't hear properly what they were saying, but they sounded real mad!" she shook her head dramatically.

An ominous feeling crept into Chrissie's bones. There was something wrong here, she just knew it! Grabbing her last cigarette from the crushed packet, Chrissie lit it with a trembling hand. Before she had time to take another puff, the bedroom door crashed open and a furious-faced Matt filled the doorway.

"I *said*!" he roared. "Get your pretty little Irish *ASS*, down to the library! NOW!" The door slammed behind him as he stormed away.

Chrissie nearly fainted in fright at the violent outburst and

171

almost fell on top of the little maid, who rushed forward to support her. Her face drained of colour and her whole body shook uncontrollably. "W*ww*— what is it?" she stuttered miserably. "What have I done?"

Rosita held on to her as best she could, fearing that the poor girl would pass out at any moment.

"Come, senorita." She tried to encourage her. "I think it's best if you come."

Trying to lead her by the arm towards the open door, Rosita murmured words of encouragement. "Best to go now," she soothed. "Then you can eat and then get some sleep, yes? The senorita must be tired and hungry from her long journey!"

Chrissie groaned loudly as she looked down and caught sight of the dark outline of her nipples showing quite clearly through the thin blouse. "I can't go like *this*!" she wailed, tears filling her eyes again.

Feeling sorry for this pretty young girl, Rosita quickly pulled off her long black cardigan, which she had draped over her shoulders when she went down into the wine cellars to bring up the drinks for lunch, and wrapped it around Chrissie's quaking shoulders. "Here," she said kindly. "You take this."

"Thanks," Chrissie said in a hushed voice as she slid her arms through the sleeves, glad of its warmth.

Chrissie's head was in turmoil as she followed her downstairs, along a wide hallway to the doors that led to the library.

"You OK, *chica*?" Rosita squeezed her cold hand.

"Mmm," Chrissie nodded, not feeling at all OK. "Thanks."

The little Mexican maid shuffled off back down the hallway, fingering the rosary beads in her pocket as she disappeared through the low archway down a few broad stone steps and into the vast kitchen area of the villa.

Chrissie stood outside the door shivering with fear as she tried to catch some of the conversation from beyond. A deep grating voice was rising and falling in angry tirades. She gnawed on her bottom lip till it felt raw as she rested her ear against the smooth wood, desperately trying to hear what this stranger was shouting about. Her heart was pounding! But she needn't have bothered. He was speaking in Spanish anyway. Saying a quick 'Hail Mary', Chrissie straightened her bent shoulders, pulled the old black cardigan tightly around her, as if to protect herself from whatever was to befall her, raised a stiff arm and knocked timidly on the door. She had hardly lowered her hand, when the door swung open before her.

"Get in!" Matt ordered.

Chrissie glared up into his eyes, now dark with hostility, and wished she had the courage to smack his arrogant face. She didn't know what the hell was going on. She was sure she hadn't done anything wrong. All she had done was to follow Charles' simple instructions and as far as she could tell, she had. Wrinkling her nose at the thick plumes of blue cigar smoke invading her nostrils as she entered the book-lined room, Chrissie's eyes fell upon the bulky figure of Miguel Fernandez. He sat motionless in one of the over-sized brown leather armchairs that were placed on either side of the magnificent white marble fireplace; the half-smoked Havana glowed dimly between his thick fingers, as he stared unblinkingly in her direction. (He reminded Chrissie of 'Aul' Slimy', for a moment, with his fleshy jowls and lecherous expression, but Chrissie realised at once that this wasn't the sort of character you would dare to answer back.) His dark mean-looking eyes never left her face as he slowly hauled himself out of his chair and flicked the remains of his cigar carelessly on to the neatly stacked pile of logs in the deep wrought-iron firebasket.

A slight movement of his head indicated to Chrissie that she should come forward. Swallowing the lump in her throat, the terrified girl tried with all her might to un-freeze the petrified expression on her pale face. But try as she might, Chrissie could neither smile, nor put one foot before the other. She was rooted to the spot. Never in her life had she felt more afraid! Every inch of the grand room was charged with an air of imminent danger.

"You *stupid*, or what!" Matt's voice hissed. "Get over there!"

Matt O'Brien's lean fingers dug sharply into Chrissie's back as he forcefully shoved her across the room. "Will you *feck off, you eegit!*"

Chrissie had finally found her voice as the spiteful push caused her to catch her foot on one of the thick colourful rugs that were scattered around the room and almost trip headlong into the glowering figure of Miguel Fernandez. As she regained her balance, Chrissie pulled herself up and glared into the mean eyes, her breath coming in short, angry pants. Clenching her jaws till they ached, Chrissie remained silent as she stood fuming, trying to pull the cardigan back on, which had slipped from her shoulders. Her eyes were bright with unshed tears of outrage as she struggled to get her arms into the sleeves. Mad with frustration she ripped it off and flung it on the floor at his feet. Her mind raced wildly as she prepared herself for the worst. The evil expression on the fat man's sweating face, put the fear of God into her.

She flinched and gasped loudly as Miguel Fernandez slow raised an arm; she noticed dark patches of sweat in the armpit of his tightly fitting cream silk shirt, feeling even more repulsed. He grinned nastily when he saw her reaction, knowing that she must have thought he was about to strike her, but instead he merely waved his arm in the direction of the long dark wooden table in the centre of the room and murmured menacingly, "Well, senorita Chrissie?"

Chrissie frowned as she followed his gaze and cried, "Oh my *God*!"

Her suitcase lay upside down on the floor and all of her lovely new clothes and shoes were scattered over the table and across the room where they had been viciously flung! Shaking her head in disbelief, Chrissie asked in a tiny voice, "Why have you done this?"

Her legs were about to give way under her but Matt's strong grip on her elbow kept her from swooning.

"Where's the cash, Chrissie?" He spun her round to face him.

She winced as the vice-like hold he had on her increased.

"What?" she stared, horrified, into his murderous eyes.

"Listen, sweetheart!" he answered through gritted teeth. "Stop acting the fool! You're beginning to piss me off! Badly!"

"I . . . I *d* – don't know what you're talking about," she whispered back, her eyes stretched wide with terror. The swift brutal slap around her face sent Chrissie sprawling across the floor between them, shrieking in pain. She instinctively curled herself up like a wounded animal, her hands covering her face in an effort to protect herself from any further blows. Everything went deadly quiet as she cowered before them, whimpering softly and trying to work out what the hell was happening. Although her poor face was stinging like mad and multi-coloured stars flashed before her eyes, Chrissie felt her anger beginning to rise once more. 'How *dare* they treat me like this! The feckin' bastards!' she thought. Still quaking with fear, she parted her fingers slightly and peeped through them. The two men hadn't moved. She could see the two pairs of feet

174

standing dangerously close by and thinking that at any moment she may get a kick in the head from either of them, she slowly began to pull her aching body into a sitting position.

"Get up!" Matt ordered spitefully. "And you can stop the play-acting!"

Chrissie groaned loudly as she got to her knees and tried to stand up. Her back was hurting badly where she had been knocked to the floor and her right arm felt as though it had been broken! Before she could utter a word in protest Matt hauled her roughly to her feet and shook her savagely. Chrissie cried out in agony.

"You have just one minute, sweetheart, to tell us what you have done with the fucking money! *COMPRENDES?*" he finished with a roar.

Nodding her head dumbly, Chrissie's brain raced. She hadn't a clue what he was talking about, but guessed rightly that the money had disappeared somewhere between the time Charles had 'so kindly' packed her case for her and when she arrived. What was she going to tell them? There was nothing she could say and it didn't look as though they would give her any time to invent any stories either. She looked over at Miguel Fernandez where he now stood with his back to the room, by the open windows that looked out on to the terrace.

"Could I sit down? Please?" Chrissie mumbled, barely able to meet Matt's hard expression. He jerked his head towards a carved bench by the wall.

Chrissie stumbled across the room wincing with pain, stepping over the scattered clothing, as she held on to her aching arm with the other hand that was now beginning to swell and turn a funny shade of blue.

"Can I have a drink of water?" she dared to ask.

"What d'ya think this is?" Matt shouted at her. "A fucking restaurant?"

Chrissie risked a quick glance over at Señor Fernandez. He hadn't moved or spoken a word. His silence was even more terrifying than Matt's ferocious outbursts.

"Get the señorita something to drink," he mumbled unexpectedly, much to Chrissie's amazement.

"What?" Matt demanded. "You must be kiddin'?"

Miguel Fernandez turned his huge frame slightly and looked over his shoulder. "Do it!"

Matt went over and pulled a thick cord that dangled by the side of the fireplace. Within seconds the library door opened and Rosita came quickly into the room. Chrissie frowned. It was almost as if she had been outside the door all the while. Rosita's lip quivered when she saw the forlorn, dishevelled-looking figure, hunched up on the bench as she rubbed her swollen cheek.

"Si, señor?" she asked brightly, as though she hadn't noticed the state that Chrissie was in.

"Bring water!" Matt said tersely.

"Right away, señor." She smiled automatically and left the room, but her heart was heavy in her breast. She blessed herself as she hurried away to the kitchen.

Chrissie ran her hand carefully over the tender side of her face and realised that her eye was puffing up even more. She hissed softly in pain as her fingers touched the bruised flesh. The room remained silent after that, as they waited. It wasn't more than a few minutes before Rosita returned with a tall glass of icy cold water and placed the freezing glass between Chrissie's trembling hands. Looking around her, she saw her cardigan lying in a heap on the floor. Without asking permission she went over and picked it up, shook it out and went back and carefully wrapped it around Chrissie's trembling shoulders. "Don't worry, *chica*," she whispered. "Rosita will take care of you."

Chrissie looked up into the kindly face, her own eyes filled with tears. "Thank you," she managed to whisper back.

Rosita's jaw tightened as she took in the injuries on the young girl's face and cringed inwardly. It wasn't the first time she had seen such things and nothing surprised her any more concerning these so-called 'men'. But it wasn't her place to make any comments. Indeed if it hadn't been for Señor Fernandez, she would have been in jail herself for many years, or worse, have suffered the death penalty. It all seemed so long ago now, since poor Julio, her son and only child, had died in agony from a huge overdose of drugs.

Miguel Fernandez stood menacmgly close to Chrissie as she sipped the icy water, which Rosita was holding to her crushed and bleeding lips. She was too terrified to utter a single sound but she risked a quick glance in his direction. Any moment she expected to be dragged from the seat and beaten to within an inch of her life. Rosita kept a protective arm around her quaking shoulders as she cleverly managed to put herself between the young girl and her infuriated employer. She knew only too well what he was capable of when roused.

"Take her upstairs!" he suddenly ordered through gritted teeth. "And make sure she doesn't leave her room until she decides to tell me the truth!"

"Señor?" Rosita asked.

"Lock the damn door, woman!" he yelled into her astonished face.

Chrissie kept her head down away from the piercing gaze of the two men who stood motionless watching her, as Rosita helped her to her feet and she made a slow and painful exit from the room. It seemed like an eternity before they made it back to her bedroom. Rosita guided her across the room and Chrissie collapsed on to the huge bed with a loud groan. Hot tears trickled down her swollen cheeks as she looked at Rosita through blurred eyes. Sobbing quietly she allowed Rosita to remove her clothing, roll her gently over and pull a soft cover up over her naked body.

'What is your name, señorita?'

"Chrissie," she mumbled. "Chrissie O'Rourke. What's yours?'

'I am Rosita . . . Rosita Gomez."

Going into the bathroom, Rosita quickly dampened a small linen hand towel. She sat down on the side of the bed, smoothed back Chrissie's hair and gently wiped away the blood and tears from the blotchy skin.

"Thank you," Chrissie whispered, trying to smile.

"What is it you have done to make them so angry?" Rosita ventured.

"I don't *know*," Chrissie sobbed, turning her head into the pillow. "I just don't *know*."

Charles Latimer's threats to keep their 'arrangements' to themselves rang crystal clear in her mind. Chrissie didn't dare admit to this inquisitive little maid what she had come to realise had actually happened. (If only she had known then that she could have trusted Rosita with her life.)

Somewhere between London and Los Angeles the money that he had hidden beneath the false bottom of her suitcase has vanished. Chrissie hadn't dared to investigate her luggage before she left. She knew that he had obviously secreted the cash out of sight and she knew it would be more than her life was worth to interfere with it. Anyway, if she didn't actually *see* the money, she felt that she needn't feel so bad about what she was doing. Everything had seemed so simple then. But now what? What in the name of God was to become of her? They didn't look like the type of people who would believe anything she said.

"Are you really going to lock me in?" Chrissie asked as Rosita rose to leave the room.

"I'm sorry, *chica*," Rosita looked at her sadly. "I have no choice."

Chrissie winced as she tried to raise herself on to her elbow.

"But I need a *doctor*," she wailed, as the door closed quietly and she heard the key turn in the lock. "Please . . . my arm's *killing* me!"

Rosita was angry! Whatever the young woman was supposed to have done, surely nothing was so bad that they had to start beating her as soon as she arrived in the house? For years she had gone about her duties deliberately ignoring any 'funny business' in the house. Young girls came and went, some were seen a few times and then never seen again. Odd groups of men and women would arrive at the grand house, often staying for weeks at a time, getting up to all sorts. In and out of each other's rooms at all times of the day and night, partying for days on end, and Rosita was certain that it wasn't just the alcohol that made them all a little crazy. But for her this was always a good time. She was rewarded financially for her extra work, but most of all for never passing comment or acting any differently to anything she saw or overheard. (They each kept to their side of the bargain, made what seemed a lifetime ago now.)

ROSITA

When Rosita Gomez had first come to California, (heavily pregnant) from Mexico, with her dear husband Manuel Ricardo, she had been so full of hope for the future. It had taken many years of toil and hardship for the young couple to gather enough money together to make their way all those hundreds of miles to a new life. They were so full of hopes and dreams as they sat huddled together on the hard seats of the bus, as it took them further and further away from their home and families; sad to be leaving, but happy and excited at the thought of a new and more prosperous life together. Rosita had smiled contentedly as she held her husband's warm hand over her growing belly, so he could feel the movements of their unborn child. She prayed that their baby would be born healthy and strong and that it would never want for anything, and promised herself that it would never have to endure the poverty and humiliation that she had suffered as a child in the little village where she had been raised. In the small community the people were kind and generous, but when your widowed mother had to beg outside the saloon bars and in the streets for a few measly cents to feed the seven hungry mouths at home, it was more than a feisty young girl like Rosita could bear.

Manuel had caught her eye one day as she grovelled in the trash-cans behind one of the better cafes in the dusty main street. He stood watching her from a distance as he took a break from the kitchens to have a beer and a cigarette. Rosita felt a wave of shame sweep over her, as he stood silently staring at her. He had seen her at the back of the church every Sunday with her mother and the rest of the family and tried to think of a way to approach her. He guessed that she was probably only about 14 years old, but like most Mexican girls looked older, as they matured very quickly into ripe young women. He would have loved to catch up with her as the family made their way back to the lower part of the village after Mass, but by the way her protective mother glared at him, he thought better of it. So when he saw her rummaging around in the

179

leftovers, on her own that day, it was more than he could stand to see her doing such a degrading thing. Rosita stood up, holding a half-eaten taco in one hand. Glaring defiantly back at him, she tossed it back into the bin, rubbed her hands together, spun on her bare heel and marched off down the street, her hips swaying provocatively. It only took him a minute to catch up with her. "Please!" he called out to her. "Please wait!" His fingers touched her arm lightly.

Rosita paused for a moment and turned to look at him. His broad smile was so lovely that she felt her heart softening. She had been ready to curse him for making her feel so stupid, but when he gazed down at her, she felt a funny little tickle in her stomach and her young heart fluttered excitedly, so she just couldn't bring herself to say anything nasty to him. Manuel told her that he had been trying to think of a way to talk to her for a long while, but was fearful of what her mother would say especially as she was such a young girl.

"I'm not so young!" Rosita answered quickly, lifting her chin higher and with a cheeky grin on her blushing face. They both laughed and began to chat as they strolled along the hot street. She was pleased and relieved that Manuel didn't mention anything about what she was doing, searching around in the rubbish. He must have known, even if it was only by the way she was dressed, that they weren't the most well-off people in the village and at least had the decency not to mention anything.

From that day on, they would meet in secret after he had finished work in the kitchens and talk for hours about leaving Santa Eugenia. Over the years, many of the families had left and found work elsewhere. Nobody ever seemed to return and this was what the two young people hoped for themselves. They would walk hand in hand around the village in the warm dusk, holding hands and smiling into each other's eyes, quietly planning their future together. (Rosita's mother knew what was going on, but decided not to make a fuss; after all she was getting more than just a few scraps of food now each day.)

Every evening when the café had closed, Manuel would make up a package of meats and pastries for them and give them to his young love when they met up, so the fatherless children at least went to bed without their stomachs aching and rumbling with hunger. Rosita had been so thrilled one night when Manuel had told her that his boss was looking for someone to help out with the cleaning, so if she wanted to work there the job was hers. She jumped at the chance, not only of making a few dollars a week, but to be near her sweet love for more than a few hours a days. It made her young heart leap with joy!

And so they went on. Together they would put a few dollars away in an old coffee bean tin whenever they had anything to spare, and every now and then would empty it all on to the big old scrubbed kitchen table and count it out. Rosita's knuckles were raw from scrubbing the floors in the café and the endless piles of greasy dishes she scraped, washed and dried several times a day, but she hardly noticed. She only had eyes for Manuel and would make any excuse to rub past him or run her fingers through his thick blue/black hair as he concentrated on the order sheets, or slide her arms around his narrow waist as he stood by the huge stove, stirring at enormous pots of tasty foods. He tried to laugh off these intimate little moments between them, but as he lay in his bed every night, he honestly didn't know how much longer he could keep his hands from Rosita's ravishing young body. He woke up each night, murmuring her name and sweating from his erotic dreams, where their eager bodies were entwined in lustful embrace as he thrust himself into her over and over again, burying his face into the thickness of her beautiful hair as she writhed and moaned beneath him.

After years of desperately trying to deny the raging passion that was building up between them, they finally succumbed one warm and bright moonlit night to their desires. After two days of a fun-filled and joyous fiesta, when the whole village celebrated; singing and dancing in the streets and passing leather carafes of sweet heady wine between them, the two young people could no longer hold back the torrent of passionate feelings they had for each other.

Rosita had fallen into his strong arms laughing and clung on to him, her hot moist skin pressing against his damp shirt, her heart beating frantically against his breast. Weak and breathless from the wild, gypsy-like flamenco that she had abandoned herself to in the middle of the cheering villagers, she took great gulps of air as she tried to cool down. Hearing a deep groan rumbling in his chest as she lay her head against him trying to catch her breath, she lifted her eyes slowly to his and, seeing the burning hunger he had tried for so long to hide, knew at once it was no longer possible for them to control their raging emotions. Manuel took her small damp hand into his and held on to it firmly as he led her quietly away, through the noisy dancing crowds. Rosita smiled secretively to herself, as she gazed down as her dirty bare feet scuffed along the heated dusty streets and let herself be taken willingly to a place where at long last, their hearts would finally beat as one and then nothing or nobody could ever come between them.

When they eventually reached Los Angeles and were greeted with great friendliness and warmth by Manuel's Uncle Joachim at the bus station, Rosita and Manuel knew they had done the right thing.

It hadn't taken long for Manuel to find a good job in one of the new restaurants that were opening up everywhere. He had learned a lot about running a kitchen back home and had been improving his cooking skills, even inventing some of his own, well accepted, recipes.

So, after staying with his uncle and aunt for a while in their noisy, overcrowded apartment, they soon moved to a small rented house. Soon they would have enough money for a deposit on a place of their very own, they told each other. Things looked wonderful, especially after Rosita presented Manuel with a beautiful bright-eyed son, a few weeks after they moved in. Her labour was long and painful, but her handsome young husband never left her side for nearly two days and two nights. It was as though he felt each pain and spasm with her. When the dark, curly headed boy had eventually made his traumatic and extremely loud entrance into the world, Manuel had almost collapsed himself with exhaustion. The old Mexican nurse who had come to help her had been most impressed. She told Rosita that most of the men usually ran a mile at the first sight of an impending birth! Even in her weary and worn-out condition, Rosita couldn't help smiling at him. 'Poor *chico*,' she had thought, as she watched him snoring quietly in the chair beside the bed, one hand dangling over the edge of the crib, resting gently on Julio's warm little head. 'How I love you."

Two years later, everything changed dramatically. One night as Manuel walked along the darkened streets on his way home from work, whistling a happy tune to himself, eager to be home and to hear all about Rosita and Julio's day, he was caught by a ricocheting bullet, that hit him square in the head. The gun had been fired by one of a group of black youths who had just robbed a drug store and were fleeing from the scene in panic. As the ageing shopowner pulled a shotgun on them and ran out of the shop and down the street after them, they fired back crazily, whooping and yelling abuse and shooting wildly in all directions.

Nobody even noticed the shadowy figure fall heavily to the pavement, a thick fountain of blood spurting from the gaping hole in his head. Manuel Ricardo Gomez died instantly. He was dead before he hit the ground. There was no time to say goodbye to his lovely wife or to hold his son once again and tell him how much he loved him and how he would protect him forever and if need be, with his own life. Rosita grieved long and hard, hating everything and everyone around her. After the quiet sombre funeral, she had spurned any help offered by Manuel's boss, telling him she would take care of things on her own from now on. He had just shrugged and walked away, knowing that whatever he said would make no difference. He had lost his young brother in a very similar incident only a couple of years before and like poor Manuel's untimely death, nobody had ever been brought to justice.

To add to her anguish, Rosita was served with a week's notice to quit only a few weeks after burying her husband. The landlord tried to be as kind as he could, telling her that he really had no choice, but if she was willing, he had a vacant apartment in the same district that would be a lot cheaper for her. Rosita just nodded dumbly and closed the door quietly on him. When she moved into the dismal couple of rooms, Rosita wept bitterly for hours, clinging on to her bemused young son, promising him that she would soon find a job and they would move on to a lovely new house. The poor child didn't understand what his distraught mother was saying, but he held on to her, sucking his thumb and wondering, in his child-like way, where his papa was.

Rosita had so many jobs in the next few years that she couldn't count them. She never did get enough money saved up to move on to a better place, but the two of them together managed quite well. Julio went to a run-down little hut behind Saint Mary's and played happily every day with a group of children his own age, so that Rosita could do her numerous cleaning and mending jobs. There was no time for her now to have a life of her own and although the few woman she had met at her church were a friendly bunch, she refused any invitations to go to their houses for coffee or meals. After a while they gave up. Rosita felt as though they were encouraging her to go out and meet other men, but although she knew that they meant well she had vowed never to look at another man. All she wanted to do was to take care of Julio and keep him well and happy, and the thought of another man touching and caressing her made her stomach turn over.

Things jogged along for years, days running into one another, the routine barely changing from one week to another. Rosita was never fully happy again and was never seen to be enjoying life. The only time she felt any kind of warmth within her was when she and Julio had their time together. They would stay behind the locked door away from the world, content with each other's company. Many a night after her tussle-headed little boy had gone to sleep, she would sit by his bed and gaze at his peaceful round face as he slumbered, and weep silent tears of loneliness for her lost love.

Julio was a bright and eager boy and when he went to his first school, Rosita was brimming with pride when he received his first-grade reports. He had done well in all his subjects and he was well liked by all the pupils, joining in all the activities with great enthusiasm. When it was time for him to go on to his next school, Rosita felt a twinge of anxiety. She had protected him, maybe too much at times, from the neighbourhood they lived in and worried that he might start mixing with some of the rougher types she had seen gathering on street corners, drinking, smoking and generally making a nuisance of themselves. She had never allowed him to go out into the streets, mixing with the other children, so apart from his schoolfriends he really had no experience of taking care of himself. She had been terrified that something bad would happen to him, like his father, and was now beginning to wonder if maybe she had been just a little too protective of him.

The new school was a bus ride away and on his first day, Julio was so excited to be going off on his big adventure, it was all she could do to force herself not to stand waving at the bus until it disappeared around the corner of their block. Julio had laughed uproariously when she said she would take him on his first day and Rosita had to bite her lip and pretend that she was only joking. Of course he was old enough now to travel on his own!

Julio did well for the first couple of years, making friends, joining the basketball-team and generally being a good all rounder as his teachers called him, but by the time he was fourteen, Rosita noticed a change. At first she told herself that it was just his age and, of course, he wanted to stay out a little longer in the evenings, going to his new friends' houses to play music or go with a crowd from the school for burgers, but when he stayed out one night until nearly midnight, Rosita felt herself growing cold with fear as the clock ticked agonisingly away.

She paced the small apartment, reciting her rosary aloud, over and over, getting more and more anxious by the minute. A few minutes before twelve Rosita heard the sound of a noisy spluttering engine pull up outside with raucous blaring music thumping deafeningly from two huge boxes that were tied to the roof. When the babble of drunken laughing voices greeted her as she threw open the door, her face strained with tension, all her worry and fear turned in an instant to uncontrollable rage. She saw her staggering, intoxicated son lurch towards her, a stupid grin across his handsome face and she yelled a torrent of abuse at the leering youths, waving her arms crazily as she fumed and spat insults at them! Julio's so-called friends jeered and whistled as they screeched away in their battered old truck and disappeared around the corner in a cloud of thick grey smoke.

Rosita jumped back quickly as Julio stumbled into her, but before she could put a hand out to steady him, he fell flat on his face at his mother's feet, banging his head sickeningly as he crashed on to the sidewalk. Rosita stood glaring down at the heap in front of her, her bosom rising and falling as her breath came out in short angry rasps. Clenching her fists by her side and her whole body shaking with anger as she beheld the disgusting spectacle before her, she wished for the first time in her life that she was a man and could haul him to his feet and drag him up and down the street giving him the beating of his young life. As she stood there panting furiously, she glanced up and down the dark empty road and thanked God that there were no witnesses to this revolting scene. Turning on her heel, she marched through to the tiny kitchen, filled a pail with water, came back to the unconscious form outside the front door and flung the contents over the prostrate figure. Slamming the door behind her, she went back into the kitchen, heated up the pot of coffee on the old stove and sat quietly by herself until she calmed down, drinking one cup after another as tears of despair flowed freely down her cheeks.

After Rosita had vented her anger and disappointment on her seemingly remorseful son, he promised her that he would never again put her through such torment. He didn't know what had come over him and guessed that he had just got caught up with a bad crowd, joining in with their drinking and smoking. He would never mix with them again, he promised faithfully. This was not true, of course. He tried to make himself believe that he had been telling his mother the truth, but deep down, he longed for his freedom. Freedom to see who ever he wanted and do things that he had been restrained from doing for so long. Why shouldn't he? After all, he wasn't a kid anymore, he told himself, and she had no right to tell him what to do. A small part of him told him that this was all rubbish, but he ignored it.

Rosita sat night after night, looking out of the window, waiting for her son to come home, praying silently to keep him safe. She had no control over him any more and since that first time he had gone from bad to worse. School was forgotten and Rosita had long since given up all hope of him returning to his education. Some nights she would go to bed exhausted after keeping her lonely vigil and lie awake until dawn, praying for his safe return. She knew that when he eventually came home he would either be drunk or stoned. She knew that he was smoking pot now, but there was nothing she could do about that either. She had tried time and time again to make him see reason, but he just laughed and hugged her tightly, telling her not to worry so much, he could handle it! Maybe he could, she tried to console herself, but where in God's name was he getting the money to pay for it all? She tried not to think about that too much, but knew that she would have to admit that he was undoubtedly up to no good. The gang of black youths that he hung around with didn't have a job between them, she was sure of that; and at least two of them had been in and out of juvenile hall for half their lives. She had gathered this information one Sunday morning, after she had tried to leave Mass as inconspicuously as possible, for fear of being confronted by one of the other mothers, but Conchita Gonzalez had caught up with her, puffing and panting, just before she had time to turn the key in the door and asked her if she was all right. "We have all been so worried about you," she told her kindly, trying to catch her breath. Rosita had smiled wearily and told her she was fine. Knowing that Julio was not at home, yet again, (in fact she hadn't seen him for days) she felt safe in asking her friend to come in for a glass of lemonade. She felt strangely relieved to have another woman to talk to again. Since the time her son had become such a stranger to her, Rosita had hardly spoken to another soul.

She no longer stopped to chat in the local shops or take short bus rides on her own to nicer parts of Los Angeles, to admire the big houses and gardens with wonderful pools. She had an over-powering feeling of guilt and went over and over in her mind where she had gone so wrong. She knew that young people had to find their own way in life, making friends, finding work, but this was something different, she felt it in her bones. The dread of finding the police on her doorstep with news of her son's arrest was one of her biggest fears, but the dread of hearing that he was dead or dying was the most awful pain of all. From lack of sleep and constant worry, Rosita was no longer able to work. She had to leave the cleaning jobs that she had kept going for so long and couldn't even concentrate on menial sewing tasks people asked her to do. She was bone weary and beginning to look much older than she was. Deep lines etched her still attractive features and the darkening smudges beneath her once bright and happy eyes made her look like an old woman.

Conchita had put her straight about the lawless crew that Julio was associating with these days. She told her in the gentlest way she could to warn her, hoping to herself that it wasn't too late already. Rosita nodded and smiled wanly saying, "I guessed they were no good."

One of Rosita's worst fears was confirmed when at six o'clock one cold winter's morning her front door was shattered by a heavy metal bar and three police officers thundered through her small home shouting for her son. The youngest of the three burly men at least had the decency to look away as she tumbled from the bed in her old nightgown and fell to her knees on the floor. It only took a few moments to establish the fact that Julio Gomez was not at home. Nevertheless, they pulled his room to pieces, turning the neatly made-up bed on end and dragging his few clothes from the wardrobe. They searched through the box that held his small record collection and tore pages from his old comics and books that he hadn't looked at in years. The poor terrified woman wailed in protest as she stood watching them from the doorway, begging them to leave it be. They ransacked their way through the whole house and, to her utter humiliation, even rummaged through her own few personal belongings. When they had left, leaving what was left of the front door swinging on its hinges, the distraught Rosita sank to the floor and cried bitterly, punching at the splintered boards with her bare knuckles until they bled.

A couple of her neighbours, who had heard what was going on, came over later and fixed up the door for her as best they could, but told her that when the landlord found out what had been going on, she had better not be surprised to get a visit from him. She thanked them for their help and then locked herself away from the world. Hardly a morsel of food passed her lips for days on end and she barely sipped at the endless cups of coffee she made herself. On a few rare occasions she would wait until after dark and shuffle off down the street to a late-night drug store and buy a few bits and pieces to keep herself going. Living her life like a waking nightmare, Rosita was stunned one morning to see that she had only a few cents left in her purse. Her meagre savings had rapidly evaporated over the months and now she didn't know what she was going to survive on.

Sitting in her isolation behind drawn curtains, Rosita finally began to accept that she must seek help. She had heard about people going on welfare, but had always managed to avoid that way of living, preferring to do any kind of work rather than sponge off the state. But now it was necessary, for a while anyway, just until Julio came to his senses, she told herself. He would probably get caught sooner or later anyhow, doing whatever it was he was doing these days to pay for his drugs and alcohol. He would no doubt go to jail for a little while, and she'd convinced herself that when he came home again he would see how stupid it had all been, and then they could get back to living a normal life again. Maybe he would even go back to college. He was doing well there, until all this nonsense started. But deep in her heart, she knew she wasn't thinking straight any more.

So it was a good thing that Conchita knocked on her door one morning on her way to the market and asked her if there was anything she could do for her. Rosita had broken down, sobbing pitifully at her kindness and after chatting for a long while allowed herself to be shepherded down to the crowded smelly offices, where she could fill in page after page of forms so that she could claim benefits. It took weeks for everything to be sorted out in the overworked department and when Rosita received her first benefit cheque she cried with relief. She wasn't happy, though, she wondered how on earth it had all come to this. What would Manuel say if he could see her now? And what would Julio say? If she was honest, she tried to tell herself, she really didn't give a damn what Julio would say! Where was he anyway? She hadn't seen or heard a word from him since that awful morning when she had had her front door battered down. The shame of it!

Still at least now, thanks to Conchita, she wouldn't starve. Maybe she could even find a few hours' work somewhere that paid cash and no one would be any the wiser. Going about her daily routine with a heavy heart, Rosita tried to live as normally as humanly possible. She had given up hope of hearing Julio's key in the door and tried to pray to God to at least keep him safe, but she couldn't seem to find the right words. All the years of beseeching the Lord to keep her son out of harm's way seemed to have fallen on deaf ears. So what was the use? What she had been dreading for years had happened. Her son was a wanted man and she was sure that word had gone around like wildfire about the raid on her house and there was no way now that he would risk returning to his home. But would she want to see him again anyway, Rosita asked herself as she sat in front of the old black and white television that Uncle Joachim had sent over when he had got wind of her circumstances. She didn't think so. She had failed him and she had failed her darling husband. She had no right to expect any miracles. She was supposed to love and take care of her son until he made a family of his own, eventually bringing armfuls of grandchildren to her to love all over again. The question of her love for her son never came into it. She loved him with every beat of her heart and would have given her life for him, but would he have done the same for her? Rosita was hurt and angry with Julio. At least he could have got a message to her. Surely he knew that she would understand that he couldn't show his face in the neighbourhood. Didn't he care that she sat night after night all alone and frightened to death?

"Damn the little bastard to hell!" Rosita yelled at the top of her voice one evening as she tried to heat some beans on the stove and only succeeded in burning them into a solid crust. She hurled the blackened, smoking pot against the wall screaming with frustration, "I hope I *never* set eyes on you ever again, Julio Gomez!"

Although Rosita hadn't meant those awful words, she never did see her son again. Not until the day she had been taken down to the city morgue to identify him, that is. Not fully comprehending what the youthful officer was saying, the details of the one-sided conversation did not register in her brain. All she could grasp was the fact that a young man had been found dead. Her tired face slowly drained completely of the little colour she had and as the policeman stood respectfully, cap in hand, at her door his heart went out to her. He was only a fresh-faced young rookie and had silently cursed his captain down at headquarters that morning when he sent him out on his first experience of delivering the news of a fatality.

"Senora Gomez?" He tried again. "Ma'am?"

Rosita looked up at the tall figure, so smart in his new uniform, her eyes stretched wide and filled with disbelief as her quivering mouth tried to form some words.

"Do you have someone who could come with you, ma'am?" he asked gently.

"Where?" Rosita finally managed to mumble.

"Down to the morgue, ma'am," he told her again. "We must have an official confirmation of identity."

Rosita shook her head dumbly, only vaguely aware of what he was asking her.

"No, there's only me," she answered quietly. What was this man saying? she puzzled; something about her son?

Standing on one side of the glass beside the police officer, Rosita's breath came in low, dry sobs. Her arms were folded tightly around her waist as if to protect herself as she stood there, stiff limbed and terrified, staring at her own reflection in the window. Waiting for a few more agonising minutes before she gained enough courage to indicate that she was ready, Rosita prayed to the Holy Virgin that there had been some dreadful mistake and when they revealed the body behind the screen she would sink to her knees in thanksgiving that it wasn't her Julio! Heaving a deep mournful sigh of resignation, she turned slightly to the nervous officer beside her and whispered, "OK."

James Daly tapped gently on the glass to show that they were ready and the dark curtains drew silently apart.

For what seemed like an eternity, Rosita couldn't react. The blood in her veins had turned to ice and it was as though she had been frozen in time. There she was, staring into a darkened room, her eyes upon the laid-out body of her only child. Surely this wasn't real? He couldn't be dead! Why would he be dead? 'He doesn't look like there's anything wrong with him at all, that young man in there,' the poor woman tried to reason with herself as she squinted her eyes into the room. 'They've made a big mistake here, that's what they've done.'

"Ma'am?" The voice enquired softly.

"What?" she asked, not turning her head from the window.

"Please, ma'am?" Christ! He was hating this. "Is it your boy?"

"No, I don't think it is. Sorry."

"Pardon me?" He was perplexed. The young guy had definitely had his identification card on him when the ambulance had picked up his corpse from the alleyway behind Barney's burger bar. "Could you please take another look?"

"Why do we have to look from out here, officer?" Rosita asked, and without waiting for a reply walked to the doorway and made to turn the handle. "I can't see properly."

"You sure?" He frowned.

"Of course I'm sure," Rosita answered abruptly. "Don't want to make any mistakes, do we?"

It was no good! Rosita couldn't block it out any longer! Try as she might there was no way that she could pretend to herself that this wasn't her son. Looking down on the perfect features it was hard to believe. He looked so peaceful and innocent. Surely dead people were supposed to look different, somehow? She had never been allowed to view the body of Manuel. Everyone had agreed that the sight of his horrific head injury would have certainly unhinged a woman so young. She had been crazy with grief for a while when they wouldn't let her see her darling husband to make her farewell, but soon appreciated their thoughtfulness because she knew it was better for her to remember him the way he was, rather than to see him in such a terrible state.

Stretching out a trembling hand, Rosita gently stroked a cold cheek. The sorrow she felt ran so deep it was impossible to even shed a tear. Feeling a light touch on her arm, she turned her sad face to the young officer.

"¡Si!" she whispered pitifully. "¡Si, es mi unico hijo . . . my only son."

When Julio's body had been released and Rosita had stumbled

blindly through the long and painful funeral service, she went back to Uncle Joachim's house and sat in the corner of his sitting room as one after another of the friends and neighbours came and gave her their deepest condolences. Later on it was difficult for her to recall who she had actually spoken to. She had refused the kind offer of Manuel's aunt and uncle to come and stay with them until she felt a little better. Knowing that she would never feel the same again, ever, she waited for her opportunity to slip quietly away and made her own way home where she once again took up her solitary existence.

It wasn't until months later, after Conchita and some of her friends had insisted on calling at her house time and time again in an effort to get her to at least come out for a little walk with them, that it suddenly dawned on her one bright spring morning that she had never asked how Julio had actually died. As she swept away the dust she had collected from around the house and brushed it out into the small backyard, she suddenly had a terrible urge to find his death certificate. She had shoved it to the back of one of the crammed drawers in her bedroom, without a second glance. It was bad enough knowing that she would never see him again, but to read the details of his death was almost more than she could bear!

Tipping the three drawers out on to her bed, she rummaged through the contents frantically. There were old school reports, crayon drawings that Julio had been so proud to present her with from his nursery days, along with crumpled bills and letters from her family when they first moved to Los Angeles. At last her searching gaze fell upon the long brown envelope. She sat down on the side of the bed, took a deep breath and slid her fingers along the gummed edge. Gingerly she withdrew the neatly folded paper and opened it carefully. The words 'Narcotics Overdose' leapt out at her from the cream-coloured paper. All the feelings of bitter hatred that had lain dormant for so long uncoiled in her body like a venomous and deadly snake. She could feel the hot poison slowly making its way through her whole being until it reached her mind. She began to retch as thick lumps of bile lodged in her throat and cold sweat trickled down her back and formed sticky pools beneath her breasts. As though she had been punched in the stomach, Rosita suddenly lurched forward and vomited across the room. Wiping her mouth with the back of her hand she rose unsteadily to her feet, smiling grimly to herself as she looked around at the mess.

There and then, she vowed that one day, however long it took, she would find the animals who were responsible for taking the life of her son and she would send them to hell, to burn and rot forever with the rest of Satans' spawn!

Around the neighbourhood, Rosita's friends and neighbours were happily surprised to see the smiling face greeting them each day. Little did they know what was hiding behind the bright countenance.

Rosita had heard of a new job agency that was advertising for women. She had heard the gossip one morning as she sat sipping coffee with a few friends from the church and her ears had pricked up when they said they knew of a couple of ladies who had got some great work in some of the fabulous new houses that were being built along the Pacific Highway. Of course they had had to be well vetted and have excellent references before they could even apply for such a position. Conchita told her that she had heard that Mrs Morgan's daughter, Alicia, had found a wonderful position with a script writer from one of the big movie studios. Rosita sat quietly, mulling over the idea of making her way down to the offices to find out more details. Not wanting to let the other woman know that she was interested, she kept her thoughts to herself. But at the first opportunity she borrowed a telephone directory and flicked through the pages until she found what she was looking for.

Rosita made an appointment for the following week with the agency and as she sat nervously waiting to be called, she glanced at her reflection in her tiny compact mirror. She licked her dry lips carefully, trying not to remove any of her lipstick as she did so. Altogether she was pleased with her efforts.

The night before she had stripped off to her bare skin and scrubbed at her body until it glowed. Her flesh was a little saggy these days, she had to admit, but all together she didn't look too bad, considering! She spent hours washing and pressing the old black suit that she hadn't worn for years and although the waist of the skirt was more than a little tight on her now, she was pleased with the results. Her shoes were in quite good condition still and she couldn't remember the last time she had worn them. She found her black shiny bag stuffed at the back of the wardrobe and gave it a good polish. The worst thing was her hair. It had been neglected for so long that when she took the clips out of it, it hung limply around her head like an old rag. Disgusted at the sight of it, Rosita took a pair of scissors to it and lopped off about six inches. At once it felt better. She lathered and rinsed it three times until it felt clean and healthy again and only after she had rubbed and rubbed at it until it was almost dry did she dare to look in the mirror. Smiling at herself, she quickly rolled up a few curls and pinned them securely to her head.

"Well you're no oil painting now, señora," She told herself. "But you could look a whole lot worse!"

"Mrs Gomez?" The high-pitched voice called out.

Rosita jumped when she heard her name and leapt to her feet. "Yes?"

"Come in, please."

The meticulously made-up secretary looked down her nose as Rosita walked passed her into the spacious office. She had seen so many women over the past few months since they had opened that she was beginning to get bored with her job. And it showed! She had a heavy date that night and was desperate to get away to the beauty parlour as quickly as she could. A guy she had been trying to impress from the real estate company along the road had finally asked her out to dinner and she couldn't wait to impress him even further.

So for once, in a long time, it was Rosita's chance to have a little good luck come her way. Checking the clock for the umpteenth time that afternoon, Paula Kaplan turned to Rosita and said rather impatiently, "Sit down, please!"

"Thank you."

"References?" Paula held out a hand.

"Well the thing is . . ." Rosita began.

"Don't tell me," Paula smirked. "You haven't *got* any?"

Rosita tried not to show her annoyance at being spoken to by someone so much younger than herself and smiled back across the desk. "I'm afraid they were lost when my other handbag was stolen the other day."

Paula knew damn well that she was lying, like so many of the other women who had come seeking working, but this one didn't look too bad. She was clean and smart and although a little older than she would have liked, she thought that maybe she would be worth a trial period at least. The girl that she had set up for Señor Fernandez' house had been taken ill with acute appendicitis, so she was stuck. Not wanting to ruin what was fast becoming an agency with an excellent reputation for supplying honest and reliable staff she wondered if this one was worth taking a chance on. Anyway there had been numerous telephone calls over the last few days from Casa Miguel, asking when the hell they were going to be sent this wonderful housekeeper that they had been promised; so she had to come up with someone soon. Getting more agitated by the minute, Paula read Rosita's lengthy application over again for the third time. Every other minute she was checking the time on her jewel-studded watch. "Look Mrs Gomez."

Rosita leaned eagerly forward in her chair. "Yes?"

"Do you *honestly* think that you could handle the running of a big important house?"

"Of course," Rosita assured her confidently.

"The thing is, you see," Paula's scarlet lips parted widely in a practised smile, showing perfect white teeth, "I have an extremely important meeting to go to in a while and I haven't got a lot of spare time to be ringing around your previous employers to check with them that what you say is true. So if you can assure me that if I let you go for a month's trial to this wonderful position you will promise me that you will send me copies of the references. I'll leave it to you to explain to your new employer what happened to the originals."

"Of *course* I will!" Rosita beamed back. "I can promise you that!"

"There you are then." Paula handed her a sheet of paper with the address and details of the duties that her job would entail. "You start tomorrow. And don't forget it could be only a temporary position."

"Tomorrow?" Rosita frowned.

"Do you want the job or not, Mrs Gomez?" Paula stood up abruptly, her shiny blonde hair swinging around her narrow face.

"Yes, of course I do."

"Well then," Paula said sharply. "Good luck!" Without another word she grabbed her bag from the drawer under the desk, pulled a jacket from the coat rack and almost ran from the room, leaving an astonished but delighted Rosita still sitting at the desk, staring at an empty chair.

Rosita sat nervously at the back of the bus thinking about the last few dollars she had spent from her benefit cheque on the fare. She hoped that everything would go well with her new boss and that she would very soon have enough saved up to put her plan into action.

Everything did indeed go very well and Señor Fernandez' household were more than pleased with her efforts. There were another couple of very young and attractive Spanish girls who came to the villa a couple of times a week to give her a hand with the heavier work and she became very fond of the young women. They could hardly speak a word of English between them, but Rosita was delighted to be able to chat to them in their own language. Her heavy heart began to feel a lot lighter as she went about her numerous tasks and prepared wonderful meals for the señor and his guests. At first she was overwhelmed by the contents of the huge larders and well-stocked wine cellars, but soon took great delight in experimenting in all sorts of adventurous menus (including some of Manuel's!) and served up delicious and unusual meals, much to Señor Fernandez' appreciation.

Rosita was a very astute woman and as she moved quietly around the long dining table each evening, clearing away the empty plates and dirty glasses, she kept her head averted and her ears open. It was obvious to her that none of the visitors to the house had regular jobs. They appeared at all times of the day and night, and she was expected to prepare meals and snacks at the strangest of hours. Still, she didn't mind and it was none of her business anyway. She was well treated and her wages were more than she could have ever expected in her life and that was what was important to her. She hadn't taken any of the days off that she was entitled to and her new boss had agreed that she could take a week or two off in a while. He was so happy with her that he was only too glad to agree to her polite request. There was no way he was going to lose a little gem like her. As far as he was concerned, the acute attack of appendicitis had been a blessing in disguise. Paula Kaplan had been a little put out by his attitude, when he said he wasn't interested in taking the other girl back, but why should she worry, she still got her commission every month whoever was doing the job!

Only a few months after Rosita had started work at Casa Fernandez there was enough money put by for her to take a full two weeks off. As she sat in the shade of the private little kitchen garden with Nuria and Teresa, she went over and over the long list of instructions she was leaving for them. She didn't want a thing to go wrong while she was away. She couldn't bear to think what might happen if she lost her position. When she was completely satisfied that the girls understood their duties she went up to her room and collected her small bag of clothing and her handbag. After waving happily to the two girls from the back of the cab that she had treated herself to, Rosita settled herself into the seat and closed her eyes to relax. At last she could begin to get things going. She wondered what everyone back at the house would have to say if they had known what she was planning to do. She had a sneaking feeling that Señor Fernandez and his compadres had their own shady dealings going on, but she couldn't think about that; she had enough to sort out herself.

By the time Rosita had booked herself into a cheap boarding house, not too far from where she used to live, she was beginning to wonder if she really was doing the right thing after all. The feeling only lasted a moment though, when a vision of her son's prone body flashed before her.

For the next two weeks, Rosita waited until after dark each evening and then went from one stinking dive to another, trying to gather information about her son and the people he was mixing with before his death. She was either ignored or laughed at. The sight of the strange little woman dressed from head to toe in black shuffling around amongst the low-lives made a sorry sight. She was greeted by jeers and laughter time and time again, suffering threatening verbal abuse and indignation more than once, yet nothing swayed her from her mission.

She went back to her lonely little room, each time wondering if she would ever be able to find out what she needed to know. As she sat alone in the quiet of the early morning watching the streaked sky slowly turn from night to day she prayed that she would have enough strength to carry on. In her heart she was as determined as ever but her body ached wearily from the miles she had trudged all over town. The disgust and repulsion she felt each time she stepped foot in one of those vile places where the scum of the earth hung out made her want to run screaming and yelling. She wanted to rip the clothes from her body and scrub away the filth and dirt that she was contaminated with. The sights she had seen of so many young people, boys and girls, made her weep angry tears of frustration and pity, but what could she do about all of them? Nothing! All she really cared about was finding the bastards who had caused her own son's death.

Just a couple of days before Rosita was due to go back to work she was roused from a fitful slumber towards the end of a fiercely hot afternoon, by a light tapping on her door. She sat up slowly, wondering if she had imagined it. She lay back down on the crumpled covers thinking that she had imagined the sound, but as she turned over on her side she noticed a small piece of paper that had been shoved under her door. She jumped quickly up from the bed and pulled the door wide open and looked up and down the dingy corridor. It was empty. Sighing heavily she rubbed her hands across her tired face, bent down and picked up the creased paper. She closed the door quietly and went and sat by the window. The daylight was slowly fading and her eyes were so sore she had to squint down at the tattered note. She looked closely at the scrawl. 'Leroy Jones', was all it said. She turned it over to see if anything else was written on the other side. Nothing! Just 'Leroy Jones'!

"What is this?" she whispered to herself, puzzled.

Rosita sat for a long while just staring down at the note on her lap. Then suddenly, it hit her. "Dios!" she cried aloud, jumping up from her chair. "Dios! It is *him*!" By some miracle, there had been someone out there who had some decency still left in them! They had revealed to her the name of the man she had been searching for. She blessed them with ever fibre of her being as she fell to her knees weeping and thanked all the saints in heaven for this miracle!

When she had calmed down, the trembling woman went into the little bathroom, stripped off her grubby clothes and took a long hot shower. As she slowly rubbed herself dry Rosita realised that she probably wouldn't have time to carry out the rest of her plan for a while. She would first have to find out where this person lived and then she would have to try and find someone who would trust her enough to sell her a gun. And she knew *that* wouldn't be easy but somehow she would do it!

For weeks after returning to the villa Rosita could think of nothing else. She still performed her duties admirably, but now she had an almost constant little smile on her face. Incredibly, on her last foray into the dark and degrading world of dealers, prostitutes and gutter trash, she had discovered the whereabouts of Mr Leroy Jones!

He was living, if it could be called that, not half a mile from her old house. In a last-ditch effort to glean some information Rosita hesitantly approached a group of scantily clad girls, who were hanging around together on the corner of a dimly lit street near the all-night pool-rooms and once again she was greeted with jeering comments and suspicious looks. Bracing herself against the inevitable reaction she waited.

"What'cha want Leroy for then, grandma?" one of the girls sneered brazenly as she flicked her cigarette ash on to the sidewalk and blew thick smoke through shiny purple lips into Rosita's face.

Rosita looked up into the girl's black, pock-marked face without blinking, her heart pounding excitedly and answered quietly, "I need something for my son."

"Ain't he big enough to do his own errands then grandma?" one of the others cackled. Rosita took a deep breath. "Can you just tell me where I can find him, please?"

Just then the girls all swung around, peering down the road as they heard a couple of cars turn the corner and come slowly up the street.

Rosita grabbed hold of the nearest girl's arm before she could run up to the first car that had slowed down by the kerb.

"*Por favor?*" she begged. "Just *tell* me!"

"Lay off, ya stupid old bitch!" the wild faced young hooker yelled at her as she wrenched her arm free. "I'm losing business here!"

Rosita watched her sadly as she fought with the other girls as they touted for business by the cruising cars. Just then she felt a gentle hand on her shoulder. "He lives up there."

Rosita heaved a sigh of relief turning to smile into the eyes of the girl. She couldn't have been more than fourteen years old and already she was beginning to look like an old woman. Her skin was a sickly shade in the evening light, her thin stringy hair dull and lifeless and her eyes held a look of hopeless resignation. "Over the old book shop," she murmured, glancing quickly over at the group of girls. "You have to go around the back way to get in."

Rosita opened her arms and pulled the girl close to her breast, the lump in her throat nearly choking her. "Why don't you go home, *chica?*" she whispered.

The young girl pulled herself away from Rosita's encircling arms and smiled wanly.

"I wish," she answered softly, as she turned on her gold plat-formed shoes and tottered across to join the others, her skinny fleshless legs barely able to hold her up.

Señor Fernandez called his housekeeper into the library one morning to ask if she would be prepared to take on a huge task later on that week when he would be inviting a party of friends from Europe to stay for a while. It would mean a lot of hard work and even more of her special meals, of course. They were very good friends of his and he wanted to repay them for the excellent hospitality that they had shown him when he had been invited to cruise around the Meditteranean with them earlier in the year. She would naturally be free to hire some extra staff for the weekend, he told her. Rosita was only too happy to oblige, especially when he added that there would be a very nice bonus in it for her!

On the final evening before the guests' departure, Rosita sur-passed herself with the splendid meal she produced, as if by magic! Each of the five delicious dishes was greeted with great gusto as each new course was served, and by the time Rosita and her two extra hired maids walked into the dining room pushing three silver trolleys laden with huge bowls filled with fresh tropical fruits and her own homemade pavlovas topped with fresh cream and straw-berry sauce, the whole table stood up and gave her a warm, appreciative round of applause. If only they had known the blood, sweat and tears that had gone into the preparation of such a feast, Rosita smiled to herself. Still it was over now and she knew how pleased Señor Miguel was when he caught her eye and winked. ('And how proud Manuel would have been of me' she thought wistfully.)

Some time later, after the entire kitchen had been scrubbed and cleaned to her satisfaction, Rosita said a sleepy goodnight to the girls and took herself off to bed. Keeping her eyes tightly shut she tried to relax, but one jumbled thought after another raced across her exhausted mind. Once or twice she thought she heard low rustling sounds coming from outside and a murmur of voices close by, one with an unusual accent. Was that English . . .? Maybe one of the Señor's friends at dinner? She couldn't be certain.

Eventually after tossing and turning for what seemed an eternity, the weary woman dozed off into a fitful sleep, but within a very short time she was abruptly brought back to full wakefulness when a loud noise startled her. She sat bolt upright in the bed blinking furiously. Then another sound! A piercing scream! Then loud voices, some sounds she couldn't recognise and then running feet and a car engine being revved up furiously.

"*Dios!* What is it?"

Pulling the tangle of covers from her heavy limbs she sat on the edge of the bed for a moment listening. Perhaps she had imagined it? She waited for another few moments and then, hearing nothing more, she tutted to herself for being silly, stood up and went towards her little bathroom; she must have been dreaming. As she passed the open windows, she glanced out across the moonlit gardens, thinking how pretty they looked, as though everything had been painted silver and sprinkled with Stardust. She stopped suddenly and frowned. Surely she was seeing things? She was worn out, but . . . it couldn't be? Could it?

Tiptoeing silently out on to the small first-floor veranda, Rosita leaned over the low stone balcony and peered out over the length of the long narrow lawn that ran along the side of the house, where the staff were accommodated. Sprawled out below, only a short distance from where she stood, was the dark shape of a man's body. The angle he was lying at looked odd, unreal; one arm and a leg twisted grotesquely beneath him; like a puppet whose strings had broken. Rosita gasped and blessed herself quickly.

"*Madre Mia!* What is this *now*?"

She ran back into her room and pulled on her robe, thinking all the time just what she should do. She felt sure now that the noise she been woken by had been a gunshot, but was it her business to interfere? Maybe she should just close her windows and go back to bed and pray for the departed soul of whoever was lying down there. But she couldn't just sit there and pretend that nothing had happened. Maybe he was still alive? Should she go and wake the Señor? Would he thank her for doing that?

She sat clutching her old worn rosary beads, listening intently for any small sound. Somewhere on the other side of the huge villa she thought she heard a few muted sounds and a murmur of voices that barely reached her through her open windows. Deciding that she could stand the suspense no longer and made her way silently down the back stairway and into the kitchen. She waited a moment or two to see if any of the young maids had heard anything, but as she stood in the middle of the empty room there was complete silence. Pulling the heavy bolt back from the garden door she opened it just a fraction. The first light of the early dawn was beginning to chase away the night and lighten the grounds now, with its pale pink and golden streaks on the horizon, but there was no time to stand and admire the fabulous sight. Rosita walked a few paces away from the house and turned back to look up at the many windows. Her eyes scanned for any sign of movement. Momentarily she thought she noticed the slightest fluttering of a curtain from one of the bedroom windows, but she dismissed it as imagination.

Praying silently she crept over the dew-covered grass, her eyes never leaving the crumpled figure. Bending over the lifeless form Rosita gasped softly as she recognised one of Señor Miguel's guests; a thick mess of blood drenched his lovely blue silk shirt, spreading its ghastly stain on the ground beneath him. She knelt down beside him and, reaching out a trembling hand, pressed her lingers gently on his neck. If there were any chance that he may still be alive, surely she would then have to rouse someone in the house? Although the flesh was still warm there was no pulse to be found. Rosita sat back on her on heels in dismay, her eyes filling with hot tears and stared down into the blank unseeing eyes in the ashen face. What should she do? Scrambling awkwardly to her feet, she blessed herself and uttered a small prayer for the man as she hurried back into the house. Pouring a large glass of water she gulped it down as quickly as she could and then made her way silently through the house, up two flights of stairs and along a wide corridor. She stood for what seemed an age outside the Señor's bedroom to compose herself.

She considered that he had been good to her, treated her fairly, paid her very well (even when her references had mysteriously gone astray!) so at least he deserved a chance to sort this dreadful problem out for himself. She knew full well that he wasn't the normal sort of businessman and nor were any of his friends, either, but that didn't bother her. Nothing they did ever involved her or affected her in any way.

Knocking timidly on the heavy door, she waited. When there was no response the first time, she tried again, a little more loudly this time. On hearing low groans of annoyance from inside the room, followed by a flow of mumbled curses she took a step backwards; a thin film of perspiration trickled down her face from her damp hair and she lifted the corner of her robe to wipe it dry. Gritting her teeth she stood determinedly, waiting. The door opened gradually and the dishevelled bulky form stood before her, frowning moodily as he muttered hoarsely, "What in the name of God do *you* want?"

Rosita averted her eyes from the rolls of bare flesh that protruded from the gaping gown and very quietly replied, "Please, Señor Miguel, forgive me, but I think it's very important that you come with me!" Before he could answer she rushed on. "Something terrible has happened, Señor, down in the garden! Please you must come!"

The urgency in her voice took him by surprise! Without another word, he looked up and down the corridor, grabbed her by the elbow and hurried her away.

"Hmm ... you have done well, Rosita," Senor Fernandez said softly as the two of them stood looking down at the mis-shapen form, the features now clearly visible in the pale mist of the morning light. "You're sure that no one else has seen this," he nodded.

"Oh *si* Señor!" Rosita nodded back emphatically. "Only me!"

"Come then," he ordered swiftly. "You must help me."

Rosita gasped loudly as she realised that he wanted her to help him to move the body.

"Si, Señor," she sighed.

Averting her face from the glazed eyes of the young man, Rosita took a deep breath and bent to take hold of his feet. Between them they dragged and bumped him over the damp ground, down a couple of steps into the kitchen, along the floor and with an almighty effort shoved him down the steps into the dark cellars. Rosita almost gagged when she heard the sickening thud as his poor head crashed against the stone floor at the bottom.

"Shut and lock that door," her boss ordered breathlessly. "We will not be needing any wine today!"

After the door was closed he held his hand out, "Give me the keys!"

Handing over the small bunch of keys with trembling hands Rosita looked up into the sweating face. "What now, Señor?"

He chewed on his thick bottom lip before he answered and

then said, "I think now, Rosita, you must go out and see if you can wash away anything that may be out there. This must remain between us. You understand?"

"Si, Señor."

"We will not speak of this again, you understand!" he repeated, his voice grim and slightly threatening. Rosita nodded her agreement.

"Go then!" He turned and left the room abruptly.

Rosita could hardly grasp what was happening but obediently went back out into the garden and over to the place from where they had removed the body. A great crimson patch had spread widely out across the grass and the trail of blood leading to the kitchen door gleaming dully in the pale sun. Just then she heard a distant sound of an engine. Realising that it must be the team of gardeners, who always arrived early in the morning to begin their work and to avoid the blistering heat of the day, she looked around wildly. There was no time to fill great pails of water to throw over the blood, so, thinking rapidly she ran over to an assortment of terracotta pots and dragged them one by one over the dark stains. Sweating and breathless, she stood up, holding her aching back and was pleased to see that there was no incriminating evidence to be seen. (No doubt Nuria and Theresa would be wondering why they had been moved, but she would just explain that they had been in too much shade and she wanted them out in the full sunlight for a while.)

As she turned back to go into the kitchen, a glint of sunlight on metal caught her eye beneath one of the bloom-laden shrubs by the wall. She crossed over to look under the thick branches.

"Oh!" she gasped, bending down more closely. She heard the truck door slam noisily and voices of the men chatting to each other as their footsteps crunched along the gravel by the side of the house. She reached out and grabbed the gun, shoving it into her pocket, just as they came around the corner. Her hand was soaking wet with fear as she held on to the small weapon and prayed that they hadn't seen anything. "Señora?" young Sergio laughed. "So early?"

She smiled back and without answering, left them staring at her disappearing figure as she scuttled back into the kitchen.

The house remained as quiet as a morgue after the other guests had made their noisy departures. Rosita had been so relieved that none of them asked for any more than coffee at breakfast. She had never felt so tired in her life – not a wink of sleep and now she had even more to think about.

Her employer had asked her not to let anybody disturb them as he closed the dining room doors on her. He also told her to tell the rest of the staff that they could take a couple of days off. Inform them that he would be going away and wouldn't need them, he had ordered. But she was to stay for the time being . . . he needed to speak to her.

Sitting alone in the kitchen, freshly showered and in one of her own dresses, Rosita waited patiently for the internal phone to ring. She deliberately kept her back to the cellar doors and forced the image of the dead man's face from her mind. She went over the events of the last few hours in her head. From the time she had walked calmly up to her room, her hand still firmly gripping the gun in her pocket and hidden it among her laundry at the bottom of the basket until now, she had been quite amazed that she felt no panic at all.

She had decided that she would not tell Señor Miguel of her discovery. It was a Godsend and she was hardly able to believe her luck! It would save her an awful lot of trouble in having to to buy such a thing, putting herself at risk, not to mention the cost. And this way, there would be no way of tracing the murder back to *her.*

Señor Fernandez beckoned to her to come and make herself comfortable in one of the huge armchairs, as she stood a little hesitantly at the library door.

"You're sure that there is no one else still here?" he asked, as he sat down opposite her and took one of his favourite cigars from the side table.

"Of course, Señor! Even the gardeners have gone," she assured him. Then she gave a little start as the door swung open behind her.

"Oh, don't worry about Marco," he smiled benignly. "He's my right-hand man."

Marco Jimenez came over and stood silently behind his boss's chair, a muscular arm resting casually on the high back, his heavy-lidded dark eyes watching her suspiciously. Rosita guessed, quite rightly, that he was there to help with the disposal of the corpse.

"I just wanted to clear up one or two things, before you go off for a couple of days too."

Rosita was surprised. She had had no idea that he was going to give her any time off. She had wondered, in fact, if he was going to implicate her in any more strange goings on!

"What is that, Señor?" she enquired politely.

"You're sure that everything has been cleaned outside?"

"Certainly, Señor" she nodded. "When Sergio and the others left I used the big watering hose . . . for a long time! Everything is as it was."

"Good," he smiled again. Then added quickly as if to catch her out, "You didn't happen to see anything else at all, something unusual that might be laying around? Maybe hear something unusual?"

Rosita frowned as if puzzled and asked him, "Like what, Señor? I'm not sure what you mean."

He stared at her intently for a few moments and then gave a little laugh, dismissing the idea with a wave of his hand. "Oh, nothing, nothing. It's not important."

Rosita hoped that he hadn't noticed that her hands were trembling slightly and she clasped them more tightly together on her lap. "Well, Señor," she began hesitantly not sure if she should mention it.

"What?"

"It's just that I thought I heard an strange accent."

Miguel sat forward in his chair and leaned towards her. "What do you mean?"

"Well," she swallowed hard. "Like the voice of the silver-haired gentleman at dinner." Watching her even more intently for a few moments Miguel Fernandez' expression quickly changed. "Marco," he said with a broad grin. "Give this little lady here that envelope on the desk." He pointed across the room. "A little something extra." He smiled at her.

Rosita thanked him as she took the thick envelope and stood up to leave.

"Just one other thing."

"*Si?*"

"Remember what I told you!" he warned, rising from his chair and coming to stand in front of her. "I appreciate what you did last night in coming to me, instead of calling 911, but if I ever hear that even one word of this unfortunate incident, shall we say, has been repeated elsewhere, I can assure you that not only would you lose your position here, but sad to say you would also lose your life!"

Rosita gasped indignantly and drew herself up to her full height. "I am a woman of honour, Señor!"

"Sure, sure," he said with a grin. "Just remember? *OK?*"

"Huh!" she puffed as she spun on her heel and marched arrogantly from the room. "I am only going to see my sick cousin! A poor woman living alone and nearly sixty years old!" they heard her say before the door slammed noisily.

"Hey Marco!" Miguel Fernandez laughed. "She's got some *cajones*, that one!"

"Pardon me?"

"Balls, Marco! I said she's got some balls! Shame she's not a bit younger. I could do with a woman like that!" He licked his full lips lasciviously.

"Sure!" the younger man laughed, enjoying the joke.

'But Marco," he said, almost under his breath. "Keep an eye on her.'

Rosita had to think rapidly. It looked as though her plan would come to fruition sooner than she thought. She must be careful, though, to cover her tracks. Nothing must lead back to the Casa Miguel.

Rolling the gun securely inside a small, thick towel, Rosita put it down at the bottom of her small travel bag and packed a few things of her own on top of it, to stop it moving about. She jumped nervously when she heard a rapping on her door. She zipped up the bag in one swift movement and went to open the door. She looked up into Marco's smiling face.

"Yes?" she enquired.

"I thought maybe I could give you a ride into town."

"Into town?"

"Uh huh! To see your cousin?"

"Ah *si!*" She smiled innocently back. "Yes, my cousin. Thank you!"

Rosita sat in the back of the black limo in silence. Although she hadn't slept for two days, her mind was alert and focused. Where should she tell him to drop her off? It all felt unreal. It crossed her mind that her boss had told him to keep an eye on her, but she would have been even more concerned if she had known what was in the trunk, not more than a couple of feet away!

The body had been deftly removed from the cellar and wrapped in a lengthy piece of old tarpaulin and shoved unceremoniously into the back of the car, as soon as Rosita had left the library. The plan was to drive around town for a few hours, waiting until nightfall, and then dump it in a dark alleyway somewhere downtown. The cops wouldn't think twice about the discovery of a dead body, a daily occurrence in the crime-ridden area. It would be nothing new for them to come across in their neighbourhood patrols. (Some poor souls had sometimes lain for days, their foetid corpses half eaten by rats before anyone had bothered to report them missing.)

"You can leave me here, please."

Marco swung the long vehicle smoothly into the kerb.

"You sure?" he frowned over his shoulder.

"Yes, thank you!" Rosita nodded. "My cousin, Natalia, lives just over there."

Before he could say any more, Rosita almost leapt from the car and closed the door.

"*Gracias!*" she waved, smiling brightly.

Walking smartly back up the road for a short distance to the crossing at the next junction, she prayed that he would drive off without seeing where she went. It was nowhere near where she wanted to be, but Rosita was familiar with this part of Los Angeles, which was a fairly nice area compared to where she and Julio had lived and she had cleaned some of the big houses around there once or twice too. Checking her watch, Rosita knew that a bus would be along soon to take her where she really wanted to go. Not wanting to look back, to cause any doubts, Rosita crossed the road when the lights changed, walked along the other side for a few yards and then pretending to brush some hair from her face, glanced quickly between her fingers over the road to where Marco still sat. She stopped abruptly by the second gate and pushed it open. Turning to look back at the car, she smiled broadly and waved again to Marco, who had wound the window down to watch her.

"Bye . . . *gracias!*" she called out to him.

Without answering, Marco grinned to himself. The tinted glass closed and the car pulled slowly away. 'Who did she think she was kiddin'?'

As Rosita walked slowly up the path, she hoped fervently that nobody was in the house. She would have to think very quickly indeed of an excuse for being there. People were so suspicious of strangers these days. They would probably call the police and then what would she do? How would she explain the little package at the bottom of her bag?

Thankfully there was no sign of life anywhere around the house and when she stood on tiptoes and looked over the hedge and down the road, it was with great relief that she saw that the car had gone. Little did she know that Marco had merely driven around the block and was at that very moment watching her from the same side that she was on, but half concealed down a side street. The bus came into view further down the wide road and Rosita had to make a mad dash back across the road to reach the bus stop in time. She was very lucky that the lights were with her. That was all she needed, to be fined for jay walking!

Marco shook his head. 'What the fuck is this dame up to?' he asked himself.

Rosita was so sure that Marco had gone, she didn't even think to look behind as the bus continued on its journey. She was only too relieved get the first half of her plan over.

Marco stayed way back from the bus until he saw Rosita step down and walk along the sidewalk towards a scruffy looking diner. He waited for a while and when she didn't come back out he started up the engine again and drove slowly past. He knew that he couldn't be seen behind the shaded glass so he took his time and looked through the grubby windows to see if he could spot her. There she was, sitting alone by the window with a cup of coffee raised to her lips. She looked as though she was waiting for someone . . . or something! He couldn't make it out, but not wanting to upset his boss by not having a full report when he returned, he decided that he would drive a little way back and park his car up in a slightly more decent area and walk back. If she saw him, he could always say that he had some business in the area.

She was still sitting there an hour later, hunched over the table as he watched from a bar across the street. Maybe she was waiting for this cousin of hers? Maybe not? Wasn't she supposed to be sick or something? He was getting fed up with all of this and his skin was beginning to crawl as he took in some of the low-lives that came and went. Not that they bothered him in the least. He could have taken half a dozen or more of them on, all at once, and still come out alive! It was just the look and the stink of them that made his stomach turn. He had a short memory. It wasn't that long ago that this brutal, callous killer had walked similar streets to this every night. If it hadn't been for the sheer luck, if you can call it luck, of stumbling in on a party where a few friends of Miguel were were out 'slumming', and who'd taken a liking to him, he would have been in the gutter right now with the rest of these loathsome creatures!

When the yellow street-lights flickered into life, Marco realised that it was getting dark outside. "Damn!" he cursed under his breath. He couldn't believe that she had been sitting there for so long.

It was time for him to get back and pick up his car and get his own business done. He would have to leave her. As he swung his long legs around on the stool he caught sight of Rosita standing up by the diner window. 'Jesus!' he swore again. "Great timing!"

But he didn't have any choice. He would have to go back and get the car. He knew that it was moderately safe from being stolen during the day, where he had left it, but after dark it would be gone within minutes.

Standing in the darkened doorway he watched as Rosita finally left the diner and walked up the litter-strewn street towards the small chapel at the crossroads. When he saw her open the church door and go in, he shook his head in disbelief. "What the *hell* is she doing now?" He wondered how long she would stay there. Perhaps if he moved fast enough he could get back with the car before she came out, but he still had his own problem to sort out. That could have to wait until later now, he thought, as he hurriedly crossed the street and begrudgingly went into the stuffy little cab office.

By the time he got back, Rosita was nowhere to be seen. Marco didn't want to leave his car unattended for more than the few seconds it took for him to take a quick look through the chapel doors to establish that the place was empty.

"Shit!" he said loudly, as he unashamedly slammed the door in frustration.

Sometime earlier, Rosita had walked stiffly from the chapel after saying a few prayers and lighting a candle. Her legs were almost numb from sitting for so long in the diner and then spending more time on her knees praying. She walked around for a while in the darkening streets and then went into a dingy bar, walked straight through to the back, into the dirty little ladies room and took a dark raincoat and a black shawl from her bag. She unwrapped the gun and slid it into the deep pocket. Nobody even looked up as she went back outside and stood for a while looking up and down the sidewalk. The usual gaggle of drunken gangs, prostitutes and pimps were slowly emerging into their nightly routines. She reckoned it would take her at least half an hour, if she moved slowly and steadily towards her target. Keeping to the deepest shadows and out of the way of any curious stares she gradually found her way to the corner where more or less the same group of hookers were gathered together again, waiting for business. She didn't want to attract their attention this time so she shuffled along and kept her head well down, her face partially covered by the shawl. On reaching the place that the young girl had pointed out that night, she pulled the shawl back a little to get a better look. The girls up on the corner were all yelling and screaming at each other and took no notice of her.

The alleyway down the side of the derelict looking buildings was filthy and as Rosita picked her way through the stinking mess, she had to hold on to a grime covered damp wall to keep her balance. She shuddered to think that Julio could have come to this awful place. If only she had known then. But she couldn't think of that now. She was almost there. It would be all over soon.

She could barely make out the glimmer of a light bulb from a window up on the first floor of the building at the end of the alley. 'That must be the place.' Her heart skipped a beat as she caught the sound of a dull thudding coming from a radio or a hi-fi. She hid her bag under the steps and pulled an old newspaper over it. Placing her foot on the bottom rung of the beat-up flight of iron steps, Rosita gasped as a young boy ran down the steps and pushed his way roughly past her, almost knocking her backwards. Strangely enough, he turned quickly and grabbed her arm to stop her falling. Thinking that he was going to attack her she opened her mouth to scream, but he was too fast for her. Before she knew what was

211

happening he covered her open mouth with a clammy hand and twisted her face around towards the dull glow coming from the top of the stairs.

"Thought it was you, grandma!" he jeered. "You're the one that's been asking all those silly questions."

Rosita's eyes bulged in terror as she waited for the worst. She put her arm out to steady herself against the railings. She feared she would faint.

Releasing her as quickly as he had grabbed her the boy smirked, "Still looking for something for your boy?"

It crossed Rosita's mind that word sure got around quickly. She just prayed that Mr Jones hadn't got wind of anything. Nodding dumbly the poor woman tried to appear calm and in control, as she pulled her shawl back over her head.

"Up there," was all he said . . . and disappeared like a ghost into the night.

Rosita was almost on her hands and knees and she climbed the steep staircase that led to the half-open door at the top. She was sweating profusely now that the time had come. The weight of the gun knocked against her leg as she rose higher and higher. It seemed like a mountain she climbed. The dull thud of music was getting louder and uglier. She *hated* it! The flickering glow through the slit in the door told her that the room inside was lit with candles and the stench made her stomach turn over. She took the gun slowly from her pocket and tapped it against the door.

"Mr Jones?" she called out bravely.

No answer.

Nudging the door further open with her toe, she peered into the gloom. There was still no response when she called out even louder. Someone inside had turned up the sound to an ear-splitting volume. Rosita cringed as her stomach churned sickeningly and her head began to thump in time to the nauseating beat. She breathed in deeply and almost vomited when her lungs filled with the vile, sickly odour that invaded the air around her.

The door had swung wide open now and she was standing in the gloomy, narrow hallway. Ahead of her was another door, obviously a bedroom from what she could see of the pile of sheets thrown in a heap on the floor. It was difficult to see right inside the room as the light was so dim. But just then the radio, or whatever it was, suddenly stopped.

Now all she could hear were the animal grunts and groans of a man, hard slapping noises and in between soft whimpering sounds from a young voice, begging him to stop. Rosita's blood began to boil. Her whole body shook in rage as she kicked open the bedroom door and yelled, "LEROY JONES?"

"Jesus Christ!" he swore as he collapsed on top of the girl. He swung his sinewy black body over the side of the bed, and Rosita's face contorted with bitter hatred. "Who wants to FUCKING know?" he screamed back at her, wondering what the hell this old woman thought she was doing.

The girl on the bed sat upright and tried to cover herself with her hands, but not before Rosita saw the bright streaks of fresh blood trickling down her thighs. Bile rose in Rosita's throat as she raised her hand and held her arm out before her, the gun pointing straight down between his legs. The girl began to scream hysterically when she saw the hatred in the woman's face.

"Shut up and get out of here, *chica*," Rosita ordered calmly. Fifteen year-old Marlene didn't need to be told twice as she saw an opportunity to escape. She clambered from the filthy mattress, grabbing a dirty old sheet from the floor and flew past Rosita, with hot tears of gratitude streaming down her battered and bruised face.

Rosita's aim never wavered for a moment as she waited patiently, listening to the girl's bare feet pattering down the iron steps and fading into the distance as she fled down the alleyway to safety. She stood like a statue, her arm outstretched and revelled at the expression of fear and disbelief on the face of her son's killer. Looking through narrowed eyes she felt nothing but disgust and loathing as he rose to his feet and stood naked before her, trembling in terror.

"Not so brave now, eh, Mr Jones?" she sneered, slowing moving the gun up and down as if not sure exactly where she was going to shoot him.

"Whatcha want?" he managed to mumble, scratching at the cold sweat that poured over his scrawny limbs. When she didn't answer immediately, but just stood watching him, he asked, "You come to rob me?"

"Rob you?" She cackled. "You got nothing *I* want, Mr Jones."

A strange calmness came over Rosita. "I have brought you something from my son," she told him at last, sighing.

"What you talking about, grandma?" Leroy Jones shook his head, rubbing a gnarled hand over his perspiring face.

"Keep your hands up, please!" Rosita shouted, taking a step towards him.

Somewhere out in the night they both heard the distant sound of a police siren. For an instant the drug-dealing pimp thought he had a chance to overcome this crazy old woman if she was distracted for a second and do to her what she was about to do to him. But unfortunately for him, that was not to be the case. The wailing of the siren made Rosita realise that she had better get it over with. She took a deep breath, raised the gun higher and pointed it straight into his face.

"This is from my son," She told him in a whisper. "From Julio." Curling a cold finger around the trigger she closed her eyes tightly and pulled sharply. Nothing happened!

"*Dios!*" She hadn't thought to check if the gun was loaded.

As Leroy Jones realised what had happened, he made a desperate lunge at the panic-stricken woman, but she was quicker than him. In her sheer horror she squeezed the trigger rapidly, three more times. This time there were no mistakes. The bullets smashed through his skull in quick succession, blasting his brains all over the room and throwing his body back against the wall.

Rosita's legs buckled as she fell to her knees, her eyes never leaving the horrific sight before her. She gazed in terror as the faceless form slowly slithered down the wall, leaving lumps of congealing blood sticking like a grotesque collage to the tattered wallpaper, and crumple to a heap amongst the empty beer cans and trash on the floor.

The sound of loud voices from outside brought her back to her senses. Pulling herself up with all the strength she could muster, Rosita shoved the gun back into her pocket, pulled her shawl tightly over her head and turned from the room and took a few hesitant paces to the front door. Peering down into the shadows at the bottom of the steps she shuddered a great sigh of relief as she saw a group of youths pass by and carry on down the alley as they laughed and joked, sharing a bottle of liquor between them. As far as she could see there was no one else around to have heard the shots. She would have to move quickly, though, before someone did come along.

Trying not to think about what she had done and the macabre

214

scene she had left behind, Rosita picked her way carefully down the squalid alleyway and back towards the street. Just before she reached the relative safety of the sidewalk, a heavy hand fell like a dead weight upon her shoulder, and halted her in her tracks!

Cold fear gripped her rapidly beating heart as she was dragged backwards into the darkness and pushed roughly up against a damp wall. A cigarette lighter flicked on and was held close to her petrified features.

"Hey!" Marco said softly. "How's your cousin?"

Her eyes rolled back in her head as her mind whirled and she began to shake violently from head to toe. Feeling as though she was falling into a great dark pit, Rosita would have fainted away if it hadn't been for the vice-like grip he had on her.

"Come on," he growled, as he pulled her from the wall and with a firm arm around her shoulders marched her off down the street. She didn't dare utter a word as her head cleared a little and the feeling gradually came back into her limbs; she thought quickly of what she was going to tell him. Within a few minutes they turned into another dingy looking backstreet and she wasn't surprised to see the limousine parked in the shadows.

"Get in."

Without waiting to be told again, Rosita obediently clambered into the back seat. She was puzzled, but didn't say a word as they drove slowly around, but when he finally pulled to a halt alongside a derelict row of buildings, got out, opened her door and ordered her sharply to stay where she was, she began to be afraid. Hardly able to see out into the almost total darkness of the deserted street, she gasped in fright when she heard him open the trunk of the car and drag something heavy out on to the sidewalk. It could only be one thing, she thought. He was disposing of the body. Squinting through the window she could just make out his bulky shape as he dragged the corpse across the short distance, kicked open the nearest door and heaved it into the abandoned property. When the deed was done, they drove speedily though the night, in silence, each of them with their own thoughts, until they reached the Casa Miguel.

The day seemed endless as Rosita paced nervously around her room, waiting and waiting for Señor Miguel to call her upstairs. Marco had hardly spoken a word to her. All he had said when they got back was for her to go and get cleaned up and wait in her room. After she had taken a quick shower and changed into a clean dress she lay on top of her bed and closed her eyes. She was desperately tired, but of course, she found it impossible to find sleep. Rising again she went and checked again for the gun in her coat pocket. It wasn't there. How could it be? She had checked it a dozen times or more since she got back. She must have dropped it. Rosita tried to prepare herself for the worst, as she knew that whenever it was found, her fingerprints would be all over it.

The jangling of the telephone made her jump.

"Do you understand what I just said?" Miguel Fernandez asked as he sat sprawling in the huge leather chair in the library. Rosita's head was buzzing. She hadn't known what to expect when she answered the summons downstairs, uut it wasn't this! Señor Fernandez had explained quietly and calmly that he knew exactly what she had done, he didn't know why, of course, and he didn't want to. That was her business.

(While Marco had been cruising around the neighbourhood looking for a suitable place to dump the body he had, by a complete fluke, spotted Rosita creeping into the alleyway and had followed her. Then, when he saw the half-naked girl stumbling down the old iron stairway and disappear into the gloom, he crept through the shadows and waited at the bottom of the steps. A few minutes later, after he'd heard the shots, Rosita herself appeared. He pressed himself further into the darkness and waited.)

"Let me explain once again, Señora," her boss said patiently. "After this conversation, nothing more will be said about what happened *here* and what it was that *you* did either! I think you can say that we're quits now?"

She nodded dumbly in response, but then opened her mouth to speak. He held up a hand to stop her, but she insisted. "I have something I *must* tell you, Señor," she began, hesitantly, looking down at the floor.

Frowning he watched her as she took a deep breath and sat down on the seat opposite him. "You see . . . I think I have lost the . . . the . . . gun." She swallowed hard.

Much to her surprise, he burst out laughing.

"What is so funny, Señor?" she asked a little angrily, raising her head to meet his amused expression. To her it wasn't funny at all.

216

She could be sent to the electric chair for what she had done, or at least spend the rest of her life in jail.

"There's just one more thing, Rosita . . . and I want the truth!"

"Señor?"

"Where exactly did you get the gun?"

"That was another thing I was going to tell you," she answered timidly, pausing as she plucked up the courage to say, "I found it in the garden."

"I *knew* it!" Marco chimed in, from behind her chair.

Miguel Fernandez laughed again and slapped his bulky thigh. "Oh, Rosita!" he roared. "You're priceless!"

Rising awkwardly from his chair he crossed the room and slid his thick fingers down the side of garishly painted modern landscape. Rosita watched in amazement as the whole painting swung forward to reveal a small metal door behind it. Her view of the safe was hidden for a moment as he entered the combination. He turned and beckoned her over. Rosita's eyes flew wide open when she saw the gun. She knew at once it was the same one. "But how . . .?" Her brow creased.

"Let's just say that dear Marco over there," Miguel Fernandez grinned, "was the best pickpocket in the area . . . in his 'wild' days, of course!" Marco grunted from the other side of the room as he poured himself a drink. He didn't like to be reminded of those times.

She understood now. He had somehow managed to extract the gun from her pocket while he had her pressed up against the wall in the alleyway. So Señor Miguel was right. They were both quits, as he called it. She kept her mouth shut and so did he.

After she was dismissed from the library, Rosita hurried back to her room and fell to her knees and thanked God for his intervention. At least that's what she imagined it to be. She had no conscience whatsoever about what she had done and was sure that in time, He would forgive her.

Downstairs in the library, Miguel joined Marco in a toast. After he had drained his glass he wandered over to the open veranda doors and stood gazing out over the splendid view to the ocean, admiring the garden.

After a few moments he said, "Get me Charles Latimer on the line!"

17

Charles Latimer sat astride his favoured steed, looking every inch the gentlemen, and gazed out across the wild and rugged terrain of his Irish country estate. Even in winter it looked beautiful, but this morning his mind was not on the breathless sights that had previously never failed to stir him. He had been roused from his languid comfort at five o'clock in the morning by the ringing of his telephone. Cursing under his breath he had pushed himself away from the warm limbs of his new young maid, Margaret, and taken the long-distance call from Miguel Fernandez.

His initial urge was to to strangle Chrissie O'Rourke with his bare hands, but he soon came to realise that she couldn't possibly have been involved in the disappearance of the money. Reggie had confirmed that she hadn't opened the suitcase again after Charles himself had 're-packed' it for her. Anyway, why would she do a stupid thing like steal from him? He was certain, for all her bravado, that she had been sufficiently in fear of him not to risk it. But whom did that leave? Reggie had been with him for years and had on more than one occasion been entrusted with even more profitable deals that had taken place. This whole thing could ruin him if it got out! He was a well known figure in the underworld and up until now had been feared and respected.

Although it was the last place on earth he wanted to pay another visit to, especially as he had just arrived in Ireland, Charles knew that he would have to go to Los Angeles to sort it out. If he didn't catch the next available flight, he would be under suspicion himself and that was the last thing he wanted.

Miguel had been more than understanding in the past concerning the unfortunate business with that young hothead Scott Wallis when he'd accused Charles of cheating at cards. Everyone knew they had argued at the tables in Miguel's private gaming rooms earlier on in the evening, but in their cocaine-induced haze had laughed it off. He was never quite sure how Miguel had known for certain that it had been Charles who had shot him in the gardens

218

later. He thought he would get away with it. Scott had ruffled more than a few feathers that night after all, so it could have been anyone. But that was a long time ago and now there were more pressing problems to deal with.

"Home!" he ordered abruptly. Tugging on the reins he turned the powerful head and galloped off down the bracken covered tracks towards the Grange. He guided his faithful Valliant over the slippery ground with expertise and as he slowed down to a canter on reaching the courtyard behind the house, he caught sight of Margaret watching him from a high window. She gave him a cheery little wave from behind the curtain and he smiled back up at her, as though he didn't have a care in the world. Grinning to himself, he dismounted quickly, led the sweating beast into the nearest stable and handed the reins to young John, his stable boy. (If it hadn't been for the urgent business he had to see to, he would have gone straight back upstairs and pleasured himself over and over again with the lass!)

When she had come to the house, some time ago, looking for work after seeing an advertisement in the *Wicklow People* for help, she had told him she was seventeen. He didn't believe it for a minute. The over-bleached blonde hair and the amount of make-up she was wearing excited him, so he didn't care how old she was. The younger the better, as far as he was concerned! If there were ever any problems, he would just ship her off to England with a pocketful of money, for a little 'op', like he had done so many times before with others. They never returned to cause him any trouble, these stupid young women.

He had watched her with amusement the day he'd shown her around his vast property, her big brown eyes wide in amazement as she took in the wealth and comfort of the grand property. After their tour of the house and grounds, he explained that he would need her to come to the house only every now and then when he came over from London for holidays and to relax. Maybe half a dozen times a year, for a week or two at a time, he'd said. The wages he offered her were unbelievable and she grabbed at the wonderful opportunity.

As Charles took a long hot shower and then changed into fresh clothes, he thought again of how easy it was to seduce these young colleens, and laughed out loud. It hadn't taken him more than a week to get this one into his bed and she was just one in a very long line. These country girls were so very earthy, he mused as he looked at his reflection in the long mirror and brushed his damp hair into shape. He pulled himself up sharply, as he felt himself getting excited, his mind wandering back to the first night he had taken her. She had screamed in agony, feeling as though she was being ripped apart as he entered her brutally and with only one thought in his depraved mind. To quench the searing lust in his groin that had been consuming him all day. The amount of drink he had plied her with all evening only barely took the edge off the pain of losing her virginity and boy did she let him know it!

She had tried to beat him off with all her strength at first when he threw her unceremoniously on top of the downy covers and she realised what he was about to do; but it was a futile attempt against such a determined and experienced man! Afterwards, when she had lain with her back to him, stifling her sobs as she wept into the pillow and listened in disgust as he snored like a pig, oblivious to her desperate humiliation, she felt hurt, angry and disappointed with herself for being so foolish.

When she had first set eyes on Charles, Margaret had naively thought that he really was attracted to her, but then after that fateful night as she lay awake until the cold light of dawn showed itself through the slit in the heavy brocade curtains, all she wanted to do was to run off home to her mother and confess all. But she knew she couldn't do that. She would have surely been thrown out of the house and then what would she do? Margaret decided the very next morning that she would have to face up to the fact that her life would never be the same after the assault on her innocent body and accept the situation. The idea that she could very easily get herself into even more trouble by letting him have his way with her whenever he fancied it, never crossed her mind.

They were getting into a worrying position over the money at home now, since Chrissie's contributions from England had unexpectedly dried up before they had hardly started.

When Margaret had arrived back at the end of her second week at the Grange and in a taxi, no less, from Wicklow Town, carrying armfuls of groceries and gifts, she had been met with squeals of delight from the younger ones and her mother had even wiped a tear from her eye. She couldn't bear to look her mother in the face, thinking guiltily of what she had done and fearing her wrath if she got an inkling of what her daughter had been up to in the grand house. When she saw the happy faces all around her, she knew she was right. She couldn't let them down now. She would carry on doing what she was doing and eventually she would managed to get a bit of money together and when Chrissie eventually remembered to write, she would ask her if she could get her a decent job in England as well and go and join her.

So in this frame of mind it didn't take her long to get used to the arrangement; even managing to occasionally take some small pleasure from his mostly unwanted attentions. Still not sixteen years old, Margaret started to feel important and like a proper woman. They were very careful not to arouse any suspicions amongst the rest of the staff, who looked down their noses at her, and kept well away from each other until they were out of sight and earshot . . . and she delighted in the intrigue. If only she had known just how she was being used.

Now and then she wondered what could have happened to Chrissie. Why hadn't she been in touch for so long? Her poor mother was becoming more and more saddened as each week went by and there was still no reply to her letters. When Chrissie had first left, there were regular letters and after a while she sent them a few pounds, but after that they didn't hear anything. After all the promises of the grand job Chrissie had convinced them she had, too. Well, there hadn't been much evidence of it yet!

When Margaret sneaked into Charles' room and saw him packing for his trip, she pouted sulkily and asked him when he would be back.

"None of your business, my dear," he snorted, clicking the small case closed.

"Well what am *I* supposed to do then?" she asked, flopping heavily down on to the bed, annoyed by his offhand attitude.

"Do what you like," Charles answered irritably.

"Can I stay here then?" she asked brightly, not wanting to upset him for fear of losing her job and all that lovely extra money he was paying her for 'services rendered'. "Me mam's not expecting me back 'til next week!"

"As long as you don't run off with all the family silver while I'm away!" he said pointedly.

Margaret pushed herself up from her comfortable reclining

position on the bed and stood to face him, her hands placed firmly on her ample hips. "What do ya think I am? A feckin' thief or what?"

A hot flush suddenly passed over Charles' lean body as he stared down at the fuming girl. For a split second she looked the image of Chrissie! He shook his head and turned swiftly away. Chrissie could never look so 'tarty'. It couldn't be, though, could it?

"Of course not! Don't be silly!" He muttered half in answer to her question and to his own. Then another thought suddenly struck him. He had never actually asked her what her surname was. His head had been so full of thoughts of her luscious, if somewhat plump body warming his bed and succumbing to his every need, however diverse, that it had never crossed his mind to ask.

Pulling on his long dark overcoat he caught her reflection in the mirror as she sidled over and sat before the elegant dressing table. He watched her as she picked up the silver-backed brush and began to stroke the dry peroxide waves seductively, knowing that he was looking.

"Don't let anyone catch you in here," he warned.

"Course not!" She smiled innocently back at him and ran her tongue over scarlet lips.

"No, I *mean* it, Margaret!" he said more loudly. "Or I can promise you, you'll be out of here quicker than those cute little toes of yours can touch the ground, when I get back!"

The more closely he watched her, the more she began to remind him of Chrissie. Funny how he'd never noticed it before, he thought. "Go and call Michael and tell him to bring the car around," he told her. "Oh and here, take this!" He reached into his wallet and pulled out a couple of ten-pound notes. "Buy yourself something nice to wear for when I get back."

"OK!" Margaret answered with a huge smile.

As she was about to leave the room, Charles Latimer called out to her, "Wait a moment."

"Yes?"

"Come back in here a minute!"

"What?" She grinned coyly up at the tall figure, thinking that he was going to kiss her goodbye.

"It's just that a odd thought just entered my mind," he lied smoothly.

"What's that then?" she frowned.

"You know what?" he smiled at her.

"What?" she urged.

"I don't even know your name."

"What *are* you talking about?" She laughed now, thinking that he was losing his marbles.

"I mean . . ." Charles tried to sound nonchalant, because in his heart he knew exactly what he was about to hear. "Your surname," he enquired calmly. "What is your surname?"

"Oh you *are* funny," Margaret giggled like the young girl that she was as she turned away from him. "It's O'Rourke! I'm Margaret Patricia O'Rourke!" she announced proudly. She spun on her heel and walked towards the door hoping he was getting a good eyeful of her swaying hips. She paused, looked back over her shoulder for a brief moment and whispered, "And don't you forget it!"

18

Sometime during the night, when Rosita was sure that there was no longer anyone around, she crept silently up the stairs with a small tray of food to Chrissie's room. As she balanced the tray on one hip, unlocked the door and pushed it slowly open, she was greeted by the low sounds of Chrissie's sobs. Her heart went out to the weeping girl; she closed the door behind her and quickly crossed the room. The place was almost in darkness. Chrissie hadn't had the strength to reach out and find the light switch on the lamp when the sun had lost its glow and the evening had faded into night.

"Señorita" The older women spoke softly as she touched the trembling shoulder.

Chrissie blinked as the soft glow as the lamplight shone into her face. Rosita gasped when she saw the mottled bruises and swellings. One eye was completely shut now and Chrissie's nose has swollen to twice its size. Small beads of perspiration glistened on her brow and her soaking hair stuck to her head and neck in thick wet strands. Although she was shocked, Rosita knew it wasn't as bad as it looked, 'as long as the nose isn't broken,' she thought to herself.

"I have brought you something to eat, Chrissie. Come, try to sit up."

Chrissie sighed deeply as she tried her best to raise herself up. "I bet I look a real mess," she tried to joke.

"You'll be fine, *chica*. Rosita will fix you up good."

"Ouch!" Chrissie yelped as she tried to straighten her arm.

"SShh!"

"I'm sorry," Chrissie whispered, her face contorted in pain. "But I think my arm's broken or something."

"Let me see."

Examining the arm closely Rosita nodded her head. "Maybe."

"Oh no! What am I going to *do*?" Chrissie fell back against the pillows, fresh tears running down her face. Rosita picked up the tray from the bedside table and placed it on the covers.

"First, Chrissie, you must eat a little.'

Chrissie looked down at the small plate, with the daintily arranged slices of meat and cheese and groaned. "I can't!"

"Yes you can!" Rosita answered determinedly. "Here!" She picked up a small piece of ham between her fingers and held it to Chrissie's lips. Chrissie was starving and the delicious smell of the smoked ham was too much to resist. She grinned awkwardly, wiping the tears from her flushed face with the corner of the sheet. "I'll try." It was agony to chew even the smallest morsel but at her new friend's insistence she managed to swallow a couple of slices and a few tiny pieces of cheese.

"Good! Now this." Rosita held a glass of ruby-red wine to her mouth. Chrissie gulped down half the glass, only spilling a little down her chin.

Rosita reached into her apron pocket and took out a small packet of aspirin. "Here is something for the fever."

Chrissie washed them down with the rest of the wine.

"Do you think my arm is really broken?" she asked fearfully.

"I don't know, *chica,* but what can I do? If I ask the Señor if we can call a doctor he will know that I have disobeyed him and come up to your room. Remember he told me to keep you locked in here until you tell him the truth about whatever it is you have done to make him so crazy!"

Chrissie turned her head away from the light. She wished she could tell Rosita everything, but at what risk? Maybe she would take a chance. Her head was spinning now from the wine and the quick effect of the tablets on her empty stomach.

"I have to go now." Rosita stood up and gathered the things together. She shoved the bloodied cloth into her pocket and made to leave the room.

"*Please* don't go!" Chrissie whimpered.

"I have to . . . I'm sorry, *chica.*"

Chrissie was rudely awoken the next morning when the door flew open and her suitcase was hurled into the room. The door slammed closed again and she was left sitting up in the bed, blinking rapidly in the bright sunlight that flooded the room and clutching at her aching arm. She leaned back against the pillows, breathing a sigh of relief, only too glad that nobody had come in. She glanced morosely over at the messy pile of her beautiful clothes and wanted to shed more tears. Running her trembling hand carefully down the side of her face, she sucked in her breath in pain. "Bastard!" she muttered to herself through tender lips. With a determined effort she dragged herself from the bed, shuffled over to the heap of clothing, pulled out a few things to wear and made her way slowly into the bathroom. Clutching at the edge of the sink she waited a moment before she raised her eyes to look at the damage.

"Bastard!" Chrissie said when she saw the lumps and purple and blue blotches. Her nose looked so odd, that if the situation hadn't been so serious, she could have even laughed at it! It took her nearly an hour to wash herself as best she could from head to toe (she couldn't even think about getting into the lovely bath again). Throwing her new bra across the room in temper after numerous attempts to hook it up with one hand, she cursed loudly. Then struggling awkwardly into a light floral frock and a soft white cardigan she went back into the bedroom and sat down heavily on the bed, out of breath.

The light tapping made her jump. Her stomach turned over as she waited for the door to open. Nearly fainting with relief she saw Rosita pop her head into the room. "Chrissie?" she called out.

"Come on in, Rosita," Chrissie beckoned to her. "And shut the door before someone sees you!"

"It's OK, *chica*," Rosita nodded. "The Señor, he knows I'm here!"

"Really?"

"*Si*," she assured her again. "Now let me have a look at that arm!"

"What about the face?" Chrissie grinned.

"You may not think so, Chrissie, but it looks a whole lot better than last night!"

"It does?"

"Sure!" she replied, nodding. "Don't worry, the bruises will go away in a while and then your pretty face will be back to normal."

Chrissie sat on the wide stool by the window and looked down at the little gang of gardeners as they went about trimming and tidying the fabulous gardens and thought how simple their life was compared to hers. What an idiot she was, she remonstrated with herself, as Rosita tenderly examined her painful arm. How had she got herself involved with such a crazy scheme? She should have known that something like this would happen, if only she hadn't been so greedy to get her hands on a pile of cash so quickly! She should have thought it over more carefully, but the state she had been in with all the damn drinking and the blasted pills prevented her from thinking clearly! Still, she was deeply involved now. Then she wondered, not for the first time, what the hell had happened to the money she was supposed to hand over to Miguel Fernandez?

Rosita's firm fingers examined the sore arm as gently as possible.

"I know it must hurt, Chrissie, but I don't think anything is broken," she told her with a crooked smile.

"You sure?" Chrissie's face brightened a little.

"Yes, I think it is very badly bruised, that's all."

She took up a large white square of cloth that she had brought with her, made it into a sling and tied it around Chrissie's neck.

"There – that will hold it up for you. Should help to ease the pain until it is better."

"Thank you, Rosita," Chrissie said gratefully. "I don't know what I would have done without you!"

Rosita was saddened when she saw tears spring once again to the poor girl's eyes. "It's nothing!" she said, taking her hand and giving it a little squeeze.

"But Rosita," Chrissie asked. "How did you manage to persuade him to let you come up here?"

"I just told him that you may be seriously injured." She grinned at the worried expression. "And I thought that maybe if he let me have a look and see what damage had been done, there would be no need to call a doctor. I also say, that maybe it wouldn't be a good idea for a stranger to come nosing around and be asking questions."

"You're very smart!" Chrissie laughed. "Did he say anything about wanting to see me again?"

Rosita shrugged her shoulders.

"I think I'm in a lot of trouble." Chrissie sighed.

"I think so too!" The woman nodded.

Chrissie got up and began to pace agitatedly around the room. "What am I going to do?"

"I wish I could help you, *chica*, but I don't know what it is you have done." Rosita looked at her, hoping that Chrissie would trust her enough to tell her.

Chrissie chewed on her thumb as she tried to think. "You wouldn't have any cigarettes by any chance would you, Rosita?' she asked hopefully.

"Oh no, Chrissie, I have never smoked and it is very bad thing for you to be doing!"

"Oh I *know*," Chrissie felt exasperated. "But I could really do with one now!" (and I've done a lot worse than bloody smoking, she thought to herself.)

Rosita felt sorry for her and said, "Listen, you stay quietly and I will run down and see if I can get one from Sergio."

"Sergio?"

"*Si*," Rosita pointed down to the gardens. "Him."

"Oh, that would be grand!" She beamed back.

It wasn't more than a couple of minutes before she was back with half a packet of cigarettes and a small lighter.

"Oh, you're an angel!" Chrissie hugged her with her good arm.

Rosita helped her to light the cigarette and told her to sit down and wait for her to come back. Chrissie sat nervously on the edge of the bed and waited. She prayed that no one else would come in before Rosita came back. While she puffed thankfully on the cigarette she decided that when the woman came back she would tell her all about it. She felt that she owed her a great deal. If it hadn't been for her timely intervention yesterday, Chrissie was certain that she would have taken the worst beating imaginable. As she stubbed out the second cigarette Rosita appeared again with a tray filled with coffee and a huge sandwich. Without a word Chrissie devoured the tasty snack and swallowed the coffee in a couple of mouthfuls, easing her parched throat. They both giggled when she burped loudly.

"Would you mind if I told you?" Chrissie asked quietly when they stopped laughing. "About how I managed to get myself into this mess?"

Rosita put a comforting arm around her shoulder. "I think you *need* to tell me, *chica*!"

"Yes, you're right!" Chrissie nodded. "If I don't get this off my chest I think I will go crazy!"

Rosita sat on the bed beside her in total silence for a very long time as Chrissie told her the whole story. Now and then she hurriedly made the sign of the cross over her breast and shook her head sorrowfully. As Chrissie went over the months and months of what had actually led her to this nightmare situation, she couldn't believe her own ears as she spoke. She didn't dare look at Rosita's face as she came to the end of her sorry tale, for fear she would see disgust. It hadn't been too bad until she had arrived in England, she told her, then everything had deteriorated rapidly and now as she recalled all the sordid details she felt utterly ashamed of herself. As she came to the end she gave a shuddering sigh and whispered, "I bet you think I'm a real bad girl!"

Rosita had turned her face away from Chrissie and when she eventually turned back Chrissie was surprised to see tears trickling down her plump cheeks. Rosita pulled a little lace hankie from her pocket and blew into it noisily. Sniffing back more tears, she looked straight into Chrissie's eyes and murmured softly, "I think that if you knew what I had done, *chica*, you would be thinking that it was *me* that was the very bad girl!"

Chrissie gasped.

"Oh! I'm not going to tell you!" She patted her hand. "Now that would be more than *my* life is worth, for sure!"

Rosita went smartly into the bathroom and came back with a hairbrush. "Let me do something with this," she tried to joke as she grasped a handful of tangled hair.

Chrissie smiled up into the lined and kindly face. "I was thinking earlier of cutting the lot off!"

"Oh no, *chica*, it's beautiful hair!" Rosita was shocked. "You must never do that!"

Working gently but efficiently on the thick tresses, Rosita kept silent as she thought over all the things the young girl had told her, but before she had time to smooth out the last of the dry knots, they both gasped in shock and Chrissie leapt from the bed, crying in pain as the brush caught in her hair.

The roaring voice outside the door made Chrissie turn ashen.

"Get yourself downstairs!" Marco yelled. "NOW!"

"Jesus Mary!" Chrissie burst out.

"Don't worry," Rosita tried to speak calmly. "I will come with you."

They heard the heavy footsteps fade into the distance.

"Do you think he will hit me again?" Chrissie's voice was almost inaudible as she let herself be helped down the wide stone staircase towards the library.

"Not while I'm with you," Rosita sniffed.

"*You* can go!" Miguel ordered gruffly, pointing to Rosita.

"But, Señor?" Rosita smiled thinly. "The señorita is not so well. I think I should stay and take care of her."

"Just get out, will you!" he shouted back. "Don't forget I have a long memory!"

"*Si*," Rosita replied through gritted teeth. "Me too, Señor!"

Turning to the quaking girl Rosita gave her an encouraging smile. "I will go and tidy your room, little one, and then prepare something for your dinner."

Chrissie was too terrified to open her mouth and just managed to give a stiff little nod.

"You may sit," Miguel spoke quietly after the door closed. Chrissie walked jerkily over to the nearest sofa. Chewing nervously on her thumb she watched him prowling around the huge room. He seemed to be trying to make his mind up about what he was going to do. Chrissie was glad at least that Matt wasn't there.

"You feeling better?" The deep low voice startled her.

"Not really," she answered, raising her eyes to meet his as he came and stood before her. He ignored the brazenness of her response and carried on. "I have spoken to Charles!"

Chrissie gasped loudly. "And I think that maybe we have made a mistake," he drawled. "He assures me that you wouldn't do anything so stupid as to steal from him."

"No, no, I wouldn't," Chrissie muttered, wondering where all this was leading. Then she knew.

"He will be here this evening!" he announced.

"Oh?"

"Don't look so surprised," he said sharply. "We would like to know what is going on!"

Chrissie found her voice again. "Well so would *I*! You don't think that I am enjoying this, do you?" She touched her sore face. She flinched as he reached out and ran a pudgy finger over her bruised cheek, wrinkling her nose at the distasteful smell of stale tobacco.

"Oh, it could get a whole lot worse than this, if we find out that you have been up to something silly!" he threatened almost under his breath. There was a light knock on the door and it opened before he had time to answer. Rosita came in carrying a pot of

230

coffee and two cups and saucers on a deep silver tray. Without a word she placed it on the long table, ignored her boss's glare, winked at Chrissie and left the room. Chrissie tried not to grin at the audacity of the woman!

"Have you any idea at all what could have happened?" Señor Fernandez asked amiably, as he poured the drinks. Chrissie could see that he was unused to waiting on himself as he splashed coffee into both saucers.

"Of course not!" She shook her head, taking the cup in her unbound hand. "All I did was follow what Charles told me to do. And this is what I get!"

After that he didn't say any more, just sat drinking his coffee in silence and staring off into space. Chrissie began to feel a little unnerved and wondered what he was up to. She dreaded seeing Charles again, but told herself that she didn't have anything to worry about. She hadn't done anything wrong after all. The suitcase must have been interfered with back in London. She didn't have the key until Reggie was saying goodbye to her. 'God!' she suddenly thought. "Surely he wouldn't have taken the money, would he?"

Chrissie's body was aching and although she had slept well she could feel the weariness creeping over her again. Placing the cup back on the tray she murmured, "Can I go now?"

"What?"

"Can I go now, please? I need to use the toilet."

"Mmm." He nodded and waved an arm in dismissal. "Go."

Chrissie shook her head as she trod heavily back up the stairs and puzzled over what that was all about. She bumped into Rosita in the wide corridor. She had finished cleaning the room and hanging up the crumpled clothes. "You OK?" she asked.

"Yes, I'm fine thanks," Chrissie smiled. "But I'm still wondering what he wanted me for."

"I think he wanted to make sure that what I said was true, about this." Rosita pointed to the swollen eye and the bandaged arm. "I said this morning that it wasn't so bad as I suspected."

"What do you mean?"

"I think that maybe he was worried that you make a fuss over things!"

"Oh I see." But she didn't really.

231

"Go and have a little siesta," Rosita nodded towards the open door of her room. "I think that maybe tonight you will need some strength."

"What do you mean?" Chrissie was alarmed.

Rosita ushered her into the room and whispered confidentially. "I heard them talking this morning about someone who is coming from London to talk to you."

"Oh *him*!" Chrissie sneered, wishing that she had never set eyes on the bastard. "Yes, I know about that!"

"Yes and maybe he won't be too happy when he sees what happened to you!"

"I doubt if he will worry about that," Chrissie said emphatically. "Remember what I told you about him."

"I know, *chica*, but these men are very strange. They don't think like we do." Rosita nodded sagely. "Now go and rest."

The evening was warm and balmy and a light breeze from the ocean ruffled the hem of Chrissie's full skirt as she crossed the terrace to join Charles and Miguel. Rosita had helped her dress for dinner. She had chosen a rather demure white cotton dress with broad shoulder straps and a long full skirt. She had picked out one of her own scarves, a thin black one, to support her arm. Her gleaming hair had been brushed thoroughly now and was tied neatly back in a black velvet bow to match the slender belt around her slim waist. Inside she was trembling, but as the two men watched her stroll over to the table, they couldn't help but admire her confidence and beauty. Charles rose to greet her. "Good evening my de—" He hesitated and grinned. "Chrissie!"

"Good evening," she nodded.

He pulled out a chair for her. "Thanks," she said, without looking at him.

Miguel Fernandez sat back, casually admiring the young woman across from him. When he had first seen her he was too enraged to think of anything else other than the missing money, but now he had more time to look at her properly; despite the slightly swollen eye, he had to admit that Charles sure was a lucky guy! Although nothing had been mentioned, he took it for granted that they were lovers, and had been a little worried at first over Matt lashing out quite so violently. 'Sometimes that boy doesn't know his own strength,' he'd mused.

Chrissie held her hand over the top of her glass as Charles offered her wine.

"No thank you," she said pointedly, glaring at him. "I don't drink."

Hiding his amused expression, Charles said, "Very good, Chrissie!"

Her nervousness began to subside as dinner was served. She smiled up at Natalia, who frowned back at her when she saw the marks on her face and then moved away quickly. Chrissie had done her best to cover the bruises with make-up but found it too difficult to disguise them completely with one hand. After bathing it over and over again in cold water the eye didn't look so bad and even the bulge on her nose was going down.

She was touched to see that someone, probably Rosita, had cut up her delicious piece of roast lamb into tiny pieces, and picking up her fork she delicately ate it bit by tasty bit until her plate was empty. The men ate their meal in silence and all the while Chrissie was discreetly watching them and wondering when they were going to broach the subject of the missing cash. She didn't have to wait too long. When the table was cleared and she'd drained her second glass of fruit juice, Charles held out his cigarette case. "Or have you given that up too?" he smirked.

"Very funny, Charles!" she answered cheekily, almost snatching one from the case.

Miguel grinned. She sure was a lovely girl and such a delightful accent. He liked women with a bit of spunk, too. Shame she was involved with Charles.

Chrissie relaxed back into the chair and breathed in the musky nightscents of the garden as they wafted over them in intoxicating waves. She had the strange floating feeling that she was dreaming all of this and very soon she would wake up and find herself next to the slumbering figure of her little sister Margaret in Ballycross Farm. She forced down the lump in her throat and took a deep drag on the cigarette.

"So, Chrissie . . ." Charles began.

'Here it comes,' she thought, her heart giving a little jump.

She turned and looked at him. "Yes?"

"I'll be perfectly honest with you, Chrissie . . ."

"Really?" she interupted tartly, remembering vividly how he hadn't been so honest with her in the not too distant past.

"Listen, will you?" he retorted sharply. "I haven't got time for any of your amateur dramatics!"

"Huh!"

"Don't push me, Chrissie!" he warned, as he accepted a large glass of brandy from Miguel. "I'm very tired and I'm *very* upset!"

"I gathered that!"

He ignored the remark. "I have gone over everything thoroughly with Reggie and he's told me that he can vouch that you didn't open the case before you checked it in at Heathrow. So . . . where does that leave us?"

Chrissie shook her head, just as puzzled as he was. "I don't feckin' know!"

"Watch your mouth!" He warned. "I've told you about that before!"

Miguel joined in. "It doesn't suit you, Chrissie."

"Sorry," she muttered, not in the least bit sorry.

"Do you think it is possible that Maria could have tampered with the case? Maybe while you were sleeping? I know she took the night off work before you left and as far as I can make out, you didn't go out anywhere." (He already knew the answer to that question, but wanted to see if there was a chance that Chrissie really had been so foolish as to get involved.) Chrissie pushed her chair away from the table and began to walk slowly around the terrace as she thought carefully. She turned to Charles, "I don't know! Can I have another cigarette?"

Miguel Fernandez jumped up with surprising agility for such a heavy man and offered one from his gold case, before Charles had a chance to move.

Remembering the events of the last evening she had spent with Maria in the little flat, she couldn't recall anything untoward happening. They had simply shared a pizza, happily supplied by Gino as a good luck token for her new job. He hadn't even stayed to help them eat it. Had to get back to work before he was missed, he'd said. (Or the pizza was!)

"Have you spoken to Maria?" Chrissie asked.

"Not yet," Charles lied, looking away.

Chrissie went cold, knowing instantly that he was lying. She had a terrible vision of Maria's battered body lying in a heap in a dark corner somewhere.

"Why don't you let me telephone her?" she ventured innocently. "Maybe I could get something out of her."

Charles narrowed his eyes suspiciously. "I don't think that's such a good idea."

"Why not?" Chrissie asked abruptly, but she thought that she already knew the answer. He acted as though she hadn't spoken. "You should think seriously, Chrissie." He tried again. "Are you certain that you can't recall anything?"

"Like what?" Chrissie shook her head exasperated, not knowing what he wanted her to say.

"Did you have any visitors that night?" He raised his voice.

"No, of course not! We ate the pizza, had a *little* wine and then I went to bed. You know I had to get up at the crack of dawn and I didn't want to oversleep!" she told him firmly. Then a sudden dread fell over her and she spun haughtily away to cover her confusion and sauntered over to the furthest corner of the terrace, pretending to admire the beautiful purple bougainvillea cascading over the balcony, not wanting them to notice the deep flush that was spreading over her face and neck. 'How the bloody hell did he know that they had stayed in?'

'Holy Mother,' she thought, 'He's right! I did hear something!' She remembered how she had lain awake for a long time after going to bed, too excited to sleep. As she was drifting off she'd thought she'd caught the sound of murmuring voices. It hadn't crossed her mind since then as she had fallen asleep soon after and had been far too busy the next morning to think of anything but her wonderful adventure to America! But, as she recalled now, she did hear something . . . and it had been a male voice. As she fondled the silky flower petals she breathed in the wonderful heady perfume slowly and deeply to control her rising fear. 'Surely Maria wouldn't have done anything so crazy. Hadn't she warned her enough times not to upset Charles, or any of his so-called friends? But hadn't she also let her know how skint she was?'

Chrissie wandered back over to the two men and looked down at them innocently. "I'm sorry – I can't help you."

"Go up and pack Chrissie," Charles ordered harshly. "You're coming back with me tomorrow!"

"What?"

"You heard me! Go!"

"But what about the shopping trip that you promised!"

Charles burst out laughing. Even Miguel gave a titter of amusement.

"Well I think we can safely say that that is off!"

"But it's Christmas next week!" Chrissie wailed and stamped her foot like a spoilt brat.

"Enough!" Charles shouted back. "Now GO!"

Chrissie turned away from them in disgust and they watched her undulating hips stalk off. By the time she reached her room, she had calmed down and started to get worried. Very worried indeed. If Maria did have anything to do with all this and if Charles really *hadn't* been in touch with her, perhaps she could somehow get word to her and at least warn her before he got his hands on her. She racked her brains trying to remember the phone number of the Purple Parrot. Maybe she could get in touch with her that way? Chrissie thought that it was probably already too late though. Knowing something of the way he worked, it was unlikely that Charles hadn't left a stone unturned, one way or another, before he left London.

She was right! At that very moment Maria's crushed body was lying in the intensive care unit of St Thomas' Hospital, bound from head to toe in bandages and hooked up to a life-saving drip. She had been found by a couple of terrified tramps under the bushes in Hyde Park earlier that morning, when they scavenged with grime-encrusted fingers around the bins searching for breakfast.

The poor girl was completely naked and so had no means of identity on her. The police assumed that she was just another prostitute who had been beaten up by an unsatisfied customer. They weren't overly concerned. They had seen it all before. It would be soon enough, when she recovered, if she recovered, to find out who she was.

So when Billy Costello pulled up outside the flat in Bayswater tooting loudly on the horn of his brand new red Mercedes sports car, he was completely unaware of the dire consequences that his greedy and selfish actions had had on his sister.

They had arranged to get out of London that day, take a leisurely drive down towards Dover and eventually catch the ferry across to France. From there they would take a long and pleasurable drive down to Spain and go in search of a nice out-of-the-way property, where they could lie low for a few years.

Jumping impatiently from the car he ran up the steps to the front door and rang the bell over and over. He didn't have time to hang around. He'd had enough of being incarcerated behind the cold, stone walls of Wandsworth Prison. Glancing guiltily over his shoulder at the passing traffic and dreading the thought of arrest, he thumped on the door with his fist. 'Get up, you lazy bitch!' he muttered.

Just then the door was opened by one of Maria's neighbours.

"What the hell's all the noise about?" a bleary-eyed young African student asked.

"Sorry, mate," Billy grinned. "Just come to collect me sister."

The student looked dumbly back at the cheery red face.

"Maria, top floor?"

"Sorry, don't know her. You wanna go up?"

"Yeah, cheers, mate!"

Billy ran up the stairs two at a time and knocked on Maria's door. He couldn't understand what was going on. He stood for a minute scratching his head. Where the hell was she? She knew bloody well that they had to get away, pronto!

He stomped off back down the stairs mumbling to himself, 'After all that bloody persuading, don't tell me she's got cold feet.'

He drove around the block a few times and then decided to give her a few minutes. Maybe she's gone out to get herself a few things for the trip. Probably needed a bit of 'gear', knowing her habit only too well. (He had stocked up himself with a few packets to see them on their way, but hadn't trusted her enough to leave her any of the little goldmine that he had discovered!) He found a parking space near a coffee bar along the road, went in and made himself comfortable for a while.

Sipping at the frothy drink he grinned as he thought about how easy it had been to pick the lock on the suitcase. He couldn't resist it and ignored Maria's constant pleas to leave it alone. All he wanted to do was to see if her new flatmate had some bits he could sell on for a bit of cash. That's why he had made a rare call on his sister, to cadge a few quid. He'd been finding it hard to go straight since his release and nobody was keen to give him a decent job, well any kind of job, with his record.

With his nimble lingers, Billy had soon discovered the secret compartment at the bottom of the case and nearly fell over, flabbergasted at the sight of the neatly arranged bundles of notes!

"Flippin' 'eck!" He finally managed to say as he held up a wad in each hand and waved them in Maria's astonished face.

"So that's what she's up to," she whispered.

Billy paced around the room, gabbling excitedly about what they could do with so much cash.

"We'll be made up, girl, with this little lot!" he said almost proudly. "We'll never have to work again!"

"Put it back, *please* Billy!" She begged him over and over again, but her frantic pleading fell on deaf ears.

Finally, after he had calmed down a little, he said sulkily, "Well, you don't have to come if you don't want to."

"I don't know, Billy. I don't like it."

"Are you bloody mad? We'll never get another chance like this!"

"Will you be *quiet*, for God's sake!" Maria said in a hushed voice. "I'm surprised you haven't woken her already!"

When they had re-packed and locked the case they sat together for hours on the lumpy sofa drinking cups of sweet black coffee as Billy did his utmost to talk his sister into running away with him and making a new life. He didn't like the idea of her working at the Purple Parrot and tried not to think about what line of work it involved. Although they never actually discussed how she earned her money, he wasn't daft; he knew what went on in those places, but didn't feel he had the right to judge her, considering all the things he had got up to over the years.

By the time he left another cold day was dawning and Maria had reluctantly agreed to go along with his crazy plans. Maybe they would get away with it, she thought, as she waved a quick goodbye on the freezing doorstep. She watched him anxiously as he marched off down the street with the two plastic carrier bags and prayed that they would get away before anyone found out about the missing cash. She had explained carefully that they would probably only have a couple of days, at the outside, before it came to light, so they would have to move quickly.

Dragging herself back up to the top floor, Maria was shocked back to reality when she heard Chrissie already moving around her room. Closing her own bedroom door as quietly as possible she jumped into bed and pulled the covers up over her head.

A short while later she heard Reggie arrive and when Chrissie sneaked in to say goodbye she feigned sleep; feeling wretchedly guilty as she ignored the whispered farewell.

When she heard the car start up she jumped back out of bed and ran to the window. Tears sprang to her tired eyes as she saw the shiny vehicle turn the corner and disappear from view. She hoped that nothing too awful would happen to her new friend; then firmly pushing all guilt from her mind, told herself jealously that Chrissie shouldn't have been so damn crafty about what was going on. After all she'd done for her as well! Greedy bitch!

Sleep eluded her as she tossed and turned. Deciding that she had better get back to the club as early as possible that morning, before anyone arrived to pick up a few personal things, Maria hauled herself from the tangled sheets and went and took a hot bath. When she was finished and was more or less ready to leave, she counted the money in her purse. Not working the night before, she wasn't as flush as she usually was in the mornings. She counted out a few notes and cursed under her breath. She'd have to take the bus instead of a taxi to the Purple Parrot; then at least she'd have enough money left to get over to Brixton and pick up some 'stuff'.

She couldn't go to her usual local supplier as she already owed him so much money that she knew it would be sooner rather than later that he carried out his threats of violence if she didn't pay up. She was already getting cramps in her stomach and her body ached all over. She'd never last the day without a bit of 'something' to keep her going. Not for the first time Maria wished with all her heart that she had never started on the bloody drugs. 'Stupid, stupid cow!' she mumbled to herself as she half ran down the street, shivering with the cold and the need for more heroin.

By sheer luck she made it in and out of the club without seeing anyone, apart from the cleaners, over to South London and back to her flat in only a couple of hours. Feeling relaxed and confident after a satisfying 'hit', Maria allowed herself to drift off into a deep sleep, dreaming of hot sun and sandy beaches.

When she woke up she was surprised to see that it was already dark. Checking the time on the pink plastic clock by the bed she suddenly remembered that she had better call in to say that she wasn't well enough to work that night. That would give her plenty of time to get packed and have another good night's sleep before Billy came to pick her up in the morning.

When she was happy that everything was more or less ready for the getaway the next day, Maria suddenly recalled that she had a couple of pounds tucked away towards the rent that she had completely forgotten about, so she went down to the off licence on the corner and bought herself a bottle of cheap wine. She cursed Billy silently for not leaving her a least a few quid out of the money. Still, soon she would have plenty of cash to spend on whatever she fancied.

After rolling a thick joint and pouring herself a generous glass of wine, Maria put her feet up on the coffee table and lay back, thoroughly enjoying the languorous experience induced by the alcohol and marihuana. Time drifted away as she dozed on and off and just as she was about to drag herself from the couch, thinking that it was about time she went to bed, there was a loud knock on the door. Puzzled she pulled herself to her feet and staggered over to see who it was at that time of the night. And how had they got in? She hadn't heard the front door bell. Probably Gino, when he'd seen her light on.

But it wasn't Gino.

The soft whimpering from the naked girl on the floor did nothing to stir the cold hearts of the two thugs who stood looking down at her. Blood oozed from her mouth and ears and great wheals of torn flesh stood out starkly on her pale skin. They wondered at her stubbornness to reveal anything, considering the beating she had just taken. They had seen grown men cave in on less.

The call they had received from Charles Latimer earlier on had sent them rushing over to Bayswater to sort out the little problem, but it didn't look like they were getting anywhere. They had dragged her from the flat, kicking and shouting, bundled her into the back of their car with a coat over her head and driven in the early hours of the morning through the empty streets to an old riverside warehouse in Bermondsey docks. She had screamed in terror as they ripped her clothes from her thin body and proceeded to punch and slap her until she collapsed on to the slimy stone floor like a rag doll. Over and over again, they shouted abuse and demanded she tell them what had happened to the money! But she couldn't utter a word. Her eyes stretched wide in horror as they took it in turns to shake her violently and scream into her petrified face. When she hadn't responded to the first thrashing, they had automatically taken knuckle-dusters from the pockets of their smart black suits and beaten her mercilessly.

The taller one who looked like a demented ape, sneered down at her panting after his vicious efforts. "You better come up with somefin', sweetheart," he grunted, adding, "or the boss ain't gonna be too pleased!"

"What we gonna do, Alf?" He tugged on his mate's sleeve, pulling him away from the now unconscious figure. "Boss said not to finish her off!"

"Looks like she's already 'ad it, Len," Alf replied, squinting over his shoulder at the lifeless form.

"What we gonno do next then?"

"Don't look like she knows nuffin' to me, anyhow."

"Better just dump her then."

19

Chrissie tipped her bag out on the bed and rummaged through the scattered contents. Breathing a sigh of relief she picked up the crumpled card. Pulling off the sling in frustration, she winced as her bruised arm was freed. Just then Rosita came into the room without knocking and Chrissie jumped when she saw her standing there.

"What are you doing?" Rosita asked when she saw the mess on the covers. Chrissie proceeded to tell her all about what had happened at dinner and said she was going to try and get in touch with her friend to warn her.

"But that might be a little difficult, *chica*!"

"Why?" Chrissie frowned.

"The time is different in England now."

"What do you mean?"

"I don't know how it works, Chrissie, but I think you will find that it is some hours different to us!"

"Of course. I remember," Chrissie smiled thinly. "It must be morning there. But that's OK. There'll still be someone at the club. The cleaners always come in early."

"Ah *chica*!" Rosita put her arm around Chrissie's shoulder. "This is all so sad!"

"You've been very good to me, Rosita. I think we could have become very good friends."

"I thought we already were," Rosita grinned wryly.

"Yes, yes we are!" Chrissie hugged her tightly. "But now I must pack."

When everything was done Rosita asked Chrissie if she would like to come down to the kitchens with her, as she still had to clean up after dinner and then they could try to call England.

"Good idea!" Chrissie said. "At least it would set my mind at rest."

Rosita very rarely used the telephone, only to order in goods for the larders from time to time, so she left it to Chrissie. She told her that she thought you had to call the operator and get her to get the number, but she wasn't sure. Chrissie made herself comfortable on the high stool and dialled the operator. The nasally-voiced girl told her she would call right back when she had her number.

The two women sat silently waiting for the call. Chrissie snatched at the receiver as soon as it rang.

"Hello?" she said, a little hesitantly.

"Who's that?" Beth's irritable voice said.

"Beth?"

"Yes! Who is it?"

"It's me, Chrissie!"

"Huh," she sneered. "What do *you* want at this time of the day?"

Chrissie ignored the snide remark, but wondered why Beth was at the club so early herself. "I need to get an urgent message to Maria!" she told her calmly.

"Well so do *I*!" Beth snapped back.

"What are you talking about?" Chrissie's stomach tightened.

"That little bitch nicked two of my best dresses yesterday! *That's why!*" she shouted back down the phone.

"What? She wouldn't do a thing like that!"

"I know it was her! So you can stop acting so bloody innocent! Reggie told me that there were all sorts of questions being asked here yesterday and he said that the cleaners had seen her sneaking in here at all hours and leaving with a bag stuffed with things!"

"That doesn't prove anything." Chrissie was enraged by her attitude.

"Course it does, you stupid bloody cow! I even went over to her soddin' flat, nearly bashed the door down, but that bloody Italian idiot told me she wasn't there. He heard her going out in the middle of the night, shouting and screaming with a couple of punters and hadn't seen her since!"

Chrissie slammed the phone down. Her hand was damp with perspiration and her body trembled with fear. "I think he's already got to her." She turned her ashen face to Rosita.

"*Dios!*" Rosita blessed herself. "What can you do?"

Chrissie sighed deeply. "There's nothing I *can* do. Maybe it's a good thing that I am going back tomorrow. At least then I can try and find out what's happened to her!"

Rosita busied herself around the kitchen and when all was clean and tidy she took a carafe from a shelf on the huge dresser. "Why don't we go outside and finish this off?"

Chrissie grinned. "Great!"

The night air was cooling a little now and a gentle breeze brushed against Chrissie's soft skin as she sat with Rosita in the little herb garden sipping the wine.

"This is lovely. So peaceful."

"*Si.*"

"I just wish I was staying a bit longer," Chrissie sighed.

"Maybe when everything is over with you will come back again?" Rosita looked hopefully at the young woman opposite her.

"Oh, I'm sorry, but I don't think so." Chrissie shook her head emphatically. "The first thing I will be doing after I make sure that Maria's OK will be to buy a ticket back home!"

"That is a very good idea," Rosita leaned across the small wrought-iron table and patted Chrissie's hand. "Your family will be so happy to see you!"

Chrissie nodded. "Mmm." She stood up from the table saying, "I think I'll take a walk around the garden."

"I'll come with you."

The silvery moon cast enchanting lacy patterns over the vast expanse of lawns, trees and shrubs, making the whole scene slightly unreal.

"It looks so pretty in this light," Chrissie said quietly as they strolled together along the narrow gravel paths and around the edges of the swimming pool.

"Beautiful!" Rosita agreed, averting her eyes from the 'special' rose bush that she had planted over by the weeping willow. (Every day she said a prayer for the young man who died there.)

Turning back towards the house Chrissie thought how wonderful it would be to live in such magnificent surroundings.

"I know what you are thinking," Rosita said softly. "But believe me, with all the strange things that go on here, you wouldn't want to stay so long!"

"That sounds very mysterious," Chrissie whispered.

"Ah, don't listen to me," Rosita said abruptly. "I think I'm getting too old for all this!" She spread her arms widely then pointed a finger to her temple: "Going a little 'loco' too!"

"Don't be silly," Chrissie laughed. "Of course you're not and you're not 'old' either. You're still a very attractive woman."

As they came closer to the house, Chrissie raised her head indicating the terrace. The two men were still there, talking and laughing.

"Don't they ever sleep?" Chrissie snorted.

"Only when the sun rises!" Rosita replied scornfully.

"I wonder what they are finding so hilarious?" Chrissie mumbled as thunderous laughter filled the still air. "I'm going to listen!" Chrissie grinned at Rosita's shocked expression.

"No, señorita. Leave them!"

"Don't be daft, it'll be funny!"

"Maybe it won't!"

"Come *on!*" she urged, creeping forward under the cover of dense foliage. "I could do with a laugh!"

"You will be in more trouble if they catch you," Rosita warned quietly, but of course Chrissie wasn't listening.

Lifting her long skirt so it wouldn't rustle along the grass, she kept to the deeper shadows under the terrace. She looked back once or twice and saw that Rosita was following some distance behind her. Pressing her back against the cool stone wall directly under the terrace where the men sat, Chrissie put her fingers to her lips as Rosita's shoe made a crunching noise on some dry twigs and came beside her.

She needn't have worried. They didn't hear a thing. After almost a bottle of brandy between them, they were in a jovial mood and seemed to be sharing the greatest of jokes, their laughter ringing out into the night.

Chrissie stood motionless as she heard chairs scraping on the tiled surface and footsteps coming across to the balcony. Holding her hand over her mouth to stop herself giggling, she waited. Feeling Rosita's tight grip on her arm she looked at her. Rosita mouthed to her that she should come back now, but Chrissie shook her head. If they moved now, they would surely be seen. They would have to wait until Charles and Miguel moved further away. She thought for a fleeting moment that it *was* rather a silly thing to have done, but feeling reckless after everything that had happened, she was in one of her rebellious moods.

"So you're telling me that you haven't got *this* one into your bed yet Charles?" Miguel Fernandez guffawed. "And you expect me to believe you?"

Chrissie's eyes widened. She knew instinctively that he was talking about *her*. What was Charles going to say?

Charles' voice was a drunken slur as he replied, "I just *told* you, my friend, the sister's enough for me!"

Chrissie thought she was hearing things! What in the name of God was he lying about now? Rosita's grip tightened on her arm as she tried to pull her away. Chrissie shrugged her off, glaring back at the frightened woman.

"Yeah, sure, sure!" Miguel laughed again, adding. "Does Chrissie know about the sister? What was her name?"

"Course not! Don't be ridiculous man!"

The blood in Chrissie's veins seemed to have turned to ice. She stood as though turned to stone, hardly breathing, but her mind raced. There must be some mistake? Who were they talking about? This was all too crazy. She hadn't heard right! They couldn't be talking about *her*? But if they were, who was the *sister*? Minutes later her suspicions were confirmed.

"I tell you, my friend, that young lass Margaret has the greatest arse that I've seen for a long time!" Charles laughed again. "And, boy, does she know how to use it!"

The footsteps and laughter gradually faded as the two men made their way back into the house out of the damp night air, still coarsly discussing Margaret's lush young body with its many attributes and her expertise in the bedroom.

Rosita tugged urgently on Chrissie's arm. "Come," she whispered shivering. "We must go *now*!" She had heard what had been said and prayed it didn't mean what she thought it meant. All she knew was that Chrissie's mischievous air had vanished and been replaced by a frozen, stunned expression. The bitter loathing startled her as Chrissie turned to face her.

"Did . . . you . . . hear . . . that?" She spoke jerkily.

"No, *chica*!"

"Don't lie Rosita!" Chrissie's voice grew louder. "You did!"

Rosita didn't wait to hear any more. Grabbing Chrissie's stiff hand in hers, she clenched it firmly and pulled her away from the wall and led her back through the gardens and into the warmth of the kitchen. Chrissie stumbled zombie-like behind the panting woman and allowed herself to be pushed gently down on to the nearest seat.

"Here!"

Rosita poured her a large glass of water and held it to her dry lips. "Drink!"

Chrissie drank the whole glass without realising just what she was doing. Rosita sat across the table from her, worried by the vacant look in her eyes.

"What is it, *chica?*" she eventually asked when she could bear it no longer.

Chrissie blinked a few times and shook her head as the numb feeling faded slightly.

"I'm not sure," she managed to utter. "I don't think I could have heard properly."

Rosita knew exactly what *she* had heard and if she wasn't mistaken it seemed to her that this Charles person had defiled Chrissie's sister! She didn't know when or where, but by the look that came over Chrissie's face she was going to find out.

"I just don't know what to think, Rosita," Chrissie said through gritted teeth. "I don't understand. How in the name of Christ could he have got near her?"

She got up and began to pace agitatedly around the room, the pain in her arm and her face now forgotten. As she walked round and round she tried to get her thoughts in some kind of order. 'It *had* to be her Margaret he was boasting about!' she reasoned, as she chewed on her nails, drawing blood. Hadn't she always said she was going to get herself a job in one of the big posh houses down there in Wicklow. So many of the English gentry had bought up the grand estates over the years, it would have been easy for her to get some kind of employment . . . when she finally got up off her lazy arse, that is! She stopped abruptly in the middle of the room. Her skirt swished against her nylons as she turned to face Rosita, who had been sitting nervously watching her.

"I'm going to kill him," she announced, almost under her breath. "I'm going to kill the bastard!"

Rosita swooned. She felt her head go light as the vision of Leroy Jones's body sliding down the wall in a mess of blood and tissue once again swam crystal clear before her. "No!" she cried, leaping from the chair and throwing herself against the rigid figure. "You must not *do* this!" she wailed.

"I have to," Chrissie replied calmly. "It's my fault, you see." She smiled inanely. "If I hadn't been so damned eager to leave my family I would have been there to look after her. So you see, I *have* to kill him!" She pulled herself away from the distraught woman and said gently, "Don't worry, I'm not going to do anything tonight. I will go to bed like a good girl and then tomorrow . . . well, we'll see what happens tomorrow." She smiled sweetly down at Rosita and kissed her tenderly on her wet cheeks. "Goodnight."

Rosita thought that the girl had gone a little crazy. The strange light in her eyes frightened her. She guessed that was what she must have looked like herself all those years ago, and as she made her own weary way upstairs she had to admit to herself that if she were in the same position as Chrissie she would probably do the very same thing! For the first time in many years, Rosita recalled how Miguel had shown her the gun in the safe that day. She wondered vaguely if it was still there.

It was!

After everything that Chrissie had told her about Charles and the events that had led up to her trip to the States, Rosita wrestled with her conscience for hours as she thought them over. She tossed and turned in her bed wondering if Chrissie dared to do the thing that she was considering. She had taken such a liking to the young Irish girl and felt that if there was some way she could help her to get out of the dreadful mess then she would. She had a terrible fear that very soon something horrific would happen to Chrissie. It sounded as though her friend in London had already been dealt with and Chrissie would end up the same way, if she wasn't very careful indeed. She got up and dressed herself swiftly. In a few short hours it would be morning, so she must soon come to a decision. The house was silent now as she made her way down to her own domain and brewed herself a pot of strong coffee. She sat calmly at the big table and sipped on the hot sweet drink. She went over and over her plan.

If she could manage to get the gun from the safe, would Chrissie be prepared to take it with her? But did she have the right to even offer it to her? Could she put the girl in that position? Maybe she would get caught and spend the rest of her life in jail. No! She couldn't risk it, she decided. To encourage another person to commit murder, for whatever reason, surely was not the right thing to do. She must try to dissuade her from doing anything so dreadful. Maybe there was another way, something not quite so drastic and dangerous. But Rosita understood completely how Chrissie had become carried away with thoughts of revenge when they had overheard the conversation between the two men. Just then the kitchen door opened and Rosita spun guiltily around.

"Couldn't sleep," Chrissie grinned.

Rosita jumped up and got another cup. "Here, drink this."

Chrissie sat down beside her and drank. "Thanks."

"You look a little better," Rosita told her. "Very tired, but not so crazy." She tried to joke.

"Oh, I'm just as crazy!" Chrissie shot back, her eyes still full of venom.

Rosita sighed deeply. "But tell me, *chica,*" she began softly. "You didn't mean what you said."

"About killing him?" Chrissie asked coldly.

Rosita just nodded.

"Of course I meant it!"

Chrissie held her hand up as Rosita opened her mouth to protest. "Listen, Rosita," she spoke determinedly. "That man is an utter bastard! I'm sorry to curse in front of you, but you don't know what he is capable of."

"Yes I do," she replied, under her breath.

Chrissie carried on; "I must have been completely out of my head to get involved with all this and now look where my greed has got me. I could have still been at home with my family and living the life of Riley. All I had to do was to get myself a decent job in Dublin and forget all about my grand ideas of going to England and making my fortune. But you see I had it in my mind since I was just a kid. All I wanted to do was to get away. Always felt I was too good for the place. Always thought that it wasn't good enough for *me*! What a fool! Well, it's all ruined now and I don't care what happens to me any more, especially after what has happened to Margaret."

Rosita sighed sorrowfully. "You think that now, *chica,* but when you are back with your mother and all your family, maybe you can speak seriously to your little sister and make her understand what she has been doing is very wrong! You don't have to actually *kill* him!"

"You don't think that he is going to let me go that easily, do you? I know too much about him and what his so-called friends get up to. Apart from that, when I discover what has happened to Maria, and I'm damned sure something really bad *has* happened to her, what do you think he's going to do about me? Let me walk away? I don't *think* so!"

Rosita didn't know what to say.

Chrissie got up and paced around the room. "Do you know what? I think that her brother was in the flat that night." She suddenly announced.

"Her brother?" Rosita said.

"Yes, yes. Billy. He has only been out of prison a few months and by all accounts he is a little sh— I bet he took the money!"

"You think so?"

"I know Maria is a bit of a girl, but I don't think that she would go into my suitcase and steal anything. Besides I didn't have the keys to open it until Reggie gave them to me at the airport. Yes, that's it. I'm sure that's the answer. She told me once that he could open all sort of locks and that's how he got caught last time. They found his fingerprints all over the safe in the office that he burgled."

Rosita pulled open one of the drawers in the table. "Here, *chica.*" She held out a packet of cigarettes. "I get Natalia to buy them for you yesterday, when she went into the shops."

Chrissie's eyes lit up. "You're an angel!" She gave her a quick hug.

She continued to pace around the room, stopping now and then to look at the lightening sky through the windows, puffing heavily on her cigarette. "Do you know what time we are supposed to leave today?" she asked.

"No."

"Well, it can't be too early," Chrissie snorted, "Or he'd be banging on my door by now."

"Why do you ask?" Rosita got up and went to rinse the cups out. "You like some more coffee?"

"Well, I was just thinking that I would need time to think of a plan."

"Please, *chica*," Rosita begged. "You must be so careful."

"Oh, I *will!*"

Rosita came and stood beside her at the window, her arm around the girl's waist. "What are you going to do?"

"I'm not sure yet, but I'll have to think of something soon." An idea suddenly sprang into her mind. "Remember that awful girl I told you about in that pub in Bermondsey? You know, Silvie? The one that gave me those pills that night?"

Rosita recalled the name and nodded.

"Well, she knows all kinds of funny people. I could tell her that someone has asked me to buy a gun for them and she would get plenty of money if she could lay her hands on one for me." Chrissie laughed when she realised what she was saying. "God, I'm beginning to sound like a gangster myself now!"

"That is a very *stupid* idea, *chica!*" Rosita said.

"Why?"

"Because then many people would get to know what you are up to. She doesn't sound to me like the kind of girl you could trust for one minute!"

Chrissie sighed in frustration; "Oh, maybe you're right. She's a crafty little minx!"

Rosita slipped her hand into Chrissie's; "Come and sit down," she ordered gently. Chrissie wrapped the silky dressing gown around herself more tightly and shivered.

"You must listen carefully to what I am going to tell you," the older woman began. Chrissie frowned. "You look so serious, Rosita."

"I *am* serious, *chica*, and I don't know for sure if this is the right thing to be doing." She blessed herself and said a quick prayer.

"What *are* you talking about?" Chrissie shook her head.

Rosita then related the whole story of her life, as Chrissie sat open-mouthed, hardly able to believe her own ears! She almost fainted when Rosita got to the part about Leroy Jones. For one of the few times in her life she was lost for words. 'How could this little woman have done such a thing? She was so sweet and caring.' Her mind whirled. Tears rolled down both their faces as Rosita concluded the sorry tale by telling her that there was a small chance that the weapon was still in the safe in the library.

Chrissie sat in stunned silence and Rosita handed her a large handkerchief to wipe her face. When she finally found her voice Chrissie asked in a gruff whisper, "How can we find out?"

"There is only one way," Rosita rose. "I will go and look, before anyone wakes up."

"Oh, I can't ask you to do that!" Chrissie jumped from the chair. "You might get caught!"

"It's OK, *chica*," Rosita shook her head. "Those lazy devils won't be up before noon."

"You sure?"

"Sure! Like you say, if you were leaving early today they would be up already."

"Well, I'm coming with you!" Chrissie said firmly.

By the look on her face, Rosita knew that she couldn't argue with Chrissie so she just said, "We must be very quiet."

"OK. Let's go then."

"No! Wait a moment!" Rosita seized her arm firmly. "Before we do this I want you *to* promise me something."

"What?" Chrissie asked impatiently.

Rosita delved into her pocket and pulled out her rosary. Thrusting them into Chrissie's hand she closed the girl's fingers tightly around the beads. "You must swear on the Holy Virgin's name that you will not kill him!" She paused for a moment staring intently into Chrissie's face. "Maybe just scare him!"

Chrissie sighed loudly in exasperation; "I'll think about it!"

"Well, think about it well," Rosita nodded slowly and seriously. "Or what you do will be on my conscience as well as yours! You understand, *chica*?"

"OK. OK!" Chrissie pulled herself free and looked down at the rosary, feeling the first twinge of guilt about what she had thought of doing. "I promise," she finally managed to utter.

A few minutes later the two women stood before the landscape picture on the library wall. Chrissie asked in hushed tones which side of the frame she should touch. "Here." Rosita pointed upwards and to the right-hand side. Chrissie ran a nervous hand down the side of her dressing gown to dry the palm. She took a deep breath. "Here goes! Wish me luck!"

Two seconds later the picture swung open and the two women gasped.

"Bugger!" Chrissie muttered. They hadn't thought about how

they could get into the actual safe! "How the hell are we going to get in *there*?"

Rosita glanced sideways up at her and winked.

"What?" Chrissie asked.

"You think I have worked here all these years without learning a little something?"

"No?" Chrissie's eyes flew open. "You don't mean . . .?"

"*Si.*"

A long time ago Rosita had toyed with the idea of getting into the safe herself and removing the evidence of her crime and fleeing from the house. She had never fully trusted the Señor when he said it was their secret and had watched discreetly over the years. On numerous occasions as she served drinks and snacks in the library during meetings between Señor Fernandez and his villainous associates, she would go about her duties with quiet professionalism, but at the same time would take advantage of any situations that arose when the safe had been opened and she could make a mental note of the numbers. Sometimes the men were a little careless in their dealings and at times she felt as though she was invisible as they continued their conversations in front of her, so it wasn't as difficult as she first imagined. It took her a while but eventually by sheer cunning she discovered the combination. It was so simple in the end. Just four numbers! She crossed to the desk and scribbled down the code.

"Here." She handed it to the astonished Chrissie.

"You little monkey!" Chrissie giggled.

"*Si.*"

Chrissie spun the small grooved wheel in quick succession to the correct numbers, listening for the little click at each turn. Surprised and amazed at her success, Chrissie clapped her hands as the door sprung open.

"Holy Mother!" she breathed.

"Shall we?"

They looked at each other.

"*Si.*"

Pulling the door wider open they could see into the steel box.

"What's all this?" Chrissie asked, as she lifted out a heavy plastic bag, filled with white powder.

"What do you think, *chica*?" Rosita answered scornfully. "Their drugs!"

Chrissie gasped. "There must be hundreds of pounds-worth of the stuff here!"

"Leave it alone, please!" Rosita reached up and held her arm. "Put it back."

Chrissie pushed the bags to one side and laughed when she saw the thick pile of dollars stacked up in neat rows. "We could have the lot," she said. "That would serve them bloody right!"

"Just see if it is there, please Chrissie!" Rosita begged, perspiration breaking out on her worried brow. "It will soon be time for the others to be getting up and the pool-man is coming today. Please hurry, *chica*!"

"Suppose you're right!" Chrissie mumbled. Reaching far back into the deep safe over the top of the cash, Chrissie's fingers wrapped around a heavy bundle. "I think I've found it," she whispered over her shoulder.

She lifted it out and unfolded the brown cloth and nodded; "Phew!"

"Come on, please!" Rosita was getting very nervous. Maybe this wasn't such a good idea after all.

"Here!" Chrissie wrapped the thin cloth back around the gun. "Hold it a minute, I want to put everything back just as it was!"

Rosita felt a shiver run down her spine as she looked down at the little bundle in her outstretched hand.

"That's it," Chrissie announced. "Let's go!"

The safe was closed and the picture pushed firmly back into place. Chrissie reasoned with herself that after all this time it would be unthinkably bad luck if Señor Fernandez suddenly wanted to check the safe for the gun. He'd probably forgotten all about it, she assured herself.

Chrissie sat on the closed lid of the toilet staring down at the gun in her lap. How had it all come to this? she wondered as she ran a finger gingerly over the cold metal. Could she go through with it? And how? Where? He deserved nothing less for what he's done! She tried to convince herself. But cold-blooded murder? She knew in her heart that what Rosita had said was right, and after all hadn't she promised her not to commit such a terrible crime? She nearly jumped out of her skin when she heard the loud rapping on the door. "We leave in a couple of hours, Chrissie!" Charles called out brusquely. "And I hope you're ready!"

Chrissie shoved the gun into the laundry basket and closed the bathroom door quickly. (She knew he couldn't actually come into the room, because she had locked the door.)

"Nearly," she called back in a remarkably controlled voice.

The door handle turned. "Why is this door locked?" he demanded.

Chrissie hurried across the room and opened it. "Because I'm fed up with people wandering in here when I'm half naked, that's why!" she answered boldly.

Charles smirked down at her. "Well that would certainly be a sight for sore eyes."

Chrissie couldn't trust herself to hold his lecherous gaze and turned abruptly away. "You should be so lucky!" she sneered over her shoulder.

Charles frowned as he closed the door on her. A worry entered his mind. He would have to make sure that Chrissie never found out about the sister. She would undoubtedly cause him a whole load of problems if she got wind of his little 'escapades' with Margaret and, knowing the temper she had on her, it could possibly get very awkward indeed. He decided that it really wasn't worth the hassle, they were ten a penny, these girls, so when he went back downstairs he made a quick call to Wicklow, rousing a very grumpy Mrs Gallagher, his housekeeper, and told her to tell Margaret that he wouldn't be needing her services any longer. He gave her permission to give the girl the wages that were due and thank her for her hard work.

With that job done, Charles relaxed on the terrace and waited for Chrissie to make an appearance. Things were bound to get nasty when they arrived back in London as she was sure to find out about Maria, and there was no telling what she would try to do. He knew she wasn't stupid and it wouldn't take her too long to discover what had happened to her friend. He would have to think of a way to keep her mouth shut. He had no idea about her call to the Purple Parrot, so was completely unaware of what she knew.

There had been no more news from his men concerning the whereabouts of the missing cash, so that was something that he would have to sort out himself as well. All they had told him was that they couldn't get anything out of the little tart and had dumped her in Hyde Park. "Bloody fools!" he muttered to himself. The whole deal would collapse if the money wasn't recovered immediately.

20

Chrissie tried to smile brightly up at Reggie as he opened the car door for her. She was bone weary after the long and tedious journey back from Los Angeles and desperately wanted to fall into bed and sleep for a week, but she knew that probably wasn't going to happen. Charles had tried to keep up a pleasant conversation with her during the first part of their journey, but soon gave up. She couldn't be bothered to answer him; she had other things on her mind!

Reggie frowned down at her, noticing the thinly disguised bruising on her face.

"You OK, love?" he asked softly.

"What do *you* think?" she grinned crookedly.

As Charles went around to the other side of the car Chrissie whispered, "Have you seen anything of Maria?"

"Sssh!" he warned. "Not now!"

"OK, but later?"

'Yeah!" he said, helping her in. "We'll talk later!"

Chrissie dozed on and off as they drove back into the centre of London from Heathrow and was annoyed when she saw that they were pulling up outside the club.

"Why are we *here*?" she asked grumpily. "I want to go home. I'm exhausted!"

"Yes, I know you are, my dear." Chrissie glared at him. "But I have a few things to check up on first and then I thought after the long journey you may prefer to be booked into a nice hotel for the night."

"*Very* thoughtful!" she said icily.

It was no good letting her go straight back to the flat. She would find out soon enough that there was no one there, Charles had decided. He would have to keep her away from the other girls as well, for the time being. They were such a canny, bitchy lot, and word would have got out by now that Maria hadn't been seen for days.

Chrissie was disgusted to find herself back in London so quickly; she'd been so excited, thinking that she would be spending Christmas in America.

As they got out of the car, a small group of carol singers dressed in traditional Victorian costume passed by with brightly lit lanterns, ringing bells and holding out collection boxes for donations for London's homeless. Chrissie thought for a terrible moment she was going ta burst into tears in the street as a vivid picture of St Stephens Green, in the middle of Dublin, covered in glittering snow, flashed before her. She could see Rosie Byrne and herself along with a group of her old school friends, joyously singing along at the tops of their voices, much to the amusement of passersby. And somewhere in the little crowd was Jimmy Dwyer, with his big red glowing cheeks and his eyes sparkling mischievously and singing the loudest of all. As usual!

If only she had known then, that Jimmy Dwyer wasn't more than a few miles away at that very moment!

Jimmy Dwyer had been shocked by his feelings when he came home that night and found that he had missed Chrissie's visit to the house. He had nearly broken his neck trying to get down to Dun Loghaire in time to see her off. As he yelled out her name, frantically calling through the swirling mists, his heart leapt as he heard her strong voice come back to him over the wailing of the ship's foghorn.

"Don't forget me!" she had called out. Jesus how *could* he? He had loved her for years! He cursed himself over and over as he and Rosie linked arms and made their way forlornly back through the dark and dismal streets, each with their own thoughts. Chrissie was right! He *was* a bloody eegit, as she had so many times told him. Why the hell hadn't he had the guts to tell her how he felt? Now it was too late!

When they eventually reached the bus stop, he bent down and pecked a tearful Rosie on the cheek. "Don't worry, she'll be OK!"

"Oh I know she will," Rosie sniffed. "She can take care of herself."

"She sure can!" He grinned.

"But what about *you*?" Rosie looked up into his big sad eyes.

"Me?" he asked cheekily. "Well, you must know after all this time I can look after meself too, don't you?"

"You know what I mean, Jimmy Dwyer!" She grinned back knowingly.

"Yeah! I think I know what you're saying!" he answered, trying not to look embarrassed. "Is it that obvious?"

"Oh for years, boyo!"

"Well, what can I do now? She's gone!"

"Don't be so soft, for God's sake man!" Rosie said sternly. "Go after her, of course!"

Jimmy pulled himself up straight and with a steely look in his eye said fervently, "You're right, Rosy, sweetheart! I *will*! I bloody well *will*!"

For all his good intentions it had taken him longer than expected to find out where Chrissie was. It was a while before he had enough money to feel he could safely go to England and not worry if he didn't find work for a while. He didn't fancy starving in a strange country!

He got in touch with his uncle in north London when he arrived and was given such a great welcome that it took him another couple of weeks to recover from the celebrations and settle down! Soon afterwards he started work on a local building site. After several attempts to reach Bermondsey he eventually found the address that Rosie had given him and found himself knocking on the right door.

When Betty had told him about the great job Chrissie had found over in Mayfair and about the lovely flat she was sharing with one of the other girls that worked there, he had been very impressed. He was so pleased that she had at last found exactly what she had been craving for over the years. He couldn't wait to see her and the expression on her face when she saw him!

He went to a lot of trouble that night to make himself look decent. What if Chrissie had got so used to the fashionably dressed men in London that she turned her nose up at him? He looked very smart in his new dark suit and blue shirt. His tie was almost a match for his eyes and when he got off the bus at Hyde Park Corner, he laughed out loud when a couple of cheeky young girls gave him a wolf whistle!

Asking directions to the Purple Parrot club he continued light-heartedly on his way. London seemed to be so alive, especially with the Christmas decorations, the lights, the trees, but mostly the incessant buzz of the traffic and the hoards of Christmas shoppers. It was a little overwhelming at first to Jimmy, but he began to take it all in his stride as he marched confidently off down the street, following the newspaper-sellers' directions.

Turning into Stone Street, he paused for a moment to light a cigarette and to calm the excitement in his stomach. As he walked slowly towards the plush entrance of the Purple Parrot, he was again impressed: "She sure has done well for herself."

"Good evening, sir!" Harry Black greeted him politely.

"Hello there!"

As the door swung open for him Jimmy hesitated for a moment. Gathering his courage, which suddenly seemed to be deserting him, he took a deep breath, nodded his thanks to the doorman and strode across the thick purple carpeting.

The sultry, dark-haired girl behind the desk smiled winningly. "May I help you?"

"I'm looking for someone," he told her a little sheepishly. The girl was such a beauty, even with her over-made-up face and the blatantly low cut of her evening dress.

"Of course you are, sir." She smiled broadly at him. "And are you a member, sir?"

"A member?" Jimmy asked, with a frown.

"Yes, sir. A member. You have to be a member to come into the club," she told him politely, trying not to sound impatient. 'God, these bloody paddies!'

"Oh right." He smiled back. "So what do I have to do to be a member?"

"Beth reached down under the desk and produced a small form. "Just fill this in please," she explained, "And then all you have to do is write me a cheque for a hundred and fifty pounds, or cash if you prefer," she added hurriedly when she saw the quizzical expression on his handsome face. "Then you may go in and 'find' yourself someone!"

"I don't think you understood me, miss," Jimmy was feeling decidedly hot under the collar now. "I'm just looking for someone who works *here*. She's a receptionist, like yourself . . . I was told," he tailed off lamely.

It had come to him in a flash, when the girl had mentioned the membership fee, just what sort of place this was. He had heard about these kind of places from his pals back home and they had warned him to stay as far away from them as possible. Not only would they rip you off with their 'fees', but would fleece you alive with the prices of drinks. Not to mention what the girls would charge you for a couple of hours of their 'time'. Apart from that, you never knew what you might catch from them!

"I'm afraid our girls are not allowed personal callers during working hours," Beth informed him haughtily, as though she owned the place.

Jimmy felt himself go cold. Pulling himself up to his full height, he glared stonily down into her arrogant face. "I don't think you get my meaning, miss."

"Oh, I think I do, sir!" Beth glared back. She had already surmised that he was looking for Chrissie.

"What's your *friend's* name?" she asked snootily.

"Chrissie O'Rourke."

Beth slid from the high stool and, placing her hands on the shiny surface of the counter, leant towards him grinning sweetly and giving him a splendid view of her ample cleavage. "I'm afraid you've missed her then."

"What do you mean?"

"She's gone away."

"What are you talking about, woman?"

Beth bristled at his tone. The smile was gone now. "She went off to America on *business* for the boss." Then she told him spitefully, "In fact, I think I heard rumours that he had gone out to join her. Bit of trouble, I believe."

Jimmy glared at her angrily, desperately quenching the desire to smack her cheeky face.

"Oh, don't worry, they'll be back in a couple of days. Mr Latimer won't leave his beloved club for very long."

Spinning abruptly on his heel Jimmy stormed out of the club, seething with a jealous rage, almost knocking an indignant looking gentleman off his feet as he barged past him into the street.

Marching off down Stone Street, without knowing where he was heading, he cursed himself over and over for being such a fool. How could he have imagined that he would find her so easily? Nothing about Chrissie could ever be simple! He should have known that she would be snapped up by some rich feller at the first opportunity. Well, that was all well and good, he tried to tell himself, but what the hell was the 'business' that snotty little madam had referred to? And the 'bit of trouble?' She had certainly implied that it was something underhand.

"Stupid bitch!" he said aloud as he paused to light another cigarette. "What in the name of God was she up to now?" He prayed that it wasn't what he was beginning to think it might be. Looking around him, he realised he was standing outside a public house and without another thought went into the crowded smoky bar and ordered himself a large whisky. He elbowed his way through the noisy room and found the only unoccupied table in a corner.

It was some hours later when he eventually found his way back to his uncle's house, much the worst for wear after getting involved with a raucous bunch of Irish lads who bought him drink after drink to cheer him up after leaving home; or so they thought.

The next morning, nursing a sickening hangover, he tried to put all thoughts of Chrissie from his mind, but he just couldn't do it. He didn't tell anyone at the house about what he had discovered, just made them laugh a lot when he gave them a great tale of how he was waylaid by a gang of lads from Limerick and had never even found the club!

All day he pondered on what he should do. The more he thought, the more he worried about what was going on. Surely there was some way of getting in touch with her. Then suddenly, he remembered. Didn't Rosie tell him that Chrissie was supposed to leave another address with Betty in Bermondsey, for any letters from home to be posted to? Jumping up from the armchair by the fire, he grabbed his heavy overcoat and called out to his Aunt Mary; "Just going out for a while, Aunt. Won't be too long."

"Right you are, love!" the voice called from the kitchen.

Before anyone had time to ask him where he was going, he rushed from the house, slamming the door behind him.

Betty looked a little surprised when she saw Jimmy once again on her doorstep.

"Sorry about this, Mrs," he grinned shyly.

"Come on in, lad," Betty smiled broadly. "You'll catch your death out there."

Jimmy looked up into the darkening sky and blinked as a few snowflakes tickled his eyelashes.

After explaining to Betty that it appeared that Chrissie was off sick for a couple of days with a cold, he had remembered that she might have a forwarding address for her and wondered if she would give it to him.

"I think I have it here somewhere," Betty told him as she rummaged through one of the kitchen drawers. "But it's been such a while since we've had any post for her I thought she had probably got in touch with her folks to tell them her new address herself!"

Jimmy held his breath as he watched her pulling out all sorts of junk from the drawer.

"Ah! Here it is," Betty smiled.

Breathing a sigh of relief Jimmy took the crumpled piece of paper and little bundle of letters from her.

"That's great," he beamed. "Thanks a million!"

"Sit yourself down and have a drink before you go."

"No thanks! I think I'd better be on my way."

"Good luck, then," Betty said as she opened the front door, to be greeted by an icy gust of wind. "Give her our love!"

"I will and thanks, Mrs Carter." He smiled his winning smile. "And have a great Christmas."

"You too, love."

"Excuse *me*!" Silvia said, grinning, as she collided with the tall figure on Betty's doorstep.

"Sorry, miss," Jimmy said to the tarty-looking girl, whose face looked as though it had been made up by a clown. "My fault."

"Ooh, I wouldn't say that," she whimpered.

"What do *you* want?" Betty asked tersely. "You know you're not welcome here!"

Jimmy glanced quickly at the two women and decided immediately that he didn't want to get involved with anything that was going on here. Looks like there's bad blood between these two for sure, he told himself as he made a quick escape. "Bye, ladies!"

"Well?" Betty asked again as she watched Silvia staring off into the distance at the disappearing figure.

"Bloody hell, he was *gorgeous*!" Silvia gushed as she pulled her pink, fake-fur collar up tighter around her neck. "Where'd he come from?"

Betty ignored her question and asked again. "I said, what do you want?"

Silvia pouted sulkily. "I only wanted to know if you'd heard anything from Chrissie, that's all!"

"No I haven't," Betty said firmly. "But I'm sure she's fine. Just been a bit busy with her great new job."

"Oh I *bet* she has," Silvia sneered.

"What's that supposed to mean?" Betty asked angrily, stepping out on to the doorstep.

"Nothing!" Silvia backed away, fearing a slap in the face from the irate woman, and scurried off down the road in the direction of *The George*.

Betty shivered as she slammed the door and went back into the house. She went into the little front room and poured herself a large sherry. She was glad to be alone in the house for a few hours, as funnily enough, she had been thinking about Chrissie all day and had indeed wondered why the girl hadn't been in touch with her. She didn't want her husband or Daisy to know how worried she was getting, so she hadn't mentioned it to them. With Christmas only a couple of days away now she had felt sure that Chrissie would have found time to make at least one quick visit. It wasn't like her at all. Betty had thought of dropping a quick line to Maggie O'Rourke to see if she had heard from her, but then had second thoughts. It would only upset her.

With her feet resting comfortably on the brass fender, Betty relaxed in front of the blazing fire and sipped on her sherry. Everything would be OK, she told herself. She wouldn't take any notice of that little madam, Silvia, just a jealous little bitch, she was! No need to worry so much. She was pretty sure that a decent girl like Chrissie wouldn't get mixed up in any nonsense.

Charles Latimer gripped Chrissie's elbow firmly and ushered her straight through the club and into his office. Beth's eyes opened wide as she watched them pass by and wondered what was going on. She would have to find out!

Sinking gratefully on to the nearest sofa, Chrissie laid back and closed her eyes, totally exhausted. Within moments she had fallen asleep. Charles perched on the edge of his desk, slowly drawing on one of his long cigarettes. He couldn't help thinking how young she looked as she slumbered innocently before him. A knock on the office door brought him quickly back to reality before his fantasies got the better of him.

"She looks just like a kid," Reggie said softly as he handed his boss a pile of correspondence.

"Mmmm," Charles agreed, dragging his gaze away from her. "What's all this?"

"Oh, just some stuff that came for you while you were away."

Charles threw the envelopes on to the desk. "I'll see to them later."

"OK," Reggie said, and made to leave the room.

"Hang on a second," Charles said. "Sit down."

Reggie closed the door gently.

Charles was extremely tired himself from the long journey and couldn't wait to get his head down for a few hours, but before he could he had to go over a few things with Reggie and some of the others. He poured two large bourbons.

"Thanks," Reggie took his glass and carefully lowered himself on to the opposite end of the sofa to Chrissie, trying not to disturb her.

"Don't worry about *her*," Charles laughed. "She's out for the count!"

They talked for a while about what they thought could have happened to the money and agreed that Chrissie had nothing to do with its disappearance. Then in very hushed tones Reggie told Charles that Maria was still in a serious condition although she had improved a little over the last day or two. She had been taken off the life-support earlier that day.

"How do you know?" Charles asked harshly, but a little relieved to know that she wasn't actually dead. That was all he would need. She would have eventually been identified, of course, and that would have led the police directly to him. He was confident that he could talk his way out of any situation, especially as he had had more than a few of the vice squad, in his pocket for years. But then again, there were still a number of decent coppers around, so you never could tell!

"Because when those two apes bragged to me about what they had done to her I called around all the hospitals and morgues till I found out where she was, that's how!" Reggie growled.

"All right old man, keep your hair on!"

"Well," Reggie continued. "She's not a bad kid and she didn't deserve what they did to her."

"Oh, *really*," Charles shot back nastily. "You should know by now, old boy, that I don't take lightly to *anyone* ripping me off. I don't care *who* they are."

"But we don't even know if Maria had anything to do with it!"
Reggie was still fuming at his boss's attitude. He swallowed the rest
of his drink and stood up. "I'd better get back outside. We're fully
booked tonight and have a couple of special 'turns' coming in
later. Could get a bit out of hand if I don't keep an eye on things."

"Right, carry on then," Charles nodded. "But come back in a
while if things are running smoothly and you can run 'madam'
here over to the *Monarch*. I've booked her in there for a couple of
days until I decide what to do with her."

"What do you mean?" Reggie frowned. "*Do* with her?"

"Oh, use your brains, man," Charles snorted. "We'll have to
think of something to keep her quiet. She's not exactly the retiring
type now, is she?"

Without answering, Reggie left the room with a cold feeling
running through him. 'Surely Charles wasn't going to do anything
stupid?' he asked himself, putting a false smile on his face as he
greeted a small group of clients. 'No,' he tried to assure himself.
'Knowing his boss the way he did, he would have done something
already!'

Neither of the two men had noticed that Chrissie had stirred
once or twice during their conversation. To her it seemed as
though she was merely having a muddled dream and the muffled
voices were coming from way off.

Chrissie sat bolt upright in the bed. The last rays of the afternoon
winter sun were streaming through the hotel window and she
covered her face against the glare. Rubbing her eyes and blinking
wildly to adjust to its brilliance she gazed round the room, wondering where the hell she was. Flopping back down on to the
crumpled pillows, she groaned loudly when she remembered that
Charles had told her he had booked the room for her. Still it *was*
very comfortable, she reluctantly admitted, and sliding further
down under the cosy sheets she closed her eyes again. God knows
she had needed the rest! Before she had time to drop off to sleep
once more a polite knock on the door and a small voice informed
her of 'room service'.

"Bugger!" she groused. "Come on in."

Chrissie polished off the delicious three-course breakfast with
gusto, without really thinking about anything. She thought for a
minute that it was a strange time of day to be having a breakfast,

but who cares? All she knew when she lifted the huge silver lids from the plates and smelled the delicious aroma, was that she was absolutely starving. She could have eaten a horse! By the time she had gulped down the second cup of steaming coffee, she felt great. Now all she had to do was to have a bath, get dressed and go back to the flat. She had had enough excitement to last a lifetime. She had to have some time to herself to get things straight in her mind and find out what Maria had to say.

Then it hit her! What was she thinking of! Her eyes darted around the room frantically, searching for her suitcase.

"Jesus!" she cried out loud. "My suitcase? The fecking g—?" She stopped herself just in time, as the young maid knocked and entered the room again.

"Thank you," Chrissie managed a stiff smile. "That was grand!"

As the door closed behind the girl, Chrissie jumped from the side of the bed and ran wildly around the room, pulling open doors and cupboards. She ran into the bathroom and gazed around in despair. As she caught sight of herself in the mirrored tiles, she felt like bursting into tears as it dawned on her. Where the hell were her clothes? Where was her luggage, with its incriminating contents and even more to the point ... who the bloody hell had undressed her? The thin pale-blue fabric of her nightdress left nothing to the imagination. Where had that come from?

Now what was she supposed to do? She couldn't get dressed, so she had no chance of making her escape. She strode back into the bedroom and tugged on the bedclothes. Falling to her knees she looked under the bed and almost fainted with relief when she saw her handbag. She sat on the side of the bed again and opening it sighed loudly when she saw that at least she had some money in her purse.

"Shite!" she cried loudly, as she pulled out a thick wad of dollars. "Now what?"

Chewing on her thumb she paced around the room, thinking of what she could do to get herself out of this mess. God, she'd kill for a cigarette! Then it came to her. She would use the phone to call down to the room-service girl. While she was waiting she went over to the window and gazed down at the scene below. The skies were darkening now and huge snowflakes swirled and danced before her.

This time it was a smartly dressed young lad who answered her call. Chrissie grabbed at the top cover on the bed and hastily wrapped it around herself when she saw the deep crimson flush spread over his youthful face.

"Yes m-m-miss," he stammered. "How can I be of service?"

Chrissie held out the bundle of dollars and smiled sweetly, admiring the cut and style of his scarlet pageboy uniform with its two rows of gleaming gold buttons and his little gold braided pill-box hat.

"Do you think you could get these changed for me, please? I'm afraid I forgot all about it at the airport."

"Certainly, miss." He blushed even more furiously as he took the money in his sweating hand. "I'll be back in a tick."

He left the room grinning to himself as he thought about the fabulously formed body on the great looking creature in room 101.

Chrissie ran a hot bath and waited impatiently for him to return. He was no time at all. When she heard the tapping on the door, she opened it only slightly, not wishing to cause them both any further embarrassment and thanked him profusely as he handed over the cash.

"Thank you so much."

"That's OK, miss." He grinned back awkwardly. "Is there anything else I can do for you?"

"Yes, there is," she replied. "You can ask that girl that came up with the food to come and see me. I would like her to do a little errand for me."

"Certainly, miss."

Evette, the young housemaid, couldn't believe her good fortune, as she tucked the five-pound tip into her apron pocket. The young lady had been so kind and all she had had to do was to go down to the nearest ladieswear shop and pick up a new outfit for her. What a shame that all her luggage had been lost on the way back from her holidays.

Chrissie wrinkled her nose as she examined the brown woollen suit and the clumsy looking shoes. The creamy blouse and the skimpy underwear seemed adequate but not exactly what she would have chosen herself, but what did it matter?

She still had a few things in the flat, so they would have to do for now, until she got her suitcase back. She tried not to think what would happen if Charles decided to go through her belongings.

Bathing and dressing as quickly as she could, Chrissie looked at herself in the wardrobe mirror and grimaced. Not the most attractive of suits but at least it was warm enough for now. She would soon be back at the flat where she could sort things out. Taking a quick peek out from the high window, Chrissie saw that the snow was falling more heavily now and the view across the park from her window was wonderful, but she didn't have time to stand admiring the view. She had to get out of the hotel as quickly as possible and make her way to Bayswater, before Charles put in an appearance, or she would be in trouble. Chrissie didn't have a clue where she was but got the impression from the scene outside that she wasn't too far from the club. Checking the money she had left in her purse, she realised that she didn't have an awful lot left. Only a few pounds, in fact. Walking smartly through the lobby, Chrissie smiled at the girl on the desk and asked if she could call a taxi for her.

21

Chrissie's feet were numb as she stood on the doorstep rummaging in her bag trying to find the door keys that Maria had given her. There had been no answer when she rang the bell half a dozen times. It seemed as though the whole house was empty. Hopping from one foot to another in the deepening drifts of snow she swore silently to herself. Just as she was about to give up her cold fingers closed around the small fluffy keyring.

"Thank God for that!" she muttered to herself.

The house was creepily cold and dark as Chrissie made her way slowly up the three long flights of stairs. On each tread she felt herself growing colder. Not just from the freezing temperature of the old house, but something inside her was telling her that things were not quite right. By the time she let herself into the musty smelling empty flat Chrissie was sure that there was something dreadfully wrong. Flicking the light switch just inside the door, Chrissie felt like crying when the lights didn't come on.

"Oh shite!"

She knew that there was an electric meter somewhere, but hadn't been at the flat long enough to know where she could find it. She cursed loudly again.

Shivering in the dank atmosphere, Chrissie fumbled once again in her bag. Thankfully she found a small match book that she had taken from the hotel room and struck one of the pink-tipped matches. Remembering that Maria had several candles around the room, Chrissie quickly found a few of them and lit them. Feeling a little more cheerful in the flickering glow, Chrissie took one of the candles from the mantelpiece and went in search of the electric meter. Breathing a sigh of relief when she quickly located it up on the wall just over the door of her room she slid a shilling into the slot and felt like cheering when all the lights in the flat came on and the radio started blaring out a carol concert being broadcast live from Trafalgar Square.

After making herself a quick cup of black tea, Chrissie took a cigarette from the packet that Evette had bought for her, lit it and sat down on the lumpy settee. She switched the radio off. She couldn't bear to hear all that merry stuff, when she was feeling so alone.

As her eyes roamed around the small room, she noticed for the first time that one of the smaller chairs by the fire was tipped sideways and the old worn rug that usually lay neatly in front of the two-bar electric fire was crumpled and dirty. Frowning she got slowly up from the seat and went over to straighten the little mat. As she bent over to catch up the corners her eyes fell upon one of Maria's red stilettos, shoved underneath the toppled chair. She pulled it out and stood looking at it, puzzled. Chrissie's heart began to beat faster! Now she just *knew* there was something badly wrong. Panic struck her! Stubbing out her half-smoked cigarette she rushed into Maria's room and looked around. The bed was crumpled and messy, clothes were strewn all over the floor and 'Jesus Mary!' she groaned loudly. 'Was that blood streaked down the wall?' She flew into her own little room. It was in the same condition. Her few belonging were flung everywhere and the little borrowed bed had been turned upside down.

Chrissie bit down hard on her bottom lip to stop herself from screaming. What the hell had happened here? God, she could do with a drink! She went back into the little sitting room and found the half bottle of vodka that she hoped was still tucked behind the row of books on the shelf. Good old Maria, Chrissie tried to joke to herself. With a shaking hand she wrenched the top off and took a long, deep swig.

The more she looked around the more she began to realise that the whole place was a real mess. Maria would never have deliberately left it in such a state. In fact, Chrissie thought fearfully, it looked as though there had been a bit of a scuffle. Well, more of a fully fledged punch-up really!

Still gulping down the neat fiery liquid Chrissie went back into Maria's bedroom. As she stood looking down at the mess, her eyes carefully avoiding the dark red stains on the wall, her gaze fell upon a Harrods carrier bag that looked as though it had been flung across the room, its contents spilling out over the bedside cabinet. Chrissie leant over the bed and pulled the bag towards her.

"Beth's dresses," she breathed, shaking her head. She recognised them immediately.

Gritting her teeth until her jaw ached, Chrissie cursed Charles Latimer from the bottom of her heart. There was no doubt in her mind that he had something to do with all this, but then again he more than likely had *everything* to do with whatever had become of Maria. What could she do, though? Where could she go for help? How could she find out anything? That bitch Beth wouldn't help her, she was sure of that! Who could she turn to?

Chrissie was beginning to feel a little woozy from the alcohol, so she sat quietly for a while and tried to sort things out in her mind. She wasn't quite drunk, but with the shock of realising that something awful could have happened to her friend she couldn't think too clearly. Maybe she should make some strong black coffee? She stretched out on the settee for a few minutes until she could make up her mind as to what to do next. Deciding against the hot drink, Chrissie swigged back the remaining vodka and put her feet up higher on the cushions. She tried to force her eyes to stay open but felt her lids begin to droop. The fatigue she felt as a result of the fear, anger and the neat vodka threatened to overwhelm her, but then, just as she was about to doze off, her eyes suddenly flew wide open as it came back to her! What was it Reggie had said the night before? They'd talk later? She got hastily to her feet, grabbing at her cigarettes. Pacing around the room she puffed on one after the other.

He *must* know what's happened, she told herself. But how could she get in touch with him, without that other bastard finding out? Shivering, she did the buttons up on her new jacket, grumbling about the rough material. She would have to risk it. Checking the change in her purse and making sure she still had 'that *damned* card' (the one that had started the whole chain of events), Chrissie snatched up the Harrods carrier bag and shoved the dresses back inside. She left the flat without a backward glance. As she hurried down the gloomy staircase she started nervously as Gino's cheery voice greeted her in the semi-darkness. With a brief hello, she attempted to pass him on the second landing, but he caught hold of her sleeve.

"How is Maria?" he asked, his voice low and secretive.

"What do you mean?" she asked in the same hushed tone.

"Well . . ." He hesitated for a moment, looking over the banisters as they heard the front door opening. "It's just that I haven't seen her for a while and she promised to come down to the restaurant and have a Christmas drink with us. And after all the noise they were making up there last week, I was wondering if there was something wrong."

"What do you mean . . . noise?" Chrissie gathered that he must have heard the fight or whatever it was, but wanted to hear what he had to say about it.

"It seems like there was an argument," he told her, not sure if he should say anything else.

"Who was up there?" Chrissie pressed him urgently. 'Did you see who went up there? Did you recognise anyone? Any voices?"

"Oh no, Señorina," Gino replied. He had said enough. He couldn't risk getting involved with anything that might bring himself to the attention of those in authority. And he had a feeling that the young lady upstairs had got herself into some kind of serious trouble. And he knew what that meant. Somewhere along the line, the police would be involved. He had been long enough in the country to know that you kept yourself to yourself. Especially when you didn't have a work permit.

"Oh, don't bloody tell me, then," Chrissie shot back grumpily. "But I *will* find out!" She finished emphatically as she shoved her way passed and let herself out into the cold evening air. Brushing the thick snowflakes from her eyes, she squinted down the dark street, stepping carefully over the freezing paving stones. She was sure that she had seen a telephone box somewhere nearby. Where the hell was it? Turning into Bayswater Road she smiled to herself through chattering teeth, as she caught sight of the orange glow further down the street. "Thank God for that" she muttered.

Holding on to the railings. Chrissie steadied herself. The ground was becoming more and more treacherous with each faltering step. Just as she put her hand out to open the door of the red telephone box, the screeching of brakes right behind her made her spin round. The door flew open as the wheels mounted the slippery pavement, crunching over the glittering snow. Before she knew what was happening a pair of rough hands lunged at her. Dragging her kicking and screaming across the icy surface, Reggie Dixon threw her forcefully into the back of the vehicle.

"Just *shut* up, will you, Chrissie!" he hissed into her ear. "I've got to make this look good!"

"What are you fecking talking about, you arsehole?" Chrissie yelled back.

"Orders" he told her under his breath. "Now be quiet!"

As the car bumped its way over the kerb and sped off into the busy stream of traffic, causing several near collisions, Chrissie pushed herself into the furthest corner of the back seat as she could, puffing and panting as she tried to recover from the shock. Reggie sat rigidly, staring out of the window. The driver, whoever he was, glanced once or twice in his rear-view mirror, but made no comment as he drove smoothly through a fresh fall of snow.

Chrissie felt the first real fear in her life. What was going to happen now? She groaned inwardly. Her stomach clenched into a tight ball of dread as she turned to look at Reggie's stony countenance. He looked so hostile! And to think that she was just about to call him and ask him to come and meet her. She had really thought that she could trust him.

Summoning up her courage, she finally asked in a tiny whisper, "What's going on? Where are you taking me?"

The driver's head turned slightly. He had heard her. When Reggie didn't reply, Chrissie asked again, even more timidly.

"Just be quiet!" Reggie answered brusquely. "You'll know soon enough!"

"But . . .!"

He turned towards her, reached out and gripped her sore arm painfully. "SHUT UP!"

Chrissie winced as the pain shot through her arm up to her shoulder; but her eyes widened hopefully catching the sly wink he gave her as he mouthed 'sorry'.

They drove on for what seemed an eternity. When Chrissie looked out of the window she noticed that the streets were becoming less busy with traffic. In fact, as they turned down a very narrow road there were hardly any cars to be seen and there were only a few straggling pedestrians making their way carefully along the dangerously slippery pavements. Her heart began to race again and she felt herself growing hot and cold. Folding her arms tightly around herself she tried to gain comfort in their support. The lovely meal she had enjoyed so much earlier on, was threatening to come up at any moment. Reggie glanced over at her feeling like a complete rat. The poor girl looked terrified, scared out of her wits.

When the barked order had come from Charles to go and 'pick' her up, as soon as he had discovered that she had left the *Monarch* Hotel, Reggie began to fear the worst. He thought for a while that Charles had discovered that Chrissie had indeed had something to do with the missing cash, but when he went into the club to hand over the night's takings to be put into the safe, Charles let him know exactly what was going on.

"Look at this!" he scowled, pointing down into the open drawer in his desk. He hadn't intended to tell him anything, but then decided he should put him in the picture.

Reggie leaned over to see what he was talking about. "What?" he said, when his gaze fell upon the small weapon lying on top of a sheaf of papers.

"*What?*" Charles almost spat back.

"Well, I don't know what you want me to say, boss!" Reggie shrugged. "Why are you showing me it? It's not the first time I've seen a gun."

"I know that, you fool!" Charles breathed hotly. "But I found the damn thing in that bloody little bitch's case!"

"No? You mean Chrissie?"

"Of course I mean Chrissie!" Charles' face was becoming redder by the minute. Any air of control had gone. "I forgot to send it over to the hotel with her, but then, I don't know why, I decided to check it again, just in case I had overlooked something and yes I *had*! This!"

"Where did she get that from . . . and what was she going to do with it?" Reggie shook his head; not believing what he was hearing and seeing.

"That is precisely what I want you to find out!" he yelled. "I've just called the hotel and they tell me that she left there hours ago. So she must have gone back to the flat somehow. And you know what that means."

Reggie nodded.

"It won't be long before she realises that Maria is on the missing list and then all hell will break loose!"

"Do you think she knew about it?" Reggie asked. "I mean . . . perhaps somebody put it there?"

"Oh, stop talking through your fucking arse, man!" Charles was almost beyond reason. His face contorted in rage and the long scar stood out lividly on his purple flesh as he paced frantically around the room, running his long thin fingers through his damp silver hair. Reggie had never seen him in such a state.

"She knows just what she's doing, that one and believe me, given half the chance she could cause us a whole heap of trouble! She must have got her hands on it in Miguel's place! Just *how* I don't know, but I'm damned sure I'm going to find out!"

"You still want me to bring her in?"

"Reggie," Charles tried to bring his temper under control. "I have already told you to do just that *and* . . . make sure she talks."

Reggie Dixon shrugged. "If you say so, boss."

"Just *go*, will you?" Charles slumped down into his chair, head in his hands.

Before he closed the door behind him, Reggie asked, "Do you want me to bring her back here?"

Charles looked up slowly. "Do you know, Reggie, I think you're being deliberately obtuse." (Charles hadn't missed the fact that Reggie seemed to have a soft spot for the girl.)

Reggie frowned. Charles waved his hand dismissively.

"Take her to the usual place."

"Reggie?" Chrissie asked in a small voice.

"Mmm?" He couldn't look at her.

"Where are we going?" Chrissie was trembling all over and the nauseating feeling in her stomach was getting worse by the minute. She was terrified! Cold sweat poured down her quivering body, her damp hair sticking to her head and neck like a freezing-cold, heavy wet rag. Before he could answer her the car slowed down to a crawl as they turned into a cobbled side street that ran down to the river. Reggie tapped the driver on the shoulder. "This is far enough."

"But the boss said . . ."

"Never mind that, he changed the plan," Reggie lied.

"Whatever you say."

Reggie helped Chrissie from the car by hauling her to her feet and, thinking that she looked as though she would pass out, he clasped her firmly around the waist. Struck dumb with terror Chrissie allowed herself to be held tightly as they stood in silence watching the car reverse from the narrow street and back on to the road.

Her legs felt like jelly as she took in her surroundings. There

275

wasn't a soul about and the silence was almost deafening. Glancing sideways she noticed a steep slope and gasped in horror when she realised that the slowly moving dark sludge she could just about make out at the bottom of the steep incline was the river.

"Come on," Reggie said, gripping her even more securely.

"W-where are y-y-you taking m-me?" she managed to stammer, fearing now for her life.

"Not far."

The freezing dampness seeped through her clothing and into her very bones as Chrissie stumbled alongside Reggie for a few minutes. Their footsteps were silent on the thick snow and her new shoes were sodden with icy slush. But as they walked on Chrissie took small comfort from the fact that they had turned away from the river and were heading back towards the road. She had truly thought for one terrifying moment that he was going to throw her into the depths of the River Thames. Reggie paused on the corner, releasing his grip on her. "Wait here!" he ordered.

"W-w-what?" She shivered violently.

Propping her up in the doorway of the derelict factory he said, "Stay there, I won't be a minute."

Chrissie felt as though she was living a nightmare as she watched him vanish around the corner.

"Oh mam!" She wailed. 'What have I *done*?" She swore to God and all the saints in heaven, that if she ever got out of this mess, she would run home as fast as she could and never, ever, leave the comfort of her family again! How many times had she said that? But she honestly meant it this time, she told herself. As Reggie disappeared from sight, Chrissie prayed fervently that he wouldn't run off and leave her there. She was so confused and scared she couldn't understand what was going on. It *was* obvious to her though, even in her befuddled state, that Charles had found out that she had left the hotel and sent Reggie over to the flat after her. He knew she would make for Bayswater, there was nowhere else she could go, and he knew that she was anxious to ask Maria a few questions. But what had led to all this?

Chrissie tried to move her feet to get some life into them, but they were completely numb. Peering stiffly out from the gloom of the doorway, Chrissie screamed in fright as she came face to face with a couple of drunken, burly looking seamen.

"Hello darlin'," one of them slurred. "Want a bit of business?"

He reached out and made a grab at her. The other almost fell on top of her in his drunken stupor.

"GET OFF ME, YOU DIRTY BASTARDS!" Chrissie yelled, her lungs fit to burst.

A searing hot flush rushed through her veins as she kicked and screamed, fighting with all her new-found strength to ward of her assailants. Struggling and lashing out with all her might she lost her footing and fell flat on her back, calling out pitifully as her head hit the hard cobbles with a sickening thud.

"Come on girl," Reggie said gently, tapping her burning cheek again. "Wake up, will you?"

Chrissie mumbled something incoherent and Reggie sighed with relief. She was beginning to come round at last. He had been concerned for a while that she wasn't going to recover conscious- ness and that would mean calling in a doctor. (He knew a couple of dodgy GPs, but the less anyone knew about what was going on the better.)

Chrissie's eyelids fluttered and then opened. "Oooh . . . my head!" she moaned.

Chrissie blinked and looked towards the voice. Her vision was slightly blurred but she could still make out the bulky frame of Reggie standing over her. "What's happened? Where am I?" she croaked, her throat parched and sore. She tried to raise herself up on her elbows.

"Wait a mo, let me give you a hand."

"Thanks."

"Here, drink this." He held a glass to her mouth.

"What is it?" Chrissie asked suspiciously.

"Water," he grinned. "Just water."

"You sure?"

"Yeah, I'm sure."

Supported once again by Reggie's strong arm, Chrissie gulped at the cool drink.

"Slowly," he warned. "Or you'll choke yourself."

She sunk back down, wiping the back of her hand over her cracked lips.

"How you feeling now?"

"My eyes feel funny and my head hurts," she groaned. "Well every bit of me's hurting, if you must know."

277

"I'm sure it does. You landed with quite a bang!"

"What are you talking about?"

"Don't you remember what happened back there?" Reggie frowned.

"Where?"

"I think you should try and get some rest," he told her. "Then you can try a bite to eat. It's nearly ready."

Chrissie sank gratefully back down on to the pillows holding the palm of her hand over her forehead, wishing that the thumping would stop. It was worse than having a bloody hangover, she thought morosely. She tried to force herself to fall asleep but her mind was in turmoil. As she lay there listening to Reggie busying himself in the next room, her muddled thoughts were gradually forming into some kind of order. Opening her eyes a little she was relieved to see that her vision was clearing. She felt her face turn scarlet when she realised that she was stark naked under the covers and pulled the thick quilt up to her chin. How had this come about?

Reggie came flying back into the room when her heard her let out an agonising scream.

"What's wrong?"

She was sitting up in the bed, her breasts unashamedly fully exposed, her eyes wide and wild as she held her arms out to him. Everything that had happened to her over the past week or so came rushing into her head like a great torrent. Reggie hesitated for only a moment before he gathered the sobbing girl into his comforting embrace. Gently stroking the thick knots of her tangled tresses he uttered soothing words and sounds until the poor young thing had finally shed the last tear. Sighing from the bottom of her heart, Chrissie let herself be lowered gently back on to the bed. Reggie pulled up the cover and tucked it in around her.

"Better?" He grinned down into the blotchy face.

"Yes," she murmured very quietly. "Thanks."

"Are you hungry?"

"I'm always hungry," she grinned crookedly.

"Good. Do you want it on a tray or can you manage to come to the table?"

"I'll get up," Chrissie said, making to pull the covers off and then quickly changed her mind.

"Wait a minute," he winked. "I'll find you something."

As they sat together in the neat little dining room, eating a huge mound of spaghetti, Reggie explained how he had come back with the taxi, just in time to deal with the two men who had attacked her. They were so drunk, he told her grinning broadly, that they hadn't put up much of a fight and he had left both them sprawling face down in the snow to sleep off their hangovers.

She pushed the empty plate away from her and wiped her mouth with the dainty serviette and asked him, "Why did you do all this for me, Reggie? You hardly know me, after all."

She kept her fingers crossed on her lap, where he couldn't see them, and hoped sincerely that he wasn't going to come out with any nonsense about being in love with her or anything so daft.

"Would you like some wine?" Reggie picked up the Chianti, avoiding her eyes.

"No thanks. I'm not drinking any more."

"Sure?"

"Yes. I'm quite sure, thanks. That's what got me into all this bloody mess in the first place. Well, that and a few other things." she finished guiltily.

"What do you mean?" Reggie was curious.

"You still haven't answered *my* question," she said, watching him as he poured a glass of the wine for himself. "Why *are* you doing all this for me?"

Reggie thought for a while and then decided that it was only fair to tell her. As he went through the events, he was upset to see her pale complexion gradually turn a sickly shade of grey. He told her that he was getting more than a little fed up with Charles' attitude towards the girls who worked for him, so easily disposable, he had said once. When Charles ordered him to go and get Chrissie, Reggie decided that he had had enough.

His bank account had built up healthily over the years he had worked at the Purple Parrot and it was about time that he got away from the sordid life he'd been involved with for so long. Time for pastures new, he told her. He fancied somewhere warm and sunny all year round. A Greek island, perhaps. He could handle the dealings with other members of the criminal fraternity, but when it came to the women, it turned his stomach. And to be honest he was fed up with the whole scene.

Chrissie listened intently and said, "Do you mean that he wanted you to torture me, or something?"

"Well not exactly *torture* you, Chrissie. Just find out where you got the um . . . well, you know, where you got the gun from," he finished quickly.

"Have you got a cigarette?" she asked abruptly.

Reggie brought a packet from the kitchen and gave it to her.

"Have these, I'm trying to pack it in!"

Chrissie looked around. "Is my handbag here?"

"Your bag?"

"Yes. I had it before you jumped on me," Chrissie tried to make light of her abduction.

"I'm sorry, love. It must have been lost in all the commotion."

"Oh, never mind. That's the least of my worries."

Chrissie sat with her elbows on the table and wondered if she should tell him everything. He had been very good to her and she felt that the least she could do was to confide in him. She was sure that he had been mixing with all sorts of undesirables over the years if he had been working for Mr Charles Latimer, so perhaps whatever she decided to tell him wouldn't come as much of a surprise. Before that, though, she had to ask him. He placed a mug of hot chocolate in front of her. Looking directly up into his eyes she said boldly, "From what you've told me, it sounds as though you know what might have happened to Maria."

Reggie took a deep breath and, not beating about the bush, answered, "She's in hospital."

"Oh my God!"

"Don't worry." He sat down beside her at the table and patted her arm. "She's OK. She's out of danger now."

"What did you do to her?" Chrissie asked gravely.

"No, no, Chrissie," Reggie became alarmed. "Not me! I had nothing to do with it!"

Chrissie believed him. "Was it *him?*" she asked with a cold sneer.

"No, of course it wasn't. Apart from the odd slap, he gets others to do the dirty work for him."

"Well, anyway," Chrissie sighed. "As long as she's on the mend, I don't think I want any more details!"

She got up and wandered around the room admiring the little ornaments that were daintily arranged on glass shelves and thought how strange it was that such a macho man as Reggie should have such lovely, pretty things everywhere. And those little serviettes, they looked like handmade lace. She had another thought. "Did he really think that Maria had taken the money?"

"Well he did at first, but after the beating she took from those two animals ... Shit! Sorry love." He bit his lip when he saw Chrissie's face begin to crumble. "You OK?"

She nodded.

Reggie held out the lighter, flicking it open. "It's your turn now!" he said. "Come and sit down and tell me all about it!"

It was hours later when Chrissie finished her tale of woe. Reggie hadn't said a word from beginning to end. His expression had never altered as she related one event after another, from the chance meeting on the *Princess Maud* to her trip back to London from America. He had heard some stories in his time, but this one, well it was mind-boggling.

"Aren't you going to say *anything*?" Chrissie prompted when he sat there staring off into space. Finding his voice he said, "Well, you have completely confirmed the fact that I have made the right decision, about leaving London, for good."

"So you're going to desert me then," Chrissie smiled weakly.

"No love, of course not." He squeezed her hand. "We'll think of something."

The thunderous hammering on the door made them jump from the sofa, their hearts pounding!

"My God! Who's that?"

"Give you two guesses!" Reggie muttered furiously.

Before they could move the door was taken off its hinges and smashed to the floor with an ear-splitting crash.

Chrissie sank to her knees and wailed like a banshee. "Jesus Christ! Not *again!*"

Charles Latimer and his two henchmen stormed into the room. Charles made a lunge at Chrissie, snatching her up from the floor in one movement, shook her violently and then smacked her repeatedly around her face. The other two men set about Reggie, punching and kicking him unmercifully.

As Reggie Dixon lay unconscious in a heap on the floor, Charles Latimer sneered down into Chrissie's battered and bleeding face. "So, my *dear*! You thought that you could get away from me, did you?"

Chrissie wanted to die, as she felt the hot liquid trickle down between her legs.

"You do well to be afraid, my *dear*." He pushed her away in disgust as he noticed the pool of urine at her feet.

The scalding tears poured down her face, stinging the cuts and scratches. "*Please! No more!*" she begged.

"I haven't even started yet," Charles hissed into the pleading face as he pulled a hanky from his breast pocket and wiped his hands. "Get her out of here," he said tersely turning to the thugs. "Take her to *my* place!"

"What about him?" one of them asked, grinning moronically.

"Leave him."

"What boss?"

"You heard me, you great baboon. Leave him where he is. I think he's learnt his lesson. Besides I might have a use for him later."

Charles Latimer wouldn't have been so sure of himself if he had known what Reggie had learnt about him in the last few hours.

Chrissie thought she had finally gone crazy! There she was, sitting in the warmth and comfort of Charles Latimer's luxurious home, listening to the pleasant jingling sounds of Christmas carols coming from all around her, dressed in a beautiful red velvet evening gown, with a narrow trim of fur around the revealing neckline and wearing the most fabulous string of pearls with matching earrings she had ever set eyes on. Her hair gleamed with health and lay in soft waves around her shoulders and down her back, almost reaching her narrow waist.

When the two animals had brought her back in a state of severe shock to his place, they had left her in Charles' hands. They had had enough and were anxious to get away and spend their generous bonus on some last-minute Christmas presents for their wives and string of kids. Chrissie had been locked in one of the many bedrooms for days without a drink or a morsel of food. She didn't care! She only managed to stagger stupidly to the en-suite toilet a couple of times to relieve herself. (Completely unaware of the fact that she been disturbed from her enforced sleep by someone sneaking into her room to 'top' her up with yet another dose of heroin.)

She couldn't even summon up one ounce of energy to kick up a fuss. Only once she glanced lethargically into the mirror, merely shrugging when the deranged looking girl stared back at her.

When the dark-skinned woman unlocked the door and came into the room that night, she was a little shocked to see Chrissie sitting up and looking around her. Chrissie gazed at her without registering any surprise.

Dorothea Jones had thought she would have a struggle to wake the girl at all, but here she was, sitting there as though she had been waiting for her. She had been told to give her a little less of the drug each day, but she hadn't thought that the girl would come around so quickly. But she was still looking like a zombie, so Dorothea didn't worry too much. With a swift movement she covered the little metal tray containing the syringe and held it behind her back.

"Good evening, madam." Her perfectly white teeth gleamed in her round black face. How was she going to do it tonight? she wondered, as she went into the bathroom and turned on the bath taps, after she had concealed the tray under a fluffy white hand towel.

"Hello," Chrissie nodded as she passed by.

"Come." The woman poked her head out of the bathroom door.

Chrissie stood up slowly from the side of the bed and giggled when her legs felt decidedly wobbly. "Whoops!"

Dorothea came out and led her into the bathroom, where Chrissie allowed herself to be stripped of Charles' silk crimson kimono and helped into the deep, perfumed water, by a complete stranger. The steam rose all around her as she lay passively, without a hint of embarrassment and allowed the woman to lather her all over with the soft soapy sponge. When she tipped her head forward and the woman began the long process of washing the dirty, matted hair, she didn't even call out when the shampoo stung her eyes.

"Oh, before I forget," Dorothea said innocently when she had finished and wrapped Chrissie's head in a turban-style towel.

"What's that?" Chrissie blinked and wiped the soap from her eyes.

"I have to give you a little shot!"

"A what?" Chrissie frowned.

"An injection, madam," she explained calmly. "You haven't been very well and as I am a trained nurse the doctor instructed me to give you a little pain relief now and then." The lies came so easily to this practised woman.

"But I'm not in pain. I don t need anything."

"Oh, there's no need for you to worry, madam, and you don't want me to get into trouble, do you?" She chuckled as though they were sharing a big joke and thought to herself, 'I'm sure you're not in any pain, with all that stuff inside you.'

"Of course not," Chrissie said and screwed her eyes up when she saw what was under the cover on the tray.

Hissing loudly as the needle pierced her tender skin, Chrissie opened her eyes a little and watched as the small amount of golden liquid entered her vein. She noticed then for the first time, that on the insides of both of her arms there were a number of different coloured bruises and scratch marks. She didn't have time to make any comment about this. Within seconds a great whoosh of heat seared through her whole body, followed by the most wonderful feeling of euphoria that enveloped her as she felt herself climbing higher and higher as if she was about to reach the sky. Then, just as she was about to reach out and touch the shimmering rainbow she began slipping deeper and deeper into the beautiful, safe and glowing warmth of a place where no one or nothing could ever harm her again. Or so she thought!

The maid left her for a while as she pulled the plug from the bath and rubbed her roughly all over with the huge bath towel. No good trying to get her out of the bath in that condition. A while later when Chrissie began to stir she coaxed her into standing up and getting out of the bath.

Chrissie looked around inanely as the woman led her out to the bedroom and sat her, naked, before the dressing table. Humming lightly to herself, Dorothea took a great deal of care drying and brushing Chrissie's lovely hair. It took an age to get out the dreadful mess of knots and tangles but the woman was more than satisfied with the results when she stepped back to admire her handiwork. Then she told Chrissie to stand up while she dressed her in brand new sheer black underwear and then, slipping the long gown over her body, she stood back once again to admire the results.

"What do you think, madam?"

"Very nice, thank you!" Chrissie smiled back with a daft looking grin on her face. She was too far gone to worry about anything now.

"The master says you are to wait here for him." With that Dorothea left the room.

"OK" Chrissie nodded, wondering vaguely who the master was.

Chrissie perched on the stool before the dressing table stroking the softness of the lovely dress fabric. As her hands ran over the wonderful texture her thoughts wandered here there and everywhere, jumping alarmingly from one mad scene to another. Although her thoughts were muddled and vague, it didn't take her too long to be certain of one thing, at least. She must be in Charles Latimer's house. She looked more closely at her reflection and tried desperately to remember where she had got all the injuries. The lumps and bruises on her face and shoulders stood out lividly against her pale skin.

When she heard the door open and their eyes met in the mirror, it all came flooding back to her.

"Ready for supper?" he asked.

Chrissie rose on stiff legs and turned to face him. She knew that she should be flying at him and trying to rip the eyes from his face, but somehow the edge had been taken off the murderous loathing she felt for him. The thought that she had planned to do him some lethal damage made her tremble. Why should she go to hell for all eternity for a stinking rat like him, anyway? She would wait and when she felt better she would find a way, somehow, of destroying him. She still had to think of a reason to give him for having the gun. That was enough to deal with at the moment. Perhaps she could tell him she found it somewhere and was going to give it to him later. That excuse sounded ridiculous, even to her, but it was all she could think of for the time being.

"Yes," she answered quietly, deciding to play along with him for now.

"Will that be all, sir?" Dorothea asked politely, when she'd served the meal and filled their goblets with sparkling wine.

"Yes, thank you," he replied. "You can go now."

When they were alone Chrissie picked at the food, pushing it round and round her plate, only nibbling at tiny morsels. Her normally voracious appetite had deserted her, but she did her best to make it look as though she was enjoying the delicious looking roast beef with all the trimmings.

"Not hungry, my dear?" he enquired.

"Not much, no," she had to admit when she saw he was watching her closely.

"Well, you must try and eat a little, my dear. You haven't been well for some days. In fact you were in quite a mess when I found you."

Chrissie lowered her eyes and carefully sliced a sliver of meat, wishing that she had the nerve and the energy to hurl the knife across the table at him! She didn't even dare to look at him. Surely, the cunning bastard didn't think she had lost her memory? Finally she gave up all attempts at trying to eat the food and pushed the plate away.

"Sorry," she muttered. "But I've had enough."

"That's OK, and don't look so worried," he replied calmly, as though they were in the most normal of situations. "You can make up for it tomorrow."

Raising his glass he said, "Cheers!"

Completely forgetting her vow of abstinence, Chrissie lifted her own drink. "*Slainte* . . . and Merry Christmas!"

Charles laughed. "Christmas?"

Chrissie frowned. "What's so funny?"

"I'm afraid, Chrissie, you've missed Christmas for this year!"

Chrissie couldn't make out what on earth he was talking about. "What do you mean? Missed Christmas?"

"You've been practically out for the count for the last couple of days, my dear," he explained. "And besides . . . the doctor said it was better to leave you to sleep."

Chrissie swallowed the whole glass in one go and held it out for a refill. Her head was spinning and she just couldn't make sense of anything. After she had taken a deep drink from the fresh glass she managed to say, "I feel OK now. I think it's about time I went home."

"Oh no! That's not a good idea at all," Charles answered hastily. "You need to rest up for another few days at least. Then we will see."

'It *is* a good idea!" she insisted, rising awkwardly from the chair. "I want to go *now!*"

"Sit down and calm down, will you?" Charles tried to keep his annoyance at bay. "You can't go anywhere at this time of night. Let's see what you feel like tomorrow, shall we?"

Chrissie could see by the determined look on his face that there was no point in arguing with him, so she slumped back heavily on to the seat. "Give me another drink then."

"Charming," he muttered as he rose to get another bottle from the sideboard.

The alcohol seemed to be going to her head even more quickly than it normally did, Chrissie thought, but somehow it didn't really bother her too much. She welcomed the warm hazy feeling it gave her and it wasn't too long before she was holding out her empty glass for yet another refill. The effect of the mixture of drink and drugs was starting to give her a bit of courage. Squinting her eyes up at him across the table she asked abruptly, "How's Maria?"

Charles had known that it wouldn't be long before she started asking questions and was prepared.

"She's fine, Chrissie," he smiled benignly back. "Should be back at work in a couple of days."

"That's not what I heard!" She clenched her jaw.

"Well, I don't know who's been putting those ideas in your head, my dear." He lit one of his long cigarettes and blew the smoke towards the ceiling. "I can assure you she has come to no harm."

Chrissie felt the rage tear through her. She snatched up the glass from the table and hurled it with all her might towards his arrogant head. Screaming at the top of her voice she cried, "YOU FECKIN' LIAR!"

Charles dropped the cigarette into the ashtray and was beside her in a flash. Grabbing at her flailing arms he pinned them to her side and spat into her face. "Listen, you stupid little bitch! She got everything she deserved! And you'll get the same, if not worse, if you don't shut that foul mouth of yours right now!"

But there was no stopping her. Struggling and kicking she fought like a wildcat to get out of his grasp. Twisting and turning in a ferocious effort to free herself, she finally got the better of him when she landed a vicious blow to his shin and he roared in agony!

Running to the door she yanked it open, but before she had time to escape to the relative safety of the bedroom he was upon her. Grabbing her lovely dress he hauled her savagely back into the room, ripping the garment from neck to waist. He spun her round and smacked her across the face with tremendous force, and she lunged at him, her nails raking across his cheeks, leaving trails of dripping scarlet.

Charles looked down in disbelief as the blood trickled down his face and neck and seeped into the ruffles of his evening shirt. The flashback was terrifying. All he could see was the insane look on the face of that other young Irish bitch, so long ago now, who had gone for him with one of his own blades. (He had had plastic surgery in Paris, but it hadn't helped much. They told him the wound was too deep.) She'd ended up encased in a block of concrete and dropped off the coast of Galway somewhere. He didn't know where and he couldn't have cared less. She got everything she deserved. But it didn't stop the nightmares!

Chrissie didn't see the vicious backhander coming; she was beside herself with the worst, blinding rage she had ever felt in her life. The blood pounded in her head and the rasping, panting of her own breath drowned out every other sound.

Charles smashed into her face as though she were a fully-grown man, tearing an ugly ragged cut down her flushed cheeks with his heavy gold ring. He had always known that Chrissie could become a bit of a handful, but this was beyond endurance!

Shocked and stunned by the traumatic blow Chrissie was sent reeling backwards, crashing into the wall. The violent attack came so suddenly that she had no time to cry out. Charles strode across the room and spitefully grabbing at a handful of her hair, hauled her to her feet as she began to slither down the wall.

"Leave me . . . please," she managed to croak almost choking on a mouthful of blood and mucus.

"I haven't even started yet!" he breathed menacingly into her terrified face, tightening his grip on her hair and twisting it viciously. "If that little knock hasn't sent you into dreamland, then I know what will."

The room, his face, everything, swam before her. As her legs buckled beneath her Charles let her drop to the floor. He stood over her, seething. He would show this little troublemaker a thing or two. If she'd imagined she could get the better of him, she could think again!

He was sure that Chrissie had nothing to do with the disappearance of his cash, but Charles had recognised the *gun* immediately when he had discovered it wrapped in several layers of her clothing in the case. He couldn't quite work out how she had come by it, but that was of no consequence now. He had it back! But he had wondered for days just exactly what she thought she was going to do with it. Perhaps she was going to try and sell it? Blackmail him? But how would she have known it had been his? He had no idea. He had scoffed at the idea that she might be going to actually use it on someone. 'What, a good *catholic* girl like her? No way.' But he would get to the bottom of it he had assured himself.

He snorted in disgust when he saw the mess she was making on the carpet. Blood oozed from her mouth, the fresh wound on her face and her nose and ears, and would leave unsightly stains if he didn't clean away the evidence of their little *fracas*, as soon as possible. There would be some explaining to do the next day. Dorothea liked to keep a clean and tidy house. He leaned over and caught hold of a great length of her hair, now sodden with congealing blood. The wound from the night when she had slipped on the icy pavement, had reopened and was gushing profusely. He stared at it for a brief moment and then without another thought, took hold of a sticky clump of hair in both hands and dragged her lifeless form out of the room, along the corridor and into the bedroom. As he bumped her across the floor, he felt suddenly wearied by the whole thing. Dumping her in the middle of the room, he pulled a cover off the bed and threw it on top of her.

By the time Charles had cleaned up the mess in the other room, he was satisfied that he could pass off the faded marks as wine stains. He knew Dorothea wouldn't ask any silly question; maybe tut and fuss for a while, but soon make short work of removing all traces.

Before Charles could retire for the night, he just had one more little task to perform.

Chrissie hadn't moved from the spot where he had left her. Her breathing was laboured and every now and then she would give out a little moan, as if she was having a bad dream. Charles pulled off the cover and turned her over. The torn dress was bunched around her and the top half of her innocent young body was exposed. The lacy brassiere that he had had sent around from *La Femme* had almost been ripped off. Charles frowned when he saw her injuries.

"Must have sensitive skin," he mumbled uncaringly as he left her lying there for a few minutes while he went into the bathroom and prepared her 'medication'.

"Still," he grinned nastily. "This should ease the pain for a while!"

22

Jimmy Dwyer had never felt so helpless in all his life! He'd made three unsuccessful attempts to contact Chrissie, but was still racking his brains to come up with an idea of how to get in touch with her.

Gazing out morosely across the river, through the sheets of falling snow, his thoughts went back to their school days in Dublin. It seemed like another lifetime now and for a moment the desperate feeling of homesickness came over him, but he forced his mind back to more urgent matters.

Oblivious to the near arctic conditions around him, he sat rigidly hunched up on the lonely bench for nearly another hour considering his next move.

He had gone to the address that Betty had given him, fully confident that he would find her there and he wasn't too put out when he was unlucky the first time, but when he returned for the second and third time he got the terrible feeling that he would never see her again. On his final visit the evening before, one of the neighbours had told him that he hadn't seen her or the other girl up there, for weeks. It was then that the cold gnawing feeling began in his stomach. He wasn't mistaken, was he? Hadn't that lippy girl at the club told him that she was due back within days? Where was she then? And where was the other girl the neighbour had mentioned? Something was very wrong!

He gave a great shuddering sigh as the booming chimes from Big Ben announced the passing of another hour. What should he do?

He didn't fancy the idea of going back to the club again, but as he sat there staring at the twinkle of reflected lights in the slow-moving water, he grudgingly decided that this was precisely what he would have to do. It was the only link he had. Maybe there would be another girl on the desk, he told himself. One that wouldn't get his back up with her snooty attitude.

Rising slowly and stiffly, on legs that were almost numb with the cold, he shuffled off along the deserted embankment, desperately trying to convince himself that things would work out all right. He comforted himself with the thought that after all this there would be a simple explanation . . . and that he had been worrying himself sick for nothing.

With growing frustration, he stamped along the pavements, in an effort to get the blood circulating again and tried time and again to hail a taxi to take him to Mayfair; cursing loudly as yet another passed by. It was impossible! He would have to bloody walk!

Over an hour later and after asking directions about a dozen times, Jimmy finally found himself back at the Purple Parrot. He braced himself, as Harry smiled his welcome, pulling the door wide for him to enter.

"Looks like we're in for a real blizzard tonight, sir."

"I think you're right!" he replied with a wry grin.

As he entered the warmth, Jimmy sighed audibly with relief when he saw the rather slight redhead perched on the high stool behind the desk.

"Evening, miss," he smiled.

"Good evening, sir," she purred back, delighted by the handsome new face. "How can I help you?"

Trying a different approach, Jimmy replied. "I heard that my cousin was working here, so I came to drop off a Christmas present from her people back home."

"A little late for that, aren't you?" she grinned cheekily.

"Yes, I know, but I've only just found out where she's working."

"Who is it you're looking for then?" Jeanette asked, flicking her long hair over her narrow shoulders.

Jimmy took a deep breath; "Chrissie O'Rourke," he told her, the broad smile never leaving his face.

Jeanette's attitude changed immediately. She at once became extremely nervous and began to fiddle with a pile of membership cards on the counter. Not daring to meet his intense gaze, she said quickly, "No one here with that name, I'm afraid, sir."

Jimmy had had enough! Glancing swiftly over his shoulder he could see that he and the girl were alone in the lobby. As quick as lightning he reached out and grasped the girl firmly by her slender wrists. Pulling her towards him at the same time, he pushed his face so close to hers that he could smell her fear!

"I know you're lying, so listen! And listen good!" he hissed. "I've had enough of the old run around from the other feckin' eejit that I met in this bloody place! I *know* that Chrissie works here and I want *you* to tell me right *now* where she is! You understand?"

"You're hurting me!" the girl whimpered. "Let me go or I'll scream for security!"

"You can scream your feckin' head off for all I care, my girl!" Jimmy was incensed and increased the vice-like grip. "Just *tell me!*"

"Let go then!" Jeanette mumbled nervously, her eyes darting around, checking that they were still alone.

Jimmy could see that the girl was terrified, confirming that he was about to hear something he'd rather not.

"You won't do anything silly?"

She shook her head. "Promise."

He released her and stood back a little and waited, his stomach in knots. "Well?" He peered down into her pallid features. Just at that moment Harry pulled the door wide and a noisy group of men entered the club.

"Look," Jeanette whispered. "I can't talk now, but if you can hang around for a few hours, we can have a chat. Wait over there." She nodded towards the plush chairs by the wall.

Recognising the men, she put on her best smile and held out the book for them to sign.

Within minutes they had all passed through the lobby and into the piano bar. Jimmy stalked back over to the desk and muttered through his clenched jaw, "I don't have time to hang around, *miss!*"

"You'll have to," she told him. "I don't get a break until ten o'clock."

"Well, I'm not sitting here like a dummy!" Jimmy said irritably.

"You haven't got a choice," Jeanette replied abruptly. Then added a little more kindly. "But you could go down the road to that pub on the corner and have a few drinks to calm yourself down. You could wait for me there."

Jimmy leaned over the desk again. "You won't disappear?"

"No."

"Sure?"

"Yes."

"Right you are then, I'll go." He didn't know why, but he believed the girl. "Meet me down there at ten, OK?"

Jeanette nodded.

When he looked around the bar, Jimmy was relieved to see that the gang of lads from that other night were not in. In fact the place was half empty. Probably gearing themselves up for the New Year celebrations at the weekend, he mused, as he made himself comfortable in the corner of the snug.

Picking up a copy of the *Daily Mirror* that someone had discarded, Jimmy did his best to concentrate on the news and gossip of the day as he flipped through the pages. He hardly read a word. His thoughts were all over the place. Patience was not one of his strong points and by the time he had finished scanning the crumpled paper and had knocked back a third whisky, he found that he couldn't sit still any longer. Glancing up at the clock over the bar, he was annoyed to see that it was only 9.15. A sudden thought made him jump from the seat and make towards the door. Perhaps he'd been mistaken about her.

Suppose she was going to give him the slip! Suppose she has no intention of meeting him. Jimmy couldn't bear to think about it. With his hands shoved deeply down into his pockets, he kept his head lowered and walked as swiftly as he could. The blinding snowstorm that had intensified while he was in the pub was whipping great flurries of snow along the street to sting his face and eyes, until he could hardly see.

It wasn't a great distance, but in his panic Jimmy thought he would never get there. Squinting his eyes against the clouds of swirling flakes, he could just make out the dull illumination coming from the club's entrance further down the street. There was hardly any traffic at all and the road was eerily quiet, but as Jimmy neared the Purple Parrot, he heard the smooth hum of the expensive car as it swept by and came to a halt outside the club with a soft swish into the deepening drifts in the gutter. He paused for a moment, then stepped sideways, partially concealing himself in a doorway. He didn't want the embarrassment of bumping into anyone.

The ever-increasing harshness of the weather drove the snow in frenzied waves along the street and Jimmy pushed himself harder up against the door for shelter. Pulling his thick collar up against the icy particles that tore against his face, he turned his back to the street and groped through his pockets for his cigarettes. His fingertips were numb as he struggled to light one. He swore out loud when the matchbox fell into the growing heap of snow at his feet. As he fumbled in the slush to retrieve the matches he glanced up as he caught the sound of voices coming from the vehicle.

"Come along, my dear," Charles coaxed. "You know you'll enjoy yourself."

"No!" Chrissie shouted. "I *won't* enjoy myself! I'm feckin' freezing and I want to go home."

Jimmy nearly fainted! The power completely left his body and he found that he was unable to stand up from his crouching position. The shock of hearing her voice had stunned him. It was the last thing he had expected. With all the energy he could muster, he grabbed hold of the brass doorknob in front of him and forcibly hauled himself to his feet. Screwing his eyes up against the great flakes of snow that swirled around his head in a crazy dance he opened his mouth to call out. Nothing happened! He tried to move, but was rooted to the spot!

"Get out now!" Charles ordered. "It's damn freezing out here!"

"I don't care if you freeze your feckin' bollocks off!"

"Delightful!" Charles scoffed.

(Yes! That was definitely Chrissie a voice in Jimmy's befuddled brain said.)

With his heart beating in his chest fit to burst, try as he might, Jimmy couldn't move another muscle. He just stood there in a daze, clinging to the door for support and watched in horror as Chrissie was dragged from the car.

"That's enough, you little bitch!" Charles shouted. "You've got work to do tonight and if you don't then you know what will happen!" he finished with a sneer. As Chrissie was hauled to her feet on to the pavement, Jimmy finally found his voice and let out an animal-like roar! "CHRISSIE!"

They both turned together and watched in amazement as Jimmy stumbled towards them, his arms outstretched. As he came closer Chrissie's eyes widened in disbelief.

"No?" He groaned. "That couldn't be Chrissie O'Rourke!" She looked nothing like the image he had carried around in his mind for so long. He could make out the gaunt, haunted features even through his obscured vision. The wildness of her eyes and the wraith-like figure put him in mind of a picture he had once seen of a deranged woman that was supposed to haunt the corridors of Dublin castle.

"Jesus Christ!" She wiped the snow from her eyelashes and blinked rapidly. "*Jimmy?*"

Then he knew it was her.

"Get back in the car!" Charles spun her round and pushed her into the back seat.

"Let me go, you BASTARD!" Chrissie tried to lash out at him, but in her drug-induced haze, couldn't fight him off for long. The burst of energy quickly dissipated.

Jimmy reached the car just as Charles slammed the door shut and ordered the driver to go.

"Where to, boss?" he asked dumbly opening the window.

"The usual place, you fool!" Charles hissed, two inches from the pock-marked face. "I'll get Len to meet you there."

Lurching forward Jimmy made a grab at the handle and twisted and turned it frantically, but, of course, it was locked from the inside and his fingers were so cold that it was impossible for him to keep a grip for more than a few seconds. As the car pulled away from the kerb, it dragged him along for several yards before he was forced to release his hold and he fell face down on the frozen, gritty surface.

Charles Latimer gave the prone body a cursory glance, resisting the urge to give him a swift kick in the head, before he turned and strode into his club to make an urgent phone call.

Harry Black shook his head. Something else to tell the 'missus' later!

Jeanette had seen the spectacle from where she had been pacing around the lobby, deciding just what she should tell this 'cousin' of Chrissie's. She had only seen the girl once, so she had no idea what sort of person she was or what game she was playing, but Maria had been a good friend and she knew that somehow the two of them had become involved in something dodgy. She was petrified of Charles and his henchmen. She had experienced a few punishments when she first started work at the club and knew what they were capable of. So she stayed on their 'good side'. But when the girls had all got together and found out, one way or another, what had happened to Maria, they had risked the wrath of Mr Latimer and his cronies and had secretly taken it in turns to pay her visits at the hospital. Jeanette, above all, had been horrified at the extent of her friend's injuries and had actually gone into the little chapel in St Thomas's to light a candle for her; a thing she hadn't done since she'd left home about five years previously.

After she regained consciousness, Maria had wept bitterly, when she saw her friends coming one at a time to her bedside, but however much they tried to persuade her to tell them what it was all about, she wouldn't say a word. For a while she silently swore vengeance on her brother for causing her so much pain and anguish, but she also had a small corner in her heart that hoped he had got away safely.

Jeanette scooted back to her place behind the desk when she saw Charles approaching, with an expression on his face as though fit to kill! She smiled pleasantly and wished him a good evening. He didn't even glance in her direction. He had more important things on his mind. When she heard his office door slam, she jumped up again and rushed outside into the unrelenting snowstorm. By this time, Harry had helped Jimmy to his feet and was brushing down the sodden overcoat as best he could.

"Better get yourself off home, son!" was his advice.

Jimmy shook his head to clear his mind. He felt as though he was going crazy! He couldn't believe what he had just seen.

"Bring him in," Jeanette spoke rapidly. "Take him through into the kitchen, down the side way." She nodded over her shoulder.

"Do you think that's wise, miss?" Harry frowned.

"No, I don't, Harry," she replied through chattering teeth. "But we can't leave him out here, can we?"

By the time they led him into the warmth of the kitchen, the feeling was creeping back into his limbs.

"Take that off and drink this."

Jimmy obediently removed the sodden coat and handed it to her, then gratefully accepted the glass of brandy. She left the bottle beside him. The two French chefs glanced at him briefly, shrugged and then carried on with their extensive food preparations.

"You'll have to wait here now, until I've finished," Jeanette told him firmly. "*He* never comes into the kitchen, so you should be OK." Jimmy swallowed the burning liquid in one go and mumbled his thanks.

Jeanette went swiftly back to her position at the desk, glad to see that no other clients had arrived. The next half an hour dragged by as she sat impatiently waiting for her break. She passed the time by exchanging a few pleasantries with Harry who had made himself comfortable just inside the doors, in his huge porters chair. There was no way he was going back outside in this weather. Neither of them mentioned the incident.

When Beth strolled nonchalantly through the lobby, at least ten minutes late, Jeanette mumbled a disgruntled, "Where the hell have you been?"

"Keep your hair on!" Beth shot back. "I've been having a little chat with Mr Latimer."

"Oh?" Jeanette wondered if he had said anything about what had happened.

Beth knew what she was thinking when she caught the guilty expression and sneered, "Looks like our friend Chrissie has got herself into a whole lot of trouble!"

"Really?" The other girl feigned ignorance, as she stooped to pick up her long black velvet cape and handbag. Just then a cold breeze blew across the lobby as Harry opened the door to admit a few more people.

"Don't look so sodding innocent," Beth said under her breath, as she took up her position behind the desk, smiling politely at the same time at the new arrivals.

Jeanette turned away swiftly, her cheeks burning. How was she supposed to get that bloke past Beth now? she fretted as she walked off as calmly as she could. She had thought she could pass him off as a 'quickie' client that she was going to entertain during her break, but Beth was a wily cow. If she got a suspicion of who the bloke was, she would run and tell Charles. Jeanette guessed that during the conversation they'd had he must have told her to look out for him in case he came back into the club and started trouble. She was right.

Jimmy was still sitting at the table where she had left him. The ashtray in front of him was piled high with dog-ends and the brandy bottle was half empty by his elbow. He looked tired and despondent, but at least he was dry she thought. She had decided that she would take him back to her place, which luckily enough was only around the corner. (Very high rent, but she could afford it now. Miraculously, she didn't have any bad 'habits' like the majority of the other girls, she didn't even smoke, but she was very good, she was very good indeed, at her job!)

"Come on, mister! Get your coat on. We're leaving."

"Right," Jimmy sprang from the chair, his weariness leaving him as he felt renewed hope on seeing her again.

As they rose swiftly to the fourth floor in the lift, Jimmy glanced sideways at the girl. She hadn't uttered another word since she had grabbed his arm and ushered him out through the back door of the kitchen, along the alleyway and out into the street. The snow was falling on a light breeze now, but the ground was frozen solid. She held on to him for support as they picked their way slowly over the crunchy surface for five minutes until they reached a very exclusive apartment block around the corner.

She was quite a nice-looking girl, he thought, as he admired the half hidden face beneath the wide velvet cowl. It was a shame about the slightly crooked nose though.

"Do you want something to eat?" Jeanette asked him as she threw off her cloak and indicated that he should take off his coat and sit down.

"No thanks." Jimmy tried to smile as he pulled off the coat and hung it on the rack that she showed him, "I couldn't eat a thing."

"OK, but I'm making myself a sandwich. I'm starving. Won't be a tick."

Jimmy looked around the very comfortable apartment and thought that she must be earning a fortune to be living in such a great place.

Jeanette was back in no time with a plate piled high with ham sandwiches and a glass of water. She offered him the plate.

"No, really." He shook his head. Taking a deep breath he said uneasily, "I thought we were going to have a little chat, as you called it?"

Jeanette sat opposite him on a low, leather-padded stool and wondered where she should start. Playing for time she chewed slowly on her sandwich.

"Well?" he prompted, beginning to get impatient, but dreading at the same time what she was going to tell him. She swallowed hard and said, "OK, but go and help yourself to a drink first. Over there, on that side table."

Jimmy didn't know how much more of this stalling he could endure, but nevertheless, went and poured himself a glass of red wine from the decanter. "Right! Let's have it then!" he said curtly as he sat down again.

"What's your name first?" she asked.

"Jimmy Dwyer. What's yours?"

"Jeanette Phillips."

"Well." He stared at her. "That's got the introductions over with."

"Was that the girl you were looking for?" She asked quietly. He knew what she meant. Jimmy clenched his hands tightly together. "Yes, I'm afraid it was."

"Well, to be honest with you, I don't really know a whole lot about what's going on between her and the boss. I just know that she seems to have got herself mixed up in some funny business, and whatever she was up to it involved a very good friend of mine. The one she shared the flat with. Maria."

"What do you mean? Funny business?" Jimmy was becoming more agitated.

"I can't tell you that because I don't know, but it must have been pretty serious because Maria ended up in hospital on a life-support machine."

"Oh, God!" Jimmy jumped up and started pacing around the room, running shaking hands through his thick hair. "Did she die?" he asked in a whisper.

"Almost," Jeanette answered sadly. "But she's on the mend now. They told me yesterday that she should be out next week, if she keeps on improving!"

Jeanette went on to tell him that she had only met Chrissie briefly and had thought what a great-looking girl she was. Too good for the Purple Parrot, she admitted. She was also very surprised to hear, from the other girls, that Chrissie was due to go out to the States very shortly after she had applied for the job at the club. They were all as jealous as hell about it!

"Not so great-looking now," Jimmy scowled. "What on earth has happened to her?"

This handsome man appeared to be very naïve, Jeanette thought to herself, but she realised that if he was sincere about helping Chrissie out of the awful situation she was in, she had better tell him what she thought. "You might not like to hear what I am going to say," she warned him.

"Just say it, will you?" Jimmy breathed hotly, even more afraid now, coming to stand in front of her.

"I think she's got herself into a really heavy scene, if you know what I mean?" She replied, looking up at him.

"No." Jimmy prayed that she wasn't going to say that she had become a prostitute.

"For God's sake, man!" Jeanette was getting annoyed by his apparent blindness.

"Couldn't you see by the state she was in? She's a bloody drug addict! A junkie, you fool!"

Jimmy felt his head go light and the room swam before him. Had he heard right? A junkie? No! Not Chrissie? Not his Chrissie?

"I'm not saying it was *her* decision to go down that road," she said, a little more gently. "But our dear boss has ways and means to deal with people who upset him, if you know what I mean."

"I think I'm getting the picture," Jimmy muttered as he swung around and helped himself to another drink, barely able to contain his rage. Jeanette checked her watch. "I've got to get back soon," she told him. "What do you want to do?"

"I take it that character I saw earlier on with her was the dear boss?"

"Yes."

"I'll tell you what I want to do then, shall I? I'd like to go back there right now, drag him out into the street, throw him in the gutter where he belongs and kick the feckin' shit out of him!" He had a cold insane look in his eyes.

"That would be a very stupid thing to do, Jimmy, believe me!"

"But it would give me great satisfaction." he smirked.

"I know that, but it wouldn't do Chrissie any good, would it?" She tried to placate him. The last thing she wanted was for Charles Latimer to put two and two together and come to the conclusion that she had been gossiping to strangers.

"Where do you think she is?"

"Probably at his place, but I'm not sure."

"Where does he live?"

"Now *that*, even I can't tell you!"

"But everyone must know!"

"I wouldn't say that exactly. He's very security minded when it comes to his own safety. The only decent one who might be able to help is Reggie, the manager of the club, but come to think of it, he hasn't been seen for a while either."

"What about your friend? Maria was it? Maybe she would know?"

"I don't think so," Jeanette answered quickly. "Besides I think she would be very reluctant to give you any information after the treatment she got."

"Yeah, you're right. Wouldn't be fair."

Jeanette excused herself for a minute to go and freshen up. "I've got to go now," she told him when she came back. "Otherwise Beth will be throwing a fit!"

Jimmy was sitting on the couch with his head in his hands. Jeanette felt sorry for him. "Do you want to stay the night?"

"No thanks." He sprung from the seat.

"Oh, don't look so scared!" She laughed. "I don't mean as a 'paying guest'."

Jimmy blushed furiously.

"N-n-no, I meant I have to get back to my uncle's," he stammered. "I'm staying with the family and anyway," he grinned crookedly. "I'm supposed to be at work tomorrow!"

"Really?"

"But it goes without saying, they can forget that! I won't be hauling bricks up ladders for a while! Not until I get this mess sorted out." He tried to make it sound light even though his heart was filled with vengeance and bitter hatred. Jeanette scribbled her phone number down for him. "Take this in case you need to get in touch, but don't, whatever you do, call me at work!" she warned.

"Thanks." He shoved the little card into his top pocket.

"Here's my uncle's number!' He wrote it on the back of his empty cigarette packet. "You call me too if you've any news, OK?"

"Sure." She smiled back.

When they reached the street again they were pleased to see that there were only a few random snowflakes drifting through the air now.

"Bye then, and good luck," Jeanette said as she turned the corner. "Let me know how it goes."

"Bye," Jimmy waved as he watched her go, amazed at how she could walk on such high heels, especially in this weather. "And thanks a million," he called out.

The treacherous surface was a nightmare to navigate. More than once Jimmy almost fell flat on his face as he made his way cautiously along the deserted pavements towards the cab rank that

Jeanette had mentioned. He wanted to cry with relief when he saw the line of taxis with their 'for hire' signs blazing.

As he sat in the back of the taxi, Jimmy's mind was working overtime. He was desperate to find a solution. He'd heard awful stories about girls that had gotten themselves into the same situation that Chrissie was now in, but what could he do? His heart was breaking as the vision of her staggering around the street in the snow flooded though his mind. If it were the last thing he did, he would pay back that evil bastard for what he had done to her! But then the most horrifying thought of all came into his head and his heart skipped several beats. It suddenly came to him that Charles had obviously known they knew each other and that was why he had bundled her back into the car. What would he do to her now? "Jesus Christ!"

"What's that, mate?" the cabbie asked.

"Sorry, just dropped me wallet!" Jimmy lied quickly.

"Don't wanna do that mate," the cabbie joked.

An idea came to him. "Can you pull over please?"

"We're not there yet, mate."

"No I know, but I've just remembered I was supposed to call someone!"

"Hang on a mo then," the cabbie said. "There's a phone box down here somewhere."

"Right . . . Grand . . ."

"Bird is it?" The driver grinned, showing a big gap in his front teeth as he turned to wink at his passenger.

"Yeah, something like that!" Jimmy winked back. "Can you wait for a minute?"

"Course mate, but don't do a runner on me, will ya?"

"No I won't do that. Just wait here," Jimmy answered, a little offended. "I'll be right back."

He couldn't believe how easy it had been to call the Purple Parrot and get Reggie's home phone number. He had tried to speak in an English accent as he explained to Beth that he was an old friend of Reggie's and was only in town for a few days and had forgotten to bring his address book. Beth was so busy dealing with a crowd of drunken, over-excited men out on a stag night that she quickly dealt with the call. Not for one second did she realise who she was speaking to. If she had, she wouldn't have been so ready with the information and would have saved herself a broken nose, multiple cuts and bruises and a lengthy visit to the casualty department!

"Are you all right?" Reggie called out from the sitting room.

Jimmy splashed his face with cold water and prayed that he wasn't going to vomit again. What Reggie had told him had put the fear of God in him and had scared him so much that he completely lost control. When Reggie had seen the ruddy complexion turn to a sour shade of yellow then to pure white, he hurriedly ushered the distraught friend of Chrissie's into the bathroom.

He had been shocked by the appearance of Jimmy Dwyer at his newly repaired front door, but when he listened to what he had to say, he asked him in. He could tell that he was dealing with an honest man and wanted to do everything he could to help him. It wouldn't make any difference now what he divulged. So, after he listened while Jimmy told him about Jeanette and what had happened outside the club, he told him everything that he knew himself. From beginning to end.

His suitcases were packed. His tickets and passport were tucked away in his new suit and all his savings had been transferred to an account in the Bahamas. He'd changed his mind about Greece. (Too easy to track him down there.)

The flat had been sold and very soon he would be on his way to a new life. Bobby would be waiting for him at the airport and they could finally lead the life together they had been keeping under cover for so long! No more blackmailing from Charles Latimer. No more threats to reveal the true nature of his sexuality. Freedom!

Jimmy crept sheepishly back into the room wiping his mouth on the back of his hand.

"OK?"

"Mmm," Jimmy replied. "Sorry about that."

"Don't give it another thought. I've seen a lot worse!"

"Well, I know it all now," Jimmy said morosely, slumping back into the seat.

"I've only told you the stuff I know about, Jimmy."

"Don't you think that's enough, man?"

"There's plenty more, but I'm sure Chrissie will fill you in on all that when you see her."

"But I still don't know where she is." Jimmy shook his head in despair. "You certain she's not in his place?"

"As certain as I can be. I told you he's not so stupid or careless as to leave her alone in his house. She was probably there for a while, but now . . . I just don't know, and he wouldn't let her go back to Bayswater, that's for sure."

"I'm sure I heard him tell whoever was driving the car to take her to the 'usual place'."

"What?" Reggie burst out, leaping from his chair and grabbing hold of Jimmy's bent shoulders. "What did you say?"

Jimmy repeated, "He told him to take her to the usual place." Then he frowned anxiously. "Doesn't that mean back to wherever he lives?"

"No, old man," Reggie shook his head gravely. "I'm very sorry to say that it doesn't mean that. It doesn't mean that at all!"

Jimmy felt his stomach begin to churn again and could barely mutter, "What *does* it mean then?"

Reggie didn't answer for a long while. Finally he said, "I have a phone call to make. Sit tight for a minute.'

"Right."

When he came back into the room he was wearing his long black overcoat.

"You going out?"

"Yes, and I want you to stay here."

Jimmy bounded from the chair. "No way!"

"There could be trouble if you come too," Reggie tried to warn him.

"I don't feckin' care what trouble there is!" Jimmy shouted back. "I'm not sitting here like a mug all night wondering what the feckin' hell's going on! She could be half-dead by now for all I know!"

"Just calm down, will you?" Reggie spoke evenly. He knew that there was no way this highly agitated young man could remain inactive when he had to rescue a damsel in distress, or even worse; so against his better judgement he reluctantly agreed to let him go with him.

As Reggie drove carefully through the slush and ice of the friendless streets, Jimmy sat stiffly beside him, staring straight ahead and praying to all the saints that they would get there, wherever that was, before anything worse happened to Chrissie.

If they'd had an inkling of what was actually going on at that very moment, Reggie Dixon wouldn't have driven quite so slowly over the slippery roads.

23

Chrissie crouched in a far corner of the dank, gloomy warehouse and shivered uncontrollably. The agonising pains that shot through her body were sending her crazy. She had already been sick down her clothes and had torn off her short black velvet jacket in disgust. The nauseating stench coming from the pool of vomit by her feet made her heave convulsively. Almost choking in an effort to keep her pitiful sobs subdued, she covered her mouth with both hands and tried not to draw attention to herself.

After Charles had sent her sprawling into the back of the car, she had screamed in violent protest, banging on the dividing glass to the driver, demanding vehemently that she be let out of the car! She shouted and swore at him, threatening him with everything she could think of, but, of course, he completely ignored her. She sat there, on the floor of the car, panting like a caged animal, cursing Charles Latimer to hell and back and wishing the seven deadly plagues to rain down on him! All together! As her outburst gradually subsided, silent tears erupted and gushed down her burning cheeks.

"Oh Jimmy," she moaned.

Gathering what little strength she had left she pulled herself painfully up on to the seat and tried to make sense of what was going on. She couldn't believe that Jimmy Dwyer was actually here, in England. And even more puzzling was what was he doing at the club? Her brain couldn't take it all in. Nothing made any sense any more. Her whole life had been turned upside down and the worst and most degrading thing of all was she had come to realise, in the last few days, that Charles had somehow led her into the vile, corrupting world of drug-taking.

"Jesus, the shame of it!" She wiped fresh tears away.

Her arms ached from the puncture marks that ran up and down her veins and she ran her thin fingers tentatively up the sleeves of her new jacket over the tender flesh. She remembered the horror of when she finally realised what he had done to her. She had caught him filling the syringe in the bathroom at his house one morning, after she had been complaining of stomach pains. The acrid smell she'd noticed after he'd gone to get her a little something from the medicine cupboard baffled her. She'd never smelt anything like it in her life. On wobbly legs she'd peeped through the crack in the door and watched in amazement as he heated some white powder in a spoon until it turned to liquid and then placing it carefully on the edge of the sink, proceeded to fill the syringe with it.

"What's that?" she'd demanded, pushing the door wide open.

Charles spun around guiltily. "Something for the pains in your stomach," he told her smoothly.

"Why can't I just have some pills?" she'd asked suspiciously.

"Too late for pills," he'd sneered, grabbing her with his free hand and dragging her back to the bed.

Chrissie was too shocked to protest. She watched in silent horror as he squeezed her arm until one of her veins stood up, bright and purple, let go quickly and shoved the needle into her arm.

"Lie down!" he ordered sharply.

Chrissie didn't have any choice; the terrific rush to her head sent her reeling backwards and she collapsed on to the pillows.

During the next week or so she didn't bother to protest any more. He was right. Her little 'top-ups', as he liked to call them, took away all her aches and pains and, in fact, the euphoric glow was wonderful, for a while anyway.

Chrissie risked a quick glance over at the two animals guarding her. They were sitting on a couple of upturned crates under a hanging light bulb, with their backs to her, and although they kept up a mumbled conversation between themselves she couldn't make out a word they were saying. She wondered what was going to happen to her next. Guessing the way the two brutes earned their living, Chrissie had expected a good hiding, at least. She was surprised that all they did was to force her down on to the filthy stone floor in the furthest corner of the creepy old warehouse and tell her to keep her mouth shut.

Turning her face away, she pulled her knees up and wrapped her thin arms tightly around them. Resting her weary, befuddled head against the mildew-covered brick wall she shuddered violently. If only the pain would go away! As she screamed silently for some relief, she knew in her heart that the only way the excruciating cramps all over her skinny, bruised body would ease, would be when Charles appeared. In utter repulsion, she felt herself praying that it wouldn't be too long before he put in an appearance. The 'animals' were obviously waiting for him.

Trying to force her mind away from the wracking pains, Chrissie strained to think about something else. Jimmy Dwyer! Rosie! Betty! Daisy! Old ma Murphy! Anything! But it proved too difficult. Her thoughts came and went in frightening flashes that left her even more confused. Every now and then a tiny idea of trying to make an escape broke through the mental anguish, but she couldn't keep hold of that idea for more than a few seconds. She didn't have the strength to run anyway.

The scraping of the wooden crates on the bare stone flags made her jump. The tall sinister figure of Charles Latimer was outlined against the dull orange glow from the open doorway. He slammed it behind him and strode in.

"Get out of here!" he said to Alf and Len who were hovering around, not sure what he wanted them to do.

"Right, boss."

And they were gone. Charles walked slowly to the far corner where he had located the soft whimpering.

Chrissie was too terrified to meet his menacing gaze as he loomed over her, staring down in disgust at the woeful, bedraggled sight. The light was so dim that he couldn't make out her features clearly, but the stench that was coming from her was enough to turn his stomach. The anger was still raging inside him. This little bitch had caused him enough problems and it didn't take him long to decide what course of action he would take to rid himself of her infernal interference in his affairs.

He had decided, on his way over to the docks, that he would interrogate her first, to find out where she had got the weapon. He had thought it over and decided that the only likely explanation was that she had stolen it from Casa Miguel, but he wanted Chrissie to confirm this. Nothing had reached him from Miguel Fernandez, so it was likely that he hadn't yet discovered its disappearance.

The morning after he'd had the altercation with that thieving young fool, somebody had obviously found the gun in the garden where he had carelessly flung it in temper. He'd been as high as a kite on a heady mixture of the finest cocaine and alcohol that night and when he had, some time later, received the call from

Miguel soon after his return to Ireland, he'd breathed a sigh of relief and vowed he would be forever in his debt. Death Row was not an appealing thought!

The other thing that was worrying Charles now was that he wasn't a hundred per cent sure any more that she was as innocent as she had made out concerning the missing cash. (Trying to get anything out of Maria now was impossible. The hospital was obligated to inform the police about her injuries and he didn't want to contact his 'friend' in the vice squad, as he'd heard rumours that he was 'going straight'. 'Once a cop, always a cop,' Charles ruefully admitted to himself when he heard. 'Still, we had a good run!'

Charles bent over and prodded Chrissie roughly on the shoulder. "Get up!"

Chrissie swallowed hard and made a futile attempt to get to her feet.

"Stop messing about and do as you're told!" he shouted.

"I c-c-can't," she stammered. "My legs hurt!"

"Stand UP! You stupid bitch!" he yelled, yanking her to her feet. Groaning pitifully she stared up in horror into his barbaric expression and waited for the blows to rain down. His fingers dug spitefully into her tender flesh as he breathed hot fumes of rage into her terrified face. Shoving her up against the wall, he released his vicious grip on her arms and clutched her throat in both hands in a grip that was so tight Chrissie thought she was about to die! Loosening his fingers slightly, when he saw her face turning purple, Charles spoke in menacing undertones, "Where did you get the gun? And what were you going to do with it?"

Chrissie's eyes bulged under her purple swollen lids as she fought for breath. Knowing that if he didn't give her some air she would probably pass out, Charles slackened his hold and without another word let her drop back to the floor, where she landed in a coughing, sobbing heap, her face and hair skimming the edge of the pool of vomit.

"You bastard!" she croaked, half hoping he wouldn't hear her. "Why are you doing this to me?"

But, of course, he did hear her. Lashing out with a well-aimed kick he sent her sprawling backwards along the slimy ground. She screamed out in agony as she crashed against the brick wall. "Because, you little whore," he yelled maniacally. "You could have landed me in more trouble than you could ever imagine, in that screwed-up little brain of yours! Now tell me where you got it!"

Chrissie didn't care any more. There was nothing more he could do to her. Defenceless and spiritless, she dragged herself to a sitting position and shook her head. What did it matter now? He was probably going to kill her anyway. Where was the great bloody Jimmy Dwyer now? In a pub somewhere, getting pissed out of his brain, she supposed. So revolted by the very sight of her, that he was drowning his sorrows in a vat of whisky before he leapt on to the boat back home. Sod him anyway! Eegit!

"I'm waiting!" he said in a low threatening voice.

Chrissie ran her tongue over her cracked lips as she peered at him through her swollen bloodshot eyes. He paced around in front of her, his footsteps echoing eerily around the tall empty building. "Can I have a fag?" she dared to ask.

"No, you can't," he replied nastily. "Not until you tell me everything I want to know."

"Pig!" she shot back.

He just laughed as he drew his cigarette case from his pocket, took out a king-size, lit it and then came over and blew the smoke into her face.

"Pig!" she repeated with more bravado than she felt.

"I hate to tell you this, Chrissie." He sneered down at her. "But right now you look and stink more like a pig than I ever will."

"Well, whose fault is that then?" she sniffed loudly, tears filling her eyes and pouring down her battered face. "I wouldn't be in this state," she shivered convulsively, "if it wasn't for you!"

"I'm getting bored with this, my dear." He crushed the half-smoked cigarette out by her foot. Before she realised what he was doing he had pulled the gun from his pocket, knelt on one knee and pushed it roughly into the side of her face. "Well?"

"Rosita gave it to me!" she yelled, before she could stop herself.

"You damn liar!" He drew back his arm as if to strike her and then thought better of it. "You stole it! Right?"

"Yes, yes, OK, OK! I bloody stole it!"

"That's better." He patted her on her wet cheek, stood up and wiped his hand on the side of his trousers. Chrissie leaned further back against the wall as if she could distance herself from him. What was he going to do now? Dropping her thudding head into her hands she wept uncontrollably. What had she ever done to deserve all this?

The torturous feelings were unbearable, not only from the terrifying thoughts of her impending doom, but also the increasing agony throughout her body that was sending her demented. When he didn't speak for a while, she finally found the courage from somewhere deep inside her to plead with him. "Charles?" she managed to whisper.

"What?"

"Can you give me something?"

"Hah!" he scoffed, taking out and lighting another cigarette. "You really are the limit, my dear! Tell you what," he said smoothly, coming closer and passing it to her. "You tell me what I want to know and then . . ." He slid his hand into his breast pocket and pulled out a long narrow silver box and waved it in front of her. "We'll see."

Chrissie snatched at the cigarette, took a deep drag and spluttered and coughed until she was red in the face. With every gasp an agonising jolt shot through her crushed ribs. "OK," she agreed, when the outburst had subsided. "Anything you want to know, just ask." Her greedy eyes never left the container.

In her desperately shameless state Chrissie blurted out almost everything. Once she started she couldn't stop. At times she was almost incoherent as she rambled from one disclosure to another. One of the parts she left out was the real reason that she stole the weapon. She had skated nervously around that part by telling him she took it for her own protection. She thought that living in London and working at the club might get a bit scary at times. She wasn't even bothered when she told him that she thought that it was probably Maria's brother Charlie who had taken the money from the case that night. Balls to the lot of them! she'd thought. The quicker she got it over with the quicker her nightmare would end. With one small 'top up', her life would become bearable again and maybe somehow she could get back on his good side.

"Good girl!" Charles smiled pleasantly as he helped her to her feet.

The touch of his hand so cold on her arm made her cringe, but she tried to smile back at him, her face a pitiful grotesque mask. "Come and sit down over here, under the light."

311

Chrissie held up the long skirt of her dress and shuffled slowly and painfully after him on legs so weak that they barely held her up. Her whole body was covered in a film a cold sweat and her teeth chattered noisily as she took one tiny step after another towards the wooden crates that he had straightened up. Her vision was blurred by the puffiness around her eyes and she had to squint to see where she was going. Charles watched her as she came towards him and thought briefly, "Pity. Could have had a good thing going there!"

Chrissie was unrecognisable from the innocent, yet brazen, young woman who had first entered his life such a short time ago. The barefooted, broken girl crept towards him; her once glorious tresses clung to her bony shoulders in lank greasy clumps and the bright sparkle that once shone from those bold brown eyes was gone and had been replaced by dull, defeated acceptance.

She was no good to him anymore, he thought. Everything had taken the wrong turning. Still, there were plenty more where she came from. Shame though, he could have made a lot of money out of her, one way or another.

He had all the information he needed now, to hell with the police. He would risk a discreet night visit to St Thomas's and by the time he'd finished with Maria Costello she'd wish she'd never been born. Not to mention that damn brother of hers. With his contacts, though, it shouldn't take too long to track young Charlie boy down!

Violent tremors ran through her body as Chrissie lowered herself on to the splintered wooden crate and held out her arm. Her body swayed as she sucked in her breath and watched in morbid fascination as the dark amber liquid entered her bloodstream. In her poor befuddled condition, Chrissie was completely unaware that Charles had administered a far stronger amount of the noxious substance than he usually did. Her head fell backwards as the searing heat surged through her, reaching her brain in an instant and he just managed to catch her with one hand before she slithered unconscious on to the cold unyielding surface at his feet. Leaving her in a helpless heap, he quickly replaced the syringe in its box and put it back into his pocket.

The next part of his plan was to get her, unseen, from the old warehouse and drag her down to the river. He found the chore distasteful, but had decided that if there were to be no snags he would have to do it himself. Reggie had let him down badly and he didn't trust any of the other 'goons' enough to carry out this little operation . . . and to keep quiet about it.

Turning her over with the toe of his shoe. Charles gazed down at the broken body. 'She looks like a dirty old rag doll that has been tossed aside, that nobody wants to play with any more,' he mused coldbloodedly, as he pulled on his black leather gloves. Bending over her, he pulled her upright and then, putting his hands under her armpits, dragged her backwards towards the door. The only thought in his head now, as he bumped the lifeless form over the uneven cracked slabs, was to get this over with as quickly as possible, get back to the house and pick up his luggage. The thought of his idyllic country retreat in County Wicklow was becoming more inviting by the minute.

Dropping Chrissie carelessly back on to the floor, he swiftly opened the slatted wooden door and glanced briefly up and down the deserted street. He looked up at the sky and cursed softly on seeing the thickening fresh fall of snow, dancing and swirling up and down the narrow street. The light at the other end where the street met the main road was barely visible through the heavy blanket, but Charles was relieved that he could just make out that there was nobody else around. 'What damned fool would be out on a night like this anyway?' he asked himself, shivering as he withdrew into the gloomy interior.

"Come on, my dear," he smirked. "There's no one to save you now. Let's get this over with, shall we?"

Confident that he was completely unobserved, Charles propped open the door with a loose brick that he noticed and pulled her roughly over the step.

He wouldn't have felt so sure of himself if he'd been remotely aware of the imminent arrival of two men who cared a great deal for Chrissie. (One of whom had every intention of putting an end to Charles Latimer's reign of terror and depravity once and for all!)

24

"Is it much further?" Jimmy asked, as he peered out through the steamed up windows.

"Couple of minutes," Reggie answered gruffly.

"You sure she'll be there?"

"Yes."

"And him?"

"Certain."

The driving conditions were worsening and Reggie was forced to slow the car down to a crawl. The last thing that they needed was for the vehicle to slide out of control on black ice.

"Can't you go any faster, man?" Jimmy asked, his voice rising with impatience.

"Calm down, will you, for God's sake? We'll be there any minute now."

"Sorry."

Within seconds Reggie pulled up at the kerb in a deep drift of snow.

"We here?" Jimmy asked softly.

"Not quite, but I think we'd better walk the rest of the way."

"Why?"

"Because . . ." Reggie tried to keep his voice calm. "Firstly, we don't know who exactly will be there and secondly that street is so steep and narrow, that there will be no way of making a quick getaway if we get stuck."

"Oh, right," Jimmy nodded.

"You ready?" Reggie looked at him steadily.

Taking a deep breath Jimmy answered, "Ready."

Reggie left the the engine running. If they were going to succeed in their mission, they would need to flee the scene with the utmost speed. He looked up and down the empty streets. Nobody was in sight. He would risk it. Even the car thieves would surely take the night off in weather like this! "Let's go!"

Jimmy stumbled from the car into the puddles of slush and ice and followed Reggie around the corner, pulling up the collar of his overcoat in an attempt to shield himself from the cutting blasts of freezing particles that ripped at his face. Clinging on to the wall with one hand for support he called out to Reggie, who was striding ahead with amazing surefootedness. "Hang on!"

Reggie spun around and waited for him to catch up. "Shut up, you fool!" he hissed.

Jimmy shrugged his apology.

Just then, over Reggie's shoulder, he noticed a vague shadowy movement further down the street. "Am I imagining it, or is that someone down there?" he whispered, close to Reggie's grim face.

Looking quickly around Reggie screwed up his eyes and peered through the veil of falling snow.

"Get back!" He grabbed Jimmy's arm and pulled him hard up against the wall. "Don't move," he ordered under his breath. Barely able to breath, Jimmy did what he was told. The two men waited and watched. Although their vision was obscured by the relentless blizzard, they could see the dark shape of the back of Charles Latimer's limousine.

"Stay here," Reggie's voice was barely audible.

"No way!" Jimmy replied, not quite so quietly.

Reggie heaved a sigh of frustration. "Stay behind me, then."

"Right."

Trying to keep a foothold on the slippery surface Jimmy obediently crept along behind him, down the increasing incline of frozen cobbles. As they neared the dark, bent figure, they could just make out, through the dense swirling flurries, that he was dragging and bumping what looked like a body down the street.

"Oh no!" Reggie gasped. He had thought that Charles would get her into his car and then after that would do whatever he was going to do with her. It hadn't occurred to him that he would try to dispose of her quite so quickly. There couldn't be anyone else with him though, he guessed, with relief, or he wouldn't be doing his own dirty work.

"What? What is it?" Jimmy asked frantically, even more alarmed now by his tone.

"He's taking her to the river!"

"Jesus Christ!"

Without another thought in his head, other than saving his darling girl from certain death as she was flung into the murky depths of the river, he hurtled down the street, screaming and yelling. "YOU FECKIN' BASTARD! LEAVE HER ALONE!"

Charles Latimer was stunned for a moment when he heard the vehement outcry. But only for a split second did he hesitate. Taking a firmer grip on the dead weight, he quickened his backward pace as he hauled the stupefied girl savagely down towards the turbid waters. No one was going to stop him now! He'd deal with these idiots next!

Reggie and Jimmy were almost upon him as he reached the edge of the concrete steps. "STOP!" Reggie and Jimmy both screamed together.

Charles threw Chrissie callously on to the top step and then stood and twisted around to look at the two men who were racing towards him. Pleased with himself for having the foresight to re-load his old and almost forgotten gun, he slipped his hand into his pocket and pulled out the weapon. Pointing the gun directly at them he called out, "Stay right there!"

Jimmy's eyes nearly popped out of his head when he saw what Charles was holding.

Reggie and Jimmy slithered to a halt only a few feet before him. Jimmy groaned loudly as he caught sight of the crumpled body lying so still and so dangerously close to the forbidding black water, her arms outstretched, as though inviting death.

Reggie wasn't at all surprised. Just what he'd expected of his old boss. But he had to think quickly now, or they would be in serious trouble. "Don't be stupid, Charles." His voice was calm and reason-able. "How do you think you'll get away with this?"

"Oh, I don't think, old man," he sneered back. "I *know!*"

Jimmy was seething with such a boiling rage that he felt as though his brain would explode. He'd never experienced such feelings in his life! Gasping to catch his breath he clenched his fists so tightly the skin felt as though it would tear from his bones, his eyes never leaving the prostrate form. "You evil swine!" he hissed though gritted teeth. "I'll kill you for this!"

"Huh!" Charles' face was contorted with fury as he waved the gun before them. "I doubt that, you ignorant paddy!"

In one swift movement, Charles spun around, lifted his foot and with a vicious kick sent Chrissie O'Rourke sprawling headlong down the short flight of steps into the darkness of the waiting river! Reggie called out in horror, screaming and begging him to stop, but he was beyond reason. As Jimmy saw him lift his foot, he knew exactly what he was about to do. An instant later he was upon him, but it was too late to stop him! The loud splash of Chrissie's body as it hit the water completely unhinged him. Jimmy lashed out with uncontrollable rage and without a thought of the weapon that had been brandished so boldly in his face a second or two ago, he threw himself at Charles Latimer and felled him with a ferocious blow to the side of his head. As he crashed to the ground screaming in agony, Jimmy kicked him mercilessly all over his body, again and again, until he could hardly draw breath.

Reggie caught him by the shoulders and tried to drag him off but his strength was no match for Jimmy. "Jimmy! Jimmy! Stop it! You'll kill him!" he begged, as he seized hold of his thick hair and yanked his head backwards.

'Good!" Jimmy screamed insanely.

But finally, with great reluctance, Jimmy relented and stood back, panting like an animal as he glared down at the cringing being before him.

"Look!" Reggie suddenly cried out, pointing towards the river. "I think I can see something! She's caught on a metal pole or something."

"What!" Jimmy spun around, his eyes wide and disbelieving. "Where?"

"Come on! For God's sake!" Reggie was already halfway down the steps. Jimmy was close on his heels as they peered through the gloom. "Over there!"

"Jesus!" Jimmy ripped off his coat, shoved Reggie out of the way and plunged straight into the icy water.

As Chrissie had rolled into the river, somehow her long hair had become entangled on an old piece of railing that jutted out, close to the water's edge. She was floating face upwards, her arms and legs extended as though she was performing a strange dance.

"Over *there*! Over *there*!" Reggie yelled, as he too ran down the slippery steps.

"Where? I c-c-can't see her!" Jimmy spluttered and coughed, choking on the foul-smelling waters.

If it hadn't been for the whiteness of Chrissie's floating limbs in the unlit stretch of water, it would have been impossible to see her, but as Jimmy struggled frantically to keep his head above the surface he caught a fleeting glimpse of an outstretched arm that appeared to be beckoning him. With a frenzied spurt of energy, he propelled himself through the numbing black water towards her. Almost hysterical with fear he made a grab at Chrissie's hand and tried to pull her away from the iron rod.

By this time Reggie had edged his way along the narrow path that ran alongside the river and was lying in the thick mud and leaning out sideways over the low wall. As they both fought to free her tangled mass of hair from the sharp metal pole, Jimmy was suddenly overwhelmed by fear. "I can't do it!" he gulped, swallowing another mouthful of the turbid river.

"Just hold *on* to her!" Reggie cried, as he momentarily released his grip on her and rolled over, plunging his hands into his pockets. He prayed that it was still there. He found it! Swearing at the top of his voice, he made a valiant effort to open the blade on his pocket knife, but his fingertips were so cold that there was barely any feeling left in them as he tried over and over to pull the knife from the case. After what seemed like an eternity, the blade was free and he called out to Jimmy, "Here! Take this."

"W-w-what? What is it?" Jimmy was almost blind with panic as he stretched out his hand.

"Cut her free! For Christ's sake! Before you both drown!"

Snatching at the small knife, Jimmy held on to the wall with one hand and reached out with the other. Clasping it with frozen fingers he set about hacking at Chrissie's hair. Tears streamed down his face as he cried out with each stroke of the knife.

"I'm sorry! I'm so sorry, my darling girl!"

After what seemed like an age filled with dreadful anguish and despair, Jimmy finally cut through the remaining twist of snarled-up hair and Chrissie was free.

"I've got her! I've got her!" he spluttered, as he caught hold of her around the waist and pulled her possessively towards his heaving chest. He swore to all the angels and saints above that he would never, ever, let her go again.

Reggie threw himself down again on to the slippery ground and stretched almost full length over the side, reaching out to Jimmy.

"Here! Take my hand!" he cried through chattering teeth. The powerful strength in his arms had them both ashore in moments.

Jimmy gathered Chrissie's limp body to himself as he squatted on the freezing ground, rocking and crooning to her as though she were a little baby. Her breathing was so shallow that he could barely hear it and he prayed fervently that she wasn't going to die in his arms.

"Get up, for God's sake, man!" Reggie jerked on the slime-covered jacket. "We have to take her to the hospital!"

Jimmy suddenly came to life and leapt from the cold earth in one swift movement, pulling Chrissie up with him. "Yes, yes." he nodded. "Course we do."

"Follow me," Reggie ordered. "And be careful, this place is treacherous."

Sweeping Chrissie up in his arms Jimmy stepped carefully in Reggie's footsteps. In the near total darkness, he groaned and shivered as exhaustion threatened to jeopardize the rescue, but he forced himself to concentrate intensely on keeping upright along the slippery narrow path, and although it was only a short distance back to the cobbled street, it seemed like a million miles away.

With heartfelt relief they reached safer ground and turned into the street once again. Coated from head to foot in thick black slime from the river, Jimmy shuddered and barely managed to stutter, "W-w-what about him?" He nodded down at the dark shape on the ground that was now almost covered with snow.

"What are you worried about him for, for fuck's sake?" Reggie snorted. "Just get her up the road and into the car before anyone starts nosing around!"

"Right," Jimmy said firmly, lifting Chrissie higher to get a firmer grip on her. A rasping sigh, so faint Jimmy wasn't sure that he'd heard it, came from Chrissie's blue lips.

"There's a blanket on the back seat. Put that around her. I'll be there in two minutes and we'll get her over to the hospital. Hurry *up*!" Reggie ordered with urgency.

"OK!" Jimmy was already striding up the street through the light snow shower, his energy returning as he kept a firm hold on his dear girl. He didn't really give a damn what was going to happen to Charles Latimer, but he had a pretty good idea! "We'll soon get you right," he told her confidently, as he reached the car.

Finding it awkward to open the door, he gently lowered Chrissie's feet to the ground and propped her up against the side of the car. As he pulled open the door a welcoming blast of hot air blew into their faces. Jimmy started as he felt Chrissie twitch convulsively

319

and let out the feeblest of moans. Almost weak with relief he tenderly lifted her into the back seat and raised her legs on to the comfortable cushions. As he wrapped the thick woollen blanket around her, from head to toe, he whispered gently, "There. You'll be all right now."

Closing the door quietly, Jimmy looked around to see if Reggie was coming. He knew now that it was desperately urgent that they get Chrissie to the hospital. Going back to the corner of the street he looked down the steep incline towards the river. The snowstorm had eased at last and soft flakes were fluttering gently to the ground on a light breeze ... and he could see quite clearly. He thought his eyes were deceiving him when he saw Charles Latimer's car slowly and silently rolling towards the river. No! He knew exactly what was going on! Smiling grimly to himself, he turned and walked back to the car, opened the passenger door and slid into the warmth of the front seat. His new suit was stuck to him with the filth and mud from the river, but he didn't care. His throat was raw and painful from all the yelling and his stomach churned with the amount of mucky water he had swallowed. He'd lost his coat, but that didn't bother him either – and where the hell were his shoes? All that concerned him was getting Chrissie well again. Well enough to take home.

"Here," Reggie said, as he opened the car door and threw Jimmy's coat over his knees. "You forgot something."

"Thanks," Jimmy mumbled, not meeting his gaze. "Everything OK?" he asked innocently.

"Perfect!" Reggie answered smugly as he put the car in gear and sped away from the kerb. Risking the icy conditions on the road to get Chrissie to the hospital as quickly as possible, he kept his foot down hard as they sped towards St Thomas's.

Jimmy sat in the corridor shivering self-consciously; the thin dressing gown that the nurse had given him barely covered his burly naked body, and he stared morosely down at his big bare feet which were a strange shade of purple and still caked in mud.

The sight of Chrissie's battered body in the bright and blinding light of the hospital had caused such a terrific shock to his already panic-stricken mind, he almost dropped her to the floor. Reggie Dixon grabbed hold of him and kept him upright as the team of emergency staff rushed towards them and guided them into a side room.

"Drink this," Reggie said quietly, handing Jimmy a steaming cup of tea.

"Will she be all right, do you think?" Jimmy asked in a whisper, peering up at him through bloodshot eyes.

"I don't know," Reggie answered honestly. "But she's in the best place."

When the duty sister had seen the state of the three characters entering the casualty department, she'd shaken her head in despair. The girl looked as though she was on her last legs. God only knew how she's got herself into such a dreadful condition. Still, that was none of her business. With professional authority, she ordered them, brusquely, to go with her nurses. Following them into the small room she took control of the situation.

"Put her on the trolley, young man," she said firmly, "And then you can go in there." She nodded to an adjoining room, "and get out of those disgusting clothes. When you're ready you can go and wait in the corridor. You too," she nodded to Reggie, screwing her face up at the sight of his ruined clothes. He mumbled something and shook his head.

"Very well, young man, but on your own head be it." She turned swiftly away saying "We'll take over from here!"

The two men spent most of the next four hours in silence as they either perched nervously on the bench by the wall or paced up and down the corridors, waiting anxiously to hear if Chrissie was going to survive her terrible ordeal. Much to their relief, nobody had come near them to enquire as to what had befallen the poor young woman they had brought into the hospital. They had discussed it briefly in the car on the way over to the hospital and had agreed to say, if asked, that they had found her unconscious in the street and it was their guess that she had been to a party and had too much to drink, then slipped on the ice and hit her head. Reggie had said that they would have to deny any knowledge of drug abuse if questioned, as that would have to involve the law. To them, she was a perfect stranger after all and they were only doing the good Samaritan bit by bringing her in to the casualty department.

Jimmy's heart leapt as the thick plastic doors of the emergency treatment room swung open and the duty sister walked through, sighing and shaking her head.

"What? What is it?" Reggie asked uneasily.

"Is the girl OK?" Jimmy tried to sound casual.

"Well, she's alive anyway!" Sister Jones tutted. "God only knows what these young creatures think they're doing to themselves, when they start on all that stuff."

"What do you mean?" Reggie asked innocently.

Her weary eyes gazed at him and she held her hand up to stop him saying anything else. "Please!" she began. "Don't insult my intelligence by telling me you have no idea who she is or what's happened to her tonight."

"But . . ." Jimmy muttered, blushing scarlet.

"Listen carefully, young man," she gave a small, tired smile. "Your friend will be all right, eventually that is, but at the moment she is a very sick young woman and will have to stay with us for a few weeks."

"A few weeks," Jimmy whispered to himself.

"She will be going to one of our special wards where we have qualified staff to deal with her problem."

"Can we see her?" Reggie asked quietly.

"No, I'm afraid that's not possible at the moment," she answered firmly. "Maybe in a couple of days. You can call to enquire after her, naturally, but I'm very sorry visits are completely out of the question for the time being."

Jimmy's head was swimming with relief to hear that Chrissie was going to be all right and he grinned sheepishly at the jaded nurse. "Thanks a million!"

"I suggest you both get off home and try to catch a few hours' sleep." She smiled back.

They both nodded in agreement and made to turn away.

"Just a minute . . ."

"Yes?" Jimmy asked.

"I also suggest you make yourself decent first!"

Jimmy grinned stupidly down at the gaping dressing gown. "You're right there!" he mumbled, unable to meet her amused expression. Just then a young nurse turned the corner of the corridor carrying his clothes.

"Here," she tried to keep a straight face. "They're not very clean but at least they're dry!"

"You're an angel," he grinned crookedly.

"I know!" she answered cheekily, giving him a quick wink, "And I'm not even going to ask you where your shoes are!"

"No, don't!" he muttered quickly as she turned swiftly away in response to sister's stern voice calling her back to her duties.

25

Jimmy woke a few hours later to the sound of the alarm clock beside the sofa. His head thumped painfully and his throat felt as though he had swallowed razor blades!

Forcing his eyes open, he mumbled his thanks as Reggie called out for him to come and get some breakfast. Every bone in his body was stiff and sore and he groaned loudly as he dragged himself from the bed and pulled on Reggie's dressing gown. Shuffling along like an old man he made his way out to the kitchen and slumped down on to the nearest chair.

"Sorry about the early wake-up call, but like I told you last night I have to get off to the airport," Reggie said, his voice a little tense. He was worried about Jimmy but there was nothing on this earth that was going to make him change his mind about his plan.

"No, no," Jimmy answered gruffly, as he reached for the mug of steaming coffee before him. "I don't know what I'd have done without you!"

"I've tried to clean that bloody muck off your clothes but they're beyond hope. Anyway, I've sorted out a few old things of mine, we're more or less the same size, so you'd better get into them as soon as you get your head together." He checked his watch again. "Eat some of that," he pointed at the plate of toast.

"I couldn't, sorry," Jimmy mumbled. "I feel like I've still got half of that rotten filthy river down me gullet!"

"By the way," Reggie said over his shoulder, as he went into the bedroom to get his suitcase. "I didn't see a wallet or anything in your pocket."

"Shite!" Jimmy shook his head.

"Don't worry, I'll give you a lift back to your place. By luck it's more or less in the direction I'm going"

The two men stood on the pavement outside Jimmy's uncle's and grasped hands firmly.

"I don't know how I can ever thank you for what you did for Chrissie," Jimmy said quietly.

"Me?" Reggie laughed. "It was you that risked your life to save her!"

"Oh not just that," Jimmy shrugged. "All the other stuff . . . you know."

"Forget it!"

"I can't!"

"I *mean* it, Jimmy!" Reggie said seriously. "Forget it! It's over! Done with!"

Jimmy heaved a great sigh. "Right you are then!"

"Just promise me one thing."

"What's that?"

"That you'll take good care of that girl of yours. Get her out of this godforsaken place."

Jimmy clenched the other man's hand firmly, "Oh, you can be sure of that!"

"Better go then, or I'll miss my flight!"

"Good luck, Reggie!" Jimmy felt a lump in his throat.

"And you too," Reggie answered sincerely as he reluctantly released Jimmy's hand and turned back to the car.

"Funny thing that," Jimmy smiled broadly to himself as Reggie wound the window down to wave and call out his final farewell. 'I've never had a swimming lesson in me life!'

For the next few weeks Jimmy called the hospital religiously every morning to see if there was any improvement in Chrissie's condition. The first week he was a nervous wreck as he dialled the number with trembling fingers, only to be told that she was 'stable' or 'comfortable'. When he dared to ask for more details he was told officiously that only the next of kin could be informed of her condition, but when the nurses began to recognise the familiar, caring voice, with its soft Irish brogue, they relented little by little, especially young nurse Joy, who had joked with him about the missing shoes. Whispering confidentially into the mouthpiece, she gave him as much information as she dared about his friend's progress.

"When do you think I'll be able to see her?" he ventured nervously on the Monday morning of the fourth week.

"We're hoping to move her into one of the general wards this afternoon," she said quietly, glancing over her shoulder to check if sister was within earshot. The other end of the line was silent. "You still there?"

Jimmy swallowed the huge lump in his throat and then answered gruffly, "Yes . . . thank you, miss."

"Sorry, have to go!" Joy said brightly. "Maybe see you later?"

"You can be sure of that!" Jimmy replied, brushing the scalding tears from his cheeks.

Jimmy was sweating profusely with nerves and excitement as he waited impatiently for the lift to reach the fifth floor. (The girl on the reception desk had checked her list and told him that Chrissie was in St Theresa's Ward.) Clutching the enormous bunch of red roses he followed the signs along the wide and almost deserted corridors. Taking a deep breath he pushed open the doors of the ward and stood for a moment, his eyes scanning the rows of beds on either side of the long room. He couldn't see her! Small groups of visitors gathered around most of the narrow iron beds and blocked his view of the far end of the room. He felt as though every eye was on him as he walked slowly and deliberately down the centre of the ward, his eyes searching. Just as an awful panic was about to descend on him he caught the briefest glimpse of a small form huddled deep down under the covers, in the last bed on the right. His heart leapt as he quickened his pace and made straight towards her. He stood awkwardly some feet from the bed and it was all he could do to stop himself from crying out in anguish. The curled-up figure under the light covers looked so child-like that his heart went out to her. He moved silently to the bedside and swallowed the huge lump in his throat as he gazed down sadly at the pale face that lay so peacefully on the pure white pillow. Somebody had cut her hair into a short, cropped style and he grinned ruefully when he thought she looked more like a young boy now.

"Would you like me to put those in a vase for you?" a gentle voice asked behind him.

Jimmy started and turned to the nurse. "Oh! Yes, please. That would be great." Taking the pretty bunch of flowers Nurse Joy smiled to herself when she saw Chrissie's long eyelashes fluttering. Without asking permission from the ward sister she dragged the long curtains around the bed to give them a little privacy.

"Jimmy?" Chrissie whispered weakly, barely able to believe her ears. "Is that really you?"

Jimmy's head spun around as he heard the plaintive voice. His heart pounded in his chest and for a moment his breath caught in his throat. Her huge dark eyes were almost pleading with him as she held out a trembling hand. Before he knew what he was doing he was on the bed beside her, gathering her possessively to his heaving chest.

"Oh Chrissie!" he mumbled as he buried his face in her freshly washed hair and sobbed like a baby. Her thin arms wound themselves slowly around his shaking shoulders and she clasped him to her, never ever wanting to let him go again. This is what she had dreamed about for so long now, as she had lain in her lonely bed recovering slowly but surely from her dreadful ordeal. With one half of her she so desperately wanted to see him and with the other she was terrified that he would reject her completely when he saw the state she was in. But each day, when Joy had come and whispered his messages to her, her hopes began to soar. She was still very weak and Chrissie knew it would take a very long time for her to recover.

As they clung wordlessly together and their hot tears mingled they couldn't find the right words to say. The feelings they both had, each for their own reasons, ran far too deep. But for the time being it was wonderful to feel the comfort and love that flowed between them. When they heard the swishing of the curtain being pulled around the bed, they finally and with great reluctance drew slowly apart.

"I'll get you both a nice cup of tea," Nurse Joy said brightly and winked at Jimmy.

Both unable to find their voices they just nodded and smiled at her.

"There's some paper hankies in the cupboard," Chrissie eventually managed to say.

Jimmy let go of her thin hand and fumbled about in the little cabinet. Pulling out a wad of tissues he held them out to her. "Here."

"Thanks," Chrissie sniffed, unable to meet his gaze.

"You're looking great," Jimmy grinned crookedly.

"Liar!" Chrissie grinned back, glancing shyly up at him through damp lashes, fiddling with the sodden hankies.

"Well, better than last time I saw you anyway!"

"Jesus, anything would be better than that, according to what I heard," she answered a little dispiritedly.

"Let's not talk about that, eh?" Jimmy answered gruffly. He wanted to forget everything now and make a new beginning for them both.

"But there's things I need to tell you."

"No! No, you don't!"

After Nurse Joy had brought them a tray with their tea and biscuits, she wished them good luck. Off duty now she was going away to visit some friends in the country. Chrissie kissed her warmly on the cheek and thanked her for everything she had done for her. The young nurse turned quickly away before they could see the unshed tears in her eyes and called over her shoulder, "You take good care of her now! You hear me? Or you'll have me to answer to!"

"I hear you!" Jimmy laughed, as they sat and watched her march smartly off down the ward and disappear through the end doors.

They huddled together and chatted quietly about things not really concerned with the awful events since Chrissie had left Ireland. Jimmy gently told her how he had written to her mother and told her all about the terrible attack of pneumonia that had put Chrissie in hospital. She had lost a bit of weight but was doing well now after convalescing down at the seaside.

He told her that he had been to see Betty Carter and explained all about her illness and said that they shouldn't worry too much. She nearly burst into tears again when he took the little crumpled pile of letters from home out of his pocket that Betty had given him.

The loud clanging of the bell announcing the end of visiting made them both jump. Chrissie's heart thumped wildly as she asked in panic, "Will you be coming again?"

"I'd stay the night, if they'd let me," he grinned cheekily.

"Huh! Some chance," she grinned back. "Will you come tomorrow?"

"Try and stop me!"

"I *won't*!"

"I *know*!"

Rising slowly to his feet, Jimmy ignored the glares from the ward sister and bent down to leave a lingering gentle kiss on Chrissie's upturned face.

"Jimmy?" Chrissie's voice was so small he had to lean over her to hear what she was saying.

"Yes?" he frowned. "What's wrong?"

"Chrissie chewed nervously on her bottom lip for a few moments before she answered him. "Will you . . . will you . . . will you take me home?"

When he didn't answer immediately the fear began to rise in her. Perhaps she was wrong, maybe she had made a terrible mistake! Perhaps he didn't feel the same way as she did after all? If she had only known what he had been thinking at that very moment! If he could have had *his* way, he'd have dragged the covers from her, pulled her from the bed, thrown her over his broad shoulders and marched straight out of the hospital with her!

"Well?" she asked again, her voice quivering, her wide eyes holding his determined gaze, still unsure of what he would say.

He hesitated only for a second and then, grinning broadly, his eyes sparkling roguishly he replied, "Well, what else would I be doing with you, me darlin' girl!"

THE END . . . well for the time being anyway!

TANGLED WEB

Florence GILLAN

POOLBEG

Published 2024 by Crimson an imprint of Poolbeg Press Ltd.

123 Grange Hill, Baldoyle, Dublin 13, Ireland

Email: poolbeg@poolbeg.com

A catalogue record for this book is available from the British Library.

ISBN 978178199-520-4

Also by Florence Gillan

Let Them Lie
The Forfeit

About the author

Florence Gillan is a retired teacher who divides her time between her native Sligo and her home in Newry, County Down. She lives with her husband Eugene, and two dogs. Her passion for reading as a child led her to write and tell stories from an early age. She has written two previous novels, *Let Them Lie* and *The Forfeit*.

Acknowledgements

I can't believe I've written my third book. The last few years have been a crazy adventure. None of it would be possible without Paula Campbell from Poolbeg. I will always be appreciative of her.

My patient editor, Gaye Shortland, has once again guided me through the complexities of editing with patience and encouragement and, for that, I am truly grateful.

Thank you to David Prendergast and the team at Poolbeg for their hard work on this book.

Once again, I'd like to express my heartfelt gratitude to my first readers: Maureen Gillan, Madeleine Skoronski, Fiona O Murchú, Rachel Hanna, David Hanna, Mark Hanna, Sarah Hanna and Eugene Hanna. Your patience and support have been invaluable. Each of you has played a unique role in this journey, and I couldn't have done it without you.

Thank you to my lovely extended family, which includes brothers, sisters, in-laws, nieces, nephews, cousins, and my witty godmother Annie Walker, who have shared in my adventure and been encouraging and supportive of me.

Thank you to my fantastic friends, who have been there for all the special times in my life, not least this continuing adventure.

Special thanks go to Madeleine Skoronski and Fiona O'Murchú. They were among my first readers, reading and rereading the text for me. They were always available to calm and steady me.

My four children were, as usual, incredibly helpful. They took time out of their busy lives to offer suggestions and improvements. They are, as always, at the heart of everything.

Finally, Eugene, none of this would have been possible without you. Thank you!

Dedication

To my children, Rachel, David, Mark and Sarah

Prologue

When the call came from O'Flaherty's, she cancelled her plans. The package was waiting in reception. She paid her bill and shook hands with the man at the front desk. She placed the neatly wrapped package on the passenger seat of her car. On the long drive home, she planned how to dispose of its contents and smiled grimly. She had been looking forward to this moment for a long time.

When she finally unlocked her front door, her sense of anticipation heightened. But all pleasures are intensified by delay, so she poured herself a large glass of wine and then took the package upstairs. She smiled as she entered the bathroom. She lifted the toilet lid and wondered how many flushes it would take. Carefully, she removed the box from its wrapping and admired the tasteful images of ferns and autumnal flora. Opening it, she carefully tipped some contents into the toilet bowl. They landed with a discreet splash, but some ash adhered to the bowl. The first flush was satisfying, and she watched as the wet ash began to disappear, but heavier clumps sat stubbornly in the bowl. She used the toilet brush to whisk them up and flushed them again. It took a surprisingly long time and numerous flushes but, eventually, the box was empty, as was her wine glass.

'Rest in shit!' she whispered as she pulled the handle for the final time.

Chapter 1

Sligo 2010

She couldn't evade him. Wherever she turned, he appeared looming out of the darkness, or she sensed his presence behind her, causing her nerve-endings to jangle unbearably. Everywhere she ran, his smirking face confronted her.

'You can't escape me, Eimear. You're mine, and you'll always be mine. Don't fight it, pet. You know we're meant to be together.'

On and on she raced, screaming. Then, just ahead of her, she saw her mother. She ran towards her eagerly and flung herself into her arms. Her mother's warm embrace and soothing voice comforted her, and the terror eased. It was going to be alright now.

Then, the arms around her increased their grip, painfully so, and she struggled to free herself.

'*Mam, let me go! You're hurting me!*'

She pushed her mother away from her and stared up into Donal's empty eyes. She screamed so loudly that her ears hurt. Desperate to escape, she raced down endless corridors, pursued by him. All the while, her screams echoed and bounced off the walls.

Then the sounds changed, grew more insistent and sharp, and she was pulled out of the dream and sat up, her body coated in sweat and her heart thumping painfully. It's only a dream, she reassured herself. Everything is OK.

Then she heard it clearly, the ringing of the doorbell.

She turned on the bedside light and looked at her phone. It was three in the morning. Again, the insistent blaring of her doorbell. Who could be at the door at this time? She had left her friends in the pub at midnight, telling them she was shattered and ready to collapse into bed. Her mother was spending the night with Meg. Could she have come home after all? Lost her key?

She pulled on her dressing gown and slippers and hurried downstairs. She hesitated, afraid to open the door at such an hour. The doorbell rang again. It sounded like a finger was pressed hard against it. Urgent.

She called out, '*Who's there?*'

'*Eimear, it's me, Alec. Look, I need to talk to you.*'

With trembling hands and a pounding heart, she unlocked the door and opened it, to reveal Alec and another Garda standing on the front doorstep.

'What is it, Alec? What's wrong?'

Her friend Alec, in his Garda uniform, looked deadly serious.

'We'd better go inside, Eimear.'

His serious tone and sympathetic look frightened her, but she led him into the kitchen, which still retained a faint remembrance of warmth.

Alec couldn't quite meet her eyes.

'You're scaring me. Why are you here?'

He didn't speak, but his eyes looked at her with compassion. She felt her legs dissolve into jelly and she clutched the worn kitchen table for support.

'It's Mam, isn't it?' she whispered through lips that suddenly seemed incapable of forming the shapes required for speech.

He led her to a chair and sat beside her.

'Eimear, there's been a car accident just outside town. Your mam's car went off the road and crashed into a wall. I'm very sorry to have to tell you that your mother died at the scene and your Aunt Meg is in hospital.'

She stared at him stupidly, her mouth opening and closing.

The female Garda stood on the other side of her and tried to take her hand.

Eimear snatched it away.

'You've made a mistake, Alec. She drove Meg home hours ago – she'd been meeting friends in Doran's pub, and I was there too. She told me she'd stay the night with Meg. She must be there now.'

He took her hand. 'I'm so sorry, love, but it's true. I was at the scene.'

Eimear clung to his hand, but her mind couldn't process his words. She pulled away and jumped to her feet. In a strange disembodied voice, she said, 'But it can't be true. She planned to help me paint my bedroom. We even bought the paint.'

A rational part of her brain realised the pointlessness of fixing on the task she and her mam had planned to undertake. But it seemed imperative to explain to Alec that her mam couldn't be dead because they'd planned to paint a bedroom.

Alec said nothing but made her take a seat again and sat beside her silently. He listened patiently as she asked the same questions over and over, trying to make sense of the devastating news that her mother was no longer part of her universe. Then the tears came and Alec squeezed her shoulder, offering warmth and something solid to cling to now that her world had shattered into pieces.

She was vaguely aware of the other guard moving around the kitchen, and she heard the clink of dishes and the purring of the kettle, normal sounds that seemed out of place, almost profane. The woman returned as she slumped at the kitchen table, and a cup of tea was pressed into her hands.

Eimear gulped some down, glad of the familiar comfort.

Then she burst into a frenzy of words. 'We need to go now, I want to see her, where have they taken her?'

'Easy, Eimear. There's no point in rushing to the hospital. Wait until morning. They took her straight to Sligo General.'

'But, Alec, I don't want her to be alone. I want to be with her.' Her sense of urgency propelled her to her feet. 'I need to get dressed. Come on, Alec, we have to go.'

'Eimear, sit down. You don't understand. They won't let you see her tonight. It will be a wasted journey. But I promise you that we'll go early in the morning.'

Then she remembered. 'You said Meg was with her. Is she badly hurt?'

'She was semi-conscious when she was found. The paramedics checked her out, and thought she had escaped with minor injuries. Your mother's side of the car took the brunt of the impact. Of course there's the possibility of concussion and the doctors won't want her to be disturbed. But she'll need you in the morning when she wakes.'

Suddenly, the urgency and energy evaporated, and Alec held her as she sobbed like a child. 'I'll call Jen and ask her to stay with you,' he said.

'*No!*'

Alec and the other Garda started at the violence of her tone.

'Come on, Eimear, you can't be alone tonight, and Jen is your best friend.'

'She *was* my best friend,' Eimear said, her voice flat.

'Eimear, I know you had a falling-out, but she would want to be with you now. And she was very fond of your mother.'

'No, I don't want her. But I'll call Lana and she'll keep me company.'

Alec sighed. 'You promise?'

'Yes, I promise.'

'OK, Eimear, I must go, but I'll leave Garda Peters here until Lana arrives.'

The Garda at his side nodded and smiled brightly. 'I'll be happy to sit with you, Eimear.'

Eimear shook her head. 'Please, you're very kind but I think I'd like some time on my own.'

'Are you sure, Eimear?' Alec said.

'Yes. I am.'

'OK so,' he said. 'Look, how about I meet you at the hospital at nine tomorrow? Lana can drive you in.'

Eimear nodded and, reluctantly, Alec and his partner left.

She waited until she heard the door slam shut, then allowed hot tears to course down her cheeks in stinging streaks.

There were people she should ring, friends of her mam who would want to know. But there was no point in disturbing anyone this early.

Besides, she needed to see her mother before finally accepting she was gone.

———— *ell* ————

At eight, she showered and dressed and drove to the hospital. Alec was in the hospital foyer waiting for her.

'Did you contact Lana?' he asked.

'No. There was no point in disturbing her in the middle of the night. Can I see Mam now?'

Alec led the way down long corridors, and Eimear was reminded of her dream. There was horror at the end of this corridor, too.

A pleasant woman in a white coat greeted her and took her into a room where her mam's shrouded body lay. Her face looked cold and remote, not like her mam at all. All that had been her had long departed. Her warm liveliness, quick smile and deep chuckle were no more. All that remained was this stiff, cold container of her spirit. Eimear shuddered, reluctant to touch the body but feeling that somehow it was expected of her. Briefly, her fingers stroked the waxy cheek, but its chill stung her fingers. She recoiled and turned to leave.

Outside the room, Alec was waiting, his pale face creased with concern. He started to speak, but she forestalled him.

'What happened? Was there another car?'

'No, Eimear. We have to make our investigations but it seems your mam may have been going too fast and lost control of the car. It was on a stretch of road with sharp bends. Meg might be able to tell us more when we speak to her later today.'

'I'd like to see Meg now.'

'I'll see what I can do. She might still be asleep.'

'Does she know that Mam has died?'

'I don't think so. She was only semi-conscious at the scene, and the hospital staff won't have told her.'

They walked to the reception and asked for Meg Curran's whereabouts. They were given directions to Female Medical.

Again, Alec took the lead and explained the circumstances to the nurse at the ward's reception. The nurse bustled off to find out about Meg.

A few minutes later, Eimear was looking down at her aunt's sleeping face.

'Do you want me to stay and tell her, Eimear?'

'No, I'll tell her. Thanks, Alec. I'll be fine now, really I will.'

'Promise you'll call me if you need anything.'

Eimear nodded.

Barely aware that Alec had left, she sat by the bed and stared at her aunt. Meg lay under the starched sheets, her eyes closed and her forehead marred by livid bruising. Eimear winced as she gazed at her. She looked so young and fragile – much younger than her forty years. But, as she looked at her lying there, she was suddenly consumed by rage. Why hadn't Meg died instead of her lovely mother? It wasn't fair! She needed her mam.

Instantly, she felt ashamed. Meg loved her and had always been especially good to her. The age gap between them wasn't big – thirteen years – and all through her childhood and teenage years Meg had been her confidante, the fun grown-up she could confide in without all the usual lectures that an adult insisted on delivering.

Meg would be devastated by the death of her sister. Like all siblings, they bickered sometimes and occasionally fell out, but they were family and always there for each other.

As if hearing her thoughts, Meg opened her eyes. She smiled at Eimear, puzzled. 'Why are you here, pet?'

Then Eimear watched as awareness of her surroundings and memories of the night returned. Her face turned pink and then white. She tried to sit up and groaned with the effort. Falling back on her pillow, she turned alarmed eyes towards Eimear.

'The crash, we were in a crash. Is – is Claire OK?'

Eimear froze, unable to form the sentence that would turn Meg's fear into a horrible certainty.

'Tell me what happened, Eimear ... please ... please ...'

'I'm sorry, Meg. She didn't ... she's gone,' Eimear whispered through numb lips.

Meg stared up and her small, round face crumpled, her blue eyes swam with tears.

'*Oh, God, no, please no!*'

Eimear grasped her hand and sobbed out, 'She's dead, Meg!'

Meg grimaced, and then she cried in loud, guttural bursts of pain.

Eimear sat on the side of the bed and they embraced.

'*I wish it had been me, Eimear! It should have been me! It's not fair!*'

Eimear said nothing. She just held her.

Later, when Meg had calmed down, a nurse came in with tea and biscuits and left them on the tray table at the end of the bed.

Eimear rose to pull the tray table towards her aunt and sat on the bedside chair again.

'Can you bear to tell me what happened, Meg? Alec thinks she was driving too fast and misjudged the road.'

Meg took a sip of tea and sighed. 'It's all a blur but, Eimear, you know your mam – she was like a young one when she got behind the wheel of that bloody sports car. Your father bought it for her, and she wouldn't hear of it being sold despite its age She said it reminded her of him,' Meg smiled sadly, 'but, really, she loved the way it made her feel – young and free. She'd have the top down in all weathers and she always drove it fast. And Alec is right. It's such a dangerous stretch of road, full of sharp bends, and all I remember is her swerving and the sound of crashing, and then everything is hazy.' Meg bowed her head, and the tears slid silently down her face. Then she clutched Eimear's hand. 'It was my fault. She was taking me home. If it weren't for me, she'd be alive now.'

'Meg, stop that. Of course it's not your fault. Mam would be furious with you for that kind of talk. She had the accident because she was driving too fast. At least she didn't harm anyone. Thank God for that. So please, no more talk of blame. Now, you need to get well. I'm going to find out when you can leave here.'

Meg nodded, and Eimear went to find a doctor. When she returned, she had some good news.

'Right, they X-rayed you last night, and you have no broken bones. They are also satisfied that you aren't suffering from concussion. So, hopefully, I can take you home after the doctor does his morning rounds. But you need to take it easy. You're bound to be stiff and sore for a while.'

Later that morning, Eimear collected Meg from the hospital and insisted on taking her back to Claire's house to recuperate. After getting Meg settled on the couch, she started the round of phone calls. Claire didn't have any close relatives – her parents were dead, and Meg was her only sibling. But she did have a few cousins. It was brutal having to break the news of her death, but her mother's closest friend, Nuala, offered to let everyone know. It was a relief for Eimear not to have to break the news to anyone else. Dealing with the shock and pain of others was more than she felt able to bear.

In the afternoon, the hospital rang. Claire's body would be released the following morning. Eimear rang the undertaker's and asked him to collect the body and bring it to the house for waking. The undertaker later called to the house and helped them compose a piece to put in the papers and on the online website, detailing the funeral arrangements. He would bring the remains to the house the following evening.

Chapter 2

The phone rang nonstop, but they managed to persuade friends and family to leave them in peace until the next day when Claire's remains would come home. The business of death, although painful, had the advantage of keeping them occupied. The suddenness of Claire's death and the manner of it had so many ramifications. Two Gardaí called to the house and took Meg's statement. They issued formal words of condolence. They were nice but baldly stated that Claire was driving too fast for the road conditions. This led to her swerving at a bend, veering across the road and slamming into a wall.

Eimear felt a burn of anger that her mother's irresponsible driving had robbed them of her. That bloody little sports car offered little protection. If she had been driving her Audi, she might have had some chance of survival.

Tiredness caught up with them eventually, and Meg suggested going to bed.

'It's no good, Meg. I won't sleep.'

'I know you won't, love, neither will I, but we can cuddle up in the bed and comfort each other until morning, and at least we'll be warm.'

Eimear nodded, relieved not to be left alone.

The long night passed, accompanied by tears and whispered words of comfort. When sleep came, her dreams were filled with dark shadows.

It was a relief to be awakened by the daylight seeping into the room. For a moment, she felt puzzled by the presence of Meg. Then it all came back ... the accident and the terrible crippling loss. The brutal ache in the pit of her stomach caused her to cry out.

Meg woke instantly, and they clung to each other.

'Oh God, this is so awful!' Meg whispered.

'I know. Mam loved you so much. She thought the world of you.'

'It's so hard to believe she's gone.' Meg got out of bed and stood staring blankly at the window.

'Why did she have to be so irresponsible?' Eimear said. 'She wasn't a boy racer—she was a middle-aged woman in her fifties. Why couldn't she act like one?'

Meg shook her head, and they both dressed without speaking.

Eventually, the grim realities of the coming days propelled them into action. They cleaned the house and ordered sandwiches and scones from the deli and bakery. They discussed where to put the coffin. The idea of people tramping through her mam's bedroom sickened Eimear. It had been her sanctuary. In the end, they decided to put the coffin in the big room at the back of the house, which your gran used to call the drawing room.

Eimear checked the room was presentable and opened the heavy curtains that screened the French windows. As she looked out at her mother's garden she thought how it would have pleased her to see it in full bloom.

She wondered if any family members would turn up at the funeral. There were so few. She felt her loneliness keenly.

Meg joined her.

'You look as though you're trying to solve a puzzle,' she said.

'I was just realising how few relatives I have – just elderly relatives of Dad's and a few middle-aged cousins I never see. I suppose Gran's sister Agnes will want to attend the funeral. She and Gran never got on. I don't think Gran even visited her when she went into the Home. But didn't she come to Gran's funeral Mass?'

'Of course she did. She's old school and, even though they hadn't spoken for ten years, she still felt it her duty to attend the funeral. Horrible old bitch!'

Eimear glanced around at all the signs of her mam's presence, a book lying face down on the window seat. She could even see the faint indentation of her mother's body on the soft cushions resting there as though awaiting her return. She thought about plumping them up but couldn't. It would feel like she was erasing her mother from this home that she had filled with love.

They heard the sound of tyres on gravel. It was the undertaker.

Meg patted her shoulder. 'Ready?' she asked.

Eimear nodded, and they opened the door.

The next day passed in a blur of people, handshakes, endless sandwiches and awkward embraces. The house was filled to the brim with all the people who loved Claire and the family and friends of Meg and Eimear.

Eimear's friends shuffled in awkwardly, uncertain how to be around her. She had lost touch with many of them while going out with Donal. She couldn't put all that on Donal. She had been happy to let friendships slide and then, after she broke off the engagement, it seemed hypocritical to seek their comfort and her pride refused to let her. But they had shown up then and now, and she was grateful.

Jen came too, and they just nodded to each other – too many sharp words had been said on both sides, and there were divided loyalties. Jen was Donal's sister and her best friend. When her engagement ended, her friendship with Jen also ended.

_____ *ele* _____

The day of the funeral was cloaked in clouds, and the rain mizzled down, making the mourners damp and despairing.

Eimear grasped her aunt's hand. Meg squeezed her fingers and the two women watched as the first sods of clay were symbolically thrown on the coffin. Gulping back tears, they waited as the procession of people grasped their hands and offered words of commiseration.

The day seemed interminable, and she was relieved when she was finally ensconced in Meg's car.

'I need to go home, Eimear. Do you want to stay with me, or will I drop you back at your place?'

The thought of being on her own felt unbearable – the emptiness too achingly awful to bear. 'Yes, I'll stay over with you. Is that OK?'

'Of course, pet. I'll be glad of the company.'

They didn't talk on the short trip to the house where Meg and her mother had grown up. Eimear's grandmother, Della, had left it to Claire and Meg when she died but Claire, of course, had her own house – the house she had inherited after the death of her husband.

Della's house was a two-storey manor building, its walls gripped by ivy, and the windows peered down at them like friendly eyes. Eimear had always loved the house. It was a welcoming place, especially when her grandmother was alive. When she visited as a child, Della made it such fun, organising trips to the cinema and rides at the local stables. Della was known locally as 'the doctor's wife'. Even though he was long dead, she retained the title in perpetuity. Not that she wasn't a force to be reckoned with in her own right. She was a stalwart of the local church, belonged to the Vincent de Paul and was active in the choral society.

Everything looked the same. Meg had made no changes to the old-fashioned décor, at least not yet.

The house was warm. The old AGA still did its best, and the kitchen was cosy and welcoming.

'I could do with a drink – will I pour you something?'

'I'd love a glass of wine. But only if you have a bottle open – just a small glass.'

They sat sipping their drinks and talking about the people who had come to the funeral. It felt strange to Eimear to talk about a funeral as though it were the afters of a party. But that's what it was – a party for someone who couldn't be there except in spirit, if you believed in that sort of thing.

'You look miles away, Eimear. What are you thinking about?'

'Nothing much. I suppose it feels so final. Nothing will ever be the same, and oh Meg, I feel so lost without her!'

'*Aww*, love, so do I, but we've got each other, and you know you can always count on me.'

'Thanks, Meg. I know.' She had always been able to count on Meg. 'Do you remember how Mam used to be ripping when I always put your opinion on clothes and boys over hers?'

Meg grinned. 'Even though that led to some questionable fashion choices. Do you remember when you dyed your hair orange? I can still see the look on your mother and Gran's faces. Of course, they blamed me, your favourite aunt!'

'Well, you hadn't too much competition in the favourite-aunt stakes, seeing as mam only had one sister and Dad's sisters were ancient and smelled of mothballs.'

They smiled reminiscently and then, at Meg's suggestion, they pored over the family photograph album. Eimear pointed to a photograph of her mother on her wedding day. She looked beautiful and, even though her father was fine-looking, her mother dazzled from the picture with Hollywood glamour.

'Your mother always looked lovely, but never more so than when she married your father. Even though I was only ten, she made me her bridesmaid. Your gran wasn't pleased because she thought I was too young for the honour. But Claire insisted that she wanted me for the job and only me. She made such a fuss of me that day. She spent longer getting me all dolled up than she spent on herself. I was such a brat, I thought it was all about me.'

'I don't know why I've never asked you before – but, did Gran mind about Dad being so much older than Mam?'

'I think she did at first, but she could see that he was devoted to your mother and could give her a good life and financial security. Your gran knew all about worrying about money after our father died.'

'It was sad they didn't have much time together before Dad had the heart attack. Mam was heartbroken – we both were."

'You poor pet, I was that sorry for you. You were so young, and I wasn't much use to either of you. I'd just started in the hotel, and they had me working night shifts, so I hardly saw you.'

'I'm sure that Mam understood, and Gran was great – she practically lived with us for months. I think being widowed young herself, she understood how Mam felt. But it seems like our family has had so much loss. It sounds pathetic as I'm an adult, but I'm an orphan now. I keep forgetting you are, too.'

Meg smiled. 'The idea of being an orphan suggests poor little children out in the snow, all alone and lost. Well, we are neither poor nor alone – nor in the snow! We have each other and never forget that I'm at the other end of the phone – call me, and I'll be there. Speaking of which, I'm going to cancel my Europe trip.'

'*What?* No way, Meg, I'm not a baby! If you cancel on account of me, I'll be furious. You've been looking forward to it for ages.'

'That's as may be, but I think now isn't a great time to be heading off. I can go any time I like.'

'Right, if you cancel your trip that's us finished, Meg! I'll be mortified. You're going, and that's it!' Eimear glared at her aunt.

Meg threw up her hands, 'OK, OK, you win! I'll go. You're a fierce young one. But to tell the truth, I've lost my excitement for the trip. It all seems a bit pointless. I can't seem to work up any enthusiasm for it.'

'God, I keep forgetting you were involved in a serious accident. Apart from the pain of losing Mam, you have to cope with the after-effects of the crash. How are you feeling, Meg?'

Meg absentmindedly twisted the Claddagh ring on her finger. 'I'm fine. Just a few aches and pains. I was lucky to have got off relatively unscathed, but you're right. The crash has left me feeling very vulnerable. A reminder that I'm not invincible.'

'Look, you don't have to decide anything now. Just keep an open mind, and we'll talk about it again.'

'Thanks, love. I'll likely go, but I just don't feel up to making any decisions now.'

Eimear squeezed Meg's hand. 'You know what, Meg, I think I could do with a change myself. I've been thinking for a while now about moving away. It's not just Mam dying, it's everything.'

'I never heard you talk of leaving before now. Is it because of Donal?'

'Yes, Donal is part of the reason, but I've been getting fed up with work for a long time. I don't want to spend the rest of my life in some back office doing wills and conveyancing. I'm so bored sometimes that I could scream.'

'I understand – and you could get a job anywhere with your qualifications – but perhaps now isn't the right time to move. I mean, right after your mam dying. This isn't the time to make changes.'

'You may be right, but I'm just so fed up. Maybe a change is what's needed. I'd love to live somewhere different, to make a fresh start and shake myself up. It mightn't be the wisest choice, but I feel like a change.'

'Eimear, perhaps the shock is influencing you. The crash was a freak accident that suddenly took Claire from us. I think you shouldn't rush into anything too soon – promise me you won't.'

'Don't worry – I'm not going to rush into anything just yet. Besides, solicitor jobs are scarce at the moment. This recession has hit hard.'

The harsh ring of the doorbell interrupted their discussion.

'God, it's very late. Who could that be?' Meg said.

She went to answer the door.

Eimear was surprised to hear raised voices. Meg sounded like she was having a full-on argument with a man. She jumped up and hurried out to see if she needed help.

Meg was standing in the porch. She was trying to prevent a tall man from entering the house.

Eimear's heart jolted with the shock of recognition. Donal, all six feet two of him, stood in the doorway. Her limbs refused to move, and she was forced to stand helplessly as he pushed past Meg.

'*I'm calling the guards if you don't leave immediately!*' Meg shouted at him.

Still, Eimear couldn't move. He stood in front of her and tentatively touched her arm.

'Eimear, please, I just want to talk to you for a minute.'

'What do you want?' she said through dry lips.

'Listen, love, I'm so sorry about your mother. I would have come to the funeral, but I didn't want to upset you. Jen told me I shouldn't go, that you wouldn't want me.'

Eimear listened in disbelief to the reproach she could hear in his voice. 'She was right. I don't want you anywhere near me.'

'Eimear, everyone has poisoned you against me, yes, even your mother, but I wanted to be here for you. You know how I feel about you, don't you?'

'Yes, I know.' Suddenly, Eimear started shaking uncontrollably.

Meg pushed her way between them. She held her mobile phone in her hand and, despite her small frame, pushed Donal back towards the door.

'I'm warning you, Donal. Get out now, or I'll call the Gardaí.'

Donal ignored her and appealed to Eimear. 'Come on, love. Is that what you want? I love you, and I want to be here for you. Tell her it's OK, and then we can talk.' He gazed at her with soft, pleading eyes.

'Right, this is my home, and I'm telling you to get out now!' said Meg.

They could hear a voice on the other end of the phone, saying: 'Sligo Garda station, what can I do for you?'

Meg and Donal locked eyes.

His fell, and with a last scorching stare at Eimear, he muttered, 'OK, I'm going.'

When he left, Eimear fled to the bathroom, and was violently sick.

Afterwards, Eimear sat dumbly as Meg ranted about Donal.

'The bastard! How dare he call here after everything he did to you! The bloody neck of him!'

Eimear let the torrent of words wash over her, but she concentrated on not letting the pain through. She couldn't let Donal get to her. She had done so much to shut him out and set up a barricade to keep him out of her thoughts.

'Meg, please, I can't bear it. Please stop talking about him. I can't bear it anymore.' The words escaping past her lips suddenly unleashed a flood of tears.

Meg stared at her with stricken eyes. 'I'm so sorry, love. I'll be quiet now.'

Gulping down sobs, Eimear smiled weakly at Meg. 'I'm OK, really I am. I wasn't expecting him to appear like that. I was half afraid he'd show up at the funeral, but he didn't and I was starting to relax and think he'd finally got the message that I wanted him out of my life. But then he shows up here, and I was just unprepared.'

'Should we let the Guards know that he's back harassing you? Haven't they warned him off? I thought he couldn't come anywhere near you?'

'No, leave it be. I don't think he'll be back. With Mam out of the way, I expect he thought he could weasel his way back into my life. And perhaps it's good that he called. Finally, what I was dreading all these weeks has happened. He was here, and you know what? I'm OK. He can't get to me anymore. I refuse to live my life worried that he'll show up. Screw him! He's not taking up any more space in my head. If he comes anywhere near me again, I'll contact the Guards. The good thing about my job is I know all the local Gardaí, and they'll watch out for me. And if he keeps being a nuisance, I'll contact his boss. I doubt if he wants to lose his nice, cushy accountant job. So, if he bothers me, I'll make life hot for him.'

'Wow, Eimear, where did all that fire come from?'

'I don't know, perhaps I'm channelling Mam. But, anyway, I'm not letting him make me live in fear any longer. I wish I'd said my piece to him when he was here. But enough is enough. He had better keep out of my way. You know what, Meg, he has more to fear from me than I have from him. I could ruin his reputation. No one will want to do business with a stalker, no matter what lies he spins. I have records with the Guards that he was harassing me.'

'I'm so proud of you, girl! If you hadn't found out what he was up to, perhaps you'd be married now, and he'd be making your life a living hell.'

'Yeah, I should be grateful. Mind you, I didn't see it that way then. When I discovered what he was up to, I saw no silver linings. Maybe it took Mam dying for me to grow up and not let that gobshite have any more power over me. And you know what? Donal's turning up here has convinced me. I'm definitely looking for a new job. I'm sick of him haunting me. I'm tired of having to justify to his sister and others why I want nothing to do with him.'

'I guess you're right. A fresh start, yes – that may be what's needed.'

They headed to bed, and despite all the emotions of the day, Eimear slept deeply and dreamlessly.

Chapter 3

Over the next few weeks, Eimear started the process of getting back into her life. Everyone was very kind at work, especially Mr Holland, her boss, and it was good to have a routine again. She moved back into her home. It was strange being alone in the house without her mam, but she was able to push through the loneliness. She filled in the long hours at night, updating her CV and applying for jobs. Meg kept in regular contact. It was nice to know she was there to lean on whenever loneliness overwhelmed her. They made a point of having a meal together twice a week. It allowed them to talk about the aching loss at the centre of their lives, but it also allowed them to discuss their plans and buoy each other up when they were becoming disheartened.

Meg contacted the printers and placed an order for memorial cards. Eimear chose a recent picture of her mother. Claire looked so vibrant, so happy, that it hurt to imagine it on a card memorialising her death. But the finished product was lovely and Meg insisted she send one to everyone who attended the wake and funeral. Eimear supplied the addresses of her friends from college.

They visited the solicitor's to see the will. Everything was straightforward and Eimear was well provided for between property and investments. With careful minding, it would offer Eimear security. There was a generous legacy to Meg as well.

After visiting the solicitor's, Meg treated them to lunch in a new café. The food was good, and they concentrated on enjoying it.

Then they ordered coffee and began to talk.

'Well, love, now you don't have to worry about money. And Claire left you her share of Mother's house – and her own house. What do you think you'll do? Will you sell up? You could get yourself something smaller and more modern.'

'Probate will take a while, so I won't do anything definite yet. I'll wait and see what the market is like. House prices have plummeted, so now may not be the best time to sell.'

Meg looked at her with anxious eyes. 'How are the job applications going? Any more developments?'

'Things are progressing nicely. I've got a few interviews lined up. Some of my college friends suggested a few firms that might be a good fit for me. They're all in Dublin, so it would be a fresh start, a new beginning. What do you think?'

'I think that you should follow your instincts – but, Eimear, what about friends? You don't know anyone in Dublin. I'd hate to think of you lonely.'

'Listen, Meg, I'm a big girl now. I'll be grand.' She quickly changed the subject. 'But what about you and your travel plans?'

Meg took a sip of coffee and sighed heavily. 'Oh God, I'm finding it so hard to get motivated. It feels strange not to be planning this with Claire. You know we'd planned she would meet up with me at some points on the trip. It seems wrong to be doing this without her. You know how she loved city breaks.'

'*Aww*, Meg, I know this must be so difficult for you.'

Meg sighed heavily. 'The truth is, I've also been finding it hard to cope with memories of the accident.'

Eimear reached across the table and placed her hand over Meg's. 'I can only imagine how hard that has been for you.'

'This week my doctor suggested I get some counselling. But, you know me, Eimear, I've never been one for navel-gazing. But I think a break from everything – from all the reminders might help.'

'God, Meg, getting counselling after a traumatic accident isn't navel-gazing! Come on!'

'You're right, but not right now. Let's see what an adventure and a complete change of scene can do for me.'

'I think a trip abroad will be a great distraction, and you'll regret it if you put it off. So tell me – what exactly have you got lined up?'

'Well, as you know, I've always had a yen to explore Europe. I've only been to Paris and Spain. So, I've decided to get an Interrail Pass. I know it's mad that I'm finally doing what college students do in their early twenties at the ripe old age of forty. *Am* I mad?'

'I think it's brilliant. I expect you to send me postcards from all the lovely places you visit and I insist on long newsy emails and lots and lots of pictures. Your phone has a decent camera, so no excuses. But I'd love letters, a kind of travelogue if you still remember how to write them. But I suppose your generation still has the skill.'

Meg laughed. 'Cheeky! I'm not much older than you, my girl, but I'll see what I can do. But if I manage more than one letter, it'll be a miracle.''

'Where will you fly to first?'

'I have no idea. I feel like doing something mad, like arriving at the airport and taking the most interesting flight available!'

Eimear laughed. 'Great idea! It's what a college student might do!'

'Yeah, but maybe I'll pass up on the youth hostels and find some nice, inexpensive hotels.' Meg raised her eyebrows and grinned.

'Definitely the way to travel! But will you be OK for money, Meg? I can lend you some until Mam's money comes through. My bank account is fairly healthy.'

'Don't be daft! I've been saving for this.'

'What about your job?'

'The hotel will have no trouble finding another receptionist – they may even hold the job for me when I return. So, we are both stepping into the unknown. But I promise you that if you need me, I'll be back on the next plane.'

'I'll be OK – don't worry about me. And I think it's great for you to have an adventure.'

The weeks flew by. Meg got a tenant for her house, someone who was building locally and needed somewhere to stay until their home was ready. She booked an Interrail Pass and talked excitedly about her itinerary, interspersed with tearful moments of guilt for moving on with her life. Eimear knew how she felt. It seemed wrong to make plans when the person most important to you had gone. It felt like a betrayal.

Eimear got two job offers and decided to go with an established firm of solicitors. It was a mid-sized firm, and she knew she was lucky to get a job there – so many of the people she graduated with were let go from their firms in the aftermath of the economic crash. The head of the practice was a man called Philip Jolly and, by a wonderful coincidence, his name suited him. He was about fifty and had a friendly open face and massive eyebrows that sat comically atop dancing eyes. He had a proper belly laugh, and everything wobbled when he chuckled, from his chin to his belly. She couldn't imagine him as a sober, serious solicitor – he looked more like an enthusiastic primary-school teacher. She briefly met some of the ancillary staff, who seemed friendly, but it was all so quick she didn't get any real impressions of them. She was to start at the beginning of September, so she needed to find somewhere to stay.

The long slog of trying to find an apartment wore her down and there were times when she was tempted to take anywhere as her start date at work was looming. Then, just when she was about to give up hope, an estate agent took her to see a nice place in Rathmines. It was a newly built block and the apartments were either one or two beds. The one she saw was a one-bed with a small but immaculate kitchen, and the living room looked out onto a small park. She stepped out onto the tiny balcony and saw that the trees that dotted the park were starting to turn russet. She loved the thought of looking out onto a blaze of colour in a few weeks when autumn really took hold. She told the estate agent that she wanted it. The cost per month was high, but the place was perfect. It wasn't a big distance from work, and it had parking. She was lucky to be the first to see the flat, and the next day she signed the lease and paid her deposit.

It was exciting to be moving into her new apartment. All her previous experiences of apartment-living were student accommodation and shared flats. She looked forward to making this place her own, styling it to suit herself.

The empty flat was soon filled with all her familiar things. Pride of place were the photographs of her parents. As she put a recent photograph of herself and her mam on the sideboard, she thought how much she looked like her mother. They both were dark-haired and dark-eyed, and had the same pointed chin and small, uptilted nose. Eimear wished she had her mother's height and grace. She thought enviously of how clothes hung so beautifully on her, whereas Eimear had to shop carefully if she didn't want to look swamped or like a little girl playing at dress-up.

Meg came to stay for a few days and helped with the unpacking. The day before her trip coincided with Eimear's first day at her new job. Eimear felt excited and a little apprehensive.

Philip Jolly introduced her to her new colleagues, and his rich laugh boomed out joyously with each introduction. They were two solicitors in their early thirties, and they seemed nice. John Kirk, from Kildare, was married with a young family, was very soft-spoken, and had a restless presence. He had spikey ginger hair, cut very short, which gave him a slightly startled air. Toby Cox, the other solicitor, was his opposite, extremely talkative and inquisitive. He reminded her of a friendly spaniel. She liked him but not his habit of asking very direct questions. He was only a few years older than her and at the end of the first day he invited her to go for a drink after work. The staff had decided to have a welcome drink for her, if she had the time. Eimear appreciated the gesture. Chatting with her new colleagues in a less formal setting would be really nice.

The pub was packed, but Toby found them a space at the back. Kate the paralegal, Hannah the secretary and Iris the receptionist came along too. They seemed nice. Kate was pale and dark with a distinctive Donegal accent and vivid blue eyes that darted constantly as though worried that she'd miss something. Hannah was the prettiest and a true Dubliner. Her family were born and raised in the Liberties for several generations. She had wavy blond hair and a curvy figure that Eimear suspected probably fluctuated from slim to chubby throughout the year. She spent most of the time peeping at Toby when she thought no one was looking and laughing hard at anything mildly witty that he said. Iris had made a reference to Hannah's boyfriend but it was clear to Eimear that she was keen on Toby. Not that Eimear blamed her, because he was a good-looking man, in a sporty, muscular way. He had thick, black, wavy hair that fell over his forehead. Eimear imagined that many girls would be keen to sweep it to one side, all the better to see his spaniel-brown eyes. But she felt safe from him as after Donal she wasn't in the market for boyfriends. Relationships were messy and fraught with misunderstandings and, for now, she wanted a quiet life free of the stresses of a new relationship. Iris was a tall, extremely thin girl. She looked stern until her laugh rippled out like an explosive Santa. Although she was from Carlow, she had a slight English accent from her years working in London as a receptionist for a hotel chain.

After one drink, Eimear made her excuses and returned to Rathmines. On the bus home, she got a call from Donal. She let him have it before he even got a chance to talk, and he barely got a word in. She didn't even care that the entirety of the bus heard her lambaste him. It felt good. Then she hung up and blocked his number. This was her third attempt, but he kept using different phones to contact her. But perhaps now he would accept she meant business and give up.

Meg had prepared steak and salad, and Eimear had the foresight to purchase a nice bottle of red.

After dinner, they sat sipping their wine.

'I hope the new job works out for you, pet. You deserve a bit of peace after the last year. Suddenly losing your mam was terrible but, before that, you had breaking up with Donal and dealing with his nasty antics. I've meant to ask you, has that fecker been in touch since he showed up at the house after the funeral?'

Eimear sighed. 'Yes, he rang me just as I was coming home on the bus. It was good because I let him have it and told him I'd make his life miserable if he contacted me again.'

'How did he take that?'

'I think I got through to him. He didn't like that I threatened his job, and I think he had never seen me so tough. It took Mam dying to make me realise that I'm no pushover and can stand up for myself. When I think back, I was such a dope. I let him away with so much while we were going out. When he cheated, he did me a favour because I saw what he was really like. Then, as if cheating wasn't bad enough, he had to lie about it and follow me around for weeks, only stopping when Alec told him to back off. But, look, Meg, let's not waste our last night together talking about that gobshite.'

'OK, love. Tell me about your first day. What are the people like?'

'I had a quick drink with the younger staff. They seem nice, and Philip Jolly is a pet – he suits his name. Do you know what, Meg? I think I'll be happy there. I really do.'

Meg raised her glass. 'To fresh starts and new adventures!'

They smiled delightedly at each other.

Meg glanced at her watch. 'God almighty, will you look at the time? I'd better get to bed. My flight is at nine, and I need to be at the airport by seven at the very latest.'

As she jumped to her feet, Eimear caught her hand, 'Hey, give me a shout before you leave. I need to get up early, too. I want to get a handle on the work in the office, so I plan to be in before anyone else.'

Meg grinned. 'OK. I've booked a taxi for six thirty, so I'll pop my head around your door.'

Eimear got up and hugged her aunt.

'I won't have time in the morning, Eimear, but I want to remind you to call me if you ever need to talk or if Donal bothers you again.'

'Meg, please don't be worrying. Donal is history, and it's a case of out of sight, out of mind. Besides, I'm the one who should be worrying about you off on your solo travels. You will take care, won't you?'

Meg grinned at her. 'I'm the auntie. I'm supposed to do the worrying, but we'll keep in contact, and I'll be back before you know it.'

<hr>

The next morning, as promised, Meg stopped at the couch where her niece was sleeping and kissed her forehead.

Eimear stirred and started to get up.

'No, stay where you are. I'm heading to the foyer to wait for the taxi.'

'Don't you want to have a slice of toast before you go?'

'No, thanks, I'm going to have something at the airport, so grab a few more minutes of snooze before the alarm rings.'

Eimear drifted back to sleep. At seven, the harsh ring of the alarm clock pulled her from sleep. Sitting on her couch bed, she looked at the flat door and felt bereft. She would miss Meg. Without her, the last few months would have been even worse. But now was the time to start embracing her new life.

Chapter 4

The next few weeks of work were challenging. She had to get used to working in a bigger firm than Holland & Byrne. Instead of just Mr Holland and a secretary, she now had half a dozen colleagues and, although Philip Jolly was very nice, he was also quite exacting. But he wasn't a control freak, and she felt he trusted her to do her job. The other two solicitors were competitive for business. The firm felt the economic downturn but was holding up its end. Still, she was able to hold her own, and in the weekly business meeting she made sure she wasn't sitting silent but tried to make her interjections thoughtful and pertinent.

She particularly liked Kate, the paralegal. Kate had moved to Dublin five years before. Her boyfriend, Joe, was a Dub, and they were saving to get married. She was full of ready smiles and sharp quips.

From the beginning, she was delighted that the girls made her feel welcome to their usual Friday evening chill-down. Usually, it was a bit of a bitch-fest as Hannah and Iris found the workload from the younger solicitors a bit much. But she liked the girls and was glad they had included her in their craic. She had been worried that they might have decided that, as a solicitor, she would not fit in with them. She wanted to go out with them partly for fear that if she didn't go they'd think her stuck-up. But she soon realised that she relished the warmth and the company of being part of a crowd of friends.

On the last Friday in September, they were ensconced in their usual corner of Lennon's. The pub was packed to the doors. The girls had to shout to be heard, but the din of the customers and the rattle of glasses gave an air of privacy. Unlike some evenings, no one was hurrying to get home. Iris had just broken up with her boyfriend. Her skinny frame shook with laughter as she regaled the girls on details of a recent blind date. Joe, Kate's fella, was out with his mates, and Hannah and her man had had a row, so everyone, including Eimear, was happy to stay late.

When Hannah was at the loo, Iris leaned closer, and in the quietest shout she could make and still be heard, she said, 'You know, now that Hannah and Paul have had their latest fight, it might be Hannah's opportunity to get together with Toby.'

Kate shook her head. '*Aww*, come on, Iris! You're exaggerating. Her Paul is a bit dull, but he's mad about her. He treats her like a princess. Maybe that's the problem – he's too keen on her and there's no challenge. Hannah always starts silly fights with him, and he never stands up to her. Maybe if he did they'd get on better. But I can't see her jeopardising her relationship because she's got a crush on Toby.'

'True, but I see how she looks at Toby, just like Philip eyeing up a nice cream doughnut!'

The girls giggled at Iris's image. Philip looked positively creepy when sizing up a plate of pastries.

'Toby is a looker, I grant you,' said Kate, 'but he's looking more upmarket than our Hannah. He's keen on Jolly's young one. Did you not see him flirting with her when she came to meet her dad for lunch the other day? He'd like to be part of the family. They're loaded.'

'I didn't know Philip had a daughter,' Eimear said.

'Yes, her name is Camilla, Cami to her friends.'

'Who the fuck calls their child Camilla?' giggled Iris.

'Hetty, short for Henrietta Jolly, does. Philip is down to earth, but Hetty has her notions, and the name Camilla fits in with where they live better than something old-fashioned like Concepta.' Kate smirked and waggled her eyebrows.

They giggled at the idea of Concepta Jolly from Howth.

'Has he any chance with her?' Eimear asked.

Kate shook her head. 'Philip Jolly is too protective of his Cami. He wants someone more mature for his precious daughter, especially as she'll be dropping out of Trinity. She failed her first-year exams and barely got the repeats. She hardly ever attended lectures, so it was no surprise she was failing.'

'How do you know so much about Camilla Jolly?' Eimear asked Kate.

'My cousin is studying law with her and says she's useless. No, you can depend on it. She'll be dropping out soon.'

The conversation ended when Hannah came back. Her bouncy blond curls were freshly brushed, and she had freshened up her make-up. She looked like a plump, big-eyed Crolly doll.

'You guys look cheerful. What are you talking about?' she asked as she resumed her seat beside Eimear.

'Nothing much, Hannah. We were discussing our weekend plans. Did I tell you that Joe and I are going to dinner at Revels tomorrow night?'

'You did not. That will set you back a fortune. Did your numbers come up?' teased Iris.

'I wish. It's a present from Joe's family for his birthday. I bought him tickets to Oxygen and I'll give them to him tomorrow at dinner. He moaned so much about missing last year's festival, so this should make him smile.'

'Will you look at the time? It's well past time I was off,' said Eimear. 'I still haven't unpacked all my boxes, and I need to find a frying pan at least. I've been living on takeout and toast.'

She reached for her coat, said goodbye to the girls and left the pub.

———— *ele* ————

She caught a bus home. She rarely brought her car to work as parking was in short supply near the office and, besides, she only needed the car when she was heading to Sligo. The bus wasn't too busy, and she got to read her novel and relax.

The bus stopped across the road from the flat. The weather had turned nasty. Sheets of rain hit her face, so she pulled her blue coat over her head and raced to the apartment block.

She was about to go upstairs when she decided to check her post-box. Perhaps there would be something from Meg. She had sent lots of texts and a postcard. There were four letters – three were bills, but she realised one was from Meg as she recognised her sloping handwriting and saw a French stamp. She smiled in delight. Meg had kept her promise.

Intriguingly, there was also a large A4-sized envelope. The postmark was the city centre and her name and address were typed. Must be something official – she couldn't think what.

She hurried up to her flat, put on the kettle and made tea. Then, tea in hand, she sat on the couch to enjoy the letter from Meg. It was nice, long, and full of descriptions of the people she had met on her travels and the beautiful sights of Paris. Being Meg, she had also described her culinary experiences. The woman did love her food. Meg joked that now she had fulfilled her promise but Eimear wasn't to expect any more letters as her hand was unused to the effort and strain. When she finished reading, she put the letter back in the envelope to read later whenever she needed a dose of her aunt's good humour and warmth.

She glanced at the bills and decided to deal with them later. Then she picked up the large envelope and pulled the flap open.

She stared at the contents. Photographs. She tipped the envelope and several large photographs slipped out. She spread them out. They were all of her. In them, she was pictured outside her office, coming back from the local Deli with Kate, and finally and most disturbingly entering her apartment. Her heart thumped. What the hell?

She remained frozen to the spot and, then, as though released from a horrible spell, she turned them over and looked to see if there was anything written or printed on the back – perhaps an address of where they had been developed. Nothing. She checked the envelope, looking for a note. Nothing.

She replaced the photos in the envelope.

Someone was surreptitiously taking photographs of her. Was it Donal? Who else could it be?

She picked up her phone and called Lana, her friend from school. Lana picked up immediately.

'Hey, stranger, how nice to hear from you! How's the new job?'

'Fine, all good. Listen, Lana. Can you tell me something?' She didn't feel up to fielding questions, anxious to get to the point. 'Do you know if Donal is still in town? I mean, has he made any recent trips to Dublin?'

'Oh God, he's not bothering you still, is he?'

'No, no. But do you know if he's left Sligo since I got here?'

'I don't think so – he's still going to work. I've seen his car parked in the usual spot.'

'What about at the weekend? Has he been around?'

'Well, he's been in the pub every Saturday despite the evil eye he gets from us all. He treated you so badly, and your real mates don't forget.'

'What about Jen? Has she been about?'

'She's by his side like his protector, deflecting the death stares we're sending him.'

'I see. Thanks, Lana.'

'Hey, hold up, girl! What's this about? He's been bothering you again, hasn't he? I thought after Alec had a word he cooled his jets.'

'No, no – I haven't heard from him. It's just ...'

'Just what, Eimear?'

'I just wanted to make sure he was still in Sligo.'

'And he's not harassing you?'

'No. Perhaps everything is going too well, and I'm a bit spooked.'

'Are you telling me everything?'

'Yes, I'm fine. Work is going great, and hopefully I'll make it down for a visit and we can all go out together and have a bit of craic. Tell me how everyone is doing.'

Eimear listened with half an ear while Lana filled her in on all the gang. Eventually, she was able to end the call.

She stared at the envelope. It was like what Donal would do: take pictures of her to make her feel scared and vulnerable. He had bombarded her with texts and messages when she broke up with him. He sent her numerous pictures on Facebook and, even after she blocked him, he continued to send her emails. It was like he wanted to remind her that he was still there, waiting in the wings, ready to pounce. But if he was in Sligo, who took the photos? She pulled them out of the envelope again. She was wearing a dark green scarf in the picture of her leaving the office. It had belonged to her mam. She wore that only a couple of days ago. In the photograph of her entering the flat, she wore the blue jacket she had bought to keep her warm now that winter was closing in. Yesterday was the first day she had worn it. Christ, he was keeping tabs on her! Lana thought Donal was still in Sligo, but she didn't know for certain. For all she knew, Donal could have slipped up to Dublin on the train and be tailing her all over town. She shivered at the thought.

She stared at the photos. This whole thing smelled of Donal. Could he have someone else take the pictures? What should she do? In the past, when Donal was being a dick, she had contacted Alec. One time, during an evening out with friends in the local pub, he had mortified her by having a very public row, alternatively wheedling and guilt-tripping her and ultimately verbally abusing her. It was the first time that he frightened her. He was no longer just a pest or a nuisance.

The persistence and, above all, the way he looked at her and the violent ugliness of his words scared her. Alec had stepped in and put him straight. And things had got better. Alec was convinced that Donal would stop bothering her. But was this a new campaign from a safe distance? After all, she couldn't prove it was Donal.

But if it wasn't Donal, who else could it be? She had no enemies as far as she knew. As a teenager, she had a few frenemies, but that was all kid stuff and long in the past. It scared her – the thought of someone taking her picture when she was out and about. She shivered at the thought of someone watching her, following her. For feck's sake, this was not what she needed. Bloody Donal, it had to be him, however he did it. Well, she wasn't going to let him get to her. It was probably just his last futile attempt to rattle her. Screw him!

Taking a breath, she picked up her phone and called Alec. She needed to put a stop to this craziness, and Alec would know what to do. He answered on the second ring.

'Hey, Alec, I hope I'm not bothering you at a bad time. Are you at work, or can you talk?'

'I'm just pulling into the driveway. My shift just finished. Is everything alright? You sound worried.'

'Yeah, well, I got something in the post that upset me.'

'What the hell? Is that bastard bothering you again?'

'The thing is, I'm not sure, but I suppose it has to be him. I got several photos in the post, and they are all recent pictures of me coming and going to work and arriving at my apartment. There's no note, but it's creepy, the idea that someone is following me, taking pictures and knows where I live. I rang Lana, and she thought Donal was in Sligo all week, saw his car around – but obviously, she couldn't be certain.'

'That proves nothing. He could have got someone to take the photos. Didn't he go to college in Dublin? He might have got a friend to take them.'

Eimear sighed angrily. 'Christ, I'm sick to death of this, Alec. I thought if I got away and made a fresh start, he'd leave me be. What should I do?'

'Right, first thing tomorrow, call to the local Garda station and tell them what's happening. They'll not do anything, but at least you'll have alerted them. In the meantime, I'll pay Donal a visit, give him hell, and tell him the Guards in Dublin are on it, too. That should soften his cough. He'll not be too worried about me, but the idea that the Dublin lads are involved might give him a fright.'

Eimear thanked Alec and ended the call with his reassurance ringing in her ears. She felt better for calling him, but the lovely, happy mood Meg's letter had created was tarnished. Her stomach growled, and where she usually ordered a takeaway on a Friday evening, she couldn't be bothered tonight. Instead, she opened a tin of beans, heated them on the gas hob and toasted some bread. She sat in front of the TV and ate her frugal meal. The telly couldn't distract her from the contents of the envelope. She decided to catch up on some paperwork and opened her laptop. The work was tedious, but it occupied her until it was time for bed.

Surprisingly, she managed to fall asleep quickly. Then, in the middle of the night, she woke with a start, her heart pounding. She listened intently, but all was quiet. She sank back into the welcoming warmth of the bed but, instead of its comfort lulling her to sleep, she tossed and turned until morning.

Chapter 5

It had taken her a while to accustom herself to the rhythm of her new job. In Holland and Byrne, she had been used to a slower pace, but in the city there was a greater sense of urgency and the variety of the work was stimulating. Her mainstay was still mainly compensation cases, wills and a little conveyancing, but she could see that there would be opportunities to get involved with some business clients, too. Of course, Toby and to a lesser extent John had most of the big clients, but she could see that there would be opportunities for her, too.

As the weeks passed, she took pains to be meticulous and thorough in her work and Philip Jolly was giving her more opportunities. This was clearly putting Toby's nose out of joint, but that couldn't be helped. At the weekly business meetings, Philip called on her more frequently, and she could see that he believed she had a future in the firm.

ele

It was mid-October, and she was well settled into the job, so well settled that she had forgotten to set her alarm on Monday morning and arrived at the office slightly late. She hated rushing and had an early client that she wanted to be prepared for. She was switching on her computer when Mr Brown walked in. Thankfully, it wasn't a very demanding meeting.

She was going through some probate issues of his mother's will. But it left her feeling out of sorts and behind with the day. She felt she was playing catch-up all morning. She worked through her lunch, eating a bar of chocolate and drinking pints of coffee to keep her going.

Now, at six o'clock, she felt ravenous but the thought of having to cook a meal when she got home drained her already ebbing energy. So when Iris suggested they grab a bite in the pub around the corner, she agreed with alacrity. It had the bonus of allowing the rush-hour traffic to dissipate, and she would have an easier journey home.

The Snuggery was aptly named. It was a small establishment with three snugs enclosing an open bar area. The girls found a free alcove and ordered a large pot of tea, burgers and chips. The food was simple with no frills, but it tasted good, and they set to eating with gusto.

Eimear debated mentioning the photos to Iris. But she was hesitant. She liked Iris. She was fun and very helpful with any extra work that needed doing. But she was a bit of a gossip. It wasn't a good look to have it known that she had a stalker who was taking sneaky pictures of her and her workmates. No, better not say anything. Philip Jolly wouldn't appreciate the drama.

Iris looked at her quizzically. 'What's up? You look worried?'

'Nothing, I'm just tired and slept in this morning – that always messes with my head.'

'How are you finding things at work? Are the two lads treating you OK? I know they can be hungry for the big jobs, but they can't just be divvying them up between each other. John is a decent lad, but he's got a wife and kids, and I suppose he's keen to do well, but I don't think he'd do you down. But Toby is a different kettle of fish – a real barracuda.'

'What, Toby? He seems harmless.'

'You are kidding? He's about as harmless as a snake. Our Toby is all charm on the outside, but he'd sell his granny if he thought it would help him. Look how he's treating Hannah. He knows she's keen on him, so he's getting her to do extra work and praising her to keep her eager to please. It's pathetic the way she laps up everything he says. She's not wise, that girl. So you watch out. He'd look you straight in the eye and lie to you without blinking.'

'God, Iris, I didn't know you disliked him so much.'

'I don't dislike him. I think he's great craic and good company on a night out, but I don't fool myself that he's my pal. Toby is out for Toby and more power to him. But I wouldn't like to see him pulling a fast one on you. The last guy who joined us only lasted six months because Toby made him look inept, so watch your back and make sure he doesn't try to muscle in on any of your clients. He's great at offering help and advice and then taking over. So be warned.'

'Thanks, Iris, I appreciate the heads-up. Things have been tough recently, and I appreciate knowing I can rely on someone.'

Iris smiled at her encouragingly and, before she knew it, she was confiding in her about her mother's death and a little about Donal. She managed to stop herself from mentioning the postal delivery. Later, while waiting for her bus, she regretted being so open. Iris was nice, but she wasn't a friend.

Back at the flat, as the long evening stretched ahead, she thought about contacting some of her college friends. Several had come to the funeral. She had neglected them when she was with Donal and, when things went wrong with him, she was too ashamed to reach out to them.

She considered ringing them and was just about to do so when she looked at the clock. It was nine o'clock. Two of her friends would probably be putting their children to bed, and the single ones were probably out socialising. Besides, it felt false to turn to them now when she had neglected them for the last four years.

She missed Meg. The postcards she sent brought some of the sunshine from where they originated into her life. In the six weeks since she had started her travels, Meg had sent three postcards and the letter. Eimear looked at the fridge where the postcards were pinned. The most recent was from Vienna. and it announced her intention to travel to Budapest to visit a buddy who was working at the international school there. Meg was having a great time. She deserved it. Claire always encouraged her sister to travel and would be delighted that, finally, she was taking her advice. It was just a pity that she wasn't around to go on a travel adventure with her. Eimear pictured her mam and Meg as two hippies wandering around Europe. Although, Claire was too glamorous to pass as a hippie.

Staring at the splashes of colour on the fridge door, she realised that it was high time she took her life in hand. All work and no play was making her a very dull girl. She was struck by how small her social life had become. It was time she kicked ass and started getting involved in life. She had always had an active social life, well, she had until she hooked up with Donal. She needed to make a life for herself here in Dublin – make new friends and develop new interests. After all, she was young, free, and single. Who knew what possibilities were out there? OK, she wasn't ready to start a relationship, but she wanted a bit of fun, a bit of lightness in her life. There were so many ways to meet people and she had always been an active person.

Trouble was a lot of the things she liked doing had associations with Donal. For example, she loved hiking, tennis, and squash. All those things they had done together. Since they broke up, she had given them up. She gave herself a pinch. Wake up, you can't let that fecker rob you of all the things that you loved. You must join a health centre, attend classes, join a book club, or a gym. There were lots of things to do, and she had no one to please except herself. She mustn't sit like a drip in her flat and let life pass her by.

Yes, a gym would be a good idea. Something new, something active … something that had nothing to do with Donal. Instantly, she felt better. Tomorrow, she would check out gyms and go on from there. It felt good to have a plan, to make a start on her new life.

The thought of the photographs and her watcher still hovered at the back of her mind, but she was determined to shut them down.

***

The next morning, she decided to take her car to work. Philip was away, so there would be space in the car park. She hopped into the car, relieved when it started immediately – sometimes, it misbehaved and had to be coaxed into cooperation. She glanced in her rear mirror and gasped, and the car jolted to a halt. The word DIE was written in capitals in lurid red on her rear window. She pulled open the car door and ran to look at it. Who the hell would do this? Was it blood? She shook herself – wise up, it must be paint. She nerved herself to touch the viscous material and smelt it. With relief, she could see it was ordinary paint. It dripped down the rear window and spread over the car's metal. If she waited to call the guards, the paint would dry and cost a fortune to remove. It had only just been done. Desperately, she grabbed the packet of tissues from her glove box and used them to wipe away the paint. It made a vivid mess. She'd never be able to see out of the window. Scanning the yard, she saw a water butt and filled a battered tin she found in a bin and started splashing water over the back window. It took an age but, with the addition of washing-up liquid, she cleared up most of the mess. She rang work, explaining she had car trouble and then dropped the car off at a garage to be valeted. The guys there were disgusted on her behalf and speculated which local lads might be responsible. She shrugged and left them, hoping they'd eliminate any paint residue.

When she got on the bus at ten, she was annoyed that she had forgotten to photograph the damage. If it happened again to her or anyone in her building, she wanted pictorial evidence to show the guards. At work, she apologised for being late and decided against telling them what had happened. Instead, she said she had a flat tyre and had left the car at home.

When she returned from work that evening, she called to the local Garda station and told them about the incident. They promised to look into it, but she wasn't about to hold her breath judging by the lacklustre response to her complaint. She reminded them about her report of the photographs she had received in the post. She took note of the name of the Garda who dealt with her.

Was this connected with the photographs she received? It seemed such a bizarre thing to do. If her tyres had been let down or her door keyed, she would have put it down to ordinary vandalism that could be directed at anyone. But someone had gone to the trouble of buying paint and writing DIE on her rear window. That didn't seem like a random act, but a deliberately targeted one.

Was Donal behind it? But it seemed too vicious for him. But who else could it be? Well, Jen was ripping with her because she dumped Donal. She had accused Eimear of blackening Donal's name all over town. Jen was fiery, but this was way over the top. She loved her brother, but this would be an unhinged overreaction.

Back at the flat, she checked her post-box to see if there was another postcard from Meg. There was only one letter in the box: an A4-sized envelope. Her heart sank.

Chapter 6

Making threats is dangerous for your health. Sleep well while you can. It won't be long now!

The words bounced off the page and hit her with their vicious tone. The sentence **'It won't be long now'** was underlined so hard it had torn the paper. Her mouth dried up, and her skin prickled. This was scary. Who was doing this to her? God, she had only arrived in Dublin two months ago and, apart from the guys in the office, she knew nobody. Had she done something to upset someone? But even if she had, this reaction was messed up. Again, she thought of Donal. But how? It seemed over the top that he had hired someone to vandalise her car. The photos, even this note, could be from him, but it was so melodramatic. Maybe it had nothing to do with Donal. It seemed bizarre that two people, Donal and a mysterious other, should have it in for her.

Could it be a case of mistaken identity? If so, how had it happened? And what should she do? How do you convince an unknown enemy that they were wasting their efforts on the wrong person?

She looked at the printed note, noticing again how a pen had been scored hard against the page, almost ripping it. That was more threatening than the actual words. It indicated intense feelings. Eimear stared at the note. It was crazy how marks on a page could scare her.

Should she mention it to Philip or one of the others? But she had just started at the firm and didn't want them to think she had enemies. A solicitor's firm likes to maintain an image of respectability. As nice as Philip Jolly was, she didn't think he'd be impressed that his latest hire was attracting such negative attention. She was still on probation. It would be months before she would have any real job security. John and Toby would probably express sympathy, but she knew they'd use the information to make her look bad and solidify their positions. If she told the girls, she would have to depend on their discretion and, anyway, what could they do?

She put the note with the photos in the pink lockbox where she kept all her important documents. OK, she could do nothing right now and needed to eat something. Perhaps she could think more clearly after eating and decide what to do. She microwaved a ready meal, something green with chicken and had a glass of wine.

Later, after finishing her rubbery meal, she stretched out on the couch and watched some telly. But it failed to grab her attention. She picked up her phone, and there was a text from Meg, suggesting they Facetime now if she was free. The thought of speaking to Meg lifted her spirits. Rapidly, she texted her agreement, and in a few minutes, the call came through. Meg's friendly face filled up the screen of her phone.

'Well, hello, darling! Aren't you a sight for sore eyes?'

'*Aww*, Meg, it's great to see you. Where in the world are you now? Come on, make me jealous!'

'It's great to see you, and I'm dying to hear all the craic. I'm just back from the shops, and I totally lost the run of myself. I've bought more clothes than I'd need for a lifetime – and how am I going to carry them about with me as I travel? I'm nuts! But, you know what, I don't care. It was such fun.' She held a bright-blue dress with splashes of orange against her body. 'What do you think, Eimear? Does it suit me?'

'Very chic, Meg. It's good to see you wearing such vibrant colours, they really suit you. It's high time you started treating yourself. You deserve it. So where are you?'

'I'm still in the lovely Budapest. My friend Alice came here to teach in one of the international schools, fell in love with a Hungarian and never left. When I called to say hi, she and her husband insisted I stay for a few days. They've been absolute dotes, but you know the saying that, like fish, guests go off after three days, and I've been here nearly a week, so I'm heading off tomorrow. I thought I'd hire a car, drive around the country and take in the sights.'

'So are you becoming addicted to travelling? Will you be off around the world next?'

Meg laughed. 'Maybe!' Then she paused, looking a little downcast. 'You know, sometimes I feel a bit disoriented. I'm thinking that all this travelling is just a way of avoiding thinking about Claire and the accident.'

'God, yes, the accident must still haunt you. Do you want to come home, Meg? You know that you can stay with me until your renters give you back your house or stay at Mam's.'

'Thanks, love, but I'm not ready to come home yet. Yes, maybe I'm running away from things, but I think on the whole being on the move is helping.'

'So where are your wandering feet taking you next?'

'Next week, I'll travel to Germany, Poland, and Denmark. I've never been to Berlin, and I'd like to visit Krakow.'

'Wow, that's exciting! You're going to be exhausted once this trip is over.'

'Well, I'm going to take a break from travelling when I get to Denmark. I plan to go to Copenhagen and stay a while. I've been checking out some websites. Do you know, if you're willing to do a bit of pet-sitting and plant-watering, you can get to stay in some nice places free of charge? It's a win-win for everybody concerned. I plan to see if I can find a nice apartment in the centre of the city.'

'Meg! You shouldn't have to look for jobs to make ends meet! I told you – if you need a loan, I can help.'

'Minding a few cats and throwing water on some flowers hardly counts as work! And I'm grand for money. I just prefer staying in someone's home rather than a soulless hotel. So stop worrying about me.'

'Well, if you're sure ...'

'I am. I'm not borrowing from my niece – besides, the Taylors gave me a generous deposit to rent the house so I'm rolling in it, honestly. But I will take you up on your offer to put me up for a few weeks when I eventually wend my way home.'

'You know I'd love to have you here, and you can pay me in nice dinners when I come home from work.'

'Well, I had good training looking after your gran all those years. Now, enough about me. Tell me everything that you've been up to. First, how's the new job?'

Eimear filled Meg in about the office and delighted her with her pen portraits of Philip Jolly and the others who worked there.

'That Toby buck seems interesting. You certainly painted him as a bit of a lad and a hunk to boot. Do I detect the stirrings of romantic interest?'

'Indeed you do not. That fellow has eyes on better fish than me. He's after the boss's young one. He's one with an eye to the main chance. But although he's a bit of a rogue, he's alright, really.'

'So everything is going fine!' Meg paused, looking awkward. 'Look, Eimear, I was just wondering if Donal has been bothering you.'

'No. Why do you ask?' She realised her voice sounded too sharp.

'It's just that he was so scary that night, the way he behaved at the house. I'm worried about you.'

'Thanks, Meg, but moving away was the best thing, and it's a case of out of sight, out of mind. I think threatening to tell his boss was a good move. In fact, I've been so busy I haven't given him a thought.'

'And here I am, bringing him up again. Sorry, pet.'

'That's fine. I appreciate your concern; really I do. But all's good.'

'Have you any more gossip for me? Any news from home?'

'Not a bit. But, hey, you'll be glad to hear I plan to join a gym. There's one that's handy for the flat and, if I meet people through it, that would be a bonus. They also offer yoga and judo classes, so I might give that a go. I'm also thinking of starting to play squash again, so soon I'll have a jam-packed social calendar.'

'Well, good for you! I'm so glad you're getting out and about again. But I hear my hosts returning from work, so I had better go. I promised them I'd cook a typical Irish dinner for them.'

'God, not bacon and cabbage?'

'No – they requested Irish stew.'

'They must think we eat nothing else. OK, get to work! Love you!'

Meg blew a kiss, and the connection ended.

Eimear felt bereft. It was nice to chat with Meg, but it made her feel her absence more keenly. Should she have told her about the unpleasant postal deliveries and the damage to her car? No, it would only upset her. Knowing Meg, she'd have insisted on getting the next plane home, and if she thought Donal was responsible for upsetting her niece she'd go for him and wouldn't hold back. There was no need to worry her. At least not yet.

It was high time Meg had a little fun. She was always minding others. Eimear wondered why Meg never married. Vaguely, she recalled Meg dating a few guys but never for more than a few months. Well, who knew, she might meet someone on her travels. That would be one wedding she'd be happy to go to.

She pondered over what Meg had said about Donal. Mam and Meg had tried to warn her about him. They thought he was possessive and jealous. But she hadn't listened. She was so flattered that this amazing hunk fancied her. She ignored all the red flags, the times he made her cancel arrangements with friends, the way he needed to know everywhere she went and who she met. She had even been flattered by his jealousy, however ridiculously misplaced. At a later point, Meg had suggested that maybe, once they got engaged, he might be more sure of her and less possessive. She desperately wanted Meg to be right. It was the one time her aunt had steered her wrong. Her mam was very upset that she had got engaged and begged Eimear to have a long engagement.

But Eimear thought him perfect, the most wonderful man alive. That should have warned her. No one is perfect unless they're playing a part. She should be grateful for the girl he was playing around with. If she hadn't seen him kissing her with her own eyes, she might be married now. Mam and Meg had been kind and supportive. There had been no 'I told you so' from either of them. They just gave her shoulders to cry on. She didn't think she'd have been as understanding in their place.

Glancing at the time, she decided to take a shower before bed. Then afterwards, she made herself a cup of chocolate. She picked up Jane Austin's *Pride and Prejudice*, a book she had read several times but never tired of. She read a chapter and then, feeling her eyes droop, switched off her bedside lamp.

She was drifting off to sleep when she thought about Meg asking if Donal had been in touch. Then her mind turned to going over the horrible recent incidents. She thought about the note and its warning about her making threats. Well, she had threatened to tell Donal's boss he was harassing her. So now he was warning her off.

She sat bolt upright in the bed, her somnolent state shattered.

She lay back again but couldn't quieten her mind and, as she tossed and turned, she went down a tunnel of dark memories. Her dreams were nightmarish and confused. It was a relief when her alarm clock sounded in the morning.

Chapter 7

The next week passed in a frenzy of activity. Philip gave her a lot more work, which was great, as it meant he rated her. But she could see that Toby had his nose put out of joint. He had hoped for the McMahon business, which landed on her desk. He gave her an engaging smile that she knew was as fake as her handbag and offered to help if she felt overwhelmed. Iris and Kate were fighting back smirks as she thanked him for his generous offer but said she'd thought she'd manage. Hannah caught the sarcasm even if Toby didn't. She hoped Hannah wouldn't hold it against her that Toby wasn't getting all the plum jobs.

On the social front, she joined the gym close to where she lived. Kate had recommended it as her boyfriend often worked out there. The staff were helpful, but once they saw she knew what she was doing, they let her get on with it. Over the weeks, she recognised the regulars who went from work straight to the gym like her. It pleased her that it attracted nearly as many women as men. It felt like a safe, friendly environment. She had also booked a few yoga sessions in the Health Centre and put her name down for squash. Perhaps someone from the gym might fancy a game sometime. All in all, she was feeling more optimistic. The anonymous postal deliveries continued to be a niggling worry. She still wasn't sure they had come from Donal. If it was him, how had he managed to get her address? Well, she had passed it on to a few people. Meg naturally, but also a few friends and her previous employer so they could forward any mail to her. Could one of them have told Donal? It seemed unlikely.

Apart from her apprehension when she checked her post-box each evening, all was well in her world. She finally believed that she was moving forward. The loss of her mother still reduced her to tears at odd moments. Sometimes, when something nice happened, her immediate thought was to tell her mam all about it, and then she would remember, and sadness would grip her tightly. But she felt that she was starting to live her life and find pleasure again in the small things, like exercising and meeting the girls at work for a drink or a trip to the cinema.

It had been two weeks since she last received the disturbing missive, and she was hopeful that if it were from Donal, he would have realised that she wouldn't talk to his boss unless he continued to harass her. A spring was in her step as she ran up the stairs to her flat. Her post-box contained only a postcard from Meg. She made tea and glanced at the postcard. It was from Berlin. Why did the sky in postcards look so impossibly blue? Even the ones from Ireland that she saw in the local post office were lush and dazzling. Meg had packed the maximum words into the space on the back of the card.

Getting lost in Meg's shiny, sunny world was wonderful, especially when the skies outside her window were grey and venturing outside without an umbrella was foolish. It made her long to plan a holiday. She'd see what was available online. It would be late spring before she could go anywhere, but it would be nice to dream. Perhaps Lana would like to go with her.

She was getting ready for bed when she heard it. The sound of a child crying. It was coming from outside her flat. She was surprised because, as far as she knew, the flats were occupied by single people or couples, and she had never seen any children. Maybe it was a visitor to one of the apartments. She shrugged, got into bed, and was soon asleep.

A loud banging on her door awakened her. She sat up in bed, her heart racing. The hammering continued unabated. Pulling on a dressing gown, she ran to the door barefoot. What time could it be? Her phone was somewhere in the kitchen and she never wore her watch to bed. Glancing through her balcony doors, she could see it was pitch dark. The banging continued, but now she heard the screams of a baby and a woman's voice pleading to be let in.

Paralysed with fear, she stood at her door. What should she do? The woman sounded terrified, and she couldn't just ignore it. She had to do something. Steeling herself, she unlocked the door. Puzzled, she looked out into the hallway, and it was empty. But then she noticed a package on the ground. She bent down to see.

He came out of the shadows, a balaclava obscuring his face. Before she could react, he grasped her by the throat and she was dragged backwards into the flat. He kicked open the door of her bedroom and threw her on the bed, where she lay incapable of movement. Everything slowed down, and he seemed to stare at her for an eternity. That was when she opened her mouth to scream. He hit her twice across the face, and the scream died in her throat.

'Please, don't hurt me,' she begged through frozen lips.

He lay down on top of her, and she felt his hot, sour breath on her skin through the mouth-hole of the balaclava. He ran his hands roughly over her body. Her arms were trapped, and she lay helpless underneath him. His masked face was inches from hers. His eyes bored into hers. He sighed, and she felt something cold rest against her cheek. With horror she realised it was a knife.

'I have money, it's in my bag in the kitchen, take what you want, but please don't hurt me!'

The masked man continued to stare at her silently. She couldn't drag her eyes from his. They were hard eyes, small and vicious. He was going to kill her. She believed it and started to pray, to call on her mam to save her. He grasped her hair, pulling her head upwards. Her hands were still trapped under the weight of his body. Still staring into her eyes, he took the knife and held it against her neck. She gulped and felt the cold knife slide along her throat. Something warm trickled down her neck. He's going to kill me now, she thought.

Suddenly, he rolled off her, and roughly turned her over on her front and grasped her hair, pulling it tight. Horrified, she heard a sawing noise and realised he was cutting her hair. The pillow absorbed her sobs, and she waited to die. Then his weight was off her, and she realised she was alone.

Sobbing hysterically, she slid to the floor. She heard the flat door slam. But she still couldn't trust that he was gone. She sat quaking with terror, desperate to get to her phone in the kitchen and yet afraid to leave the relative safety of her bedroom. But eventually, carrying her bedside lamp with her as a weapon, she walked into the kitchen. The flat was empty. With trembling hands, she checked that her door was shut and that the snib was in place. She found her phone lying on the kitchen counter and dialled 999. Her sobs made it difficult for the operator to understand her, and she forced herself to breathe and calm down. It took a few attempts before her dried-up mouth would cooperate. She asked for the gardaí. When she was put through, she managed to give her address and explain something about what happened. Although if any sense was made of her sobbing, hiccupping account, she didn't know.

Chapter 8

The gardaí arrived. Two officers, a man and a woman. They were very kind and waited patiently until she calmed down. The woman held her hand and spoke soothingly while the male officer made tea. He had sweetened it, which she disliked,   and, although she appreciated his reasoning regarding sweetened drinks and shock, it was impossible to drink. The female officer introduced herself as Garda Maureen Collins, and her colleague was Garda Shane Owens. He took notes while she explained to Collins what had happened. They checked outside for the package on the ground, but it was gone. They promised to check for fingerprints the next day and asked if she would be willing to have her prints taken for elimination. Eimear knew this was probably a waste of time as she told them with a shiver that the hand gripping her throat was gloved. But the guards said it would be no harm to check. Collins asked if she wanted to be checked out in the hospital. She shook her head. Apart from the cuts to her throat and the red marks from the blows she had received, she was OK. If OK meant terrified and shaken to her core. When she'd looked in the mirror while she waited for the gardaí, she could see the fine line drawn by the blade on her neck. It still throbbed uncomfortably.

'Look, you need to get that injury to your neck checked out,' Garda Owens said. 'I know it's not deep but you may need a tetanus shot to be on the safe side. We'll drop you off at the hospital. At the very least, someone will talk to you, and counselling will be available when you feel up to it.'

Rather than putting up any resistance, it seemed easier to give way, and she submitted to being taken to A&E. She had her wound cleaned. Thankfully, it was superficial and, after she got her shot, she was keen to get away from the hospital. The guards were very kind and dropped her back at the flat.

Collins asked if she had a friend who could stay with her. Eimear hesitated. She could stay with one of the girls from work. Kate was becoming a bit of a mate, but she feared everyone at work finding out. She didn't want it to interfere with her job. That was the one space where she felt safe. Shaking her head, she insisted she would be fine.

'Tell me, Eimear, did you notice anyone following you recently?' asked Collins. 'Have you been anywhere where someone might be able to learn your habits?'

'I joined a gym a few weeks ago. But I never noticed anyone. I haven't been talking to any one person in particular.'

Garda Owens broke in. 'It's beginning to sound opportunistic, but what is surprising is that nothing was taken and, apart from roughing you up, he didn't seriously harm or assault you. You're a solicitor – is there any possibility that a client might have a grudge against you?'

'No, I've only been there a short while, and all my clients seem happy with my efforts on their behalf. But I reported a few things recently to your station.'

She listed all the ugly things that had happened to her over the last few weeks – the photographs of her, the anonymous notes and the damage to her car. She fetched the note and photos from her lockbox.

They looked at them and the Garda Owens placed them in an evidence bag. 'We'll have them fingerprinted, but it's unlikely to be useful as most poison-pen writers know to wear gloves.'

'Eimear, if the letter, the photographs, the vandalism of your car, and the attack are connected, it looks like someone has a serious grudge against you,' said Garda Collins. 'Can you think of anyone at all who has reason to want to hurt you? Of course, the other incidents may be unconnected to the attack on you, but honestly it seems an unlikely set of coincidences, and I'm not a great believer in coincidences. So, I think we'll assume they are all connected. So, if you have any suspicion at all, tell me now.'

Eimear hesitated but made up her mind. 'There is someone. My ex-fiancée and I parted on bad terms and, for a long time afterwards, he followed me around, sent me nasty texts and generally made a nuisance of himself. I reported him to the gardaí in Sligo, and he eventually got the message. He left me alone for weeks but, after my mother died in August, he called at my house and made a nuisance of himself. I threatened to inform his boss if he bothered me again. It seemed to have worked. It's just that the note mentioned me threatening someone.' Eimear paused. 'You know what? Donal was a dick, but even he wouldn't go this far. Besides, the man who broke in looked nothing like him.'

'I thought he wore a mask?' Collins said sharply.

'Yes, he did, but his eyes were different, and even though he spoke in a whisper, it didn't sound remotely like Donal's voice.'

Owens stared at her intently. 'So, Eimear, what's your theory then?'

'I don't know, I really don't. I've only been in Dublin for a couple of months. I hardly know a soul. I live a pretty quiet life – all I do is go to work, have occasional drinks with the ones from work, and go to the gym.'

'What about your work colleagues? Have you any problems with any of them, the men or the women?'

'No, I get on fine with them all. I'm not there long enough to have been a threat to anyone. It makes no sense.'

'What about at the gym? Have you noticed anyone watching you or someone always hanging around when you are there?' he said.

Eimear racked her brain. Usually, she wasn't aware of anyone when working out—she was focusing on her programme. Try as she could, she had no memory of any unwanted attention, or at least no more than any young woman would experience. The trainers were all pleasant and professional. She never got any bad vibes from them. She shook her head.

'Have you threatened someone apart from your ex? Is there a colleague who might perceive that you plan to get him or her into trouble?'

'No, definitely not. Could this be a mix-up? Perhaps I'm being targeted by mistake.'

'Or someone has deliberately set you up and made some thug think you are threatening their business. Does your firm deal with many criminal cases?' asked Collins.

'Again, no. Most of our work is compensation cases, probate, and conveyancing. We have a few clients with dubious reputations, but I don't deal with them. Oh God, I don't know! This is all surreal. I don't have enemies. Donal is the only person I've fallen out with, and I can't believe he's behind this.'

The officers got to their feet.

'I think you should find somewhere else to stay tonight, or get a friend to come here,' Collins said.

'Well, there's not much night left, is there? It's after five now. I'm not dragging someone over here now. Besides, I'll soon be getting ready for work.'

Collins stared at her in concern. 'Eimear, you're not fit to go to work today. Take my advice and ring in sick. You need to take time to recover. What has happened to you is very traumatic. You must talk to people and get the support of family and friends. There is nothing to be gained by going to work and then getting overwhelmed and having to leave.'

Eimear nodded slowly. Collins was right. She looked at her hands, and they were still trembling. 'Perhaps you're right. I don't want to get upset at work and have to come home, and I feel very shaken.'

'Of course you do.'

'OK, I'll call in sick, but I don't want them to know about this, at least not yet.'

Garda Collins walked to the door, followed by Eimear. 'OK, and Eimear, when you feel up to it, come into the station to make a full statement. You never know what you may remember about the assailant. It's amazing what can suddenly pop into your head, which might just cast light on all these things happening to you. By the way, we've noticed you have some CCTV cameras in the foyer, and we'll see if they can shed any light on the identity of your assailant.'

At the door, Shane Owens, who had been looking around the flat, joined them and said, 'I've checked around the place, and I recommend you make a few changes to your security. For starters, you need a spy-hole, a chain so the door can't be fully opened, and a deadbolt. Also, I'd recommend you secure your windows at night and bolt the balcony door.'

They fixed a time for her to visit the station and arrange for the flat to be checked for fingerprints later in the day. Then they said goodbye.

After they left, the flat echoed with silence. Eimear forced herself into action. She longed to clean the flat and strip the bed but knew she needed to leave things as they were until after the gardaí checked it.

She went into the bathroom and examined her hair. Peering at it in the bathroom mirror, she saw it retained its bob shape from the front. She positioned a hand mirror to see the back of her head. It looked horrible. A big hunk of her hair had been hacked close to the scalp. How in the name of God could she disguise it? She would have to go to a hairdresser and get it sorted, but it would mean cutting it very short.

She sat in the kitchen, drinking coffee until it was time to call the office. She told Iris that she had a stomach bug and wouldn't be in to work until the next day and asked her to reschedule all her appointments. She forced herself to listen to Iris's words of sympathy and then hung up.

Finding a hairdresser salon to fit her in when she wanted was difficult. They all seemed very busy. But eventually, at the fourth salon, she arranged an appointment for the next day. Great, she could get it sorted after work. In the meantime, she'd try to cobble a bun together, but it would look odd. Shit! What would the bastard do with her hair anyway?

Would he dump it or keep it as a trophy? She felt sick at the thought of him perving over it.

She kept her appointment at the station, had her prints taken for exclusion and read over the statement she had made to the two officers who called at her flat. As she was leaving, she met Maureen Collins, who told her the security camera in the foyer of her building was being checked to see if they could identify her assailant. She promised to contact her when they had examined it.

After she left the Garda Station, she visited a locksmith's and arranged for them to call and put in the additional security she needed. She was in luck, and they promised to call that afternoon. She hoped the gardaí would be finished checking for prints by then.

When she returned to the flat, she was met at the door by two officers who took her key and did their tests. They promised to be finished by two, so she took herself off to a coffee shop and had a sandwich. She didn't feel like eating but realised she needed to keep her strength up. She got a call from the guards to say they were finished with the flat and would put her keys in the post-box.

When she entered the foyer, she noticed the discreet camera and hoped it would help. She was opening her post-box when a neighbour from the flat above her collared her.

'Do you know anything about all the gardaí swarming around?' he asked.

She shook her head, muttered something about having to make a call and fled upstairs.

Every surface in her flat seemed to be covered in powder residue. Sighing, she set to work, dusting down all the surfaces and sweeping all the dust into a dustpan. She wiped everything with disinfectant spray. When the kitchen and living area were restored to order and cleanliness, she braced herself to enter her bedroom. Flashbacks of what had happened here infiltrated her head, and she felt dizzy and sick with fear. She forced herself to strip the bed and put fresh sheets on it. But she wasn't sure if she could sleep there again. It felt contaminated.

The locksmith arrived just as she finished cleaning. She sat on her couch and tried to read while he got to work. After he had left, she felt a bit more secure.

As the night drew in, she checked and rechecked the locks. At seven, she ordered a pizza. Her intercom buzzed, it was the pizza delivery service. She buzzed him into the building. But, even so, when he reached her door and knocked, she stood quaking behind it. Eventually, putting on the security chain, she peered out, and when she saw it was indeed the pizza delivery. She paid for her meal and locked up immediately afterwards.

She ate with relish; for the first time since her attack, she felt real hunger. She had a bottle of wine left over from the weekend. She sniffed it – it smelled bitter, but what the hell? She needed a drink. Besides, the pepperoni would disguise the taste. She watched a little TV, couldn't get caught up in any of the plots but continued watching. She didn't want to have to face going to bed yet.

Eventually, at midnight, she knew she'd have to get some sleep, or she'd be useless at work in the morning. Gritting her teeth, she walked into the bedroom. It looked immaculate; she had dressed the bed in her favourite duvet and squirted perfume around the room. But when the time came to go to bed, she stood frozen at the bedroom doorway. Over and over, she kept reliving the horror of the night before. The weight of the man's body, his mean little eyes, the sour smell of sweat, the pain of his hand on her throat and the terror that he would kill her. Stifling a sob, she backed away. Then she marched back into the room and pulled the duvet and pillows off the bed. She couldn't face the room tonight. Instead, she made up a bed for herself on the couch.

Before she lay down, she squirted some of her mother's favourite perfume on her pillow. Mam will keep me safe, she told herself. Amazingly, it worked, and she slept soundly the whole night until the insistent ring of her alarm pulled her back to the conscious world.

Chapter 9

Fixing her hair was challenging, but whatever magic was in her mam's perfume continued to work wonders. A new strength and resilience coursed through her. She wasn't going to let the bastard who attacked her rob her of her peace and turn her into a fearful victim. Tonight, she would sleep in her room and to hell with him. She was pleased when she completed her hairdressing attempts and had the perfect excuse for styling it that way should anyone enquire. The next step was dealing with the marks on her neck and face. The ones on her neck she could disguise with a scarf, and she piled on a copious amount of foundation to cover the yellowing marks on her face. Now, she was ready to face the world, or at least the office.

When she arrived, Iris was the only one in. She was at the reception desk, turning on her computer and checking for messages. She did a double-take when she saw Eimear.

'Jeeze, girl, what happened to you?' she said.

Eimear grinned. 'I had a small accident with the curling tongs and had to cut a lump out of my hair to free myself. But don't worry, I'm going to the hairdresser to get a cut after work.'

'*Aww* no, I liked your bob. What are you going to do with it?'

'I'm getting it chopped short. I'm bored with this style anyway, so no harm done.'

'Are you over your stomach thing?'

'Yeah, I think I ate something dodgy, but I'm OK now. Were the clients OK with rescheduling my appointments?'

'Yeah, in the main, but that old devil Harrison groused, so I'm afraid I booked him in at five. Is that OK?'

'No bother at all. What's the rest of my day like? Will I get lunch, or am I booked solid?'

'No, you're grand. Maybe you'll take a shorter break, but it'll work out.'

'Thanks, Iris, you're a star. See you later whenever I get my head up for air.'

Eimear was pleased with how she handled things with Iris, and because she was snowed under with work, she could avoid the others. She ate lunch at her desk or drank it as all she had was coffee until she found a packet of biscuits in the little staffroom. But she was pleased. The day was productive; she felt reasonably up-to-date.

Her evening appointment with Mr Harrison was trying, as he was one of those men who were only happy if they had something to complain about. He spent ten minutes complaining about the inconvenience of his appointment being cancelled, and even though she sorted out everything he asked her to, it seemed only to annoy him more. His was a face and a personality that only his mother could love. But eventually, he left, and she was able to finish up and say goodbye to Iris. The other solicitors and staff had already left.

She went to a fast food place and sat at the counter, eating slowly to pass the time until her hair appointment at seven. From the counter, she picked up a newspaper another customer had left behind. The articles interested her, and the time flew by. When she glanced at her watch, she realised she had only five minutes to get to the hairdresser. She had better hustle, or she'd be late.

The stylist was horrified at the state of her hair, and she was glad she had thought up her curling tongs story. They pored over some style books but, with the damage to her hair, it would have to be a pixie cut. Eimear sat nervously on her chair as hair rained down on the floor. She was afraid to look in the mirror and tried to keep reading her magazine.

The stylist tapped her on the shoulder.

'What do you think?'

Eimear blinked. She looked so different. It was strange; she always had either long or mid-length hair. This was some change, and she discovered she liked it.

'You have a look of Twiggy or Audrey Hepburn. What do you think?'

Eimear grinned. 'I love it!'

She was shown the style from the back and sides and couldn't stop grinning. Her head felt different and lighter; it made her feel younger and freer. *Wow* was the word that kept popping up. She had never really believed in the power of a haircut to transform. But she did now. Gathering her belongings, she paid her bill and left Louise, her stylist, a very generous tip. She smiled all the way back to Rathmines.

The reaction at work the next day gave her an added ego boost. It didn't hurt to see the admiration in Toby's eyes. Philip was gallant and of course the girls exclaimed over her hair and regaled her with disasters they had suffered at the hands of hair-styling appliances. The change in her cut had the advantage of making her feel different. With this brave new cut, she could take on the world.

She was determined to make a few changes. For starters, she wasn't going to act like a victim. She was going to take action to preserve her safety. When she got home tonight, she'd pop over to the fitness centre and sign up for a self-defence class. If she was in America, she could probably buy a gun. But the idea of having a lethal weapon in her home made her shiver. No, she would take sensible precautions, and hopefully the gardaí would have identified the man on the CCTV cameras. Before she left work, she would try to find out if they had any news for her. Garda Collins had given her a number to call.

The rest of the working day flew by and, just as she was about to leave, her phone rang.

It was Garda Collins.

'Well, how are you feeling today, Eimear?'

'I'm on the mend, but I still feel shaken up. Do you have any news for me?'

'We went through the camera footage. We do have an image, but it's difficult to identify him. I thought we would drop over tonight around nine and show you the stills from the camera. But I wouldn't hold out high hopes of identifying him. Still, it's worth a try. Does that time suit you?'

'Yeah, that's fine, but I could drop by the station on my way from work to save you a trip.' Eimear was worried about uniformed guards being seen at her flat again. She didn't want to have any more inquiries from her neighbours.

'No, it's fine. We have to be in the area anyway. So see you then.'

Eimear's previous optimistic mood dissipated somewhat. She felt a sense of nervous anticipation. It was doubtful that she would recognise the man who entered the building. Perhaps he was wearing the balaclava when he arrived, in which case identification would be impossible.

After getting off the bus, she hurried into the flat and grabbed her gym clothes. Ten minutes later, she was pounding her stresses out on the treadmill and exhausted herself lifting weights. Her body was slowly getting accustomed to her workouts, but she ached in places she didn't realise she had muscles. But her head felt clearer, and the feeling of strength buoyed her up. She signed up for a programme of self-defence classes, and the positive feeling stayed with her until she was outside her flat door.

She hadn't changed the locks to enter her apartment. Now, she wondered if she should. She was more concerned about someone breaking in while she was in the flat, rather than when she was out. But perhaps it might be a good idea to do it anyway. The locksmith who had installed a deadbolt on the floor and a bolt on the top of the door had been puzzled by her need for so much internal security, joking that he thought this was a nice area to live in. She smiled inanely at him, unwilling to explain the need for so much internal security.

Once inside, she put on the safety chain and bolted the door top and bottom. Then she had a hot shower and made herself something to eat. She was reading when she heard the buzzer sound.

Recognising Garda Collins' voice, she buzzed her in.

When they got to her door, she looked through the peephole and rechecked it was them. She felt a bit foolish, but she needed to establish this as a routine.

When she let them in, Owens commented on her new security approvingly.

'I'm sure that will give you some peace of mind. Always check who is outside and make any tradesmen show their identity card before you fully unlock the door.'

'Don't worry. I'm taking extra care until you catch the man who attacked me. So, do you have any news for me?'

She offered them a seat, and they refused tea.

Maureen Collins smiled at her encouragingly.

'I can't say we've got anyone in the frame yet, but as you suspected, the only prints in the flat belonged to you and one other person. They were everywhere, so I assume they were from a regular visitor who stayed over, not the assailant.'

'Yes, they would be my aunt's – she stayed with me when I moved in. She's the only person who's been here. I'm only starting to get to know people.'

'Is it possible that the person who previously lived in this apartment was the intended target?'

'God, I never thought of that. I suppose it's possible. I'll check with the landlord.'

'Don't worry about that – we'll make enquiries on your behalf. OK, as I told you when I spoke on the phone, we have isolated an image of a man entering the flat at two in the morning. As you know, the foyer door is operated by a buzzer for security.'

'Oh god, so someone buzzed him in. I'm so stupid. He couldn't get in unless he buzzed one of the flats.'

'We have no way of telling who let him in. So we plan to call on all your neighbours to discover if their flat was buzzed on Tuesday night and if they allowed access to the building and why.'

'I know you must do this, but could you please not say I was involved? I've just moved here and don't want to be an object of talk or speculation.'

'Don't worry, we won't mention you. Do you know how many flats are occupied?'

'I'm not sure. There are ten post-boxes with names attached and two blank ones, so I assume those are empty flats.'

'Great, well, it's just after nine, perhaps my colleague could do a quick visit to as many flats as possible and see if he has any luck. It's not too late, and you said there are no children in the building, so I think it would save time if he does it now.'

Eimear nodded, and Garda Owens left to make his enquiries.

Garda Collins put a manila envelope on the table, removed two black-and-white images and passed them to Eimear.

The pictures were fuzzy. In the first one, a man wearing a hoodie obscuring most of his face could be seen entering the building. The second image was slightly clearer; in this, he was heading for the stairs, but he kept his head down and very little of his face could be seen. Eimear sighed. It was impossible to recognise anyone from this.

'Is he familiar? Perhaps you've seen someone like him in the gym?' Collins probed.

'No, it's no use. I'm sorry.' Eimear's hand shook as she stared at the man who attacked her. She felt sick.

'OK, no problem. There was only a slim chance that you'd recognise him. He waited to put on the balaclava until he got to your door, but he was careful when he entered and left the building to keep his face hidden from the CCTV cameras. Look, you're as white as a sheet. Why don't I make us both a cup of tea while we wait for Shane to return?'

It turned out that Maureen Collins was entertaining company. She was from Longford and, although only in her mid-twenties, a mother to two kids. They bonded over their shared love of Bruce Springsteen – both had been to see him when he played in Dublin.

When Garda Owens returned, he had little to report. He had spoken to six of the eight occupants, and no one admitted to letting the man in. He told Eimear that he would check the remaining apartments later.

'One young lad did admit that sometimes he buzzed in people late at night who claimed to have forgotten the door code. But it isn't too hard to watch someone putting a code in, so the guy could have got the code just by waiting around and pretending to tie his shoelaces. It's not exactly a complex code, is it? And people are careless. So we're no further on.'

And on that disheartening note, the gardaí left.

Chapter 10

It had been nearly two weeks since she had spoken with Meg. Of course, there were lots of texts and pictures of the various cities she travelled to, but she missed seeing and hearing from her. When Meg Facetimed her on Sunday, Eimear had been having a particularly low day. Seeing her aunt's friendly face lifted her spirits. She felt sorely tempted to confide everything that had happened to Meg. But that would be selfish. She would insist on coming back to stay with her. It wasn't fair.

Because she was hiding so much from Meg, the call felt awkward and stilted, at least on her side. But she was determined to protect Meg from all the drama in her life. There was nothing she could do, so it felt cruel to alarm her.

Meg looked happy. The sun had given her skin a nice glow, and her brown hair was lightly streaked with grey. At home, she seemed slightly dowdy but looked younger and prettier with her sun-bronzed skin and sparkling eyes.

'*Wow!* I love the new hairdo. It's very chic. I didn't know you planned such a dramatic change. As long as I've known you, you've had long or mid-length hair.'

'*Aww*, I just felt like a change. I was bored with my bob and decided to go for a radical change. Do you really think it suits me?'

'Absolutely – it's very young and cool.'

'Thank you!'

'Any nice plans for next weekend?' Meg asked.

'I plan to head home. I thought I'd make a start on sorting out some of Mam's things',

'*Aww*, pet, don't be doing that on your own. Time enough for that when I come back from my travels.'

'I need to go home. I haven't been back since Mam died, and I think I need to do this. But I'm only going to make a start on clearing things. When you come back, we can finish sorting things out.'

'OK, but make sure you arrange to have friends about you. Grief can be overwhelming.'

They didn't speak for a while, both silently thinking of their loss.

Then, to lighten the mood, Eimear said, 'Enough about that – your last postcard was from Berlin. Where are you now?'

Meg grinned. 'Well, I'm nicely fixed up here in Copenhagen. I got a wee job house-sitting for an English couple who moved here to be close to their daughter, who married a local. I get free accommodation – all I have to do is feed their fish and water their plants for the next week. Eimear, you have to visit this city. It's so fabulous, full of art and culture. You'd love it!'

'And handsome Vikings,' Eimear added.

Meg laughed a deep, rich chuckle and winked at her. Eimear experienced such a wave of longing for her aunt that it caught her breath. She looked so much like her mother. The same wavy hair and dark eyes and the same way her nose crinkled when she smiled.

'What's wrong, love?'

Eimear forced herself to grin. 'I'm grand, keeping busy – and I took your advice – I've been joining things, right left and centre. I go to the gym four times a week and have joined a fitness class.' She decided not to mention the fitness class was self-defence. She didn't want to arouse any concerns with her aunt. 'Aren't you proud of me?'

'I'm more than delighted, but I notice none of those things you mentioned involve social activities. I hope you're making friends.'

'I am. The girls at work are lovely, and I plan to go out for a drink with two girls I met at the gym during the week. Then, I'll head to Sligo to check out the house and meet up with a few college mates, too. So, you don't need to worry about me.'

Meg grinned at her. 'I know I'm an awful nag but, now that Claire is gone, I feel that I should keep an eye out for you for her sake.'

'I miss her so much.' Eimear's voice cracked, and she went silent.

'I know love, so do I. She was some woman. There was no one like our Claire.'

'You're so right. Mam was a true original. Do you remember the time she took up flying? Gran and I were so worried about her. But she was brilliant and so proud when she got her licence. I can still see her grinning from ear to ear as she waved it at us when she came home. I think it was her happiest moment.'

'No, love, having you was her happiest moment. I can tell you that. You meant the world to her. As much as she loved your dad, Gran and me, you always came first with her.' Meg smiled reminiscently. 'I remember when she told me she was expecting you. She was so excited. But then, of course, poor James was diagnosed with cancer almost as soon as she discovered she was pregnant.' She sighed. 'Still, he hung around long enough to see you start primary school.' '

Eimear nodded. 'I wish I could remember him better. I have only a few memories of him reading to me and playing with me. But at least I have those.'

'Yes, it's wonderful that you had those years with him. Those were precious years for me, too. I was so young when you were born and, as soon as I saw you, I was mad about you. So, Eimear, never forget that. And if you ever need me, I'm there instantly.'

Eimear laughed. 'Good job that all is well with me then. So enjoy Copenhagen and the handsome Vikings, and keep sending me postcards. I love getting them. My fridge door is a sea of sunshine and blue skies, but I still have room for a few more.'

In the background, Eimear heard Meg's doorbell. 'OK, Meg, I'll let you get that. Bye.'

As she stared at the dark screen, Eimear felt desolate. After her call with Meg, the weight of loneliness oppressed her. It was ridiculous, but she really was alone. While she dated Donal, she neglected all her relationships, and he didn't encourage her to keep in touch with friends. He jealously guarded their time together. At first, she had been flattered that he was so besotted with her. When what friends she still retained tried to warn her that he was too possessive, she cut them off. She wasn't proud of the way she had behaved. She accused them of being envious that their boyfriends didn't care so much about them. She blushed when she remembered how she had acted. She was lucky that a few stalwarts like Lana and Alec had held fast, waiting in the wings until needed.

She might be married to him now if it weren't for his silly mistake. He had sent her flowers for her birthday, but when she opened the card attached to the bouquet, it said, *For Susan with love*. Of course, he blamed the florist for the mistake but, although she said she believed him, it awakened her suspicions, and she wondered about discrepancies in things he said.

But one day everything became clear. She was out trying on wedding dresses. Meg and her mam were with her. They had narrowed it down to a style that suited her and made an appointment to call back to the shop the following Saturday. Claire suggested they drive to the new hotel on the outskirts of town to celebrate their successful day. It was early, so they managed to get a table. They had a lovely meal, and Eimear was happy when she left the hotel.

As she was crossing the carpark, she spotted Donal's car. She flew over to greet him. Then she saw that he wasn't alone. A girl with masses of curly brown hair was in the front seat. She couldn't make out her face as Donal was kissing her. She stopped, frozen with shock, beside the car.

When he finally noticed her, he flushed bright red and jumped from the car as if the seat had burned him. He stared helplessly at her.

The girl opened her car door and came to stand beside him. She smiled boldly at Eimear, saying, 'Come on, Donal love, why don't you introduce me?' When Donal gazed at her dumbly, she beamed and said, 'I'm Susan, nice to meet you.'

Those few words were all it took to shatter Eimear's illusions, finally.

Eimear backed away from the car. Donal came after her.

'Wait, Eimear, please, let me explain!'

She stopped and stared at him. 'Well, explain it to me, Donal. Explain why you're snogging a girl while I've been spending the day trying on wedding dresses for our wedding?'

He was only a few feet from her, but it was as though they were separated by continents. He looked foolish and pathetic somehow, not the strong, confident man that she'd thought loved her and wanted to make a life with. He looked guilty – like a small boy caught out in wrongdoing and shamed by being caught.

'So, you have nothing to say?'

He continued to stare silently. Then he moved towards her and tried to touch her hand. She reacted as though he had scalded her.

'Keep away from me, Donal. We're finished.'

'Eimear, love, whatever is the matter?' Her mam reached her side, her face creased with concern.

'*Why don't you ask him?*' she shrieked and burst into tears.

She was dimly aware of her mam and Meg leading her away, her body unresisting and with no volition of its own.

The following days passed in a dull blur. She refused to see him. Mam took her engagement ring from the bin where she had flung it, parcelled it up, and posted it back to him. Meg cancelled all the wedding plans.

Donal recovered his energy and kept up a barrage of phone calls and texts, and banged on the door of her mother's house night after night. She couldn't bear to see him. Her mam and Meg guarded her. Her friends called around, but she was too ashamed to see them. She had made her choice and chose Donal over them. She felt she didn't deserve their comfort now.

Meg told her she was foolish, cutting off her nose to spite her face. But Eimear couldn't bear to be an object of pity. She was just grateful that the preparations for the wedding were so recent that she hadn't even chosen bridesmaids.

But Donal was persistent, if nothing else. One night, he pushed past her mam and insisted on seeing her. Claire stood guard and refused to leave as he begged Eimear for a second chance. He said that nothing had happened between him and Susan. He claimed she was obsessed with him, and he was flattered by her attention. He even had the gall to suggest that he wouldn't have glanced at another girl if Eimear had been a better girlfriend. Eimear, he insisted, had made him feel insecure. That was when the final scales dropped from her eyes, and she saw him for who he was. She told him she never wanted to see him again. Her mam finally managed to hustle him out the door. She could still see the impotent fury in his face when he realised he couldn't change her mind.

But his campaign continued. He sent flowers, cards, and letters to her home and workplace. Mr Holland was very understanding, but seeing Donal's car across the street was unnerving when she left the office in the evening. She had to change where she went for lunch because he constantly showed up. Her mam and Meg went to see him, warning him that if he continued harassing her, they would inform the gardaí. Even then, he persisted. He followed her car, parked outside the house and tried to talk to her whenever she was in town. She was frightened of him. Now, she was grateful that he had been unfaithful to her as she shuddered at the thought of being trapped in a marriage with him.

His sister Jen, who also happened to be her best friend, was caught in the middle. But blood won out, especially when Eimear threatened to report him to the gardaí. They had a colossal row, and a decade-long friendship was ended. Even at Claire's funeral, Jen didn't break her silence. Eimear was surprised that she had even turned up.

In the end, she went to Alec. She told him everything and showed him the pile of cards, letters and texts Donal had sent her. She listed all the times he had accosted or followed her. Alec took notes and he went to visit Donal. He warned him that if he persisted in harassing Eimear, they would encourage her to take a barring order out against him. It worked for a few months, but then she saw him waiting in his car outside the restaurant when she went on the first date since they had broken up. She had no interest in dating, but Meg persuaded her against her better judgment. She told her that sitting around brooding on Donal was bad for her and she could do with the ego boost of a date. So she went. The guy was nice, flatteringly attentive, but there was no spark. It was too soon. Donal followed her and her date back to her home. The poor guy she was with was freaked. Even more so when Donal threatened him. That was the last straw. Eimear called Alec, and he started the process of the barring order. But she couldn't quite go through with it. But she left the paperwork ready should Donal continue to harass her.

Could there be a connection between what happened with Donal in Sligo and what was happening to her now? OK, her assailant wasn't Donal, but he could have hired some thug. It all seemed far-fetched. Besides, she thought Donal would never pay someone to do his dirty work, would he? But he did like the idea of keeping her under control. He might even get a kick from sending her the photos and the threatening letter. But the other things, the damage to her car and the attack on her seemed unlikely somehow. Surely Donal couldn't hate her enough to set that animal on her. Could he?

Chapter 11

Work was intense, and she had a new client. His name was Tommy Brennan. He was a small, dapper man dressed like he was about to attend a wedding. There was nothing casual about him. He spoke in short, clipped sentences and stared just past her shoulder when he talked to her. His accent was hard to place, but there was a hint of Glasgow somewhere.

He told her he had been referred to her by a friend but couldn't recall his name. Despite his short, sharp sentences, he took quite a while to come to the point. The point eventually was that he wanted to contest his mother's will. He claimed that she had been subjected to undue influence by his sister, and she had received the bulk of the mother's not inconsiderable estate.

'Miss Martin, it's not the money. I'm not short of a few bob, but I don't particularly appreciate being made a fool of. My sister thinks she can have everything her way, and, well, I want to teach her a lesson.'

'I see, Mr. Brennan. Could you tell me all the relevant details, and I'll give you my opinion?'

Brennan looked at her incredulously. 'I don't care about your opinion. I want you to bring this to court, whether you think it's a good idea or not.'

Eimear stared at him, perplexed. When she read over her notes, she doubted he could win and was bewildered by his motivation for bringing the case.

'Mr Brennan, before we proceed, I have to tell you that your chances of winning this case are small. If we involve a judge and brief lawyers, costs could go against you.'

'That's OK, I'm not short of money.'

'But even if you win, the legacy will have disappeared in lawyers' fees.'

'Look, are you prepared to take this on or not?'

Eimear sighed. 'I will do my best for you, Mr Brennan.'

'Right, now I've got a few men in mind to represent me in court. I've dealt with them before, and they did the job.'

She stared at him when he mentioned the names of two top barristers. Could he be serious? She excused herself for a few minutes and popped into Philip's office. He whistled when he heard who her new client was. She explained the lunacy of the lawsuit.

Philip grinned. 'Well, fools and their money are soon parted. But at least we know he can pay up, and he must have something against that sister if he's willing to blow a fortune to keep her from inheriting. But go for it, girl. His business will be a feather in our cap, and you never know he might pull it off. But this is only the tip of the iceberg. He could bring us a fortune in business. The main thing is to keep him happy.'

'I feel sorry for the sister,' she muttered.

'We're not counsellors, Eimear. We're here to fulfil our clients' wishes and give them sound advice, which you did. But they don't have to accept it.'

Eimear returned to Tommy Brennan and took down a few more details. When she was finished, they arranged another meeting and shook hands. She walked him to the door.

Toby was at the front desk talking to Iris when they passed. When she had seen Brennan off, Toby whistled. 'Was that who I think it was? The notorious Tommy Brennan, aka Tommy the Terminator.'

'Why do you call him that?'

'Because he's notorious for bringing cases against anyone he perceives to have crossed him. He's got deep pockets, so he can keep appealing cases until his opponents run out of money. He's made quite a few people regret ever having crossed his path. *Who*a, well done for snagging him!'

'God, he sounds like a vindictive ghoul.'

'Don't let Philip hear you saying that. You'll be the golden girl for bringing him in. How did you manage it?'

'He claims I was recommended to him, but it makes no sense; most of my work has been low-profile. And he won't say who gave him my name.'

'Whoever it was, they did you a favour. You owe them a pint. Look at the time. It's heading home time. How about we go for a drink and celebrate you bringing in Mr Moneybags?'

Eimear wasn't sure she wanted to go for a drink with Toby. They got on alright, but she caught him watching her once or twice with a calculating look in his eye. He saw her as the competition. John Kirk, the other solicitor, stuck to what he did best and, although ambitious, he was a bit dull and preoccupied with his little family. But Toby was keen to succeed. Eimear wondered if he was still pursuing Camilla Jolly.

It was a dangerous game because Philip was a protective father and, if he thought Toby was messing with his girl, he would make his displeasure felt. But what the hell, she didn't fancy a long night at home and decided to accept his drink offer.

'OK, give me a chance to finish my notes, and I will join you for one.' She turned to Iris. 'Do you want to come along?'

'No chance. I have a date with a pizza, and I'm getting out a nice mushy film and then having a long soak. Maybe next time.'

When Eimear joined Toby in the foyer, she saw Hannah glaring at them.

'Hey, Hannah, do you fancy joining us?' she asked.

Hannah snapped, 'No, I have plans.'

Eimear glanced at Toby. He shrugged and held the door open for her. Surely, Hannah couldn't be jealous of her and Toby?

The pub was packed, and they were lucky to find seats. Toby fetched the drinks, a gin and tonic for her and a pint of Guinness for him.

At first, they chatted about their favourite films and books they enjoyed, and Toby enthused about sports. He played Gaelic at the weekend with a few mates but missed the competitive side of things.

'I wasn't good enough to progress, but my mates and I still train and compete in a lower league. It keeps me fit, and it's good craic to meet up with the lads I went to school with. What about you, Eimear? What do you do to amuse yourself?'

'Well, I go to the gym regularly and, recently, I've taken self-defence classes.'

'*Ooh*, should I watch my p's and q's with you or risk lying on the flat of my back if I step out of line.'

'I shouldn't worry too much, Toby. I'm just starting, so you're not in too much danger from me.'

Toby leaned in, placed his hand lightly on her knee, and squeezed gently.

'Maybe I wouldn't mind being on the flat of my back beside you.'

Eimear stiffened and pushed his hand away. To his credit, he got the message, but she was unnerved to see the nasty expression on his face when she rejected him. She was disappointed in him for trying it on with her. He had moved uncomfortably close to her and he now awkwardly withdrew, giving her more space

Out of the corner of her eye, she spotted Hannah and a guy she guessed was her boyfriend, Paul, at the bar and waved to them. Hannah stared sourly at her. Eimear felt a flash of irritation. Who did Hannah think she was giving her dagger eyes? Even if she was interested in Toby, it was no concern of Hannah's. She had a bloody boyfriend. Irritated, she glanced at her watch. She picked up her bag.

Toby noticed. 'Hey, you're not leaving already? The night is young.'

'Sorry, Toby, I'm bushed. I'll buy you a pint, but I can't stay.'

'*Nah*, get me some other time. It's probably time I made tracks, too. After all, tomorrow is a work day, and I need to up my game now that you're attracting wealthy clients.'

'Don't be silly, Toby. He'll probably realise how junior I am and decide he wants the boss to take over. Right, I'm off.'

Eimear waved to Hannah when she was leaving, but the girl blanked her. This was annoying. She had got on with Hannah and found this jealous act hard to deal with. It brought back memories of Donal, and she didn't want to waste any more time thinking about him.

On the bus home, she debated going to the gym. It didn't close until ten, and she could have a workout to clear her head. But, when she got off the bus, the thought of walking to and from the gym in the dark made her nervous. She cursed the bastard who attacked her for robbing her of her peace of mind. But the seed of fear had been planted, and she decided to pick up a Chinese takeaway instead and lounge in front of the telly. The thought of the food cheered her up. The nearest restaurant to her flat wasn't far, so she called in and made a substantial order. Anything she didn't eat tonight, she'd have tomorrow.

The food in its aluminium containers smelled so good she felt giddy with hungry anticipation. It lived up to its promise, and she ate so much that her stomach hurt slightly. She spent the rest of the night watching forgettable television and dozing off. At midnight, she awoke feeling cold and smelling of Chinese food. Unable to face clearing up the mess from her meal, she left it until the morning. She filled a hot-water bottle for her bed. Soon, the warmth of the bed and the fullness in her stomach made her drowsy.

She was about to fall asleep when she sat up, worried she had forgotten to bolt the door. After getting out of bed and reassuring herself that it was indeed bolted, she was wide awake again. Lying in bed, she tossed and turned all night, but sleep eluded her.

Chapter 12

Tommy Brennan proved to be a major pain for Eimear. He was demanding, impatient and, at times, completely unreasonable. But Philip was keen that she keep him happy, and even though she knew his case was ridiculous and vindictive, she had little choice but to pursue his agenda. That agenda appeared to be making his sister's life a living hell. What did she ever do to him in the name of all that is good and holy? But hers not to reason why but to proceed with his instructions, and letters flew back and forth between all parties involved.

Hannah was like a frost descending whenever she came into the room. She spoke to Eimear only when necessary and then as briefly as possible.

In exasperation, Eimear snapped at her one morning after she was particularly Baltic. 'Look here, Hannah, have I done something to offend you? You've been short with me lately.'

'I don't know what you mean. Are you complaining about me again?'

'What the hell, Hannah? When have I ever complained about you?'

Hannah tossed her mane of blond hair and rolled her eyes. She was about to head for the door when Eimear called her back.

'Listen, Hannah, I don't know what you think I've done to you. But come on, let's talk about it, and I'm sure we can sort it out.'

'I have work to do, Miss Martin, so if you don't mind I better get on with it. If you have a problem with that, take it up with Mr Jolly.'

She turned and left the office, closing the door with exaggerated care. Eimear returned to her desk. She was baffled. She and Hannah usually got on, at least until recently. OK, she didn't know her as well as Kate and Iris, but they could pass the time together and have the odd natter. What was rattling her cage?

The only thing she could think of was that Hannah was jealous of the time she had spent with Toby. But that was nuts. How did she make it clear to the silly mare that she was about as interested in Toby as she was in watching paint dry? And why on earth was Hannah implying that she had complained about her? She had never spoken to Philip Jolly about Hannah or anyone else. It made no sense. There must be an explanation somewhere. It occurred to her that Iris or Kate could shed some light on Hannah's odd behaviour. She decided Iris was the best person to approach. With that in mind, she invited her for lunch in the Snuggery.

The place was crowded, but Iris spotted two seats near the door. It was chilly, but they had somewhere to sit and eat. They ordered, and Eimear let Iris chatter about her plans for the weekend. Eventually, she managed to bring the conversation around to work.

'Iris, have you noticed anything strange about Hannah? She's being really cool with me, and I was wondering if something is wrong. Like, if she thinks I'm making a play for Toby. I mean, are she and Paul still together?'

'I think the romance is still going on, and she's certainly not mooning about Toby, so maybe she's over her crush. But honestly, I've been swamped at the moment, and we haven't had a good chat in ages. But it's not like her to be cool. If upset with you, she'd be more likely to have a stand-up row than give you the cold shoulder. Our Hannah doesn't have many filters.'

'Well, I can't understand it. I tried talking to her this morning, and she implied that I had complained about her. I assume she means to Philip.'

'Well, did you?'

'Of course I bloody didn't. I mean, Hannah is a bit erratic at times, but I've no complaints and, anyway, I'd have spoken to her first if I had a problem with her work. Where did she get the idea that I've been complaining about her?'

'Look, leave it with me, and I'll get to the bottom of it. Now, tell me, what you are up to for the weekend? Do you have any nice plans?'

'I'm heading home to Sligo. Philip is letting me rearrange clients so that I can get away early. You know what rush hour is like on a Friday. I'll be an age leaving town if I wait until five-thirty. If I can persuade my afternoon appointments to reschedule, I'll get away just after three.'

'Well, good for you. Is there anyone of interest in Sligo, a lad who is pining for your return?' Iris teased.

Eimear flushed as Donal's face flashed before her. 'No one at all. I'm a free agent and not looking for anyone either.'

'Focusing on the career then. But, Eimear, don't forget to have a little fun. It doesn't do to be too consumed with work. Live a little, girl.'

Eimear laughed, and the conversation turned to other things.

—— *ele* ——

The rest of the day flew by. Her appointments were agreeable to being changed. She packed up her belongings and headed for the small car park at the back of the building. It was shared with the accountant next door, but she drove in early that morning to ensure a space. She had packed lightly because she still had most of her clothes at home. It was weird to think of the house in Sligo as home, now that her mam wasn't there to share it with her. But Eimear was determined to face up to things, and there was nothing like returning to an empty house to make her accept the enormity of her mother's death. Her new job and her worries were a distraction from dealing with her grief. Despite getting away before rush hour, the drive out of the city was still hectic, but soon the open road lay ahead of her. She fiddled with the radio stations, looking for music or news to distract her from her thoughts, but no matter how she tried, her mind fixated on the nightmare events infiltrating her world.

At night, thoughts and memories stole her sleep. When she closed her eyes, the man with the pebble eyes glared down at her, and her chest tightened, and she felt as though she were drowning. At least during the day, the busyness of work acted as a distraction. But driving freed her mind to endure all she wished she could escape. She struggled to shake off intrusive thoughts but, even when she succeeded, they were replaced by the deadening pain of grief. Her heart ached for her mam.

It had been months since she had last been home. At seven, it was dark, and for the first time in her memory, there wasn't a light glowing in the house. It looked abandoned, and sadness and weariness fell over her like a heavy coat. She was reluctant to leave the warmth of the car, but it had to be done.

She took her holdall from the boot of her car, unlocked the front door, switched off the alarm and rapidly turned on as many lights as she could to dispel the gloom. There was plenty of oil in the tank, so she turned on the heating. It would take an age for the house to heat up, and she debated lighting a fire, but the thought of going outside in the cold and dark for coal deterred her. She carried her bag upstairs and turned on the electric blanket in her bed. She stared across at her mam's room but couldn't bring herself to open the door. That could wait till morning. She realised from the rumble in her stomach that she was hungry.

In the kitchen, she found some bread in the freezer, which she could toast. There was hard cheese in the fridge that she could melt over the bread. It would be warm and comforting, and also, in the freezer, she found a packet of sausages. She defrosted them in the microwave and popped all six under the grill. She was thankful that she had the foresight to bring a pint of milk from her flat. It was still nice and cold from the car boot. So, she had all her dietary needs taken care of.

When she carried her meal into the living room and switched on the TV for company, she felt comforted, if not cheerful.

She enjoyed watching a detective show and surprised herself by getting lost in the story. It was a long time since television had proved much of a distraction. Mam loved her TV shows and always tried to find something they could both enjoy. Eventually, they settled on *Morse*, and Eimear and Claire both fell a little in love with the irascible detective. She remembered how her mother cried at the final episode's closing scene. They both had. They had watched and enjoyed the series' spin-off *Lewis* but, as much as they enjoyed it, Inspector Morse was king. Mam wouldn't read any of Colin Dexter's Morse novels because she always wanted to try to puzzle out the villains by herself. She never did, but she enjoyed Inspector Morse's mental dexterity.

At eleven, Eimear headed upstairs. Her bed was warm and cosy, and she switched off the blanket. She read the final pages of *Pride and Prejudice*. It never mattered to her that she knew the ending. She just loved the characters and the world Austen created. If she was an Austen character, who would she be, she wondered? She wished she was like Elizabeth Bennet, but she had a feeling that the only trait they shared was poor judgement of people. On that thought, she fell deep into sleep.

Chapter 13

She had forgotten to draw the curtains, and the morning light woke her. Glancing at her watch, she saw that it was nearly nine. She sprang out of bed. There were lots of things to do. First, she needed to pick up groceries. It would be a good idea to buy some provisions to freeze for future visits. Her meal last night, although filling, was neither healthy nor really to her taste. Then, she would tackle the task she came home to do. She would set about going through her mam's clothes and belongings.

The local SuperValu provided her with everything she needed for the weekend. She bought pork chops and vegetables for dinner and stocked up on soups and sliced bread that she could freeze later. While queuing for the till, she met one of her mam's friends, Mary Boyle. She squeezed Eimear's hand and told her how she missed Claire, and she hoped that now that she was home, she would call over to the house.

'In fact, why not come for lunch on Sunday?' she suggested.

'I'd love to, but I plan to head back to Dublin on Sunday.'

'How early? We can do lunch for one and have you on the road well before dark, if that suits you. Alma and the boys would love to see you. What do you say? Can I count you in?'

Eimear was torn. Her mam had liked Mary, and meeting up with the Boyles would be fun. They had lost touch since secondary school, but she had always liked Alma, and her brothers were good, solid lads. But she had hoped to get away early on Sunday. Then she could almost hear Meg urging her to reconnect, and she thanked Mrs Boyle and said she'd love to come for lunch.

Back at the house, she put the groceries away and tidied up the breakfast things. She put on a wash as the laundry basket in her room was full of dirty clothes. She put it on a fast cycle and hoped that if she put the clothes on the drying rack, they would dry in the warmth of the house. She put the heating on again, as she wanted to be warm when tackling her mam's bedroom.

When she could no longer put it off, she went upstairs with half a dozen black bin bags. Stepping inside the room, she could still smell the faint fragrance of her mam's perfume. It rooted her to the spot. She wasn't prepared for how her mam's room hadn't changed. The bed was made, but her mam's nightdress peeked out underneath a pillow. It still smelled of her. As she sat on the bed, holding it close to her face and inhaling the scent, she felt the tears prickle in her eyes. Replacing the nightdress, she walked over to the dressing table. Claire loved cosmetics; the table was cluttered with all her lotions and potions. She opened a jar of face cream and could see the indent of her mother's finger. Hurriedly, she replaced the cap.

Pulling open the wardrobe, she was again enveloped in the scent of her mother. But this time, she was prepared. She lifted armfuls of clothes out and threw them on the bed. Mam was a dedicated fashion-lover, but she had honed her style. She was a tall, slender woman who loved the feel of clothes. Quality mattered to her, and she bought infrequently but carefully. Her colour palette was simple; she wore greens, olives, and browns but also loved splashes of orange. Eimear was surprised to discover how many shoes she owned. There must be at least fifty pairs; almost all had a high heel. Once, she had confided in Eimear that although heartbroken by the death of her husband, at least now she could wear high heels. Eimear's dad was a short man, and Eimear took after him. She was only just over five feet. Staring at her mother's beautiful clothes, she realised none would fit her. She could take the hems up, but the waist would be in the wrong position. They wouldn't suit Meg either. Meg wasn't much taller than her, and the clothes would swamp her.

Eimear reckoned the charity shop in town would be doing very well. She filled five bin bags with coats, dresses, blouses, scarves, and jumpers to donate to Vincent de Paul. The one thing of her mother's that she could wear was her beautiful cashmere coat. It was camel-coloured, and although long on her, she could easily have it taken up without altering the style. The shoes, sadly, were too large, but maybe they might fit Meg. She set some shoes, scarves, and a pile of jumpers aside for Meg to try on. She wondered if Nuala would like a keepsake. Her clothes would never fit Claire's old school friend, but perhaps she'd like something else. She made a mental note to contact her.

Mam had a lot of jewellery, all gifts from her father. To Eimear's knowledge, Mam never bought herself a piece of jewellery. She would offer Meg her choice. She spotted the little gold St Briget's cross that Claire put on almost every day. Eimear tried it on, and this time the tears poured down. She had considered offering it to Meg, but it had such associations with her mam that she knew she could never part with it. But the thought of wearing it was too painful – maybe someday she'd be able to put it on without crying. She put the little cross in the zipped pocket of her handbag to take back to Dublin

There, she had done enough. Her tummy started to rumble and, although it was a little early, she decided to see about preparing a meal. The thought of spending any more time clearing her mother's room was unbearable. But at least she had made a start on the things that had to be done. She'd go through the rest of her mother's belongings when Meg came home. Meg had planned to be away for three months, which meant she'd be home by early December. Perhaps they could book a week in the sun in Tenerife or Lanzarote and escape Christmas altogether. Mam was like a child about Christmas. Meg said it was because she had only one child and wanted to make it as magical as possible.

She forced herself to eat at the table in the dining room. It wasn't easy because it reminded her so much of her mother and how she liked to set the table carefully and often lit candles. Her mam insisted on using cloth napkins, which Meg and herself found silly as it made for washing and ironing. Meg teased, calling her Lady Claire, but Mam just smiled and said why shouldn't I take trouble over all the people I love? So Eimear set the table with the best dishes and crockery and took a linen napkin from the drawer in honour of her mam. It was a pity the food didn't live up to the setting. But it was adequate; the meat was a little overcooked, as were the vegetables. But Eimear ate every bit.

After clearing up, she sat listening to the music Claire loved. She was an opera fan, and Pavarotti's dulcet voice filled the room. Eimear closed her eyes and lost herself in the glorious voice. She had been drifting off to sleep when she heard the loud ring of the front door. The sound was insistent. She looked at the mantelpiece clock, and it was nearly eleven. Who would be calling at this time? Nervously, she got to her feet and stood uncertainly in the hallway. There was no peephole, so she couldn't see who was outside. She had been asleep, so she had no idea if a car had driven up to the house. Could it be the neighbours? They lived a quarter of a mile away but might have been concerned if they saw the lights in what they knew to be an empty house. Meg had asked them to keep an eye on the place. The ringing sounded again. Arming herself with one of Mam's golf clubs which sat where she had last left them in the porch, she opened the door.

Chapter 14

Donal stared at her out of the gloom. She started to shut the door, but he managed to stick his foot inside. He was tall, and she was slight, and he could push his way inside. Her heart was hammering against her chest. But she was determined not to let him know that she was frightened of him.

'What are you doing here, Donal? You know there's a world of trouble for you when you come here. Meg and I made that perfectly clear. If you clear off now, I'm willing to forget this ever happened.'

'Eimear, please, I just want to talk. I never see you on your own; from the moment things went wrong with us, your mother or that aunt of yours have kept us apart.'

As he spoke, he glanced at the golf club in her hand. She tightened her grip.

'That thing that went wrong between us was you seeing another girl while we were engaged. And you managed to try to blame your unfaithfulness on me. So I'm really not interested in what you have to say.'

'OK, OK, you're right; I know I was out of line. I've thought about it. I should have admitted I was wrong, but I didn't want to lose you. Can't I come in, and we can sit down and talk things over? I want to explain.'

'Well, I have no interest in hearing your explanation. Look, Donal, it's over; it's been over for months, and I now realise that we were never right together. You messed around with that girl – well, you did me a favour. It made me see that we would never have worked. So, no hard feelings if you go now.'

'Please, Eimear, I still love you. The other girl was a mistake. I admit I was totally in the wrong. Can we start again, and I'll show you I've changed?'

'Donal, I don't want to start again. I don't love you – in fact, I'm heartily sick of you. I wish we had never met. Now get out of my house, or I'll make sure the guards and your boss know that you are making a nuisance of yourself again.'

Donal's face reddened. 'So you're still making threats, are you?'

Eimear stared at him. 'What did you say?'

'I said, you fucking bitch, that I'm sick of you threatening to lose me my job.'

Each word was said slowly and viciously, and his spittle hit her cheek. Gone was the wheedling, apologetic manner. This was the real Donal.

Seeing the look on her face, he backed down again.

'*Aww*, Eimear, why do you do this to me? You wind me up, and I say hard things. I want you to understand we're meant to be together – someday, you'll see that I'm right, and then you'll be sorry.'

Her heart pounded, and her fingers were slippery with sweat as she clutched the golf club tightly. 'Please go. Can't you just accept that we're over?'

'If we're over, why do you keep trying to involve me in your life, Eimear? All these lies you've been telling your pet cop about me. Is it some coded way of telling me not to give up on you?'

She stared at him in disbelief. Nothing had changed. When she broke it off with him, he had blamed her for his infidelity, and now he was suggesting that she was so anxious to get him back that she was inventing stories. In his warped mind, everything he did wrong was her fault. He stood there immovable, determined to make her turn back the clock. He was beyond reasoning.

She felt a suffocating sense of panic. What if he wouldn't go? She was all alone here. Her body started to tremble. It took all her will to control it. She believed he would force his way in if he knew how terrified she was. She held his gaze.

'Donal, I'm tired. You need to go now. Please go!'

He showed no sign of moving, and then she had a moment of inspiration. She looked past him and shouted, '*Hey, come here! Now! I need you!*'

Donal spun around, and she used all her strength to push him out the door. It only worked because he was slightly off balance. She slammed the door and bolted it. She listened to him hammering on it as she picked up her phone.

She called Alec.

He was with her in minutes. She paced the floor while she waited for him to come. Barely waiting for him to get out of his car, she rushed to explain what had happened.

He led her back inside and they sat side by side at the kitchen table.

'OK, Eimear, this is an escalation; we need to frighten him. He's been warned about the consequences of approaching you and chooses to ignore it. We gave him a chance to do the right thing, and now it's time to take serious action. I'm going to visit him at work and inform his employer that he's been harassing you, and in the meantime, we'll stop him from approaching you or contacting you.'

'But suppose he loses his job and blames me? Oh, Alec, I'm worried. I've been getting threats in Dublin.'

Trembling with emotion, she told him about the threatening letter and the attack in her flat. He listened, horrified.

'Eimear, do you think this is related? Do you think Donal is behind this?'

'I don't know, it seems mad. The man who broke in wasn't Donal. It seems difficult to believe that he hired someone to attack me and how could he give them access to my flat? Hardly anyone knows where I live. I don't know what to believe.'

'Why the hell didn't you tell me all this before now? I thought it was just the photographs, and that was bad enough. This is seriously disturbing behaviour.'

'I know, I should have contacted you, but the guards in Dublin seemed really helpful. I didn't want to keep bothering you. I told them about Donal and they know that I've complained about him to the guards here in town. And I suppose I've been unwilling to believe Donal could be responsible for all these things that have happened to me. Eimear ran her hands distractedly through her hair. 'Do you know, he even had the cheek to suggest I've been making up things to keep him part of my life?'

'The man is clearly deluded,' said Alec, shaking his head. 'Right, this is what's going to happen. Tomorrow morning, you visit the station and make a statement about what happened here tonight. Then you put the gardai in Dublin in touch with me, and we can see if there's any connection between what happened in your flat and Donal.'

'OK, that makes sense.'

'Now, do you have anyone to stay with? You can't be on your own tonight.'

Eimear promised to call a friend to come and stay. He told her to turn the alarm on when she went to bed, and then he left. After he had gone, she locked up and set the alarm. She thought about ringing Lana or one of the girls from school. They would be happy to keep her company. But the thought of going through everything that happened with them made her feel sick. Besides, it would get back to Jen, and she didn't need Jen contacting her on Donal's behalf. It was simpler to stay stum and let Alec handle things. She put a chair against her bedroom door handle. The radio kept her company until she eventually fell into a deep sleep.

ele

In the morning, she visited the station and made a statement. She was asked if she wished to proceed with the barring order. She nodded her agreement.

Back at the house, she packed her car. She rang Mary Boyle and explained that she had a stomach bug and couldn't come for lunch. Then she set off for Dublin.

Chapter 15

She arrived just after two. Her head ached from tiredness and yet she felt restless. She had a long day to get through but didn't risk napping in case she couldn't sleep at bedtime. She didn't want all this chaos to affect her work. Her life was messy enough as it was. Around and around in her head, she tried to figure out who was responsible for all the sinister things happening. It had to be Donal. There was no other explanation. But although she believed him capable of violence, she just couldn't see him outsourcing it. But after last night she felt really scared of him. It was a relief to have made her statement at the local Garda station. She hoped that Alec would put the frighteners on Donal and that he'd finally wise up and leave her in peace. Alec mentioned that he'd also have a word with Donal's boss. He would hate that.

She opened her laptop and checked her emails. Then she emptied out her holdall and changed the sheets on her bed. There was nothing nicer than the feel of fresh sheets against your skin. She turned on the TV, but it failed to hold her interest. She felt restless as the day dragged on. The flat felt more like a prison than a refuge, and she was desperate to get out into the fresh air. It was a cold, damp day, but she preferred to be oppressed by the wide grey sky than the walls of her flat, which seemed to close in on her.

Outside, the gloom had intensified, and the damp seemed to seep into her bones, but still, it felt better to be free from the confines of her flat. As she emerged from the flat, she saw a woman, a runner, standing across the road, staring at her building. She wondered idly whether to take up running. The intensity of her workouts was beginning to have an impact, and her back and legs ached from all the punishment she was subjecting them to. Perhaps she should be more careful. She didn't want an injury. When she crossed the road, the runner had left, and she could see her in the distance pounding her way towards the park.

Eimear walked briskly around the perimeter of the park. There weren't many people, just a couple of runners and a woman with a pram. She put on her iPod earbuds and listened to Tina Turner. She needed that powerful, upbeat sound to lift her spirits. It worked. By the time she returned to her flat, she felt better or at least less defeated.

—— *ℓℓ* ——

The next morning, the office was a hive of activity. She barely came up for air. The others were equally occupied, and at eleven she popped into the little kitchenette to make a cup of coffee. Hannah shot her a dagger look, and Iris looked uncomfortable and avoided her eyes. God, she didn't need any more drama. There was no milk, so she took her coffee black. She couldn't face passing the lobby and seeing Hannah, so she took a break sitting at the small table where the staff ate their lunches. Most people ate in the office from Monday to Thursday, and on Friday nearly everyone headed out to treat themselves to something tasty. She had enjoyed the Friday routine, and usually everyone except Philip went to the Snuggery or Lennon's. It was a nice way to end the working week, but it made everyone sluggish on Friday afternoon and reluctant to work.

Glancing at the wall clock, she thought guiltily of the mountain of work that awaited her. Mr Brennan was coming in at two, so she had better be well prepared, or the old grouch would not quit moaning. She managed to scuttle back to her office, only to find Brennan installed. He wasn't in a good mood, pacing up and down, looking at his watch and blowing a gale of sighs.

'At last you deign to appear, missy. I've been waiting ten minutes.'

'I'm sorry you've been waiting, Mr Brennan, but your appointment was for two. Look, I'll show you.'

She opened the work diary and saw that Brennan's two o'clock appointment had a line drawn through it and an arrow pointed to eleven. She stared at it, confused. She hadn't changed the time.

'I'm sorry, Mr Brennan, but there seems to have been a miscommunication. When did you reschedule the appointment?'

'What are you talking about? You sent me an email and changed the time. It was a great inconvenience, but I agreed to your request. I rang that receptionist and told her how annoyed I was.'

'One moment, please. I need to check something.'

As Eimear left him muttering about incompetence, she hurried to Iris at the reception.

'Hey, Iris, do you know anything about Mr Brennan's change of appointment time? He claims I emailed the change, and he spoke to you about it.'

Iris stared at her stonily. 'Yes, he rang and harangued me for fifteen minutes about how he had to rearrange his schedule and how his time cost money. What's the problem?'

'The problem is I didn't change the appointment time.'

'Are you saying I did?' Iris snapped.

'No, of course not. I just want to find out where the miscommunication originated.'

'Fine, I'll pull up your emails. Put in your password.'

Eimear did so, conscious that Brennan's mood wouldn't improve with all this delay. Iris keyed his name into the search engine, and there, in deleted emails, she found the email sent to Tommy Brennan from her account. A rather curt one at that. Except she hadn't sent it.

She stared at Iris. 'I don't understand. I never sent that email.'

'You clearly did, and I put a note in your diary to remind you of the new appointment time. Are you accusing me of messing up?'

'God no, of course not. I just can't understand it.'

Eimear hurried back and the appointment went from bad to worse. She couldn't find the document he had given her to study. She had planned to work on it this morning and have it ready for him in the afternoon. Where the hell was it? It had been on her desk when she left on Friday evening. He was incandescent, shouting about it being an original. She tried to calm him down but only seemed to inflame him further. He glared at her in exasperation and then stamped off, shouting abuse at her and demanding to see Philip Jolly.

'What's the point of talking to the monkey when it's the organ grinder I want?' was his parting shot.

Luckily, Philip was out, so Brennan stormed out. The force he used to slam her door shook her office and the reception. She stood staring at the closed door.

There was a gaggle of excited chatter in reception, which ended abruptly when she entered. Hannah pointedly turned her back. Iris pretended to be looking through files.

'Iris, I can't understand what happened. I didn't send that email.'

'Are you accusing me of sending it? I don't have your password, so you needn't mind blaming me for your cock-up.'

'Come on, Iris, I'm not blaming you.'

'Then what are you doing? You can try complaining to Philip, but the girls will back me up. I never changed that appointment; if you forgot, that's your lookout. I put the reminder in your diary; all you had to do was look for it. Is there anything else you want to blame me for? No? Well, I have work to do.' With that, she picked up the phone and proceeded to punch in a number.

Eimear stared at Iris in confusion. Why was she being this way? Usually, Iris was her ally, always sympathetic. Why was she behaving as if she had done something terrible to her?

In the afternoon, things got worse. Philip had returned, and Brennan got to him before she could explain what had happened. He entered her office without knocking, his usually friendly face stern.

'I'm very disappointed with you, Eimear. It was unprofessional to change appointments without filling the staff in and leaving them to deal with a client's annoyance.'

Eimear tried to explain what happened, but Philip raised his hand.

'Eimear, you're a little too fond of sending emails. You complained to me about Hannah's work, and now you're trying to get Iris into trouble for your mistakes. The poor girl is very upset.'

Eimear stared at him, open-mouthed. 'I never said a word about Hannah. I've always found her work good, and I certainly don't blame Iris for what happened. I'm baffled by it all. Please can you show me this complaining email?'

'Fine, come along to my office now.'

Silently, she followed him into a spacious chamber that she had only seen once, and that was when he interviewed her. He tapped on his computer, and she looked over his shoulder. There was an email from her. It outlined several mistakes Hannah had made in preparing documents and suggested that she had a poor attitude to work.

'I never sent this. Surely I would have spoken to Hannah first and talked to you in person if I had a complaint?'

'I did wonder why you approached the matter the way you did. When I responded to your email, I asked you as much. In your reply, you explained that you had spoken to Hannah, but she was rude and unwilling to change her way of working, and you felt you had to progress the matter.'

'I never spoke to Hannah about her work.'

'So she told me, and I'm afraid I thought she was lying, but it seems you were the one lying, not her.'

'Mr Jolly, I repeat, I did not send those emails. This is mad.'

Philip stared at her. 'Sit down, my dear.'

At the change in tone, she slumped onto the chair before his desk.

'I know your former employer, Frank Holland. He gave you glowing references, partly why you got this job. But Frank told me about your mother's death and the ending of your engagement, and he said the young man in question caused you a lot of trouble. He said he harassed you, and you were on the verge of getting a barring order against him.'

Eimear stared dumbly at Philip.

'He wasn't being a gossip and was genuinely concerned about you. But he recommended you for the job because you were an excellent solicitor and felt you needed a fresh start. He was very sorry to lose you. Now I think that maybe you needed more time to recover from the traumatic year that you've experienced.'

'Everything you say is true but, Philip, I didn't write those emails.'

'Then who did and why?'

'I don't know.' Suddenly, Toby's face flashed across her mind. 'Toby'– The look on Philip's face quelled her.

'Are you seriously suggesting that a fellow solicitor would do such a thing? Who will you be accusing next? I recently spoke with Toby, and he very reluctantly said that the atmosphere has changed since you arrived to work here. It is no longer the convivial, happy office it had been. He mentioned that you are difficult to work with and inclined to be suspicious of offers of help.' Philip hesitated and then, looking embarrassed, added, 'He also said that you made a pass at him in the pub a few nights ago. When he rejected you, you stormed out.'

'That's a lie – Toby hit on me. *He's* the one who was sore about *my* rejection.'

'Please, Eimear, don't let yourself down any further. Hannah saw everything and backed up what Toby said. In fact, he very reluctantly admitted that you have been giving him a lot of unwanted attention. He tried to let you down gently, but you were becoming more blatant and even inappropriate in your behaviour towards him.'

Eimear blushed red to the roots of her hair. 'That's bloody ridiculous and a total lie. I've never once shown him any more attention than I would to another colleague. Where is he? I want to hear him make those accusations to my face.' Her body trembled with rage, and she knew that her raised voice could be heard in reception.

'Calm down, Eimear, Toby is working with a client, and I will not have him disturbed. But he has reported hearing you speak most disrespectfully about everyone in this firm, including me. I confess that I'm very disappointed in you, Eimear.

Eimear gasped, struggling to interrupt. Philip raised his hand to silence her.

'You need to understand that I run a happy ship here. We have always rubbed along well—that is, until recently. I don't understand what is happening with you, but I can't have it interrupting a contented and productive workplace.'

Eimear stared helplessly at him. Tears of frustration pricked her eyes.

'Please, Philip, I need you to believe me. I don't know what's happening or who's playing tricks on me. But I never did or said those things.'

Philip sighed and leaned back in his chair. 'OK, Eimear. I'm willing to believe that you sincerely think you didn't send those emails, but they could only have been sent by someone who had your password. Did you give it to anyone in the office?'

Eimear shook her head.

'How about you take a few days off, see your doctor, maybe go on sick leave for a while and get your head together. I'm sure when you get the help you need, everyone will be delighted to welcome you back.'

'If I take time off, it will be admitting I've done something wrong.' She got to her feet. 'And I bloody well didn't.'

'Eimear, I'm afraid you have no choice. I spoke to Mr Brennan on the phone, and he was on the point of terminating his business with us. I could only assure him that young Toby would do an excellent job and that I would personally supervise his efforts. He eventually agreed but insisted that he didn't want to set eyes on you for the duration of his business with us. He showed me the email you sent him, and it was extremely abrupt. I think it would be better for the harmony of all concerned if you take a short break. Understand me, Eimear, I don't want to sack you. Remember, you are still on probation. So take my advice and see your doctor and sort out whatever is causing this erratic and paranoid behaviour.'

Numbly, Eimear left his room. In her office, she sat staring at her computer screen. She couldn't find any record of her sending those emails until she checked her deleted mail. There they were: the email to Tommy Brennan, which bordered on rude, and several more unpleasant ones she sent to Philip complaining about Hannah and even having a dig at Iris.

It made no sense. She never wrote those emails, yet they were all sent from her email account. She sat dazed at her desk. Despite all the chaos in her life, her job was the one sure place she felt safe. But now her boss thought she was crazy, and Hannah and Iris despised her. Who was responsible? Could Toby have got into her account? It was possible, but she was careful about her password and always turned off her computer whenever she left the office. What could have motivated him? Perhaps he was jealous because she impressed Philip with her work or hurt pride because she rejected his clumsy pass. But to tell all those other lies about her, he must really hate her.

She tried to remember whether Donal might know her password. Stupidly, she tended to use easy-to-remember passwords relating to birthdays and the names of old family pets. Donal would know this, and she supposed he could have figured out her password by trial and error.

Or could Hannah be involved? But that was mad. She had never complained about her work. And yet the evidence was there that she had done these things. Eimear even began to doubt herself. Could she have done these things in some fugue state? Was it possible? It was true she was under a lot of strain. She looked again at her deleted emails. The phrasing in them didn't sound remotely like her. They were almost comically formal, especially the one complaining about Hannah. There was an element of truth in the complaints; Hannah had a bit of an attitude when asked to do anything. But she rarely made errors in documents. She read the email.

I regret to inform you that Hannah has been responsible for numerous errors in documents she has been tasked with preparing. Her presentation of work to be sent to clients is slapdash. When tasked with redoing work, her attitude is surly and uncooperative. I regret to say she is sometimes rude in her dealings with clients.

Respectfully yours,

E. Martin

The response to Philip's email asking her if she had spoken to Hannah about her work was even snarkier.

I have attempted to address these failings with Hannah, but she was unwilling to take constructive criticism, and her manner during our conversation was rude and disrespectful. I would appreciate it if you pointed out that this attitude toward her work can no longer be tolerated.

If it remains unchecked, I fear it will spread to other staff members. Iris has been a little short with clients lately, and although she is usually a good worker, I fear Hannah's example will influence her. I think this issue needs to be addressed in a timely manner.

Respectfully yours,,

E. Martin

She stared in disbelief. These emails were almost archaic in their formality. But they were written using her email. Someone with access to her password wrote them. She reread the emails. They all were signed off with the phrase, 'Respectfully yours'. That was not how she ended her emails. She checked the one she supposedly sent to Tommy Brennan. It also used this sign-off. There was no way she sent those emails. She considered pleading her case again with Philip, but she didn't think it would do any good. She closed down her computer and gathered up her few belongings.

The foyer was eerily quiet. Iris was at her post, pretending to be busy.

Hannah came out of Toby's office, smirking with satisfaction.

'Hannah, I know you think I've complained about you to Philip. But I promise you I didn't and will prove it.'

Hannah just stared coldly at her. Eimear turned to Iris.

'Please, Iris, you must believe me. None of this is true. What you've heard isn't true – really, it isn't. Please try to keep an open mind. Someone is playing tricks, and I promise I will get to the bottom of it.

Her voice wobbled dangerously, and she hated how pathetic she sounded. But she forced her head up and walked out the door into the cool afternoon air.

Chapter 16

It wasn't until she got back to her flat, bolted the door, and put on the safety chain that she could finally release the tears of pain and frustration. She howled, kicked over a chair and smashed a plate. Then the storm was over. The thought of food was repulsive, and the only thing to drink was the dregs of a bottle of wine. She debated going out and buying booze in the local off-licence but realised she couldn't afford to indulge herself. She was Claire Martin's daughter and would not let whoever was messing with her head win.

She wasn't about to take Philip Jolly's advice and see her doctor. That would be admitting that she was losing her mind. She knew she hadn't written those emails. She would use the next few days to figure out how to clear her reputation. She was convinced that Toby was responsible for all this insanity. He had told Philip hideous lies about her. If he hadn't sent the emails, he certainly capitalised on them. But as she brooded on exacting revenge on him, she wondered if everything happening to her was connected. On the surface, it seemed impossible. The notes she got happened when she had only just started her job. She was no threat to anyone at work at that point. How could those letters and the attack on her relate to either Donal or Toby? Was it possible that she had two different enemies operating independently? Or more likely, working hand in hand to destroy her life. What did she do to incite such hatred?

Her head felt like it was melting. She wished she had someone to talk things over with. The only person that sprang to mind was Kate. Well, what about it? They always got on well – maybe she could convince her that someone was setting her up. But could she trust her? Kate had known Iris, Toby, and Hannah for years, so why would she take her word against colleagues she had known for years? Unable to deal with another rejection but unwilling to sit staring at the walls of her flat, she headed out.

Her self-defence class was at seven, so she had brought a change of clothes in her rucksack. It was just five now, but she was desperate for a change of scene, to be surrounded by people. There was a little pub not too far from where she had her class. It was quiet inside, and she found a corner at the back and ordered coffee and a sandwich.

She wished she had brought a book to read. After eating, she ordered a glass of beer and was determined to sip it slowly until it came time to attend her class. She found an abandoned newspaper and hoped it would deter any man from deciding it was his duty to save a poor female from her own company. It didn't, but a few well-chosen words made the gallant men depart with muttered curses. The word 'bitch' currently seemed to be a popular one to describe her.

She left for her class a little early but was restless and needed to keep moving. The room where the session took place was chilly, and she shivered, but that would change once they were put through their paces. The instructor got her students to change partners regularly to keep things fresh.

At the end of the class, Eimear waited and helped Fiona, the instructor, put the mats away.

'I'd like to do more classes; you just do the two here, right? Do you do sessions anywhere else?'

'I do a few in the city centre in one of the community centres. It's rough and ready regarding the facilities, but the class is smaller, so we get through more. If that suits you.'

'Can you sign me up for two more sessions? It can be afternoon or early evening, at least for the moment.'

Fiona looked at her quizzically. 'Is there any reason for taking all these classes? I mean, you're not in any bother, are you?'

'No more than any other woman,' Eimear responded tartly.

Fiona nodded. 'OK, then. So you do Mondays and Wednesdays here. What about Thursday evening and Saturday afternoon in town? You're lucky, but I've had a few dropouts recently, so I have room. But I hope it won't be too much for you.'

They finished clearing up, and Eimear headed back to the flat. She kept a watchful eye in case someone was following her, and when she reached her block of flats, she could see it was deserted. Thankfully, there was nowhere for someone to lie in wait out of sight. Even so, she walked briskly to the door, put in her code and ran upstairs. She locked her door and replaced the safety chain. She got a Coke from the fridge. Glancing at her phone, she saw a message from Meg asking her to Facetime at eight. It was closer to nine now, but she decided to try and see if she could get in touch with her. She was in luck, and soon Meg answered. Her face was even more bronzed, and she grinned happily at her.

'OK, make me jealous and tell me where you are now?' Eimear asked.

'Not so far away. I finished my plant-watering duties and have come to Scotland. I'm staying in a little guest house in Edinburgh. Tomorrow I'm touring the city and the first port of call is the Castle, then on Friday I'm taking a train to London, and I'm staying with an old school friend, who is taking a few days' holiday to show me the sights. I've been to London before when I was young with your mother, but it was a flying visit, and I barely remember what we got up to. I plan to do everything. But the good news is that I'm finally putting a halt to my gallop and hope to come home in the next couple of weeks. I'm so looking forward to seeing you and hearing all your news. And listen here, young one, I think I will have to feed you up a bit – you're looking tired and peaky. I hope they're not working you too hard.'

Eimear laughed. 'I'm just exhausted listening to all your plans. But I'm delighted that you're coming home soon.'

'Do you remember when last we spoke about my coming home? I mentioned staying with you for a few days. Is that still OK?'

Eimear hesitated.

Meg noticed and added, 'If it's awkward, I can just head back to Sligo. The Taylors will still be renting my place, but I can easily stay with my friend Annie.'

'Don't be silly, Meg. Of course you can stay with me here in Dublin as long as you like. I have that sofa bed, and I'm in and out so much we'll be like ships that pass in the night. Then, if your renters are still in situ, move into Mam's house. I'm hardly ever there, and you can make yourself at home.'

'I may take you up on that, but I'm so glad you're getting out and about. That's what I hoped for you. When I stay over, I will pay for my keep by preparing tasty meals for when you come home every evening. Honest to God, Eimear, I've put on so much weight, all my clothes are about to fly off me. But the food was so good, I had to do it justice. I'll enjoy trying out some new recipes on you.'

They chatted for a while, and then Eimear pretended she was expecting a call, and they said goodbye.

She was glad Meg was coming home but fervently hoped she would be back at work by the time she arrived. It made it imperative that she sort things out as quickly as possible.

Meg was coming home. The thought that she would have an ally, someone she could trust and rely on and open her heart to, eased her misery. But fond and all as she was of Meg, she wouldn't be of much help. Apart from a friendly ear, she would have no solutions to offer, and she'd only be someone to worry about. The idea of Meg fussing over her would be an irritant rather than a help. Perhaps by the time Meg had returned from her travels, she'd have got to the bottom of all the chaos surrounding her.

Chapter 17

Thursday was a work day, but not for her. She knew it was important to keep busy, so she sorted through her laundry and put on a wash. But she couldn't stop her thoughts, and the events of the previous day played in the movie theatre of her mind. Her cheeks burned as she recalled the anger and contempt in the eyes of Iris and Hannah and the look of pity on Philip's face as he told her she needed to see a doctor. Shame washed over her body in a burning wave. She surrendered to it, slumped on the couch, and buried her face in a cushion. Then she visualised her mother scolding her, urging her to get up and show some backbone. She almost heard her say, "Feeling sorry for yourself never fixed anything." Feck it, she wasn't a quitter, and there was no way she was letting her life be ruined. Today, she would keep busy and go for a brisk walk, followed by a workout in the gym. Then she planned to contact Kate. She had to find out what was happening at work. Clearing her name was a priority.

She dressed and walked briskly around the park for an hour, and the fresh air worked magic. The park was a popular running spot, mainly men today, but she spotted a lone female. It was the woman she had seen outside her flat a few days ago. She had a strong, almost mannish build with muscular legs, and she could certainly run. Maybe she should take up running, too. She certainly had the time. Exercising hard made it harder to be plagued by intrusive thoughts. And maybe whatever thoughts she did have would be more focused and less inclined to wander down avenues in the past that didn't need revisiting. The runner glanced at her as she ran past. Their eyes met briefly and, for a moment, she thought the woman hesitated as if she were about to stop and greet her. Then she was gone, pounding down the path. Eimear turned and looked after her, for some reason feeling slightly uneasy. She shook the feeling off. She was becoming paranoid. A woman merely glanced at her and she felt threatened? Now she was imagining threats where none existed.

She turned and walked on.

Back at the flat, she checked the time. It was ten minutes to nine. Kate would be in the office now. She pictured her settling down to deal with all the legal work the firm sent to her. She rang her mobile. The phone rang out for so long that she was about to give up, certain Kate didn't want to speak to her.

But then Kate answered. Her voice sounded guarded.

'Hi Kate, this is me, Eimear. Can you talk?'

'Give me a minute. I'm busy right now, but call me back in ten minutes.'

Eimear was relieved that Kate was at least willing to make contact with her. Impatiently, she waited for the time to elapse and then called again. This time, Kate answered promptly.

'Kate, listen, I don't know what you've heard, but you've got to hear my side of things, please.'

She could hear Kate's even breath and, after a pause, she spoke.

'I'll tell you what has been told to me. Hannah says you've been going behind her back to complain about her work; Iris says you cancelled an important appointment with Brennan and then pretended you hadn't and tried to blame her for your mistakes. Philip doesn't confide in the likes of a lowly paralegal, but Toby said that a lot of your work was shoddy and that you tried to steal his clients, and that you are always bitching about us to him. Is that close enough?'

'Kate, none of that is true. I need to talk to you to explain. I want to clear my name.'

'Eimear, I like you. But I've known the girls and Toby for three years – why should I take your word against theirs?'

'I'm not asking you to, but I would like to meet and explain my side of things.'

Kate was silent for so long that Eimear feared she had hung up.

'OK, I'll meet you tonight after work. But not the Snuggery or Lennon's. There's a pub on the corner, just past the traffic lights on the left-hand side – do you know it? I think it's called Hughes, and we can talk there.'

'Thank you so much, Kate. I really appreciate it.'

'Don't be too grateful; you're buying the drinks. I'll be there shortly after half-five. OK, got to go now.'

She hung up with renewed hope. If Kate was willing to see her, there was a chance she could sort all this madness out.

Eimear tidied the flat, did some household tasks that needed doing, and when everything was spick and span, she changed into her workout gear.

The gym was quiet. Not too many people worked out so early in the day. She noticed the runner from the park lifting weights. Eimear was impressed as she was lifting heavy weights effortlessly. The woman suddenly turned her head and stared at her. Eimear hurried past. There was something odd about that woman.

She went through her usual routine but pushed herself a lot harder. It had the effect of quieting her mind. When she returned to the flat, she took a long hot shower to help ease the aches from her workout and washed her hair. Getting it cut short had been a good idea; it was much easier to manage, but today it made her feel like one of those shriven women, punished for consorting with the enemy. She applied make-up to rid herself of this self-image and instantly felt better. Mam always said that putting on a bit of lippy was akin to getting into a suit of armour. With the right shade of lipstick, a girl was ready for anything.

A wave of ravenous hunger almost floored her. She hadn't eaten since the night before, and a glance in her fridge and cupboards didn't offer anything to tempt her. It was time to get shopping and stock up on provisions. She had been eating too many takeaways recently, which had to stop. It wasn't healthy, and she needed all her wits about her.

The supermarket, like the gym, wasn't busy. She picked up a few lamb chops and some fresh fruit and vegetables and stopped by the drinks section where she picked up a bottle of vodka. She knew it probably wasn't wise to keep drink in the flat, but then again, why not?

When she returned to the flat, she put away the groceries, stuck the chops under the grill and cooked a few veg. She hadn't the patience to wait for spuds to cook, so she made do with extra carrots and broccoli.

She forced herself to eat the meal slowly. It tasted good but she found her mind kept drifting off to dark places.

After her meal, she cleared up. There were still a couple of hours until she was due to meet with Kate. Finding the flat oppressive, she decided to head into town early. Luckily, she remembered to take a change of clothes for her self-defence class later that evening. Fiona had given her directions, and the class was at seven. So when she finished meeting Kate, she could head there straight away.

She caught a bus into town and wandered around the shops until it was time to meet Kate. It didn't take long to locate the pub. It was handy for Kate, near the office, and she'd pass it on her way to the bus stop. It was a small, proper local pub; most clientele were elderly men. She found a table at the window and ensconced herself there.

Kate arrived at a quarter to six. Eimear waved to her, and Kate joined her. She ordered a G & T for Kate and a slimline tonic for herself from a passing barman. Kate raised her glass in salute and took a sip. She looked uncomfortable, and Eimear noticed that she avoided eye contact.

'Well, I suppose my name is dirt at work,' she said to break the ice.

'You could say that. Eimear, what were you about? I never thought of you as underhanded. I mean, anyone can forget an appointment. But blaming Iris was out of order.'

Eimear flushed. She wanted to rush into an angry denial but knew she had to use reason and logic to explain what happened and make her case.

'OK, I can see why Iris might have felt I was blaming her, but it was all a confusion. Look, I'll forward you the emails I supposedly sent to

Brennan and the ones to Philip when I supposedly complained about Hannah. The sign-off is completely different when you compare them to other emails I've sent. I always end an email with 'Kind regards, Eimear', but these are signed, 'Respectfully yours'. I only sign that way in formal letters – if ever. Why would I suddenly start doing that in an email?'

'So what are you saying? That someone else using your email address sent emails purporting to be coming from you. Why in the name of god would someone do that to you?'

'I don't know, Kate, but I need to find out.'

Kate didn't look convinced. 'What about all the bitching you've been doing to Toby about us. He says you're nice as pie to our faces but sniggering about us when we're out of earshot.' She glared at Eimear, her brown eyes sharp with suspicion.

'I can only say that that is completely untrue. If anyone is making nasty comments, it's Toby. Don't tell me you haven't heard him making little digs about Iris and Hannah. I know you have.'

She could see that she had given Kate pause for thought.

'Are you suggesting that Toby sent those emails just to get rid of you?'

Eimear sighed. 'I wish I could but, although Toby would like rid of me, I don't think he'd go that far. He's just taking advantage of the shit I'm in. But you should have heard the things he said to Philip about me. He accused me of sexually harassing him, behaving inappropriately and making a pass at him. Come on, Kate, you know I have no interest in Toby; there's no way I'd have been perving over him as he suggested.'

'Well, he certainly thinks he's irresistible to all women. But I know that you've never shown any interest, at least not openly. I admit that carry-on doesn't sound like you.'

'Well, thanks for that, Kate, a sex pest I'm not.'

'So, if you don't think Toby is behind the emails, who are you accusing? Iris, Hannah, me?'

'Kate, I'm not blaming anyone but, you see, there's something you don't know.'

'Well, tell me, Eimear, if you want me to understand.'

Eimear hesitated and then, taking a breath, briefly described everything that had been happening to her and even mentioned Donal.

'Christ, that's a lot.' Kate stared at her. 'Have you contacted the guards?'

'Yes, I have, but they are having difficulty getting anywhere. Do you believe me?'

'Eimear, I don't know what to believe. Do you think all these things happening at the office are connected? Do you think it's your ex?'

'I honestly don't know. But how did someone get my email password?'

The two girls stared at each other. Then Kate looked at her watch.

'I have to get a move on. It's my turn to cook tonight.'

"Kate, tell me, do you believe me now?'

Kate stared at her. 'Put it this way, I don't disbelieve you. But you have to admit it all sounds very far-fetched.'

'I know, but all I ask is that you keep an open mind.'

The girls hugged awkwardly, and then Kate left. Eimear gathered her sports bag and headed to the community centre where her class was due to begin.

The class was much smaller than her usual one, and the women were friendlier. Fiona mentioned that for some women, defence classes weren't just a precautionary thing but something they did to stay alive. It was a sobering thought. The women made her welcome, although they did slag her for her country accent. She left tired and happy.

She rang a taxi as she didn't feel like a bus commute. The happy mood lasted until she stood at the door of her flat. Across the door, in red paint that dripped like blood, was the word **BITCH** written in block capitals.

Chapter 18

Garda Collins promised she'd be with her in less than half an hour, but Eimear couldn't open the door and wait in the flat. She was afraid of what she might find inside. Instead, she leaned against the wall until the weakness in her legs forced her to sit leaning against the wall. There was another tenant in a flat on this floor, and she hoped they wouldn't show up. She wasn't up to answering questions from anyone except the guards. Eventually, closer to an hour than the promised half hour, Collins and her colleague Shane Owens turned up. They took pictures of the graffiti and asked if it was similar to the paint daubed on her car a month ago. Eimear wasn't sure but thought it was likely.

Collins made her coffee and took some notes. She was sympathetic, and Eimear could see that the garda was upset for her. Collins was impressed when she heard Eimear had been coming home from self-defence classes.

'I wish all women would learn these skills. It would at least give them time to get away from an attacker and get to safety.'

'It's a pity we must go to those lengths, though. Isn't it?' Eimear said.

'Yeah, I know, Eimear, but this is the world we've got, and we all have to figure it out for ourselves.'

They sat in silence, and Eimear wondered if she should tell her about what was happening to her at work. But what if Maureen Collins thought she was some nut who attracted trouble by her behaviour? No, she'd keep shtum for the moment.

'We do have something. At least we'll have CCTV footage of him getting into the building. The paint is still quite sticky, so it can't have been that long ago. Shane is getting hold of the tape now, and we may have something tomorrow. I'll call you when we have anything.'

The two officers left, and Eimear tried to scrub the drying paint off her door. It took ages, and when she was finished, she still wasn't convinced she had obliterated the graffiti. Was it her imagination, but could she still see the visual echo of the word bitch on the door? Gritting her teeth, she scrubbed the door so hard that the original black paint was scoured away, revealing the wood underneath. She rang Alec and filled him in on what happened. He was very concerned and promised to find out if Donal was in Sligo when the door was vandalised.

Sleep was impossible, so she didn't even bother going to bed. She watched mindless TV, and when she had enough of that, she paced her flat, counting out the steps like a prisoner measuring their cell. Eventually, at nine, she was so exhausted, she lay on the couch and fell into a deep, dreamless sleep. When she opened her eyes and checked the time, it was three in the afternoon. She had slept for six hours. Her head ached, but she felt better for the sleep even though it left her groggy. She splashed cold water on her face and was patting it dry when her phone rang.

'This is Garda Collins. I wonder if you can pop down to the station this afternoon.'

'Good, do you have news?'

'I think it would be better if you called to see us, and we can discuss our findings. Can you get away from work?'

'That's OK, I'll get down to the station. See you shortly.'

Did she imagine it, or was Collins a bit unfriendly on the phone, cold even? No, now she was getting paranoid.

_____ece_____

She passed a young man accompanied by a garda in the station foyer. He smirked at her, which was unnerving. She went to the front desk and asked to see Garda Collins.

She was brought into a small, windowless interview room. A chair was chained to the floor, and the table looked like it was welded to the ground. She shivered – despite having accompanied clients to many Garda interviews, she never got used to the feeling of vulnerability they induced. Interview rooms were meant to be intimidating.

Collins and Owens entered, and she smiled warmly at them, but the smile died as she met the chill emanating from the officers, particularly Collins.

'Have you any news? Have you got the person responsible for what happened?'

'Yes, we have,' said Collins.

'That's fantastic! Well done! Did he say why he did it? Was someone paying him? Was it Donal?'

A knock on the door and another uniformed officer entered the room and handed Collins a sheet of paper. She showed it to Owens, and he stared at Eimear, his eyes hard and calculating. What the hell was going on? Why were they being so hostile?

'Ms Martin, I wonder why you have been wasting our time. Don't you think we have enough to do without dealing with this crap?'

Stunned by how Collins spoke to her, Eimear got to her feet, her face flushed with anger.

'What the hell are you talking about?' she demanded.

'Sit down, Ms Martin. We have information to give you. The boy we saw on the CCTV camera is known to us. He has been lifted several times for petty crime, nothing serious, but he's a nuisance. Today, when we picked him up, he first denied everything, but eventually, when confronted with the CCTV camera evidence, he sang like the proverbial canary. He told us that someone had indeed paid him to daub paint on your door.'

'Great, who was he?'

'Not he, but she, and you know what? He gave us a detailed description. The woman had a West of Ireland accent, very short hair, and a small mole on her left cheek.'

Eimear stared, mesmerised, and raised her hand to her face.

'In fact, a mole just like yours. She also wore a coat that was a very distinctive blue colour, very like the one you are wearing right now.'

Eimear forced herself to speak. 'You are taking the word of a thug for hire. Why wouldn't he know what I look like? He has probably been following me!'

'Come off it, Eimear. I asked my colleague to walk the boy past you just now, and he didn't hesitate to identify you. I'm impressed that you held your nerve when you saw him,' said Collins.

This can't be happening. The two guards stared at her with hard eyes.

'What about the break-in at my flat? The man terrorised me and cut off my hair. You saw the bruises on my neck and face. How do you explain that?'

Owens leaned forward and stared at her. 'Well, Eimear, I've been thinking about that. Someone let that man in, and every flat occupant denied doing it. One lady I spoke to said you were very odd and apt to accuse people of making noise, and your fellow tenants find you unpleasant. As for the marks on your face, you must admit they were very superficial; perhaps you did them yourself or got your masked friend to do it.'

'This is insane. I've barely spoken to the tenants in the building, never mind complaining about them. Why in hell's name would I be doing all this to myself? You must think I'm mad.'

Owens smirked. 'Maybe you need to see a doctor about that, but I think it's a basic case of attention-seeking.'

Eimear turned pleading eyes towards Garda Collins.

'Come on, you can't believe I'd do this to myself. You can't really believe it of me, can you?'

Collins didn't answer, her face closed and hostile.

'You do realise, as a solicitor, how much trouble you're in?' said Owens

Eimear glared at him. 'Can't you see I've been set up?'

'Really, just like your work colleagues have set you up?'

Eimear's face blanched.

'Yes, we tried to reach you at work today and had a very interesting chat with your boss. It seems you are causing trouble wherever you are.

Unfortunately, it seems to have rebounded on you.' Collins's voice was icy with disdain.

Eimear lost all power of speech; she just kept shaking her head. Collins stared at her.

'Look, Eimear, I'm willing to take a charitable view; perhaps this looking for attention has some medical term. Your boss said he told you to see your doctor. I think that's good advice. I hope you take it. But I won't be as understanding if I hear from you again. Now we have real crimes to deal with, so push off.'

Fighting back tears of humiliation and rage, she walked out of the station. Someone very clever was trying to destroy her life. But how had they got hold of her coat? She had bought it in a department store, and there must be many similar ones. Someone was going to an insane amount of trouble to either frame her or drive her mad. And by fuck she wasn't going to let them.

If things got much worse, she would lose her job and, without a decent reference, she could kiss goodbye to her career. Who was doing this, and why?

Chapter 19

She would have to confide in Meg. Tonight, she would contact her and ask her to come home. There was no way she could handle this on her own. Whoever was playing games with her life was so many steps ahead that she was helpless to defend herself. She badly needed to regroup and come up with a plan. Mam would know what to do, and in Mam's absence, Meg would step in.

She texted her, and Meg agreed to Facetime that evening. While waiting for Meg to call her, she drank so much coffee that her nerve endings vibrated. As she paced the floor, she wondered how much she should tell Meg. She didn't want to alarm her, but at the same time, she didn't feel equipped to handle all this insanity on her own. She doubted that Kate would be willing to see her side of things, not after the gardaí had called to the office. That would be the final nail in the coffin.

At eight, Meg called. The familiar warm feeling of home crept over her as she looked at her aunt's friendly face.

'Well, pet, how are you doing?'

'Grand, Meg, but I'm dying to see you. When did you say you were coming home? I want to have everything nice for you.'

'Well, I've just arrived in London to stay with my friend for a week or so, but I'm coming home possibly, the weekend after next, so if that offer of a place to stay still holds, I'll take it up.'

'Aww, that's great news, Meg.'

Eimear's relief at Meg's words suddenly turned into an avalanche of tears. Looking at Meg's alarmed face, she forced herself to calm down. She debated about telling Meg an edited version of what happened, but it all spilt out. Meg looked shocked, and Eimear could see her frustration at not being there to offer comfort and support.

'Oh my god, this is terrible. Why didn't you tell me sooner instead of leaving me here enjoying myself and thinking that all was well with you?'

'There was nothing you could do, Meg, and I didn't want to worry you.'

'Right, I'm coming straight home. I can't believe you haven't told me all this before.'

To Eimear's consternation, her aunt's voice wobbled dangerously.

'If Claire knew I left you to face all this alone while I've been off gallivanting, she'd never forgive me.'

'Please, don't be at that, Meg. I wanted to tell you, but really, what could you do? I thought the guards had it in hand until they turned against me.'

'The cheek of them, to believe a young gurrier like that over you! They must be mad.'

'Calm down, Meg – I'm not alone or at least I won't be for long. I've been thinking about getting a private investigator on it. Then I might finally get to the bottom of everything.'

'Well, that's a good idea. We can't just sit back and let whoever is doing this destroy you.'

'Thanks, Meg.'

'Thanks for what?'

'Well, for believing me, for not assuming that I've either lost the plot and am doing things unbeknownst to myself or else I'm an attention-seeking vengeful psychopath.'

'Listen, girl, I've known you for your entire life, and although you may have been a bit of a brat at times and refused to listen to your elders, a more sane and balanced human being I've never met and I'll beat the head off anyone who says otherwise.'

Eimear started to laugh as she looked at Meg's fierce face.

'I'm glad I have you on my side, Meg; I wouldn't want to get on the wrong side of you.'

'Do you remember that little brat, Johnny what's his name, who used to pull your hair and call you names in primary school? Well, he learnt his lesson after I tore strips off him in front of his pals at the community centre.'

'So that was why he stopped hassling me. I never knew.'

'Your mother did, and she egged me on because she was too much of a lady to put him in his place properly. So you can count on me. Together, we'll get to the bottom of things. I promise you.'

'Thanks, Meg. I feel so much better knowing I have you in my corner.'

'You know what? I'm going to get a flight out tomorrow

'Don't be silly. As long as I know you're coming soon, I'll be grand.'

'Well, if you're sure, it's just that I committed to minding my friend's cats while she is away at a work thing. But if I can sort out a cattery, I'll be home much sooner.'

'The weekend after next is fine, Meg. Don't be changing your plans. I mean it.'

'You need to find someone you trust to stay over with you in the meantime. Do you have anyone you can ask?'

Realising this was the only way to reassure her aunt, she lied and told her she'd stay at a friend's place. She pretended that she'd met a nice girl at the gym and that she would be delighted to have her stay with her. Meg looked a bit happier, and they ended the call.

As she switched off her phone, Eimear felt more hopeful and filled with a new purpose. It was time to start fighting back.

With that thought in mind, she called Kate, but there was no answer. She left it an hour and then called again – no answer. So Kate had given up on her, too. She poured herself a generous measure of vodka. She drank deeply. It helped.

Shaking her head, she walked over to her desk. She took out her legal pad. Right, remember your training. Think about all this logically. Write out all the facts and try to make sense of it all. There must be some way to figure out who was doing this to her. If it were Donal ... she'd make sure he'd live to regret it. But for now, she would deal with all the facts. All the things that had happened to her in Sligo and everything that had happened here in Dublin. She was smart. Even Toby and Philip had to give her that. Well, she'd use some of those smarts to figure this out. She'd make Maureen bloody Collins sorry for doubting her.

Over the next hour, she wrote down only facts she knew were true. Then she read what she had written.

SLIGO

1. *Discovery that Donal is having an affair. This is verified by my seeing Donal with the girl and by his reaction to said discovery.*

2. *I break off the engagement.*

3. *Donal starts a campaign of harassment – texting numerous times every day, calling me on the phone, showing up to my place of work, following me, showing up when I'm on a date.*

4. *Donal warned to stop harassing me by local guards.*

5. *Showing up at Mam's house after the funeral despite being warned off by Alec, showing up again when I was alone in the house and scaring me.*

6. *Alec to inform Donal's boss of his behaviour and give Donal a final warning.*

7. *The process of a barring order begins.*

DUBLIN FLAT

1. *Photos taken of me since I moved to Dublin and sent to me in the post. The postmark was the city centre.*

2. *The word DIE scrawled across my car*

3. *A letter warning me not to go through with my threats. Does this mean my threat to inform Donal's boss?*

4. *A man breaks into the flat and assaults me.*

5. *The word Bitch painted on my door.*

6. *The guards arrest someone they claim I hired to vandalise my doorway – why did he lie? Or does he really believe I paid him to do this?*

WORK

1. *Email purporting to be sent by me to Philip Jolly complaining about Hannah.*

2. *Email sent changing the appointment with Tommy Brennan*

3. *Missing document*

4. *Staff turned against me.*

5. *Toby lies about me – is this opportunistic, or is he part of the conspiracy?*

SUSPECTS
DONAL
MOTIVE:

- *Anger at being rejected and publicly humiliated.*

- *Persecution complex – sees himself as the victim.*

PRO:

- *While safe in Sligo, he could have hired someone to do his bidding. Did he have any contacts in Dublin who might be willing to help him?*

CON:

- *According to Lana, he was seen in Sligo at least some of the times I have been targeted.*

JEN
MOTIVE:

- *Anger at how her brother had been treated.*

PRO:

- *She has been bad-mouthing me to everyone in Sligo.*

CON:

- *She is not a psychopath. An angry sister, yes, but a rational person.*

TOBY
MOTIVE:

- *Jealous of my success in the firm.*

- *Angry at me for rejecting him when he made the pass.*

- *He told lies about me to Philip and the girls at work.*

- *He had the opportunity to access my email account,*

- *He may have contacts in the criminal underworld who could have been responsible for some of the things that had happened to me.*

CON:

- *Unlikely to take any real risks that could land him in trouble.*

- *And he has no known link with Donal.*

HANNAH:
PRO:
- *Crazy about Toby and might have been willing to tell lies about me out of jealousy or to help Toby.*

- *Furious at the complaints she believes I made against her.*

CON:
- *Unlikely to be vicious enough to do me serious harm.*

PHILIP JOLLY, IRIS, KATE – no reason for them to want to harm me.

She stared at what she had written. It didn't give her any answers but helped sort everything out in an orderly way.

She looked at the time and decided to try and get some sleep. She wasn't optimistic, but her body was tired, even if her mind was whirring like a clockwork toy. She made up a bed on the couch, and after double-checking that the door was bolted, she turned the TV on low for the company. If someone broke in tonight, there was no way in hell she could call the guards. She doubted if they'd come, and if they did, they'd probably arrest her for wasting their time.

Chapter 20

Eimear awoke, if not refreshed, then filled with fresh determination to deal with the circumstances she faced. She had always been a logical, organised person, but all the things that had happened to her lately had unbalanced her and made her emotional. She needed to think of the chaos surrounding her as a puzzle to be solved. It was important to try and think dispassionately as though she were working on behalf of a client.

The first plan for her day was to take a brisk walk around the park to clear her head. She had always done her best thinking while walking and, who knew, perhaps she'd come up with some idea to solve her problems. She dressed warmly as it was a bitterly cold November day. Walking through the park, she allowed the solitude to ease into her. The trees were bare of colour, and even the green of the grass was muted, and the whole world, from the heavy grey skies to the faded grass, suited her subdued mood. She didn't need nature's carnival of beauty right now. Fittingly, it was as though the world was acknowledging her pain and showing empathy by reflecting her suffering.

'Hey, cheer up, smile!'

The greeting from the middle-aged man in a brown duffel coat jerked her from her reflections. She pulled up.

'What did you say?' she asked as a warm heat rose across her body.

The man paused and grinned at her through gapped teeth. 'I said cheer up!' He stood grinning at her inanely.

Eimear walked over to him and looked him straight in the eye. 'Why don't you just fuck off and mind your own business!'

The man looked startled. 'Now look here, I was only saying ...'

'In what universe do you think I or any woman would care to get advice from a Neanderthal in a poxy donkey jacket?

No sooner had he hurried off than a wave of shame swept over Eimear. There was no excuse for her overreaction. Her mother would have been ashamed of her. The guy was harmless and didn't deserve such a mouthful of insults. What the hell was happening to her? This was not who she was – a vicious virago. She needed to take herself in hand; she couldn't afford to lash out like that.

Back at the flat, she checked her phone. There was a message from Alec asking her to ring him. Perhaps he'd have news. At least he'd tell her how he got on with Donal. She rang immediately. It was his private phone, and he answered straight away.

'Well, Eimear, how's tricks?'

'Grand, Alec, look, I'm busy at the moment. Could you fill me in on what's happening with Donal?'

'Sure thing, Eimear. Well, I went to see him at his place of work. His face was a picture when he saw me. He hurried me into the cubby hole he called his office and told everyone in earshot that he wasn't to be disturbed. I cautioned him and informed him that you had made a statement about his behaviour. Of course, he denied doing anything wrong. He claimed you called him and invited him over and then went psycho on him. It's a classic case of 'he says, she says'. But with the confirmation of your aunt and the list of behaviours he embarked on since the engagement was called off, then we have a good case with the judge.'

'Did you find out if he was away from Sligo when my car was vandalised and my door was daubed with paint?'

'He claims to have been in Sligo when your car was damaged. It was confirmed by one of his colleagues. But his alibi for the evening your door was defaced is trickier. He claimed to have been sick with the flu and was in bed. He says his mother can confirm as she called to see him. But I'm not sure how much faith we can put in her confirmation as she will stick up for her son no matter what.'

'Thanks so much, Alec. Did you speak to his boss?'

'I didn't, as he was away on a business trip. But it's no harm to have that hanging over him. It'll keep him ripe with worry. What about at your end? Do the lads in Dublin have any more information on what's happening? I can give them a ring to stop them dragging their feet. I trained with a few men from that station so I could encourage them to get a hustle on.'

Eimear hesitated. Should she tell Alec that she was persona non grata with the gardaí here? If he contacted them, perhaps he'd lose faith in her, and she couldn't bear to lose him as an ally. No, she had to keep him on her side, and she couldn't risk him doubting her.

'Well, Eimear, do ya want me to have a word?'

'No, Alec, leave things be. They've been great, and I don't want them to think I'm checking up on them. But I'll let you know if things change. OK?'

Eimear asked after Alec's mother and congratulated him on his football team's success. Then, she ended the call.

She spent the rest of the morning reviewing her list from the previous night. Should she hire a private investigator? She wasn't short of money. Maybe she could contact some of the friends she did law with? Some of the barristers who worked on criminal cases might be able to recommend someone suitable. It was one line of attack anyway, and it would make her feel like she was doing something practical to help herself out of this mess.

She also needed to make some decisions about work. She was off nearly a week, and Philip had insisted she attend her doctor, so she would do just that. It was important to cover her absence from work, or Philip would use it as an excuse to get rid of her. He probably would anyway. She rang her GP in Sligo and asked to speak to him when he was free. The receptionist arranged for her to ring at half four as Dr Murphy would have finished his afternoon clinic by then.

To fill in the time, she headed to the gym. Her workout was intense and allowed her mind to quieten. She glimpsed her park runner doing press-ups; the woman was very fit. She had muscles Rocky would be proud of.

Back at the flat, she showered, had a cup of strong coffee, and thought about what to say to her GP, Dr Murphy. He was her family doctor. He had looked after her since she was a baby, and she was fond of him. She rang reception in his surgery and was put through to his office.

'Hello, Dr Murphy, it's me, Eimear Martin.'

'Well, how are you, my dear? I was so sorry to hear about your mam. She was a lovely lady, and I missed the funeral as we were on holiday, but I hope you got our Mass card. Edel wrote a little note for you and Meg.'

'I did, thank you. Give my best wishes to Mrs Murphy.'

'Will do! Now, Eimear, what can I do for you?'

'Doctor, I've been going through a bad time. I suppose you know about my broken engagement and, on top of it, Mam's death, and well, I'm finding it hard to cope here at the new job. I'm feeling overwhelmed.'

Without intending to, Eimear started crying, and the doctor made concerned noises.

'It sounds like you should have taken more time to grieve for your mam and, of course, your break-up. Starting a new job so soon and away from all your friends and support wasn't a great move. Edel tells me that Meg has gone off travelling, too. I'm sure that can't help. So listen, I'll send a prescription for a mild antidepressant to the usual pharmacy, and you need to collect it when you're back at home. In the meantime, I'm giving you a two-week cert so you can get back on your feet.'

'Oh, doctor, I hate taking work off, but I haven't been able to go to work all week. I kept bursting into tears, and I was mortified. So, I wonder, could you give me a cert from last Monday?'

'I will surely, Eimear. So, if you need more time after two weeks, call to see me, and we'll work something out. I don't usually do phone consults, but you're never sick. But when you come home, make an appointment to see me. The tablets will take a few weeks to kick in, and we may need to increase the dosage, but I'll need to see you to discuss a treatment plan. I'll send the cert in the post, and you can pass it on to your employer.'

They said goodbye. Eimear felt shitty for manipulating the doctor. He was a good man. But anyway, she hadn't lied and needed more time off work to get to the bottom of everything happening to her.

Chapter 21

When the medical cert arrived, she posted it to work. She wondered what the work crowd would say about her continued absence. No doubt they would take this as confirmation that she was a crazy lady with a malicious streak. The thought that she would make them eat crow when she proved her innocence kept her spirits up. She would do it, if it were the last thing she would do.

That evening, she contacted a friend from law school and got a list of names of private investigators. She explained her need for one by mentioning she was dealing with a complicated compensation case. It was nice to get in touch with one of the old crowd from her days in Blackhall Place where she trained as a solicitor. She was tempted to confide in one of them. Her best mate from among the Dublin crowd was Joan. They had always got on well, and she had even contemplated asking her to be a bridesmaid before everything with Donal imploded. Joan worked for her father's firm in Kildare. She had dropped Eimear a nice letter after her engagement ended, and she had gone to Claire's funeral. Her finger hovered over Joan's name in her phone. But the thought of explaining everything to her forthright friend caused her to hesitate. Deep down, she was afraid that Joan might not believe her either.

Instead of calling Joan, she called three of the detectives recommended, but only one was free to start work on her case, and she hesitated to make an appointment. He sounded bored and impatient, so she decided to put off making an appointment with him. She needed someone who would believe in her and whom she could trust. This man did not tick any of those boxes. Depressed, she poured herself a glass of vodka. It didn't quite hit the spot, so she had another and another. She fell asleep on the couch.

On Tuesday, she got a call from Philip Jolly. He had on his fake friendly voice and, after he asked her how she was feeling, she realised he was checking that she was taking sick leave. He cut off any attempt to explain that she had done nothing wrong. He mentioned the visit of the Garda, obviously bursting to find out what was going on.

'Eimear, I'm afraid I had to be frank with the two officers who called here last week about the reasons for your absence from work. Perhaps you would be happier working somewhere else where you can make a fresh start with new colleagues. I fear you have rather burnt your bridges here.'

'Mr Jolly, I have just obtained a cert for two more weeks and posted it to you. I hope you're not dismissing me when I'm on sick leave.'

'Not at all, Eimear. I'm glad you've taken my advice and seen your GP and, of course, we all wish you a speedy recovery. But, Eimear, sometimes it's better to move on when things have taken a bad turn — make a fresh start, so to speak.'

'Philip, I'm not ready to give up so easily. I'm determined to prove that I did nothing wrong. Sometimes, appearances can be deceptive. '

'I see, well, I hope you feel better soon, and now I must go. I'll watch out for your certificate in the post.'

It took all her willpower not to snarl at him, but she realised that she had better not give him any more excuses to get rid of her.

A punishing session in the gym worked off some of her rage. Was she overdoing it at the gym? She trained mainly to put in the time but also because she wanted to be ready. The feeling she had when she was attacked in her flat was overwhelming. She had never felt so powerless, her body so feeble. So maybe her obsession with getting strong was unhealthy, but she hoped it would keep her safe. It had to. In the changing room, she rubbed some ointment onto her shoulders to keep the soreness at bay. She hoped the nagging pain in her lower back wasn't indicative of a serious injury.

On the way back, she stocked up on cleaning supplies. She was running through all her cleaning products at a fierce rate. Boredom had turned her into a very thorough cleaner. Then, after ensuring she was safely locked in, she napped on her couch. When she awakened, it was time to head out to her self-defence class. This was one part of her routine that she enjoyed. The gym was fine, but it was, in the main, a solitary activity. But the self-defence classes were fun, and she got to know some of the women who attended and their stories, too. There were some people in bad situations out there. But realising that other people's lives were also fucked up didn't make her feel any better about hers.

Her confidence grew as she practised holds and learned how to disarm attackers. When these classes were finished, she planned to take up martial arts. The one good thing that had come out of all the shit that had rained down on her was how her confidence in her body had grown.

Sometimes, when she headed home after a session, she almost wanted someone to attack her. She thought about all the moves she had learned in her class. If only she had known how to defend herself when ... She bit her lip to distract herself from the memory of that night. If only she had the skills then that she now had acquired. But then again, maybe terror would have paralysed her. She needed to keep practising until the defensive moves became automatic.

The next two days passed, and she tried to keep busy. Finally, she decided to make an appointment with the private detective. She was just about to ring when she got a call from Alec.

'Hi there, Alec. How are you?'

'Fine, listen, Eimear, I think we need to talk. Is there any chance you will come back to Sligo? I need to see you.'

'What's up, Alec, you're scaring me. Tell me, what's up?'

'It would be better if you came home. I mean it, Eimear. Try to make it soon.'

'OK, I can drive down tomorrow; I was planning to head home on Thursday anyway, so a day early won't make much difference to my plans. Do you want me to call at the station?'

'No!' Alec said sharply.

'Well, where then?'

'I'll call to your house tomorrow afternoon. I have a few hours off as I have a late shift. Say around four. Will you be there then?'

'Yes, I'll be there, Alec, but can't you tell me what's happening?'

There was no reply. Alec had hung up.

That night, she tossed and turned, finally falling into a deep sleep at four in the morning. Her alarm was set for nine, and she dressed quickly. The sooner she got on the road, the sooner she'd discover why Alec was so mysterious. It wasn't like him to keep her in suspense. He knew how freaked out she was. In the end, she didn't get on the road until after one; her car had a puncture, and the wheel nuts were impossible to get off, so she rang the AA and had to wait ages for them to arrive.

When she drove up the avenue to her house, it was almost four, and the November daylight was ebbing away. The leafless trees in her mother's garden looked like brooding giants. She had always loved them and had spent happy summer days as a child high in their leafy canopies, but today, they seemed unfriendly, even sinister.

She unlocked the door and turned the alarm off. The house was loud with silence, and her mind whirred with anxiety. She turned on the heating and boiled water for some tea as she was parched.

Alec would be here soon, and she would hear what he had to say. It couldn't be good when he wouldn't talk to her on the phone.

She drank her tea and kept watching out for Alec's car. Eventually, she heard the sound of tyres on gravel, and then his car pulled up at the front door. She hurried out to greet him, but the welcome smile faded from her face when she saw the hard look on his. It reminded her of how Maureen Collins had looked at her, and her stomach churned.

'*Get inside!*' he snapped.

'Alec, what's wrong? Why are you being like this?'

'That's rich coming from you, Eimear Martin. Now get inside and shut the fuck up because I'm doing the talking now.'

He pushed past her and into the kitchen. The rigid line of his shoulders scared her more than anything he said. This wasn't her old friend Alec. This was a hard, cold man, a man wearing a uniform. Her heart sank.

Chapter 22

Alec stood in the kitchen. He'd always pull his hat off when he met her, but he stood in the kitchen in all his Garda regalia looking at her with hard, contemptuous eyes. Suddenly, she had enough of it.

'*What the fuck is eating you?*' she demanded, giving him glare for glare.

'Well, you've got a neck, Eimear, I'll give you that.'

'Are you going to get to the point and tell me why you're acting like an angry wasp?'

'Fine, where do I start? Aww, yes, first, I hear from one of those garda who, according to you, have been looking into your so-called attack. I did wonder why you didn't want me to bother them. Imagine my surprise when they told me about your antics in Dublin. They weren't best pleased with you.'

Eimear interrupted. 'Alec, please, you have to believe me!'

'You know what? I don't have to believe a rotten word that comes out of your mouth. I can see now that you're a manipulator. I don't know your game, but I'm on to you now.'

'Please listen to me –'

He raised his hand to silence her as she implored him to listen.

'No, you listen. I was fool enough to believe all the nonsense that you fed me. Poor little Eimear, her fiancée betrayed her, and after she dumped him, he stalked and harassed her. Well, now I know that it's all lies.'

'*Alec!*' she pleaded.

'Sergeant O' Driscoll to you. Now, just shut up and listen. I realise now that everything you accused Donal of was a case of your word against his. And I was fool enough to believe every line you fed me. OK, he sent you a few nasty texts and followed you around, but the rest is all lies. I know that because he showed me the letter you sent him and the present.'

Eimear could feel the room spinning. She tried to speak, but nothing came.

'Lost for words, Eimear, well, that makes a change. But let's be fair. Donal gave me the note and the present to show you. Here!'

Alec reached inside his jacket and tossed an envelope on the table. Her hands shook so much she couldn't open it. Eventually, she managed to grope inside and pulled a card out. In what looked like her handwriting were the words '*All is forgiven, call over*'.

'Is that your handwriting?' Dumbly, she nodded. He continued to glare at her mercilessly.

In a faint part of the brain, a memory was dredged up.

'I wrote that ages ago after we had a row. He's just manipulating you.'

'Know what, that's almost funny, and I'm impressed how you can think on your feet. The lies keep on coming. But that's not all. Look in the envelope.'

Inside the envelope was a little gold cross—her mother's cross. It couldn't be, but it was. It was identical to the cross her mother always wore.

'Is that your mother's cross?'

'It looks like the one she wore, but it can't be it. I've got it here. Look, I'll get it.'

She raced upstairs and searched her mother's jewellery box. All her pieces were there except the cross. Damn! She had put it in the zipped pocket in her handbag to take back with her to Dublin. It must still be there. She ran downstairs and located her bag on a hook in the cloakroom. The cross wasn't there. But, of course, she wouldn't have left it there. She would have taken it out of her bag and put it somewhere in her own dressing table in Dublin. She vaguely remembered doing so. Slowly, she walked back into the kitchen, where Alec waited.

'Donal received this in the post the day he called to your house. He claimed you gave it to him. The poor bastard has been through hell and back. He nearly lost his job over you. Are you so warped that it wasn't enough dumping him, but you had to make his life a living hell to punish him?'

'Alec, please, I don't understand any of this. *You must believe me.*'

'No, Eimear, I'm done being the instrument of your warped desire for revenge. If it weren't for my respect for your mother and aunt and our friendship, I'd run you in for what you've done. I asked Donal if he wanted to press charges, and you know what? He didn't. He's a better man than I'd be in the same circumstances. So, Eimear, this is the last piece of friendly advice I'd give you. Get some help for yourself. There's something deeply wrong with you, and I never want to see or hear from you again.'

Alec walked out of the room, and Eimear, her legs weak, slumped in a chair. She heard him start his car and drive away. She couldn't move, couldn't cry. Walls of despair towered around her, and she felt like she was suffocating. Her heart pounded furiously in her chest, and she could hardly catch a breath. She was convinced she was about to die. Somehow, she staggered to the window and opened it, letting the cold evening air wash over her.

She knew she wasn't fit to drive back to Dublin. Maybe everyone was right, and she was mad. Perhaps she was doing all the things to herself. It was a simpler explanation than her paranoid belief that everyone was out to get her. She longed for Mam and whispered her name over and over. She walked into Mam's room and reached for her dressing gown. She needed to feel close to her, and the dressing gown would feel as though Mam was folding her into her arms.

The house phone shattered the silence with its harsh ring. She walked slowly into the hallway and stared at it, terrified and unwilling to pick it up. Pulling Mam's dressing gown tightly around her body, she inhaled the lingering scent.

The ringing stopped, and she let her breath escape and started to walk away. The phone rang again. This time, she staggered on jellied legs to answer it.

'Well, my love, I'm off the hook. It was nice of you to send me the cross. I knew it meant that you wanted us to be together. But, you have to stop with the mixed signals. Alec was horrified when he saw how you set me up. I found that nice card you sent me after we argued over some silly thing. It really convinced Alec. Eimear, I want you to know that I forgive you. There's nothing to come between us now. But you must stop playing games. See you soon, my love.'

She dropped the phone like a hot coal and slumped on the floor. She watched as the last vestiges of light were consumed by darkness, and the air became chill.

Chapter 23

She was terrified all night that Donal would turn up at the door or break in. She was too exhausted to face a long drive back to Dublin. So she checked all the windows and doors, put on the alarm, and barricaded herself in her room. Donal's threat echoed repeatedly – '*See you soon,*' he had promised. Because that's how it was: he now could harass her with impunity. So, it was Donal behind everything, and she had never credited him with the intelligence to mastermind all that was happening to her. The persistence, yes, but the intelligence, no. Of course, she could be going mad. Did she do all these things unaware of what she was doing? Was it possible that she sent those damming emails, paid someone to attack her and sent Donal the cross?

Unable to look at the cross and chain, she replaced it in her mother's jewellery box. All its happy associations with Mam were now twisted and warped by Donal's handling of it. No, whatever else she knew, she wasn't mad. There was no way she did all those things. That level of self-harm was inconceivable. The guards in Dublin and Alec had accused her of attention-seeking. But they were wrong. All she ever wanted was to lie low, to deal with her grief over Mam and the pain of her disillusionment with Donal in peace. The new job was to be a fresh start.

Everywhere she turned led to dead ends and more confusion. She thought about contacting Lana and some of her old friends, but Alec would probably have told them she wasn't to be trusted. Soon she would be a pariah, and everyone would believe she was a vindictive bitch out to make trouble for Donal. She couldn't bear any more rejection or see the disillusionment on the faces of her friends. The way Alec looked at her made her insides shiver and curdle. If he didn't believe her, then why should anyone else? Maybe even Meg would turn against her, and then she really wouldn't be able to go on.

She sat hyper-alert for sounds of someone breaking in and robbing her of peace or sleep.

Eventually, at four in the morning, she could bear it no longer and took the long, lonely road to Dublin. As she drove, she was sustained by the thought of arriving at the flat and having the comfort of food and sleep. But the flat wasn't home; it was where she hid out and hunkered down, and now her mother's house was no longer home. The words of her old religion teacher, Miss Doyle, entered her head: 'a wandering Aramean'. Her teacher explained it as a reference to Abraham, but for her, it represented a lost soul searching for a home, for belonging, but now she realised there was no home. She was destined to wander, hopelessly lost.

Christ, she was getting dark. This train of thought wouldn't help. There was only one thing to do. She would have to get Meg to talk to Alec to convince him that she wasn't making everything up. At least Meg could confirm that Donal behaved aggressively towards her. But no doubt he wouldn't believe Meg and think she was standing up for her niece. But her aunt was a sensible, intelligent woman. She would see some way out; at the very least, she would support and believe in her. At the moment, there were vanishingly few people who did that.

When she pulled up in the car park at the back of her flat, she sat paralysed, reluctant to enter the building. What fresh disasters awaited her there? With dread, she tapped in the door code and walked with heavy feet up the stairs to her first-floor flat. At her door, she was convinced that she could still see the faint outline of the word bitch. Steeling herself, she unlocked the door. But all was quiet. She locked and bolted the door behind her. There was still some milk in her fridge that didn't smell poisonous, so she made tea and ate some toast. After her frugal meal, she considered trying to get some sleep but knew it was unlikely; better keep going until night-time and hope for the best then.

How best to pass the endless day? She could go to the gym. But she felt a deep aching tiredness sweep over her, not a tiredness that embraces sleep but a sick, restless ache. Suddenly, she was fed up with it all. The relentless wave of disasters was too much to cope with, and she wanted to surrender to self-pity and despair. Fuck it! She was tired to the bone of trying to figure things out.

Getting to her feet, she knew what she needed was oblivion. She pulled on her coat and headed for the off-licence. She had never been a big drinker, at least not before all this nightmare had engulfed her. But she needed to pass through the day and night with the anaesthetic magic of alcohol. At the off-licence, she bought two bottles of wine and a bottle of vodka to replace the one she had depleted. Tonight she knew that wine alone wouldn't take her to the place she needed.

She set about it methodically, drinking the vodka like medicine. She was getting nicely pissed when she remembered that she hadn't checked her post-box in several days. At first, she shied away from the thought of going near it, but then a surge of alcohol-fuelled courage geed her up. It was only a post-box; she'd open it, and besides, what more had she to lose? Her job, home, friends, and credibility were long gone. She giggled as she imagined what credibility would look like if it had a physical form. Getting to her feet, she staggered downstairs to the lobby. At the post-box, she dropped her key and fumbled with the tiny keyhole in the box, dropping her key again. When she picked it up, she became aware of the woman looking at her disgustedly.

'What are you looking at?' she slurred.

'You're drunk!'

'Wow, what a clever bunny you are!'

'I'm sick of you. We never had any bother until you came, now we have the police calling at all hours and you playing music half the night. We're all sick to death of you.'

'Wadda ya mean? I wasn't playing any music.'

'Oh, come off it! You were blasting it out the other night. The woman with the misfortune to live above you said she banged on your door, but you wouldn't answer. You were probably dead drunk, like now.'

Eimear stared. Suddenly, the fog of drunkenness lifted. She went over to the woman, who shrank back in fear. She grabbed her arm.

'When was the music playing? What night? Please, it's important.'

'The night before this, Wednesday. Can't you remember? Were you so out of it? It wasn't the first time either.'

Eimear stared stupidly at her. The woman glared and turned on her heel. Eimear picked up her keys and opened the post-box. It was empty.

Chapter 24

She was in Sligo on Wednesday – in Sligo and not here playing music at top volume. Someone had access to her flat and was doing their best to alienate her neighbours. What other reason for blasting music out in the small hours? But why? What was the reasoning behind destroying her friendships, making her a pariah at work, and now turning her neighbours against her? Was she to be driven out of her flat? Well, she certainly played into their hands by letting that old biddy see her hammered out of her tree. Donal couldn't have done this. Who hated her so much that they wanted to destroy her life, isolate her from everyone and potentially drive her mad?

The sense of security she had in her flat was shattered. Someone had keys to it and went about causing whatever havoc they liked. OK, the bolts she had put on her door kept her safe from intruders, but it never occurred to her that they had access to her home when she was away. It meant she wasn't secure in her flat. Thank god she had bolts on the door, but the idea of someone wandering around her flat when she was out, touching her things, terrified her. She couldn't bear it anymore. The air of the place seemed to emit menace.

She pulled on her coat, and before she left, she filled a flask with coffee and laced it with a healthy dose of vodka. It would taste vile, but she couldn't face sobriety yet. Outside, the cold air hit her like a slap, turning her cheeks red. Pulling her collar up, she headed for the park. She tried to keep walking, but her feet didn't cooperate fully, and she lurched from side to side. Giggling, she decided that sitting on a park bench was the best option.

She poured some coffee/vodka mix into the flask's cup. She debated what to call her invention—a *cafodka* or a *vocaffe*. She liked the sound of both names, even if she didn't particularly like the taste of the concoction. The park was empty due to the late November chill; all sensible people would be at work or beside cosy fires—not like her, all alone. Giggling again, she sang tunelessly. '*I'm nobody's child.*'

It was comforting to keep all her thoughts at bay. She was so hammered she forgot why she had been so upset. The memory was there but just out of reach. Why didn't she get drunk more often? It was great. But she wasn't alone in the park. A runner was doing a circuit. As the person drew near, she recognised the woman as the park runner who went to her gym. When the woman ran past, she looked at her. Was that amusement in her face? Eimear didn't care, and she closed her eyes. Her winter coat was thick and warm, and the *cafodka* made her sleepy.

'*Woah*, are you OK?'

Eimear jerked her eyes open and stared at the stocky woman with ruddy cheeks staring down at her. Squinting, she recognised her.

'Hey, I know you, you go to my gin, I mean my gym.'

The runner held Eimear's arm. 'You were sliding off the bench.'

'I'm grand,' she slurred and began to get unsteadily to her feet.

'Wait, are you Eimear Martin?'

Eimear stared at her goggle-eyed.

'I'm Anna French – we went to St Philomena's. We were in the same year. Don't you remember me?'

Eimear stared at her, bewildered. She shook her head and started to wander off.

'Hey, wait, you don't look too good. Look, why don't I give you a lift home?'

At the word home, Eimear began to laugh. She giggled and sang in a warble, '*I'm nobody's child*', then giggled and walked off.

'Wait! I can't leave you like this! Let me take you back to where you live.'

'Don't want to, I hate it.'

'Right, I'm staying not too far from here. You're coming with me. My car is near the park.'

Eimear let herself be led out of the park. It felt good to be looked after, to give up. She didn't care where this Anna was taking her.

She led her to a small black Fiesta and pushed her into the passenger seat. Eimear sat passively while the woman reached across and put on her seat belt.

Eimear pointed to her flask and asked, 'Do ya want a caffodka?' Then she giggled.

The woman took the flask from her and said, 'I think you've had enough caffodka for today.'

Eimear dozed off in the warmth of the car. Then, her delicious slumber was spoiled by someone insistently shaking her. It was that annoying runner person, Miss Iron Muscles, from the park. The woman yanked her out of the car and led her down steep steps.

'Be careful, my love. The steps are slippery. I live in the basement flat.'

Eimear stared stupidly about her, her body sagging against the wall. The woman unlocked her door and pushed Eimear inside.

'OK, Eimear, I will make a supreme sacrifice and give you my bed. Whatever you do, please don't puke or pee in it; it's a brand-new mattress.'

Anna took Eimear's coat, skirt, and half-dragged her to the bed. Eimear dropped onto it and Anna removed her shoes and tights. It felt soft and comfy, like being hugged by a giant sheep. Vaguely, she heard Anna telling her where the loo was, and then she fell fast asleep.

Chapter 25

The sun stabbed her eyes as she awoke, blinking into the light. Everything hurt; her skin felt tender and her stomach queasy, but the torture inside her skull minimised all those discomforts into mere peccadillos. She closed her eyes against the brutality of the light. Where was she? The room was an interior decorator's delight, that is, if they despised minimalism. Here, the wallpaper was a dazzling explosion of colour and foliage. Even the pictures adorning them competed with the flaming flora, but in them animals from the darkest jungles stared insolently from their wooden frames instead of flowers and plants.

Eimear shuddered. She remembered the park, the woman who claimed to know her, and assumed that she had been brought here by this Anna person. She swung her legs out of bed. Staring at her bare legs, she wondered where her skirt was. She was peering around hopelessly when a knock on the door was followed by its opening, revealing a brunette with curly hair and a round smiling face.

'Well, good morning to you. There's a towel at the bottom of the bed, and the bathroom's across the hall. Shower and get dressed, and I'll meet you for coffee and croissants in the kitchen.'

Eimear did as bidden. The shower helped a little. When she staggered back into the bedroom, she saw a glass of water and two paracetamol were sitting on her bedside locker. She swallowed the tablets and drained the glass of water.

She dressed slowly, reluctant to join Anna in the kitchen. At the doorway, she hesitated but, steeling herself, walked in. Anna had set the small kitchen table for two. There was coffee, orange juice, toast and croissants awaiting her. The smell of the coffee made her shudder.

'Take a seat, Eimear. I'll be with you in a minute; I'm just putting the bin out. Help yourself to whatever you feel like.'

Eimear was sipping orange juice and hoping she could keep it down when Anna returned.

'Well, do you remember me now?'

Eimear stared, 'Tell me your name again?'

'Anna French.'

Eimear still drew a blank.

'OK, maybe you remember me better as 'Stenchy Frenchy'. Does that ring any bells?'

It did. Then, superimposed on Anna's face was a plump, spotty one and an untidy school uniform instead of a tracksuit.

'God, of course. I know you now. I didn't recognise the name.'

'No, Stenchy French was what you and your mates called me.'

Eimear flushed. She remembered the plump girl who smelled of BO, and she remembered the mean nickname.

'Don't look so upset. I got over all the name-calling calling, and you weren't the worst; you mostly ignored me.'

'God, Anna, I'm sorry.'

'Don't worry, I got over it, and as you can see it hasn't done me any harm. I can't say the same for you. Eimear Martin of the Big House, I'd never have expected to find you paralytically drunk in a Dublin park. We all expected big things from you. I thought you were a barrister or an accountant.'

'I'm a solicitor.'

'Well, what happened to you yesterday – so pissed you nearly fell off the park bench. Was it some man who messed you around?'

Eimear got to her feet. 'Thanks for helping me yesterday. But I'd better get moving. I'm going to call a taxi and head home. I think I'll go outside and get some fresh air while waiting. But thanks again.'

Eimear went to the doorway. Her eyes were blind with tears. She was groping her way up the steps to the street when Anna caught up with her.

'Hey, look, I'm a tactless gobshite, don't mind me. Look, please let me drop you home.'

Eimear shook her head dumbly and struggled to escape Anna's grip.

'For God's sake, come back in. You haven't even got your coat, and I'm thinking that's where your phone is.'

Gritting her teeth, Eimear had no choice but to re-enter the apartment. She found her coat, and when she checked her phone, it was as dead as a doornail.

'OK, you have two choices. We can wait while we charge your phone – I have a charger, or I can drive you home. Which will it be?'

In answer, Eimear handed over the phone.

Anna took it, found the charger and then led Eimear back to the kitchen table.

'Now, while we wait, let's get reacquainted. I'll tell you my story and fill you in on all the exciting chapters in my life, and then perhaps you'll do the same for yours. So here goes. After leaving school, not being of an academic bent, I got office work and was trained as a secretary. I loathed it and went off travelling, first in Europe and then further afield. I paid my way by working in pubs and restaurants. I did that for several years, and then I moved to England. As a mature student, I took the opportunity to train as a physiotherapist in Manchester and discovered that I liked it well enough to stick to it. I moved to Dublin about a year ago. My friend offered to sublet her apartment to me until I found somewhere better or until she returned from Australia. That's my potted history – no man or woman in my life, at least not at the moment, but I'm open to offers. I had one or two relationships, but nothing stuck.'

Seeing that Eimear wasn't going to respond, she continued, 'Seriously, I have no hard feelings about the school days. You were actually fine to me. So, there's no need to feel guilty, and I've long got over it. Besides, I did stink; hygiene wasn't big in our house; the parents had their issues. But after Dad died, Mam got help, and she's in recovery now. So that's all, folks, as they say on all the best TV programmes. Now it's your turn – tell Auntie Anna all!'

Eimear tried to speak. Instead, she just howled like a dying wolf.

'For fuck sake, Martin, what's wrong? Christ on a bike, I didn't mean to upset you.'

'It's fine, I'm sorry, I just ....'

The words wouldn't form, and Eimear continued sobbing hysterically.

'Right, stop trying to talk. I can see you're in trouble. You don't have to tell me anything. But, Eimear, I'm not one to be superstitious or all *woo-woo*, but maybe our meeting yesterday was meant. Maybe you needed someone to confide in, and hey presto, I dropped into your path. So, take a breath. I will head out to the shops and pick up something for lunch, and if you're still here when I come back, I'll be ready to listen. I know I made my life sound easy, but it wasn't. I had some shitty times, too, and I know that it does help to talk, and I'm a brilliant listener. Now, I'm going to shut up and leave you to think. OK, my love?'

Eimear kept her head in her hands and only lifted it when she heard the door bang. She jumped to her feet. Her phone was probably charged enough. She unplugged it; it was half-charged. She stood indecisively at the door, phone in hand. She keyed in the number for the taxi company she used. But instead, she hesitated and then put the phone back to finish charging. The thought of returning to the flat, of dealing with angry tenants who had probably complained to the landlord, reduced her to helpless despair. What more did she have to lose? She would talk things over with Anna. She was a stranger, yet not a stranger. She wouldn't be affected by anything she said, and she might have some idea of what to do – offer a fresh perspective. But at the very least, talking to someone sympathetic would be a relief. She was sitting at the table when Anna returned an hour later.

Chapter 26

Anna insisted they walk to clear their heads and took her for a stroll along the canal. It was cold, but it did help to shake some of the cobwebs from her head. Anna chatted about her travel experiences and shared funny anecdotes, often at her own expense. She had no difficulty laughing at herself. Eimear said little and appreciated having the time to let Anna's words wash over her like a soothing stream. But after a while, Anna led them back to her basement flat.

Eimear sat looking at a bird table suspended from a tree a few feet from the kitchen window. She watched as a fat robin ate hungrily from the ball of seeds hanging from one of its spikes. A blackbird chased the poor thing away. Anna called Eimear to the table for soup and crusty bread.

'Sometimes I regret putting that bird table up. It doubles as both a bird table and the lunch menu for the neighbour's cat. I'm convinced he watches from a distance as though deciding on his daily appetiser.'

The soup smelled delicious, and Eimear realised she was ravenous. They ate in silence.

'How come you're not at work today?' she asked Anna.

'I'm working privately. A few friends and I rent out space in town, and I see some private clients. Most of my work is in the afternoons and evenings. That's why I can run and go to the gym when it's quiet. I do enough to pay the bills. Eimear, I'm not very driven by money – so long as I can get by, I'm happy, and if I get the wanderlust again, it's easy to up and go.'

'I can see how it must be nice to be free, but don't you get lonely too?'

'*Nah*, I have plenty of friends; I like my own company, and I'm happy for the moment. I try not to plan too far into the future. My philosophy is to enjoy what's happening now and let the future take care of itself. Hey, why don't we sit on the couch? We can watch the action on the bird table and hopefully repel any murderous impulses from the cat.'

They sat side by side on the couch, but the light easiness between them had ebbed away, leaving Eimear tense and anxious.

'Eimear, I don't want to pressure you, but if you want to talk about what's bothering you, I can listen. I can't promise to improve things, but maybe you'll feel less alone.'

Eimear looked at Anna – her plain round face, muscular frame, and practical clothes. The weight of her loneliness bore down on her. Anna was offering to share the burden, if only for a short time. Taking a deep breath, she began.

To her ears, it sounded fantastical, paranoid, even unhinged. She stared at her hands while she spoke. Occasionally, Anna asked a question, but she mainly let Eimear talk. Finally, when she told her everything from Donal's unfaithfulness, his stalking, her mother's death, the vandalism to her car and door, the photos, the threatening letter, and the attack on her in the flat.

Then she stopped. So far, she had Anna's sympathy, but if she continued, Anna would think she was deluded or worse. It suddenly occurred to her that Anna might know Donal. He would have been at all the pubs she and her friends frequented, so there was a good chance that Anna knew him, too. She paused uncertainly.

'Do you know Donal? Do you remember him from when you went to school?

'Was he the tall skinny lad who hung out with the boys from the college? I remember he had the coolest sunglasses, which he wore all the time. He towered over everybody but managed to look cool and sophisticated. But I never would have dared to speak to him. He was the lad all the Leaving Cert girls wanted to take to their Debs. If you remember, Eimear, I didn't do much socialising back then so I only knew of him.'

'Yeah, that's Donal.'

'I'm sorry he turned out to be such a jerk.'

'Well, at least I found out what he was really like before we got married.'

'What else? There's something more you're not telling me.'

Eimear hesitated and then took a leap of faith. She told about the emails, about the guards believing that she orchestrated the vandalism and attacks on herself and then, in a broken voice, she spoke about Alec and her mother's cross. Finally, she came to a halt. She didn't dare look up to watch suspicion cloud Anna's face. She was certain she would regret inviting her to stay and share her story. Soon, Anna would tactfully pretend she had to go out or was expecting a friend, anything to rid herself of her crazy guest.

'Is that everything?'

'Yes, I'm sure you think I'm crazy, but it's all true.' Still, she couldn't look at Anna's face.

'Well, it sounds so impossibly crazy that it must be true.'

Eimear looked up. 'What? You believe me?'

'Well, you could have lost all grasp of reality and been doing all these things to yourself subconsciously, but you know what, I have a better solution.'

'What's that?'

'I think someone is trying to drive you out of your mind. The question is, who hates you enough to do that?'

Eimear felt some of the pent-up tension ease from her body. Anna acted as though she assumed she was telling the truth, and relief made her momentarily lost for words. Then, pulling herself together, she said, 'I don't know. Donal was angry with me but couldn't pull off everything that happened to me. He's not that smart, and he has a job in Sligo. It keeps him busy, and it provides him with a good income. He would never jeopardise that.'

'Well, then perhaps he has help. What are the names of the people you work with? Look, you need to write all this down so we can get a clearer picture of what is happening.'

'I did write it all down, or most of it. It's back at the flat.'

'Right, let's go there.'

'What, now?'

'There's no time like the present. And you know what? I'll stay over with you tonight. We can talk it over and try to figure this out.'

Eimear stared at her. 'Why are you doing all this?'

Anna grinned. 'Do you think I'm all part of the sinister plan?'

Eimear looked at her searchingly. 'I don't know who to trust anymore. And I don't see why you want to get involved. If everything I'm saying is true, you're getting mixed up in a dangerous situation, and if I'm lying or delusional, that'd be dangerous, too. So why are you willing to get involved?'

Anna sighed. 'OK, a long time ago I needed a friend. I was an outcast; no one wanted to sit beside me at school; they called me names and whispered behind my back. The teachers didn't know how to help and, in many ways, made things worse. But one day, when everyone refused to sit beside me because I stank, you did. No one forced you to, but I think you saw the misery on my face and sat beside me, and we worked on a project together. Don't get me wrong, we didn't become friends, but you saw I needed help that day and gave it to me.'

'I don't remember doing that. Are you sure it was me?'

'It was you. And I never forgot it. To you, it was no big deal, but it mattered to me. So that's partly why I'm willing to help.'

'And the other reason?'

'I love a good mystery.' Anna winked. 'Come on, let's head.'

Chapter 27

They sat up late into the night. Eimear ordered takeaway food, and they gorged themselves. Anna pored over the account Eimear had written and questioned her minutely about everything. The only interruption was at eight, just after the food had arrived. The sharp rapping unnerved her. Anna walked with her to the door. Her landlord stood outside. He looked stern. She invited him in, but he insisted on standing in the corridor.

'Ms Martin, I've had a complaint from one of your neighbours about you playing loud music late at night. And another tenant accused you of being drunk in the foyer of the building, and I have heard reports of the guards visiting here regularly, and now I see that the door to your flat has been defaced.'

Before Eimear could get a word out, Anna pushed her way forward and, in a bolshy voice, said, 'Now, hold on a second – my friend Eimear here has been the subject of a vicious attack from a former boyfriend. She approached the Garda as was her right. The man wrote something rude on her door. She washed it off and, of course, will get the door repainted. She didn't want to bother you with her problems. And as for the loud noise, that was my fault. She was called out to attend to a sick relative in Sligo, and I happened to be visiting her. I'm her cousin from London.

It was me who had the music blaring. I'm a little deaf, so I didn't realise it was so loud and disturbing others. As for Eimear being a bit jarred, surely she can be upset when she gets bad news. Her relative died.'

Anna said this in a very loud voice. Whenever the landlord spoke, she insisted he needed to speak up. By the end of the conversation, the poor landlord was apologising to her for disturbing them.

When the door closed behind him, they dissolved into laughter.

'You are such a liar, Anna French!'

'Yeah, well, at least it'll get him off your back for a while. And do get that door painted. It looks disturbing. Tomorrow we'll buy paint and do it ourselves. I don't have to work until two, so we should get it well in hand.'

The next morning, Eimear went out and bought black paint. When she arrived back, Anna borrowed an old top, and they set about painting the door. The results weren't bad for a pair of amateurs. Eimear admired their efforts as she waved Anna off on her way to her first client of the day. It felt good to fix something, even if it was only a minor part of the mess in her life. Since Anna came into her life, she felt a sliver of hope. It was nice to have someone to talk to about everything happening to her. Having someone believe she wasn't mad or criminal was still nicer. But even with Anna helping her, she didn't see any way out. She could find a detective to look into things, but she was reluctant to explain herself all over again and perhaps see the look of contempt or pity on their face. It was a miracle that Anna believed her, but that might not last.

Meg was her best hope. Meg could back up her account of Donal's stalking her. But even then, apart from his unpleasant emails and visiting the house after Mam's funeral, it was still a case of her making accusations without much corroboration. But with Meg and Anna on her side, she would feel less lonely. It was great that Meg was coming at the weekend, but she worried she was putting her aunt in danger by involving her in all the chaos surrounding her. Maybe it would be better if she stayed at a safe distance from this. Should she put her off coming back to Ireland? She could still give advice on how to proceed. But she knew Meg. There was no way she'd sit on the sidelines and let her face things without her. So, when Anna called this evening, they would contact Meg. Three heads were better than one, and Meg would be relieved she wasn't alone.

As she crossed the road to the gym, she was suddenly reminded of the evening she saw Anna outside her flat. She had been looking up at the building. Why? And then there was the time she seemed to be about to stop and say something to her but didn't. That suggested she might have known who she was – but when she finally spoke to her in the park she behaved as if she suddenly recognised her. In fact, Anna had made her feel uneasy from the start. Now that thought bothered her all the time she was working out.

Her energy was low, but she persisted with her programme. Then she called to the locksmith's and arranged for someone to call the next day to change her locks. She would have to let her landlord know and give him a spare set of keys, too. On her way back to the flat, she bought a large frozen pizza and a few salad items to feed Anna and herself. It would be nine before Anna finished all her work sessions.

When Anna arrived at the flat, she had the food ready. Anna ate more than her fair share, as she liked her food. Eimear forced herself to eat, as Anna's disapproving gaze pierced her whenever she faltered.

'Why were you at my flat the other day? I saw you when I was crossing the road,' said Eimear abruptly.

Anna raised her eyebrows. 'So I was looking at your apartment building -so what. I often look at apartment buildings. At some stage, I will have to move out of my friend's place, and your building isn't too far from mine. I like the area. There's no big mystery, Eimear.'

'Look, you can't blame me for wondering. I mean, I see you outside my flat, and then all of a sudden, you are involved in my life.'

'Well, I hope my answer satisfies you. Look, Eimear, if you don't trust me, that's fine. I understand.'

'I'm sorry, Anna, it's just that I've been let down by everyone I trusted lately. I can't let my guard down.'

Anna wiped her mouth with her napkin. 'I get it. Look, do ya want me to leave?'

Eimear shook her head. 'No, I'm being paranoid. I don't want you to go. Besides, I wanted to tell you about Meg. I was hoping to contact her this evening. The great news is she's coming home this weekend.'

'I'm keen to meet this aunt of yours.'

'Yeah, Meg is sound. She's always had my back. Look, let's call her now.'

There was no answer when she tried calling Meg, so the girls cleared up the meal and made tea.

After ten minutes, Meg Facetimed back. 'Sorry, Eimear, I was in the shower. Is everything OK? God, has something else happened?'

Meg stared at her, her eyes wide and worried.

'I went to Sligo since I last spoke to you. Alec wanted to see me.'

'Why did he have to drag you down to Sligo?'

'I think he wanted an opportunity to bawl me out in person. He made contact with the guards in Dublin, and they told him I was a liar and a fantasist who was causing trouble at work and was likely given the sack.'

Meg started to interrupt, but Eimear continued rapidly.

'He also went to see Donal, and Donal showed him a note I had sent him telling him all was forgiven. It was a note I wrote ages ago that he held on to.'

'Well, Alec must realise that!'

'Wait, there's more. He showed Alec a gift I sent him. Do you remember Mam's little Saint Brigit's cross? Well, he showed it to Alec.'

'I don't understand. How did he get the cross?'

'I don't know. I brought it back with me to Dublin. I know I did. But somehow Donal got it.'

'Oh my God, this makes no sense!'

'Well, the upshot is that Alec thinks I've been manipulating him to wreck Donal's life. It was horrible, Meg, the way he looked at me with such contempt.' Eimear's voice shook as she recalled the scene in her kitchen.

'Wait until I get to talk to him. I'll make him see sense. Although how he could take the word of that pup Donal over yours, I cannot credit!'

'Well, he had all the evidence he needed, and I didn't help by not telling him about what happened with the guards in Dublin.'

"Right, I'm coming straight home – you can't be alone to deal with all this.'

'Calm down, Meg. I'm not alone.'

'You're not?' Meg stared at her, puzzled.

'I've met up with an old school friend, and she's offered to help. I've brought her here to meet you.'

Meg looked startled as Anna leaned in.

'Anna, Meg, Meg, this is Anna.'

'Hello, Meg. Eimear has told me all about you, and I promise that I'm here to help. I'm on her side. I think someone is deliberately making her life hell, and my money is on Donal.'

Meg seemed to be searching for words, still recovering from this sudden surprise.

Anna grinned.

'Listen, Meg, you've had a lot to take in, and I think you and Eimear need to talk alone. So, I'm going to head off now, and later we can all meet online or in-person to plan a strategy.'

Ignoring Eimear's protests, Anna picked up her belongings and headed out the door.

She had barely shut the door when Meg began talking.

'How well do you know that girl?'

'Not that well. We were in St Philomena's together.'

'I don't ever remember meeting her.'

'Well, we weren't close.'

'And now she suddenly shows up, offering to help you?'

'It wasn't exactly sudden. I saw her running in the park and at the gym. I didn't recognise her. It was only because I got drunk one day and she saw me in the park that she stopped to help me and we realised we knew each other from school.'

Meg threw her hands in the air. 'Hold on a sec! What do you mean you "got drunk"? You were drunk and alone in a park? Are you out of your mind?' She glared at Eimear. 'I can't believe you'd put yourself in such danger.'

Eimear felt herself flush. Oh God, she thought. I shouldn't have let that slip.

'Calm down, Meg, I was fine, and Anna swooped to the rescue.'

'*Swooped to the rescue?* You mean you were so drunk that a passer-by could see you needed help? *What?*'

'You're right. I know. It was a foolish thing to do. I promise you it'll never happen again.'

'God, Eimear, I don't know what to say. How could you be so irresponsible? Someone is threatening you, and you decide to make it easy for them?'

'You're right, I know. I'm sorry, but everything just got to me. It was like I had to release a valve, and the drink helped me. But I get it. I was an idiot. Now, please, can we let it go?'

Meg bowed her head and Eimear could see her taking a few deep breaths.

'Meg – I'm sorry.'

Meg raised her head and looked at Eimear. 'All I can say is thank God I'm coming home. You should have told me you were in such a state of mind.'

'I didn't want to worry you.'

'Worry me? I've lost Claire – have you any idea what losing you too would do to me?'

'I know, Meg. I do. I just felt you didn't need more stress.'

'What are you talking about, girl? That's what I'm here for – having your back.'

'Thank you, Meg. You're the best. But look, some good has come of my stupidity. Anna has pulled me out of my depression and I have another ally now.'

'Well, thank goodness there's someone sensible to watch out for you. I suppose I should have thanked her for minding you, but every time we talk there seems to be some fresh disaster befalling you, so I'm suspicious of everyone.'

'So am I. I was even suspicious of Anna.'

'But I've been thinking about all the things that happened to you – I definitely think it's all down to Donal Carty.'

'I'm not sure it is Donal. How does he manage to feck up my life here in Dublin?'

'Could he know someone in your office, someone jealous of you, or threatened in some way?'

The image of Hannah and Toby appeared in her mind. Hannah hadn't the smarts or the guile to ruin her career, but Toby had. Could it be possible that Donal knew Toby? If that were so, then everything would make sense, or at least some of it would. But why would Toby go to all this trouble to hurt her? OK, he was annoyed that she was impressing the boss and that she had rejected his advances, but still, this was a stretch. It certainly wasn't Toby who attacked her! But, then again, Toby had some shady clients. He didn't represent them in criminal court cases but worked on other business areas for them. Could he have contacts with thugs who would do anything for money? She remembered Philip bringing up concerns about some less respectable clients Toby was dealing with. He was worried about the firm's reputation, but Toby managed to reassure him, at least in part.

Meg could see that she had stirred up something in Eimear.

'What are you thinking?'

'You may have a point about Donal's connection with someone from work. I think I might know how I can find out.'

Meg looked alarmed. 'You're not planning on doing something stupid, are you?'

'Of course not. But I think I can see a way of getting information. I have no intention of taking any risks, Meg, I promise you.'

Meg sighed with relief. 'Glad to hear it. But Eimear, it's great that you have someone on your side, but don't be too trusting. It's early days and, remember, you hardly know the girl.'

'I will be careful, but I can't see why she would want to harm me. Anna barely knew Donal, and she's been working abroad for ages."

'Look, love, I'm not saying that Anna is a bad person, and maybe she does want to help. But be careful – that's all I'm saying. She's in a position to know everything about you, all your plans. Perhaps take a step back. Check her out before you trust her too much.'

'But Anna has already made a difference. She calmed the landlord down and took responsibility for the loud music. She even helped me paint the bloody door!'

Seeing Meg's puzzled look, she filled her in on the most recent developments and related how Anna had talked down the angry landlord.

'Well, fair dues to her. She sounds like my kind of girl. I'd loved to have been there to see her in action. By the way, what are you doing about changing the locks to your flat? Someone got in to turn the music up. What other tricks might they be playing? You told me about someone writing emails. Suppose it wasn't done at the office. You have a laptop. It has your work emails. All anyone has to do is use your laptop when you're out and write anything they like. God, Eimear, love, you need to change your locks. You're not safe!'

Meg sounded panicked, and Eimear rushed to reassure her.

'I've booked a locksmith to change the locks, but at least I'm safe once I bolt myself in. So, no need to panic. You should see the locks I have. It's like I live in New York.'

'Well, bolt it now. Right now. I mean it. I need to know that you're safe.'

'OK, I'm doing it now.'

Eimear went and put on the safety chain and bolted the door to keep Meg happy.

'Good, at least I know you're safe for the moment. Now, I will contact my friend and tell her I have to leave earlier than planned, and Pixie and Trixie will have to find new cat-sitters.'

'I don't believe anyone calls their cats Pixie and Trixie?'

'Well, Jill does, and stop changing the subject. I'm coming home immediately. And I'm not going back to Sligo. You can give me your bed, but I'm staying with you. So don't raise any objections.'

'Meg, I wouldn't dream of it. I'm dying to see you and so glad you're staying with me. But please keep to your schedule. I've things I want to do before you get here.'

'What things? Please tell me you won't tackle Donal or do anything dangerous.'

'I promise, Meg. I just need to sort out some things relating to work. Nothing dangerous, I promise.'

Eimear wasn't sure that Meg believed her, but she didn't want her to rush around changing plans. Once Meg arrived, she would be more constrained.

Smiling cheerfully at her, she added, 'Text me your flight times, and I'll pick you up at the airport.'

They said goodbye, and she felt lighter after she ended the connection. The only shadow was the doubts that still lingered in her mind about Anna.

Chapter 28

The next morning, the man arrived to change her locks. She felt a lot more secure when he handed her the new keys. She also changed all her email passwords. Although she hadn't sent too many emails since leaving work, it was no harm to take precautions.

She puzzled over how someone could have managed to gain access to her flat and turn her music on so loudly that it would disturb the neighbours. She was careful with her keys, but then again, she had kept them in her bag at work, and it wouldn't be too difficult for someone to lift them and get them copied—someone like Toby, perhaps.

Her head felt muzzy, and she desperately needed fresh air – a brisk walk around the park was what was needed. When she passed the bench where she had met Anna, she stopped and sat down.

She felt uncomfortable as she remembered Anna staring up at her building. Her explanation did make sense, but ... Eimear's head hurt with all the contradictory information battering her brain. What possible motive could Anna have for wanting to harm her, or what could have made her ally with Donal? And what could she possibly gain from interfering in her life? No, the whole thing made no sense. She was in danger of being suspicious of everyone. Getting paranoid wouldn't help. Her thoughts continued on a spiralling loop of wild conjecture. Perhaps

Anna believed that she was deliberately damaging Donal's life, telling lies about him, and getting him into trouble; if she did know Donal, she might want to protect him. Eimear's head began to spin. She would either have to keep Anna at arm's length or take a leap of faith and trust that Anna meant only the best for her. Her head ached with the worry of it all. Should she see if she could find out more about Anna? Perhaps ask Lana to make enquiries.

Her thoughts turned to work. She needed to make some decisions about her job. Should she resign, and hope Philip Jolly would be charitable, and not destroy her professional reputation? He was a good man, but she wouldn't put it past Toby to whisper against her. To make sure she didn't get to work in any firms where he had contacts. The thought of being driven out of Dublin infuriated her. If Toby wasn't behind all the things that had gone wrong for her, he had certainly benefited from them. He had lied to Philip and the girls about her. He had cast her as not only a nasty person, undermining her colleagues, but as a love-sick obsessive too. Meg suggested that perhaps Donal knew someone at her workplace; it could be Toby. There must be some way she could find out if there was a connection between them. It was a pity that Kate still refused to respond to her calls. She had liked her, and she would have been a great ally. But Toby and Hannah, combined with the visit from the gardaí, would have turned Kate against her.

Being out of work made the days hard to fill, and the tendency to brood was hard to resist. Anna was supposed to call around this evening. On impulse, she texted her, leaving a message that she had to go out but would be in touch tomorrow. This would give her some breathing room and time to determine how much she could trust Anna. She even considered following her and seeing if she met with Donal or Toby. God, she really was in danger of losing her mind, afraid to trust anyone.

Back in the apartment, once again, the walls seemed to press in, and she desperately needed to get out of their enclosure. In fanciful moments, it seemed to her that the walls were alive, and at times, she even thought she could hear them breathe. God, she needed to get away. She put on a heavy jacket and some gloves, and just as she was about to leave, she had a sudden idea. She ran into her bedroom and, after digging around in a few boxes, found what she was looking for. Grabbing her car keys and some money, she left the flat. The Mini looked OK. There was no sign of sinister messages, and her tyres looked undamaged.

She started the car. It was time to stop passively waiting for someone to rescue her, whether Meg, Anna, or the gardaí. She would figure a few things out herself. First, she would visit Kate. She had never been to her home, but she knew the address because it was easy to remember: Duck House, Dolphins Barn, Flat 1. She overheard Kate giving it to a taxi driver after a boozy session in Lennon's.

She pulled up close to the flat, down a little side street. She was probably parking in someone's space, but to hell with that. At the building, she pressed the doorbell. When Kate's musical voice answered, she crossed her fingers and spoke.

'Hi Kate, it's me, Eimear. Can I come up?'

There was a long silence, and Eimear was about to speak again when the buzzer went. In a minute, she was standing outside Kate's flat. She stared at the cream door uncertainly, wondering what she would say. She didn't get a chance to knock.

Kate opened the door, her face cold.

'What do you want, Eimear?'

'You haven't answered my texts or calls. I needed to talk to you.'

'Look, Eimear, I don't see the point of you coming here. Your name is mud at the office, and when I tried to stick up for you, they all started turning on me. God, but you're one unpopular girl!'

'But do you believe them? Do you think I would do all those things, basically self-sabotage myself? I was doing well until those emails and the mess with Brennan. Why would I do that to myself? Look, can I come in?'

Kate nodded and stepped aside. She pointed to the couch and lifted a pile of clothes, and Eimear sat down. The apartment was a mess. This wasn't how she expected Kate to live. She was so tidy and organised at work.

Seeing her glance around, Kate shrugged.

'Joe has moved out. We had a row, and I've let things slide.'

'I'm sorry, you and Joe seemed good together.'

'Yeah, well, appearances can be deceptive. Look, I don't see what I can do for you. I'm not convinced you're the demon incarnate, but as for self-sabotage, Toby said all your work was a mess, and your clients were furious with you.'

'That's not true, Kate, you know me. You know how hard I worked for my clients. I was never sloppy.'

'Well, I'm inclined to agree. I think Toby wanted some of your plum clients, and he probably lied to Philip to be seen as the man who saved the day.'

'So you believe me?'

'Aww, now let's not run away with ourselves. I don't necessarily believe you, but I wouldn't put it past Toby to stir things up to make you look even worse.'

'OK, don't believe me, but I just want to know if you've ever seen Toby with a man named Donal Carty. He has sandy hair, is clean-shaven, and is over six feet tall.'

'Come on, Eimear, that describes half the guys in Dublin.'

'Well, have a look at this photo.' Eimear had found a picture of Donal in an old scrapbook from the first holiday she took with him. She had thought she had burned all her pictures of him, but this one had escaped. It wasn't very clear, but maybe it would jog Kate's memory.

'Is this your old boyfriend?'

'Yes, I think he's behind some of the stuff happening to me.'

Kate stared at the picture and then, shrugging, handed it back.

'I don't know, I can't be certain.'

'Will you at least show it to the girls at work? Say someone dropped it in the office. It might jog a memory.'

'Why should I do this for you, Eimear? How do I know you're not a nut job out to cause trouble?'

'You don't but, if I'm not a nut job but an innocent victim, how are you going to feel if you don't help me?'

There was a long silence, and then Kate got to her feet.

'You have to go now, Eimear. I won't make promises, but I'll hold on to the picture and see what I can do.'

'Thanks, Kate, that's all I ask. And I'm truly sorry about Joe.'

'You shouldn't be. If I weren't so pissed at Joe and men in general, I wouldn't give you the time of day. But right now, I'm subscribing to a theory.'

'What's that?'

'That all men are bastards, and I wouldn't put anything past them.'

With those words, she shut the door on Eimear.

Chapter 29

The drive home gave her time to reflect. Was there a chink of light? Kate wasn't an ally, but she wasn't an enemy either. There was a possibility she could discover something. If she could find something linking Toby and Donal, she could at least approach the gardaí in Dublin and show them that there was possibly a conspiracy against her. But again, why? Why would Toby pay someone to attack her and vandalise her car and home? It was a considerable risk to take. And for what? A few clients. There had to be more to it. What possible reason would Donal and Toby have to join forces? OK, Donal had his warped reasons for wrecking her life. She had dumped him and reported him for harassment. But for Toby, she wasn't any real threat. None of it made sense.

She racked her brains to try and discover who might hate her enough to go to all this trouble. Whoever it was, they were very clever. The rest of the evening passed slowly. She was too tired for the gym and couldn't face her self-defence class. The idea of practising falls and moves to thwart attackers made her feel exhausted. No, she needed an evening off, an evening of distraction. Reading had always been her escape, but she couldn't shut her thoughts off tonight. She thought about going to the cinema but realised it would be futile. She wouldn't be able to switch off her thoughts.

She decided to embark on a major cleaning of her flat. She emptied the cupboards and cleaned her oven and fridge. She washed and ironed every item of her clothing apart from what she was wearing, and still, she couldn't close off the sharp, intrusive chatter in her head. On a nightmarish loop, she rehashed everything. Over and over, she thought about the disaster her life had become. Then, she had a moment of clarity. It was all Mam's fault. Everything that had happened to her happened because Mam had died. If her mam were alive, she wouldn't have left Sligo. But Mam had to drive like a lunatic and get herself killed. And now she was on her own. Waves of self-pity and rage consumed her, and the sight of her tidy, spotless flat irritated her beyond reason.

She started pulling cupboards out, emptying them on the floor, kicking chairs over and even tearing the sheets from her freshly made bed. While she ripped and tore, her brain felt mercifully quiet. She was all rage and fury, and then she stopped, and the crying began.

Hours later, she restored some order to the flat, and after checking that she was securely locked in, she made herself a warm drink. She threw the duvet back on her bed and got underneath it. The emotional storm had left her exhausted, but her mind still whirred. Her outburst of rage embarrassed her, but perhaps it was necessary to let some of the pressure out.

As she lay on the bed, she began to look on the positives in her situation. She had made some progress, and Anna and Meg were on board. Both believed her and were willing to help. Anna had a hard time at school but seemed grateful for her kindness. Eimear couldn't even remember the incident she spoke about. But Anna insisted it happened.

But then again, it didn't have the same importance for Eimear that it did for Anna, who faced the cruelty of teenagers daily.

Giving up trying to work things out, she turned on her side. Mam always told her to think about pleasant things when she couldn't sleep, but there seemed to be a dearth. Eventually, she drifted into a restless sleep. But her dreams were disturbing. A menacing stranger chased her through foggy streets that echoed with pounding feet.

The next morning, to make up for her laziness yesterday, she went to the gym before breakfast and worked longer and harder than usual. It gave her a real break from her head. One of the guys, a regular in the gym on the weekends, smiled at her when she passed and tried to engage her in conversation. He was cute, and his body was lean rather than muscular. She'd have flirted with him at any other time in her life. But now she had no room for anything but solving this toxic mystery engulfing her. She didn't need another player clogging the field and distracting her mind. But she couldn't seem to shake him off. Several times, they headed to the same machine, and she knew it wasn't an accident. He tried to engage her in conversation, but she was curt and avoided eye contact. He seemed to take her coolness for encouragement, and she tensed. She thought about cutting short her session but felt furious that he should make her feel so intimidated.

She moved to a different part of the gym and started lifting weights. She was bent over, reaching for a heavier kettlebell, when she felt a hand on her shoulder. She reacted instinctively, and he landed flat on his back on the floor.

'You crazy bitch, why did you do that?' he gasped as he struggled to his feet.

'You shouldn't have kept bothering me.'

'God, you're a psycho!'

He pushed past her, his face red with anger and humiliation. One of the trainers came over and asked if she was alright. She mumbled something and then fled.

When she got home, she showered and dressed but could not face food. Was this going to be the end of her going to the gym? OK, he was a pest, but she could really have hurt him. She was so wound up that she might lash out anywhere, anytime. For the first time, she was scared she might be a danger to others. The thought troubled her.

Her phone beeped; glancing at it, she noticed a message from Kate and a missed call. The message gave little away but filled her with hope. It said: **Got some news. Meet me for a drink at six in Hughes' bar.**

What did it mean? What could Kate have discovered? Should she call Anna and ask her to come along? She hesitated. Maybe she should meet Kate and hear what she had to say, and then she could fill Meg and Anna in later.

At six, she arrived at the bar. It was packed, but eventually she located Kate sipping a glass of beer as she perched on a bar stool. Kate waved and pointed to a second bar stool that she had been guarding.

Eimear gave her drink order and asked her if she wanted another. Kate shook her head.

'No, I haven't time. I'm meeting dickhead tonight to sort out the household bills.'

'OK, you said you had some information for me. I appreciate any help, Kate.'

'Right, first a bit of office gossip. Hannah, the big dope, is still salivating over Toby. She thinks he was a big hero to stick up for her against big bad you. She still thinks you're the devil incarnate, but Iris feels guilty. Since you left, Toby has been lording it over everyone and has taken to bossing Iris around. As you know, Iris will do anything if you ask her nicely, but if you start bossing her, then suddenly she's on a go slow. So I think she's on the verge of giving you the benefit of the doubt.'

'You mentioned you might have some information for me.'

'I haven't much that's solid, but Toby and this guy Donal have a connection. He was an old college buddy. Did Donal go to UCD?'

'Yes, he did. He graduated in 2001.'

'Well, that sounds right. Toby lived with some lads from down the country – one of them was called Donal. I don't know about the surname.'

'How did you find out?'

'Good question; it was by accident. The two lads, Toby and John, were comparing notes about the social life in the colleges they attended. John went to UCC, and Toby said he went to UCD. I asked him if he stayed at home, seeing as he's a Dub. He said his parents had bought a house near the college, and he moved in and found a group of lads to rent the place. He was there to keep an eye on things in case it was trashed and turned into a party pad. Anyway, he mentioned that he shared with three lads from Sligo. I asked how he coped living with a load of culchies. Well, he made one of his weak cracks about civilising the country yokels by his refining presence.'

'God, that's interesting. But did you get any more information from him?'

'Hold on, I'm getting to it. I asked him if he kept in touch with any of the lads. He said the Donal lad, and he kept in touch. Then he laughed and said Donal had had a bit of girl trouble, but he was getting it sorted. I didn't like how he said it. It was a bit creepy. But anyway, it does fit in with some of what you were saying.'

Eimear sat up, electrified. 'This is wild. Toby shared a house with Donal and is still in touch with him. Oh my God, this could explain so much. Thank you so much, Kate.'

'Now hold your horses, and don't get too carried away. This doesn't prove anything.'

'I know it doesn't prove anything, but at least I have a lead as to why all these things may be happening to me. There's so much I'd love to tell you but it will have to wait. But this helps. I wish I could make Philip and everyone else believe I haven't done anything wrong.'

'All I know is that the boss has been looking at Toby oddly lately. I think he's finding that the golden boy isn't all he's cracked up to be, and I know that a few of your clients were disappointed not to have you working for them anymore and weren't very happy with Toby.'

'That's good to know.'

'Maybe you should call Philip. I think he'd be more receptive to believing you now.'

'I'm going to wait until I can fully clear my name. But I appreciate the encouragement. Tell Iris I was asking for her.'

'No way. Look, I don't mind helping you out, but I'm keeping my head down. I don't want anyone in the office to know that I've met with you. I've enough on my plate as it is.'

'Yes, I understand.'

Kate drained the last of her beer and leaned over to hug Eimear quickly. 'Good luck,' she whispered.

Anna was waiting at her door when she arrived back.

Chapter 30

Eimear made tea and filled Anna in on what Kate had told her. The comfort of having a friend who believed in her made such a difference.

'Well, at least your theory about Toby and Donal is confirmed. They do know each other. Your man, Toby, believed whatever story Donal fed him about your break-up. He must have painted himself as the victim and you as the cruel femme fatale. It probably suited Toby to do you down as a favour for his pal and a benefit to himself.'

'That makes sense, but I can't see Toby arranging to have me attacked. He's a shit but hardly a psychopath.'

'Then maybe Donal arranged the attacks on you.'

'Maybe ... but I can't see how he could have known any goons for hire unless he asked Toby, and even Toby would hesitate to get involved with criminals; it would be career suicide. He doesn't mind doing a few dodgy business deals for them, but no way he would jeopardise his position in the firm.'

'Would Donal have the money to hire someone? I mean, is he likely to have the cash?'

'He makes good money as an accountant and comes from a well-off family, so in theory, money wouldn't be a problem.'

I wonder what the going rate for vandalism and breaking into someone's home and attacking them is? 'Think back to that night. Did you notice the man's accent? Was he from Dublin?'

'He didn't say anything.'

'Is there any chance it could be Donal? I mean, you didn't see a face, did you?'

Eimear tried to imagine the night again. It was horrible, but she forced herself to go over everything in slow motion: the door opening and the package on the ground. Then, being rushed and thrown on the bed. She remembered with sickening clarity the man's body lying on top of her and his warm breath on her face. Was it Donal's body? The man's build was similar to Donal's, and the height was comparable. It was possible, but no, the eyes were wrong. She'd have recognised Donal's eyes anywhere. It wasn't him.

'No, it wasn't Donal. It could have been someone he sent, but I'm certain the man who attacked me that night wasn't Donal.'

'OK, let's leave that for the moment. Your door was vandalised, and the lad was arrested and claimed you paid him for doing the damage. Was he convincing? Do you think he believed you paid him, or was he lying?'

'Of course, he was bloody lying.' Eimear glared at Anna. 'I thought you believed me.'

'Calm down. I believe you, but I wonder if the boy was tricked into believing you paid him or if he was paid to lie.'

'What difference does that make?'

'A huge difference; if the boy was convinced that you were the one paying him, then …'

'There's a woman involved, someone made up to look like me. I did wonder, if he just gave a description of my coat or if someone actually dressed up like me to pay him to paint the message on my door. I've gone back and forth about it. But I suppose it makes more sense if someone did disguise themselves as me to arrange it with him.'

'Exactly, think about it: you had just got a distinctive haircut, the woman was wearing a coat like yours, and all she'd need was a short funky wig. Those things would fool the boy. So, he'd identify you and get himself off the hook.'

'So now I just have to figure out who this woman could be.'

'Afraid so.'

They stared at each other.

'Oh god, this keeps getting worse, bad and all as it is to think Donal hates me enough to harm me - now I have to add in a female accomplice. Am I such a hateful person that so many people want to harm me?'

'Look, this woman could be a friend of Donal's. What about the lassie he had the fling with? Could she be involved too?'

'I don't know too much about her. Donal claimed she had a thing for him and was pestering him. The poor pet only fell for her wiles because I was being difficult and neglectful.' Eimear's voice was laced with sarcasm.

'Are they still an item?'

'I honestly don't know or care. When I caught them together, I dumped him, and to be honest I think she did me a favour as I had doubts about Donal. I didn't like how he monopolised me and bossed me around. Seeing them together just made it easier to end things.'

'So, you could claim the moral high ground and still be the one who did the dumping.'

'That's a bit harsh.'

'Well, I believe in calling a spade a bloody spade. You have to admit it was convenient to discover his affair. It saved you from a disastrous marriage.'

Eimear thought over what Anna said. It had a strong element of truth.

'OK, that's probably true. I was upset and betrayed by Donal, but you're right. Deep down, I was glad to have a decent excuse to end things. He and his family were well respected in our town, and I knew I'd be demonised if I broke up with him. We had booked a wedding venue and told all our friends. It was humiliating for all of us, but after what he did, nobody could blame me for breaking our engagement. This way, even his parents had to accept my decision. Even Donal's mother had to accept her darling son was a sinner.'

'So, this mystery woman. Could she be behind this? Working with Donal's knowledge to cause you harm?'

'But why? She's got what she wanted if Donal was what she wanted.'

'But has she? He stalked and harassed you for months and was clearly obsessed with you. Then you turned on him and started to make life hot for him. Perhaps she was jealous because, even with you out of the way, he's still dancing to your tune.'

'No, this is too far-fetched.'

'Maybe, but say, after Donal got angry with you for threatening to tell his boss about his behaviour, and you threatened a barring order, she saw a way of helping him get back at you. She joined him in his obsession with you, but this time to destroy you. Think about it. It's a win for her. She gets to be his collaborator and consolation and has the advantage of seeing you ruined, and Donal is finally free of you.'

'But that's mad!'

'What do you call what's happening to you? Either you are a fantasist, a paranoid crazy bitch, or someone is out to get you.'

'Which do you think I am?'

'I wouldn't be here if I thought you were the former. I've experienced being bullied and gaslighted by people, and I recognise the signs in you. So, I think you're perfectly sane. A bit annoying, but as sane as most of us anyway.'

Eimear's eyes filled up. 'That's the nicest thing anyone has said to me in ages, insults and all.'

She opened a bottle of wine. Her phone beeped; it was a text from Meg saying that she wanted to FaceTime. But Eimear didn't feel up to talking with her. She'd contact her aunt later.

'Right, so what do we do next?' Anna asked.

It felt so good that she said *we*, not *you*, that Eimear's heart warmed.

'What do you suggest?'

'I think you need to find out who this mystery woman is. The locals must know. You need to head back home to Sligo and make enquiries.'

Eimear hesitated. 'I'm not too popular back home. Donal will have spread the word that I have been wrongly accusing him. And he did say he'd be seeing me. I think he was warning me that he could call to the house anytime he likes. I'm scared. At least here in the flat, I feel relatively safe.'

'How about I come down with you?'

'Look, that's good of you. But you have a job, and pretty soon I won't have one. So, no to coming down with me. But you're right, I do need to go. However, I don't know who would want to help me. Especially if Donal has told everyone that I had been attacking his character, trying to get him in trouble with the guards and attempting to get him fired. I'll be persona non grata. But you're right I have to at least try.'

'Hold up, I could come down with you at the weekend, and together we might make progress, and you'll have back-up.'

Eimear grinned at her. 'Thanks, Cagney.'

'I'm Lacey, actually. She was my favourite—a strong woman, a detective of sound values and common sense. Cagney was more of a loose cannon.'

'But I'm only going down for a couple of days. Besides, Meg is hoping to get a flight home soon, so perhaps I'll delay things until she gets back.'

Then, almost as though she knew Eimear was talking about her, she got a text message from Meg. 'Well, speak of the devil - Meg can't get the bloody cats she's minding sorted out until Saturday, so she won't be back until Saturday evening. I'll tell her to fly into Knock airport, and I'll pick her up from there.'

'So when are you going to Sligo then? Are you waiting until your aunt gets in?'

'Mmm, tell you what, Anna, I'll go down tomorrow, and you can come at the weekend. I'll keep a low profile and see where I stand with the locals. If Donal's mother and sister have whipped up a mob of angry villagers, you and Meg can sweep in and save me!'

Anna furrowed her brow. 'Are you sure it's safe, Eimear? I mean, you are more defenceless in Sligo.'

'Not so defenceless. My dad kept a shotgun, I don't think it works, but hopefully any intruders won't know that.'

Anna wasn't too happy with Eimear's decision to leave for Sligo and tried to persuade her to wait until she could join her at the weekend. Eventually, she gave up and headed back to her little basement flat.

Chapter 31

Meg was horrified when she told her about her plan to go home.

'Are you mad, Eimear? There is some lunatic out there wishing to harm you, and here you are making it easy for them.'

'I know it seems mad, but we have a theory that Donal may be working with this woman he had an affair with. Together, they are succeeding in turning everyone against me. We think it's about time that I found out who she is. Then, at least, I can work out a way to stop them.'

'I suppose Anna put you up to this?'

'I know you are suspicious of her, Meg, but I'm certain she's on my side. What possible reason could she have to want to harm me?'

'You said yourself that she was bullied at your school. Maybe she thinks of you as one of her tormentors and is just pretending to like you.'

'Please, give it a rest, Meg. Anna doesn't even want me to go to Sligo. She suggested waiting until the weekend when you and she can be there.'

Meg sighed. 'Well, that's something, I suppose. And are you going to take her advice, even though you won't take mine?'

'I'm going down tomorrow. I'll only be there two nights before you get in. So please try not to worry.'

'I don't understand why you can't just wait a couple of days until I can be with you?'

'I know it would be more sensible, but I need to feel like I'm doing something. At least I can make a few inquiries about this girl Donal was seeing behind my back. I can find out if they're still seeing each other. It's so frustrating just waiting for things to happen.'

'What did she look like? By the time myself and Claire arrived she had gone back to sit in the car and we were too busy looking after you to take any notice of her.'

'Yeah, I got a good look. She even had the gall to introduce herself. Once she said her name, I remembered it from a card Donal had sent me by mistake. She wasn't very tall, and she had long brown curly hair. She was very made-up, like she was going for a night on the town. I remember thinking afterwards that she didn't seem like Donal's type. He always hated girls who wore a lot of make-up. After that, I was too busy shouting at Donal to pay her any more attention.'

'Didn't you ask Donal who she was? Surely that was the natural thing to do.'

'Well, I didn't know there were rules for when your fiancé cheated on you. I didn't care who she was. I was just raging that he cheated and made a fool out of me.'

Meg looked chastened. 'Aww, pet, I'm sorry. I feel so helpless and afraid for you. I've let you and Claire down. She must be turning in her grave at how I've left you to cope with all this alone.'

'Meg, I didn't want to spoil your adventure, so I didn't tell you about it. At first, I thought I had the gardaí on my side to help, but then things just escalated. I think I was paralysed with anxiety about the whole situation. Besides I didn't think there was anything that you could do except be freaked out.'

'Well, I'm able to help now.'

'Did you get Pixie and Trixie sorted?'

'Eventually, but only after contacting practically every cattery in London, but finally I got them sorted. To tell you the truth I was seriously thinking of just abandoning them and letting Jill come back from her trip early. But anyway, I'm dropping them off on Saturday morning and I've managed to get a flight to Knock that evening. It's getting in at seven-thirty. Will you be able to meet me?'

'I'll be there on the dot. I'm looking forward to seeing you.'

'OK, that's great, but please, Eimear, I wish you'd stay put until we can go home together. People will probably talk to me easier than to you. So why not wait? It's only a few days.'

'I tell you what, Meg, I'll think about it.'

'That's just code for – I'll say anything to get you off my case.'

Eimear laughed, 'You know me so well.'

They ended the call with Meg warning her to put the alarm on when she was in the house and not be alone with Donal for any reason.

⁂

Eimear threw a few things in a bag the next morning and headed for home. It was just after the morning rush hour, and the traffic was light. She played the loudest, most upbeat music on the drive, anything to distract her from what lay ahead. She still didn't know how to get the information she needed, but there was bound to be someone she could persuade or trick into revealing who the woman was. When she tired of the music and intrusive thoughts returned, she listened to an audiobook, desperate to keep her mind off the shit storm that was her life. It worked, and for a couple of hours, she was lost in the world of *Rebecca* by Daphne Du Maurier.

As she drove up the long driveway to her old home, she was struck anew by its bleakness. The place looked abandoned. All the usual signs of occupation were absent. Her mother would have been busy pruning the garden for the coming of spring, but instead, everything was overgrown and neglected. The windows Mam kept shiny with the aid of the local window cleaner were grimy. Weeds were forcing their way through the gravelled walkway. If a house could look dispirited or despairing, that was how it appeared. Mam would be sad to see this air of neglect, especially in the garden, which was her pride and pleasure.

Eimear made a mental promise to do something about the neglect. The place needed to be maintained. It deserved it. After she turned off the alarm and made herself a coffee, she called Alf, the window cleaner and arranged for him to call the following day. The gardener, a grumpy old man named Matt, was less cooperative. He insisted that he was very busy with all his regular clients. She knew he was making a dig at her for not booking him earlier.

'Sorry, Matt, I know how keen everyone is to get you working on the gardens, but since Mam died, I've been away, and when I came home today, I was shocked at the state of the garden. Mam would be heartbroken. You know how she loved her garden.'

'Aye, your mam was a good gardener for an amateur. We didn't always see eye to eye on plants, but she was a lovely lady. Look, I'll see what I can do. How about I call around in the morning to have a look? Then I'll see if I can fit you in. For your mam's sake.'

'Matt, that would be great. I'll be around all morning, but sure, even if I'm not, you can look and see what needs doing.'

That afternoon, Eimear did some household chores, hoovering the floors and washing the windows inside the house. Alf used to do the windows inside and out for Mam, but Eimear didn't fancy anyone wandering through the house. Then, a thought struck her. All the cleaning she was doing reminded her. Marie O'Brien used to clean for her mother. Once a fortnight, she gave the place a thorough going over, lifting furniture, washing skirting boards and cleaning out the kitchen cupboards. Eimear's mam had given her a key and the alarm code. After Claire died, Marie didn't return them. The idea of the keys to her house being out there was disturbing. Marie was a decent woman but careless. What if Donal got hold of her keys? The idea made her heart hammer uncomfortably. She needed to get them back or at least know they were safe. She found her number in the address book her mother kept by the telephone. There was no answer. She tried to dampen her anxiety. An hour later, she tried the number again. On the third ring, it was answered.

'Hi Marie, this is Eimear Martin here.'

'Aww, Eimear, how nice to hear from you. I was that sorry to hear about your poor mam. Jim and I were at the funeral to pay our respects.'

'I know, Marie; thank you so much. Mam appreciated all your hard work over the years for her.'

'That's nice to know. Are you looking for me to do a cleaning for you?'

'I'd love that, Marie. Perhaps we could arrange something soon, but I'm calling because I've lost my front door key. It's probably somewhere in the garden, but it means I can't properly lock up. I know that Mam gave you the keys so that you could easily come and go. And I was hoping you'd still have them.'

'No, love. Don't you remember you sent me a wee note and asked me to drop the keys in the post-box at the door?'

'I'm sorry, I don't remember doing that. Are you sure?'

'Positive, sure, it was just a few days after the funeral. I figured that with your mother gone, you were planning to sell up. Didn't you get the keys, then?'

'Marie, do you still have that note from me?'

'I'm sorry, Eimear – do you not believe me?' Marie's usually friendly voice suddenly sounded terse.

'Of course I do. It's just that lately I've realised I made many decisions in haste. It was a confusing time for me if you recall. With the wedding cancellation and then my mother dying, I was a bit all over the place. I just wanted to see what I wrote. God knows what else I did.'

Eimear realised her explanation for wanting to see the note was weak, but she hoped that if Marie still had it, she might recognise the handwriting. But instead, she had offended Marie, and it was ridiculous to think she'd have hung on to the note.

'Aww, love, you've had it hard. You were too good for that pup.'

'Marie, please don't answer if you'd rather not, but do you know if the woman my ex was with is still around? I'd hate to run into her.'

'No idea, darlin'. No one seemed to know who she was. She was a bit of a mystery woman, but your man, Donal, doesn't seem to be hanging around with anyone in particular. As for the note, it's long gone. You thanked me for all my help over the years and asked me to drop off the keys. I didn't do wrong, did I?'

'Not at all. Thanks again, Marie.'

'But are you locked out, pet?'

'No, I have a back door key, thank goodness.'

She ended the call. That could explain how the cross and chain might have disappeared from her mother's jewellery box ... but she was certain she had taken it back to Dublin in her handbag.

Impulsively, she ran outside to check the post box at the end of the drive. Usually, the postman drove up to the house, but when Mam was away, she didn't like the idea of the letters piling up by the door. It was she believed an invitation to thieves that the house was unoccupied. The box wasn't locked. Mam was hopeless about keeping it locked, forever losing her key for it. The postman only used it when she told him she was going to be away. It contained junk mail and nothing else. Someone had dropped a note to Marie telling her to drop off the keys. Marie didn't know her handwriting, so she would have just done what was asked of her in the note. Could it be Donal or this mystery woman he had an affair with? The idea that Donal could wander into her house terrified her. It was too late to do anything about changing her locks today. The shops would be shut. But tonight, she would barricade the door and look out her father's shotgun.

There was a heavy dresser in the hallway, and with a struggle she slid it into place across the front door. She scratched the wooden hall floor, but that couldn't be helped. The dresser would stay there, and she would enter and leave the house through the back door. She stared at the alarm. Marie had the code. She cleaned for several people in the area. Some of them had alarms. Where did she keep those alarm codes? Could they be easily accessed? But then again, Donal had seen her enter the code dozens of times. He probably even used the code himself. Feeling nervous, she turned on the alarm and went to bed in her mother's bedroom.

Chapter 32

The following morning, the window cleaner arrived and cleaned all the windows. He was there for nearly two hours. She replenished his bucket with hot, soapy water a couple of times. After he had finished with the windows, she made him a cup of tea and listened as he shared nice memories of her parents. When he left, she could see the difference he had made. The sad air of neglect was lifted, and the place was brighter. She knew she was being fanciful, but the house seemed happier somehow. Matt arrived at lunchtime, and she invited him into the kitchen, made him coffee and supplied him with biscuits. She had to listen to many silly yarns before he would even look at the garden. Matt certainly liked to talk. After he had his fill and gave a little speech about what a fine woman her mother was, he walked the garden with her. As he looked around, he tutted about the neglect.

'Your mother wouldn't have let things get this bad; she'd have had me over to set things right months ago.'

'Yes, I'm sorry, but I've been busy.'

'Well, there's a bit to do. I'm busy for the next week, but I should be able to fit you in the next Wednesday if that suits you. The job should take about a week and I'll need to order a skip.'

'That'll be great, Matt. I'll probably not be here, but you can work away, and I'll fix up with you when I'm next down. Will that be alright?'

They shook hands, and she felt lonely as she watched Matt leave. But at least she had done her duty by Mam by making sure her garden was going to get the care it needed. Determined not to allow herself to be gloomy, she decided to take a trip into town. She needed to buy supplies anyway, and there wasn't much to eat. Yesterday, she had dined on fish fingers and beans. Besides, she needed to arrange to have the locks changed.

On impulse, she rang Lana. She was surprised to hear from Eimear but sounded pleased, too. They arranged to meet the following day for coffee at eleven in the central hotel.

The next morning, Eimear drove into Sligo town and parked in the Connaughton Road car park. She strolled into the hotel and chose a window seat overlooking the Garavogue River. The whoosh of the river as it rushed by acted as a soothing balm to her nerves.

Lana arrived right on time. Her slight figure was wrapped in a heavy winter coat. She took it off, freed her fair hair from her beanie and grinned at Eimear.

'I was so pleased you called me, Eimear. I'm owed a bit of time off, so I was able to arrange an extra-long morning break. Unfortunately, I have to be back at twelve.'

Lana worked for a travel agency. She was its backbone, and Eimear reckoned her employers were terrified she'd leave them. So they'd be willing to bend over backwards to keep her.

'It's lovely to see you, Lana. You look great.'

It was true. Lana glowed with wholesome prettiness.

'Thanks, Eimear. You always look good, but I have to say you look a little thin and tired. Are you OK? I know you've been through a lot. It must be hard losing your mam so suddenly.'

'Yes, it was, but at least she didn't suffer.'

'How's Meg? I helped her plan her big trip. At first, she planned to book a complete package, but in the end she decided to take it at her own pace. It turned out that she had people to stay with, in the different cities. How's it going for her?'

'She's having the time of her life. I was glad to see her getting away. Mam's death and the accident hit her very hard. It was nice for her to get away from all the memories and still have friends to call on. I think it was the best of both worlds for her.'

'I'm delighted for her. She was so good to us when we were teens, picking us up from the pub when we were the worse for wear and hiding our condition from your mam when I stayed over. She was a legend!'

Eimear ordered coffee for them both. When it arrived, Eimear decided not to waste any more time on small talk.

'Lana, you know how Donal and I broke up?' she said abruptly.

Lana looked startled. 'Yes, Eimear, we were all gutted for you. But the guy didn't deserve you.'

'Yeah, well, I know that I had a lucky escape. But I wonder if you happened to know the girl he was seeing behind my back?'

Lana looked uncomfortable, and Eimear reassured her. 'No, I'm not seeking revenge. It's just that I've recently encountered a girl who looks like the girl I saw with Donal. She has curly brown hair, and I think her name is Susan. Does that ring any bells with you?'

Lana still looked uncertain.

'Hey, Lana, I don't hold anything against this girl. In fact, I owe her my thanks. Donal and I would never have worked.'

'Eimear, I don't know how to tell you this, but there's a rumour going around in our group that you have been trying to make life tough for Donal, trying to make him lose his job and get him in trouble with the guards. I don't want to open any old wounds.'

Eimear flushed. 'Lana, I'm not vindictive. I don't care about Donal. I want nothing to do with him. But I have a special reason for asking about this girl. I promise you that I don't mean either Donal or her harm. Don't you believe me?'

Lana looked into Eimear's face. 'The Eimear I know is a decent human being, and I'd be willing to bet that anything Donal has to say is not to be believed. But I really don't know very much. This is all I know: her name is Susan Crossley. She was a client in the firm Donal works for. I suppose that's how they met. I don't know if she knew about you, probably not.'

'Are they still seeing each other?'

'I'm not certain, but one of the girls from work, Katherine, said she saw them together in a restaurant recently. They weren't exactly cuddling up, but they did seem to be having fairly intense conversations.'

'Thanks, Lana. I appreciate you telling me, and I promise you I have no desire to hurt either of them. All I want is to be left alone.'

Lana nodded and then blurted, 'Have you seen Jen recently?'

'Jen doesn't talk to me anymore. She blames me for the break-up with Donal and couldn't understand why I wouldn't give him another chance.'

Lana leaned forward in her seat and took a breath.

'Jen is spitting bricks about you and badmouthing you to anyone who'll listen. She said that you were on a mission to ruin her brother. She said the most awful things. I had to avoid her because she has become so toxic.'

'That's a pity. I was very fond of Jen.'

'We all were, but lately, she's become really hard. It's difficult to talk to her. If I were you, I'd keep well away from her.'

'One more thing, Lana. Do you remember a girl called Anna French from school?'

Lana closed her eyes and wrinkled her forehead as she cast her mind back a dozen years. Finally, she opened her eyes. 'Yes, I remember her. She had a bad time at school. I'm afraid she was bullied horribly – she was given a mean nickname.'

'Stenchy Frenchie.'

'Yes, some of the girls were really nasty. But I'm ashamed to say none of us were particularly nice to her. I think there were lots of problems at home. She left school the year before her Leaving Cert. Why do you ask?'

'I've met up with her recently. Lana, can you remember if I was mean to her?'

'Eimear, you were too busy studying and daydreaming about Mr Lynch to bother anyone. Don't you remember we all fancied him but you used to write his name in your copybook over and over and combine it with yours.'

'God, I had forgotten all about him! What happened to him? Is he still in St Phil's?'

'No, he's a principal at some school in the midlands now. Where did you come across Anna French?'

'I met her in the park one day. She seems happy now.'

'I'm so glad. Wait, I've only just remembered ... Anna had a breakdown. And I think that was what was blamed for her attack on Ginny Adams. That's why she left before her Leaving Cert. Ginny was giving her a hard time, and Anna attacked her and beat her up pretty badly.'

'How did I not know about that?'

'Well, I think the nuns hushed it up. The Adamses weren't happy to have Ginny's behaviour made common knowledge, so Anna left the school and the incident wasn't publicised.'

Eimear sat for a moment thinking about Anna. It explained a lot about her. Eimear remembered Ginny. She was in the group she hung about with in school. They weren't close but they did go to the same parties and hung out with the same crowd. She tried to remember if she witnessed any of Ginny's bullying behaviour towards Anna. But at that time she was totally caught up with herself, and her crush on Mr Lynch to notice much else. When Ginny left, her close friends were very mysterious about it. But she assumed her dad had got a transfer – he was a bank manager. She was aware of the rumours about Anna having a breakdown, but was ashamed to realise she barely gave her a thought.

It was disturbing to think how completely self-absorbed she was at that time. She finished her coffee and saw Lana glancing at her watch.

'Thanks, Lana, and thanks for meeting up with me. I appreciate it. You're a better friend than I deserve.'

'It was my pleasure. Now, look at the time; I had better get back to work. Thanks for the chat and the coffee.'

Eimear sat thinking over everything Lana had told her. It raised interesting possibilities. Donal was still involved with Susan Crossley, and his sister Jen was badmouthing her. Was it possible that either Jen or Susan were working hand in hand to ruin her life? But it all seemed so madly far-fetched. Sighing with frustration, she paid for her coffee and left the hotel.

Sligo was quiet. The shops were half full, which suited her, as there was less chance of bumping into people she knew. She got the few items she needed in the supermarket – just a few things to tide her over. When Meg came home, she'd do a big shop for her and let her stay in Mam's house until her renters moved out. She reminded herself that she needed to go to the locksmith. But first, she ran into the pharmacy to pick up some painkillers. The pharmacist reminded her that there was a prescription for her too. At first, she was puzzled and then remembered Dr Murphy had prescribed antidepressants. She had better get them filled; it was easier than trying to explain that she didn't need them.

While waiting to pay, a woman pushed past her. Donal's mother. The woman's face flushed bright red when she saw Eimear.

'You have some cheek to show your face here after what you put my Donal through!'

Eimear was uncomfortably aware that the entire shop could hear the woman practically bellowing at her. She grabbed the package the pharmacist handed her, put what she owed on the counter, and tried to retreat from the shop.

But the woman got between her and the door.

'Yes, you might well look shifty, the state of you. My Donal was lucky to have got away from you.'

'Please let me pass, Mrs Carty.'

'I'm not stopping you, or will you accuse me too? You're great at the false accusations, aren't you?'

The customers were openly gawking at her, and Eimear felt her face burn with embarrassment. Desperate, she pushed past the shouting woman and fled the shop. She hurried off as fast as she could in case the mad witch would follow her. She was relieved to get in her car and put distance between herself and the angry woman. Her plans to arrange for a locksmith to call were forgotten until she was on the outskirts of the town. Should she go back? She would feel safer if she could change the locks. That's all she seemed to be doing lately: changing locks. But she still didn't feel any safer. A curious listlessness assailed her. She was just so tired of it all. Mrs Carty's verbal attack on her was the last straw.

When she got home, she called the locksmith's, and someone promised to call the following afternoon. She put the groceries away and prepared a quick meal. The house phone rang, startling her. Who could be ringing her? Who knew she was home? Steeling herself, she answered it.

'Hello, love, I was just wondering how you're doing?'

It was a relief and a pleasure to hear Meg's warm voice.

'I'm grand. I just finished dinner. How are you? '

'All good here. I'm just cleaning the flat so that it looks nice when Jill returns. What about you? Is everything OK? Donal hasn't been near you, has he?'

'No, I haven't seen Donal. But I met up with Lana and she filled me in on a few things. But we can talk when you get in the day after tomorrow. Looking forward to having a proper chat.'

'Me too, then we can properly get to the bottom of everything.'

'Listen, Meg, I have to go. I've left a tap running, and I think I left the stopper in the sink, so I better go in case there's a flood.'

Eimear disliked lying, but she wasn't sure she could keep up a pretence that all was well against Meg's probing. She could never hide things from Meg. She knew her too well.

The phone rang out again, causing her to jump. Probably Meg ringing her back to find out if the sink had overflowed.

'It's OK, Meg, there's no flood.'

'Eimear.'

Her fingers tightened on the phone's receiver when she heard his voice. 'What do you want, Donal?'

'Mother said she saw you in the chemist today. I hear she gave you a nice welcome back.'

'Leave me alone, Donal.'

'Or what, Eimear? What will you do? Set your friendly garda on to me. No, I didn't think so. He knows you've been a naughty girl, so I don't think the gallant Alec will be rushing to the rescue, do you?'

'Why are you doing all this to me? I know about how you and Toby shared a flat in Dublin. I know that with his help, you managed to turn the office against me. But setting thugs on me is a bit low even for you.'

'So, it's true you are completely delusional. Alec said as much. He tried to explain away your behaviour as a mental breakdown. He worried I might press charges against you—poor little Eimear. But you know what? I impressed him by taking the higher moral ground and not being vindictive. I don't have the slightest idea of what you're accusing me of this time. But you really must stop blowing hot and cold with me. One time, you're begging me to come to you – the next, you're acting all terrified. How about I drop by? Then we can discuss all your crazy theories and persecution complexes.'

'I don't know what you're talking about, Donal, but I've changed the locks, so don't think about it. I promise you'll regret it.'

There was a long sigh. 'Come on, Eimear, stop playing games. I'm getting tired of it. Perhaps next time, I won't bother to join in. I care about you. You know I do, but I don't like you messing with my head.' Then, in a soft, coaxing voice, he added. 'Eimear, I know I messed up. I let you down. But you've made me suffer for it long enough. Remember how good we used to be together. Remember Italy.'

Images filled her mind, technicolour memories of wandering through sunlit streets, gondola rides at sunset, and lazy afternoons sipping wine and making love. It was another world when everything was simple, and they were achingly in love. His voice broke the spell.

'Come on, Eimear, you know we were so good together. Don't throw it all away by being angry. Let's start again.'

'Donal, that was the past, it's over. We're over!'

'If it was about me cheating, I promise it will never happen again.'

'It was more than the cheating; it was all the other things. Donal, we were never right together. Please leave me alone.'

'That's so funny, Eimear. Let me leave you alone. The whole place knows about your vendetta. There's hardly a person here who doesn't know about the games you've been playing.'

She listened to his harsh laugh and the sarcasm in his voice. He was delusional. He had to be. 'Donal, there's no point in talking anymore.' She replaced the receiver as he started to argue.

But his wheedling voice, with its empty promises, was stuck in her head. What had he meant by her vendetta against him? It was typical of him to gaslight her and pretend she was messing with him. He had even convinced Alec. But it worried her. For a brief moment, she thought. Maybe it's me. Maybe I'm doing all these things, self-sabotaging and lashing out. Maybe Mam's death coming so soon after the breakup with Donal has unhinged me.

She searched the drinks cabinet and found a bottle of her mother's best whiskey. It wasn't her favourite drink, but any port in a storm. She poured herself a good measure. As the liquid hit the back of her throat, it braced her. Doubting herself was falling into Donal's sick plan. Someone was doing their best to wreck her life, and she was damned if she was going to help them by starting to doubt her sanity.

Should she head back to Dublin? But he could be waiting outside, calling her on his mobile phone. He could be lying in wait for her right now. No, she'd stick it out. She was locked in and had barricaded the door. Then she had an even more terrifying thought. What if he was already in the house? But no, that was impossible. The dresser hadn't been moved, and he didn't have a key for the back door, not if he was using Marie O'Brien's set. She was almost certain that Marie's set was only for the front door.

But to ease her mind, she armed herself with her mother's golf club and went from room to room. All were empty. Well, everything seemed secure upstairs. She was about to return the golf club to the bag with the rest of the clubs when she thought better of it and decided to keep it handy just in case. She left it in the living room.

She found her father's shotgun locked in a box in the cloakroom. She took it out. It wasn't loaded, but she knew there were cartridges in the scullery up high on a shelf beside the fuse box. Balancing on a stool, she located a box of cartridges. She wasn't sure if she could load the gun. She was only five when her father died, so she had never learned how to shoot. Her mam hated guns but couldn't bring herself to get rid of them because her father liked them. She'd have a go loading it later. Maybe there'd be instructions online as to how to do it safely. She was nervous about guns and was half afraid she'd accidentally shoot herself.

She settled down on the couch and watched some YouTube videos on loading shotguns. The guns in the videos were different models from her Dad's gun. But she hoped the methodology was similar. She practised loading and unloading the gun. It wasn't exactly a smooth operation, but she managed it. She felt nervous keeping a loaded shotgun beside her, but the alternative was even more unnerving. It was better to be sure than sorry.

She made a bed for herself on the sofa in the living room. It felt safer than going upstairs – at least she'd be able to hear any sound of Donal trying to enter her home. She lay on the couch watching TV and tried not to jump at all the creaks and rustles that were part of the fabric of such an old house. Eventually, she dropped off to sleep.

Chapter 33

Eimear didn't know what had awakened her. But her body was tense, and she strained to hear. Her first thought was that someone was trying to get in through the front door, and her barricade was hampering them. But no, the sound was coming from the kitchen. She had locked the back door she was sure. But there was a sound of footsteps coming from there. The pounding of her heart and the blood pumping fiercely through her veins made it difficult to hear. Maybe it was all a dream. Then she heard the sound of the kitchen door opening into the hallway.

It was the signal to leap into action. There was no time to call the guards for help. She picked up the shotgun, her hands shook uncontrollably. They were slick with sweat, and her heart felt like it was trying to break free of her chest. Terrified, she heard footsteps coming down the passageway and stopping outside the living room. Her body felt hot and cold simultaneously.

'*Whoever is out there, I've got a shotgun, and I'm going to fire as soon as you open the door!*' she screamed, hating the panic in her voice. '*I mean it, I'm so scared I won't hesitate!*'

There was no response. How difficult was it to shoot a gun? In movies, they spoke of recoil or misfiring, which meant the gun backfired. She could end up killing herself. Mesmerised, she watched as the handle turned slowly. Not daring to breathe, she waited, paralysed with fear. Her sweaty fingers slipped over the trigger. The door opened.

'Eimear, it's me, you said ...'

'Keep away, Donal, I mean it. I'll fire if you come a step closer.'

'Look, I'm tired of this game you're playing. Put the gun down, and we can talk.'

'Don't come any nearer, Donal. I mean it!'

'Come on, Eimear, you don't know how to use that thing. You look more scared of it than of me.'

Then he moved rapidly and snatched the shotgun from her grasp and made it safe. She stood staring at him, unable to move. Think, she told herself, you've been training for this for weeks—all those self-defence classes. Don't be a helpless victim. Don't make it easy for him to hurt you. She could hear her teacher Fiona's voice: 'Use his strength against him.' She stood still, waiting for him to make his move.

He reached out and grasped her shoulders. Moving back rapidly, she rammed the heel of her hand hard against his nose. He squealed and dropped to his knees in pain. She bolted past him for the door. She headed for the front door, forgetting momentarily it was barricaded. She froze, and he grabbed her by the shoulders, spinning her round. She elbowed him violently in his stomach and kicked at his knee cap, unfortunately she wasn't wearing shoes and though it caused him to buckle it didn't disable him. Already he was back on his feet. Terrified, she went for the stairs, but by the time she started to run up them, Donal was hard on her heels, still clutching his bleeding nose.

'*You fucking bitch!*' he roared.

Frantically she raced up the stairs and heard his ragged breathing as he followed her. She knew he would gain on her before she got to the top. He grabbed her ankle, and she fell. He pulled her around to face him and raised his hand to strike her. She braced herself, trying to plan her next move. Donal loomed over her, and then she heard a loud smack. Donal stared glassy-eyed at her as he slowly slid to the ground. His body fell heavily against her, and he moaned. She looked over his shoulder and saw Meg wielding her mother's golf club high over her head. She brought it down again across Donal's head, leaving a dinge that sent blood flying, spattering globs of it and brain matter against her face. Horrified, she watched as Meg was about to strike again. She dragged her body free of Donal's and pulled the club from her aunt's grasp.

Meg grabbed Eimear to her and hugged her hard.

'I thought he was going to kill you!' she sobbed.

Eimear stared down at Donal's prone body, lying motionless. 'I think he's dead,' she whispered through dry lips.

They stood clinging to each other, frozen in place. Eimear buried her face in Meg's shoulder, unable to look at Donal. Everything seemed to have slowed down. She tried to speak, but her lips were stiff, and her tongue too heavy for speech.

Then, with a gigantic effort, she pulled herself free of Meg. She looked back at Donal's body sprawled across the stairs.

'We better get the gardaí and an ambulance,' Eimear said, surprised by how steady her voice was.

'I'll call them, Eimear. But I think we both need a drink.'

She pushed Eimear toward the kitchen. As she dragged herself on leaden feet into the warm room, she heard Meg asking for an ambulance and the gardaí. What was she doing here? What did Meg tell her to do? Then she remembered she had to get them drinks. She got Mam's whiskey from the cupboard. Her hands trembling uncontrollably, she tried to pour whiskey into two glasses; some of the liquid spilt onto the table. She was staring at it, mesmerised, when Meg returned.

'The gardaí are on their way. I called for an ambulance, too. Before the guards arrive, we need to talk. But Eimear, first, will you do something for me? Will you double-check that Donal is dead? I want to know that he wasn't just stunned, and we could do CPR or something.'

Seeing the fear and reluctance on Eimear's face – she added. 'Please, love, I really can't face it.'

'Christ, Meg, he looked well beyond help. But I'll check.'

Bracing herself, she walked with dragging feet to where Donal's body lay; one of his shoes had come off, and his nose and mouth were stained with blood from where she had hit him. Thankfully, she couldn't see the damage to his skull. His eyes were open, and he stared sightlessly at the ceiling. She resisted an insane desire to put on his shoe, as though by restoring it, everything would return to normal. It was pointless, but she rested her fingers on his wrist to check for a pulse. Nothing.

She returned to the kitchen. Meg was topping up her glass.

'OK, drink first, talk later.'

Eimear took a gulp; it tasted rough, but she wasn't used to whiskey. She stared at Meg. 'You saved my life.'

Meg smiled weakly. 'Well, I did one good thing with my day anyway.'

'But Meg, how are you here? You were supposed to be in London. How did you get here?'

'Did you think I was going to let my only niece return to this house all alone while a deranged lunatic was stalking her? Please, what sort of aunt do you take me for?'

'God, I'm so grateful you were here, but where were you? How did you get here? I spoke to you only yesterday.'

'Well, it's a very long story, and perhaps now is the time that you understand everything. But, Eimear, you don't look well at all - you look like you are about to faint.'

As if through a fog, Eimear stared at her aunt. Her legs felt like jelly, and her head swam. She allowed Meg to help her to her mother's armchair. She badly wanted to tell Meg not to take her there. This was Mam's chair, and the outline of her body was still etched on the cushions. But she felt strangely helpless, like a passive child. Was this shock? She felt strange.

Meg hushed her as she tried to speak. 'Here, have a little more whiskey; it will help clear your head.'

Eimear shook her head, but Meg insisted that she take another gulp. Her head felt cloudy, and her whole body felt as though it was wrapped in cotton wool. Nothing was getting through. She closed her eyes and then felt the harsh sting of a slap, and then another and another.

PART 2

MEG

Chapter 34

Appearances are deceptive. Here I am, on the surface the fun auntie, the helpful co-worker, the devoted daughter – good old dependable Meg. But the other Meg was hiding in plain sight – watching and listening. I wasn't always this way. I was once exactly as I appeared, that is, until that day – the day when the scales dropped from my eyes, and I saw everything clearly. I was born with blinkers on, only able to see what I was allowed to see. But when I finally learned the truth, so many things made sense. It was like everything was illuminated, and all the dim spaces were exposed to the light.

It had started as such an ordinary day. As usual, I was pining for my big sister Claire. At least I shared that in common with my mother: we both missed Claire. I can't remember what I was doing – probably trying to avoid annoying Mother. She and I didn't get on well. I was a disappointment to her, an irritant. I had given up trying to understand why I pained her so much. Her face generally looked sour when she saw me, like she had a bad taste in her mouth. Since Claire married, we had been thrown together more than we liked. She and I lived alone. Daddy died when I was a little girl, and then Claire went off to college. Then, after a short stint working locally as a teacher, she married James and moved with him into the big house outside the village. When I complained about how little I saw of her, Mother snapped, 'What do you expect?' Claire was a married woman and had no time to waste on the likes of me. So Mother and I put up with each other, each missing Claire and resenting each other.

On the day of enlightenment, when the world shifted on its axis, I was just thirteen, a miserable hormonal mess. I was recently released from boarding school in Galway and was home for the long summer holidays. I kept out of Mother's way, a mutually agreeable tactic. But the cold weather drove me inside in search of a tasty snack or at least an apple to take to my bedroom, where I could curl up and read my book. I was passing through the hallway en route to the kitchen when I heard voices from the drawing room. If I had kept walking, everything might have been different, but I didn't. Mother only brought her special friends into the drawing room – the solicitor, the doctor, their wives and, of course, the priest. The kitchen wasn't good enough for them.

Despite my mother's efforts to cure me of the habit, I was always a curious child. 'Curiosity killed the cat,' she would say whenever I asked too many questions. The door was slightly ajar, and I stood there ready to indulge my curiosity, undeterred by criticism. I could glimpse Mother in her perfectly ironed dress, her hair tightly curled and in regimented waves as she squatted on the edge of her armchair. Mother never slouched or sank into a chair; she perched as though ready to take off. The other occupant was her sister Agnes. I was surprised to see her here as the sisters had a frosty relationship. My curiosity intensified. Something juicy was coming; I just knew it. Agnes was possibly the ugliest woman I ever saw – to describe her as homely would be an injustice to the plain. The overall impression she gave was a sky before rain. Her hair, clothing, and face had an ashen cast. And, of course, several grey hairs sprouted from the moles, liberally decorating her face. Some days, I amused myself by counting them.

I was just about to give up and head to the kitchen to nab some biscuits from the larder when I realised they were talking about me.

'Della, you really should tell the girl. It will all come out sometime, and it's better she knows the truth from you than hear from someone else.'

My skin prickled with excitement.

'Don't be ridiculous. There's no way she could find out – only the three of us know what happened.'

'What about the father? Why the big secret? I mean, it's not as if I'm going to say anything. Come on, Della, who was he?'

'It really doesn't matter now. The point is Claire refused to tell us anything.'

'But, surely, she can't have had that many opportunities, to well … you know.'

'I think your obsession with knowing who was Meg's father is unadulterated nosiness.'

'Well, excuse me, I just thought whoever he is, he might be a bit curious about how his child turned out.'

'Well, I have no idea who he is, and I really see no purpose in talking about it.'

'Don't worry, I'll not ask again, but I think you know more than you're letting on. I've known you all your life, and I can tell when you're being mysterious. But I'll hold my tongue.'

'That will make a change. You have never been known for holding your tongue.'

'Well, I may as well hold it because you never listened to me anyway. If you remember, at the time, I told you that Claire should have had the child adopted, instead of that ridiculous plan of pretending the baby was yours. I still can't believe how you pulled the wool over everyone's eyes.'

'You know well that that's what I wanted, but Claire wouldn't hear of it! I was afraid she was going to brazen things out and parade her bastard around the village. You know my solution was the only compromise that she accepted.'

'What did Patrick think about it? Becoming a father again in his fifties.'

'Look, I really don't know why you're bringing all this up now. The important thing is that Claire didn't have to have her whole life ruined by a foolish mistake.'

My heart pounded so loud and hard against my chest that I was afraid they could hear it. Everything slowed down – my breath, my thoughts – all I could do was listen. What did this mean? I was so frozen with excitement that I almost missed them moving to the door. I fled, but I was certain that Mother had seen me.

I ran outside to the garden shed. It smelled mouldy and damp, but I didn't mind. I needed to think. Could it be? Was Claire my mother, not my sister? I sat on an old car tyre and tried to make sense of things.

I loved Claire; she was my big sister, my comfort when I was sad and the one person in the world that I truly loved and who loved me. That she was my mother overwhelmed me. But it all made sense. The woman I called mother all my life was cold, critical, and impossible to please. The only thing we agreed on was our devotion to Claire. I was dazzled by happiness. My real mother loved me, and my pretend mother was my grandmother. It all made sense. I knew Mother didn't like me. She insisted I call her 'Mother', not mammy or mam like my friends addressed their mothers. Yet, she let Claire call her 'mammy'. I always wondered why she would always correct me if I called her anything but Mother. Yes, it made sense. She disliked me because I was a *bastard*. The word lodged in my throat, uncomfortable and strange. It was a dark word, a term of abuse, and yet it thrilled me to be Claire's bastard.

I vaguely wondered about this mysterious man who was my real father. But I wasn't interested. He had abandoned me, but Claire had kept me close. I counted back the time. Gosh, she was only slightly older than me when she got pregnant. I was so proud that though she couldn't keep me herself, she never abandoned me. All my thirteen years, Claire had watched over me. She listened to my tales of woe; she defended me against Mother's scoldings and punishments. When she married James, she included me in everything, insisting I be her bridesmaid, even though mother said I was too young and would spoil the wedding photographs. But by then, Claire had done the unthinkable; she had got engaged to James Martin, rich and old. At least to me, he was old, but Claire seemed to like him. Even for Mother, Claire could do no wrong, not even having my ugly mug spoiling her wedding photographs.

This was the most unsettling news but also the most wonderful news.

I watched from the shed as Aunt Agnes waddled off down the drive to catch the bus into town. It was lunchtime, and I headed for the kitchen. Mother glanced at me out of the corner of her eye when I sat down to eat the lunch she had prepared. We both sat waiting. It was a war of nerves as we each waited for the other to break the silence. I was determined to hold fast.

'You know, Meg, that eavesdroppers seldom hear anything good of themselves,' she snapped finally.

For a moment, I didn't know what to say. I nearly bottled it and pretended I didn't know what she was talking about, but I had enough of her and her lies. Courage swept away my fear.

'What's a bastard, Mother?'

She flushed. 'Tell me what you heard. Out with it, Meg.'

I took a deep breath and stared boldly back at her. 'Claire's my mother, you're my granny.' I could see that me calling her granny had no more appeal for her than calling her mammy.

'You mustn't listen at doors – you get the wrong end of things. Your aunt Agnes and I were talking about someone else.'

She said the words, but they sounded unconvincing. It made me bolder.

'I know what I heard, but I can always go and ask Claire. She'll tell me the truth.' It was satisfying to watch her face flush brightly.

'Don't you dare or ...'

'Or what, Granny?'

She reached across the table and grabbed my arm roughly. '*You're to say nothing, my girl!*'

I pulled away from her and got to my feet, sending the chair flying. 'I'll do as I please, and the one thing I'm glad of is that I'm not your girl. I'm Claire's girl, and I'm going to live with her. Don't pretend you won't be glad, you've never liked me!'

I ran out of the house, dizzy with newfound freedom. '*Claire is my mammy*' rang like a bell in my head. Over and over, I recited it. Everything seemed brighter in the world. Finally, everything was clear, and I had a new freedom. I didn't have to feel guilty for disliking Mother. She wasn't my real mother. My real mother loved me. She was too young to mind me when I was a babby, but she kept me close, refusing to let me go.

It was only two in the afternoon. Claire would be at her house. Hopefully, James wouldn't be around. I longed to talk to her, discover everything, and tell her how happy I was. Her home was miles away, and I was desperate to see her. I couldn't wait until the five o'clock bus, which would have dropped me close to the house she shared with James. No, I would ride my bike to her home. If I left now, I could be there in an hour and a half, maybe two if the hills slowed me down. Nothing could stop me from seeing her. I heard Mother shouting for me. I ignored her and lifted my bike from under the sour apple tree. I wheeled it as quietly as possible around the front of the house, mounted it, and cycled as fast as I could down the drive.

Dimly, I could still hear her shouting.

All the long cycle, the heady refrain '*Claire is my mammy*' played on a loop of pure joy.

I made good time, fired by the twin engines of adrenaline and happiness. And I was in luck; James's Mercedes was gone, and Claire's little MG was parked in the driveway. She saw me from the sitting room and hurried to meet me as I threw open the back door and burst into the kitchen. Her face lit up like always when she saw me, and my heart skipped excitedly.

'Meg, what are you doing here? God, you're as red as a beetroot. Have you cycled all the way here? Your timing is great because I've only just got home.'

I was hot and out of breath and momentarily tongue-tied. So overwhelmed with happiness that I hadn't thought about how I would tell her of my discoveries.

'*I know you're really my mother!*' I finally blurted.

Claire stared at me, her expression frozen in shock. She didn't speak, she just stared at me. I rushed into her arms.

'Oh Claire, I'm so glad! I always knew that Mother never liked me, and now I understand. We don't have to have secrets anymore.'

Still, Claire said nothing, and I became afraid. Maybe I got everything wrong.

At last, she spoke, 'Meg love, let's sit down. We have so much to talk about. James will be back any minute, so come upstairs to my bedroom, and I can explain.'

She led me up the long stairway and opened the double doors into her huge bedroom. She then led me to a sofa thing she called a loveseat. We sat, and she held my hand. She was silent for so long that I became afraid again.

'Claire, it's true. You're my mother, aren't you?' My voice wobbled as I asked. If she denied it, all my joy would disappear.

She stroked my cheek. 'Yes, love, it's true. I don't know how you discovered it, but yes, it's true.'

'I overheard Agnes and Mo–' The name froze on my tongue. 'Are you glad I found out, Claire? I thought you'd be glad.'

'Of course I'm glad. But I didn't want you to find out this way. You do understand, don't you, why I couldn't claim you as my own?'

'Tell me. Please. They were talking about me and how I was really your daughter. Aunt Agnes said I should be told the truth, but *She* wouldn't tell me anything. *She* tried to pretend I had misheard and they were talking about someone else. But it is true, isn't it, Claire?' I stared at her, desperate for confirmation.

Claire sighed. 'Yes, loveen, it's true. It was so long ago, and I was barely fifteen. My parents were horrified. It was such a scandal. Things are getting better now, but in 1970, having a baby when you weren't married was a big deal. The names they called girls who got in the family way were cruel. They wanted to send me away to the nuns and then to have you adopted. But I wouldn't agree. Even before I met you, I loved you, Meg. You must believe that. But there was such stigma, and my parents were proud people. But I refused to give way. Eventually, Mammy agreed to pretend to be pregnant and pass you off as her child. I was a slim girl, and I didn't show until early summer, which was the holidays from school. I pretended that I was going to stay with my father's family in England. Instead, I stayed in a home for unmarried mothers. Meanwhile, my mother pretended to be pregnant and arranged to have the baby in Dublin. She made up a story about it being a risky pregnancy, which at her age wasn't surprising. It helped that Daddy was a doctor. No one knew the truth except my parents and Mammy's sister Agnes.'

All the time she spoke, she continued to hold my hand. I was afraid to talk to interrupt the story of how I began. I was thrilled. It was like I was being rebirthed.

'As soon as you were born, Meg, I knew I had made the right decision to keep you. I loved you instantly. But I couldn't acknowledge you. That was the deal I struck with my mother. In the eyes of the world, she was your mother, but in my heart I claimed you. I looked after you like any mother when you were a baby. I fed you, and you slept in a basket by my bed. I got up with you at night and cared for you except when I was at school. My parents made me promise that I would get a good Leaving Cert and go on to college. I didn't want to leave you, but I knew I needed an education to get a job and look after you eventually. When I was eighteen, I went to Dublin and trained to be a teacher. I pined for you, but it was all part of my plan to become independent and take you to live with me.'

'Why didn't you? Why leave me with...?' I couldn't call that woman 'Mother' anymore.

Claire looked uncomfortable. 'I met James, and we fell in love. So I couldn't take you to live with me.'

I was shocked. 'Did he say no?'

'I couldn't tell him, love.'

'But he's mad about you. If you explained, he'd have let me live with you.'

'It's not that simple. James is twenty years older than I am, and he's of a different generation. I was afraid of losing him. I kept waiting for the right time to tell him about you, but after we married I knew I left it too late. I was scared he might think I had tricked him into marriage. He might have understood if I had told him at once, but I was afraid of how he would react to my deceiving him. I'm so sorry. I tried to persuade him to let you live with us as my sister, but he couldn't understand. You see, he wanted children of his own.'

'But you can tell him now! Maybe he'll be glad to have me as a stepdaughter – after all, you never did have children.'

Claire let go of my hand. 'Oh love, that's just it. James and I are going to have a child.'

I stared at her, confused. I wasn't sure how to react, but I said, 'Then I'll have a little sister or brother, and we can be a proper family.'

'No, love, I can't do that to James. He'd be devastated that I've kept a secret from him. He's very religious, and he'll be horrified. Oh love, this can be our lovely secret. But you mustn't tell anyone else. '

I stared at her, uncomprehending. 'You want me to keep pretending you're my sister?'

'Yes, love, just for the time being. James would be devastated, but he's so happy now. I don't want to spoil it for him.'

I jumped to my feet. 'What about me? Don't I matter?'

'Of course you do. But I can spend even more time with you, and when the baby comes, you can be her very special auntie.'

I stared stupidly at her. She put her arms around me, but I pushed her away. 'I'm not keeping your dirty secrets. I'm going to tell everyone. Then you'll have to admit that I'm your daughter.

Claire started to cry, but I didn't care. I ran outside, got on my bike, and cycled away. The refrain that had filled me with joy now mocked me. '*Claire is my mammy.*'

Chapter 35

I didn't go home that night and spent the night in a hayshed. My eyes were red and sore from crying, and I could hardly see through them. Eventually, exhausted, I slept. Claire and Mother found me early the next morning. Claire was white, and looked exhausted, and Mother was furious.

'You stupid, selfish girl! Don't you realise Claire could lose her baby because of all the fuss you've created?'

'*Good, I hope she does!*' I screeched.

The smack I received across the face knocked me sideways.

'Stop it, leave her be!' Claire begged. 'Aw, love, please listen to me. I'm so sorry. This must be so very hard for you.'

She tried to pull me towards her, but I drew back and glared at her.

'Meg, why don't the two of us go off somewhere for a few days, and then we can really talk.'

'You're just afraid I'll tell your precious James that you're a tramp!'

Claire's face blanched even more.

Mother interrupted. 'Be careful, you ungrateful whelp, that I don't teach you a lesson you won't forget in a hurry!'

'You can't keep me quiet, I'll tell everyone!' I said triumphantly.

Mother lunged at me again, but Claire pulled her away.

They spoke at the door of the shed, and then Mother gave me one last vicious look and left.

'Meg, please, you have every right to tell whoever you want, but I just ask that you hear me out. There's something else that I haven't told you.'

'Oh, what a surprise! Claire Martin is keeping secrets!' I snarled.

'I know you're angry, but there's another reason I want to keep it secret. But first, I want you to know that I'm proud you're my daughter, and I always have been.'

'Doesn't look like it though. Does it?'

'James is ill. He's got cancer. That's why I don't want him to learn about our relationship. He's so happy about the baby, and I don't want to tell him how I deceived him. Please, Meg. The cancer is terminal. He's only got a year or two if we're lucky. I want to make him happy. He's been so good to me. And to you, too. He paid for all our trips away and the new clothes I bought you.'

I stared. 'Is that the truth? Is James really going to die?' Claire flinched at my words, but I didn't care. 'I'm sorry about that, and I'll keep our secret, but you have to promise me that after he dies, you tell everyone about me. Do you promise?'

Claire looked at me, her eyes shining with gratitude. She pulled me into her arms. I let my body relax, but I was still hurt that she put James before me.

'Oh, love, thank you! But at least we can be together more often, and when the baby comes ...'

'*My sister!*' I snapped.

'Yes, your little sister – or brother – but we must keep things quiet until ...'

'Until James is dead,' I said baldly. I admit I was glad when I saw her wince. I was glad that I hurt her. After all, she hurt me. 'Then, it occurred to me that there was so much more that I needed to know. Things that could make a huge difference to me.

'Who's my father?' I asked and I held my breath as I waited for her to tell me.

''He was just some boy I knew when I stayed in Dublin. He was only a kid. I never told him about you. Mammy tried to trace him, but he disappeared.

'What was his name?'

'His name was Mateo. I called him Matt. He wasn't from Ireland. He was a Spanish student here for the summer to learn English. To be honest, Meg, it was such a difficult time for me; I didn't want to think about him anymore. I was more concerned with finding a way to keep you. It took a lot to figure out a way. Things are easier now, but back then, to have a baby out of marriage was considered a terrible thing. But I loved you, Meg, and between us, Mammy and I found a way. I had to grow up fast. But I was so delighted to have found a way to keep you close.'

'But isn't there any way I can find out about my dad?' I loved the shape of the word in my mouth. The man I thought was my father died when I was little, and he was daft as a brush. I kept out of his way.

'Please, love, you're wasting your time wondering about him. I put him out of my head. I don't even remember his surname; it was such a mouthful.'

Reluctantly, I went back home with Mother. She barely spoke to me for the rest of the day, which suited me. I'd be happy if we never spoke again. At least now I was free to hate her. Before, I tried so hard to make her care about me. I went around pathetically, trying to please her. The relief of knowing that I didn't have to anymore was like being set free. I didn't have to feel guilt for all my angry, hateful thoughts because she deserved every single one.

After a while, I got used to the new reality. Very little changed, at least on the surface. I continued to live with Mother, but the rules were no longer the same. I no longer felt the need to obey her or keep her rules. It suited me. I could see that she hated this change in our relationship. The control had shifted. If she complained about my behaviour or my refusal to do the jobs she gave me, then I just sighed and talked about having a little chat with James or Father Brown. That soon shut her up.

I saw Claire more often than before. I sensed James wasn't too happy with how much time I spent with his wife. But I didn't care. He wasn't getting it all his way, cancer or no cancer. At times, I wondered if he was ill at all. He certainly didn't spend too much time in bed. But he did have a lot of hospital appointments.

Claire had got very big. My new sister or brother was growing inside her, feeding off her like a fat tapeworm and trying to take her from me.

One day, when Claire was styling my hair for a local dance, she smiled at me in the mirror.

'How would you like to be the new baby's godmother?'

'Oh, are you serious? I'd love that.'

Claire beamed delightedly at me, and for a while I stopped hating the intruder. I was willing to share Claire and excited for the day when I could call her mammy. Sometimes, when we were alone, I used that name, but Claire looked nervous when I did. I suppose she worried about James overhearing.

At the end of the summer, I was packed off to boarding school. I pretended I hated going, but it was a relief. Living with Mother felt like being on a battlefield where both sides were afraid to fire the first shots. At times, the tension was so bad that we stopped eating together. When I carried my meal on a tray to watch in front of the TV in the living room, she wrinkled her nose in disgust, but deep down, she was relieved to see me go. Food tasted better for both of us when we didn't have to sit eye to eye.

The baby was born at the end of December. I was home for my Christmas holiday. I visited Claire in the hospital. She proudly showed me the little tapeworm. I have to admit, she was pretty — all pink, soft cuteness. I liked how tightly she grasped my fingers. She was strong, fierce like me.

Claire whispered in my ear. 'How do you like your little godchild?' I was hurt. Why didn't she say little sister? Then I realised that making me godmother was just a sop to me, and I hardened my heart against the little worm.

'What shall we call her?' Claire asked.

'Alice. I like the name. Let's call her Alice, from *Alice in Wonderland*.'

'That's lovely, Meg. I didn't know you read that book. I loved it when I was a child, too.' She grinned at me delightedly. I went home happy. I felt that maybe things might just be alright, and I could eventually grow to love my little sister Alice.

The next day, Claire came home from the hospital, and I wasn't allowed to see her. Mother spoke of Claire needing peace to establish breastfeeding. That sounded repulsive and brought back to mind my image of a bloated parasite. But after a week, I was allowed to see Claire and baby Alice again. I only had a few days left before I had to return to school, and I was determined to spend as much time as possible with them.

The house was transformed. It smelled of babies, a mixture of talc, and Sudocrem. Piles of nappies sat on chairs, and pretty little playsuits and tiny pink dresses were scattered on every surface. Mother sat on a chair, folding nappies and stared suspiciously at me as I entered the kitchen. James was sitting in an armchair holding little Alice. He looked happy but frail, and for a moment, I almost felt sorry for him. He wouldn't get to enjoy his baby daughter for long. Then he smiled and beckoned me towards him.

'Well, Auntie Meg, how do you like your new niece Eimear?' he said in the silly fake jolly voice he always used when he spoke to me.

I stared at him, puzzled. 'Sorry, don't you mean Alice? Claire said I could choose the name, and I picked Alice.'

James laughed. 'Aww, my dear, I'm afraid I overruled you. I hate the name Alice, and besides, I want to call her after my mother – Eimear.'

Claire came into the room and saw my face. I stared at her accusingly.

'You said she'd be called Alice—you promised!'

Claire squirmed. 'Look, love, We can still use Alice as a second name.'

I glared at her and headed straight for the door.

Claire followed me, and I could hear James and Mother telling her to let me get over it. James shouted something about me being a spoiled brat. I kept on walking, a lump of disappointment overlaid with rage embedded in my throat.

Claire caught up with me in the garden. She caught me by my arm, but I shrugged her off.

'Please, Meg, don't be angry. Can't you see how ill he is? His mother meant the world to him, and I had to let him have his way.'

'But you promised me!' I screamed at her. *'What about me? Why does he always have to come first?'*

'Look, love, I promise when we're together, you can call her Alice and later when ...' she faltered.

'You mean when he's dead, then I can call her Alice, and you'll tell everyone you're my mother.'

'Yes, of course, ' she said eagerly. I desperately wanted to believe her.

Chapter 36

Every time I returned from boarding school, the Worm got bigger. I couldn't bring myself to call her Eimear or Alice, so in my mind she reverted to the Worm. Despite myself, I have to admit she was pretty. At her christening, James and Claire organised a big party. I did my bit in the church. The Worm roared all through the ceremony. Back at the house, food was laid on, and pink balloons and a big banner stretched across the ceiling to welcome Baby Eimear. I wanted to be sick. Even the cake was pink.

James beamed from ear to ear, like he had the most perfect child in the world. I had the satisfaction of watching Mother and Claire exchange nervous glances. As well they should. I could blow up this happy occasion with one word. But I held my peace. You see, I still loved Claire, and I believed she would do right by me. Over that day, as I wandered through the rooms filled with well-wishers and looked at the piles of gaily-wrapped presents for the Worm, I wondered about the day I was christened. I bet there was no cake, no celebration. It was probably more like a funeral.

The christening buoyed James up for a while, but gradually he grew weaker. He had to spend more and more time in the hospital, and Claire was torn between minding the baby and being with him. Mother wasn't fit to be much help; she had arthritis flare-ups and found it hard to manage the new baby. Whenever she did mind her, it turned my stomach to hear her drooling over her and talking silly baby talk. I knew she never would have bothered with me when I was a baby. No, I was a stain, a blot on perfect Claire's perfect life. If she could have erased me, she would have.

On one of my rare weekends home from school, I offered to babysit so Claire could spend more time with James. I could see she was reluctant to let me mind her precious Worm, but she eventually agreed. Before leaving, she wrote me a list of instructions and insisted I ring Mother if I was worried about anything.

It was nice to be alone in Claire's house. It was huge. There was an enormous kitchen, a scullery, a drawing room, a dining room, a library and James's study, which he always kept locked. Upstairs, there were seven bedrooms. Claire's room was massive, with a dressing room and a private bathroom. It was nice to have a proper snoop around. Our house wasn't as big or fancy, and we were better off than most people around us. Mother thought herself and Claire a cut above the locals or yokels, as she referred to them when she was talking on the phone with her posh friends. But this house dwarfed ours. The furniture was old world, not reproductions like Mother had. No, this was all the real thing. All the chairs, tables and mirrors were probably there from the time of James's parents and even further back. I imagined coming to live here after James was dead. Which room would be mine? At least I'd have first dibs, as the Worm wouldn't be able to put in any preference for quite a while.

The Worm slept for an hour and then started to cry. I was watching a movie, so I turned the sound up, but it was useless. The noise penetrated, spoiling my enjoyment of the film, and I had to go upstairs to her. She stank. I knew what to do as I had changed her before under Claire's supervision. I cleaned the disgusting mess away and put her down again. She didn't sleep, so I got her a bottle and shoved it in her mouth to shut her up. But she spat it out and screamed even harder. Sighing, I picked her up. Still she roared. I paced the floor, jiggling her fiercely. I would miss my film if she didn't shut up soon. I would miss all the exciting bits. In exasperation, I shook her and shouted at her to shut up.

That's when Claire walked in. I didn't hear her return with all the noise the Worm made. Claire glared at me and snatched the baby out of my arms.

I went downstairs and watched the rest of the movie. It was hard to follow what was happening as I had missed so much of the action.

'Meg, we need to talk.' Claire's voice interrupted me.

Sighing, I glanced up at her. 'What now?' I demanded.

Instead of answering me, she turned off the television.

'Hey!' I protested. 'I was watching that!'

'Meg, I want you to realise how dangerous it is to shake a baby. I know you were frustrated with her crying, but there's no excuse for what you did.'

I realised that I had upset her, and I was sorry. She loved the Worm, and I had better learn to accept it.

'I thought you loved little Eimear ...'

She paused, and I waited.

'I know you love your baby sister, but I can't trust you to mind her if you lose your temper with her.'

I mumbled apologies and promised to do better. 'How's James?' I asked not because I cared but because I thought it best.

She started crying. 'Oh, Meg, he's so poorly, the doctors want to move him to the hospice.'

I rushed to hug her and told her how sorry I was and that I would pray for James. But secretly, I was delighted. With James gone, the three of us could be a proper family, and I would be a great big sister to the baby. Everything would change. I could see that my response made Claire happy. She hugged me tightly. I felt excited as I thought of the wonderful times we would have as a proper family in this lovely house. I even decided which of the bedrooms I would choose – the room with the flowery blue wallpaper and the cast-iron bed. I just had to learn to be patient. Not long now!

Of course, James rallied and came home again. I tried to hide my disappointment because Claire was so happy. She explained that the doctors in Dublin decided to try one more treatment. It wasn't a cure, but it would give him more time. I pretended to be pleased, but I ached with jealousy. When would it be my time? I was tired of waiting.

The Worm grew and, I admit, she was fun. As she got older, I could play with her, and surprisingly, she was always delighted to see me. Absence made her heart grow fond, and my rare visits caused her to clap her hands delightedly. I tried to make the best of things. Claire made a fuss of me when I visited, but it felt forced, and she rarely called to see me and the old woman.

Mother was getting stiffer and found it hard to manage the stairs. She hated having to ask me to help link her to bed.

Eimear was five by the time James finally died. He had survived for so long that I had almost given up hope. I was eighteen. He was a big man in the community, and the house was filled for two days with lines of people coming to pay their respects. The funeral was concelebrated with five priests and the Knights of Columbanus in attendance. James had been a proud member of the Knights and a devout Catholic. He was buried with all honours. Mother gripped Claire's arm tightly and watched over her devotedly. She did her best to keep me away from Claire. But I bided my time. Mother was old – really old, and soon I'd be free of her too, and then it would be just me and Claire, my mammy, and, of course, the child. I didn't mind sharing her with Eimear, not anymore. We could be proper sisters – she would always look up to her big sister, and I would watch out for her. But I was getting impatient for my new life to begin.

Mother kept giving me dirty looks and warning me not to upset Claire. But I knew things were hard for Claire; she missed James, and I wanted to give her time to get over him. I mean, she always knew he was going to die. It was hardly a surprise, but I was willing to be patient.

My time at boarding school was over. I wasn't sad. The friends I made there were like me, a bit disconnected from their homes, and while at school we were close. But I never confided in them. I entered a world of games and academia in school and didn't shine at either. My report cards described me as average. What an insulting word to describe a person or their abilities! But it was obvious that I wasn't college material. Mother wanted me to apply for nursing, but I was suspicious she wanted me to end up as her carer. Instead, I applied for work at the Cassidy Hotel. I started as a dog's body, doing a bit of everything, but I had my eye on the receptionist's job. They seemed to like me in the hotel. It was nice to be appreciated.

I forced myself to be patient and waited a couple of weeks before discussing things with Claire. I wasn't a monster, I gave her time to get over him.

The back door was locked and, after I banged on it, she let me in. When did she start locking the back door? Usually, it was on the latch, and I called in whenever I felt like it. Of course, she must be sick of visitors traipsing in and out to offer sympathy for James. So if she didn't lock the door, she'd get no peace.

She looked very pale; her eyes had a wrung-out appearance as if all her tears had been sucked out of her. If she had been a bit friendlier, I might have said nothing. But the tired, cold look she gave me cut me to the quick. I thought she'd be delighted to see me.

'Sorry, Meg. It's not a great time. I haven't been sleeping, and I planned to have a nap. Can you call tomorrow? I'll be in better shape.'

I ignored what she said and instead walked past her into the kitchen.

'Where's Eimear?' I asked.

'She's with the childminder. I needed some time to myself, and I didn't have the energy to keep her entertained. Sandra's little one loves to play with Eimear, so I thought she'd be better off there than with me.'

'I'm glad Eimear isn't here. It'll give us a chance to talk, to plan.'

'Meg, I'm really tired. Can't we talk tomorrow about whatever plans you have? But I'm sure we can arrange a summer holiday if that's what you mean.'

I stared at her. Could she really think I was talking about holidays?

'Claire, I'm not talking about holidays. You must know why I'm here.'

Her face flushed, and she looked away. 'Meg, please, not now, not today. It's too soon.'

I could feel my rage build up. I had been so patient. Five years' worth of patience was bubbling like burning lava inside me. The wave building in my chest was like a scream. I gritted my teeth to hold it in.

'I'm sorry you're tired, Claire, but I'm tired too. You promised that after James died, you would tell everyone I was your daughter, and we would live together like a proper family.'

Claire walked past me and slumped on a kitchen chair. 'Please, Meg, not this again. Not now. I'm not able to bear it.'

'*You're not able to bear it!*' the sarcasm shot out of my mouth, whipping her to attention. 'What about me? What about all I have to bear – the lies, the pretence, hiding who I am? And why? To protect your precious James. Well, I kept my part of the deal. Now, I want you to do your part.'

Claire backed away as though I had struck her when I mentioned bloody James. I stared her out. I wasn't backing down this time.

'Meg, please, give this up – you're a grown-up now. Why do we have to broadcast our private family business?'

I stared at her, unable to believe what I was hearing. She got to her feet and touched my arm appealingly.

'Look, Mammy will be upset if all this comes out now. She's old –– don't bring all this scandal on her now,' she begged.

'You want me to wait till that witch who made my childhood miserable dies before you finally acknowledge me as your child. Or will you make more excuses then?'

'I just don't want to cause upset.'

'What about my upset and my feelings, don't I count?'

Claire looked at me with eyes brimming with tears, and I realised she was never going to acknowledge me. She had just strung me along. She didn't love me. I was her mistake. A mistake that she regretted making and, most of all, regretted keeping. I knew without a shadow of a doubt that if she could have gone back in time, she'd have given me away or got rid of me. Fury, disappointed rage coursed through me. I wanted to hit her and kick her skinny body to a pulp of bruised flesh. But I had a better revenge. I walked slowly to the back door and opened it.

Then, just before I left, I smiled at her, saying each word as I poured icy water on the coals of my hatred.

'Well then, if you won't, I will. I am fed up with keeping who I am as some dirty little secret. What is it the Bible says? The truth shall set you free. Well, I'm going to get busy spreading the word.'

Then I left.

I stole every penny I could find in the house. Mother squirrelled cash away everywhere. I must have found a couple of hundred. It was enough to give me time to think and not have to see any of their treacherous faces until I decided exactly what to do. I went to Dublin and did all the bad things my religion teacher, Miss Doyle, warned me against. It was three months of drink, drugs and sex. How I didn't get pregnant, I don't know. I stayed in a small hotel and visited the nicer hotels to pick up decent prospects. I found most of the men boring as fuck. But I did meet one or two people who would become very useful to me, although I didn't realise it then.

Over the weeks I grew reckless, and I didn't care what happened to me anymore. I obviously wasn't worth anything, only whatever value I put on myself, which amounted to enough cash to buy cheap booze and get a little hit from the weed the stringy teenagers sold down dark alleyways. If I ran out of money, I found other ways to persuade them to give me what I needed.

One night, I got out of it with drink and weed, and the man I was with started to push me around, and I lashed out at him. He wasn't used to being resisted. He set to teaching me what he helpfully called a lesson. The lesson might have killed me if it weren't for Tommy. I don't know what impulse he had to come to my rescue. Tommy isn't a man who does acts of random kindness. But for whatever reason, he saved me that night. The man who beat me lost a lot of teeth and Tommy gave me one as a souvenir.

He took me to a small hotel and got a doctor to check me over. I expected to pay him back somehow but, oddly, he left me in peace to recover. When I was better, he offered me a job. He owned a lot of small businesses, including the hotel he had brought me to. He put me to work in the bar, and some nights he'd order brandy and buy me one, too, and we'd chat. Well, he did most of the talking. Eventually, he got curious about the little culchie he had rescued. He was easy to talk to because he didn't care; he just liked stories, so I told him mine.

Eventually, I got bored and was ready to go home. Tommy told me to keep in touch and to let him know if I needed to earn extra cash. ' A fresh-faced wee country girl might be useful to me from time to time,' he said, staring at me with his cold assessing eyes. We parted on good terms, and I accepted his offer of future work. He gave me a wad of cash as a parting gift, but this time I knew the gift would come with strings. I was able to make myself useful to Tommy over the years and took several trips abroad on his behalf. I noted grimly that neither Claire nor Mother tried to find me. Perhaps they hoped they'd seen the back of me. Well, tough luck!

Mother was furious when I showed up unannounced. She demanded her money back. I just smiled at her and said, didn't she realise there was a price on silence? That shut her up. As for Claire, my lovely mammy, she pretended to be glad to see me, but I knew she was scared of me, of what I would do. The only one truly glad to see me was Eimear. She squealed with delight and hugged me tightly as though she never wanted to let me go. It was a sweet revenge. I could see how it worried Claire. But I was nice to her. I acted like I was willing to accept the status quo. She was desperate to know where I had disappeared, but she knew she hadn't the right to ask. After all, she wasn't my mother, was she?

They were all afraid that I'd open my mouth. I realised that was my currency. As soon as I told people, they'd stop noticing me. But they'd sit up and take notice as long as I held the threat. Besides, I enjoyed holding it over Mother. I'd drop little hints when the priest or any of her snooty friends visited her. It was such fun. But deep inside, it hurt, and I desperately wanted to believe that, eventually, Claire would acknowledge me. That's what a sucker I was. Even then, I still clung to the dream.

Chapter 37

At first, I had no real interest in finding out about my father. Claire had told me very little. I was so desperate for her to acknowledge me that an absent father barely seemed to matter. But over time, I became curious about who he was. If Claire wouldn't recognise me as her daughter, the least she could do was tell me about my father. The man I used to call father died when I was five, and I never liked him. He smelled of cigarettes and sat drooling and reciting poetry, not proper poetry like in books; it was more like nursery rhymes. I now know that he had dementia, but then, he scared me, and I kept away from him. It was a relief to know that he wasn't my real dad. But I became curious about my biological father, what he was like and why he left Claire to manage with me alone.

I challenged her one day after she had called to see Gran. That was one good thing about Eimear's arrival. It was acceptable for us all to call the old witch Gran now. Claire looked tired, and her usual mobile face tensed when she saw me waiting for her.

I stopped her just as she was leaving the house. 'I want to talk, Claire,' I demanded.

'Please, Meg, I'm bushed. Can't it wait until tomorrow?' she pleaded weakly.

But I was adamant. 'No, I want to ask you something.'

Wearily, she ran her fingers through her hair. I realised with surprise that it was sprinkled with streaks of grey. I always thought of her as young. She was still in her thirties but seemed to have aged after James died.

She pointed to her car, and I got into the passenger seat. It was cold, so she turned on the engine.

'Let's go for a drive. I've been indoors too much lately,' she said.

I didn't ask where we were going; I composed my thoughts. The silence in the car wasn't pleasant. Claire was nervous, afraid I'd make more demands of her.

We drove to Lissadell, pulling in on the green overlooking the shore. The sea had the stillness of a lake, and the mountains and woods held it snugly in a calming embrace. For a short while, we sat in the car contemplating the view. It was soothing when I was so churned up inside.

'I want to know about my father.'

'I told you already, Meg, he was a foreign language student.'

'You told me his name was Matteo, but there must be more. I mean didn't you know where he lived? For God's sake, you must have had somewhere to go. I wasn't the bloody Immaculate Conception, was I?'

'Why are you so fired up about this now? You never showed much interest in knowing before.'

'Well, maybe he will want to know about me.'

'Meg, I've told you it's complicated,'

I snorted in derision. 'I don't care anymore. I want to know who my dad is. It's the least you can do.'

Claire sighed deeply and held the silence for so long that I feared she would remain clammed up, but suddenly, she spoke in a rush, almost as though she had rehearsed it. I suppose she knew this day was coming—the day when I wanted to know everything.

'Your father was a nice boy. We met when I was up in Dublin, staying with friends. We had a little romance. We were both very young. When I came home, I felt ill. I didn't know what was wrong with me. It was months before I realised that I was pregnant.'

'Didn't you contact him, tell him about me?'

'Meg, he was only a boy. He wasn't from Ireland. He was a foreign language student. I had no way of contacting him; even if I did, he couldn't do anything. He was only a few months older than me.'

'But he's not a teenager now. Can't you find out where he stayed? The people who boarded him might have his address or the language school he attended.'

'It was so long ago. It's no good, Meg. I never saw where he stayed. We met at his friend's house, and I never knew the friend's name.'

'Well, what was he like? Do I look like him? Where was he from?'

'Mateo was Spanish, from Seville. He was a nice boy, very happy and kind.'

'But didn't you want to keep in touch? I thought you cared about each other?'

'We did, but I lost his address. Mammy washed my jeans, and it was in the pocket.'

'Why didn't he write to you?'

'I was supposed to write first, and then he'd reply, so when he never heard from me, he must have thought I didn't want to keep up contact.'

I had many more questions, but Claire had little more to tell me.

'Do I look like him? I know Spaniards are darker-skinned and brown-eyed. Why don't I look more Spanish?'

'I don't know, Meg. I guess you take after me.'

'Mateo, what? What was his surname?'

'I really can't remember Meg.'

'You can't remember the name of the boy who knocked you up?'

Claire flushed at the derision in my voice.

'Did you shag so many boys that the names are blurred?' I could see that I was hurting her, and I was glad. She deserved to feel discomfort and shame for how she had treated me. I forced myself to speak more calmly. 'It was a foreign name. You must know. Please, Claire, I have a right to know.'

'Meg, you're angry and hurt, but you must understand. It was my first time with a boy, and I was so young. I knew nothing about contraception. I didn't intend for it to happen. I thought he loved me. But even before we parted, I knew it was a mistake. He was going back to his family and his life in Spain. We were both so young, playing at being grown-ups. His name was Mateo Garcia, something - it was a double-barrelled name. I really can't recall it. But apart from him coming from Seville, I know nothing about him. We were only together for a few weeks and spent so little time together. The Coyles, the family I stayed with, were cousins. They were hosting a Spanish student, a girl called Maria. It was through her that I met Mateo, and she only knew him because she attended the same language school. Please, Meg, don't try to find him; it will only cause heartbreak for everyone concerned.'

'That's for me to decide!' I snapped.

276

There wasn't much to go on, but I was determined to find my real father. I didn't know where to begin.

'What about the Coyles? They might still be in contact with the Spanish girl, or they will at least know the name of the language school. The school might have kept records?'

I felt growing excitement at the thought of this Spanish father. He never got a chance to be part of my life. But maybe he'd be glad to know he has a daughter. My heart filled as I thought of all the Spanish relatives I might have. I felt exotic and special; those long-lost relatives beckoned like a bright star—a beacon for the loneliness of my life.

'Meg, please don't approach the Coyles. Let me try to find out. I'm still in touch with Stella, my cousin, and she might be able to help.'

I wasn't sure how hard Claire would work to find out about my father, so I thought I'd give her an incentive.

'Claire, if you do this, I promise I'll keep quiet about you and Mother, but I better get results quickly.'

Claire nodded, started the engine, and drove me back home. She didn't come in and left me to go back to her brat. Watching her drive away, I thought about my handsome Spanish father. There must be some way I could discover who he was. I felt excited at the thought.

Later that night, as I lay in bed, my excitement dampened. If Claire, my mother, refused to acknowledge me, why would a man who never even knew of my existence possibly care? But I nourished a thin flame of hope that someday we would find each other and someone in this world would be proud to call me their child. Then, I would have found a home.

Claire called to see me one wet November evening. She was dressed beautifully, effortlessly elegant. I looked like a small lump of dough in a sack beside her. But she seemed tense. She had lost weight, and her dress hung loosely from her body. Mother told her to eat more and get rest. She never bothered with my appearance except to disparage it.

Claire whispered to me to follow her into the hallway.

'Meg, come into the drawing room. We can be private there.'

How fitting, the room of revelations it was turning out to be. But I was excited. Perhaps she had news about my father.

'What have you found out? Did you contact your cousins?' I could barely breathe with excitement.

'Yes, I contacted Stella.' Claire spoke slowly and kept her eyes on her hands, which were twisting the folds of her skirt.

'Well, what did they say? Come on, Claire, don't keep me in suspense.'

'Meg, I'm sorry I don't have much news. Stella told me the school was called The Begley Language School and was based on Grafton Street.'

'Well, that's a starting place, at least.'

'No, I'm sorry, you see, the school closed fifteen years ago. It went bankrupt. I asked Stella if she was in touch with Maria, the language student who had stayed with her. She told me that they only kept in touch for a few months, and she hasn't a clue where she is now.'

'And my father, what about him?'

'She has no idea what became of him. She said the people he stayed with returned to England, but she couldn't remember their names. I'm so sorry, Meg. I know you wanted me to have better news.'

My eyes stung with the bitterness of my disappointment. 'You're lying. You don't want me to find him. You're afraid it'll all get out that lovely Claire Curran was a bit of a slut.'

Claire flinched. 'Meg, I know you feel I'm against you, but I'm not. If you don't believe me you can talk to Stella yourself. Please believe me, I want to help you.'

I glared at her, but what could I do? There was no point in talking to this Stella person. She'd say whatever Claire told her to. Tears of disappointment stung my eyes. The door to my past remained firmly shut.

Chapter 38

Mother got ill when I was twenty-five. She had breathing difficulties and took to her bed for large parts of the day. A lifetime of smoking had caught up with her. I enjoyed watching her power ebb and her ability to wound become impaired. I relished her dependence on me. She hated being so helpless. She begged Claire to take her in, but Claire's house was being renovated, and workmen were in and out. So it was impractical for her to stay with her beloved Claire.

I took leave from my job as a receptionist at the hotel. They were sympathetic and eager for me to return to work whenever I could. It was nice to be appreciated by someone. The manager was a bit sweet on me and suggested I go on hotel management courses, but I was content to keep my life simple.

Of course, now I had my responsibilities to Mother to occupy me. I got an allowance from the state for my work as Mother's carer, and her state pension helped me save money for my future. It supplemented my infrequent but substantial earnings from Tommy.

Caring for Mother was a challenge for her more than for me. She could never be sure of me. Oh, I didn't harm her; well, maybe I delayed giving her painkillers at times and ignored her when she needed help going to the bathroom. I enjoyed the daily little humiliations she suffered. They were some small balancing of the pain she inflicted on me as a child. But my hate for her paled beside what I reserved for Claire. She spent a lot of time with Mother, holding her hand and speaking words of comfort. Sometimes, she looked at me strangely, as though she didn't recognise me. Neglect and denial have consequences – a lesson Claire was learning at last.

My relationship towards Eimear had continued to flower. Despite my earlier indifference, the child seemed besotted with me. At first, it irritated me, but after a lifetime of being starved of affection, I was seduced. Seeing someone's eyes light up whenever they saw me was nice. So soon, I became her wonderful Auntie Meg. The person who took her to the cinema, brought her nice clothes and always took her side. I knew that my relationship with Eimear worried Claire. She was suspicious of my motives, as well as she might be. I was the worm in the apple of her life. The more distant Claire and I grew, the warmer my relationship with Eimear.

Life went on. Resentment fuelled me, but to all outward appearance I had accepted my role in the periphery of Claire's life. Eimear and I becoming so close was the perfect way to punish Claire. She stole my birthright, and I was going to steal her child. So, I cultivated Eimear. I was her ally during her teenage years, siding with her against Claire on the teenage/parent battlefield. Claire was helpless to do anything. When Eimear gushingly said I was like a sister to her, not an aunt, how I laughed. But it became fun. Fakery became such a way of life that sometimes I almost forget my hatred. Almost.

Eimear had the life I should have had, and I resented her for it. I watched how she was treated like a little princess for her First Holy

Communion. For her confirmation, Claire insisted she take the name Alice – a blatant sop to me – but it was too little and too late. I watched the big celebration for her sixteenth birthday, the money spent on clothes, the holidays and most of all, the pride that shone from Claire's eyes as she looked at her daughter. She had no such pride or joy in me, her firstborn. I was her dirty secret, her shame.

But it was hard to be angry with Eimear. Like me, she was innocent. The thirteen-year age gap between us lessened over time. I listened to her dating woes and advised her on clothes and make-up. I was her cool auntie. If there was anything that she wanted to wear that Claire objected to, I backed her up. But I was careful not to cause a breach. I wanted Claire to be wary of me but not so afraid as to keep me from Eimear.

Eimear had cause to be grateful to me. I helped her sort out a bullying problem at school. When she turned sixteen, I offered to take her on holiday to Spain as a birthday treat. She had done well in her Junior Cert, and I wanted to show her how proud we were of her. Claire hated the idea but could do nothing. I was her loving godmother, after all. She tried to persuade Eimear not to go, and when that didn't work, she pathetically suggested that we all go together. I turned to her, my eyes wide and hurt and said, 'Don't you trust me, Claire?' So, she could do nothing, and I was a hero in Eimear's eyes.

The holiday was a great success. It served a dual purpose: a treat for Eimear and allowed me to do a little business on Tommy's behalf. He had a lot of associates living close to our resort. But to Eimear, I was the cool aunt who allowed her freedom to go and enjoy the nightlife and allowed her to have her first taste of alcohol. I helped her deal with her first hangover and her first holiday romance. Unlike boring Mam, she thought I was so amazing to give her all the freedom she wanted. I confess as she teetered out in her fake tan, revealing teenage clothes and high heels, I did hope for the worst, but the child was annoyingly compliant with curfews and never let boys get too familiar. Annoyingly, she was in bed before midnight most nights. But, for her, it was the most amazing adventure and, in the end, we solemnly promised that what happened on tour would stay on tour. Maddeningly, nothing did happen.

The time away from her precious Eimear must have seemed endless for Claire. It pleased me that she pined for her over the long week we were away. When we arrived home, it was to hear that Mother had taken a turn for the worse. I was prepared to get back into nursing duties, but Claire and Eimear stuck to her bed like limpets, and I barely got the woman to herself. But when she was close to the end and well-drugged up, I told her what I planned to do to her. To this day, I treasure the look on her face.

Claire was a bit difficult about my decision to cremate the old bitch, but I had the advantage. After all, how could she refuse my request to arrange a cremation when she had refused me so much over the years? Cremations were unusual in rural Ireland back then. The only other person we knew who was cremated was an elderly man who died in England, and the family cremated his body and brought the ashes home. I insisted to all and sundry that it was our dear mother's dying wish as she had a horror of being buried. So, after a funeral mass, the remains of Agnes Curran were brought to Dublin for cremation. Claire was upset and convinced that her mother would have preferred a conventional burial, but what could she do?

I relished every moment, from collecting her ashes to triumphantly flushing them down the toilet. 'Rest in shit,' I said as I watched her go. It was the most satisfying moment of my life. I had carried through my promise to the bitch I was forced to call Mother. And now she rested in the sewer where she belonged. The ashes I gave Claire were from the kitchen fire. The local priest arranged to have them interred in the family plot. I could barely contain my laughter.

With my so-called mother dead, I wondered what excuse Claire would make to avoid telling the world or at least the local community that I was her daughter. When I challenged her, she muttered mealy-mouthed words about not wanting to upset her precious Eimear. *Isn't it enough that we both know our relationship with each other, darling?* That was when I knew for certain that Claire was ashamed of me. It pleased me to know she was a little afraid of me, too.

The years crept by, and I had a life to live. I enjoyed my job in the hotel. It helped me to understand the world a little better. I was a watcher. I saw how people interacted with each other. I learned how to please people, to get them to like me. I began to realise that was my superpower. I was the best friend, the supporting actor. My job was to make the stars shine. It helped that I was what one might call pleasant-looking, unremarkable. I didn't threaten the women, and the men thought I should be delighted by any attention from them. So, in work, I developed a friendship group, and I amused myself by seeing how I could manipulate them for my pleasure. I played games where I turned friends against each other, broke up relationships and staged grand reconciliations. It amazed me how unobservant people were. Unaware that the catalyst for a break-up was also the loving friend who occasionally reunited the parted lovers.

Eimear went off to college and trained as a solicitor. Claire was delighted and proud. I think she was glad Eimear was away from my influence, too. She made regular forays to Dublin to take her to shows. I bided my time. I knew Eimear was a home bird. But with her gone, I thought Claire and I could spend more time together and return to our former closeness. I suppose, even after everything, I still wanted my mother back, the one I lost as a baby. It was pathetic! But it shows how hard it is for hope to become fully extinguished. But Claire invented reasons to avoid my company, except when others were around. Aware that she was afraid of me, I wasn't entirely displeased. If I couldn't have her love, I at least had her attention.

Eimear returned to Sligo and got a job with Holland and Byrne. It wasn't the most exciting job. I doubted whether Eimear would stick it for long. But then she fell for Donal Carty. I knew he was trouble. He had a reputation for being a bully – a subtle bully mind. He played with girls' affections and routinely cheated on them. But to my surprise, he seemed genuinely keen on Eimear. I wondered if it was the money. Her father left Eimear money, and Claire's will would make her a comparatively wealthy girl. Although, the money may have made her a more attractive prospect, I could see that he was crazy about her. Eimear was quite a catch; she didn't have Claire's height and grace but was very pretty, full of life and good humour.

Claire was suspicious of him from the very beginning. She had heard the same rumours as I did. Claire made the mistake of letting her dislike of Donal show. They argued about him. I knew I would have to be subtle, so I neither encouraged nor discouraged the relationship overtly. But I did persuade Eimear to talk about him.

Like a typical bully, Donal did his best to isolate Eimear, turn her off friends, and demand her complete attention. He rained gifts on her and showered her with compliments. It was manna for a sheltered girl like Eimear. He was her first big love. I was interested to find out how things would work out. I had my ideas but decided not to interfere. There would be time enough for that later. In the meantime, I wanted her to tell her Auntie Meg everything.

I was visiting Eimear when I overheard Claire on the phone talking to her solicitors about making a will. She was approaching her fiftieth birthday, so maybe it made her think about her morality. Gibney, her solicitor, offered to come to the house so she could tell him what her wishes were, and then he'd draft it up properly, and she could come to the office to sign it. I bet he didn't make too many house calls, but then Claire was a valued client, and I think the old goat fancied her.

They were in Claire's study. I listened just as I did all those years ago. As I stood watching through a crack in the door, I hoped against hope that, in her will, she would finally acknowledge me. She listed small bequests to friends and items of jewellery she wished to leave as keepsakes. They listed the charities she wanted to remember in her will. Then she got to the main part. The last drops of hope were squeezed from my heart as she said: '*To my only daughter, Eimear, I leave my jewellery (except those pieces mentioned as bequests to friends), my savings, stocks and shares and my share in my mother Doloros (Della) Curran's house, and this house, with all its land and outbuildings.*'

My heart was pounding. I waited to hear her mention my name. Finally, she did: *'To my sister, Meg Curran, I leave the sum of twenty thousand in the hope that she will spend it on travel.'*

I left the house without her ever realising I was there.

Chapter 39

It's not that I ever really believed Claire would do the right thing. Over the years, I have given her every opportunity. No one can say that I wasn't patient. But now I had enough. To her dying day, she was never going to acknowledge me, and there were fewer and fewer people who could prove my case. Mother was dead, and Agnes, her sister, whom I had overheard revealing my secret, was in her dotage and barely knew what day it was, never mind my parentage. There were no other witnesses to the fraud perpetuated against me. So Claire felt safe. Safe enough to leave as her final legacy, a document owning me not as her daughter but as her sister. It was too much to bear.

I said nothing. What was the point? The time for words was over. But my pain festered, an open sore that would never heal. But everyone's life went on. Eimear and Donal got engaged despite Claire's misgivings. I watched as Eimear, besotted by Donal's looks and charm, surrendered herself to him. She let him choose her clothes and pick the music she listened to. He was an artist. I had to admire how he made her believe every word that came out of his mouth. He was the playbook for control. Gradually, he insinuated his way into all aspects of her life. He took away her confidence, subtly undermined her friendships, made her suspicious of friends she had known since childhood and encouraged her to drift away from them and socialise with his friends. He used his jealousy as proof of his love and devotion. Poor Eimear was constantly tying herself up in knots, trying to please him. I told her that after they married, he would finally feel secure. He needs to know you are fully committed to him. I felt a little guilty for saying that, but I was angry with Claire.

I watched from the sidelines. I discovered his affair by accident. One evening, I was leaving work late. I came in on my day off to cover for a colleague who was sick. I saw him in the car park, locking lips with some young one in his car. He didn't see me, but I made it my business to keep tabs on him. I knew his type – now that he had Eimear locked down, he was getting bored. He wanted fresh meat to keep him stimulated. I debated what to do. Of course, I couldn't let her marry him. She needed to find him out, but I wasn't in any hurry to tell her what he was up to. I didn't want to be the bearer of bad news. But Donal was a dope; he was getting sloppy, and he sent her flowers for Valentine's Day and put the wrong name on the card. I could see Eimear was getting suspicious, but he reassured her. It's amazing the lies one is willing to believe when you're desperate to avoid the truth. I should know.

She was forced to open her eyes the day she spotted him and his little friend. Once she saw it, it was like the light had poured in, and she realised what a narrow escape she had. Donal first tried to deny he had an affair, then blamed her for what had happened. He even tried to guilt her into apologising for his infidelity. I could barely keep a straight face when he explained that she had made him feel insecure and unloved, and that was why his head was turned. I have to award him marks for having a brass neck. But Eimear finally developed a backbone.

I could see how this made her irresistible to him. Like a child denied the best toy, he was prepared to use any means to attain it. Eimear was even more appealing now that she was unattainable. He started a campaign to win her back. He sent her gifts and letters and inundated her with pleading text messages. He hung around outside her office at lunchtime, desperate to speak to her. He couldn't handle her rejection. His fragile pride couldn't take it. But Eimear stood firm. She was on the brink of taking legal action against him. I took him to one side and convinced him to back off and give her time. Alec thought he was the hero who made him cool his jets, but I knew how to handle the Donals of the world. I had plans for Donal, but the time wasn't ripe yet.

Claire was beside herself with worry. I supported her, and she was grateful I had her back and, by extension, Eimear's. We spent many nights strategising how to help Eimear overcome all this pain. We became closer. The shadow of our shared secret didn't impinge, and we even settled into an easy companionship. Claire believed our mutual love of Eimear had healed our rift. I took on the task of cancelling all the arrangements for the wedding. It wasn't difficult; not much had been planned, but they were grateful to me. But everything was about to change. Neither of us had any foreboding.

We went to the pub that night, all three of us. Eimear was still reeling from the shock of Donal's betrayal and burning with humiliation. Initially, she was reluctant to go out with us, but we convinced her that the longer she stayed away from her local, the harder it would be. We both checked that Donal was away for the weekend and wouldn't be in the pub. We had such a lovely time, and I think of it now as Claire's wake. Claire and I sat with our friends, and although Claire was sorry for Eimear, she was relieved, too. Her girl was safe. So we watched Eimear crying into her drink about what a bastard Donal was. Her few remaining girlfriends were holding her hand and sympathising with her. They told her what a jerk he was and what a lucky escape she had. Her idiot friend Alec was there to pat her back and offer undying support. The fool had it bad for her, and she couldn't see it. It never fails to surprise me how people can never see the obvious. Donal's sister Jen entered the pub, and as soon as she saw Eimear, she turned on her heel. Eimear darted off to the loo to enjoy a good cry about losing a fiancé and her best friend. Claire wanted to go to her, but I persuaded her to leave it to Eimear's friends to comfort her.

But despite her worry about Eimear, Claire looked happy and carefree. With Donal out of the picture, I suppose she felt her precious daughter was safe. As I sat in the pub surrounded by Claire's friends and Claire's daughter, I continued to torture myself. Why was she so resistant to acknowledging me as her child? I mean, it was 2010, and no one gave a damn anymore. Eimear would probably be delighted to know that I was her sister. It made no sense.

As for the story she told me about my Spanish father, I was beginning to have doubts. When she first told me, I was thrilled and kept asking her more and more questions about him. But over time, there were changes in her answers. First, she told me he was from Seville; later she said Barcelona, and her description of how he looked changed with retelling. The only thing she consistently got right was the name, Mateo. I began to wonder if there was more to my origin story. Maybe my father was a local man, or perhaps someone married. There had to be more to it. It was convenient that the only means of tracing him were shut down. I was beginning to think it was all a pack of lies.

At eleven o'clock, I told her I wanted to go home. Claire hadn't been drinking, but she was reluctant to go. I think she was enjoying the company of her friends, and although she felt sorry for Eimear, she was hopeful that her girl would be happy again. We called out our goodbyes. When she fretted about Eimear getting home. The gallant Alec offered to drive her. Claire was glad to have her daughter in the safe hands of a garda. I bet he'd have liked to get those same hands on her precious Eimear, but of course, he was too much of a gentleman.

On the drive back to my house, Claire kept up a barrage of chat about everyone she met in the pub. I interrupted her harshly.

'I know the terms of your will!' Even in the car's darkness, I could see her flush. 'You really shouldn't have private conversations when I'm around, Claire. Don't you know I have a history as an eavesdropper?'

'Meg, please. This has to end. I know you want me to tell everyone who you are, but I'm sorry, I can't.'

'Can't or won't, Claire? Over the years, you gave me different reasons why you couldn't tell anyone. It would hurt James, Mother, and even Eimear. But now, James and Mother are dead. Eimear is grown up and already looks on me like a sister. No one cares anymore about illegitimacy. There's nothing but sympathy for the women who got pregnant in the seventies. Why are you keeping this secret?'

'Meg, please, It's better this way. I promise you.'

'It makes no sense, and there's no one around to care. The only reason that you're doing this is because you hate me.'

'That's not true. Meg, I could have given you up for adoption, but I wanted you despite –'

'Despite what? I don't believe that Spanish lad was my father. Was my father a local man, someone married with children? Please, Claire, at least give me the means of finding out who he is?'

She stared stubbornly ahead at the road.

'Right, if you don't tell me, then I'll do a DNA test. There are loads of sites online that can help you find out about your heritage. If you don't help me, I'll find out for myself. All I have to do is spit, and they'll give me the answers or help me get to them.'

'Please, Meg, you mustn't. Please, I beg of you, let it go.'

'That's so easy for you to say. You don't know what it's like for me—living a lie, not knowing who I am. You have to tell me!'

Instead of answering, Claire started crying. I wasn't having any of it. I grabbed her arm, causing the car to slide across the road.

'*Stop it!*' Claire screamed.

'Not until you tell me.'

We were both screaming now. And then, she told me.

That was when I grabbed at the steering wheel. In slow motion, I watched as the ditch seemed to come at us. The air was filled with screams, groaning metal and shattered glass. I must have lost consciousness for a few minutes. When I came to, Claire was clutching the steering wheel, and blood was pouring from her head. She was dead. Mammy was dead, and finally, I knew the truth.

PART 3

Chapter 40

Rubbing her sore cheek, Eimear stared up at Meg. Shaking her head, she struggled to understand. Meg smiled down at her. But this was a Meg she had never seen before. Her face was hard. She flinched when Meg stroked her cheek.

'I don't understand,' Eimear whispered through parched lips. 'What's happening to me?'

'You're dying, pet.' Meg smiled kindly at Eimear. 'You really haven't a clue, have you?'

'Please, Meg, what's going on? What did you do to me?'

'My dear, I've done nothing, and when the gardaí come here, they'll understand exactly what happened. By the way, it may be a while. Did you like my performance earlier?' She mimicked a panic-stricken voice. *'Please, please, operator, we need help. We need an ambulance and the guards.'* Meg grinned at her. 'Poor dear, I have to break it to you. No one is coming. Well, at least not until I've finished all my preparations. So we have just enough time to talk. After you slip off, I'll tidy up and leave, only to return with reinforcements when I cannot enter your house. I love the barricade. You have done half my work for me. But save the talking. I have so much to tell you, and I think you have a right to know.'

Meg touched her finger to Eimear's lips as she attempted to speak.

'We don't have too much time, and you're becoming sleepy. Soon, it will be too late. So you need to pay attention. I'm sure you have lots of questions for me. But I can see that your poor little brain is a bit cloudy, so how about I ask the questions for you? I suppose the first question you'd like answered is, who is behind everything that's happened to you? It's such a long story. I don't have time to give you all the details. I suppose you'll have to make do with the highlights. You know, I was quite a broken person, not that you ever noticed, being young and cossetted. Your mother broke my heart, and it never mended. I put plaster over the cracks, but the pain kept seeping through. I might have given up and ended my pathetic little life if it weren't for Tommy. I met him in Dublin when I was in a very dark place – thanks again to your mother and her broken promises. I went what is politely called off the rails. Not that Claire cared. She was glad to see the back of me. But then I met Tommy. You know Tommy, don't you – Tommy Brennan?'

Eimear whispered, 'Tommy Brennan?'

'Yes, pet, Tommy Brennan. I sent him to you. He once came to my rescue – a regular knight in shining armour. He was good to me when no one else, least of all Claire, cared about me. And he accepted me. I wasn't a looker like you or Claire, but I think I amused him, and like me, he had his story, and he could see how badly I was treated. He made me realise that you had to play the hand you were dealt and make anyone who hurt you pay. His credo was – hit hard and hit often. When I was concocting my little plan, he told me about the connection between Donal and Toby. Tommy has so many contacts in so many places, and Toby likes to walk on the wild side, so let's just say Toby owed him a favour. It worked so nicely that he could persuade Toby to turn everyone against you. Toby even contacted Donal and offered to make things hot for you in the office. I suppose the poor sap hoped you'd come running home to him when you got the sack. He was such a hopeless romantic, the idiot. But he wasn't a nice boyfriend to you, was he?'

Eimear moved her head slowly from side to side, trying to shake off the awful lethargy that was starting to overwhelm her. She stared helplessly as Meg talked on. It was hard to take in the words. Meg took her by the shoulders and shook her hard.

'Keep alert, girl! Where was I? Ah yes, how did I turn the office against you? It was child's play. When you were out at your relentless gym workouts, I found your laptop and sent off a few choice emails to make you look unhinged. I was always careful to delete them so you wouldn't see them on your email stream. You really should have changed your password; most careless of you.'

Meg's light-hearted tones jarred with the words she was speaking.

'Dear Tommy was a great help to me. It was thanks to him and his contacts that I was able to send you all my lovely postcards and organise the nasty surprises you experienced recently. He introduced me to one of his associates — Brendan, your late-night caller who did a little hairdressing job on you.'

Eimear opened and closed her mouth. She couldn't formulate the words, but she moaned and struggled to get up.

'I was very impressed about how stoic you were about not telling nice Auntie Meg that you were in such trouble. I was quite proud of you for that. I expected to have to come rushing to the rescue a lot sooner.'

Meg grinned at her in delight, like a child talking about how clever they were being. She's mad, quite mad, Eimear thought. It was a struggle to understand what was happening, her brain didn't seem to be working properly. She felt tired, oh so tired. Another stinging slap brought her back to alertness.

'Come now, Eimear. You don't want to die without knowing everything, do you? So keep awake, or I'll have to hurt you. I mean, I was always very fond of you – even against my will at times. You were such an endearing little one – you quite stole my heart away.'

Even through the fog of drugs, Eimear felt stomach-clenching fear. She tried to speak, but Meg shushed her.

'Where was I? Yes, I hired an associate of Tommy's to vandalise your car – sorry about that – I know how much you liked your motor, but no lasting harm done, eh?' Meg stroked her cheek tenderly. 'Then, when the time was right, I found another little operator to use his graffiti skills on your door. The poor lad really did believe it was you who hired him. I hacked up an old wig, styled it like yours, and borrowed your nice blue coat when you were out.'

Eimear moaned and tried to get to her feet. Meg smiled and pushed her back on the armchair.

'I know you're secretly impressed or would be if you weren't about to die. You see, I never left the country. I rented a room just above yours and made a copy of your keys when I stayed with you. So I could come and go whenever I liked. It was all such fun. I was frustrated with how slow the Dublin cops were to figure things out and contact Alec. Poor Alec, he was so shocked when Donal showed him your mother's cross. I came by it quite by accident when I was poking about in your dressing table in your flat. I always liked it, and I thought you'd give it to me. But I think Donal appreciated it even more. Oh Eimear, Eimear! You have a knack for making people believe in you, thus making their disillusionment with you even more painful. But once you were marked down as vindictive, no one wanted anything to do with you. It was fun dressing up and spinning yarns to the other tenants about you. Once or twice, you almost caught me, but my luck always held. You see, Eimear, it was like it was meant to be.'

Another scalding slap shook Eimear out of her daze.

'Come on, girl, no sleeping. You'll have all the time in the world for that shortly.'

Again, Eimear struggled to pull herself up, but it was hopeless. Her body was disconnected from her brain.

'Now your next question might well be, why, dear Auntie Meg, are you doing these terrible things to poor little me? Would you like to know? But you really need to keep alert. It would be disappointing if you missed the key motivation for all my actions. You know how you love to read all those mystery novels, but you will never have read one so engrossing. '

Eimear stared glassily up at Meg. Then she felt a sharp sting in her arm. '*Aaaah!*' she shrieked.

'Don't worry, I just want to give you a little dart to keep you alert. I found a needle in Claire's sewing basket. Now, where was I? Ah, yes, you probably recall that Mother and I never got on. But no matter how mean she was to me, I didn't mind because Claire was so good. No big sister could have been nicer. She took me everywhere, even let me be part of the wedding of the century to rich James Martin.'

Eimear watched through half-closed eyes as Meg paced back and forth. She looked feverish with excitement.

'Everything became clear for me when I overheard that bitch I called Mother having a chat with her sister. What a surprise I got when I heard what they were saying. When I challenged her, she admitted that I was the bastard child of her daughter. To save Claire from the shame and stigma of being an unmarried mother, she, with the help of her husband, pretended I was a late baby. Unbelievably, it worked. Now I could finally understand why she disliked me and constantly threw up to me what a perfect child Claire was. She saw me as Claire's one mistake. A mistake that hadn't been dumped off to be adopted or aborted – a mistake that was in full view, an unexploded bomb.'

Meg leaned over Eimear and laughed.

'You can imagine my delight when I discovered that Claire was my real mother. Everything made sense. No wonder I never felt any love from the woman I called Mother. She sometimes looked at me with such loathing, and I could never understand why. Now I understood. I realise now that she hated me so much because I reminded her of my father.' Meg made a sound, part laugh and part sob. 'But I was so happy then because I loved Claire. Although we no longer lived together, she always showed me love and encouragement. I saw all the ways she had demonstrated her love to me in the presents she showered on me and the trips she took me on. I was desperate to see her. I needed to be certain it was the truth. It seemed too wonderful to be true. I went to see her in the big house she shared with your father. Luckily, he was out. I asked her if it was true. She was shocked, but she admitted it. She refused to talk about my real father, at least not then. She told me a fairy story about a sweet Spanish boy and a teenage romance. I was willing to forgive her for the deception, forcing me to live with Mother. I foolishly assumed she would acknowledge me and let me live with her. Boy, was I wrong!'

Meg glared at Eimear. ' Wake up!' she said, delivering another scorching smack across Eimear's face. 'You need to hear this. My wonderful mammy, the perfect Claire, said it wouldn't be fair to James to acknowledge me. He was ill, dying, and she didn't want to upset him. No one cared about my being upset. Then she told me she was pregnant with you. She thought I'd be delighted.' Meg laughed, a raucous sound. 'She went on and on about how she loved me. I was her precious child, but it must be our secret. I screamed at her. I left her and went back to that bitch I had to call mother. I didn't speak to any of them for three days. Claire tried to bribe me into forgiving her, but she wasn't willing to do the one thing I wanted.'

Meg paced the floor, her face white with anger.

'But I was smart. I would never forgive them, but they didn't have to know that. That's when I started hating you. You were the golden girl, and Claire doted on you. She loved you far more than me. Oh, she tried to appease me with nice holidays and trips abroad. But I knew she'd rather be with you. You had the life that should have been mine,'

Meg's voice was loud with anger, and she walked back to Eimear and shook her hard to jolt her back from the unconsciousness that was overwhelming her. 'Instead, I was a spectator at the feast. And I had to pretend to be happy about it. But I was torn. I really did want to be part of your lives, but not as a pretend sister to Claire and a pretend aunt to you. I wanted my rightful place. I wanted to be seen. I was more than just a mistake. Claire kept stringing me along, giving me false hope. It wasn't until I heard her discussing the terms of her will that I really knew it was all lies. In her final act, she denied me. 'She left it all to you, her *only* daughter. That's what she put in her will,'

Meg's voice rose higher and higher, and as Eimear watched in fascinated horror, she leaned in closer and poked her viciously. 'She left you *everything*, even her share in my home. That was when I finally accepted my place – as her mistake. You were the only one who mattered to her. Then, all the hate I kept back came rushing at me. I was filled with darkness and pain. The only thing to kill the pain was to destroy you all.'

She lifted Eimear's eyelids. 'It'll be over soon. I mixed your antidepressant with a few of dear old gran's Valium, quite a few.'

Again, Meg laughed, but Eimear was slipping away. She was dimly aware of Meg's voice washing over her, the violence of her words no longer having the power to hurt.

'Right, Eimear, I'm afraid I'm losing my audience, so I'll hurry my story. It isn't fair that you die without understanding the perfection of my plan. I did hope we'd have more time together, but ah, well. Poor Donal was a goof. He really was besotted with you. I sent him taunting texts from your phone to get him riled up. He showed them to Alec to convince him what a bitch you were. Then, to mess with his head, this evening, I sent him a final text message from you, begging him to come here and expressing remorse for all the harm you caused him. You even told him you would leave the back door unlatched so he could drop by any time. I deleted the message so you wouldn't see it,'

Meg laughed delightedly. 'Oh, Eimear, I really wasn't sure he'd even show up. But it couldn't have worked out any better. After you went for your snooze, I unlocked the backdoor and, like a fly entering a web, he walked into the trap. But when the guards see his phone, they'll know what a fucked-up homicidal girl you are,'

Eimear barely heard. She was slipping further and further into an enveloping warm darkness. She flinched as the needle stabbed her arm and opened her eyes, blinking slowly.

'Poor Donal, whom you lured here and attacked him with a golf stick. Finally, overcome with remorse, you took your own life. I plan to call on your cleaning lady, and with her help, we'll discover you tomorrow morning. Too late, of course, to save you.'

Everything was fuzzy; the horror of Meg's words and actions seemed to be happening to someone else. Blessedly, she drifted off to a place free of all this horror. Another stinging slap pulled her back.

'One more thing I must share with you. Claire told me who my real daddy was.'

Again, Eimear heard the raucous sound of Meg's laughter.

'You'll never guess. No wonder Claire and dear gran wanted to keep it a secret.'

Meg pulled up Eimear's eyelid and poked her eyeball. The pain shook her back to painful consciousness, and she was forced to listen.

'*Wakey wakey!* I don't want you to miss the final exciting instalment. I really do wish we had more time.'

Eimear once again felt the sharp pain of the needle in her thigh and moaned.

'On our little car journey, Claire finally admitted that my daddy was her daddy. I didn't take that well, I assure you! With fatal results!'

Again, that awful laughter seemed to bounce around Eimear's skull.

'Claire never went to a mother and baby home. She was kept in the house while dear Mother paraded herself around the place with a cushion stuffed up her skirt. It must have mortified her to go to Mass and meet her beloved Father Brown while living a lie. Claire gave birth to me, her little bastard, and guess who delivered me into the world – it was dear old Dad. Is that a first, a doctor delivering his daughter and granddaughter simultaneously? Isn't that hilarious? The old bastard lived for a few years after I was born. No one else knew the whole truth. They're all dead and rotting in hell now.'

Meg released her and patted her cheek gently. 'OK, now you know it all, you can rest.'

Eimear began to slip down a long tunnel into blackness. She was glad to give up the struggle. This nightmare reversed everything she knew and believed to be true. Meg, whom she loved, was this monstrous, hateful creature. It couldn't be true, and yet it was true.

A loud banging interspersed with shouts briefly shook Eimear back to consciousness. She was dimly aware of Meg cursing and her shoulders being shaken violently.

'Who knows that you're here?' Meg snarled, her nails digging brutally into Eimear's wrists.

Eimear couldn't speak; her lips were numb, and her tongue was too big for her mouth.

'Shit!' Meg hurriedly picked up the glass and held it to Eimear's lips. She poured the liquid down Eimear's throat, holding her nose to force her to drink. She spluttered and choked over the partially dissolved tablets and whiskey mixture.

In some part of her brain, Eimear knew there was an opportunity for survival. Meg's panic energised her. She closed her lips tightly even as Meg tried to force them apart. But Meg's fingers held her nose and blocked her airway, and she knew that she would have to submit to the urgent need to open her mouth and breathe, even though it would mean death. When she gave up and the poisonous liquid poured down her throat, her faint grip on consciousness deserted her, and she fell into blissful darkness accompanied by the sound of breaking glass.

Chapter 41

Everything hurt; her throat and stomach were screaming out with pain. She fell in and out of consciousness. When she opened her eyes, Anna was holding her hand.

'Hello, love, you've been through the wars. How are you feeling?'

Through parched lips, Eimear whispered, 'Like someone has taken a scourer to my throat,' She tried to say more, but it hurt too much.

Then she remembered.

'Donal, is he...?'

'Yes, he's dead. According to Alec, it was instantaneous.'

Eimear forced herself to sit up, even though everything hurt. Her stomach muscles ached with violence she had never experienced, even after the most brutal workout. Anna helped her up and placed an extra pillow behind her shoulders.

'Don't try to talk yet. Wait until I get you some ice cubes. The nurse said having your stomach pumped feels like hell. We don't have to talk if you aren't able. I can let you rest and come back later.'

'No, please, don't go. Just give me a bit of time. Everything is still fuzzy.' Her voice rasped past her lacerated throat.

'What day is it?'

'It's Sunday morning. You got here in the early hours of Saturday, more dead than alive. You scared the life out of me, girl. They worked on you pretty fast, and you've been out of it ever since. Christ, you are one lucky girl. You might never have made it if we hadn't got you here so quickly.'

'I owe my life to you, Anna.'

'We got lucky if my friend hadn't followed Donal and called me ...'

They both remained silent. Words seemed inadequate for the enormity of what had happened. Then Eimear whispered through dry lips.

'Do they think I killed Donal?'

'I think at first nobody knew what to believe. Donal was covered in blood, and to tell the truth, I feared you had lost the plot entirely and run amok. I called the guards and your friend Alec came. I think when he saw you, he assumed that you had killed Donal and were now attempting to kill yourself.'

Eimear started to shudder. No, she couldn't bear this, to have everyone believe she was to blame. Her chest felt tight, and her body bathed in sweat. Was she having a heart attack?

'It's OK, Eimear, no one thinks you killed Donal. Alec very reluctantly gave me the lowdown. He wouldn't say very much, as it's an ongoing investigation, but he insisted you weren't under suspicion. The person in his sights is Meg. He said there were forensic indicators that made it unlikely you attacked Donal. And there was evidence of you being forced to take all those tablets.'

'I was. It was Meg. She was behind everything. It's all messed up and confused, but she hit Donal, and then she tried to kill me. She drugged my drink.' Hot tears slid down Eimear's cheeks, and she shuddered. 'Meg hates me. She acted like I was her enemy. How did I not see it? But she was always so loving. How was I so blind?''

Anna reached for her hand and squeezed reassuringly. 'You're safe now, love. The guards are questioning her. I saw her hightailing it out the backdoor just after we broke in. She'll have a lot of questions to answer, not least why there was a sewing needle stuck in your leg.'

'God, I remember her trying to keep me awake so I could hear more of the sick things she was telling me. Then, when I thought it was all over, I could hear banging sounds, and she started to panic and forced more whiskey down my throat.'

'Well, that was the cavalry to the rescue. I'm just sorry we waited so long. Meg, in her panic, spilt whiskey all over you to make you swallow. Also, there were signs of bruising on your face, but what exonerated you was Meg's behaviour. She said she was trying to save you. When she heard us breaking into the house, she claimed to have panicked and decided to run for help. But she looked as guilty as hell.'

Eimear stared at Anna. 'Please slow down, my head isn't working properly yet.'

'Sorry. I told the guards that the last time I saw Meg she was still in London and not due to fly into Ireland until Saturday evening. When my statement was read to her, she claimed that I was lying and that you had confided that you were afraid of me.'

Eimear took a deep breath. 'I suppose I was suspicious of you. I worried about seeing you outside my flat, and I know it's mad, but I even wondered if you secretly resented me for what happened to you at school.'

'Well, considering all the things happening to you, it's hardly surprising that you were wary of everyone who came into contact with you.'

'Except Meg,' said Eimear.

They both relapsed into silence.

Then Eimear said, 'How did you get to the house? My god, Anna, you saved my life.'

Anna grinned. 'That was a bit of detective work on my part. I was worried about you and unhappy with you returning to your house alone. So, I changed my work schedule and came down to Sligo. My mother still lives in town. I asked a friend of mine to keep an eye on you. I didn't want you to see me spying on you. He found that too boring, so he took to following Donal instead. When he saw him heading to your home, he called me. I was out late-night shopping, with my mother. I sent her home, and met him at the house.'

Eimear was listening, wide-eyed.

'My mate, George – I'll introduce you properly when you're feeling better – he told me he saw Donal enter the house and didn't know what to do. Everything was quiet and then we saw a light in the kitchen. I crept up to the window and peeped in.' Anna took a deep breath. 'I could make out a figure lying across the staircase. I rang the gardaí, but I was terrified of what was happening. I couldn't tell who was lying on the stairs and was frantic that it might be you. That's when we started banging on doors and then broke a window and climbed in. You don't know how lucky you are to be alive. I battered the face off of you to try and keep you conscious. At the hospital, they pumped your stomach. That's why you're so sore. We could tell them what was in your system from the bottles scattered on the kitchen counter. We sent them off in the ambulance with you.'

Eimear put a hand to her throat as she swallowed painfully. Anna quickly poured some water from the jug on the bedside table, helped Eimear take a few sips, then replaced the glass.

'Where was I? Oh, yeah, while trying to keep you conscious, I heard someone stumbling about in the garden at the back of your house. The back door was wide open, so Meg must have skedaddled out just as George and I got inside. Of course I didn't know then it was Meg. That's when the cops and ambulance arrived. I told your friend Alec that someone had just left the house and was making their escape through the garden,' Anna grinned at her. 'It was like something out of a movie. I swear someone may even have blown a whistle, and then the kitchen was filled with beefy guards who poured out of the door into the garden. They eventually located Meg limping across a field a good distance from the house – she'd been taking a shortcut, running for help, when she twisted her ankle badly – or so she said. When they brought her back to the house, she started spinning a story of how she had been trying to save you and then panicked and ran for help. It was all so confusing that it was hard to know who or what to believe. But the fact that she was legging it out the back instead of helping you made me very suspicious, that and the small fact that her clothes were covered in blood! And there was something sketchy about her behaviour – like she was playing a part. I knew the bitch was lying, but I couldn't prove it.'

Eimear shuddered, 'This is all so surreal, It's like something out of a horror film. But that's what the last few months have felt like for me – a waking nightmare.'

'You know what? At one point, I thought they were going to let Meg travel in the same ambulance as you to get her ankle checked out. But Alec wasn't having any of it. He took her straight to the station with him.'

'Where is she now?'

'Sitting in a cell, I hope. According to Alec, she's awaiting her solicitor. By the way, he wants to talk to you. He'll need a statement about what happened. I gave him a good telling-off for not believing you. In the end, I felt sorry for the poor man.'

'Anna, I can't believe this of Meg. I loved her. She came top of the list of all the people I trusted.'

'Well, you don't expect your auntie to have homicidal tendencies towards you, do you?'

'Anna, that's just it. It's coming back to me now. Meg isn't my aunt – she's my sister, my half-sister. At least that's what she told me. Could it be true?'

Then, the hot tears rolled down Eimear's face, followed by hacking sobs. A nurse rushed into the room, scolded Anna for upsetting her patient, and insisted she leave.

Throwing up her hands to admit defeat, Anna agreed to go.

'Look, Eimear, you need to sleep and process everything that's happened to you,' she said. 'I'll tell Alec to wait until tomorrow to talk to you. You try to rest in the meantime.'

Eimear slept, occasionally waking because her throat hurt, but eventually she fell into a deep, mercifully dreamless sleep.

Chapter 42

The morning light edged under Eimear's eyelids, and she opened them reluctantly. The world of sleep felt safe, and she was wary of leaving it. It still felt like an upside-down world. Did she dream of Anna's visit? Could she trust her memories? A friendly woman arrived with a tray containing tea, toast and a pot of strawberry yoghurt. She sipped the tea, but it was too hot, so she left it to cool. She shuddered at the toast, knowing that her still-tender throat would be lacerated by it. She opened the yoghurt pot eagerly, suddenly ravenously hungry. When did she last eat? She searched her mind. She vaguely remembered eating something for dinner back at the house but couldn't drag what it was from the depths of her brain, however hard she tried. She kept on trying; anything was preferable to remembering what happened afterwards. Whenever her mind lit on a memory from that night, her guts twisted in agony, and so she worked determinedly on recalling what she had eaten for her last meal. It assumed ridiculous importance. But she needed to postpone the lancing of her memories that she would soon have to endure.

After her breakfast, she lay dozing. She opened her eyes, vaguely aware of a presence. It was Alec.

'Hi, Eimear. Sorry to disturb you, but I wonder if you're up to talking about everything that's happened.'

She stared at him in silence, taking in her old friend. His broad shoulders were encased in the uniform of a Garda Sergeant, and his plain, wholesome face stared down at her.

She struggled to sit up, and a nurse entered to place extra pillows at her back.

'Now, mind that you don't overstay your welcome and tire the poor girl out. She's been through a lot.'

Alec nodded his agreement. After the nurse left, he looked at her awkwardly.

Eimear smiled weakly at him.

'Hi, Judas,' she said.

Alec blanched, 'Eimear, I don't know what to say.'

'I'm not going to lie, Alec, I was gutted when you turned against me. It felt like there was no way out when even you stopped believing in me.'

Alec's face looked intense. 'I need to say I'm sorry. I should have believed you, but I didn't. There's no changing that.'

'Yes, you should have, but then again, I know that you were manipulated too, and there was so much pointing to my being unhinged and obsessed with Donal.'

Alec shook his head. 'I feel so bad, Eimear. I wasn't a good friend. I should have given you the benefit of the doubt.'

'Come on, Alec, let it go. We were all fooled one way or another. So how about we get the legalities over with, and then we can work on everything else?'

Alec nodded. 'OK, I've taken a statement from your aunt, and now I need to hear from you?'

Eimear pointed to the glass of water on the tray at the bottom of her bed.

'Push that tray up to me, Alec. It's a long story, and I'll need a few sips of water to keep me going.'

Eimear began. She told Alec everything that had happened to her in Dublin. Alec flushed when she mentioned how he had turned against her. Then, she related the events of the night of Donal's death. She started crying as she described Meg bringing the golf stick down repeatedly on Donal's head. She drank some water and continued to explain how Meg had fooled her into thinking she had called for help and instead drugged her.

'Alec, she told me she was my half-sister. She was so full of hate. It was like someone had taken over her body, and she wasn't my Meg anymore but a creature full of rage. I don't even know if what she told me is the truth.'

'It must have been horrific,' he said.

'What happened after I passed out?'

'Well, as you know, Meg was apprehended in a field some distance from the house, with a supposed twisted ankle. The ankle was fine, as it turned out – which didn't lend credibility to her claims that she was running for help. When we brought her down to the station, she told us that you had been talking in a very disturbed way for quite a while. The last conversation she had with you alarmed her, and she decided to see if you were alright. When she arrived at the house, she claimed that the front door was wide open, and when she entered, she saw Donal's body covered in blood on the stairs. She checked to see if he was alive. When she realised he was dead, she approached the kitchen, where she heard loud sobs. She discovered you crushing tablets and putting them into a glass there. She tried to stop you, but you were hysterical and kept screaming that Donal got what was coming to him.'

'Oh God, this is unbelievable!'

'She said you were beyond reasoning and, after struggling to take the glass from you, she became concerned for her safety and ran out the back door. She said she never heard the sirens because she was too upset and wanted to get away from you to call for help.'

Her heart pounding furiously for one awful moment, she wondered if Alec could still believe Meg's lies.

'You do believe I didn't kill Donal, don't you?'

'Of course I do. Maybe, if Meg had more time, she could have rigged the crime scene to frame you, but she ran out of time. For a start, she couldn't have got in through the front door as she claimed because it was barricaded. Then we discovered the pill bottle was covered in her prints. Her story that she was trying to wrestle it from your hands was belied by the absence of any of your prints on the bottle or the mortar and pestle used to crush the tablets,' Alec pulled his chair closer to the bed. 'She got you to put your hands on the golf stick, but they're all wrong for someone using it to strike. More importantly, the blood spatter on her clothes showed she was the person who struck him. When we examined your clothes, the blood splatter showed that you were in front of him and possibly lying down. Again, she didn't have time to change her clothes. They were covered in Donal's blood. Eventually, we got her to admit she killed Donal, and she claimed she was protecting you – saving your life.'

'That's true, he was attacking me. If she hadn't arrived when she did, I'm convinced he'd have really hurt me; he looked beyond reason,' she said, shuddering.

'We've checked his phone, and there are several messages from you taunting him and disparaging his sexual prowess. For a man like Donal, they enraged him. He showed me some of them when I went to see him about harassing you. It made him seem like the victim, not you. I'm sorry, Eimear. I thought you were disturbed, especially after I heard from the guards in Dublin.'

'So that's why he attacked me. He thought I was messing with his head.'

'Donal was a disturbed man. We accept now that he was stalking you, and I think that he was manipulated by Meg pretending to be you in such a way as to enrage him.'

'Why are you sure I didn't send him the messages?'

'We couldn't be certain, but when we checked your whereabouts when the messages were sent, we have you on CCTV in Quinn's pharmacy arguing with Donal's mother. It's tight, but it seemed unlikely that straight after a blazing row, you would be texting him to come round for a visit. But it was possible, and it did muddy the waters for you.'

'I forgot my phone that day. God, it all seems so long ago,' she said, closing her eyes for a moment. Then, with a quiver in her voice, she asked, 'So, do you think I sent those messages?'

Alec smiled at her reassuringly. 'When Meg realised the evidence was mounting against her, she began talking. I don't say she cracked; I just think she was dying to tell someone how clever she was. Unbelievably, she kept giving out about you not listening to her when she was describing everything she had done.'

'So, am I in the clear, Alec? I can't bear to always be under suspicion.'

'We have a few things to clear up. But there was no stopping Meg from telling us how clever she was. She told us that she never went on her trip. Instead, she rented a flat in your building, and she was able to enter and leave your flat when you went out. That was how she got into your emails and sent texts on your phone. She boasted about how she deleted everything and left no trace.'

'And the postcards were sent courtesy of Tommy Brennan and Co.'

'Yes, she wrote all the cards and Tommy got his associates to post them. He keeps his business under the radar, but it's likely he has contacts all over Europe, both for his legal dealings and the dodgy one too.'

Eimear shook her head. 'She always seemed so genuinely fond of me, Alec. Was it all a pretence?'

'I think she was conflicted. When I interviewed her, she asked after you like she cared, and then she acted as though you were her enemy. It was hard for me to separate the nice Meg Curran that I had known all my life from this murderous woman.' Alec hesitated. 'Look, all this can wait, Eimear.'

'No, Alec, please tell me as much as you can, or I'll never sleep.'

'So she never cared about me at all.'

'In her warped way, she did, but I think she was intensely jealous. She believed her whole life was a pretence and that you were the golden child. You always came first with Claire. I know your mother had her reasons, but I think jealousy and the pain of rejection sent Meg over the edge of

317

sanity. In interrogation, she kept comparing her life with yours, and she was full of resentment.'

After Alec left, hot tears scalded her cheeks. She gave in to them until she was drained dry, and then she told herself she was done crying.

Chapter 43

The trial was short. Meg was charged with manslaughter, attempted murder, harassment and incitement to violence. Meg's solicitor had persuaded her to enter a guilty plea to all the charges. The mitigating factors of her early guilty plea and traumatic and dysfunctional family background explained her motivation but did not excuse her actions. Various psychiatric experts gave evidence as to her mental state. But the fact remained that she had hit Donal not once but twice, that she had orchestrated a terror campaign against Eimear and attempted to murder her. This took planning and deliberation. It couldn't be explained away by mental instability alone. So, with the mitigation of an early guilty plea and the support of a very expensive barrister, she was sentenced to 15 years.

Eimear wondered who paid the brief. Was it Tommy Brennan? She noticed that his name was never mentioned in the court. Alec said that she retracted everything she had said about him in her original statement and refused to implicate him in what happened. Perhaps that was the price of an expensive lawyer, or maybe she was afraid of crossing him.

Eimear kept away from the court. As Meg had pleaded guilty, she didn't have to give evidence. But she did supply the court with a victim impact statement, as did the Carty family. She hid out in Anna's flat until the worst of the publicity was over. The papers had their frenzy, and there was no shortage of locals to give their impressions and recollections of Meg to keep journalists well supplied with copy. But Eimear was protected by an army of friends and neighbours who showed where their loyalties lay. For the kindness she was shown, she was grateful. Not everyone was kind. Donal's mother gave vent to her pain and anger, and Eimear decided to give her a pass. The poor woman was driven demented by her grief.

One day, she met Jen in the street. She stopped, but Jen strode past her as if she didn't see her. That meeting made her realise that she needed to move away; there were too many painful memories, not just for her but for the Carty family, too.

Philip Jolly had been in touch and offered her, her job back whenever she was well enough to return. Iris, Kate, and even Hannah had sent her messages of support. When the role Toby played in her ordeal came out, he was encouraged to find employment elsewhere. She still wasn't sure she wanted to go back to Dublin. It sounded fanciful, but she felt she needed to heal her soul. So perhaps taking time out and going travelling might be what she needed. Anna had offered to join her whenever she wanted company.

When the dust had settled, and the worst of the gossip had died, she returned to her mother's house. She still felt the lingering remnants of fear whenever she had to open a door. Her therapist said it would take time, but eventually it would ease, and she would feel safe again.

Anna asked her if she planned to visit Meg in prison. She suggested that it might bring closure. But Eimear knew seeing Meg would just be opening the door to a nightmare she needed to put behind her. Seeing

Meg was never going to be part of her healing. Besides, she knew that was what Meg wanted, and there was no way she was ever going to let her inside her head again.

Shortly after her return home, Alec called. They sat in the garden. It was just as Mam would have appreciated: everything in full bloom, heady with fragrance and a dazzling blaze of colour.

'I'm surprised to see you back here, Eimear. I thought this place would be full of dark memories for you.'

'It had bad memories but plenty of good ones, too. Mam and Dad were happy here, and I had a wonderful childhood. It's just that I have to separate all the memories connected with Meg. But I think I'll put it on the market later in the year.' Eimear sighed and stared back at the house. 'Alec, what happened to her was wrong. My mother and Gran wronged her. They lied to her about who she was, and then when she found out the truth, they insisted she continue the lie. For a teenage girl, that must have been a terrible rejection.'

'You almost sound sorry for her after all she did to you.'

'I can see the injustice of how she was treated and feel for her suffering, but I don't forgive her. I'm not sure if I ever can. But my mother and grandmother sowed the seeds of all this when they treated her like they did. Secrets, unless exposed to the light, are corrosive. The secrets buried inside Meg were like a tick consuming her.'

'According to things she said in interrogation, your grandmother did her best to make Meg feel she was worthless, and that was even before she learned the truth.'

'Alec, I've been torturing myself about this, but I think she was responsible for what happened to Mam. She told me something awful. I was so far gone that I'm not even sure if she really said it. It's so horrific. Please, Alec, it mustn't go any further – but I think Meg said that in the car just before the crash Mam confessed that her father, my grandfather, was responsible for her pregnancy. And that she, Meg, had caused the crash.'

'I don't know, Eimear, and best not to torture yourself thinking about it. She can't harm you now.'

'But, Alec, she'll get out someday, won't she?'

Alec shrugged. 'Best not to think about that,' he said.

THE END

Printed in Great Britain
by Amazon